The Adventures of

PEREGRINE PICKLE

TOBIAS SMOLLETT

The Adventures of

PEREGRINE PICKLE

in which are included

MEMOIRS OF A
LADY OF QUALITY

Edited with an Introduction by

JAMES L. CLIFFORD

OXFORD UNIVERSITY PRESS

LONDON   OXFORD   NEW YORK

1969

Oxford University Press

LONDON OXFORD NEW YORK
GLASGOW TORONTO MELBOURNE WELLINGTON
CAPE TOWN SALISBURY IBADAN NAIROBI LUSAKA ADDIS ABABA
BOMBAY CALCUTTA MADRAS KARACHI LAHORE DACCA
KUALA LUMPUR SINGAPORE HONG KONG TOKYO

First published in the OXFORD ENGLISH NOVELS series
by Oxford University Press, London, 1964

First issued as an Oxford University Press paperback, 1969

PRINTED IN GREAT BRITAIN

CONTENTS

INTRODUCTION   xv

NOTE ON THE TEXT   xxx

SELECT BIBLIOGRAPHY   xxxi

A CHRONOLOGY OF TOBIAS GEORGE SMOLLETT   xxxiii

I. *An Account of Mr. Gamaliel Pickle—The Disposition of his Sister described—He yields to her Sollicitations, and retires to the Country*   1

II. *He is made acquainted with the Characters of Commodore Trunnion and his Adherents ; meets with them by Accident, and contracts an Intimacy with that Commander*   4

III. *Mrs. Grizzle exerts herself in finding a Proper Match for her Brother ; who is accordingly introduced to the Young Lady whom he marries in due Season*   12

IV. *The Behaviour of Mrs. Grizzle at the Wedding, with an Account of the Guests*   16

V. *Mrs. Pickle assumes the Reins of Government in her own Family ; her Sister-in-law undertakes an Enterprize of Great Moment ; but is for some time diverted from her Purpose, by a very interesting Consideration*   18

VI. *Mrs. Grizzle is indefatigable in gratifying her Sister's Longings. Peregrine is born, and managed contrary to the Directions and Remonstrances of his Aunt, who is disgusted upon that Account ; and resumes the Plan which she had before rejected*   24

VII. *Divers Stratagems are invented and put in Practice in order to overcome the Obstinacy of Trunnion, who at length is teized and tortured into the Noose of Wedlock*   32

VIII. *Preparations are made for the Commodore's Wedding, which is delayed by an Accident that hurried him the Lord knows whither*   36

IX. *He is found by the Lieutenant ; reconducted to his own House ; married to Mrs. Grizzle, who meets with a small Misfortune in the Night, and asserts her Prerogative next Morning ; in consequence of which her Husband's Eye is endangered*   41

v

Contents

x. *The Commodore being in some Cases restif, his Lady has recourse to Artifice in the establishment of her Throne; she exhibits Symptoms of Pregnancy, to the unspeakable Joy of Trunnion, who nevertheless is baulked in his Expectation*   46

xi. *Mrs. Trunnion erects a Tyranny in the Garrison, while her Husband conceives an Affection for his Nephew Perry, who manifests a Peculiarity of Disposition even in his tender Years*   51

xii. *Peregrine is sent to a Boarding-School, becomes Remarkable for his Genius and Ambition*   54

xiii. *He exercises his Talents at the Expence of the School-Master, whose Character and Business declining, he desires to be recalled*   58

xiv. *The Commodore takes Peregrine under his own Care. The Boy arrives at the Garrison;—is strangely received by his own Mother; —enters into a Confederacy with Hatchway and Pipes, and executes a Couple of waggish Enterprizes upon his Aunt*   63

xv. *The Triumvirate turn the Stream of their Wit upon the Commodore, who by their Means is embroiled with an Attorney, and terrified with an Apparition*   68

xvi. *He is also by their Device engaged in an Adventure with the Exciseman, who does not find his Account in his own Drollery*   72

xvii. *The Commodore detects the Machinations of the Conspirators, and hires a Tutor for Peregrine, whom he settles at Winchester School*   77

xviii. *Peregrine distinguishes himself among his School-fellows, exposes his Tutor, and attracts the particular Notice of the Master*   81

xix. *He is concerned in a dangerous Adventure with a certain Gardener; heads an Insurrection in the School; takes the Field with his Adherents, marches up into the Country, and fixes his Head Quarters at an Inn*   85

xx. *The Governors tamper with their Pupils, Peregrine is deserted, prevailed upon to return, and submit to Correction; sublimes his Ideas, commences Gallant, and becomes acquainted with Miss Emily Gauntlet*   91

xxi. *He inquires into the Situation of this young Lady with whom he is enamoured; elopes from School; is found by the Lieutenant, reconveyed to Winchester, and sends a Letter with a Copy of Verses to his Mistress*   97

Contents

XXII. *His Messenger meets with a Misfortune, to which he applies a very extraordinary Expedient that is attended with strange Consequences*   103

XXIII. *Peregrine is summoned to attend his Uncle, is more and more hated by his own Mother; appeals to his Father, whose Condescension is defeated by the Dominion of his Wife*   108

XXIV. *Trunnion is enraged at the Conduct of Pickle. Peregrine resents the Injustice of his Mother, to whom he explains his Sentiments in a Letter. Is entered at the University of Oxford, where he signalizes himself as a Youth of an enterprising Genius*   112

XXV. *He is insulted by his Tutor, whom he lampoons; makes considerable Progress in polite Literature; and in an Excursion to Windsor meets with Emilia by Accident and is very coldly received*   117

XXVI. *After sundry unsuccessful Efforts, he finds Means to come to an Explanation with his Mistress; and a Reconciliation ensues*   123

XXVII. *He atchieves an Adventure at the Assembly, and quarrels with his Governor*   130

XXVIII. *He receives a Letter from his Aunt, breaks with the Commodore, and disobliges the Lieutenant, who, nevertheless, undertakes his Cause*   135

XXIX. *He becomes Melancholy and Despondent; is favoured with a condescending Letter from his Uncle, reconciles himself to his Governor, and sets out with Emilia and her Friend for Mrs. Gauntlet's House*   140

XXX. *They meet with dreadful Alarm on the Road, arrive at their Journey's End. Peregrine is introduced to Emily's Brother; these two young Gentlemen misunderstand each other. Pickle departs for the Garison*   144

XXXI. *Peregrine is overtaken by Mr. Gauntlet, with whom he fights a Duel, and contracts an intimate Friendship. He arrives at the Garison, and finds his Mother as implacable as ever. He is insulted by his Brother Gam, whose Preceptor he disciplines with a Horsewhip*   150

XXXII. *He projects a Plan of Revenge, which is executed against the Curate*   155

Contents

XXXIII. *Mr. Sackbut and his Pupil conspire against Peregrine, who being apprized of their Design by his Sister, takes Measures for counterworking their Scheme, which is executed by Mistake upon Mr. Gauntlet. This young Soldier meets with a cordial Reception from the Commodore, who generously decoys him into his own Interest* 159

XXXIV. *The two young Gentlemen display their Talents for Gallantry, in the Course of which they are involved in a ludicrous Circumstance of Distress, and afterwards take Vengeance on the Author of their Mishap* 165

XXXV. *Peregrine has an Interview with his Sister Julia. Is interrupted and attacked by his Mother, and relieved by his Friend Gauntlet. Julia is settled in the Garison, and Trunnion affronted by his old Friend Gamaliel Pickle* 170

XXXVI. *The Commodore sends a Challenge to Gamaliel, and is imposed upon by a waggish Invention of the Lieutenant, Peregrine and Gauntlet* 174

XXXVII. *Peregrine takes leave of his Aunt and Sister, sets out from the Garison, parts with his Uncle and Hatchway on the Road, and with his Governor arrives in safety at Dover* 178

XXXVIII. *He adjusts the Method of his Correspondence with Gauntlet; meets by Accident with an Italian Charlatan, and a certain Apothecary, who proves to be a noted Character* 181

XXXIX. *He embarks for France; is overtaken by a Storm; is surprised with the Appearance of Pipes; lands at Calais, and has an Affair with the Officers of the Custom-house* 186

XL. *He makes a fruitless Attempt in Gallantry; departs for Boulogne, where he spends the Evening with certain English Exiles* 192

XLI. *Proceeds for the Capital. Takes up his Lodging at Bernay, where he is overtaken by Mr. Hornbeck, whose Head he longs to fortify* 197

XLII. *They set out in Company, breakfast at Abbe Ville, dine at Amiens, and about Eleven O'clock arrive at Chantilly, where Peregrine executes a Plan which he had concerted upon Hornbeck* 201

XLIII. *He is involved in an Adventure at Paris, and taken Prisoner by the City-guard. Becomes acquainted with a French Nobleman, who introduces him into the beau monde* 204

Contents

XLIV. *Acquires a distinct Idea of the French Government; quarrels with a Mousquetaire, whom he afterwards fights and vanquishes, after having punished him for interfering in his amorous Recreations*   210

XLV. *Mr. Jolter threatens to leave him on Account of his Misconduct, which he promises to rectify; but his Resolution is defeated by the Impetuosity of his Passions. He meets accidentally with Mrs. Hornbeck, who elopes with him from her Husband, but is restored by the Interposition of the British Embassador*   217

XLVI. *Peregrine resolves to return to England, is diverted with the odd Characters of Two of his Countrymen, with whom he contracts an Acquaintance in the Apartments of the Palais Royal*   223

XLVII. *He introduces his new Friends to Mr. Jolter, with whom the Doctor enters into a Dispute upon Government, which had well nigh terminated in open War*   229

XLVIII. *The Doctor prepares an Entertainment in the Manner of the Ancients, which is attended with divers ridiculous Circumstances*   233

XLIX. *The Italian Marquis and German Baron are disgraced; the Painter is persuaded to accompany Pickle to a Masquerade in Woman's Apparel; is engaged in a troublesome Adventure, and with his Companion conveyed to the Bastile*   241

L. *By the Fidelity of Pipes, Jolter is informed of his Pupil's Fate. Confers with the Physician. Applies to the Embassador, who with great Difficulty obtains the Discharge of the Prisoners, on certain Conditions*   247

LI. *Peregrine makes himself merry at the Expence of the Painter, who curses his Landlady, and breaks with the Doctor*   251

LII. *Pallet conceives an hearty Contempt for his Fellow-traveller, and attaches himself to Pickle, who, nevertheless, persecutes him with his mischievous Talent, upon the Road to Flanders*   257

LIII. *Nor is the Physician sacred from his Ridicule. They reach Arras, where our Adventurer engages in Play with two French Officers, who next Morning give the Landlord an interesting Proof of their Importance*   262

LIV. *Peregrine moralizes upon their Behaviour, which is condemned by the Doctor, and defended by the Governor. They arrive in Safety at Lisle, dine at an Ordinary, visit the Citadel. The Physician quarrels with a North-Briton, who is put in Arrest*   267

Contents

LV. *Pickle engages with a Knight of Malta, in a Conversation upon the English Stage, which is followed by a Dissertation on the Theatres of the Ancients, by the Doctor*   272

LVI. *An Adventure happens to Pipes, in Consequence of which he is dismissed from Peregrine's Service. The whole Company set out for Ghent in the Diligence. Our Hero is captivated by a Lady in that Carriage; interests her spiritual Director in his Behalf*   277

LVII. *He makes some Progress in her Affections; is interrupted by a Dispute between Jolter and a Jew; appeases the Wrath of the Capuchin, who procures for him an Interview with his fair Enslaver, in which he finds himself deceived*   283

LVIII. *He makes another Effort towards the Accomplishment of his Wish, which is postponed by a strange Accident*   287

LIX. *They depart from Ghent. Our Hero engages in a political Dispute with his Mistress, whom he offends, and pacifies with Submission. He practises an Expedient to detain the Carriage at Alost, and confirms the Priest in his Interest*   290

LX. *The French Coquet entraps the Heart of the Jew, against whom Pallet enters into a Conspiracy; by which Peregrine is again disappointed, and the Hebrew's Incontinence exposed*   295

LXI. *Pallet, endeavouring to unravel the Mystery of the Treatment he had received, falls out of the Frying Pan into the Fire*   299

LXII. *Peregrine, almost distracted with his Disappointments, conjures the fair Fleming to permit his Visits at Brussels. She withdraws from his Pursuit*   307

LXIII. *Peregrine meets with Mrs. Hornbeck, and is consoled for his Loss. His Valet de Chambre is embroiled with her Duenna, whom, however, he finds Means to appease*   312

LXIV. *Hornbeck is informed of his Wife's Adventure with Peregrine, for whom he prepares a Stratagem, which is rendered ineffectual by the Information of Pipes. The Husband is ducked for his Intention, and our Hero apprehended by the Patrole*   316

LXV. *Peregrine is released. Jolter confounded at his mysterious Conduct. A Contest happens between the Poet and Painter, who are reconciled by the Mediation of their fellow Travellers*   320

Contents

LXVI. *Peregrine renews his Inquiries about his lost Amanda, in the Course of which he is engaged in an Intrigue with a Nun, which produces strange Consequences*   325

LXVII. *The Travellers depart for Antwerp, at which Place the Painter gives a Loose to his Enthusiasm*   332

LXVIII. *Peregrine artfully foments a Quarrel between Pallet and the Physician, who fight a Duel on the Ramparts*   336

LXIX. *The Doctor exults in his Victory. They set out for Rotterdam, where they are Entertained by two Dutch Gentlemen in a Yacht, which is overturned in the Maes, to the manifest Hazard of the Painter's Life. They spend the Evening with their Entertainers, and next Day visit a Cabinet of Curiosities*   343

LXX. *They proceed to the Hague; from whence they depart for Amsterdam, where they see a Dutch Tragedy. Visit a Musick-house, in which Peregrine quarrels with the Captain of a Man of War. They pass through Haarlem, in their Way to Leyden. Return to Rotterdam, where the Company separates, and our Hero, with his Attendants, arrives in Safety at Harwich*   348

LXXI. *Peregrine delivers his Letters of Recommendation at London, and returns to the Garison, to the unspeakable Joy of the Commodore and his whole Family*   352

LXXII. *Sees his Sister happily married. Visits Emilia, who receives him according to his Deserts*   358

LXXIII. *He attends his Uncle with great Affection, during a Fit of Illness. Sets out again for London; meets with his Friend Godfrey, who is prevailed upon to accompany him to Bath; on the Road to which Place, they chance to dine with a Person, who entertains them with a curious Account of a certain Company of Adventurers*   362

LXXIV. *Godfrey executes a Scheme at Bath, by which a whole Company of Sharpers is ruined*   366

LXXV. *The two Friends eclipse all their Competitors in Gallantry, and practise a pleasant Project of Revenge upon the Physicians of the Place*   370

LXXVI. *They distress the Housekeepers of Bath, by another mischievous Contrivance. Peregrine humbles a noted Hector, and meets with a strange Character at the House of a certain Lady*   376

Contents

LXXVII. *He cultivates an Acquaintance with the Misanthrope, who favours him with a short Sketch of his own History*   383

LXXVIII. *A Treaty is concluded betwixt Cadwallader and our Hero ; in Consequence of which divers pleasant Adventures occur, until the young Gentleman is summoned to the Garison on a very interesting Occasion*   388

LXXIX. *Peregrine arrives at the Garison, where he receives the last Admonitions of Commodore Trunnion, who next Day resigns his Breath, and is buried according to his own Directions. Some Gentlemen in the Country make a fruitless Attempt to accommodate Matters betwixt Mr. Gamaliel Pickle and his eldest Son*   391

LXXX. *The young Gentleman having settled his domestic Affairs, arrives in London, and sets up a gay Equipage. He meets with Emilia, and is introduced to her Uncle*   396

LXXXI. *He prosecutes his Design upon Emilia with great Art and Perseverance*   400

LXXXII. *He prevails upon Emilia to accompany him to a Masquerade, makes a treacherous Attempt upon her Affection, and meets with a deserved Repulse*   404

LXXXIII. *He endeavours to reconcile himself to his Mistress, and expostulates with the Uncle, who forbids him the House*   410

LXXXIV. *He projects a violent Scheme, in consequence of which he is involved in a most fatiguing Adventure, which greatly tends towards the Augmentation of his Chagrin*   413

LXXXV. *Peregrine sends a Message to Mrs. Gauntlet, who rejects his Proposal. He repairs to the Garison*   419

LXXXVI. *He returns to London, and meets with Cadwallader, who entertains him with a curious Dialogue*   423

LXXXVII. *Crabtree sounds the Duchess, and undeceives Pickle, who, by an extraordinary Accident, becomes acquainted with another Lady of Quality*   426

LXXXVIII. *The Memoirs of a Lady of Quality*   432

LXXXIX. *Peregrine amuses his Imagination, by slight Incursions upon the Territory of Vice and Folly ; reforms a backsliding Brother, and sends a celebrated Sharper into Exile*   540

Contents

XC. *He persuades Cadwallader to assume the Character of a Magician, in which he acquires a great Share of Reputation, by his Responses to three Females of Distinction, who severally consult the Researches of his Art*   551

XCI. *Peregrine and his Friend Cadwallader proceed in the Exercise of the Mystery of Fortune-telling, in the course of which they atchieve various Adventures*   558

XCII. *The Conjurer and his Associate execute a Plan of Vengeance against certain Infidels who pretend to despise their Art; and Peregrine atchieves an Adventure with a young Nobleman*   568

XCIII. *Peregrine is celebrated as a Wit and Patron, and proceeds to entertain himself at the Expence of whom it did concern*   575

XCIV. *Peregrine receives a Letter from Hatchway, in consequence of which he repairs to the Garison, and performs the last Offices to his Aunt. He is visited by Mr. Gauntlet, who invites him to his Marriage*   583

XCV. *Peregrine sets out for the Garison, and meets with a Nymph of the Road, whom he takes into Keeping, and metamorphoses into a fine Lady*   596

XCVI. *He is visited by Pallet; contracts an Intimacy with a New-market Nobleman; and is by the Knowing-ones taken in*   603

XCVII. *He is taken into the Protection of a Great Man; sets up for Member of Parliament; is disappointed in his Expectation, and finds himself egregiously outwitted*   608

XCVIII. *Peregrine commences Minister's Dependent; meets by Accident with Mrs. Gauntlet; and descends gradually, in the Condition of Life*   618

XCIX. *Cadwallader acts the Part of a Comforter to his Friend; and is in his Turn consoled by Peregrine, who begins to find himself a most egregious Dupe*   626

C. *He is indulged with a second Audience by the Minister, of whose Sincerity he is convinced. His Pride and Ambition revive, and again are mortified*   632

CI. *Peregrine commits himself to the Publick, and is admitted Member of a College of Authors*   637

CII. *Further Proceedings of the College*   645

CIII. *The young Gentleman is introduced to a Virtuoso of the first Order, and commences Yelper*   660

Contents

CIV. *Peregrine finding himself neglected by Sir Steady Steerwell, expostulates with him in a Letter ; in consequence of which, he is forbid his House, loses his Pension, and incurs the Reputation of a Lunatick*   666

CV. *He writes against the Minister, by whose Instigation he is arrested, and moves himself by Habeas Corpus into the Fleet*   676

CVI. *Pickle seems tolerably well reconciled to his Cage ; and is by the Clergyman entertained with the Memoirs of a noted Personage, whom he sees by Accident in the Fleet*   691

CVII. *He is surprised with the Appearance of Hatchway and Pipes, who take up their Habitation in his Neighbourhood, contrary to his Inclination and express Desire*   735

CVIII. *These Associates commit an Assault upon Crabtree, for which they are banished from the Fleet. Peregrine begins to feel the Effects of Confinement*   743

CIX. *He receives an unexpected Visit ; and the Clouds of Misfortune begin to separate*   748

CX. *Peregrine reconciles himself to the Lieutenant ; and renews his Connection with Society. Divers Plans are projected in his Behalf ; and he has Occasion to exhibit a remarkable Proof of Self-denial*   754

CXI. *He is engaged in a very extraordinary Correspondence, which is interrupted by a very unexpected Event*   758

CXII. *Peregrine holds a Consultation with his Friends, in consequence of which he bids adieu to the Fleet. He arrives at his Father's House, and asserts his Right of Inheritance*   765

CXIII. *He performs the last Offices to his Father, and returns to London, upon a very interesting Design*   770

THE LAST. *He enjoys an Interview with Emilia, and makes himself ample Amends for all the Mortifications of his Life*   773

NOTES   783

INTRODUCTION

Peregrine Pickle, Tobias Smollett's second novel, has never been as popular as his first, *Roderick Random*, or his last, *Humphry Clinker*. Although he clearly intended it to be a more extensive and finished work, with wider appeal, various circumstances combined to defeat his ambition. The novel received little contemporary acclaim, and has ever since had a mixed reception.

Just when it was begun is not certain. After the appearance of *Roderick Random* in January 1748, Smollett may at once have thought of writing a second novel, but more likely the real impetus was provided in February 1749 by the spectacular success of Fielding's *Tom Jones*. Copy for the first volume was probably completed by June 1750, when Smollett moved into his new house in Chelsea.[1] Then during the summer of 1750, Smollett journeyed, like Peregrine in the novel, to Paris and the Low Countries. Could the expedition have been designed to gather local colour for the novel? Many have thought so. If not specifically so planned, the trip did provide much material for his second volume.

In Paris Smollett undoubtedly visited most of the places described in the novel. We know that he met an English painter—vain, ostentatious, and ignorant—who provided some qualities for the character Pallet, that he saw something of his future biographer, Dr. John Moore, and that he became acquainted with some exiled Scots. After a short visit to the Low Countries, he was back in London by September, concentrating on the concluding portions. Thomas Birch wrote to his patron, Philip Yorke, on 10 November:

> The Author of Roderick Random is printing another Sett of Adventures which, I presume, are of the *low* kind, if Mr. Fielding will allow me the Use of that Word; for the name of the Hero of this new piece is Jeremiah Pickle.

Working at top speed, Smollett still had to put together the last two volumes. From references in Richardson's letters it seems evident that at least the first three volumes were in print by December.

---

[1] For biographical details see the standard authority, Lewis M. Knapp, *Tobias Smollett: Doctor of Men and Manners* (1949). Other works mentioned will be found listed in the select bibliography which follows.

Introduction

On 23 January 1751 the *General Advertiser* carried the announcement that the whole work would speedily be published.

Rumours had been flying about London of the inclusion in Smollett's new novel of some scandalous recollections of a well-known lady of fashion, more noted for her amours than her probity. For rival journalists such an opportunity was too good to miss, and Dr. John Hill dashed off a competing publication—*The History of a Woman of Quality: or, The Adventures of Lady Frail*—advertised as 'by an Impartial Hand'. This was published on 8 February. The day before, on the 7th, Smollett had inserted in the *General Advertiser* a warning to unsuspecting readers, appended to an advertisement of his own coming work.

That the publick may not be imposed on, we are authorized to assure them, that no Memoirs of the above Lady, that may be obtruded on the World, under any Disguise whatever, are genuine, except what is comprised in this Performance.

But it was not until 25 February that *The Adventures of Peregrine Pickle* finally appeared, in four compact volumes, at the price of 12s. bound, or 10s. 6d. in boards.

In addition to Hill's rival memoirs, Smollett was plagued by quarrels with the booksellers, perhaps because of his insistence on keeping exclusive copyright for himself. Although there was a Dublin piracy the same year, and French and German translations two years later, the overall sale was disappointing.

It was the sensational 'Memoirs of a Lady of Quality' which kept alive whatever interest there was in the new novel. In March two pamphlets appeared: *A Letter to the Right Honourable the Lady V—ss V— Occasioned by the Publication of her Memoirs in the Adventures of Peregrine Pickle*, a severe attack on the lady by a near relation of one of Lord Vane's henchmen, insisting that she had omitted all the worst parts of her conduct; and *A Parallel Between the Characters of Lady Frail and the Lady of Quality in Peregrine Pickle*, pointing out the chief resemblances between the two, and inferring the truth of the more damaging points made in Hill's version. Not until July was there any reasoned defence. In *An Apology for the Conduct of a Lady of Quality, Lately Traduc'd under the Name of Lady Frail ... In a Letter from a Person of Honour to a Nobleman of Distinction*, which purported to include further anecdotes 'never before made publick', Lady Vane was absolved of crude sensuality. Her troubles, the writer insisted, were caused by the ill-usage of her husband and her own indiscretions.

Readers were divided, both as to the ethics of publishing the memoirs and as to their style. Lady Luxborough commented to the poet William Shenstone:

Peregrine Pickle I do not admire . . . but the thing which makes the book sell, is the History of Lady V—, which is introduced (in the last volume, I think) much to her Ladyship's dishonour; but published by her *own* order, from her *own* Memoirs, given to the author for that purpose; and by the approbation of her *own* Lord. What was ever equal to this fact, and how can one account for it?

When her correspondent apparently objected to her taste in reading, Lady Luxborough added:

As to Peregrine Pickle, I hired it, and that merely for the sake of reading one of the volumes, wherein are inserted the Memoirs of Lady V—; which, as I was well acquainted with her, gave me curiosity. The rest of the book is, I think, ill wrote, and not interesting.

Samuel Richardson, perhaps not an unbiased witness as a rival novelist, called it 'the very bad Story of a wicked woman'; and Mrs. Delany found it 'wretched stuff'. Thomas Gray wrote to Horace Walpole: 'Has that miracle of *tenderness and sensibility* (as she calls it) lady Vane given you any amusement?' 'Peregrine, whom she uses as a vehicle, is very poor indeed with a few exceptions.'

On the other hand, a few did find something to praise. In the March issue of the *Monthly Review* there was a long, favourable analysis by John Cleland, author of *Fanny Hill*, who seriously discussed the new fiction and its connexion with biography. Mrs. Elizabeth Montagu, the 'Queen of the Blue-Stockings', wrote to her sister: 'I recommend to your perusal "The Adventures of Peregrine Pickle". Lady Vane's story is well told.' And Lady Mary Wortley Montagu commented:

I think Lady V's memoirs contain more Truth and less malice than any I ever read in my life. . . . Her style is clear and concise with some strokes of Humour which appear to me so much above her, I can't help being of opinion the whole has been modell'd by the Author of the Book in which it is inserted who is some subaltern admirer of hers.

What struck most observers was the astonishing fact that a lady should actually publicize the story of her own infidelities. Horace Walpole, who had years earlier characterized the Lady as 'Liquorissa', at once passed on the news to Sir Horace Mann:

> My Lady Vane has literally published the memoirs of her own life, only suppressing part of her lovers, no part of the success of the others with her: a degree of profligacy not to be accounted for; she does not want money, none of her stallions will raise her credit; and the number, all she had to brag of, concealed!

For the remainder of the year, as Fred W. Boege has shown, Lady Vane continued to be a sure target of poetasters and periodical satirists. In the *General Advertiser* of 16 March and in both the *London Magazine* and the *Universal Magazine*, there were harsh verses by Richard Graves entitled 'The Heroines: or, Modern Memoirs', where Lady Vane is yoked with two other recent female writers.

> Not so of modern wh—s th' illustrious train,
> Renown'd Constantia, Pilkington, and ——,
> Grown old in sin, and dead to am'rous joy,
> No acts of penance their great souls employ;
> Without a blush behold each nymph advance,
> The luscious heroine of her own romance;
> Each harlot triumphs in her loss of fame,
> And boldly prints and publishes her shame.

Even by the end of 1751 there were references in the periodicals. One jingling set of verses ended:

> Let me, mamma, now quit this chain,
> And but for this once try;
> I'll have my lords as well as V—e,
> Or know the reason why.

But the Lady of Quality was not the only source of controversy. Many readers were offended by various personal attacks on well-known people. It is possible for us to see that Smollett's vicious slaps at Garrick, at Lord Chesterfield, Lord Lyttelton, and the actor Quin, were motivated by the long years of frustration over his play *The Regicide*. And we can properly evaluate his hearty dislike of Fielding and Akenside. There is some evidence that Smollett thought Fielding in *Tom Jones* had plagiarized from *Roderick Random*, and Akenside's pompous manner, together with his scornful attitude toward Scotland, must have irritated the thin-skinned expatriate. Here was an opportunity to repay old scores, one that Smollett could not resist. The result was such characters as Mr. Gosling Scrag, Mr. Spondy, the physician met at Paris, and the other fairly obvious satirical portraits.

Other readers deplored the blatant vulgarity of many of the episodes. In the *Monthly Review* Cleland cited as instances Peregrine's chastisement of his tutor and an episode where the youth had bored holes in his aunt's chamber-pot, but defended their inclusion as part of the picaresque tradition. Not many were so ready to excuse this side of Smollett's work.

Evidently Smollett himself had some qualms, for almost seven years later, near the end of 1757, he set to work to expurgate his own work—to take out or soften the bitter personal attacks, and to remove some of the 'low' passages. By this time he had become reconciled to Garrick, and Fielding was dead. His resentment over other slights had cooled. To reprint the original version as it stood would have been embarrassing. So he omitted the ridicule of Garrick's acting, the sneers about Fielding's marrying 'his own cook-wench', and the cruel parody of Lord Lyttelton's elegy to his wife. Deleted, too, were the perforated chamber-pot episode, a long tasteless intrigue of Peregrine with a nun, and some of the horse-play and amorous philandering on the Continent. There were also a few changes in the memoirs of Lady Vane, made, it appears, at her ladyship's request. The revision was almost entirely a matter of excision, new transitions to cover the large omissions, and some breaking up of long sentences and changing of words and phrases. In all, the rewritten version was some 79 pages shorter —now 106 chapters rather than 114.

Undoubtedly the new edition—the one universally read since 1758—is a better-written work, which did present Smollett to the world in a somewhat more appealing guise. Yet because the original version represents the essential early Smollett in all his acerbity and violence, the decision has been made to reproduce it in this series. No cuts have been made, and the text is given just as it was presented to readers in 1751.

In the two centuries since its appearance the reputation of *Peregrine Pickle* has undergone strange variations. Because attention at first fastened almost exclusively on its sensational aspects, the genuine merits of the novel were obscured. There was little comment on Smollett's vigorous style and his remarkable skill in characterization. Yet *Peregrine Pickle* continued to be read, and by the turn of the century it was accepted as a masterpiece, even if a scandalous one. The author of *The Lounger's Common-Place Book* thought Smollett superior to Richardson and

Fielding, and insisted that *Peregrine Pickle* was the best of his novels.

Many of the great Romantics—Wordsworth, Coleridge, Leigh Hunt, and Lamb—were youthful admirers of Smollett (De Quincey alone disagreeing), the perpetual argument being over his place compared to Fielding's. Coleridge and Hazlitt preferred Fielding; Keats, and Lamb, for the greater part of his life at least, backed Smollett. It was with the greatest difficulty that Hazlitt was able to convert him. Scott, perhaps for patriotic reasons, was in the Smollett camp, as was Dickens later on. The question of who was adjudged the greater is of little importance to us today; what is interesting is the fact of the intense rivalry, that the two could be rated so evenly, and that Dickens, as is reported, could actually have preferred *Peregrine Pickle* to *Tom Jones*. And even those who rated Fielding higher were admirers of his rival. Reminiscing once over events twenty years past, Hazlitt wrote: 'I knew Tom Jones by heart, and was deep in Peregrine Pickle.' To this he added, 'I do not think any one can feel much happier—a greater degree of heart's ease—than I used to feel in reading Tristram Shandy, and Peregrine Pickle, and Tom Jones.'

It was another displaced Scot in the next generation who continued the affectionate praise of Smollett. With deep emotion Carlyle once confessed, 'I remember few happier days than those in which I ran off into the fields to read "Roderick Random". . . . To this day I know of few writers equal to Smollett.'

True, the tone of much of this praise is retrospective—remembering boyish enthusiasm. Smollett, one gathers, was the author for young readers, and often there is a slight suggestion that his novels are a little 'off-beat', not quite good form. The immorality and sordidness of much of *Peregrine Pickle*, even in the cleaned-up version, was becoming more and more offensive to nineteenth-century taste. As early as 1812 John Wilson Croker in the *Quarterly Review* could comment 'In Tom Jones, Peregrine Pickle, and Amelia, we have a most accurate and vivid picture of real life; but it is, if we may venture to say so, *too* real . . . we are convinced that the gay immoralities, the criminal levities, and the rewarded dissipation of Tom Jones and Peregrine Pickle have contributed to inflame, and we will venture to add, to debauch many a youthful imagination.' Two years later Croker added, 'We do not believe that any man or woman was ever improved in morals or manners by the reading of Tom Jones or Peregrine Pickle.'

Judged by such standards, it was inevitable that Smollett's fame should decline. By the last decades of the nineteenth century, it was at rock bottom. 'Peregrine Pickle', one writer commented, 'is an ill-conditioned Tom Jones and more dissolute.' Another insisted, 'As a novelist, Smollett's reputation, once very high, is growing less every year with the best portion of the reading world, and must continue to do so as a love of moral purity shall continue to increase.'

Happily Smollett can today be judged more objectively. Our concern is not so much with his vulgar brutality, but with his claims to serious purpose. Is *Peregrine Pickle* anything more than a mere succession of sensational episodes? Does it have any depth and subtlety? These are the questions which now are being raised.

That Smollett was a moralist is today generally accepted. Even Henry James, not too sympathetic to Smollett's type of fiction, saw clearly that his aim was 'to instruct and to edify', as well as to amuse. But what of his method?

It has been customary to sneer at Smollett's lack of artistic form, to describe his novels as haphazard, to say that they represent nothing more than a sequence of farcical adventures, strung together with clever journalistic skill, and interspersed with taste-less jokes and amorous scenes. But this apparent formlessness, critics now insist, was quite deliberate. Underneath there is more structure than has hitherto been realized.

That Smollett was consciously experimenting with earlier techniques is obvious, but it is not easy to decide which ones, or in what combination. Was Smollett essentially producing a realistic *Bildungsroman*, the story of a young man's acquisition of experi-ence, enlivened with some satirical touches? Or was he trying to combine the literary tradition of the Spanish picaresque with that of formal Latin satire? Or was he really using the structure of melodrama, with comic overtones? Among recent scholars who have studied *Peregrine Pickle* there is no general agreement; each tends to stress a different approach, or a special combination of factors.

In describing his first novel, *Roderick Random*, Smollett wrote to a friend that it was 'intended as a satire upon mankind'. But could this have been merely to claim more serious purpose than was actually there? Certainly by the time he came to his third major work of fiction, *Ferdinand Count Fathom*, he was ready to attempt a definition.

A Novel is a large diffused picture, comprehending the characters of life, disposed in different groups, and exhibited in various attitudes, for the purposes of an uniform plan, and general occurrence, to which every individual figure is subservient. But this plan cannot be executed with propriety, probability or success, without a principal personage to attract the attention, unite the incidents, unwind the clue of the labyrinth, and at last close the scene by virtue of his own importance.

The disorder, the aimless ramblings, the revolting episodes, according to the author himself, are all there in order to create the illusion of life. This is realism with a serious moral tinge.

Still the question may be asked—why choose such a loose narrative form for his serious social commentary? A simple answer might be that it was what he knew best. One must remember that in 1748 he had completed an English translation of Le Sage's *Gil Blas*, and was working on another of *Don Quixote*. He was saturated with picaresque theory. Moreover, he must have seen that this kind of narrative was admirably suited for satiric and comic effects. From the beginning, picaresque fiction was intended as a protest against the unreal conventions of aristocratic romances. Instead of a hero of good birth and noble sentiments, the chief character, the traditional picaroon, was often a bastard or a scheming servant. Throughout his endless wanderings, his assumption of one role after another, his sufferings at the hands of capricious fortune, he learned to see through the normal hypocrisy and self-deception of mankind. He came to have few illusions and rarely any twinges of conscience. Instead, he tried to get what he could out of the world as he found it.

The early picaresque narratives were only incidentally satirical. Though sordid and unromantic, life was still to be enjoyed. The typical picaroon rarely became misanthropic. The earlier writers saw no reason to be over-depressed by the natural depravity of man, or to moralize about it. But Smollett had been nurtured on the serious satires of Pope and Swift, and was incapable of writing a simple story without serious overtones. Vice was something to be exposed, using all the weapons of wit and rhetoric at one's command. Among his earliest published compositions, which preceded *Roderick Random*, were a number of Popian satires in heroic couplets. In *Advice* and *Reproof* he had castigated society, and lashed out at individual sinners. Is it too much to think that in turning to prose fiction he carried with him some of the same aims and techniques, and that he deliberately chose the picaresque form because it so easily allowed him to do so?

One might point out that the Latin *satura* was ostensibly a medley or ragout. Although carefully planned to attack some one vice, it was often on the surface a rambling assembly of vicious types. Thus essentially it had something of the same loose structure as picaresque fiction. As Smollett must have seen, there was no reason why the two could not be effectively combined. The well-known brutality and tastelessness, so Ronald Paulson argues, 'the cracked skulls, the excremental, and the gratuitously cruel', in Smollett's novels may thus be explained as the natural result of just such a fusion.

Moreover, the vulgarity and harshness, according to this inter-pretation, may also be traced to Smollett's literary ancestors. Satire, as understood in the late sixteenth and early seventeenth centuries, involved punishment. 'I'll send abroad a satire with a scourge', George Wither exclaimed. 'Not one shall 'scape him that deserves the lash.' The traditional satirist was always full of rage, continually talking of whipping his enemies, achieving revenge by metaphorically beating and purging evil-doers. Could Smol-lett's heroes, then, be essentially fictional representations of the satiric persona, with the physical punishment of sinners as their principal function? The vicious practical jokes, the chastisement inflicted by Peregrine on those he dislikes, are part of his literary heritage. Much that has disturbed later readers could thus be explained by an analysis of Smollett's satiric intention.

It is well to remember, too, that Smollett's indecent humour is that of an extrovert—never erotic or sniggering. He is scarcely ever pornographic or sensual. Many of his violations of good taste, like those of Swift, have to do with the waste products of the body, with human needs which are in themselves not considered shame-ful. Like Rabelais, he merely finds comedy in places where society prefers to draw the curtain.

According to this kind of analysis, *Peregrine Pickle* has a serious purpose. Moreover, so Rufus Putney shows, it follows a clear-cut plan. What Smollett intended was to satirize a major element of eighteenth-century life—high society. In *Roderick Random* he had given a realistic picture of poverty and ordinary existence. In his second novel he meant to show the shams and false pretensions of the aristocratic and wealthy. He stressed the hollowness of titles, the triviality, the affectation and meanness of the upper classes. To bind all this together according to his general theory, he must have a central character, who would for a time be an active partici-pant in the *beau monde*. Peregrine is designed specifically for this purpose. He is given most of the vices being satirized, but at the same time it is always clear that he is naturally generous and good-hearted. If he is often capricious, cruel, proud, and dissolute, he is also basically benevolent and well-meaning. Within him there is a constant warfare of conflicting passions. He reacts to powerful inner drives, at first to passion, pride, and self-love, and only gradually to reason and benevolence.

The plot, says Putney—and he rightly insists that there is a well-designed plot—is essentially one of conflict and final reformation. Not only is there the ancient traditional device of a spectacular rise and fall, having the usual ending with reversed fortune, but there is a carefully worked out progression of events. The episodes are not thrown together in a loose fashion just as they came into the author's mind. There are gradations, slow changes of value, differences of point of view. Peregrine's faults progress gradually from mere high spirits, to venial crimes, and only at last to viciousness and debauchery. His disintegration of character does not come all at once. Each section of the novel has a specific satiric purpose, and the action serves to reinforce one basic moral lesson.

Given an excellent upper-class education and all the money he needs, Peregrine is enabled to move easily in fashionable life in London, Bath, and the Continent. His natural uncontrolled pride and his strong passions lead him into one rash act after another. For a time he is successful, triumphant over all his rivals, but the false values of the aristocracy eventually force him into one unforgivable act. From then on everything goes wrong. Although for a time he still seems to be on the heights, soon one disaster after another plunges him into the depths. Everything appears to be lost. It is at this point, when his disillusionment and bitterness have taken over completely, when he has apparently lost any desire to live, that he is saved by the loyalty of Pipes, Hatchway, and his other devoted companions. Although the fashionable world may be corrupt, there is still love and affection among true friends. Thus Peregrine is taught by adversity and is forgiven. Then like Tom Jones, having achieved some wisdom, he receives his reward.

These critics thus assume a purpose which is based on a pessimistic view of mankind. But not all of *Peregrine Pickle* is satiric. In places, for the most part in the love scenes, Smollett appears almost to adopt the popular contemporary cult of sensibility. In others he resorts to pure melodrama. Of course, melodrama has often been successfully joined with satire. There is the same contrast of opposing forces: bad men are shown triumphing over good. But there is a basic difference. Unlike satire, where the fictional assumption is that folly and vice are triumphant, melodrama makes clear that the villains are ultimately punished and there is restitution to those who have suffered; and this violent turn of fortune can only be secured through powerful wrenching of probability and distortion of character. Nevertheless, melodrama can arouse a powerful response in the ordinary reader, who, almost against his will, becomes emotionally involved in what appears to be an ill-balanced struggle. With each succeeding atrocity, his sympathy for the victims increases, and his indignation builds up to such a point that he is ready to accept almost any favourable resolution.

Is *Peregrine Pickle*, then, fundamentally a melodrama? The well-meaning characters do eventually triumph. The evil conspirators are punished or displaced. All ends happily. It is true, also, that the book includes a large number of 'good' characters—Trunnion, Hatchway, Pipes, and the heroine Emilia. There is no doubt that melodrama does play a significant part in the structure of the novel. But is it the dominant factor?

It is well to remember that formal satire also contains some elements of praise, designed as contrast to the harsh attack. Pope had his share of benevolent characters in the *Moral Essays*, though they tend to be forgotten in our shocked fascination with Sporus and Atossa. Perhaps the crucial point is the overall impression left on the reader. In *Peregrine Pickle*, is it optimistic? Is there any convincing suggestion that the bulk of mankind is really virtuous and that right will always prevail? Generations of readers have not found it so. Many, even, have thought Smollett's view of mankind almost as disillusioned as that of Swift. His virtuous characters, it has been argued, are meant to be exceptions. They are a few admirable 'sports' in a degraded world.

To sum up: Is the basic pattern of *Peregrine Pickle* satire, realism, or melodrama? Or a combination of all three? The most sensible answer is to say that Smollett was not a careful rhetorician, working within well-defined limits. A gifted story-teller, he took what he wanted from many diverse techniques, not always caring whether they were completely fused. What gives Smollett his own particular flavour is the mingling in his novels of so many diverse traditions—the picaresque, classical formal satire, comedy, melodrama, the new sensibility, and at times stark realism. Yet his fertility is so great, his vigour of presentation so appealing, that the reader simply does not care. The story drags him headlong through every slough and side road.

How, then, explain the inclusion of Lady Vane's memoirs and the account of the Annesley case? Neither is essential to the story of Peregrine and his progress. Why should Smollett break his narrative twice with interpolations of this sort? At the time there were rumours that he was well paid by Lady Vane for publicizing her story. Yet there is no conclusive evidence that Smollett ever received anything from the Lady of Quality. Indeed, it is more likely that he had somehow met her and been impressed by her story. To him she may have symbolized the rebel condemned by society. Her very frankness in admitting her many affairs, and her insistence that it was love which had been her undoing, evidently made an immediate appeal. From his point of view her error had not been criminal sensuality, but rather a daring nonconformity which flouted the rules of society. Certainly Smollett's attitude throughout is that of respectful admiration.

Who wrote the memoirs? No one seems to know. Did Smollett write them down from Lady Vane's dictation? Or were they the lady's own composition, corrected, possibly, by someone else? From stylistic evidence alone it seems likely that, whatever the source, the final version was done by the same hand that shaped the rest of the novel.

There remains the question of why Smollett should have inserted a memoir of this sort, extending to some 50,000 words, in the middle of his novel. To delay the unfolding of the plot for so long a time has seemed to most critics a mistake. There was ample precedent to support him. The long autobiographical digression was a recognized part of the classical epic formula. Smollett's innovation was merely to bring in the true story of a real lady of fashion.

His rival Fielding had successfully followed the same older tradition, with the history of Leonora in *Joseph Andrews* and the episode of the Man of the Hill in *Tom Jones*. Modern commentators make the point that Fielding used the interpolated story of the Man of the Hill in a very special way. In this disillusioned account we are shown the evil world of London in microcosm. This is a warning of what may happen to Tom should he fail to allow reason and benevolence to curb his passions. Similarly, if Smollett's chief purpose in *Peregrine Pickle* is to expose the vices and depravity of aristocratic society, then the inclusion of an actual case history may be allowed. But his attitude towards Lady Vane is ambivalent.

Although a rebel, she is also an integral part of the society which he deplores. He admires her too much to allow her story to become a bitter epitome of the hypocrisies of high society. His rage and disgust are held in restraint, so that for many later readers the mood of the memoirs does not seem to fit effectively into the serious framework of the novel. On the other hand, the story of MacKercher and the Annesley case, which represented just the kind of injustice which would have aroused Smollett's intense partisanship, does appear to have a functional value. Here, Smollett believed, was an actual instance where blatant injustice had triumphed, where truth had been overridden by the power of entrenched position. Coming as it does at the place in the narrative where Peregrine has reached his low point, disillusioned and in prison, the digression helps to emphasize the hopelessness of his position. Right does not always triumph. The fact that Peregrine is himself speedily rescued from despair merely means that his is a special case.

The problems of structure have their fascination, but for most of us the chief pleasure in reading *Peregrine Pickle* comes from its wealth of colourful characters. As a creator of vivid eccentric types Smollett is unsurpassed. Although his heroes are often mere bundles of obvious antagonisms—on the one hand energetic and uninhibited, sexually loose, and quick to seek revenge; and on the other hand lonely, alienated outcasts, with instinctive benevolent feelings—and his heroines largely stereotypes, some of his minor characters have the stamp of genius. The nautical trio of Commodore Trunnion, Hatchway, and Pipes, the malcontent Cadwallader Crabtree, and a host of lesser worthies, once met will never be forgotten. That they have at times the sharpness of caricature must at once be admitted. And that they owe much to their literary ancestors, that whole troop of gulls and braggarts and sharpers of Elizabethan comedy, is also obvious. Smollett carries on the 'humour' tradition of Ben Jonson, with the same stress on one dominant trait, the same tortured wrenching of personality, the same kind of over-emphasis. Crabtree is a descendant of the ancient family of malcontents and railers, and Trunnion's last moments, which V. S. Pritchett calls one of the great scenes of English literature, may well have been modelled on Falstaff's end.

But to stress literary indebtedness can be as unrewarding as to seek originals for characters in fiction. Of course we have ample evidence that Smollett often had living models. He was quite willing to flay unmercifully well-known contemporaries. It is also true that he may have known about the house built like a ship by

Admiral Daniel Hore, at Hull near Warrington, where the inmates slept in hammocks, and nautical language was invariably used. And he may have known personally Captain John Bover, the supposed original of Jack Hatchway, and Thomas Smale, of Pipes. But these individuals can have provided only incidental hints. Like Dickens with Mr. Micawber, Smollett could compound genuine human traits with powerfully overwrought 'humours' to form memorable characters which both embody and transcend life itself. Distortion is an artistic device which is readily acceptable today. We understand better how over-emphasis and twisting shapes can suggest deeper meanings. Artistic distortion, then, rather than caricature, may be a better term to use for Smollett. What he does with his creations is to suggest the comic vagaries of life—not so subtly as Sterne, but with inexhaustible fertility.

Smollett is at his best in the early portions of the novel, with nautical characters and with broad comical scenes. Witness Commodore Trunnion's tacking against head winds in his slow progress to his wedding. Or his ludicrous battle with an attorney, when he picks up a whole turkey to use as a weapon. It is Smollett's ability to stir up irrepressible laughter that should be stressed. If our response may often be a guffaw rather than a smile, the reason is the farcical nature of much of his comedy. But this, too, has therapeutic value. A London physician of the eighteenth century is reputed to have had a 'pleasant habit of writing on his prescriptions: "*Recipe* every day for a few hours several pages of Peregrine Pickle" ' (Knapp, p. 315).

Nothing has yet been said about Smollett's manner of writing, yet in the long run it is his robust style which carries the reader along. Nevertheless, Albrecht Strauss has shown how difficult it is to isolate the qualities which give it such undeniable vigour. At times Smollett can be pompous and ridden with clichés. He can use trite eighteenth-century diction and hackneyed periphrasis. In his early novels the sentences often run on and on with turgid elaboration, particularly when the subject is romantic love or elevated pathos. These, however, represent only occasional lapses. For the most part his style has the easy rhythm of speech, the colloquial touch of everyday affairs. Once he has the bit firmly in his teeth, with an open road ahead, and a practical joke or a comic scene to describe, Smollett's verve is irresistible. Few writers have had such gusto, such enormous creative energy.

Although the writing is largely free from abstract ideas, this does not mean that Smollett's work lacks serious purpose. He merely refuses to philosophize, to brood, or to waste time in useless intro-spection. He is a story-teller, who is also an observer and satirist, with a world of folly to expose. But the demands of the narrative always have first claim. Thus *Peregrine Pickle*, with all its arid stretches and other imperfections, remains an absorbing story, containing some of the most memorable comic characters in all British fiction.

J. L. C.

NOTE ON THE TEXT

Except for the chapter-headings and the elimination of the long 's', the present text exactly follows the first edition of 1751. This was first printed by the University Press at Oxford in 1936 for the Limited Editions Club.

SELECT BIBLIOGRAPHY

GENERAL WORKS ON SMOLLETT

The standard biographical authority is Lewis M. Knapp, *Tobias Smollett: Doctor of Men and Manners* (1949). Other studies, of varying importance, are: *The Letters of Tobias Smollett*, ed. Edward S. Noyes (1926); Howard S. Buck, *Smollett as Poet* (1927); Eugène Joliat, *Smollett et la France* (1935); Louis L. Martz, *The Later Career of Tobias Smollett* (1942); George M. Kahrl, *Tobias Smollett: Traveler-Novelist* (1945); Fred W. Boege, *Smollett's Reputation as a Novelist* (1947); Laurence Brander, *Tobias Smollett* (1951); M. A. Goldberg, *Smollett and the Scottish School* (1959). Also containing useful material are: Herbert Read, 'Tobias Smollett', *Reason and Romanticism* (1926), pp. 187–205; L. M. Ellison, 'Elizabethan Drama and the Works of Smollett', *Publications of the Modern Language Association*, September 1929, pp. 842–62; Claude E. Jones, *Smollett Studies* (1942); V. S. Pritchett, *New Statesman and Nation*, 28 February 1942, p. 145; A. D. McKillop, 'Tobias Smollett', *The Early Masters of English Fiction* (1956), pp. 147–81; Albrecht B. Strauss, 'On Smollett's Language', *English Institute Essays, 1958* (1959), pp. 25–54; Ronald Paulson, 'Satire in the Early Novels of Smollett', *Journal of English and Germanic Philology*, July 1960, pp. 381–402; Robert Alter, 'The Picaroon as Fortune's Plaything', *Rogue's Progress* (1963), pp. 58–79; Robert W. Elmer, 'Melodrama, Comedy and Satire in the Early Novels of Smollett' [unpublished dissertation, Columbia University].

EDITIONS OF *PEREGRINE PICKLE*

1st edition, 1751; 2nd, 1758; 3rd, 1765; 4th, 1769. For others see *CBEL*. Included in all editions of Smollett's *Works*, notably those by George Saintsbury (1895), W. E. Henley (1899–1901), G. H. Maynadier (1902), and by the Shakespeare Head (Blackwell, 1925). With illustrations by Henry Fuseli (1769), Thomas Rowlandson (1805; some in 1790), George Cruikshank (1831), and John Austen (1936). Translated into French (1753), Russian [first 35 chapters] (1788), German (1753, 1785), Danish (1787–95), Dutch (1815), Russian (1955). See also Joliat. The 1st edition reprinted by the Limited Editions Club (2 vols., 1936), with an Introduction by G. K. Chesterton. The later revised version included in the Everyman's Library, with an Introduction by Walter Allen (2 vols., 1956).

SPECIAL STUDIES OF *PEREGRINE PICKLE*

The most important detailed analysis of the novel may be found in Howard S. Buck, *A Study in Smollett, Chiefly 'Peregrine Pickle'* (1925), which includes a complete collation of the 1st and 2nd editions. Other special studies are: William W. Huse, Jr., 'Pickle and Pickwick', *Washington University Studies*, x (1922), 143–54; E. S. Noyes, 'A Note on *Peregrine Pickle* and *Pygmalion*', *Modern Language Notes*, May 1926, pp. 327–30; Howard S. Buck, 'Smollett and Akenside', *Journal of English and Germanic Philology*, January 1932, pp. 10–26; James R. Foster, 'Smollett's Pamphleteering

Foe Shebbeare', *PMLA*, December 1942, pp. 1053-1100; Rufus Putney, 'The Plan of *Peregrine Pickle*', *PMLA*, December 1945, pp. 1051-65, and 'Smollett and Lady Vane's Memoirs', *Philological Quarterly*, April 1946, pp. 120-6; Judd Kline, 'Three Doctors and Smollett's Lady of Quality', *Philological Quarterly*, July 1948, pp. 219-28; William Scott, 'Smollett, Dr. John Hill, and the Failure of *Peregrine Pickle*', *Notes and Queries*, September 1955, pp. 389-92; Lewis M. Knapp and Lillian de la Torre, 'Smollett, MacKercher, and the Annesley Claimant', *English Language Notes*, September 1963, pp. 28-33.

A CHRONOLOGY OF
TOBIAS GEORGE SMOLLETT

1721 (19 March)	Baptized in the parish church of Cardross, Dumbartonshire, Scotland
Dates uncertain	Attended Dumbarton grammar school, and later Glasgow University
1735 (November)	Working in a dispensatory in Glasgow
1736 (30 May)	Apprenticed to William Stirling and John Gordon, surgeons of Glasgow
1739 (some time after June)	Travelled to London
1740 (10 March)	Received warrant as surgeon's second mate in the Navy—first served on the *Chichester* in the Cartagena expedition
1741 (September)	Returned to England
1741–4	Movements uncertain. May have returned to West Indies. Married Anne Lassells, daughter of a Jamaica planter
1744 (May)	Set up as a surgeon in London
1746	Published a short poem, 'The Tears of Scotland'
1746 (September)	*Advice*, a Juvenalian verse satire
1747 (January)	*Reproof*, another verse satire
1747–8	Translating Le Sage's *Gil Blas* (in the press, Nov. 1748)
1748 (January)	*The Adventures of Roderick Random*
1749 (June)	Published *The Regicide* after fruitless struggles to get it produced
1750 (Summer)	Visited Paris and the Low Countries
1751 (25 February)	*The Adventures of Peregrine Pickle*
1752 (January)	*Habbakkuk Hilding*, probably by Smollett
1752 (March)	*An Essay on the External Use of Water*
1753 (February)	*The Adventures of Ferdinand Count Fathom*
1755 (February)	Translation of *Don Quixote* (begun at least by 1748)
1755–7	Working on *A Complete History of England*
1756 (March)	Involved in launching the *Critical Review*. An active editor until 1763

A Chronology of Tobias George Smollett

1756 (April)	Edited *A Compendium of Authentic and Entertaining Voyages* (7 vols.)
1757 (January)	*The Reprisal*, a farce, presented at Drury Lane
1760 (January)	Began *British Magazine*. In it, from January 1760 to December 1761, appeared *The Adventures of Sir Launcelot Greaves*
1760 (November to late February 1761)	In the King's Bench Prison for libel of Admiral Knowles
1760–5	Working on *Continuation of the Complete History of England* (5 vols.)
1761–5	Joint Editor of *The Works of Voltaire*
1762 (29 May to 12 February, 1763)	Editing *The Briton* in support of Lord Bute—health deteriorating
1763 (3 April)	Only child, Elizabeth, dies, aged 15
1763 (June)	Travelled to France with wife and friends, then to Italy
1765 (July)	Returned to England
1766 (May)	*Travels through France and Italy*
1766 (May–August)	Travelled to Scotland and then back to Bath and London
1768	Completing *The Present State of All Nations* (8 vols.), on which he had been working since 1760
1768 (Autumn)	Left England for Italy, finally settling near Leghorn
1769 (April)	*The History and Adventures of an Atom*, a violent political satire, probably by Smollett
1771 (June)	*The Expedition of Humphry Clinker*
1771 (17 September)	Died near Leghorn. Buried in English cemetery there
1773	*Ode to Independence*, published posthumously
1776	Translation of Fénelon's *Adventures of Telemachus*, published posthumously

CHAPTER I

An Account of Mr. Gamaliel Pickle. The Disposition of his Sister described. He yields to her Sollicitations, and retires to the Country

IN a certain county of England, bounded on one side by the sea, and at the distance of one hundred miles from the metropolis, lived Gamaliel Pickle Esq; the father of that hero whose adventures we propose to record. He was the son of a merchant in London, who (like Rome) from small beginnings, had raised himself to the highest honours of the city, and acquired a plentiful fortune, tho', to his infinite regret, he died before it amounted to a Plum,[1] conjuring his son, as he respected the last injunction of a parent, to imitate his industry and adhere to his maxims, until he should have made up the deficiency, which was a sum considerably less than fifteen thousand pounds.

This pathetic remonstrance had the desired effect upon his representative, who spared no pains to fulfil the request of the deceased; but exerted all the capacity with which nature had endowed him, in a series of efforts, which, however, did not succeed; for, by that time he had been fifteen years in trade, he found himself five thousand pounds worse than he was when he first took possession of his father's effects: a circumstance that affected him so nearly, as to detach his inclinations from business, and induce him to retire from the world, to some place where he might at leisure deplore his misfortunes, and, by frugality, secure himself from want, and the apprehensions of a jail, with which his imagination was incessantly haunted. He was often heard to express his fears of coming upon the parish; and to bless God, that, on account of his having been so long a housekeeper, he was intitled to that provision. In short, his talents were not naturally active, and there was a sort of inconsistency in his character; for, with all the desire of amassing which any citizen could possibly entertain, he was encumbered by a certain indolence and sluggishness that prevailed over every interested consideration, and even hindered him from profiting by that singleness of apprehension, and moderation of appetites, which have so frequently conduced to the acquisition of immense fortunes,

I

and which he possessed in a very remarkable degree. Nature, in all probability, had mixed little or nothing inflammable in his composition; or, whatever seeds of excess she might have sown within him, were effectually stifled and destroyed by the austerity of his education.

The sallies of his youth, far from being inordinate or criminal, never exceeded the bounds of that decent jollity which an extraordinary pot, on extraordinary occasions, may be supposed to have produced in a club of sedate book-keepers, whose imaginations were neither very warm nor luxuriant. Little subject to refined sensations, he was scarce ever disturbed with violent emotions of any kind. The passion of love never interrupted his tranquillity; and if, as Mr. Creech says after Horace,

> Not to admire is all the art, I know,
> To make men happy, and to keep them so.[1]

Mr. Pickle was undoubtedly possessed of that invaluable secret; at least, he was never known to betray the faintest symptom of transport, except one evening at the club, where he observed, with some demonstrations of vivacity, that he had dined upon a delicate loin of veal.

Notwithstanding this appearance of phlegm, he could not help feeling his disappointments in trade; and upon the failure of a certain underwriter, by which he lost five hundred pounds, declared his design of relinquishing business, and retiring to the country. In this resolution he was comforted and encouraged by his only sister Mrs. Grizzle, who had managed his family, since the death of his father, and was now in the thirtieth year of her maidenhood, with a fortune of five thousand pounds, and a large stock of oeconomy and devotion.

These qualifications, one would think, might have been the means of abridging the term of her celibacy, as she never expressed any aversion for wedlock; but, it seems, she was too delicate in her choice, to find a mate to her inclination in the city: for I cannot suppose that she remained so long unsollicited; tho' the charms of her person were not altogether enchanting, nor her manner over and above agreeable. Exclusive of a very wan (not to call it a sallow) complexion, which perhaps was the effect of her virginity and mortification, she had a cast in her eyes that was not at all engaging, and such an extent of mouth, as no art or affectation could contract into any proportionable dimension: then her piety was rather peevish than resigned, and did not in the least diminish a certain stateliness in her demeanour and conversation, that delighted in communicating the importance and honour of her family, which, by the bye, was not to be traced two generations back, by all the power of heraldry or tradition.

She seemed to have renounced all the ideas she had acquired before her father served the office of sheriff; and the æra which regulated the dates of all her observations, was the mayoralty of her papa. Nay, so sollicitous was this good lady for the support and propagation of the family-name, that, suppressing every selfish motive, she actually prevailed upon her brother to combat his own disposition, and even surmount it so far, as to declare a passion for the person whom he afterwards wedded, as we shall see in the sequel. Indeed, she was the spur that instigated him in all his extraordinary undertakings; and I question whether or not he would have been able to disengage himself from that course of life in which he had so long mechanically moved, unless he had been roused and actuated by her incessant exhortations. London, she observed, was a receptacle of iniquity, where an honest unsuspecting man was every day in danger of falling a sacrifice to craft; where innocence was exposed to continual temptations, and virtue eternally persecuted by malice and slander; where every thing was ruled by caprice and corruption, and merit utterly discouraged and despised. This last imputation she pronounced with such emphasis and chagrin, as plainly denoted how far she considered herself an example of what she advanced; and really, the charge was justified by the constructions that were put upon her retreat by her female friends, who, far from imputing it to the laudable motives that induced her, insinuated, in sarcastic commendations, that she had good reason to be dissatisfied with a place where she had been so long overlooked; and that it was certainly her wisest course to make her last effort in the country, where, in all probability, her talents would be less eclipsed, and her fortune more attractive.

Be this as it will, her admonitions, tho' they were powerful enough to convince, would have been insufficient to overcome the languor and *vis inertiæ* of her brother, had she not reinforced her arguments, by calling in question the credit of two or three merchants, with whom he was embarked in trade.

Alarmed at these hints of intelligence, he exerted himself effectually; and having withdrawn his money, which he had laid out in Bank stock and India bonds, removed to a house in the country, that his father had built near the sea-side, for the convenience of carrying on a certain branch of traffick in which he had been deeply concerned.

Here then Mr. Pickle fixed his habitation for life, in the six-and-thirtieth year of his age; and tho' the pangs he felt at parting with his intimate companions, and quitting all his former connexions, were not quite so keen as to produce any dangerous disorder in his constitution, he did not fail to be extremely disconcerted at his first entrance into a scene of life to which he was totally a stranger. Not but that he met with abundance of people in the country, who, in consideration of his fortune, courted his acquaintance, and breathed nothing but friendship and hospitality: yet even the trouble of receiving and returning these civilities, was an intolerable fatigue to a man of his habits and disposition. He therefore left the care of the ceremonial to his sister, who indulged herself in all the pride of formality, while he himself, having made a discovery of a public house in the neighbourhood, went thither every evening, and enjoyed his pipe and cann; being very well satisfied with the behaviour of the landlord, whose communicative temper was a great comfort to his own taciturnity; for he shunned all superfluity of speech, as much as he avoided any other unnecessary expence.

CHAPTER II

He is made acquainted with the Characters of
Commodore Trunnion and his Adherents;
meets with them by Accident, and contracts
an Intimacy with that Commander

THIS loquacious publican soon gave him sketches of all the characters in the county; and, among others, described that of his next neighbour Commodore Trunnion,[1] which was altogether singular and odd. 'The commodore and your worship (said he) will in a short time be hand and glove; he has a power of money, and spends like a prince—that is, in his own way—for to be sure he is a little humoursome, as the saying is, and swears woundily; tho' I'll be sworn he means no more harm than a sucking babe. Lord help us! it will do your honour's heart good to hear him tell a story, as how he lay along-side of the French, yard-arm and yard-arm, board and board, and of heaving grapplings, and stink-pots, and grapes, and round and double-headed partridges, crows and carters—Laud have mercy upon us! he has been a great warrior in his time, and

4

lost an eye and a heel in the service—Then, he does not live like any other Christian landman; but keeps garrison in his house, as if he were in the midst of his enemies, and makes his servants turn out in the night, watch and watch (as he calls it) all the year round. His habitation is defended by a ditch, over which he has laid a draw-bridge, and planted his court-yard with patereroes[1] continually loaded with shot, under the direction of one Mr. Hatchway,[2] who had one of his legs shot away, while he acted as lieutenant on board of the commodore's ship; and now, being on half-pay, lives with him as his companion. The lieutenant is a very brave man, a great joker, and, as the saying is, hath got the length of his commander's foot—Tho' he has another favourite in the house called Tom Pipes,[3] that was his boatswain's mate, and now keeps the servants in order. Tom is a man of few words, but an excellent hand at a song concerning the boatswain's whistle, hussle-cap and chuck-farthing—there is not such another pipe in the county—So that the commodore lives very happy in his own manner; thof he be sometimes thrown into perilous passions and quandaries, by the application of his poor kinsmen, whom he can't abide, because as how some of them were the first occasion of his going to sea. Then he sweats with agony at the sight of an attorney; just for all the world, as some people have an antipathy at a cat; for it seems he was once at law, for striking one of his officers, and cast in a swinging sum. He is, more-over, exceedingly afflicted with goblins that disturb his rest, and keep such a racket in his house, that you would think (God bless us!) all the devils in hell had broke loose upon him. It was no longer ago than last year about this time, that he was tormented the live-long night by two mischievous spirits that got into his chamber, and played a thousand pranks about his hammock, (for there is not one bed within his walls.) Well, Sir, he rung his bell, called up all his servants, got lights, and made a thorough search; but the devil a goblin was to be found. He had no sooner turned in again, and the rest of the family gone to sleep, than the foul fiends began their game anew. The commodore got up in the dark, drew his cutlass, and attacked them both so manfully, that, in five minutes, every thing in the apartment went to pieces. The lieutenant hearing the noise, came to his assistance; and Tom Pipes being told what was the matter, lighted his match, and going down to the yard, fired all the patereroes, as signals of distress. Well, to be sure, the whole parish was in a pucker: some thought the French had landed; others imagined the commodore's house was beset by thieves: for my own part, I called up two dragoons that are quartered upon me;

and they swore with deadly oaths, it was a gang of smugglers engaged with a party of their regiment that lies in the next village; and mounting their horses like lusty fellows, rode up into the country as fast as their beasts could carry them. Ah, Master! these are hard times, when an industrious body cannot earn his bread, without fear of the gallows. Your worship's father (God rest his soul!) was a good gentleman, and as well respected in this parish, as e'er a he that walks upon neat's leather. And if your honour should want a small parcel of fine tea, or a few anchors of right Nantz,[1] I'll be bound you shall be furnished to your heart's content. But, as I was saying, the hubbub continued till morning, when the parson being sent for, conjured the spirits into the Red Sea; and the house has been pretty quiet ever since. True it is, Mr. Hatchway makes a mock of the whole affair; and told his commander in this very blessed spot, that the two goblins were no other than a couple of jackdaws which had fallen down the chimney, and made a flapping with their wings up and down the apartment. But the commodore, who is very choleric, and does not like to be jeered, fell into a main high passion, and stormed like a perfect hurricane, swearing that he knew a devil from a jackdaw as well as e'er a man in the three kingdoms. He owned, indeed, that the birds were found, but denied that they were the occasion of the uproar. For my own part, Master, I believe much may be said on both sides of the question; thof to be sure, the devil is always going about, as the saying is.'

This circumstantial account, extraordinary as it was, never altered one feature in the countenance of Mr. Pickle, who having heard it to an end, took the pipe from his mouth, saying, with a look of infinite sagacity and deliberation, 'I do suppose he is of the Cornish Trunnions. What sort of a woman is his spouse?' 'Spouse! (cried the other) odd's heart! I don't think he would marry the queen of Sheba. Lack a day! Sir, he won't suffer his own maids to lie in the garrison, but turns them into an out-house, every night, before the watch is set. Bless your honour's soul! he is, as it were, a very oddish kind of a gentleman. Your worship would have seen him before now; for, when he is well, he and my good master Hatchway come hither every evening, and drink a couple of canns of rumbo apiece; but he has been confined to his house this fortnight, by a plaguy fit of the gout, which, I'll assure your worship, is a good penny out of my pocket.'

At that instant, Mr. Pickle's ears were saluted with such a strange noise, as even discomposed the muscles of his face, which gave immediate indications of alarm. This composition of notes at first resembled the crying of quails, and croaking of bull-frogs; but, as it approached nearer, he could distinguish articulate sounds pronounced with great violence, in such a cadence as one would expect from a human creature scolding thro' the organs of an ass. It was neither speaking nor braying, but a surprising mixture of both, employed in the utterance of terms absolutely unintelligible to our wondering merchant, who had just opened his mouth to express his curiosity, when the landlord, starting up at the well known sound, cried, 'Odd's niggers! there is the commodore with his company, as sure as I live!' and with his apron began to wipe the dust off an elbow-chair placed at one side of the fire, and kept sacred for the ease and convenience of this infirm commander. While he was thus occupied, a voice still more uncouth than the former, bawled aloud, 'Ho! the house, a hoy!' Upon which the publican, clapping an hand to each side of his head, with his thumbs fixed on his ears, rebellowed in the same tone, which he had learned to imitate, 'Hilloah.' The voice again exclaimed, 'Have you got any attorneys aboard?' and when the landlord replied, 'No, no;' this man of strange expectation came in, supported by his two dependants, and displayed a figure every way answerable to the oddity of his character. He was in stature at least six feet high, tho' he had contracted an habit of stooping, by living so long on board; his complexion was tawny, and his aspect rendered hideous by a large scar across his nose, and a patch that covered the place of one eye. Being seated in his chair, with great formality the landlord complimented him upon his being able to come abroad again; and having, in a whisper, communicated the name of his fellow-guest, whom the commodore already knew by report, went to prepare, with all imaginable dispatch, the first allowance of his favourite liquor, in three separate canns, (for each was accommodated with his own portion apart) while the lieutenant sat down on the blind-side of his commander; and Tom Pipes, knowing his distance, with great modesty took his station in the rear. After a pause of some minutes, the conversation was begun by this ferocious chief, who fixing his eye upon the lieutenant with a sternness of countenance not to be described, addressed him in these words: 'D—n my eyes! Hatchway, I always took you to be a better seaman than to overset our chaise in such fair weather. Blood! didn't I tell you we were running bump ashore, and bid you set in the lee-brace, and haul upon a wind?' 'Yes, (replied the other with an arch sneer) I do confess as how you did give such orders, after you had run us foul of a post, so as that the carriage lay along, and could not right herself.'

7

'I run you foul of a post! (cried the commander) d—n my heart! you're a pretty dog, an't you, to tell me so above board to my face? Did I take charge of the chaise? Did I stand at the helm?' 'No; (answered Hatchway) that I must confess you did not steer; but howsomever, you cunned all the way, and so, as you could not see how the land lay, being blind of your larboard eye, we were fast ashore, before you knew any thing of the matter. Pipes, who stood abaft, can testify the truth of what I say.' 'D—n my limbs! (resumed the commodore) I don't value what you or Pipes says, a rope yarn. You're a couple of mutinous——I'll say no more; but, you shan't run your rig upon me. Damn ye, I am the man that learnt you, Jack Hatchway, to splice a rope, and raise a perpendicular.'

The lieutenant, who was perfectly well acquainted with the trim of his captain, did not chuse to carry on the altercation any farther; but, taking up his cann, drank to the health of the stranger, who very courteously returned the compliment, without, however, presuming to join in the conversation, which suffered a considerable pause. During this interruption, Mr. Hatchway's wit display'd itself in several practical jokes upon the commodore, with whom, he knew, it was dangerous to tamper in any other way. Being without the sphere of his vision, he securely pilfered his tobacco, drank his rumbo, made wry faces, and (to use the vulgar phrase) cocked his eye at him, to the no small entertainment of the spectators, Mr. Pickle himself not excepted, who gave evident tokens of uncommon satisfaction at the dexterity of this marine pantomime.

Mean while, the captain's choler gradually subsided, and he was pleased to desire Hatchway by the familiar and friendly diminutive of Jack, to read a news-paper that lay on the table before him. This task was accordingly undertaken by the lame lieutenant, who, among other paragraphs, read that which follows, with an elevation of voice that seemed to prognosticate something extraordinary. 'We are informed that admiral Bower[1] will very soon be created a British peer, for his eminent services during the war, particularly in his late engagement with the French fleet.' Trunnion was thunderstruck at this piece of intelligence. The mug dropt from his hand, and shivered into a thousand pieces; his eye glistened like that of a rattle-snake, and some minutes elapsed before he could pronounce, 'Avast! overhaul that article again.' It was no sooner read the second time, than smiting the table with his fist, he started up, and with the most violent emphasis of rage and indignation, exclaimed, 'D—n my heart and liver! 'tis a land lie, d'ye see; and I will maintain it to be a lie, from the sprit sail-yard to the mizzen

8

top-sail haulyards! blood and thunder! Will. Bower a peer of this realm! a fellow of yesterday, that scarce knows a mast from a manger; a snotty-nose boy, whom I myself have ordered to the gun, for stealing eggs out of the hen-coops! and I, Hawser Trunnion, who commanded a ship before he could keep a reckoning, am laid aside, d'ye see, and forgotten! If so be, as this be the case, there is a rotten plank in our constitution, which ought to be hove down and repaired, damn my eyes! For my own part, d'ye see, I was none of your Guinea-pigs; I did not rise in the service by parliamenteering interest, or a handsome bitch of a wife. I was not hoisted over the bellies of better men, nor strutted athwart the quarter-deck in a laced doublet and thingumbobs at the wrists. Damn my limbs! I have been a hard-working man, and served all offices on board from cook's shifter to the command of a vessel. Here, you Tunley, there's the hand of a seaman, you dog.' So saying, he laid hold on the landlord's fist, and honoured him with such a squeeze, as compelled him to roar with great vociferation, to the infinite satisfaction of the commodore, whose features were a little unbended, by this acknowledgment of his vigour; and he thus proceeded in a less outrageous strain: 'They make a damned noise about this engagement with the French: but, agad! it was no more than a bum-boat battle, in comparison with some that I have seen. There was old Rook and Jennings,[1] and another whom I'll be damned before I name, that knew what fighting was. As for my own share, d'ye see, I am none of those that hollow in their own commendation: but if so be that I were minded to stand my own trumpeter, some of those little fellows that hold their heads so high, would be taken all aback, as the saying is; they would be ashamed to shew their colours, d—n my eyes! I once lay eight glasses along-side of the Floor de Louse,[1] a French man of war, tho' her metal was heavier, and her complement larger by an hundred hands than mine. You, Jack Hatchway, damn ye, what d'ye grin at? D'ye think I tell a story, because you never heard it before?'

'Why, look ye, Sir, (answered the lieutenant) I'm glad to find you can stand your own trumpeter, on occasion; thof I wish you would change the tune; for that is the same you have been piping every watch, for these ten months past. Tunley himself will tell you, he has heard it five hundred times.' 'God forgive you, Mr. Hatchway; (said the landlord, interrupting him) as I'm an honest man, and a housekeeper, I never heard a syllab of the matter.'

This declaration, tho' not strictly true, was extremely agreeable to Mr. Trunnion, who, with an air of triumph, observed, 'Aha!

Jack, I thought I should bring you up, with your gibes and your jokes. But suppose you had heard it before, is that any reason why it shouldn't be told to another person? There's the stranger, belike he has heard it five hundred times too; han't ye, brother?' addressing himself to Mr. Pickle; who, replying with a look expressing curiosity, 'No, never;' he thus went on: 'Well, you seem to be an honest, quiet sort of a man; and therefore, you must know, as I said before, I fell in with a French man of war, Cape Finisterre bearing about six leagues on the weather-bow, and the chace three leagues to leeward, going before the wind: whereupon I set my studding-sails, and coming up with her, hoisted my jack and ensign, and poured in a whole broadside, before you could count three rattlins in the mizzen shrouds; for I always keep a good look-out, and love to have the first fire.' 'That I'll be sworn; (said Hatchway) for the day we made the Triumph, you ordered the men to fire, when she was hull-to, by the same token we below pointed the guns at a flight of gulls; and I won a cann of punch from the gunner, by killing the first bird.' Exasperated at this sarcasm, he replied with great vehemence, 'You lie, lubber! d—n your bones! what business have you to come always athwart my hawse in this manner? You, Pipes, was upon deck, and can bear witness, whether or not I fired too soon. Speak, you blood of a —— and that upon the word of a sea-man: how did the chace bear of us, when I gave orders to fire?'

Pipes, who hitherto had sat silent, being thus called upon to give his evidence, after diverse strange gesticulations, opened his mouth like a gasping cod, and with a cadence like that of the east wind singing through a cranny, pronounced, 'Half a quarter of a league right upon our lee-beam.' 'Nearer, you porpuss-fac'd swab! (cried the commodore) nearer by twelve fathom: but, howsomever, that's enough to prove the falsehood of Hatchway's jaw—and so, brother, d'ye see, (turning to Mr. Pickle) I lay along-side of the Floor de Louse, yard-arm and yard-arm, plying our great guns and small arms, and heaving in stink-pots, powder-bottles, and hand-grenades, till our shot was all expended, double-headed, partridge and grape: then we loaded with iron crows, marlin spikes, and old nails, but finding the Frenchman took a great deal of drubbing, and that he had shot away all our rigging, and killed and wounded a great number of our men, d'ye see, I resolved to run him on board upon his quarter, and so ordered our grapplings to be got ready; but Monsieur perceiving what we were about, filled his topsails and sheered off, leaving us like a log upon the water, and our scuppers running with blood.'

Chapter II

Mr. Pickle and the landlord paid such extraordinary attention to the rehearsal of this exploit, that Trunnion was encouraged to entertain them with more stories of the same nature, after which he observed by way of encomium on the government, that all he had gained in the service was a lame foot and the loss of an eye. The lieutenant, who could not find in his heart to lose any opportunity of being witty at the expence of his commander, gave a loose to his satirical talent once more, saying, 'I have heard as how you came by your lame foot, by having your upper-decks overstowed with liquor, whereby you became crank, and rolled, d'ye see, in such a manner, that by a pitch of the ship, your starboard heel was jammed in one of the scuppers; and as for the matter of your eye, that was knocked out by your own crew when the Lightning was paid off: there's poor Pipes, who was beaten into all the colours of the rainbow for taking your part, and giving you time to sheer off; and I don't find as how you have rewarded him according as he deserves.' As the commodore could not deny the truth of these anecdotes, however unseasonably they were introduced, he affected to receive them with good humour, as jokes of the lieutenant's own inventing; and reply'd, 'Ay, ay, Jack, every body knows your tongue is no slander; but, howsomever, I'll work you to an oil for this, you dog.' So saying, he lifted up one of his crutches, intending to lay it gently a-cross Mr. Hatchway's pate; but, Jack, with great agility, tilted up his wooden leg, with which he warded off the blow, to the no small admiration of Mr. Pickle, and utter astonishment of the landlord, who, by the bye, had expressed the same amazement, at the same feat, at the same hour, every night, for three months before. Trunnion then directing his eye to the boatswain's mate, 'You, Pipes, (said he) do you go about and tell people that I did not reward you for standing by me, when I was hussled by those rebellious rapscallions; damn you, ha'n't you been rated on the books ever since?' Tom, who indeed had no words to spare, sat smoking his pipe with great indifference, and never dreamed of paying any regard to these interrogations, which being repeated and reinforced with many oaths, that (however) produced no effect, the commodore pulled out his purse, saying, 'Here, you bitch's baby, here's something better than a smart ticket;' and threw it at his silent deliverer, who received and pocketed his bounty, without the least demonstration of surprize or satisfaction; while the donor turning to Mr. Pickle, 'You see brother, (said he) I make good the old saying, we sailors get money like horses, and spend it like asses; come, Pipes, let's have the boatswain's whistle, and be jovial.'

This musician accordingly, applied to his mouth the silver instrument that hung at a button-hole of his jacket, by a chain of the same metal, and though not quite so ravishing as the pipe of Hermes, produced a sound so loud and shrill, that the stranger (as it were instinctively) stopped his ears, to preserve his organs of hearing from such a dangerous invasion. The prelude being thus executed, Pipes fixed his eyes upon the egg of an ostrich that depended from the ceiling, and without once moving them from that object, performed the whole cantata in a tone of voice that seemed to be the joint issue of an Irish bagpipe, and a sow-gelder's horn; the commodore, the lieutenant and landlord joined in the chorus, repeating this elegant stanza,

> Bustle, bustle, brave boys!
> Let us sing, let us toil,
> And drink all the while,
> Since labour's the price of our joys.[1]

The third line was no sooner pronounced, than the cann was lifted to every man's mouth with admirable uniformity; and the next word taken up at the end of their draught, with a twang equally expressive and harmonious. In short, the company began to understand one another; Mr. Pickle seemed to relish the entertainment, and a correspondence immediately commenced between him and Trunnion, who shook him by the hand, drank to further acquaintance, and even invited him to a mess of pork and pease in the garrison. The compliment was returned, good fellowship prevailed, and the night was pretty far advanced, when the merchant's man arrived with a lanthorn to light his master home; upon which, the new friends parted, after a mutual promise of meeting next evening in the same place.

CHAPTER III

Mrs. Grizzle exerts herself in finding a Proper Match
for her Brother ; who is accordingly introduced to the
Young Lady whom he marries in due Season

I HAVE been the more circumstantial in opening the character of Trunnion, because he bears a considerable share in the course of these memoirs; but, now it is high time to resume the consideration of Mrs. Grizzle, who, since her arrival in the country, had been engrossed by a double care, namely, that of finding a suitable match for her brother, and a comfortable yoke-fellow for herself.

Neither was this aim the result of any sinister or frail suggestion, but the pure dictates of that laudable ambition, which prompted her to the preservation of the family name. Nay, so disinterested was she in this pursuit, that, postponing her nearest concern, or at least leaving her own fate to the silent operation of her charms, she laboured with such indefatigable zeal in behalf of her brother, that before they had been three months settled in the country, the general topick of conversation in the neighbourhood, was an intended match between the rich Mr. Pickle and the fair miss Appleby, daughter of a gentleman who lived in the next parish, and who, though he had but little fortune to bestow upon his children, had (to use his own phrase) replenished their veins with some of the best blood in the county.

This young lady, whose character and disposition Mrs. Grizzle had investigated to her own satisfaction, was destined for the spouse of Mr. Pickle, and an overture accordingly made to her father, who being overjoyed at the proposal, gave his consent without hesitation, and even recommended the immediate execution of the project with such eagerness, as seemed to indicate either a suspicion of Mr. Pickle's constancy, or a diffidence of his own daughter's complexion, which, perhaps, he thought too sanguine, to keep much longer cool. The previous point being thus settled, our merchant, at the instigation of Mrs. Grizzle, went to visit his future father-in-law, and was introduced to the daughter, with whom he had, that same afternoon, an opportunity of being alone. What passed in that interview, I never could learn, though from the character of the suitor, the reader may justly conclude that she was not much teized with the impertinence of his addresses. He was not, I believe, the less welcome for that reason; certain it is, she made no objection to his taciturnity, and when her father communicated his resolution, acquiesced with the most pious resignation. But, Mrs. Grizzle, in order to give the lady a more favourable idea of his intellects than what his conversation could possibly inspire, was resolved to dictate a letter, which her brother should transcribe and transmit to his mistress, as the produce of his own understanding; and had actually composed a very tender billet for this purpose; yet her intention was intirely frustrated by the misapprehension of the lover himself, who, in consequence of his sister's repeated admonitions, anticipated her scheme, by writing for himself, and dispatching the letter one afternoon, while Mrs. Grizzle was visiting at the parson's.

Neither was this step the effect of his vanity or precipitation; but having been often assured by his sister, that it was absolutely necessary for him to make a declaration of his love in writing, he took this opportunity of acting in conformity to her advice, when his imagination was unengaged or undisturbed by any other suggestion, without suspecting in the least, that she intended to save him the trouble of exercising his own genius. Left, therefore, as he imagined, to his own inventions, he sat down and produced the following morceau, which was transmitted to miss Appleby, before his sister and counsellor had the least intimation of the affair.

Miss SALLY APPLEBY,

Madam,

Understanding you have a parcel of heart, warranted sound, to be disposed of, shall be willing to treat for said commodity, on reasonable terms; doubt not, shall agree for same; shall wait of you for further information, when and where you shall appoint. This the needful from

Yours, &c.

GAM. PICKLE

This laconic epistle, simple and unadorned as it was, met with as cordial a reception from the person to whom it was addressed, as if it had been couched in the most elegant terms that delicacy of passion and cultivated genius could supply: nay, I believe, was the more welcome, on account of its mercantile plainness; because when an advantageous match is in view, a sensible woman often considers the flowery professions and rapturous exclamations of love, as ensnaring ambiguities, or at best impertinent preliminaries, that retard the treaty they are designed to promote: whereas Mr. Pickle removed all disagreeable uncertainty, by descending at once to the most interesting particular.

She had no sooner, as a dutiful child, communicated this billet-doux to her father, than he as a careful parent visited Mr. Pickle, and in presence of Mrs. Grizzle, demanded a formal explanation of his sentiments with regard to his daughter Sally. Mr. Gamaliel, without any ceremony, assured him he had a respect for the young woman, and with his good leave, would take her for better for worse; and Mr. Appleby, after having expressed his satisfaction that he had fixed his affections in his family, and comforted the lover with the assurance of his being agreeable to the young lady, they forthwith proceeded to the articles of the marriage-settlement, which being discussed and determined, a lawyer was ordered to engross them; the wedding cloaths were bought, and in short, a day was appointed for the celebration of their nuptials, to which every body of any fashion in the neighbourhood was invited. Among these commodore Trunnion and Mr. Hatchway were not forgotten, being the sole companions of the bridegroom, with whom, by this time, they had contracted a sort of intimacy at their nocturnal rendezvous.

They had received a previous intimation of what was on the anvil, from the landlord, before Mr. Pickle thought proper to declare himself; in consequence of which, the topick of the one-eyed commander's discourse at their meeting for several evenings before, had been the folly and plague of matrimony, on which he held forth with great vehemence of abuse, levelled at the fair sex, whom he represented as devils incarnate sent from hell, to torment mankind; and in particular, inveighed against old maids, for whom he seemed to entertain a singular aversion; while his friend Jack confirmed the truth of all his allegations, and gratified his own malignant vein at the same time, by clenching every sentence with a sly joke upon the married state, built upon some allusion to a ship or sea-faring life. He compared a woman to a great gun loaded with fire, brimstone and noise, which being violently heated, will bounce and fly, and play the devil, if you don't take special care of her breechings. He said she was like a hurricane that never blows from one quarter, but veers about to all points of the compass: he likened her to a painted galley curiously rigged, with a leak in her hold, which her husband would never be able to stop. He observed that her inclinations were like the Bay of Biscay; for why? because you may heave your deep sea lead long enough, without ever reaching the bottom. That he who comes to an anchor on a wife, may find himself moored in damned foul ground, and after all, can't for his blood slip his cable; and that for his own part, thof he might make short trips for pastime, he would never embark in woman on the voyage of life, because he was afraid of foundering in the first foul weather.

In all probability, these insinuations made some impression on the mind of Mr. Pickle, who was not very much inclined to run great risks of any kind; but the injunctions and importunities of his sister, who was bent upon the match, overbalanced the opinion of his sea friends, who finding him determined to marry, notwithstanding all the hints of caution they had thrown out, resolved to accept his invitation, and honoured his nuptials with their presence accordingly.

CHAPTER IV

The Behaviour of Mrs. Grizzle at the Wedding, with an Account of the Guests

I HOPE it will not be thought uncharitable, if I advance by way of conjecture, that Mrs. Grizzle, on this grand occasion, summoned her whole exertion, to play off the artillery of her charms, upon the single gentlemen who were invited to the entertainment: sure I am, she displayed to the best advantage all the engaging qualities she possessed: her affability at dinner was altogether uncommon, her attention to the guests was superfluously hospitable, her tongue was sheathed with a most agreeable and infantine lisp, her address was perfectly obliging; and though, conscious of the extraordinary capacity of her mouth, she would not venture to hazard a laugh, she modelled her lips into an enchanting simper, which played upon her countenance all day long; nay, she even profited by that defect in her vision we have already observed, and securely contemplated those features which were most to her likeing, while the rest of the company believed her regards were disposed in a quite contrary direction. With what humility of complaisance did she receive the compliments of those who could not help praising the elegance of the banquet! and how piously did she seize that opportunity of commemorating the honours of her sire, by observing that it was no merit in her to understand something of entertainments, as she had occasion to preside at so many, during the mayoralty of her papa! Far from discovering the least symptom of pride and exultation, when the opulence of her family became the subject of conversation, she assumed a severity of countenance; and after having moralized on the vanity of riches, declared that those who looked upon her as a fortune, were very much mistaken; for her father had left her no more than poor five thousand pounds, which, with what little she had saved of the interest since his death, was all she had to depend upon: indeed, if she had placed her chief felicity in wealth, she should not have been so forward in destroying her own expectations, by advising and promoting the event at which they were now so happily assembled; but she hoped she should always have virtue enough to postpone any interested consideration, when it should happen to clash with the happiness of her friends. Finally, such was her modesty and self-denial, that she industriously informed those whom it might concern, that she was no less than three years older than the bride; though had she added ten to the reckoning, she would have committed no mistake in point of computation.

To contribute as much as lay in her power to the satisfaction of all present, she in the afternoon regaled them with a tune on the harpsichord, accompanied with her voice, which, though not the most melodious in the world, I dare say, would have been equally at their service, could she have vyed with Philomel in song; and as the last effort of her complaisance when dancing was proposed, she was prevailed upon, at the request of her new sister, to open the ball in person.

In a word, Mrs. Grizzle was the principal figure in this festival, and almost eclipsed the bride, who far from seeming to dispute the preheminence, very wisely allowed her to make the best of her talents; contenting herself with the lot to which fortune had already called her, and which she imagined would not be the less desirable, if her sister-in-law were detached from the family.

I believe I need scarce advertise the reader, that during this whole entertainment, the commodore and his lieutenant were quite out of their element; and this indeed, was the case with the bridegroom himself, who being utterly unacquainted with any sort of polite commerce, found himself under a very disagreeable restraint during the whole scene.

Trunnion, who had scarce ever been on shore till he was paid off, and never once in his whole life, in the company of any females above the rank of those who herd upon the point at Portsmouth, was more embarrassed about his behaviour than if he had been surrounded at sea by the whole French navy. He had never pronounced the word *Madam* since he was born, so that far from entering into conversation with the ladies, he would not even return the compliment, or give the least nod of civility when they drank to his health; and I verily believe, would rather have suffered suffocation, than allowed the simple phrase, *your servant*, to proceed from his mouth. He was altogether as inflexible with respect to the attitudes of his body; for, either through obstinacy or bashfulness, he sat upright without motion, insomuch that he provoked the mirth of a certain wag, who addressing himself to the lieutenant, asked whether that was the commodore himself, or the wooden lion that used to stand at his gate? An image to which, it must be owned, Mr. Trunnion's person bore no faint resemblance.

Mr. Hatchway, who was not quite so unpolished as the commodore, and had certain notions that seemed to approach the ideas of common life, made a less uncouth appearance; but then he was a wit, and though of a very peculiar genius, partook largely of that disposition which is common to all wits, who never enjoy themselves, except when their talents meet with those marks of distinction and veneration, which (in their own opinion) they deserve.

These circumstances being premised, it is not to be wondered at, if this triumvirate made no objections to the proposal, when some of the grave personages of the company made a motion for adjourning into another apartment, where they might enjoy their pipes and bottles, while the young folks indulged themselves in the continuance of their own favourite diversion. Thus rescued, as it were, from a state of annihilation, the first use the two lads of the castle made of their existence, was to ply the bridegroom so hard with bumpers, that in less than an hour he made divers efforts to sing, and soon after was carried to bed, deprived of all manner of sensation, to the utter disappointment of the bridemen and maids, who, by this accident, were prevented from throwing the stocking, and performing certain other ceremonies practised on such occasions. As for the bride, she bore this misfortune with great good humour, and indeed, on all occasions, behaved like a discreet woman, perfectly well acquainted with the nature of her own situation.

CHAPTER V

Mrs. Pickle assumes the Reins of Government in her own Family; her Sister-in-law undertakes an Enterprize of Great Moment; but is for some time diverted from her Purpose, by a very interesting Consideration

WHATEVER deference, not to say submission, she had paid to Mrs. Grizzle before she was so nearly allied to her family, she no sooner became Mrs. Pickle, than she thought it incumbent upon her to act up to the dignity of the character; and the very day after the marriage, ventured to dispute with her sister-in-law on the subject of her own pedigree, which she affirmed to be more honourable in all respects than that of her husband; observing that several younger brothers of her house had arrived at the station of lord mayor of London, which was the highest pitch of greatness that any of Mr. Pickle's predecessors had ever attained.

This presumption was like a thunderbolt to Mrs. Grizzle, who began to perceive that she had not succeeded quite so well as she imagined, in selecting for her brother a gentle and obedient yoke-fellow, who would always treat her with that profound respect which she thought due to her superior genius, and be entirely regulated by her advice and direction: however, she still continued to manage the reins of government in the house, reprehending the servants as usual; an office she performed with great capacity, and in which she seemed to take singular delight, until Mrs. Pickle, on pretence of consulting her ease, told her one day she would take that trouble upon herself, and for the future assume the management of her own family. Nothing could be more mortifying to Mrs. Grizzle than such a declaration, to which, after a considerable pause, and strange distortion of look, she replied, 'I shall never refuse or repine at any trouble that may conduce to my brother's advantage.' 'Dear madam,' answered the sister, 'I am infinitely obliged to your kind concern for Mr. Pickle's interest, which I consider as my own, but I cannot bear to see you a sufferer by your friendship; and therefore, insist upon exempting you from the fatigue you have borne so long.'

In vain did the other protest that she took pleasure in the task; Mrs. Pickle ascribed the assurance to her excess of complaisance, and expressed such tenderness of zeal for her dear sister's health and tranquillity, that the reluctant maiden found herself obliged to resign her authority, without enjoying the least pretext for complaining of her being deposed.

This disgrace was attended by a fit of peevish devotion that lasted three or four weeks; during which period, she had the additional chagreen of seeing the young lady gain an absolute ascendency over the mind of her brother, who was persuaded to set up a gay equipage, and improve his housekeeping, by an augmentation in his expence, to the amount of a thousand a year at least: tho' this alteration in the oeconomy of his houshold, effected no change in his own disposition, or manner of life; for, soon as the painful ceremony of receiving and returning visits was performed, he had recourse again to the company of his sea-friends, with whom he spent the best part of his time. But, if he was satisfied with his condition, the case was otherwise with Mrs. Grizzle, who finding her importance in the family greatly diminished, her attractions neglected by all the male-sex in the neighbourhood, and the withering hand of time hang threatning over her head, began to feel the horror of eternal virginity, and in a sort of desperation, resolved at any rate to rescue herself from that reproachful and uncomfortable situation. Thus determined, she formed a plan, the execution of which, to a spirit less enterprizing and sufficient than her's, would have appeared altogether impracticable; this was no other than to make a conquest of the commodore's heart, which the reader will easily believe was not very susceptible of tender impressions; but, on the contrary, fortified with insensibility and prejudice against the charms of the whole sex, and particularly prepossessed to the prejudice of that class distinguished by the appellation of old maids, in which Mrs. Grizzle was, by this time, unhappily ranked. She nevertheless took the field, and having invested this seemingly impregnable fortress, began to break ground one day, when Trunnion dined at her brother's, by springing certain ensnaring commendations on the honesty and sincerity of sea-faring people, paying a particular attention to his place, and affecting a simper of approbation at every thing he said which by any means she could construe into a joke, or with modesty be supposed to hear: nay, even when he left decency on the left hand, (which was often the case) she ventured to reprimand his freedom of speech with a gracious grin, saying, 'Sure you gentlemen belonging to the sea have such an odd way with you.' But, all this complacency was so ineffectual, that, far from suspecting the true cause of it, the commodore, that very evening, at the club, in presence of her brother, with whom, by this time, he could take any manner of freedom, did not scruple to damn her for a squinting, block-faced, chattering piss-kitchen; and immediately after drank despair to all old maids; a toast which Mr. Pickle pledged without the least hesitation, and next day intimated to his sister, who bore the indignity with surprising resignation, and did not therefore desist from her scheme, unpromising as it seemed to be, until her attention was called off, and engaged in another care, which, for some time, interrupted the progress of this design. Her sister had not been married many months, when she exhibited evident symptoms of pregnancy, to the general satisfaction of all concerned, and the inexpressible joy of Mrs. Grizzle, who (as we have already hinted) was more interested

Chapter V

in the preservation of the family-name, than in any other consideration whatever. She therefore no sooner discovered appearances to
justify and confirm her hopes, than postponing her own purpose,
and laying aside that pique and resentment she had conceived from
the behaviour of Mrs. Pickle, when she superseded her authority;
or perhaps, considering her in no other light than that of the vehicle
which contained, and was destined to convey her brother's heir to
light, she determined to exert her uttermost in nursing, tending,
and cherishing her, during the term of her important charge. With
this view she purchased Culpepper's midwifery,[1] which, with that
sagacious performance dignified with Aristotle's name, she studied
with indefatigable care, and diligently perused the Compleat
House-wife, together with Quincy's dispensatory,[2] culling every
jelly, marmalade and conserve which these authors recommend as
either salutory or toothsome, for the benefit and comfort of her
sister-in-law, during her gestation. She restricted her from eating
roots, pot-herbs, fruit, and all sort of vegetables; and one day when
Mrs. Pickle had plucked a peach with her own hand, and was in
the very act of putting it between her teeth, Mrs. Grizzle perceived
the rash attempt, and running up to her, fell upon her knees in the
garden, intreating her, with tears in her eyes, to resist such a pernicious appetite. Her request was no sooner complied with, than
recollecting that if her sister's longing was baulked, the child might
be affected with some disagreeable mark, or deplorable disease,
she begged as earnestly that she would swallow the fruit, and in the
mean time ran for some cordial water of her own composing, which
she forced upon her sister, as an antidote to the poison she had
received.

This excessive zeal and tenderness did not fail to be very troublesome to Mrs. Pickle, who having revolved divers plans for the
recovery of her own ease, at length determined to engage Mrs.
Grizzle in such employment as would interrupt that close attendance
which she found so teizing and disagreeable. Neither did she wait
long for an opportunity of putting her resolution in practice. The
very next day, a gentleman happening to dine with Mr. Pickle,
unfortunately mentioned a pine-apple, part of which he had eaten
a week before at the house of a nobleman who lived in another part
of the country, at the distance of an hundred miles at least.

The name of this fatal fruit was no sooner pronounced, than
Mrs. Grizzle, who incessantly watched her sister's looks, took the
alarm, because she thought they gave certain indications of curiosity
and desire; and after having observed that she herself never could

eat pine-apples, which were altogether unnatural productions, extorted by the force of artificial fire, out of filthy manure, asked with a faltering voice, if Mrs. Pickle was not of her way of thinking? This young lady, who wanted neither slyness nor penetration, at once divined her meaning, and replied with seeming unconcern, that for her own part she should never repine, if there was not a pine-apple in the universe, provided she could indulge herself with the fruits of her own country.

This answer, which was calculated for the benefit of the stranger, who would certainly have suffered for his imprudence by the resentment of Mrs. Grizzle, had her sister expressed the least relish for the fruit in question: I say, this answer had the desired effect, and re-established the peace of the company, which was not a little endangered by the gentleman's want of consideration. Next morning, however, after breakfast, the pregnant lady, in pursuance of her plan, yawned (as it were by accident) full in the face of her maiden sister, who being infinitely disturbed by this convulsion, affirmed it was a symptom of longing; and insisted upon knowing the object in desire, when Mrs. Pickle affecting an affected smile, told her she had eaten a most delicious pine-apple in her sleep. This declaration was attended with an immediate scream uttered by Mrs. Grizzle, who instantly perceiving her sister surprized at the exclamation, clasped her in her arms, and assured her, with a sort of hysterical laugh, importing horror rather than delight,[1] that she could not help screaming with joy, because she had it in her power to gratify her dear sister's wish; a lady in the neighbourhood having promised to send her, in a present, a couple of fine pine-apples, which she would that very day go in quest of.

Mrs. Pickle would by no means consent to this proposal, on pretence of sparing the other unnecessary fatigue; and assured her, that if she had any desire to eat a pine-apple, it was so faint, that the disappointment could produce no bad consequence. But this assurance was conveyed in a manner (which she knew very well how to adopt) that instead of dissuading, rather stimulated Mrs. Grizzle to set out immediately, not on a visit to that lady, whose promise she herself had feigned with a view of consulting her sister's tranquillity, but on a random search thro' the whole county for this unlucky fruit, which was like to produce so much vexation and prejudice to her and her father's house.

During three whole days and nights, did she, attended by a valet, ride from place to place without success, unmindful of her health, and careless of her reputation, that began to suffer from the nature of her inquiry, which was pursued with such peculiar eagerness and distraction, that every body with whom she conversed, looked upon her as an unhappy person, whose intellects were not a little disordered.

Baffled in all her researches within the county, she at length resolved to visit that very nobleman, at whose house the officious stranger had been (for her) so unfortunately regaled, and actually arrived in a post-chaise at the place of his habitation, where she introduced her business as an affair on which the happiness of a whole family depended.[1] But, alas! she had come too late; his lordship lamented, in very polite and pathetic terms, that he was disabled from exerting his humanity, and enjoying the pleasure he should feel in contributing to the happiness of his fellow-creatures, at such an easy rate; telling her, that he had unluckily, the very day before, sent the two last pine-apples his garden had produced, in a present to a certain lady in the neighbourhood.

Mrs. Grizzle was so affected with this explanation, that she fainted away, and was immediately carried to the public house, where she had left her horses, and where she remained inconsolable for the disappointment, which in all likelihood would have proved more fatal to her than to the person for whom she was so piously concerned, had not she in the evening, by the medium of her own servant, received a hint from the nobleman's gardener, that for five pieces she should be furnished with a couple of as fine apples as ever were seen in England. The terms (I scarce need say) were greedily embraced, the fruit secured in her possession; and she departed that very night on her return to her brother's house, where she safely arrived with her acquisition, and was most cordially received by her sister, who had been under some apprehensions on her account. Neither was his lordship forgotten in Mrs. Grizzle's benediction, when she understood from the valet who accompanied her, that he had, with his own eyes, seen above an hundred pine-apples ripe for cutting in his garden the evening of that very day on which he had assured her that there was not one left.

CHAPTER VI

Mrs. Grizzle is indefatigable in gratifying
her Sister's Longings. Peregrine is born,
and managed contrary to the Directions and
Remonstrances of his Aunt, who is
disgusted upon that Account ; and resumes the Plan
which she had before rejected

THE success of this device would have encouraged Mrs. Pickle to
practise more of the same sort upon her sister-in-law, had she not
been deterred by a violent fever which seized her zealous ally, in
consequence of the fatigue and uneasiness she had undergone;
which, while it lasted, as effectually conduced to her repose, as any
other stratagem she could invent. But Mrs. Grizzle's health was no
sooner restored, than the other being as much incommoded as ever,
was obliged, in her own defence, to have recourse to some other
contrivance; and managed her artifices in such a manner, as leaves
it at this day a doubt whether she was really so whimsical and capricious in her appetites as she herself pretended to be; for her longings
were not restricted to the demands of the palate and stomach, but
also affected all the other organs of sense, and even invaded her
imagination, which at this period seemed to be strangely diseased.

One time she longed to pinch her husband's ear; and it was with
infinite difficulty that his sister could prevail upon him to undergo
the operation. Yet this task was easy, in comparison with another
she undertook for the gratification of Mrs. Pickle's unaccountable
desire; which was no other than to persuade the commodore to
submit his chin to the mercy of the big-bellied lady, who ardently
wished for an opportunity of plucking three black hairs from his
beard. When this proposal was first communicated to Mr. Trunnion by the husband, his answer was nothing but a dreadful effusion of oaths, accompanied with such a stare, and delivered in such
a tone of voice, as terrified the poor beseecher into immediate
silence; so that Mrs. Grizzle was fain to take the whole enterprize
upon herself, and next day went to the garrison accordingly, where
having obtained entrance by means of the lieutenant, who, while
his commander was asleep, ordered her to be admitted for the joke's
sake, she waited patiently till he turned out, and then accosted him
in the yard, where he used to perform his morning walk. He was

Chapter VI

thunder-struck at the appearance of a woman in a place which he had hitherto kept sacred from the whole sex, and immediately began to utter an apostrophe to Tom Pipes, whose turn it was then to watch; when Mrs. Grizzle falling on her knees before him, conjured him with many pathetic supplications, to hear and grant her request, which was no sooner signified, than he bellowed in such an outragious manner, that the whole court re-ecchoed the opprobrious term *bitch*; and the word *damnation* which he repeated with surprising volubility, without any sort of propriety or connection; and retreated into his penetralia, leaving the baffled devotee in the humble posture she had so unsuccessfully chosen to melt his obdurate heart.

Mortifying as this repulse must have been to a lady of her stately disposition, she did not relinquish her aim, but endeavoured to interest the commodore's counsellors and adherents in her cause. With this view she sollicited the interest of Mr. Hatchway, who being highly pleased with a circumstance in all probability so productive of mirth and diversion, readily entered into her measures, and promised to employ his whole influence for her satisfaction: and as for the boatswain's mate, he was rendered propitious by the present of a guinea which she slipt into his hand. In short, Mrs. Grizzle was continually engaged in this negotiation for the space of ten days, during which the commodore was so incessantly pestered with her remonstrances, and the admonitions of his associates, that he swore his people had a design upon his life, which becoming a burthen to him, he at last complied, and was conducted to the scene like a victim to the altar, by the exulting priests; or rather growling like a reluctant bear, when he is led to the stake amidst the shouts and cries of butchers and their dogs. After all, this victory was not quite so decisive as the conquerors imagined; for the patient being set, and the performer prepared with a pair of pincers, a small difficulty occurred: she could not for some time discern one black hair on the whole superficies of Mr. Trunnion's face; when Mrs. Grizzle, very much alarmed and disconcerted, had recourse to a magnifying glass that stood upon her toilette; and after a most accurate examination, discovered a fibre of a dusky hue, to which the instrument being applied, Mrs. Pickle pulled it up by the roots, to the no small discomposure of the owner, who feeling the smart much more severe than he had expected, started up, and swore he would not part with another hair to save them all from damnation.

Mr. Hatchway exhorted him to patience and resignation, Mrs.

Grizzle repeated her intreaties with great humility; but finding him deaf to all her prayers, and absolutely bent upon leaving the house, she clasped his knees, and begged for the love of God that he would have compassion upon a distressed family, and endure a little more for the sake of the poor infant, who would otherwise be born with a grey beard upon its chin. Far from being melted, he was rather exasperated by this reflection; to which he replied with great indignation, 'Damn ye for a yaw-sighted bitch! he'll be hanged long enough before he has any beard at all:' so saying, he disengaged himself from her embraces, flung out at the door, and halted homewards with such surprising speed, that the lieutenant could not overtake him until he had arrived at his own gate; and Mrs. Grizzle was so much affected with his escape, that her sister, in pure compassion, desired she would not afflict herself, protesting that her own wish was already gratified, for she had plucked three hairs at once, having from the beginning been dubious of the commodore's forbearance. But the labours of this assiduous kinswoman did not end with the atchievement of this adventure: her eloquence or industry were employed without ceasing, in the performance of other tasks imposed by the ingenious craft of her sister-in-law, who at another time conceived an insuppressible affection for a fricassee of frogs, which should be the genuine natives of France; so that there was a necessity for dispatching a messenger on purpose to that kingdom: but as she could not depend upon the integrity of any common servant, Mrs. Grizzle undertook that province, and actually set sail in a cutter for Bologne, from whence she returned in eight and forty hours with a tub full of those live animals, which being dressed according to art, her sister would not taste them, on pretence that her fit of longing was past: but then her inclinations took a different turn, and fixed themselves upon a curious implement belonging to a lady of quality in the neighbourhood, which was reported to be a very great curiosity; this was no other than a porcelain chamber-pot of admirable workmanship, contrived by the honourable owner, who kept it for her own private use, and cherished it as an utensil of inestimable value.

Mrs. Grizzle shuddered at the first hint she received of her sister's desire to possess this piece of furniture; because she knew it was not to be purchased; and the lady's character, which was none of the most amiable in point of humanity and condescension, forbad all hopes of borrowing it for a season; she therefore attempted to reason down this capricious appetite, as an extravagance of imagination which ought to be combated and repressed; and Mrs. Pickle,

only asserts that killing is murder; an asseveration, the truth of
which, it is to be hoped, I shall never dispute.'

Mrs. Grizzle, who, sooth to say, had rather too superficially considered the clause by which she thought herself authorized, perused
the paper with more accuracy, and was confounded at her own
want of penetration. Yet, though she was confuted, she was by no
means convinced that her objections to the cold bath were unreasonable; on the contrary, after having bestowed sundry opprobrious epithets on the physician, for his want of knowledge and
candour, she protested in the most earnest and solemn manner
against the pernicious practice of dipping the child; a piece of
cruelty, which with God's assistance, she should never suffer to be
inflicted on her own issue; and washing her hands of the melancholy consequence that would certainly ensue, shut herself up in
her closet, to indulge her sorrow and vexation. She was deceived,
however, in her prognostic; the boy, instead of declining in point
of health, seemed to acquire fresh vigour from every plunge, as if
he had been resolved to discredit the wisdom and foresight of his
aunt, who, in all probability, could never forgive him for this want
of reverence and respect. This conjecture is founded upon her
behaviour to him in the sequel of his infancy, during which she was
known to torture him more than once, when she had opportunities of
thrusting pins into his flesh, without any danger of being detected.
In a word, her affections were in a little time altogether alienated
from this hope of her family, whom she abandoned to the conduct of
his mother, whose province it undoubtedly was to manage the nur-
ture of her own child; while she herself resumed her operations upon
the commodore, whom she was resolved at any rate to captivate and
inslave. And it must be owned, that Mrs. Grizzle's knowledge of
the human heart never shone so conspicuous as in the methods she
pursued for the accomplishment of this important aim.

Through the rough unpolished husk that cased the soul of
Trunnion, she could easily distinguish a large share of that
vanity and self-conceit that generally predominate even in the
most savage breast; and to this she constantly appealed. In his
presence she always exclaimed against the craft and dishonest
dissimulation of the world; and never failed of uttering particular
invectives against those arts of chicanry, in which the lawyers
are so conversant to the prejudice and ruin of their fellow creatures:
observing that in a seafaring life, so far as she had opportunities of
judging or being informed, there was nothing but friendship, sincerity, and a hearty contempt for every thing that was mean or selfish.

This kind of conversation, with the assistance of certain particular civilities, insensibly made an impression on the mind of the commodore; and that the more effectual, as his former prepossessions were built upon very slender foundations: his antipathy to old maids, which he had conceived upon hearsay, began gradually to diminish, when he found they were not quite such infernal animals as they had been represented; and it was not long before he was heard to observe at the club, that Pickle's sister had not so much of the core of bitch in her as he had imagined. This negative compliment, by the medium of her brother, soon reached the ears of Mrs. Grizzle, who thus encouraged, redoubled all her arts and attention; so that in less than three months after, he in the same place distinguished her with the epithet of a damned sensible jade.

Hatchway taking the alarm at this declaration, which he feared foreboded something fatal to his interest, told his commander with a sneer, that she had sense enough to bring him to, under her stern; and he did not doubt but that such an old crazy vessel would be the better for being taken in tow. 'But howsomever, (added this arch adviser) I'd have you take care of your upper works; for if once you are made fast to her poop, agad! she'll spank it away, and make every beam in your body crack with straining.' Our she-projector's whole plan had like to have been ruined by the effect which this malicious hint had upon Trunnion, whose rage and suspicion being wakened at once, his colour changed from tawny to a cadaverous pale, and then shifting to a deep and dusky red, such as we sometimes observe in the sky when it is replete with thunder, he after his usual preamble of unmeaning oaths, answered in these words. 'Damn ye, you jury-legg'd dog, you would give all the stowage in your hold to be as sound as I am; and as for being taken in tow, d'ye see, I'm not so disabled but that I can lie my course, and perform my voyage without any assistance; and, agad! no man shall ever see Hawser Trunnion lagging a-stern in the wake of e'er a bitch in christendom.'

Mrs. Grizzle, who every morning interrogated her brother with regard to the subject of his night's conversation with his friends, soon received the unwelcome news of the commodore's aversion to matrimony; and justly imputing the greatest part of his disgust to the satyrical insinuations of Mr. Hatchway, resolved to level this obstruction to her success, and actually found means to interest him in her scheme. She had indeed, on some occasions, a particular knack at making converts, being probably not unacquainted with that grand system of persuasion, which is adopted by the greatest personages of the age, as fraught with maxims much more effectual than all the eloquence of Tully or Demosthenes, even when supported by the demonstrations of truth: besides, Mr. Hatchway's fidelity to his new ally, was confirmed by his foreseeing in his captain's marriage an infinite fund of gratification for his own cynical disposition. Thus, therefore, converted and properly cautioned, he for the future suppressed all the virulence of his wit against the matrimonial state; and as he knew not how to open his mouth in the positive praise of any person whatever, took all opportunities of excepting Mrs. Grizzle by name, from the censures he liberally bestowed upon the rest of her sex. 'She is not a drunkard, like Nan Castick of Deptford; (he would say) nor a nincompoop, like Peg Simper of Woolwich; nor a brimstone, like Kate Coddle of Chatham; nor a shrew, like Nell Griffin on the Point Portsmouth; (ladies to whom at different times, they had both paid their addresses) but a tight, good humoured sensible wench, who knows very well how to box her compass; well trimmed aloft, and well sheathed alow, with a good commodity under her hatches.' The commodore at first imagined this commendation was ironical, but hearing it repeated again and again, was filled with astonishment at this surprising change in the lieutenant's behaviour; and after a long fit of musing, concluded that Hatchway himself harboured a matrimonial design on the person of Mrs. Grizzle.

Pleased with this conjecture, he rallied Jack in his turn, and one night toasted her health as a compliment to his passion; a circumstance which the lady learning next day by the usual canal of her intelligence, and interpreting as the result of his own tenderness for her, she congratulated herself upon the victory she had obtained; and thinking it unnecessary to continue the reserve she had hitherto industriously affected, resolved from that day to sweeten her behaviour towards him with such a dash of affection, as could not fail to persuade him that he had inspired her with a reciprocal flame. In consequence of this determination he was invited to dinner, and while he staid, treated with such cloying proofs of her regard, that not only the rest of the company, but even Trunnion himself perceived her drift; and taking the alarm accordingly, could not help exclaiming, 'Oho! I see how the land lies, and if I don't weather the point, I'll be damn'd.' Having thus expressed himself to his afflicted inamorata, he made the best of his way to the garrison, in which he shut himself up for the space of ten days, and had no communication with his friends and domesticks but by looks, which were most significantly picturesque.

CHAPTER VII

Divers Stratagems are invented and put in Practice,
in order to overcome the Obstinacy of Trunnion,
who at length is teized and tortured into the
Noose of Wedlock

THIS abrupt departure and unkind declaration affected Mrs. Grizzle so much, that she fell sick of sorrow and mortification; and after having confined herself to her bed for three days, sent for her brother, told him she perceived her end drawing near, and desired that a lawyer might be brought, in order to write her last will. Mr. Pickle surprised at her demand, began to act the part of a comforter, assuring her that her distemper was not at all dangerous; and that he would instantly send for a physician, who would convince her that she was in no manner of jeopardy; so that there was no occasion at present, to employ any officious attorney in such a melancholy task. Indeed, this affectionate brother was of opinion that a will was altogether superfluous at any rate, as he himself was heir at law to his sister's whole real and personal estate. But she insisted upon his compliance with such determined obstinacy, that he could no longer resist her importunities; and a scrivener arriving, she dictated and executed her will, in which she bequeathed to commodore Trunnion one thousand pounds, to purchase a mourning ring, which she hoped he would wear as a pledge of her friendship and affection. Her brother, though he did not much relish this testimony of her love, nevertheless that same evening gave an account of this particular to Mr. Hatchway, who was also, as Mr. Pickle assured him, generously remembered by the testatrix.

The lieutenant fraught with this piece of intelligence, watched for an opportunity, and as soon as he perceived the commodore's features a little unbended from that ferocious contraction they had suffered so long, ventured to inform him that Pickle's sister lay at the point of death, and that she had left him a thousand pounds in her will. This piece of news overwhelmed him with confusion, and Mr. Hatchway imputing his silence to remorse, resolved to take advantage of that favourable moment, and counselled him to go and visit the poor young woman, who was dying for love of him. But his admonition happened to be somewhat unseasonable; for Trunnion no sooner heard him mention the cause of her disorder

32

than his morosity recurring, he burst out into a violent fit of cursing, and forthwith betook himself again to his hammock, where he lay uttering in a low growling tone of voice, a repetition of oaths and imprecations, for the space of four and twenty hours, without ceasing. This was a delicious meal to the lieutenant, who eager to inhance the pleasure of the entertainment still more, and at the same time conduce to the success of the cause he had espoused, invented a stratagem, the execution of which had all the effect he could desire. He prevailed upon Pipes, who was devoted to his service, to get upon the top of the chimney belonging to the commodore's chamber, at midnight, and to lower down by a rope a bunch of stinking whitings, which being performed, he put a speaking-trumpet to his mouth, and hollowed down the vent, in a voice like thunder, 'Trunnion! Trunnion! turn out and be spliced, or lie still and be damned.' This dreadful note, the terror of which was increased by the silence and darkness of the night, as well as the eccho of the passage through which it was conveyed, no sooner reached the ears of the astonished commodore, than turning his eye towards the place from whence this solemn address seemed to proceed, he beheld a glittering object that vanished in an instant; and just as his superstitious fear had improved the apparition into some supernatural messenger cloathed in shining array, his opinion was confirmed by a sudden explosion, which he took for thunder, though it was no other than the noise of a pistol fired down the chimney by the boatswain's mate, according to the instructions he had received; and he had time enough to descend before he was in any danger of being detected by his commander, who could not for a whole hour recollect himself from the amazement and consternation which had overpowered his faculties.

At length, however, he got up and rung his bell with great agitation. He repeated the summons more than once, but no regard being paid to this alarm, his dread returned with double terror, a cold sweat bedewed his limbs, his knees knocked together, his hair bristled up, and the remains of his teeth were shattered to pieces in the convulsive vibrations of his jaws.

In the midst of this agony he made one desperate effort, and bursting open the door of his apartment, bolted into Hatchway's chamber, which happened to be on the same floor; and there found the lieutenant in a counterfeit swoon, who pretended to wake from his trance in an ejaculation of 'Lord have mercy upon us!' And being questioned by the terrified commodore with regard to what had happened, assured him he had heard

33

the same voice and clap of thunder by which Trunnion himself had been discomposed.

Pipes, whose turn it was to watch, concurred in giving evidence to the same purpose; and the commodore not only owned that he had heard the voice, but likewise communicated his vision, with all the aggravation which his disturbed fancy suggested.

A consultation immediately ensued, in which Mr. Hatchway very gravely observed, that the finger of God was plainly perceivable in those signals; and that it would be both sinful and foolish to disregard his commands, especially as the match proposed was, in all respects, more advantageous than any that one of his years and infirmities could reasonably expect; declaring that for his own part he would not endanger his soul and body by living one day longer under the same roof with a man who despised the holy will of heaven; and Tom Pipes adhered to the same pious resolution.

Trunnion's perseverance could not resist the number and diversity of considerations that assaulted it; he revolved in silence all the opposite motives that occurred to his reflection; and after having been, to all appearance, bewildered in the labyrinth of his own thoughts, he wiped the sweat from his forehead, and heaving a piteous groan, yielded to their remonstrances in these words: 'Well, since it must be so, I think we must e'en grapple. But damn my eyes! 'tis a damn'd hard case that a fellow of my years should be compelled, d'ye see, to beat up to windward all the rest of his life, against the current of his own inclination.'

This important article being discussed, Mr. Hatchway set out in the morning to visit the despairing shepherdess, and was handsomely rewarded for the enlivening tidings with which he blessed her ears. Sick as she was, she could not help laughing heartily at the contrivance, in consequence of which her swain's assent had been obtained, and gave the lieutenant ten guineas for Tom Pipes, in consideration of the part he acted in the farce.

In the afternoon the commodore suffered himself to be conveyed to her apartment, like a felon to execution, and was received by her in a languishing manner and genteel dishabille, accompanied by her sister-in-law; who was, for very obvious reasons, extremely sollicitous about her success. Though the lieutenant had tutored him touching his behaviour at this interview, he made a thousand wry faces before he could pronounce the simple salutation of *How d'ye?* to his mistress; and after his counsellor had urged him with twenty or thirty whispers, to each of which he had replied aloud, 'Damn your eyes I won't,' he got up, and halting towards the couch

34

on which Mrs. Grizzle reclined in a state of strange expectation, he seized her hand and pressed it to his lips; but this piece of gallantry he performed in such a reluctant, uncouth, indignant manner, that the nymph had need of all her resolution to endure the compliment without shrinking; and he himself was so disconcerted at what he had done, that he instantly retired to the other end of the room, where he sat silent, and broiled with shame and vexation. Mrs. Pickle, like a sensible matron, quitted the place, on pretence of going to the nursery; and Mr. Hatchway taking the hint, recollected that he had left his tobacco pouch in the parlour, whither he immediately descended, leaving the two lovers to their mutual endearments. Never had the commodore found himself in such a disagreeable dilemma before. He sat in an agony of suspence, as if he every moment dreaded the dissolution of nature; and the imploring sighs of his future bride added, if possible, to the pangs of his distress. Impatient of his situation, he rolled his eye around in quest of some relief, and unable to contain himself, exclaimed, 'Damnation seize the fellow and his pouch too! I believe he has sheered off, and left me here in the stays.' Mrs. Grizzle, who could not help taking some notice of this manifestation of chagrin, lamented her unhappy fate in being so disagreeable to him that he could not put up with her company for a few moments without repining; and began in very tender terms to reproach him with his inhumanity and indifference. To this expostulation he replied, 'Zounds! what would the woman have? let the parson do his office when he wool, here I am ready to be reeved in the matrimonial block, d'ye see, and damn all nonsensical palaver.' So saying, he retreated, leaving his mistress not at all disobliged at his plaindealing. That same evening the treaty of marriage was brought upon the carpet, and by means of Mr. Pickle and the lieutenant settled to the satisfaction of all parties, without the intervention of lawyers, whom Mr. Trunnion expressly excluded from all share in the business; making that condition the indispensible preliminary of the whole agreement. Things being brought to this bearing, Mrs. Grizzle's heart dilated with joy; her health, which by the bye was never dangerously impaired, she recovered as if by inchantment, and a day being fixed for the nuptials, employed the short period of her celibacy in choosing ornaments for the celebration of her entrance into the married state.

CHAPTER VIII

Preparations are made for the Commodore's Wedding,
which is delayed by an Accident that hurried him
the Lord knows whither

THE fame of this extraordinary conjunction spread all over the
county; and on the day appointed for their spousals, the church
was surrounded by an inconceivable multitude. The commodore,
to give a specimen of his gallantry, by the advice of his friend
Hatchway, resolved to appear on horseback on the grand occasion,
at the head of all his male attendants, whom he had rigged with the
white shirts and black caps formerly belonging to his barge's crew;
and he bought a couple of hunters for the accommodation of himself and his lieutenant. With this equipage then he set out from the
garrison for the church, after having dispatched a messenger to
apprize the bride that he and his company were mounted; whereupon she got immediately into the coach, accompanied by her
brother and wife, and drove directly to the place of assignation,
where several pews were demolished, and divers persons almost
pressed to death, by the eagerness of the crowd that broke in to see
the ceremony performed. Thus arrived at the altar, and the priest
in attendance, they waited a whole half hour for the commodore,
at whose slowness they began to be under some apprehension, and
accordingly dismissed a servant to quicken his pace. The valet
having rode something more than a mile, espied the whole troop
disposed in a long field, crossing the road obliquely, and headed
by the bridegroom and his friend Hatchway, who finding himself
hindered by a hedge from proceeding farther in the same direction,
fired a pistol, and stood over to the other side, making an obtuse
angle with the line of his former course; and the rest of the squadron
followed his example, keeping always in the rear of each other, like
a flight of wild geese.

Surprized at this strange method of journeying, the messenger
came up, and told the commodore that his lady and her company
expected him in the church, where they had tarried a considerable
time, and were beginning to be very uneasy at his delay; and therefore desired he would proceed with more expedition. To this
message Mr. Trunnion replied, 'Hark ye, brother, don't you see
we make all possible speed? go back and tell those who sent you,

that the wind has shifted since we weighed anchor, and that we are
obliged to make very short trips in tacking, by reason of the narrowness of the channel; and that as we lie within six points of the wind,
they must make some allowance for variation and leeway.' 'Lord,
Sir! (said the valet) what occasion have you to go zig zag in that
manner? Do but clap spurs to your horses, and ride straight forward, and I'll engage you shall be at the church porch in less than
a quarter of an hour.' 'What! right in the wind's eye? (answered
the commander) ahey! brother, where did you learn your navigation? Hawser Trunnion is not to be taught at this time of day how
to lie his course, or keep his own reckoning. And as for you,
brother, you know best the trim of your own frigate.' The courier
finding he had to do with people who would not be easily persuaded out of their own opinions, returned to the temple, and made
a report of what he had seen and heard, to the no small consolation
of the bride, who had begun to discover some signs of disquiet.
Composed, however, by this piece of intelligence, she exerted her
patience for the space of another half hour, during which period
seeing no bridegroom arrive, she was exceedingly alarmed; so that
all the spectators could easily perceive her perturbation, which
manifested itself in frequent palpitations, heart-heavings, and
alterations of countenance, in spite of the assistance of a smelling-
bottle which she incessantly applied to her nostrils.

Various were the conjectures of the company on this occasion:
some imagined he had mistaken the place of rendezvous, as he had
never been at church since he first settled in that parish; others
believed he had met with some accident, in consequence of which
his attendants had carried him back to his own house; and a third
set, in which the bride herself was thought to be comprehended,
could not help suspecting that the commodore had changed his
mind. But all these suppositions, ingenious as they were, happened to be wide of the true cause that detained him, which was no
other than this: the commodore and his crew had by dint of turning, almost weathered the parson's house that stood to windward
of the church, when the notes of a pack of hounds unluckily reached
the ears of the two hunters which Trunnion and the lieutenant
bestrode. These fleet animals no sooner heard the enlivening sound,
than eager for the chace they sprung away all of a sudden, and
straining every nerve to partake of the sport, flew across the fields
with incredible speed, overleaping hedges and ditches, and every
thing in their way, without the least regard to their unfortunate
riders. The lieutenant, whose steed had got the heels of the other,

finding it would be great folly and presumption in him to pretend
to keep the saddle with his wooden leg, very wisely took the opportunity of throwing himself off in his passage through a field of rich
clover, among which he lay at his ease; and seeing his captain
advancing at full gallop, hailed him with the salutation of 'What
chear? ho!' The commodore, who was in infinite distress, eying
him askance, as he passed, replied with a faultering voice, 'O damn
ye! you are safe at an anchor; I wish to God I were as fast moored.'
Nevertheless, conscious of his disabled heel, he would not venture
to try the same experiment which had succeeded so well with
Hatchway, but resolved to stick as close as possible to his horse's
back, until providence should interpose in his behalf. With this
view he dropped his whip, and with his right hand laid fast hold
on the pummel, contracting every muscle in his body to secure himself in the seat, and grinning most formidably, in consequence of
this exertion. In this attitude he was hurried on a considerable way,
when all of a sudden his view was comforted by a five bar gate that
appeared before him, as he never doubted that there the career of
his hunter must necessarily end. But, alas! he reckoned without his
host; far from halting at this obstruction, the horse sprung over
it with amazing agility, to the utter confusion and disorder of his
owner, who lost his hat and periwig in the leap, and now began to
think in good earnest, that he was actually mounted on the back of
the devil. He recommended himself to God, his reflection forsook
him, his eye-sight and all his other senses failed, he quitted the
reins, and fastening by instinct on the mane, was in this condition
conveyed into the midst of the sportsmen, who were astonished at
the sight of such an apparition. Neither was their surprize to be
wondered at, if we reflect on the figure that presented itself to their
view. The commodore's person was at all times an object of admiration; much more so on this occasion, when every singularity was
aggravated by the circumstances of his dress and disaster.

He had put on in honour of his nuptials his best coat of blue broad
cloth, cut by a taylor of Ramsgate, and trimmed with five dozen of
brass buttons, large and small; his breeches were of the same piece,
fastened at the knees with large bunches of tape; his waistcoat was
of red plush lapelled with green velvet, and garnished with vellum
holes; his boots bore an intimate resemblance both in colour and
shape to a pair of leathern buckets; his shoulder was graced with
a broad buff belt, from whence depended a huge hanger with a hilt
like that of a backsword; and on each side of his pummel appeared
a rusty pistol rammed in a case covered with bear-skin. The loss of

his tye-periwig and laced hat, which were curiosities of the kind, did not at all contribute to the improvement of the picture, but on the contrary, by exhibiting his bald pate, and the natural extension of his lanthorn jaws, added to the peculiarity and extravagance of the whole. Such a spectacle could not have failed of diverting the whole company from the chace, had his horse thought proper to pursue a different route, but the beast was too keen a sporter to choose any other way than that which the stag followed; and therefore, without stopping to gratify the curiosity of the spectators, he in a few minutes outstripped every hunter in the field; and there being a deep hollow way betwixt him and the hounds, rather than ride round about the length of a furlong to a path that crossed the lane, he transported himself at one jump, to the unspeakable astonishment and terror of a waggoner who chanced to be underneath, and saw this phenomenon fly over his carriage. This was not the only adventure he atchieved. The stag having taken a deep river that lay in his way, every man directed his course to a bridge in the neighbourhood; but our bridegroom's courser despising all such conveniences, plunged into the stream without hesitation, and swam in a twinkling to the opposite shore. This sudden immersion into an element of which Trunnion was properly a native, in all probability helped to recruit the exhausted spirits of his rider, who at his landing on the other side gave some tokens of sensation, by hollowing aloud for assistance, which he could not possibly receive, because his horse still maintained the advantage he had gained, and would not allow himself to be overtaken.

In short, after a long chace that lasted several hours, and extended to a dozen miles at least, he was the first in at the death of the deer, being seconded by the lieutenant's gelding, which actuated by the same spirit, had, without a rider, followed his companion's example.

Our bridegroom finding himself at last brought up, or in other words, at the end of his career, took the opportunity of this first pause, to desire the huntsmen would lend him a hand in dismounting; and was by their condescension safely placed on the grass, where he sat staring at the company as they came in, with such wildness of astonishment in his looks, as if he had been a creature of another species, dropt among them from the clouds.

Before they had fleshed the hounds, however, he recollected himself, and seeing one of the sportsmen take a small flask out of his pocket and apply it to his mouth, judged the cordial to be no other than neat Coniac, which it really was; and expressing a desire of participation, was immediately accommodated with a moderate dose, which perfectly compleated his recovery.

By this time he and his two horses had engrossed the attention of the whole crowd; while some admired the elegant proportion and uncommon spirit of the two animals, the rest contemplated the surprising appearance of their master, whom before they had only seen *en passant*; and at length, one of the gentlemen, accosting him very courteously, signified his wonder at seeing him in such an equipage, and asked if he had not dropped his companion by the way. 'Why, look ye, brother, (replied the commodore) mayhap you think me an odd sort of a fellow, seeing me in this trim, especially as I have lost part of my rigging; but this here is the case, d'ye see: I weighed anchor from my own house this morning at ten A.M. with fair weather, and a favourable breeze at south south-east, being bound to the next church, on the voyage of matrimony: but howsomever, we had not run down a quarter of a league, when the wind shifting, blowed directly in our teeth; so that we were forced to tack all the way, d'ye see, and had almost beat up within sight of port, when these sons of bitches of horses, which I had bought but two days before (for my own part, I believe they are devils incarnate) luffed round in a trice, and then refusing the helm, drove away like lightning with me and my lieutenant, who soon came to anchor in an exceeding good birth. As for my own part, I have been carried over rocks, and flats, and quicksands; among which I have pitched away a special good tye-periwig, and an iron-bound hat; and at last, thank God! am got into smooth water and safe riding: but if ever I venture my carcase upon such a hare'um scare'um blood of a bitch again, my name is not Hawser Trunnion, d—n my eyes!'

One of the company, struck with this name, which he had often heard, immediately laid hold on his declaration at the close of this singular account; and observing that his horses were very vicious, asked how he intended to return? 'As for that matter, (replied Mr. Trunnion) I am resolved to hire a sledge or waggon, or such a thing as a jack-ass; for I'll be d—n'd if ever I cross the back of a horse again.' 'And what do you propose to do with these creatures? (said the other, pointing to the hunters) they seem to have some mettle; but then they are meer colts, and will take the devil and all of breaking. Methinks this hither one is shoulder slipped.' 'Damn them, (cried the commodore) I wish both their necks were broke, thof the two cost me forty good yellow-boys.' 'Forty guineas! (exclaimed the stranger, who was a squire and a jocky, as well as owner of the pack) Lord! Lord! how a man may be imposed upon! Why, these cattle are clumsy enough to go to plow: mind what a flat counter; do but observe how sharp this here one is in the withers; then he's fired in the further fetlock.' In short, this connoisseur in horse-flesh, having discovered in them all the defects which can possibly be found in that species of animals, offered to give him ten guineas for the two, saying, he would convert them into beasts of burthen. The owner, who (after what had happened) was very well disposed to listen to any thing that was said to their prejudice, implicitly believed the truth of the stranger's asseverations, discharged a furious volley of oaths against the rascal who had taken him in, and forthwith struck a bargain with the squire, who paid him instantly for his purchase; in consequence of which he won the plate at the next Canterbury races.

This affair being transacted to the mutual satisfaction of both parties, as well as to the general entertainment of the company, who laughed in their sleeves at the dexterity of their friend, Trunnion was set upon the squire's own horse, and led by his servant in the midst of this cavalcade, which proceeded to a neighbouring village, where they had bespoke dinner, and where our bridegroom found means to provide himself with another hat and wig. With regard to his marriage, he bore his disappointment with the temper of a philosopher; and the exercise he had undergone having quickened his appetite, sat down at table in the midst of his new acquaintance, making a very hearty meal, and moistening every morsel with a draught of the ale, which he found very much to his satisfaction.

CHAPTER IX

He is found by the Lieutenant; reconducted to his
own House; married to Mrs. Grizzle, who meets with a
small Misfortune in the Night, and asserts her Prerogative
next Morning; in consequence of which her
Husband's Eye is endangered

MEAN while lieutenant Hatchway made shift to hobble to the church, where he informed the company of what had happened to the commodore; and the bride behaved with great decency on the occasion; for, as soon as she understood the danger to which her future husband was exposed, she fainted in the arms of her sister-in-law, to the surprize of all the spectators, who could not comprehend the cause of her disorder; and when she was recovered by the application of smelling-bottles, earnestly begged that Mr. Hatchway and Tom Pipes would take her brother's coach, and go in quest of their commander.

This task they readily undertook, being escorted by all the rest of his adherents on horseback; while the bride and her friends were invited to the parson's house, and the ceremony deferred till another occasion.

The lieutenant, steering his course as near the line of direction in which Trunnion went off as the coach-road would permit, got intelligence of his track from one farm-house to another; for such an apparition could not fail of attracting particular notice; and one of the horsemen having picked up his hat and wig in a bye-path, the whole troop entered the village where he was lodged, about four o'clock in the afternoon. When they understood he was safely housed at the George, they rode up to the door in a body, and expressed their satisfaction in three chears; which were returned by the company within, as soon as they were instructed in the nature of the salute by Trunnion, who by this time had entered into all the jollity of his new friends, and was indeed more than half-seas over. The lieutenant was introduced to all present as his sworn brother, and had something tossed up for his dinner. Tom Pipes and the crew were regaled in another room; and a fresh pair of horses being put to the coach, about six in the evening the commodore, with all his attendants, departed for the garrison, after having shook hands with every individual in the house.

Without any farther accident he was conveyed in safety to his own gate before nine, and committed to the care of Pipes, who carried him instantly to his hammock, while the lieutenant was driven away to the place where the bride and her friends remained in great anxiety, which vanished when he assured them that his commodore was safe, being succeeded by abundance of mirth and pleasantry at the account he gave of Trunnion's adventure.

Another day was fixed for the nuptials; and, in order to baulk the curiosity of idle people, which had given great offence, the parson was prevailed upon to perform the ceremony in the garrison, which all that day was adorned with flags and pendants displayed, and at night illuminated by the direction of Hatchway, who also ordered the patereroes to be fired as soon as the marriage knot was tied. Neither were the other parts of the entertainment neglected by this ingenious contriver, who produced undeniable proofs of his elegance and art in the wedding-supper, which had been committed to his management and direction. This general banquet was intirely composed of sea-dishes; a huge pillaw, consisting of a large piece of beef sliced, a couple of fowls, and half a peck of rice, smoaked in the middle of the board: a dish of hard fish swimming in oil appeared at each end, the sides being furnished with a mess of that savoury composition known by the name of lob's course, and a plate of salmagundy. The second course displayed a goose of a monstrous magnitude, flanked with two Guinea-hens, a pig barbecu'd, an hock of salt pork in the midst of a pease-pudding, a leg of mutton roasted, with potatoes, and another boiled, with yams. The third service was made up of a loin of fresh pork with apple-sauce, a kid smothered with onions, and a terrapin baked in the shell: and last of all, a prodigious sea-pye was presented, with an infinite volume of pancakes and fritters. That every thing might be answerable to the magnificence of this delicate feast, he had provided vast quantities of strong beer, flip, rumbo, and burnt brandy, with plenty of Barbadoes water for the ladies; and hired all the fiddles within six miles, who, with the addition of a drum, bag-pipe, and Welch-harp, regaled the guests with a most melodious concert.

The company, who were not at all exceptious, seemed extremely well pleased with every particular of the entertainment; and the evening being spent in the most social manner, the bride was by her sister conducted to her apartment, where, however, a trifling circumstance had like to have destroyed the harmony which had been hitherto maintained.

I have already observed, that there was not one standing bed within the walls; therefore the reader will not wonder that Mrs. Trunnion was out of humour, when she found herself under the necessity of being confined with her spouse in a hammock, which tho' enlarged with a double portion of canvas, and dilated with a yoke for the occasion, was at best but a disagreeable, not to say dangerous situation. She accordingly complained with some warmth of this inconvenience, which she imputed to disrespect, and at first absolutely refused to put up with the expedient: but Mrs. Pickle soon brought her to reason and compliance, by observing that one night would soon be elapsed, and next day she might regulate her own oeconomy.

Thus persuaded, she ventured into the vehicle, and was visited by her husband in less than an hour, the company being departed to their own homes, and the garrison left to the command of his lieutenant and mate. But it seems the hooks that supported this swinging couch were not calculated for the addition of weight which they were now destined to bear; and therefore gave way in the middle of the night, to the no small terror of Mrs. Trunnion, who perceiving herself falling, screamed aloud, and by that exclamation brought Hatchway with a light into the chamber. Tho' she had received no injury by the fall she was extremely discomposed and incensed at the accident, which she even openly ascribed to the obstinacy and whimsical oddity of the commodore, in such petulant terms as evidently declared that she thought her great aim accomplished, and her authority secured against all the shocks of fortune. Indeed her bedfellow seemed to be of the same opinion, by his tacit resignation; for he made no reply to her insinuations, but with a most vinegar aspect crawled out of his nest, and betook himself to rest in another apartment, while his irritated spouse dismissed the lieutenant, and from the wreck of the hammock made an occasional bed for herself on the floor, fully determined to provide better accommodation for next night's lodging.

Having no inclination to sleep, her thoughts during the remaining part of the night were engrossed by a scheme of reformation she was resolved to execute in the family; and no sooner did the first lark bid salutation to the morn, than starting from her humble couch, and huddling on her cloaths, she sallied from her chamber, explored her way thro' paths before unknown, and in the course of her researches perceived a large bell, to which she made such effectual application as alarmed every soul in the family. In a moment she was surrounded by Hatchway, Pipes, and all the rest of the servants half dressed; but seeing none of the feminine gender appear, she began to storm at the sloth and laziness of the maids, who, she observed, ought to have been at work an hour at least before she called; and then, for the first time, understood that no woman was permitted to sleep within the walls.

She did not fail to exclaim against this regulation; and being informed that the cook and chambermaid lodged in a small office-house that stood without the gate, ordered the draw-bridge to be let down, and in person beat up their quarters, commanding them forthwith to set about scouring the rooms, which had not been hitherto kept in a very decent condition, while two men were immediately employed to transport the bed on which she used to lie from her brother's house to her new habitation; so that, in less than two hours, the whole oeconomy of the garrison was turned topsy-turvy, and everything involved in such tumult and noise, that Trunnion being disturbed and distracted with the uproar, turned out in his shirt like a frantic maniac, and arming himself with a cudgel of crab-tree, made an irruption into his wife's apartment, where perceiving a couple of carpenters at work, in joining a bedstead, he, with many dreadful oaths and opprobrious invectives, ordered them to desist, swearing he would suffer no bulk-heads nor hurricane-houses to stand where he was master: but finding his remonstrances disregarded by these mechanics, who believed him to be some madman belonging to the family, who had broke from his confinement, he assaulted them both with great fury and indignation, and was handled so roughly in the en-counter, that in a very short time he measured his length on the floor, in consequence of a blow that he received from a hammer, by which the sight of his remaining eye was grievously endangered.

Having thus reduced him to a state of subjection, they resolved to secure him with cords, and were actually busy in adjusting his fetters, when he was exempted from the disgrace by the accidental entrance of his spouse, who rescued him from the hands of his adversaries, and, in the midst of her condolance, imputed his mis-fortune to the inconsiderate roughness of his own disposition.

He breathed nothing but revenge, and made some efforts to chastise the insolence of the workmen, who, as soon as they under-stood his quality, asked forgiveness for what they had done with great humility, protesting that they did not know he was master of the house. But, far from being satisfied with this apology, he groped about for the bell, (the inflammation on his eye having utterly deprived him of sight) and the rope being, by the precaution of the delinquents, conveyed out of his reach, began to storm with incredible vociferation, like a lion roaring in the toil, pouring forth innumerable oaths and execrations, and calling by name Hatchway and Pipes, who being within hearing, obeyed the extraordinary summons, and were ordered to put the carpenters in irons, for having audaciously assaulted him in his own house.

His myrmidons seeing he had been evil-intreated, were exasper-ated at the insult he had suffered, which they considered as an affront upon the dignity of the garrison; the more so, as the mutineers seemed to put themselves in a posture of defence, and set their authority at defiance: they therefore unsheathed their cutlasses, which they commonly wore as badges of their commis-sion; and a desperate engagement, in all probability, would have ensued, had not the lady of the castle interposed, and prevented the effects of their animosity, by assuring the lieutenant that the commodore had been the aggressor; and that the workmen, finding themselves attacked in such an extraordinary manner, by a person whom they did not know, were obliged to act in their own defence, by which he had received that unlucky contusion.

Mr. Hatchway no sooner learnt the sentiments of Mrs. Trunnion, than sheathing his indignation, he told the commodore he should always be ready to execute his lawful commands; but that he could not in conscience be concerned in oppressing poor people who had been guilty of no offence.

This unexpected declaration, together with the behaviour of his wife, who in his hearing desired the carpenters to resume their work, filled the breast of Trunnion with rage and mortification. He pulled off his woollen night-cap, pummelled his bare pate, beat the floor alternately with his feet, swore his people had betrayed him, and cursed himself to the lowest pit of hell, for having admitted such a cockatrice into his family. But all these exclamations did not avail; they were among the last essays of his resistance to the will of his wife, whose influence among his adherents had already swallowed up his own; and who now peremptorily told him, that he must leave the management of every thing within doors to her, who understood best what was for his honour and advantage. She then ordered a poultice to be prepared for his eye, which being applied, he was committed to the care of Pipes, by whom he was led about the house like a blind bear growling for prey, while his industrious yoke-fellow executed every circumstance of the plan she had projected; so that, when he recovered his vision, he was an utter stranger in his own house.

CHAPTER X

The Commodore being in some Cases restif, his Lady
has recourse to Artifice in the establishment of her Throne;
she exhibits Symptoms of Pregnancy,
to the unspeakable Joy of Trunnion,
who nevertheless is baulked in his Expectation

THESE innovations were not effected without many loud objections on his part; and divers curious dialogues passed between him and his yoke-fellow, who always came off victorious from the dispute; insomuch that his countenance gradually fell; he began to suppress, and at length intirely devoured his chagrin; the terrors of superior authority were plainly perceivable in his features, and in less than three months he became a thorough-paced husband. Not that his obstinacy was extinguished, tho' overcome; in some things he was as inflexible and muleish as ever, but then he durst not kick so openly, and was reduced to the necessity of being passive in his resentments. Mrs. Trunnion, for example, proposed that a coach and six should be purchased, as she could not ride on horseback, and the chaise was a scandalous carriage for a person of her condition; the commodore, conscious of his own inferior capacity in point of reasoning, did not think proper to dispute the proposal, but lent a deaf ear to her repeated remonstrances, tho' they were inforced with every argument which she thought could sooth, terrify, shame or decoy him into compliance: in vain did she urge the excess of affection she had for him, as meriting some return of tenderness and condescension; he was even proof against certain menacing hints she gave, touching the resentment of a slighted woman; and he stood out against all the considerations of dignity or disgrace, like a bulwark of brass. Neither was he moved to any indecent or unkind expressions of contradiction, even when she upbraided him with his sordid disposition, and put him in mind of the fortune and honour he had acquired by his marriage, but seemed to retire within himself, like a tortoise when attacked, that shrinks within its shell, and silently endure the scourge of her reproaches, without seeming sensible of the smart.

This, however, was the only point in which she had been baffled since her nuptials; and as she could by no means digest the miscarriage, she tortured her invention for some new plan by which she might augment her influence and authority: what her genius refused was supplied by accident; for she had not lived four months in the garrison when she was seized with frequent qualms and reachings, her breasts began to harden, and her stomach to be remarkably prominent: in a word, she congratulated herself on the symptoms of her own fertility, and the commodore was transported with joy, at the prospect of an heir of his own begetting.

She knew this was the proper season for vindicating her own sovereignty, and accordingly employed the means which nature had put in her power. There was not a rare piece of furniture and apparel for which she did not long; and one day as she went to church, seeing lady Stately's equipage arrive, she suddenly fainted away. Her husband, whose vanity had never been so perfectly

47

gratified as with this promised harvest of his own sowing, took the alarm immediately, and in order to prevent relapses of that kind, which might be attended with fatal consequences to his hope, gave her leave to bespeak a coach, horses and liveries to her own liking. Thus authorized, she in a very little time exhibited such a specimen of her own taste and magnificence as afforded speculation to the whole county, and made Trunnion's heart quake within him, because he foresaw no limits to her extravagance, which also manifested itself in the most expensive preparations for her lying-in.

Her pride, which had hitherto regarded the representative of her father's house, seemed now to lose all that hereditary respect, and prompt her to outshine and undervalue the elder branch of her family. She behaved to Mrs. Pickle with a sort of civil reserve that implied a conscious superiority, and an emulation in point of grandeur immediately commenced between the two sisters. She every day communicated her importance to the whole parish, under pretence of taking the air in her coach, and endeavoured to extend her acquaintance among people of fashion. Nor was this an undertaking attended with great difficulty, for all persons whatever, capable of maintaining a certain appearance, will always find admission into what is called the best company, and be rated in point of character according to their own valuation, without subjecting their pretensions to the smallest doubt or examination. In all her visits and parties she seized every opportunity of declaring her present condition, observing that she was forbid by her physicians to taste such a pickle, and that such a dish was poison to a woman in her way: nay, where she was on a footing of familiarity, she affected to make wry faces, and complained that the young rogue began to be very unruly, writhing herself into divers contortions, as if she had been grievously incommoded by the mettle of this future Trunnion. The husband himself did not behave with all the moderation that might have been expected; at the club he frequently mention'd this circumstance of his own vigour as a pretty successful feat to be performed by an old fellow of fifty-five, and confirmed the opinion of his strength by redoubled squeezes of the landlord's hand, which never failed of extorting a satisfactory certificate of his might. When his companions drank to the *Hans en kelderr*,[1] or Jack in the low cellar, he could not help displaying an extraordinary complacence of countenance, and signified his intention of sending the young dog to sea, as soon as he should be able to carry a cartridge, in hopes of seeing him an officer before his own death.

Chapter X

This hope helped to console him under the extraordinary expence to which he was exposed by the profusion of his wife, especially when he considered that his compliance with her prodigality would be limited to the expiration of the nine months, of which the best part was by this time elapsed; yet in spite of all this philosophical resignation, her fancy sometimes soared to such a ridiculous and intolerable pitch of insolence and absurdity, that his temper forsook him, and he could not help wishing in secret, that her pride might be confounded in the dissipation of her most flattering hopes, even tho' he himself should be a principal sufferer by the disappointment. These, however, were no other than the suggestions of temporary disgusts, that commonly subsided as suddenly as they arose, and never gave the least disturbance to the person who inspired them, because he took care to conceal them from her knowledge.

Mean while she happily advanced in her reckoning, with the promise of a favourable issue; the term of her computation expired, and in the middle of the night she was visited by certain warnings that seemed to bespeak the approach of the critical moment. The commodore got up with great alacrity, and called the midwife, who had been several days in the house; the gossips were immediately summoned, and the most interesting expectations prevailed; but the symptoms of labour gradually vanished, and, as the matrons sagely observed, this was no more than a false alarm.

Two nights after they received a second intimation, and as she was sensibly diminished in the waist, every thing was supposed to be in a fair way; yet this visitation was not more conclusive than the former; her pains wore off in spite of all her endeavours to encourage them, and the good women betook themselves to their respective homes, in expectation of finding the third attack decisive, alluding to the well-known maxim, that *number three is always fortunate*. For once, however, this apothegm failed; the next call was altogether as ineffectual as the former; and moreover, attended with a phænomenon which to them was equally strange and inexplicable: this was no other than such a reduction in the size of Mrs. Trunnion as might have been expected after the birth of a full-grown child. Startled at such an unaccountable event, they sat in close divan; and concluding that the case was in all respects unnatural and prodigious, desired that a messenger might be immediately dispatched for some male practitioner in the art of midwifery.

The commodore, without guessing the cause of their perplexity,

49

ordered Pipes immediately on this piece of duty; and in less than two hours they were assisted by the advice of a surgeon of the neighbourhood, who boldly affirmed that the patient had never been with child. This asseveration was like a clap of thunder to Mr. Trunnion, who had been during eight whole days and nights in continual expectation of being hailed with the appellation of father.

After some recollection he swore the surgeon was an ignorant fellow, and that he would not take his word for what he advanced, being comforted and confirmed in his want of faith by the insinuations of the midwife, who still persisted to feed Mrs. Trunnion with hopes of a speedy and safe delivery; observing that she had been concerned in many a case of the same nature, where a fine child was found, even after all signs of the mother's pregnancy had disappeared. Every twig of hope, how slender soever it may be, is eagerly caught hold on by people who find themselves in danger of being disappointed. To every question proposed by her to the lady with the preamble of 'Han't you?' or 'Don't you?' an answer was made in the affirmative, whether agreeable to truth or not, because the respondent could not find in her heart to disown any symptom that might favour the notion she had so long indulged.

This experienced proficient in the obstetric art was therefore kept in close attendance for the space of three weeks, during which the patient had several returns of what she pleased herself with believing to be labour-pains, till at length she and her husband became the standing joke of the parish; and this infatuated couple could scarce be prevailed upon to part with their hopes, even when she appeared as lank as a greyhound, and they were furnished with other unquestionable proofs of their having been deceived. But they could not for ever remain under the influence of this sweet delusion, which at last faded away, and was succeeded by a paroxism of shame and confusion, that kept the husband within doors for the space of a whole fortnight, and confined his lady to her bed for a series of weeks, during which she suffered all the anguish of the most intense mortification; yet even this was subdued by the lenient hand of time.

The first respite from her chagrin was employed in the strict discharge of what are called the duties of religion, which she performed with the most rancorous severity, setting on foot a persecution in her own family, that made the house too hot for all the menial servants, even ruffled the almost invincible indifference of Tom Pipes, harrassed the commodore himself out of all patience, and spared no individual but lieutenant Hatchway, whom she never ventured to disoblige.

CHAPTER XI

Mrs. Trunnion erects a Tyranny in the Garrison,
while her Husband conceives an Affection for
his Nephew Perry, who manifests a Peculiarity of
Disposition even in his tender Years

HAVING exercised herself three months in such pious amusements,
she appeared again in the world; but her misfortune had made such
an impression on her mind, that she could not bear the sight of a
child, and trembled whenever the conversation happened to turn
upon a christening. Her temper, which was naturally none of the
sweetest, seemed to have imbibed a double proportion of souring
from her disappointment; of consequence her company was not
much coveted, and she found very few people disposed to treat her
with those marks of consideration which she looked upon as her
due. This neglect detached her from the society of an unmannerly
world; she concentred the energy of all her talents in the government of her own house, which groaned accordingly under her
arbitrary sway, and in the brandy-bottle found ample consolation
for all the affliction she had undergone.

As for the commodore, he in a little time weathered his disgrace,
after having sustained many severe jokes from the lieutenant; and
now his chief aim being to be absent from his own house as much as
possible, he frequented the publick-house more than ever, more
assiduously cultivated the friendship of his brother-in-law Mr.
Pickle, and in the course of their intimacy conceived an affection
for his nephew Perry, which did not end but with his life. Indeed
it must be owned that Trunnion was not naturally deficient in the
social passions of the soul, which, tho' they were strangely warped,
disguised and overborne by the circumstances of his boisterous life
and education, did not fail to manifest themselves occasionally
thro' the whole course of his behaviour.

As all his hopes of propagating his own name had perished, and
his relations lay under the interdiction of his hate, it is no wonder
that thro' the familiarity and friendly intercourse subsisting between
him and Mr. Gamaliel, he contracted a liking for the boy, who by
this time entered the third year of his age, and was indeed a very
handsome, healthy and promising child; and what seemed to
ingratiate him still more with his uncle, was a certain oddity of

disposition for which he had been remarkable even from his cradle. It is reported of him, that before the first year of his infancy was elapsed, he used very often, immediately after being dressed, in the midst of the caresses which were bestowed upon him by his mother while she indulged herself in the contemplation of her own happiness, all of a sudden to alarm her with a fit of shrieks and cries, which continued with great violence till he was stripped to the skin with the utmost expedition by order of his affrighted parent, who thought his tender body was tortured by the misapplication of some unlucky pin; and when he had given them all this disturbance and unnecessary trouble, he would lie sprawling and laughing in their faces, as if he ridiculed the impertinence of their concern. Nay it is affirmed, that one day, when an old woman who attended in the nursery had by stealth conveyed a bottle of cordial waters to her mouth, he pulled his nurse by the sleeve, and by a slight glance detecting the theft, tipt her the wink with a particular slyness of countenance, as if he had said with a sneer, 'Ay, ay, that is what you must all come to.' But these instances of reflection in a babe nine months old are so incredible, that I look upon them as *ex post facto* observations, founded upon imaginary recollection, when he was in a more advanced age, and his peculiarities of temper became much more remarkable: of a piece with the ingenious discoveries of those sagacious observers, who can discern something evidently characteristic in the features of any noted personage whose character they have previously heard explained; yet, without pretending to specify at what period of his childhood this singularity first appeared, I can with great truth declare, that when he first attracted the notice and affection of his uncle, it was plainly perceivable.

One would imagine he had marked out the commodore as a proper object of ridicule, for almost all his little childish satire was levelled against him. I will not deny that he might have been influenced in this particular by the example and instruction of Mr. Hatchway, who delighted in superintending the first essays of his genius. As the gout had taken up its residence in Mr. Trunnion's great toe, from whence it never removed, no not for a day, little Perry took great pleasure in treading by accident on this infirm member; and when his uncle, incensed by the pain, used to damn him for a hell-begotten brat, he would appease him in a twinkling by returning the curse with equal emphasis, and asking what was the matter with old Hannibal Tough? an appellation by which the lieutenant had taught him to distinguish this grim commander.

Chapter XI

Neither was this the only experiment he tried upon the patience of the commodore, with whose nose he used to take indecent freedoms even while he was fondled on his knee; in one month he put him to the expence of two guineas in seal-skin, by picking his pocket of divers tobacco pouches, all of which he in secret committed to the flames. Nor did the caprice of his disposition abstain from the favourite beverage of Trunnion, who more than once swallowed a whole draught in which his brother's snuff-box had been emptied, before he perceived the disagreeable infusion: and one day, when the commodore had chastised him by a gentle tap with his cane, he fell flat on the floor as if he had been deprived of all sense and motion, to the terror and amazement of the striker; and after having filled the whole house with confusion and dismay, opened his eyes and laughed heartily at the success of his own imposition.

It would be an endless and perhaps no very agreeable task, to enumerate all the unlucky pranks he played upon his uncle and others, before he attained the fourth year of his age; about which time he was sent, with an attendant, to a day-school in the neighbourhood, that (to use his good mother's own expression) he might be out of harm's way. Here, however, he made little progress, except in mischief, which he practised with impunity, because the school-mistress would run no risk of disobliging a lady of fortune, by exercising unnecessary severities upon her only child. Nevertheless Mrs. Pickle was not so blindly partial as to be pleased with such unseasonable indulgence. Perry was taken out of the hands of this courteous teacher, and committed to the instruction of a pedagogue, who was ordered to administer such correction as the boy should in his opinion deserve. This authority he did not neglect to use; his pupil was regularly flogged twice a day, and after having been subjected to this course of discipline for the space of eighteen months, declared the most obstinate, dull and untoward genius that ever had fallen under his cultivation; instead of being reformed, he seemed rather hardened and confirmed in his vicious inclinations, and was dead to all sense of fear as well as shame. His mother was extremely mortified at these symptoms of stupidity, which she considered as an inheritance derived from the spirit of his father, and consequently insurmountable by all the efforts of human care. But the commodore rejoiced over the ruggedness of his nature, and was particularly pleased when upon inquiry he found that Perry had beaten all the boys in the school; a circumstance from which he prognosticated every thing that was fair and fortunate in his future fate; observing, that at his age he himself was just such another. The boy, who was now turned of six, having profited so little under the birch of his unsparing governor, Mrs. Pickle was counselled to send him to a boarding-school not far from London, which was kept by a certain person very eminent for his successful method of education. This advice she the more readily embraced, because at that time she found herself pretty far gone with another child, that she hoped she would console her for the disappointment she had met with in the unpromising talents of Perry, or at any rate divide her concern, so as to enable her to endure the absence of either.

CHAPTER XII

Peregrine is sent to a Boarding-School,
becomes Remarkable for his Genius and Ambition

THE commodore understanding her determination, to which her husband did not venture to make the least objection, interested himself so much in behalf of his favourite, as to fit him out at his own charge, and accompany him in person to the place of his destination; where he defrayed the expence of his entrance, and left him to the particular care and inspection of the usher, who having been recommended to him as a person of parts and integrity, received *per* advance a handsome consideration for the task he undertook.

Nothing could be better judged than this piece of liberality; the assistant was actually a man of learning, probity, and good sense; and though obliged by the scandalous administration of fortune to act in the character of an inferior teacher, had by his sole capacity and application, brought the school to that degree of reputation which it never could have obtained from the talents of his superior. He had established an oeconomy, which though regular, was not at all severe, by enacting a body of laws suited to the age and comprehension of every individual; and each transgressor was fairly tried by his peers, and punished according to the verdict of the jury. No boy was scourged for want of apprehension, but a spirit of emulation was raised by well-timed praise and artful comparison, and maintained by a distribution of small prizes, which were adjudged to those who signalized themselves either by their industry, sobriety or genius. This tutor, whose name was Jennings, began with Perry, according to his constant maxim, by examining the soil; that is, studying his temper, in order to consult the biass of his disposition, which was strangely perverted by the absurd discipline he had undergone. He found him in a state of sullen insensibility, which the child had gradually contracted in a long course of stupifying correction; and at first he was not in the least actuated by that commendation which animated the rest of his school-fellows; nor was it in the power of reproach to excite his ambition, which had been buried, as it were, in the grave of disgrace: the usher therefore had recourse to contemptuous neglect, with which he affected to treat this stubborn spirit; foreseeing that if he retained any seeds of sentiment, this weather would infallibly raise them into vegetation: his judgment was justified by the event; the boy in a little time began to make observations; he perceived the marks of distinction with which virtue was rewarded, grew ashamed of the despicable figure he himself made amongst his companions, who far from courting, rather shunned his conversation; and actually pined at his own want of importance.

Mr. Jennings saw and rejoiced at his mortification, which he suffered to proceed as far as possible, without endangering his health. The child lost all relish for diversion, loathed his food, grew pensive, solitary, and was frequently found weeping by himself. These symptoms plainly evinced the recovery of his feelings, to which his governor thought it now high time to make application; and therefore by little and little altered his behaviour from the indifference he had put on, to the appearance of more regard and attention. This produced a favourable change in the boy, whose eyes sparkled with satisfaction one day, when his master expressed himself with a shew of surprize in these words, 'So, Perry! I find you don't want genius, when you think proper to use it.' Such encomiums kindled the spirit of emulation in his little breast; he exerted himself with surprising alacrity, by which he soon acquitted himself of the imputation of dullness, and obtained sundry honorary silver pennies, as acknowledgements of his application: his schoolfellows now sollicited his friendship as eagerly as they had avoided it before; and in less than a twelve-month after his arrival, this supposed dunce was remarkable for the brightness of his parts; having in that short period learnt to read English perfectly well, made great progress in writing, enabled himself to speak the French language without hesitation, and acquired some knowledge in the rudiments of the Latin tongue.

The usher did not fail to transmit an account of his proficiency to the commodore, who received it with transport, and forthwith communicated the happy tidings to the parents.

Mr. Gamaliel Pickle, who was never subject to violent emotions, heard them with a sort of phlegmatic satisfaction that scarce manifested itself either in his countenance or expressions; nor did the child's mother break forth into that rapture and admiration which might have been expected, when she understood how much the talents of her first-born had exceeded the hope of her warmest imagination. Not but that she professed herself well pleased with Perry's reputation; though she observed that in these commendations the truth was always exaggerated by school-masters, for their own interest; and pretended to wonder that the usher had not mingled more probability with his praise. Trunnion was offended at her indifference and want of faith, and believing that she refined too much in her discernment, swore that Jennings had declared the truth, and nothing but the truth; for he himself had prophecied from the beginning, that the boy would turn out a credit to his family. But by this time Mrs. Pickle was blessed with a daughter, whom she had brought into the world about six months before the intelligence arrived; so that her care and affection being otherwise engrossed, the praise of Perry was the less greedily devoured. The abatement of her fondness was an advantage to his education, which would have been retarded, and perhaps ruined by pernicious indulgence and preposterous interposition, had her love considered him as an only child; whereas her concern being now diverted to another object that shared, at least, one half of her affection, he was left to the management of his preceptor, who tutored him according to his own plan, without any lett or interruption. Indeed all his sagacity and circumspection were but barely sufficient to keep the young gentleman in order; for now that he had won the palm of victory from his rivals in point of scholarship, his ambition dilated, and he was seized with the desire of subjecting the whole school by the valour of his arm. Before he could bring this project to bear, innumerable battles were fought with various success; every day a bloody nose and complaint were presented against him, and his own visage commonly bore some livid marks of obstinate contention. At length, however, he accomplished his aim; his adversaries were subdued, his prowess acknowledged, and he obtained the laurel in war as well as wit. Thus triumphant, he was intoxicated with success. His pride rose in proportion to his power, and in spite of all the endeavours of Jennings, who practised every method he could invent for curbing his licentious conduct, without depressing his spirit, he contracted a large proportion of insolence, which a series of misfortunes that happened to him in the sequel could scarce effectually tame. Nevertheless there was a fund of good nature and generosity in his composition; and though he established a tyranny among his comrades, the tranquillity of his reign was maintained by the love rather than by the fear of his subjects.

In the midst of all this enjoyment of empire, he never once violated that respectful awe with which the usher had found means to inspire him; but he by no means preserved the same regard for the principal master, an old illiterate German quack, who had formerly practised corn-cutting among the quality, and sold cosmetic washes to the ladies, together with teeth-powders, hair-dying liquors, prolifick elixirs, and tinctures to sweeten the breath. These nostrums, recommended by the art of cringing, in which he was consummate, ingratiated him so much with people of fashion, that he was enabled to set up school with five and twenty boys of the best families, whom he boarded on his own terms, and undertook to instruct in the French and Latin languages, so as to qualify them for the colleges of Westminster or Eaton. While this plan was in its infancy, he was so fortunate as to meet with Jennings, who for the paultry consideration of thirty pounds a year, which his necessities compelled him to accept, took the whole trouble of educating the children upon himself, contrived an excellent system for that purpose, and by his assiduity and knowledge executed all the particulars to the entire satisfaction of those concerned, who by the bye, never inquired into his qualifications, but suffered the other to enjoy the fruits of his labour and ingenuity.

Over and above a large stock of avarice, ignorance and vanity, this superior had certain ridiculous peculiarities in his person, such as a hunch upon his back, and distorted limbs, that seemed to attract the satirical notice of Peregrine, who, young as he was, took offence at his want of reverence for his usher, over whom he sometimes chose opportunities of displaying his authority, that the boys might not misplace their veneration. Mr. Keypstick, therefore, such as I have described him, incurred the contempt and displeasure of this enterprising pupil, who now being in the tenth year of his age, had capacity enough to give him abundance of vexation.

CHAPTER XIII

*He exercises his Talents at the Expence of the
School-Master, whose Character and Business declining,
he desires to be recalled* [1]

As the German professed himself a man of learning, and sometimes
affected to make a parade of it, by examining the younger boys on
the rudiments of grammar, which he made shift to comprehend;
Peregrine, who was advanced as far as Cornelius Nepos,[2] used to
teize and perplex him, by frequently begging his explanation of
certain sentences in that author, while the usher was engaged in
some other employment.

On these occasions he practised a thousand pitiful shifts to conceal his own nakedness; sometimes reprehending the boy for
disturbing him in his meditations, sometimes pleading the weakness of his eyes, that hindered him from considering the passage;
and sometimes remitting him to the dictionary, as a punishment for
his inattention when it was construed by Mr. Jennings. Notwithstanding these evasions, he was persecuted by his tormentor
with such perseverance, that he could find no other resource than
that of pretending to be in a violent hurry, in consequence of which
he always quitted the place; so that whenever Perry and his companions were incommoded by his presence, they had recourse to
this expedient, which never failed to expel him in a trice.

Not contented with having thus rendered him contemptible in
the eyes of his disciples, this indefatigable wag exercised his
invention in various contrivances, to plague, disturb and expose
him.

Conscious of his own defect in point of stature and proportion,
the little pedant used all the additions of art and address to improve
his person, and raise himself as near as possible to the standard
dimensions of nature; with this view he wore shoes with heels
three inches high, strutted like a peacock in walking, and erected
his head with such muscular exertion, as rendered it impossible
for him to extend his vision downwards below the preternatural
prominence of his breast. Peregrine, therefore, taking advantage
of this foppery, used to strew his way with bean-shells, on which
whenever he chanced to tread, his heels slipped from under
him, his hunch pitched upon the ground, and the furniture of his

head fell off in the shock; so that he lay in a very ludicrous attitude for the entertainment of the spectators. He moreover seized opportunities of studding his breeches with large pins, which when he sat down with a sudden jirk, penetrated the skin of his posteriors, and compelled him to start up again with infinite expedition, and roar hideously with the pain. Nay, perceiving that he was extremely penurious in his house-keeping, he spoilt many a pot of excellent soup maigre, by slily conveying into it handfuls of salt or soot, and even drove needles into the heads of sundry fowls, that from the suddenness of their death he might conclude some infection was communicated to his poultry, and dispose of them accordingly for the half of their value. But no instance of young Pickle's mischievous talents affected him with such immediate perplexity and confusion as this that I am going to recount.

Being apprized by one of his friends that a lady of fashion intended to visit his school on a certain day, without giving any previous notice of her coming, that she might be an eye-witness of the accommodation in his house before she would commit her son to his care, he ordered his boarders and apartments to be dished out for the occasion, spared no pains in adorning his own person, and in particular employed a whole hour in adjusting a voluminous tye, in which he proposed to make his appearance. Thus prepared, he waited with great confidence and tranquillity, and no sooner saw the coach appear at a distance, than he went to his closet in order to put on the periwig, which he had deposited in a box, that no accident might ruffle or discompose it before it was presented to her ladyship; but neither the box nor its contents were to be found. At first he thought it might be misplaced by some of the servants, to whom he called with great eagerness and vociferation, while he himself ran from room to room in quest of what he wanted: the domesticks could give him no intelligence of his tye; he heard the gates opened to admit the equipage, his impatience increased, he swore in high Dutch, the noise of the wheels on his pavement saluted his ears, his vexation redoubled, and tossing his night-cap on the floor, he waddled down stairs to the hall for his ordinary periwig, which he now found himself compelled to wear. How shall I describe his distraction when he understood that too was missing! he became quite delirious, foamed at the mouth, danced to and fro in the passage like one bereft of his senses, blasphemed alternately in English and French, and must have been found by the lady in that frantic condition, had not his servants conveyed him to his own chamber by force.

The noble visitant was received by Jennings, who told her that Mr. Keypstick was confined to his bed, and explained the whole oeconomy of the school so much to her satisfaction, that she resolved to honour them with the charge of her own offspring. Keypstick fell sick in good earnest, and his intellects seemed to have received a rude shock from the violence of the passion into which he had been precipitated by the roguery of Peregrine, who had concealed both periwigs in the cellar, and now having enjoyed his trick, carried them back unperceived to the places from which they had been removed.

A whole week elapsed before the master recovered so much temper as to appear decently in public; and even then his countenance was stormy, and his resentment against the authors of his disgrace so intense, that he promised a reward of five guineas to any boy that would discover the principal actor, or any of the accomplices concerned in this audacious intrigue; declaring that no consideration should screen the offenders from condign punishment, could they once be convicted of the trick.

Pickle had not conducted this *Jeu d'esprit* without participation, and some there were privy to the affair whose fidelity was not incorruptible; but their secrecy was secured by the terror of Peregrine, whose authority and influence was such as to baffle the master in all his endeavours to unravel the conspiracy.

This extraordinary reserve, and the recollection of several other mortifying jokes he had undergone, inspired him with ungenerous suspicions of Mr. Jennings, who he could not help thinking had been at the bottom of them all, and spirited up principles of rebellion in the school, with a view of making himself independent. Possessed with this chimera, which was void of all foundation, the German descended so low as to tamper in private with the boys, from whom he hoped to draw some very important discovery; but he was disappointed in his expectation; and this mean practice reaching the ears of his usher, he voluntarily resigned his employment, and finding interest to obtain holy orders in a little time after, left the kingdom, hoping to find a settlement in some of our American plantations.

The departure of Mr. Jennings produced a great revolution in the affairs of Keypstick, which declined from that moment, because he had neither authority to enforce obedience, nor prudence to maintain order among his scholars; so that the school degenerated into anarchy and confusion, and he himself dwindled in the opinion of his imployers, who looked upon him as superannuated, and withdrew their children from his tuition.

Peregrine seeing this dissolution of their society, and finding himself every day deprived of some companion, began to repine at his situation, and resolved, if possible, to procure his release from the jurisdiction of a person whom he both detested and despised. With this view he went to work, and composed the following billet, addressed to the commodore, which was the first specimen of his composition in the epistolary way.

Honoured and loving uncle,

Hoping you are in good health, this serves to inform you, that Mr. Jennings is gone, and Mr. Keypstick will never meet with his fellow. The school is already almost broke up, and the rest daily going away; and I beg of you of all love to have me fetched away also, for I cannot bear to be any longer under one who is a perfect ignoramus, who scarce knows the declination of *musa*, and is more fit to be a scarecrow than a schoolmaster; hoping you will send for me soon, with my love to my aunt and my duty to my honoured parents, craving their blessing and yours. And this is all at present from, honoured uncle, your well-beloved and dutiful nephew and godson, and humble servant to command 'till death

Peregrine Pickle

Trunnion was overjoyed at the receit of this letter, which he looked upon as one of the greatest efforts of human genius, and as such communicated the contents to his lady, whom he had disturbed for the purpose in the middle of her devotion, by sending a message to her closet, whither it was her custom very frequently to retire. She was out of humour at being interrupted, and therefore did not peruse this specimen of her nephew's understanding with all the relish that the commodore himself had enjoyed; on the contrary, after sundry paralytical endeavours to speak, (for her tongue sometimes refused its office) she observed that the boy was a pert jackanapes, and deserved to be severely chastised for treating his betters with such disrespect. Her husband undertook his godson's defence, representing with great warmth that he knew Keypstick to be a good for nothing pimping old rascal, and that Perry shewed a great deal of spirit and good sense in desiring to be taken from under his command; he therefore declared that the boy should not live a week longer with such a shambling son of a bitch, and sanctioned his declaration with abundance of oaths.

61

Mrs. Trunnion composing her countenance into a look of religious demureness, rebuked him for his profane way of talking, and asked in a magisterial tone if he intended never to lay aside that brutal behaviour? Irritated at this reproach, he answered in terms of indignation, that he knew how to behave himself as well as e'er a woman that wore a head, bad her mind her own affairs, and with another repetition of oaths gave her to understand that he would be master in his own house.

This insinuation operated upon her spirits like friction upon a glass globe, her face gleamed with resentment, and every pore seemed to emit particles of flame. She replied with incredible fluency of the bitterest expressions. He retorted equal rage in broken hints and incoherent imprecations. She rejoined with redoubled fury, and in conclusion he was fain to betake himself to flight, ejaculating curses against her; and muttering something concerning the brandy-bottle, which, however, he took care should never reach her ears.

From his own house he went directly to visit Mrs. Pickle, to whom he imparted Peregrine's epistle with many encomiums upon the boy's promising parts; and finding his commendations but coldly received, desired she would permit him to take his godson under his own care.

This lady, whose family was now increased by another son that seemed to engross her care for the present, had not seen Perry during a course of four years, and with regard to him, was perfectly weaned of that infirmity known by the name of maternal fondness; she therefore consented to the commodore's request with great condescension, and a polite compliment to him on the concern he had all along manifested for the welfare of the child.

CHAPTER XIV

The Commodore takes Peregrine under his own Care.
The Boy arrives at the Garrison ;—is strangely received
by his own Mother ;—enters into a Confederacy with
Hatchway and Pipes, and executes a Couple of waggish
Enterprizes upon his Aunt

TRUNNION having obtained this permission that very afternoon, dispatched the lieutenant in a post chaise to Keypstick's house, from whence in two days he returned with our young hero; who being now in the eleventh year of his age, had outgrown the expectation of all his family, and was remarkable for the beauty and elegance of his person. His godfather was transported at his arrival, as if he had been actually the issue of his own loins. He shook him heartily by the hand, turned him round and round, surveyed him from top to bottom, bad Hatchway take notice how handsomely he was built; squeezed his hand again, saying, 'Damn ye, you dog, I suppose you don't value such an old crazy son of a bitch as me, a rope's end. You have forgot how I wont to dandle you on my knee, when you was a little urchin no higher than the David,[1] and played a thousand tricks upon me, burning my bacco-pouches and poisoning my rumbo: O! damn ye, you can grin fast enough I see; I warrant you have learnt more things than writing and the Latin lingo.' Even Tom Pipes expressed uncommon satisfaction on this joyful occasion; and coming up to Perry, thrust forth his fore-paw, and accosted him with the salutation of 'What chear, my young master? I am glad to see thee with all my heart.' These compliments being passed, his uncle halted to the door of his wife's chamber, at which he stood hollowing, 'Here's your kinsman Perry, belike you won't come and bid him welcome.' 'Lord! Mr. Trunnion, (said she) why will you continually harrass me in this manner with your impertinent intrusion?' 'I harrow you, (replied the commodore) 'sblood! I believe your upper works are damaged. I only came to inform you that here was your cousin, whom you have not seen these four long years; and I'll be damned if there is such another of his age within the king's dominions, d'ye see, either for make or mettle; he's a credit to the name, d'ye see, but damn my eyes I'll say no more of the matter; if you come you may, if you won't you may let it alone.' 'Well, I won't come then (answered his yoke-fellow) for I am at present more agreeably employed.' 'Oho! you are? I believe so too;' cried the commodore, making wry faces and mimicking the action of dram-drinking. Then addressing himself to Hatchway, 'Prithee Jack, (said he) go and try thy skill on that stubborn hulk; if any body can bring her about I know you wool.' The lieutenant accordingly taking his station at the door, conveyed his perswasion in these words, 'What, won't you turn out and hail little Perry? It will do your heart good to see such a handsome young dog; I'm sure he is the very moral of you, and as like as if he had been spit out of your own mouth, as the saying is; do shew a little respect for your kinsman, can't you.' To this remonstrance she replied in a mild tone of voice, 'Dear Mr. Hatchway, you are always teazing one in such a manner; sure I am, no body can tax me with unkindness, or want of natural affection;' so saying, she opened the door, and advancing to the hall where her nephew stood, received him very graciously, and observed that he was the very image of her papa.

In the afternoon he was conducted by the commodore to the house of his parents; and strange to tell, no sooner was he presented to his mother than her countenance changed, she eyed him with tokens of affliction and surprize, and bursting into tears, exclaimed her child was dead, and this was no other than an impostor whom they had brought to defraud her sorrow. Trunnion was confounded at this unaccountable passion, which had no other foundation than caprice and whim; and Gamaliel himself so disconcerted and unsettled in his own belief, which began to waver, that he knew not how to behave towards the boy, whom his godfather immediately carried back to the garrison, swearing all the way that Perry should never cross their threshold again with his good-will. Nay, so much was he incensed at this unnatural and absurd renunciation, that he refused to carry on any further correspondence with Pickle, until he was appeased by his sollicitations and submission, and Peregrine owned as his son and heir. But this acknowledgment was made without the privity of his wife, whose vicious aversion he was obliged, in appearance, to adopt. Thus exiled from his father's house, the young gentleman was left entirely to the disposal of the commodore, whose affection for him daily increased, insomuch, that he could scarce prevail upon himself to part with him, when his education absolutely required that he should be otherwise disposed of.

In all probability, this extraordinary attachment was, if not produced, at least rivetted by that peculiar turn in Peregrine's imagination, which we have already observed; and which, during his residence in the castle, appeared in sundry stratagems he practised upon his uncle and aunt, under the auspices of Mr. Hatchway, who assisted him in the contrivance and execution of all his schemes. Nor was Pipes exempted from a share in their undertakings; for, being a trusty fellow, not without dexterity in some cases, and altogether resigned to their will, they found him a serviceable instrument for their purpose, and used him accordingly.[1]

The first sample of their art was exhibited upon Mrs. Trunnion, from whose chamber Peregrine having secreted a certain utensil, divers holes were drilled through the bottom of it by their operator; and then it was replaced in a curious case that stood by the bedside, in which it was reserved for midnight-occasions. The good lady had that evening made several extraordinary visits to her closet, and that sort of exercise never failed of having a diuretic effect upon her constitution; so that she and her husband were scarce warm in bed, when she found it convenient to reach out her hand, and introduce this receptacle under the cloaths. It was then that Peregrine's roguery took effect. The commodore, who had just composed himself to rest, was instantly alarmed with a strange sensation in his right shoulder, on which something warm seemed to descend in various streams: he no sooner comprehended the nature of this shower, which in a twinkling bedewed him from head to foot, than he exclaimed, 'Blood and oons! I'm afloat!' and starting up, asked with great bitterness if she had pissed through a watering can. Equally surprized and offended at the indecent question, she began to regale him with a lecture on the subject of that respect in which she thought him so deficient; but perceiving the source of his displeasure, was silenced in the middle of the first sentence; and after a short pause of astonishment, screamed with vexation.

As there was a necessity for shifting the bed-linnen, she got up with great reluctance, rung her bell, and when her maid entered, presented this new fashioned cullender, and threatened with many choleric expressions to split it into a thousand pieces on her skull. Thunderstruck at the phænomenon, it was some time before the attendant could open her lips in her own vindication; at length, however, she protested she was innocent as the babe unborn, and that the pot was sound and intire when she rinsed it in the afternoon.

Her suspicion was of consequence transferred upon Perry, against whom she uttered many menacing invectives; though she was afterwards ashamed of disclosing her resentment, and in the mean time was fain to take up her night's lodging in another apartment; while Trunnion, after a string of unmeaning oaths, which were extorted from him by his present uncomfortable situation, could not help laughing at the adventure; and Peregrine with his confederates, applauded themselves in secret for having reduced them to such ridiculous distress.

Encouraged by the impunity with which they performed this feat, our associates atchieved another, that had like to have been attended with very serious consequences. Mrs. Trunnion having one day received a sudden call which she could not help obeying, her nephew, who was always on the scout, took that opportunity of gliding unseen into her closet, and finding her case open, infused into one of the bottles a good quantity of powdered jallap,[1] which had been purchased by the lieutenant for that purpose. He had desired the apothecary, from whom he bought it, to give him as much as would impregnate two quarts of brandy, which, he guessed, each bottle might contain; and never dreamed that the patient, though left to her own discretion, was in any danger of taking an over-dose; he therefore directed Perry to convey the whole proportion into one of the full bottles that stood at some distance from that which he would perceive was in present use, that the spirits might have time to extract the virtues of the root before it should come to their turn. Every thing was done according to his prescription, and a very small hole being bored in the wainscot, through which they could reconnoitre her from another room; they observed her motions by turns, with a view of seeing whether or not she would be alarmed by the extraordinary taste of the tincture they had made.

When they had watched in this manner for three or four days, Pipes being upon duty, perceived her take the first cup of the composition, which she had no sooner swallowed, than she began to shut her eyes, smack her lips, spit and express all the marks of loathing and disgust: nevertheless, she seemed to doubt her own sense, rather than the flavour of the Coniac, the neatness of which she had already experienced, and therefore repeated the cordial, as if in defiance to her own distaste; taking care, however, to arm her palate with a large lump of sugar, through which it was strained in its passage.

Hatchway was startled when he understood she had taken such a dangerous draught of the medicine, especially as she had immediately after stepped into the coach to go to church, where he feared she might catch cold, or be otherwise affected, to the jeopardy of her person and the prejudice of her reputation. Nor was his fear altogether disappointed. The service was not half performed, when Mrs. Trunnion was suddenly taken ill; her face underwent violent flushings and vicissitudes of complexion; a cold clammy sweat bedewed her forehead, and her bowels were afflicted with such agonies, as compelled her to retire in the face of the congregation. She was brought home in torture, which was a little assuaged when the dose began to operate; but such was the excess of evacuation she sustained, that her spirits were quite exhausted, and she suffered a succession of fainting fits that reduced her to the brink of the grave, in spite of all the remedies that were administered by a physician who was called in the beginning of her disorder, and who, after having examined the symptoms, declared that the patient had been poisoned with arsenic, and prescribed oily draughts and lubricating injections to defend the coats of the stomach and intestines from the vellicating particles of that pernicious mineral; at the same time hinting, with a look of infinite sagacity, that it was not difficult to divine the whole mystery; and affecting to deplore the poor lady, as if she was exposed to more attempts of the same nature; thereby glancing obliquely at the innocent commodore, whom the officious son of Æsculapius suspected as the author of this expedient, to rid his hands of a yoke-fellow, for whom he was well known to have no great devotion. This impertinent and malicious insinuation made some impression upon the by-standers, and furnished ample field for slander, to asperse the morals of Trunnion, who was represented through the whole district as a monster of barbarity. Nay, the sufferer herself, though she behaved with great decency and prudence, could not help entertaining some small diffidence of her husband: not that she imagined he had any design upon her life, but that he had been at pains to adulterate the brandy, with the view of detaching her from that favourite liquor.

On this supposition she resolved to act with more caution for the future, without setting on foot any inquiry about the affair; while the commodore imputing her indisposition to some natural cause, after the danger was past, never bestowed a thought upon the subject, so that the perpetrators were quit for their fear, which, however, had punished them so effectually, that they never would hazard any more jokes of the same nature.

CHAPTER XV

The Triumvirate turn the Stream of their Wit upon the Commodore, who by their Means is embroiled with an Attorney, and terrified with an Apparition

THE shafts of their wit were now directed against the commander himself, whom they teized and terrified almost out of his senses. One day while he was at dinner, Pipes came and told him that there was a person below that wanted to speak with him immediately about an affair of the greatest importance, that would admit of no delay; upon which he ordered the stranger to be told that he was engaged, and that he must send up his name and business. To this demand he received for answer a message, importing that the person's name was unknown to him, and his business of such a nature, that it could not be disclosed to any one but the commodore himself, whom he earnestly desired to see without loss of time.

Trunnion, surprised at this importunity, got up with great reluctance in the middle of his meal, and descending to a parlour where the stranger was, asked in a surly tone what he wanted with him in such a damned hurry, that he could not wait till he had made an end of his mess. The other, not at all disconcerted at this rough address, advanced close up to him on his tiptoes, and with a look of confidence and conceit, laying his mouth to one side of the commodore's head, whispered softly in his ear, 'Sir, I am the attorney whom you wanted to converse with in private.' 'The attorney!' cried Trunnion, staring and half choked with choler. 'Yes, Sir, at your service, (replied this retainer to the law) and if you please, the sooner we dispatch the affair the better; for 'tis an old observation, that delay breeds danger.' 'Truly, brother, (said the commodore, who could no longer contain himself) I do confess that I am very much of your way of thinking, d'ye see; and therefore you shall be dispatched in a trice;' so saying, he lifted up his walking staff, which was something between a crutch and a cudgel, and discharged it with such energy on the seat of the attorney's understanding, that if there had been any thing but solid bone, the contents of his skull must have been evacuated.

Fortified as he was by nature against all such assaults, he could not withstand the momentum of the blow, which in an instant laid him flat on the floor, deprived of all sense and motion; and Trunnion hopped up stairs to dinner, applauding himself in ejaculations all the way for the vengeance he had taken on such an impudent pettifogging miscreant.

The attorney no sooner awaked from this trance, into which he had been so unexpectedly lulled, than he cast his eyes around in quest of evidence, by which he might be enabled the more easily to prove the injury he had sustained; but not a soul appearing, he made shift to get upon his legs again, and with the blood trickling over his nose, followed one of the servants into the dining-room, resolved to come to an explanation with the assailant, and either extort money from him by way of satisfaction, or provoke him to a second application before witnesses. With this view he entered the room in a peal of clamour, to the amazement of all present, and the terror of Mrs. Trunnion, who shrieked at the appearance of such a spectacle; and addressing himself to the commodore, 'I'll tell you what, Sir, (said he) if there be law in England, I'll make you smart for this here assault; you think you have screened yourself from a prosecution, by sending all your servants out of the way, but that circumstance will appear upon trial to be a plain proof of the malice propense with which the fact was committed; especially when corroborated by the evidence of this here letter, under your own hand, whereby I am desired to come to your own house to transact an affair of consequence;' so saying, he produced the writing, and read the contents in these words.

Mr. ROGER RAVINE

Sir,

Being in a manner prisoner in my own house, I desire you will give me a call precisely at three o'clock in the afternoon, and insist upon seeing myself, as I have an affair of great consequence, in which your particular advice is wanted by your humble servant

HAWSER TRUNNION

The one-eyed commander who had been satisfied with the chastisement he had already bestowed upon the plaintiff, hearing him read this audacious piece of forgery, which he considered as the effect of his own villany, started up from table, and seizing a huge turkey that lay in a dish before him, would have applied it sauce and all by way of poultice to his wound, had he not been restrained by Hatchway, who laid fast hold on both his arms, and fixed him to his chair again, advising the attorney to sheer off with what he had got. Far from following this salutary counsel, he redoubled his threats, and set Trunnion at defiance, telling him he was not a man of true courage, although he had commanded a ship of war, or else he would not have attacked any person in such a cowardly and clandestine manner. This provocation would have answered his purpose effectually, had not his adversary's indignation been repressed by the suggestions of the lieutenant who desired his friend in a whisper to be easy, for he would take care to have the attorney tossed in a blanket for his presumption. This proposal, which he received with great approbation, pacified him in a moment; he wiped the sweat from his forehead, and his features relaxed into a grim smile.

Hatchway disappeared, and Ravine proceeded with great fluency of abuse, until he was interrupted by the arrival of Pipes, who, without any expostulation, led him out by the hand, and conducted him to the yard, where he was put into a carpet, and in a twinkling sent into the air by the strength and dexterity of five stout operators, whom the lieutenant had selected from the number of domesticks for that singular spell of duty.

In vain did the astonished vaulter beg for the love of God and passion of Christ, that they would take pity upon him, and put an end to his involuntary gambols; they were deaf to his prayers and protestations, even when he swore in the most solemn manner, that if they would cease tormenting him, he would forget and forgive what was passed, and depart in peace to his own habitation; and continued the game till they were fatigued with the exercise.

Ravine being dismissed in a most melancholy plight, brought an action of assault and battery against the commodore, and subpœna'd all the servants as evidences in the cause; but as none of them had seen what happened, he did not find his account in the prosecution, though he himself examined all the witnesses, and among other questions, asked whether they had not seen him come in like another man? and whether they had ever seen any other man in such a condition as that in which he had crawled off? But this last interrogation they were not obliged to answer, because it had reference to the second discipline he had undergone, in which they, and they only were concerned; and no person is bound to give testimony against himself.

In short, the attorney was nonsuited, to the satisfaction of all who knew him, and found himself under the necessity of proving that he had received in course of post, the letter which was declared in court a scandalous forgery, in order to prevent an indictment with which he was threatened by the commodore, who little dreamt that the whole affair had been planned and executed by Peregrine and his associates.

The next enterprize in which this triumvirate engaged, was a scheme to frighten Trunnion with an apparition, which they prepared and exhibited in this manner. To the hide of a large ox Pipes fitted a leathern vizor of a most terrible appearance, stretched on the jaws of a shark which he had brought from sea, and accommodated with a couple of broad glasses instead of eyes. On the inside of these he placed two rush lights, and with a composition of sulphur and saltpetre, made a pretty large fuse, which he fixed between two rows of the teeth. This equipage being finished, he, one dark night chosen for the purpose, put it on, and following the commodore into a long passage in which he was preceded by Perry with a light in his hand, kindled his fire-work with a match, and began to bellow like a bull. The boy, as it was concerted, looking behind him, screamed aloud, and dropped the light, which was extinguished in the fall: when Trunnion alarmed at his nephew's consternation, exclaimed, 'Zounds! what's the matter.' And turning about to see the cause of his dismay, beheld a hideous phantom vomiting blue flame, which aggravated the horrors of its aspect. He was instantly seized with an agony of fear, which divested him of his reason; nevertheless, he, as it were mechanically, raised his trusty supporter in his own defence, and the apparition advancing towards him, aimed it at this dreadful annoyance with such a convulsive exertion of strength, that had not the blow chanced to light upon one of the horns, Mr. Pipes would have had no cause to value himself upon his invention. Misapplied as it was, he did not fail to stagger at the shock, and dreading another such salutation, closed with the commodore, and having tripped up his heels, retreated with great expedition.

It was then that Peregrine, pretending to recollect himself a little, ran with all the marks of disturbance and affright, and called up the servants to the assistance of their master, whom they found in a cold sweat upon the floor, his features betokening horror and confusion. Hatchway raised him up, and having comforted him with a cup of Nantz, began to inquire into the cause of his disorder: but he could not extract one word of answer from his friend, who, after a considerable pause, during which he seemed to be wrapped up in profound contemplation, pronounced aloud, 'By the Lord! Jack, you may say what you wool; but I'll be damned if it was not

E

Davy Jones himself: I know him by his saucer-eyes, his three rows of teeth, his horns and tail, and the blue smoak that came out of his nostrils. What does the black-guard, hell's baby want with me? I'm sure I never committed murder, nor wronged any man whatsomever, since I first went to sea.' This same Davy Jones, according to the mythology of sailors, is the fiend that presides over all the evil spirits of the deep, and is often seen in various shapes, perching among the rigging on the eve of hurricanes, shipwrecks, and other disasters, to which a sea-faring life is exposed; *warning the devoted wretch of death and woe.*[1] No wonder then that Trunnion was disturbed by a supposed visit of this dæmon, which, in his opinion, foreboded some dreadful calamity.

CHAPTER XVI

*He is also by their Device engaged in an Adventure
with the Exciseman, who does not find his Account
in his own Drollery*

HOWSOEVER preposterous and unaccountable that passion may be, which prompts persons, otherwise generous and sympathising, to afflict and perplex their fellow-creatures, certain it is our confederates entertained such a large proportion of it, that not satisfied with the pranks they had already played, they still persecuted the commodore without ceasing. In the course of his own history, the particulars of which he delighted to recount, he had often rehearsed an adventure of deer-stealing, in which (during the unthinking impetuosity of his youth) he had been unfortunately concerned. Far from succeeding in that atchievement, he and his associates had (it seems) been made prisoners, after an obstinate engagement with the keepers, and carried before a neighbouring justice of the peace, who used Trunnion with great indignity, and with his companions committed him to jail.

His own relations, and in particular an uncle on whom he chiefly depended, treated him during his confinement with great rigour and inhumanity, and absolutely refused to interpose his influence in his behalf, unless he would sign a writing, obliging himself to go to sea within thirty days after his release, under the penalty of being proceeded against as a felon. The alternative was either to undergo this voluntary exile, or remain in prison disowned and deserted by every body, and after all suffer an ignominious trial, that might end in a sentence of transportation for life. He therefore, without much hesitation, embraced the proposal of his kinsman, and (as he observed) was in less than a month after his discharge turned adrift to the mercy of the wind and waves.

Since that period he had never maintained any correspondence with his relations, all of whom had concurred in sending him off; nor would he ever pay the least regard to the humiliations and supplications of some among them, who had prostrated themselves before him, on the advancement of his fortune: but he retained a most inveterate resentment for his uncle, who was still in being, tho' extremely old and infirm, and frequently mentioned his name with all the bitterness of revenge.

Perry being perfectly well acquainted with the particulars of this story, which he had heard so often repeated, proposed to Hatchway, that a person should be hired to introduce himself to the commodore, with a supposititious letter of recommendation from this detested kinsman; an imposition that, in all likelihood, would afford abundance of diversion.

The lieutenant relished the scheme, and young Pickle having composed an epistle for the occasion, the exciseman of the parish, a fellow of great impudence and some humour, in whom Hatchway could confide, undertook to transcribe and deliver it with his own hand, and also personate the man in whose favour it was feigned to be writ. He, accordingly, one morning arrived on horseback at the garrison, two hours at least before Trunnion used to get up, and gave Pipes, who admitted him, to understand, that he had a letter for his master, which he was ordered to deliver to none but the commodore himself. This message was no sooner communicated, than the indignant chief (who had been waked for the purpose) began to curse the messenger for breaking his rest, and swore he would not budge till his usual time of turning out. This resolution being conveyed to the stranger, he desired the carrier to go back and tell him, he had such joyful tidings to impart, that he was sure the commodore would think himself amply rewarded for his trouble, even if he had been raised from the grave to receive them.

This assurance, flattering as it was, would not have been powerful enough to persuade him, had it not been assisted with the exhortations of his spouse, which never failed to influence his conduct. He therefore crept out of bed, tho' not without great repugnance, and wrapping himself in his morning-gown, was

73

supported down stairs, rubbing his eye, yawning fearfully, and grumbling all the way. As soon as he popt his head into the parlour, the supposed stranger made divers awkward bows, and with a grinning aspect accosted him in these words: 'Your most humble servant, most noble commodore! I hope you are in good health; you look pure and hearty; and if it was not for that misfortune of your eye, one would not desire to see a more pleasant countenance in a summer's day. Sure as I am a living soul, one would take you to be on this side of threescore. Laud help us! I should have known you to be a Trunnion if I had met with you in the midst of Salisbury-plain, as the saying is.' The commodore, who was not at all in the humour of relishing such an impertinent preamble, interrupted him in this place, saying with a peevish accent, 'Pshaw! pshaw! brother, there's no occasion to bowss out so much unnecessary gum; if you can't bring your discourse to bear on the right subject, you had much better clap a stopper on your tongue, and bring yourself up, d'ye see: I was told you had something to deliver.' 'Deliver! (cried the waggish impostor) odds heart! I have got something for you that will make your very intrails rejoice within your body. Here's a letter from a dear and worthy friend of yours. Take, read it and be happy. Blessings on his old heart! one would think he had renewed his age, like the eagles.' Trunnion's expectation being thus raised, he called for his spectacles, adjusted them to his eye, took the letter, and being curious to know the subscription, no sooner perceived his uncle's name, than he started back, his lip quivered, and he began to shake in every limb with resentment and surprize: nevertheless, eager to know the subject of an epistle from a person who had never before troubled him with any sort of address, he endeavoured to recollect himself, and perused the contents, which were these:

Loving Nephew,

I doubt not but you will be rejoiced to hear of my welfare; and well you may, considering what a kind uncle I have been to you in the days of your youth, and how little you deserved any such thing; for you was always a graceless young man, given to wicked courses and bad company, whereby you would have come to a shameful end, had it not been for my care in sending you out of mischief's way. But this is not the cause of my present writing. The bearer, Mr. Timothy Trickle, is a distant relation of yours, being the son of the cousin of your aunt Margery, and is not over and above well as to worldly matters. He thinks of going to London, to see for some post in the excise or customs, if so be that you will recommend him to some great man of your acquaintance, and give him a small matter to keep him till he is provided. I doubt not, nephew, but you will be glad to serve him, if it was no more but for the respect you bear to me, who am,

Loving Nephew,
Your affectionate Uncle,
and Servant to command,
TOBIAH TRUNNION

It would be a difficult task for the inimitable Hogarth himself to exhibit the ludicrous expression of the commodore's countenance, while he read this letter. It was not a stare of astonishment, a convulsion of rage, or a ghastly grin of revenge, but an association of all three, that took possession of his features. At length he hawked up, with incredible straining, the interjection ah! that seemed to have stuck some time in his windpipe, and thus gave vent to his indignation: 'Have I come along side of you at last, you old stinking curmudgeon! you lie, you lousy hulk, ye lie! you did all in your power to founder me when I was a stripling; and as for being graceless, and wicked, and keeping bad company, you tell a damned lie again, you thief; there was not a more peaceable lad in the county, and I kept no bad company but your own, d'ye see. Therefore, you Trickle, or what's your name, tell the old rascal that sent you hither, that I spit in his face, and call him *Horse*; that I tear his letter into rags, so; and that I trample upon it as I would upon his own villainous carcase, d'ye see.' So saying, he danced in a sort of frenzy upon the fragments of the paper which he had scattered about the room, to the inexpressible satisfaction of the triumvirate, who beheld the scene.

The exciseman having got between him and the door, which was left open for his escape, in case of necessity, affected great confusion and surprize at this behaviour, saying, with an air of mortification, 'Lord, be merciful unto me! is this the way you treat your own relations, and the recommendation of your best friend? Surely all gratitude and virtue has left this sinful world! What will cousin Tim, and Dick, and Tom, and good mother Pipkin, and her daughters, cousin Sue, and Prue, and Peg, with all the rest of our kinsfolks say, when they hear of this unconscionable reception that I have met with. Consider, Sir, that ingratitude is worse than the sin of witchcraft, as the apostle wisely observes; and do not send me away with such unchristian usage, which will lay a heavy load of guilt upon your poor miserable soul.' 'What you are on the cruize for a post, brother Trickle, an't ye? (said Trunnion, interrupting him) we shall find a post for you in a trice, my boy. Here, Pipes, take this saucy son of a bitch, belay him to the whipping post in the yard. I'll teach you to rowce me in a morning with such impertinent messages.' Pipes, who wanted to carry the joke farther than the exciseman dreamt of, laid hold on him in a twinkling, and executed the orders of his commander, notwithstanding all his nods, winking, and significant gestures, which the boatswain's mate would by no means understand: so that he began to repent of the part he acted in this performance, which was like to end so tragically, and stood fastened to the stake, in a very disagreeable state of suspence; casting many a rueful look over his left shoulder, (while Pipes was absent in quest of a cat and nine tails) in expectation of being relieved by the interposition of the lieutenant, who did not, however, appear; and Tom returning with the instrument of correction, undressed the delinquent in a trice, and whispering in his ear, that he was very sorry for being employed in such an office, but durst not for his soul disobey the orders of his commander, flourished the scourge about his head, and with admirable dexterity made' such a smarting application to the offender's back and shoulders, that the distracted gauger performed sundry new cuts with his feet, and bellowed hideously with pain, to the infinite satisfaction of the spectators. At length, when he was almost flead from his rump to the nape of his neck, Hatchway, who had purposely absented himself hitherto, appeared in the yard, and interposing in his behalf, prevailed upon Trunnion to call off the executioner, and order the malefactor to be released.

The exciseman, mad with the catastrophe he had undergone, threatened to be revenged upon his employers, by making a candid confession of the whole plot; but the lieutenant giving him to understand, that in so doing he would bring upon himself a prosecution for fraud, forgery and imposture, he was fain to put up with his loss, and sneaked out of the garrison, attended with a volley of curses discharged upon him by the commodore, who was exceedingly irritated by the disturbance and disappointment he had undergone.

CHAPTER XVII

*The Commodore detects the Machinations of the
Conspirators, and hires a Tutor for Peregrine,
whom he settles at Winchester School*

THIS was not the last affliction he suffered from the unwearied
endeavours and inexhausted invention of his tormentors, who
harrassed him with such a variety of mischievous pranks, that he
began to think all the devils in hell had conspired against his peace;
and accordingly became very serious and contemplative on the
subject.

In the course of his meditations, when he recollected and compared the circumstances of every mortification to which he had
been lately exposed, he could not help suspecting that some of
them must have been contrived to vex him; and as he was not
ignorant of his lieutenant's disposition, nor unacquainted with the
talents of Peregrine, he resolved to observe them both for the
future with the utmost care and circumspection. This resolution,
aided by the incautious conduct of the conspirators, whom, by
this time, success had rendered heedless and indiscreet, was
attended with the desired effect. He in a little time detected Perry
in a new plot, and by dint of a little chastisement, and a great many
threats, extorted from him a confession of all the contrivances in
which he had been concerned. The commodore was thunderstruck
at the discovery, and so much incensed against Hatchway for the
part he had acted in the whole, that he deliberated with himself,
whether he should demand satisfaction with sword and pistol,
or dismiss him from the garison, and renounce all friendship with
him at once. But he had been so long accustomed to Jack's company, that he could not live without him; and upon more cool
reflection, perceiving that what he had done was rather the effect of
wantonness than malice, which he himself would have laughed to
see take place upon any other person, he determined to devour his
chagrin, and extend his forgiveness even to Pipes, whom in the
first sally of his passion he had looked upon in a more criminal light
than that of a simple mutineer. This determination was seconded
by another, which he thought absolutely necessary for his own
repose, and in which his own interest and that of his nephew concurred.

Peregrine, who was now turned of twelve, had made such advances under the instruction of Jennings, that he often disputed upon grammar, and was sometimes thought to have the better in his contests with the parish-priest, who, notwithstanding this acknowledged superiority of his antagonist, did great justice to his genius, which he assured Mr. Trunnion would be lost for want of cultivation, if the boy was not immediately sent to prosecute his studies at some proper seminary of learning.

This maxim had more than once been inculcated upon the commodore by Mrs. Trunnion, who, over and above the deference she paid to the parson's opinion, had a reason of her own for wishing to see the house clear of Peregrine, at whose prying disposition she began to be very uneasy. Induced by these motives, which were joined by the sollicitation of the youth himself, who ardently longed to see a little more of the world, his uncle determined to send him forthwith to Winchester, under the immediate care and inspection of a governor, to whom he allowed a very handsome appointment for that purpose. This gentleman, whose name was Mr. Jacob Jolter,[1] had been schoolfellow with the parson of the parish, who recommended him to Mrs. Trunnion as a person of great worth and learning, in every respect qualified for the office of a tutor. He likewise added, by way of eulogium, that he was a man of exemplary piety, and particularly zealous for the honour of the church of which he was a member, having been many years in holy orders, tho' he did not then exercise any function of the priesthood. Indeed, Mr. Jolter's zeal was so exceedingly fervent, as, on some occasions, to get the better of his discretion: for, being an high-churchman, and of consequence a malecontent, his resentment was habituated into an insurmountable prejudice against the present disposition of affairs, which, by confounding the nation with the ministry, sometimes led him into erroneous, not to say absurd calculations; otherwise, a man of good morals, well versed in mathematicks and school-divinity, studies which had not at all contributed to sweeten and unbend the natural sourness and severity of his complexion.

This gentleman being destined to the charge of superintending Perry's education, every thing was prepared for their departure; and Tom Pipes, in consequence of his own petition, put into livery, and appointented footman to the young squire. But, before they set out, the commodore paid the compliment of communicating his design to Mr. Pickle, who approved of the plan, tho' he durst not venture to see the boy; so much was he intimidated

78

by the remonstrances of his wife, whose aversion to her first-born became every day more inveterate and unaccountable. This unnatural caprice seemed to be supported by a consideration which (one would imagine) might have rather vanquished her disgust. Her second son Gam, who was now in the fourth year of his age, had been ricketty from the cradle, and as remarkably unpromising in appearance as Perry was agreeable in his person. As the deformity increased, the mother's fondness was augmented, and the virulence of her hate against the other son seemed to prevail in the same proportion.

Far from allowing Perry to enjoy the common privileges of a child, she would not suffer him to approach his father's house, expressed uneasiness whenever his name happened to be mentioned, sickened at his praise, and in all respects behaved like a most rancorous stepmother. Tho' she no longer retained that ridiculous notion of his being an impostor, she still continued to abhor him, as if she really believed him to be such; and when any person desired to know the cause of her surprising dislike, she always lost her temper, and peevishly replied, that she had reasons of her own, which she was not obliged to declare: nay, so much was she infected by this vicious partiality, that she broke off all commerce with her sister-in-law and the commodore, because they favoured the poor child with their countenance and protection.

Her malice, however, was frustrated by the love and generosity of Trunnion, who having adopted him as his own son, equipped him accordingly, and carried him and his governor in his own coach to the place of destination, where they were settled on a very genteel footing, and every thing regulated according to their desires.

Mrs. Trunnion behaved with great decency at the departure of her nephew, to whom, with a great many pious advices, and injunctions to behave with submission and reverence towards his tutor, she presented a diamond ring of small value, and a gold medal, as tokens of her affection and esteem. As for the lieutenant, he accompanied them in the coach; and such was the friendship he had contracted for Perry, that when the commodore proposed to return, after having accomplished the intent of his journey, Jack absolutely refused to attend him, and signified his resolution to stay where he was.

Trunnion was the more startled at this declaration, as Hatchway was become so necessary to him in almost all the purposes of his life, that he foresaw he should not be able to exist without his company. Not a little affected with this consideration, he turned his eye ruefully upon the lieutenant, saying in a piteous tone, 'What! leave me at last, Jack, after we have weathered so many hard gales together? D—n my limbs! I thought you had been more of an honest heart: I looked upon you as my foremast, and Tom Pipes as my mizzen; now he is carried away, if so be as you go too, my standing rigging being decayed, d'ye see, the first squall will bring me by the board. D—n ye, if in case I have given offence, can't ye speak above-board? and I shall make you amends.'

Jack being ashamed to own the true situation of his thoughts, after some hesitation, answered with perplexity and incoherence, 'No, damme! that an't the case neither: to be sure you always used me in an officer-like manner, that I must own, to give the devil his due, as the saying is; but for all that, this here is the case, I have some thoughts of going to school myself to learn your Latin lingo; for, as the saying is, *Better late mend than never will do well*: and I am informed as how one can get more for the money here than any where else.'

In vain did Trunnion endeavour to convince him of the folly of going to school at his years, by representing that the boys would make game of him, and that he would become a laughing-stock to all the world; he persisted in his resolution to stay, and the com- modore was fain to have recourse to the mediation of Pipes and Perry, who employed their influence with Jack, and at last prevailed upon him to return to the garison, after Trunnion had promised he should be at liberty to visit them once a month. This stipulation being settled, he and his friend took leave of the pupil, governor and attendant, and next morning set out for their habitation, which they reached in safety that same night.

Such was Hatchway's reluctance to leave Peregrine, that he is said, for the first time in his life, to have looked misty at parting: certain I am, that on the road homewards, after a long pause of silence, which the commodore never dreamt of interrupting, he exclaimed all of a sudden, 'I'll be damned if the dog han't given me some stuff to make me love him.'[1] Indeed there was something congenial in the disposition of these two friends, which never failed to manifest itself in the sequel, howsoever different their education, circumstances and connexions happened to be.

CHAPTER XVIII

Peregrine distinguishes himself among his School-fellows,
exposes his Tutor,
and attracts the particular Notice of the Master

THUS left to the prosecution of his studies, Peregrine was in a little
time a distinguished character, not only for his acuteness of apprehension, but also for that mischievous fertility of fancy, of which
we have already given such pregnant examples. But as there was
a great number of such luminaries in this new sphere to which he
belonged, his talents were not so conspicuous, while they shone in
his single capacity, as they afterwards appeared, when they con-
centrated and reflected the rays of the whole constellation.

At first he confined himself to piddling game, exercising his
genius upon his own tutor, who attracted this attention, by endeavouring to season his mind with certain political maxims, the
fallacy of which he had discernment enough to perceive. Scarce
a day passed, on which he did not find means to render Mr. Jolter
the object of ridicule; his violent prejudices, ludicrous vanity,
aukward solemnity and ignorance of mankind, afforded continual
food for the raillery, petulance and satire of his pupil, who never
neglected an opportunity of laughing, and making others laugh at
his expence.

Sometimes in their parties, by mixing brandy in his wine, he
decoyed this pedagogue into a debauch, during which his caution
forsook him, and he exposed himself to the censure of the company.
Sometimes, when the conversation turned upon intricate subjects,
he practised upon him the Socratic method of confutation, and,
under pretence of being informed, by an artful train of puzzling
questions, insensibly betrayed him into self-contradiction: and at
one time he, in a most dexterous manner, set on foot a correspondence between him and the chambermaid of the house, which
ended in his utter shame and confusion.[1] The wench was handsome, Jolter was frail; and one evening, while in his cups, beheld
her with a carnal eye.

Perry, who was ever on the catch, discovered his longing, and
prevailed upon the object of his passion to feed his flame with small
favours, until it became too violent to be restrained: he then urged
his addresses with redoubled ardor, promised, vowed, bribed and

intreated; the inamorata seemed to yield, and blessed him with a declaration, that her chamber-door should be left open at midnight.

True to the assignation, he rose at the hour appointed, and full of the most vigorous expectation, in his shirt, darkling explored his way to the place of rendezvous. His heart throbbed with joy when he found immediate admittance; he saw the cap of his Dulcinea, who seemed to be asleep; he sprung into bed, and clasped in his arms————oh heavens! no other than the traitor Pipes, who, by his master's direction, personated the maid; and returned the embrace with such muscular contraction, that the unfortunate lover felt the disappointment, and the impossibility of disengaging himself, at the same time. His malicious pupil, attended by another scholar who lived in the same house, and the sly jilt who was the cause of this disaster, immediately entered the room with lights, and detected the forlorn governor in all the mortification of disgrace.

This adventure destroyed all the remains of authority which he had hitherto preserved over Peregrine; so that, for the future, no sort of ceremony subsisted between them, and all Mr. Jolter's precepts were conveyed in hints of friendly advice, which the other might either follow or neglect at his own pleasure. No wonder then that Peregrine gave a loose to his inclinations, and by dint of genius and an enterprising temper, made a figure among the younger class of heroes in the college.

Before he had been a full year at Winchester, he had signalized himself in so many atchievements, in defiance to the laws and regulations of the place, that he was looked upon with admiration, and actually chosen *Dux*, or leader, by a large body of his contemporaries. It was not long before his fame reached the ears of the master, who sent for Mr. Jolter, communicated to him the informations he had received, and desired him to check the vivacity of his charge, and redouble his vigilance in time to come, else he should be obliged to make a public example of his pupil for the benefit of the school.

The governor, conscious of his own unimportance, was not a little disconcerted at this injunction, which it was not in his power to fulfil by any compulsive means. He therefore went home in a very pensive mood, and after mature deliberation, resolved to expostulate with Peregrine in the most familiar terms, and endeavour to dissuade him from practices which might affect his character as well as interest. He accordingly frankly told him the subject of the master's discourse, represented the disgrace he might incur by neglecting this warning; and putting him in mind of his own situation, hinted the consequences of the commodore's displeasure, in case he should be brought to disapprove of his conduct. These insinuations made the greater impression, as they were delivered with many expressions of friendship and concern. The young gentleman was not so raw, but that he could perceive the solidity of Mr. Jolter's advice, to which he promised to conform, because his pride was interested in the affair; and he considered his own reformation as the only means of avoiding that infamy which even in idea he could not bear.

His governor finding him so reasonable, profited by these moments of reflection, and in order to prevent a relapse, proposed that he should engage in some delightful study that would agreeably amuse his imagination, and gradually detach him from those connexions which had involved him in so many troublesome adventures. For this purpose, he, with many rapturous encomiums, recommended the mathematics, as yielding more rational and sensible pleasure to a youthful fancy than any other subject of contemplation; and actually began to read Euclid with him that same afternoon.

Peregrine entered upon this branch of learning with all that warmth of application which boys commonly yield on the first change of study; but he had scarce advanced beyond the *Pons Asinorum*,[1] when his ardor abated, the test of truth by demonstration did not elevate him to those transports of joy with which his preceptor had regaled his expectation; and before he arrived at the fortieth and seventh proposition, he began to yawn drearily, make abundance of wry faces, and thought himself but indifferently paid for his attention, when he shared the vast discovery of Pythagoras, and understood that the square of the hypothenuse was equal to the squares of the other two sides of a right-angled triangle. He was ashamed, however, to fail in his undertaking, and persevered with great industry, until he had finished the first four books, acquired plain trigonometry, with the method of algebraical calculation, and made himself well acquainted with the principles of surveying. But no consideration could prevail upon him to extend his inquiries farther in this science; and he returned with double relish to his former avocations, like a stream which being dammed, accumulates more force, and bursting o'er its mounds, rushes down with double impetuosity.

Mr. Jolter saw with astonishment and chagrin, but could not

resist the torrent. His behaviour was now no other than a series of licence and effrontery; prank succeeded prank, and outrage followed outrage with surprising velocity. Complaints were every day preferred against him; in vain were admonitions bestowed by the governor in private, and menaces discharged by the masters in publick; he disregarded the first, despised the latter, divested himself of all manner of restraint, and proceeded in his career to such a pitch of audacity, that a consultation was held upon the subject, in which it was determined that this untoward spirit should be humbled by a severe and ignominious flogging for the very next offence he should commit; and in the mean time that Mr. Jolter should be desired to write in the master's name to the commodore, requesting him to remove Tom Pipes from the person of his nephew, the said Pipes being a principal actor and abettor in all his malversations; and to put a stop to the monthly visitations of the mutilated lieutenant, who had never once failed to use his permission, but came punctual to a day, always fraught with some new invention. Indeed, by this time, Mr. Hatchway was as well known, and much better beloved by every boy in the school than the master who instructed him, and always received by a number of the scholars who used to attend Peregrine when he went forth to meet his friend, and conduct him to his lodging with public testimonies of joy and applause.

As for Tom Pipes he was not so properly the attendant of Peregrine, as master of the revels to the whole school. He mingled in all their parties, and superintended the diversions, deciding between boy and boy, as if he acted by commission under the great seal. He regulated their motions by his whistle, instructed the young boys in the games of hussle-cap, leap-frog, and chuck farthing; imparted to those of a more advanced age the sciences of cribbidge and all-fours, together with the method of storming the castle, acting the comedy of Prince Arthur, and other pantomimes, as they are commonly exhibited at sea; and instructed the seniors who were distinguished by the appellation of bloods, in cudgel-playing, dancing the St. Giles's hornpipe, drinking flip and smoking tobacco. These qualifications had rendered him so necessary and acceptable to the scholars, that exclusive of Perry's concern in the affair, his dismission in all probability would have produced some dangerous convulsion in the community. Jolter, therefore, knowing his importance, informed his pupil of the directions he had received, and very candidly asked how he should demean himself in the execution; for he durst not write to the commodore without this previous notice, fearing that the young gentleman, as soon as he should get an inkling of the affair, would follow the example, and make his uncle acquainted with certain anecdotes, which it was the governor's interest to keep concealed. Peregrine was of opinion that he should spare himself the trouble of conveying any complaints to the commodore; and if questioned by the master, assure him he had complied with his desire; at the same time he promised faithfully to conduct himself with such circumspection for the future, that the masters should have no temptation to revive the inquiry. But the resolution attending this extorted promise was too frail to last, and in less than a fortnight our young hero found himself intangled in an adventure from which he was not extricated with his usual good fortune.

CHAPTER XIX

He is concerned in a dangerous Adventure with a
certain Gardener ; heads an Insurrection in the School ;
takes the Field with his Adherents, marches up into
the Country, and fixes his Head Quarters at an Inn

HE and some of his companions one day entered a garden in the suburbs, and having indulged their appetites, desired to know what satisfaction they must make for the fruit they had pulled. The gardener demanded what (in their opinion) was an exorbitant price, and they with many opprobious terms refused to pay it. The peasant being surly and intractable, insisted upon his right; neither was he deficient or sparing in the eloquence of vulgar abuse. His guests attempted to retreat, a scuffle ensued, in which Peregrine lost his cap, and the gardener being in danger from the number of his foes, called to his wife to let loose the dog, who instantly flew to his master's assistance; and after having tore the leg of one, and the shoulder of another, put the whole body of scholars to flight. Enraged at the indignity which had been offered to them, they solicited a reinforcement of their friends, and with Tom Pipes at their head, marched back to the field of battle. Their adversary seeing them approach, called his apprentice, who worked at the other end of the ground, to his assistance, armed him with a mattock, while he himself wielded an hoe, bolted his door on the inside, and flanked with his man and mastiff, waited the attack without flinching. He had not remained three minutes in this posture of defence, when Pipes, who acted as the enemy's forlorn hope, advanced to the gate with great intrepidity, and clapping his foot to the door, which was none of the stoutest, with the execution and dispatch of a petard, split it into a thousand pieces. This sudden execution had an immediate effect upon the 'prentice, who retreated with great precipitation, and escaped at a postern gate. But the master placed himself like another Hercules in the breach; and when Pipes, brandishing his cudgel, stepped forward to engage him, levelled his weapon with such force and dexterity at his head, that had the skull been made of penetrable stuff, the iron edge must have cleft his pate in twain. Casemated as he was, the instrument cut sheer even to the bone, on which it struck with such amazing violence, that sparks of real fire were produced by the collision. And let not the incredulous reader pretend to doubt the truth of this phæno-menon, until he shall have first perused the ingenious Peter Kol-ben's Natural History of the Cape of Good Hope,[1] where the inhabitants commonly use to strike fire with the shin-bones of lions which have been killed in that part of Africk.

Pipes, though a little disconcerted, far from being disabled by the blow, in a trice retorted the compliment with his truncheon, which, had not his antagonist expeditiously slipped his head aside, would have laid him breathless across his own threshold; but, happily for him, he received the salutation upon his right shoulder, which crashed beneath the stroke, and the hoe dropped instantly from his tingling hand. Tom perceiving, and being unwilling to forego the advantage he had gained, darted his head into the bosom of this son of earth, and overturned him on the plain, being himself that instant assaulted by the mastiff, who fastened upon the outside of his thigh. Feeling himself incommoded by this assailant in his rear, he quitted the prostrate gardener to the resentment of his associates, who poured upon him in shoals, and turning about, laid hold with both his hands of this ferocious animal's throat, which he squeezed with such incredible force and perseverance, that the creature quitted his hold; his tongue lolled out of his jaws, the blood started from his eyes, and he swung a lifeless trunk between the hands of his vanquisher.

It was well for his master that he did not longer exist; for by this time he was overwhelmed by such a multitude of foes, that his whole body scarce afforded points of contact to all the fists that drummed upon it, consequently, to use a vulgar phrase, his wind was almost knocked out, before Pipes had leisure to interpose in his behalf, and persuade his offenders to desist, by representing that the wife had gone to alarm the neighbourhood, and that in all probability, they would be intercepted in their return. They accordingly listened to his remonstrances, and marched home-wards in triumph, leaving the gardener in the embraces of his mother earth, from which he had not power to move when he was found by his disconsolate helpmate and some friends whom she had assembled for his assistance. Among these was a blacksmith and farrier, who took cognizance of his carcase, every limb of which having examined, he declared there was no bone broke, and taking out his fleam, blooded him plentifully as he lay. He was then conveyed to his bed, from which he was not able to stir during a whole month, and his family coming upon the parish, a formal complaint was made to the master of the college, and Peregrine represented as the ring-leader of those who committed this bar-barous assault. An inquiry was immediately set on foot, and the articles of impeachment being fully proved, our hero was sentenced to be severely chastised in the face of the whole school. This was a disgrace the thoughts of which his proud heart could not brook. He resolved to make his elopement rather than undergo the punishment to which he was doomed; and having signified his sentiments to his confederates, they promised, one and all, to stand by him, and either screen him from chastisement, or share his fate.

Confiding in this friendly protestation, he appeared unconcerned on the day that was appointed for his punishment; and when he was called to his destiny, advanced towards the scene, attended by the greatest part of the scholars, who intimated their determination to the master, and proposed that Peregrine should be forgiven. The superior behaved with that dignity of demeanor which became his place, represented the folly and presumption of their demand, reprehended them for their audacious proceeding,[1] and ordered every boy to his respective station; but they had gone too far to retract, and instead of obeying the injunction they had received, marched directly out of the college, with their captain in the midst of them, and halting on a rising ground at the distance of a short mile from town, held a council to deliberate on what was to be done.

This consultation was too tumultuous to end in any unanimous decision, so that Mr. Pickle put himself at their head, and proceeded straight forward till the hurry and confusion that prevailed among them should subside; while Tom Pipes, who had by this time joined the company, brought up the rear with great calmness and tranquillity, and never once inquired into the reason of this extraordinary migration. They pursued this indeterminate course for six miles, when a public-house presenting itself to their view, there was a proposal made to halt for refreshment, and they disposed of themselves accordingly, as the conveniencies of the place would permit. Having made a very hearty breakfast on bread and butter and cheese, which they took care to dilute with a proportionable quantity of ale; a motion was made for holding another board, from which the younger boys were excluded, that they might, as much as possible, avoid clamour and distraction in their counsels. Here Peregrine being invested with the supreme command, made a public speech to his constituents, wherein having thanked them for their generous interposition in his favour, and the great honour they now conferred upon him, he observed that in all likelihood, they should in a little time reap the fruits of their resolution, and be recalled with honour to the studies they had left; but as it would be necessary to persevere a little longer, that the masters might see they were not mere boys whom they had disobliged, he proposed that they should dismiss the minor brothers who were not capable of enduring a little fatigue, and deposit all their money in the hands of one person who should be chosen for that trust, and to regulate their expence upon the road; while they advanced farther into the country, and waited patiently for the terms which would undoubtedly be propounded unto them. The proposal was unanimously embraced, the money produced, to the amount of ten guineas, and put into the hands of Pipes, who was elected caterer and purser to the whole community; and the young boys being exhorted to return, the rest, to the number of five and twenty, departed under the auspices of Peregrine, who conducted them ten miles farther to a certain village, where they took up their lodging at an inn, and bespoke something hot for supper; after which they called for punch and strong beer, and indulged themselves in such intemperance, that in a little time riot and disorder prevailing, they sallied forth in quest of willing dames to crown their enjoyment, and committed many other excesses which the prudence and authority of Peregrine could not restrain.

In the morning the landlord saved them the trouble of calling for a bill, and they had the mortification to see that their night's extravagance had mounted up their expence to one half of their whole stock. They discharged the reckoning, and as few or none of them had any inclination or appetite for breakfast, put themselves in motion, and marched onwards for seven miles before they made another halt. This happened on the edge of a common, where they perceived the sign of the George, to the no small comfort and satisfaction of some among them, whose tongues by this time cleaved to the roofs of their mouths, in consequence of the debauch of last night. Here then they paused, and having moistened their throats with plentiful streams of ale, began to relish the situation, and ordered their steward to provide something for dinner. The people of the house would have gladly dispensed with their custom, as they had no great faith either in the finances or principles of their guests, who seemed too young to be possessed of much money or consideration. But as they lived in a solitary place, unprovided with defence against the insults to which they might be exposed from the resentment of such a disorderly crowd, they would not venture to signify their distrust, and lamented that there was nothing in the house with which they could entertain them. Tom Pipes, who had observed a flock of geese upon the common, and abundance of poultry in the yard, took no notice of the landlord's declaration, but went out, and in less than five minutes returned with provision sufficient to regale twice the number of his associates. The woman durst not venture to disapprove of what he had done, but after having assured him that the fowls were none of her own, very peaceably employed her whole family in preparing them for the fire, and some bacon and greens being added to the repast, our company disposed themselves in different groups upon the grass, and dined with great mirth and satisfaction, without once recollecting that another such meal would utterly exhaust their common fund. However, this sweet insensibility did not long prevail; about four o'clock they called to pay, and were very much startled to find themselves charged no less than two pounds eleven and sixpence for the entertainment they had received. They looked upon this reckoning as unconscionable, and disputed every article accordingly; but the landlady solemnly protested that the sum would barely indemnify her, and imputed great part of the charge to the unnecessary number of geese and chickens which had been slaughtered without her knowledge or consent.

Pipes, who on certain subjects, thought a little too much at large, proposed to punish her for her exorbitant demand, by marching off without paying one farthing; but this advice Peregrine declined with disdain, looking upon such an expedient as inconsistent with the dignity of the corps which he had the honour to command; and ordered that the bill should be immediately discharged. This affair being settled to the satisfaction of all parties concerned, they resumed their march, and in the evening arrived at a certain market town where they resolved to fix their quarters until they should hear tidings from the college which they had left. With this view they chose their residence at the best inn belonging to the place, and determined to manage the remains of their fortune with great frugality. But the spirits of some amongst them beginning to flag, in consequence of the fatigue of their journey, and their own reflection that now represented the folly of their design, with the uncomfortable circumstances that must in a few hours attend the consumption of their stock; this prudent scheme of oeconomy was over-ruled, a huge bowl of punch prepared, and Pipes ordered to enliven the company with a song. Their cares were in a little time overwhelmed, and the greatest part of the night was consumed in mirth and jollity; though next morning they waked in the horrors, and universal despondence took place, when they learnt that their bank was scarce able to defray the expence of their bill, which they received next their stomachs, and were obliged to discharge.

They were now reduced to a dilemma that occasioned another general consultation, in which they agreed to club their pocket-pieces and silver buckles for present support, and give notice by letters of their situation to their respective relations, taking care to ascribe their distress to the ill usage they had met with at school: on this occasion Peregrine produced the ring and medal he had received from Mrs. Trunnion, and Pipes not only presented his own purse, which was pretty well furnished, but even made a proffer of his silver whistle, with the chain by which it had for many years depended from his neck. They thanked him for his disinterested attachment, but all his sollicitations could not prevail upon the chiefs to profit by this instance of his good fellowship; because they considered him as a person whose assistance in this particular it was neither just nor honourable to use.

CHAPTER XX

The Governors tamper with their Pupils.
Peregrine is deserted, prevailed upon to return,
and submit to Correction ; sublimes his Ideas,
commences Gallant, and becomes acquainted with
Miss Emily Gauntlet

MEAN while the master, surprised and disconcerted at such an
unprecedented secession, convened all the tutors of those who
were concerned in this dangerous association, in order to concert
proper measures for recalling them; and after mature deliberation,
as it was the opinion of every body, that such a number of raw,
hot-headed boys, without money, conduct, experience or plan,
could not possibly cohere for any length of time, they resolved to
leave them to the operation of their own passions; not doubting
that as the first impulse gradually weakened, they would drop off
one by one, and the whole confederacy be thus melted down. The
return of the young boys justified the prognostic; but the masters
were not a little alarmed, when they understood that the rest had
chosen a general, submitted to certain regulations, and adopted
a determinate design. They resolved, nevertheless, to give them a
little more scope, and waited four and twenty hours for the effect
of their forbearance; when hearing no accounts from the deserters,
they began to consider this revolt as a very serious affair; and in
pursuance of their advice and direction, the governors set out in
quest of their stray pupils.

It was not difficult to discover the rout they had taken; such
a remarkable caravan could not pass unheeded; they got intimation
of their advances from stage to stage, and at night arrived at an inn
that stood on the road, about two miles short of the town where the
adventurers had settled their head quarters. From hence they
repaired in a body to the house of a neighbouring justice, who, in
consequence of their representations, granted a warrant to apprehend and secure the body of Thomas Pipes, as an idle vagabond
and seducer of youth. Thus authorised, they went early next morning to the town, and set up their horses at another inn, where they
remained *incognito*, until they had engaged the constable with
a competent number of assistants; then a person was sent to inform
Mr. Pipes, that his company was desired at the White Hart.

Tom received this message immediately after the contribution of effects, already mentioned; and imparted the contents to his master, who rightly judging that it concerned the common cause, desired him to obey the summons. He followed the messenger accordingly; and no sooner set his nose within the room to which he was directed, than the constable and his posse sprung upon him, before he had the least intimation of his design, or any opportunity of acting in his own defence.

Thus overpowered, he was made acquainted with the cause of his being arrested, which, in all appearance, did not give him a great deal of concern, and in private committed to jail, where he was left to his own meditations.

This previous measure being successfully taken, the tutors went into separate apartments, and sending for their respective pupils, each plied his own charge in particular with such arguments as he judged most conducive to dissuade him from persevering in the imprudent scheme which he had already prosecuted too far. No great eloquence was required to accomplish this aim, which was already more than half effected by their own reflections; and therefore the greatest part of them yielded to such reasonable remonstrances, and consented to return to school, provided they might be indulged with a general amnesty for what they had done. This they were impowered to promise to all of them, except Peregrine, whom, as ringleader and first cause of this disturbance, the master had marked out for a public example. For this reason he stood out against all the admonitions of Mr. Jolter, who in vain conjured him to put up with a little correction, rather than run the risk of being ignominiously expelled, and of forfeiting the friendship of his uncle, on whom he knew his chief dependance was built; till at length, seeing his adherents persuaded out of their allegiance, and himself bereft of all company and means of subsistence, he with great reluctance resigned himself to his fate; and having obtained the discharge of Pipes, was reconducted to the college, where, notwithstanding the intercession of his governor, who begged earnestly that his punishment might be mitigated, our unfortunate hero was publickly horsed, *in terrorem* of all whom it might concern.

This disgrace had a very sensible effect upon the mind of Peregrine, who having, by this time, passed the fourteenth year of his age, began to adopt the pride and sentiments of a man. Thus dishonourably stigmatized, he was ashamed to appear in public as usual; he was incensed against his companions for their infidelity and irresolution, and plunged into a profound reverie that lasted several weeks, during which he shook off his boyish connections, and fixed his view upon objects which he thought more worthy of his attention.

In the course of his gymnastic exercises, at which he was very expert, he contracted intimacies with several youths who were greatly his superiors in point of age, and who, pleased with his aspiring genius and address, introduced him into parties of gallantry, which strongly captivated his inclination. He was by nature particularly adapted for succeeding in adventures of this kind; over and above a most engaging person that improved with his years, he possessed a dignified assurance, an agreeable ferocity which inhanced the conquest of the fair who had the good fortune to enslave him, unlimited generosity, and a fund of humour which never failed to please. Nor was he deficient in the more solid accomplishments of youth; he had profited in his studies beyond expectation, and besides that sensibility of discernment which is the foundation of taste, and in consequence of which he distinguished and enjoyed the beauties of the Classics, he had already given several specimens of a very promising poetic talent.

With this complexion and these qualifications, no wonder that our hero attracted the notice and affection of the young Delias in town, whose hearts had just begun to flutter for they knew not what. Inquiries were made concerning his condition; and no sooner were his expectations known, than he was invited and caressed by all the parents, while their daughters vyed with each other in treating him with particular complacency. He inspired love and emulation wherever he appeared; envy and jealous rage followed of course; so that he became a very desirable, though a very dangerous acquaintance. His moderation was not equal to his success; his vanity took the lead of his passions, dissipating his attention, which might otherwise have fixed him to one object; and he was possessed with the rage of increasing the number of his conquests. With this view he frequented public walks, concerts and assemblies, became remarkably rich and fashionable in his cloaths, gave entertainments to the ladies, and was in the utmost hazard of turning out a most egregious coxcomb.

While his character thus wavered between the ridicule of some, and the regard of others, an accident happened, which, by contracting his view to one object, detached him from those vain pursuits that would in time have plunged him into an abyss of folly and contempt. Being one evening at the ball which is always given to the ladies at the time of the races, the person who acted as master of the ceremonies, knowing how fond Mr. Pickle was of every opportunity to display himself, came up and told him, that there was a fine young creature at the other end of the room, who seemed to have a great inclination to dance a minuet, but wanted a partner, the gentleman who attended her being in boots.

Peregrine's vanity being aroused at this intimation, he went up to reconnoitre the young lady, and was struck with admiration at her beauty. She seemed to be of his own age, was tall, and tho' slender, exquisitely shaped; her hair was auburn, and in such plenty, that the barbarity of dress had not been able to prevent it from shading both sides of her forehead, which was high and polished; the contour of her face was oval, her nose very little raised into the aquiline form, that contributed to the spirit and dignity of her aspect; her mouth was small, her lips plump, juicy and delicious, her teeth regular and white as driven snow, her complexion incredibly delicate and glowing with health, and her full blue eyes beamed forth vivacity and love: her mein was at the same time commanding and engaging, her address perfectly genteel, and her whole appearance so captivating, that our young Adonis looked, and was overcome.

He no sooner recollected himself from his astonishment, than he advanced to her with a graceful air of respect, and begged she would do him the honour to walk a minuet with him. She seemed particularly pleased with his application, and very frankly complied with his request. This pair was too remarkable to escape the particular notice of the company: Mr. Pickle was well known by almost every body in the room, but his partner was altogether a new face, and of consequence underwent the criticism of all the ladies in the assembly; one whispered, 'She has a good complexion, but don't you think she is a little awry?' A second pitied her for her masculine nose; a third observed, that she was aukward for want of seeing company; a fourth distinguished something very bold in her countenance; and in short, there was not a beauty in her whole composition, which the glass of envy did not pervert into a blemish.

The men, however, looked upon her with different eyes; among them her appearance produced an universal murmur of applause; they encircled the space on which she danced, and were enchanted by her graceful motion. While they launched out in the praise of her, they expressed their displeasure at the good fortune of her partner, whom they damned for a little finical coxcomb, that was too much engrossed by the contemplation of his own person, to discern or deserve the favour of his fate. He did not hear, therefore could not repine at these invectives; but while they imagined he indulged his vanity, a much more generous passion had taken possession of his heart.

Instead of that petulance of gaiety for which he had been distinguished in his public appearance, he now gave manifest signs of confusion and concern; he danced with an anxiety which impeded his performance, and blushed to the eyes at every false step he made. Though this extraordinary agitation was overlooked by the men, it could not escape the observation of the ladies, who perceived it with equal surprize and resentment; and when Peregrine led this fair unknown to her seat, expressed their pique in an affected titter, which broke from every mouth at the same instant, as if all of them had been informed by the same spirit.

Peregrine was nettled at this unmannerly mark of disapprobation, and, in order to increase their chagrin, endeavoured to enter into particular conversation with their fair rival. The young lady herself, who neither wanted penetration, nor the consciousness of her own accomplishments, resented their behaviour, though she triumphed at the cause of it, and gave her partner all the encouragement he could desire. Her mother, who was present, thanked him for his civility in taking such notice of a stranger, and he received a compliment of the same nature from the young gentleman in boots, who was her own brother.

If he was charmed with her appearance, he was quite ravished with her discourse, which was sensible, spirited and gay. Her frank and sprightly demeanour excited his own confidence and good humour; and he described to her the characters of those females who had honoured them with such a spiteful mark of distinction, in terms so replete with humorous satire, that she seemed to listen with particular complacency of attention, and distinguished every nymph thus ridiculed with such a significant glance, as overwhelmed her with chagrin and mortification. In short, they seemed to relish each other's conversation, during which our young Damon acquitted himself with great skill in all the duties of gallantry; he laid hold of proper opportunities to express his admiration of her charms, had recourse to the silent rhetoric of tender looks, breathed divers insidious sighs, and attached himself wholly to her during the remaining part of the entertainment.

When the company broke up, he attended her to her lodgings, and took leave of her with a squeeze of the hand, after having obtained permission to visit her next morning, and been informed by the mother that her name was Miss Emilia Gauntlet.

All night long he closed not an eye, but amused himself with plans of pleasure, which his imagination suggested, in consequence of this new acquaintance. He arose with the lark, adjusted his hair into an agreeable negligence of curl, and dressing himself in a genteel grey frock trimmed with silver binding, waited with the utmost impatience for the hour of ten, which no sooner struck, than he hied him to the place of appointment, and inquiring for Miss Gauntlet, was shewn into a parlour. Here he had not waited above ten minutes, when Emilia entered in a most inchanting undress, with all the graces of nature playing about her person, and in a moment rivetted the chains of his slavery beyond the power of accident to unbind.

Her mother being still abed, and her brother gone to give orders about the chaise, in which they proposed to return the same day to their own habitation, he enjoyed her company *tête à tête* a whole hour, during which he declared his love in the most passionate terms, and begged that he might be admitted into the number of those admirers whom she permitted to visit and adore her.

She affected to look upon his vows and protestations as the ordinary effects of gallantry, and very obligingly assured him, that were she to live in that place, she should be glad to see him often; but as the spot on which she resided was at a considerable distance, she could not expect he would go so far upon such a trifling occasion, or take the trouble of providing himself with her mamma's permission.

To this favourable hint he answered with all the eagerness of the most fervid passion, that he had uttered nothing but the genuine dictates of his heart, and desired nothing so much as an opportunity of evincing the sincerity of his professions; and that though she lived at the extremity of the kingdom, he would find means to lay himself at her feet, provided he could visit her with her mother's consent, which he assured her he would not fail to sollicit.

She then gave him to understand, that her habitation was about sixteen miles from Winchester, in a village which she named, and where (as he could easily collect from her discourse) he would be no unwelcome guest.

In the midst of this communication they were joined by Mrs. Gauntlet, who received him with great courtesy, thanked him again for his politeness to Emy at the Ball, and anticipated his intention, by saying that she should be very glad to see him at her house, if ever his occasions should call him that way.

CHAPTER XXI

He inquires into the Situation of this young Lady
with whom he is enamoured ; elopes from School ;
is found by the Lieutenant, reconveyed to Winchester,
and sends a Letter with a Copy of Verses to his Mistress

HE was transported with pleasure at this invitation, which he
assured her he should not neglect; and after a little more conversation on general topics, took his leave of the charming Emilia
and her prudent mamma, who had perceived the first emotions of
Mr. Pickle's passion for her daughter, and been at some pains to
inquire about his family and fortune.

Neither was Peregrine less inquisitive about the situation and
pedigree of his new mistress, who, he learned, was the only daughter of a field-officer, who died before he had it in his power to make
suitable provision for his children; that the widow lived in a frugal,
though decent manner, on the pension, assisted by the bounty of
her relations; that the son carried arms as volunteer in the company
which his father had commanded; and that Emilia had been educated in London, at the expence of a rich uncle, who was seized with
the whim of marrying at the age of fifty-five; in consequence of
which, his niece had returned to her mother, without any visible
dependance, except on her own conduct and qualifications.

This account, though it could not diminish his affection, nevertheless alarmed his pride; for his warm imagination had exaggerated
all his own prospects; and he began to fear, that his passion for
Emilia might be thought to derogate from the dignity of his
situation. The struggle between his interest and love produced
a perplexity which had an evident effect upon his behaviour; he
became pensive, solitary and peevish, avoided all publick diversions, and grew so remarkably negligent in his dress, that he was
scarce distinguishable by his own acquaintance. This contention
of thoughts continued several weeks, at the end of which the charms
of Emilia triumphed over every other consideration; and having
received a supply of money from the commodore, who acted
towards him with great generosity, he ordered Pipes to put up some
linnen, and other necessaries, in a sort of knapsack which he could
conveniently carry, and thus attended set out early one morning
on foot for the village where his charmer lived, at which he arrived

97

before two o'clock in the afternoon; having chosen this method of travelling, that his rout might not be so easily discovered, as it must have been, had he hired horses, or taken a place in the stage-coach.

The first thing he did was to secure a convenient lodging at the inn where he dined; then he shifted himself, and according to the direction he had received, went to the house of Mrs. Gauntlet in a transport of joyous expectation. As he approached the gate his agitation increased, he knocked with impatience and concern, the door opened, and he had actually asked if Mrs. Gauntlet was at home, before he perceived that the portress was no other than his dear Emilia. She was not without emotion at the unexpected sight of her lover, who instantly recognizing his charmer, obeyed the irresistible impulse of his love, and caught the fair creature in his arms. Nor did she seem offended at this forwardness of behaviour, which might have displeased another of a less open disposition, or less used to the freedom of a sensible education; but her natural frankness had been encouraged and improved by the easy and familiar intercourse in which she had been bred; and therefore, instead of reprimanding him with a severity of look, she with great good humour rallied him upon his assurance, which, she observed, was undoubtedly the effect of his own conscious merit, and conducted him into a parlour, where he found her mother, who in very polite terms expressed her satisfaction at seeing him within her house.

Having drank tea together, Miss Emy proposed an evening walk, which they enjoyed through a variety of little copses and lawns, watered by a most romantic stream, that quite enchanted the imagination of Peregrine.

It was late before they returned from this agreeable excursion, and when our lover wished the ladies good night, Mrs. Gauntlet insisted upon his staying to supper, and treated him with particular demonstrations of regard and affection. As her œconomy was not encumbered with an unnecessary number of domestics, her own presence was often required in different parts of the house, so that the young gentleman was supplied with frequent opportunities of promoting his suit, by all the tender oaths and insinuations that his passion could suggest. He protested, that her idea had taken such entire possession of his heart, that finding himself unable to support her absence one day longer, he had quitted his studies, and left his governor by stealth, that he might visit the object of his adoration, and be blessed in her company for a few days without interruption.

She listened to his addresses with such affability as denoted approbation and delight, and gently chid him as a thoughtless truant, but carefully avoided the confession of a mutual flame; because she discerned, in the midst of all his tenderness, a levity of pride which she durst not venture to trust with such a declaration. Perhaps she was confirmed in this caution by her mother, who very wisely, in her civilities to him, maintained a sort of ceremonious distance, which she thought not only requisite for the honour and interest of her family, but likewise for her own exculpation, should she ever be taxed with having encouraged or abetted him in the imprudent sallies of his youth: yet notwithstanding this affected reserve, he was treated with such distinction both by one and t'other, that he was ravished with his situation, and became more and more enamoured every day.

While he remained under the influence of this sweet intoxication, his absence produced great disturbance at Winchester. Mr. Jolter was grievously afflicted at his abrupt departure, which alarmed him the more, as it happened after a long fit of melancholy which he had perceived in his pupil. He communicated his apprehensions to the master of the school, who advised him to apprize the commodore of his nephew's disappearance, and in the mean time inquire at all the inns in town, whether he had hired horses, or any sort of carriage, for his conveyance, or was not met with on the road by any person who could give an account of the direction in which he travelled.

This scrutiny, though performed with great diligence and minuteness, was altogether ineffectual; they could obtain no intelligence of the runaway. Mr. Trunnion was well nigh distracted at the news of his flight; he raved with great fury at the imprudence of Peregrine, whom in his first transports he damned as an ungrateful deserter; then he cursed Hatchway and Pipes, who he swore had foundered the lad by their pernicious counsels; and, lastly, transferred his execrations upon Jolter, because he had not kept a better look-out: finally, he made an apostrophe to that son of a bitch the gout, which for the present disabled him from searching for his nephew in person. That he might not, however, neglect any means in his power, he immediately dispatched expresses to all the sea-port towns on that coast, that he might be prevented from leaving the kingdom; and the lieutenant, at his own desire, was sent across the country, in quest of this young fugitive.

Four days had he unsuccessfully carried on his inquiries with great accuracy, when resolving to return by Winchester, where he hoped to meet with some hints of intelligence, by which he might profit in his future search, he struck off the common road, to take the benefit of a nearer cut; and finding himself benighted near a village, took up his lodging at the first inn to which his horse directed him. Having bespoke something for supper, and retired to his chamber, where he amused himself with a pipe, he heard a confused noise of rustic jollity, which being all of a sudden interrupted, after a short pause his ear was saluted by the voice of Pipes, who, at the sollicitation of the company, began to entertain them with a song.

Hatchway instantly recognized the well-known sound, in which indeed he could not possibly be mistaken, as nothing in nature bore the least resemblance to it; he threw his pipe into the chimney, and snatching up one of his pistols, ran immediately to the apartment from whence the voice issued: he no sooner entered, than distinguishing his old shipmate in a crowd of country peasants, he in a moment sprung upon him, and clapping his pistol to his breast, exclaimed, 'Damn you, Pipes, you're a dead man, if you don't immediately produce young master.'

This menacing application had a much greater effect upon the company than upon Tom, who looking at the lieutenant with great tranquillity, replied, 'Why so I can, Master Hatchway.' 'What! safe and sound?' cried the other. 'As a roach,' answered Pipes, so much to the satisfaction of his friend Jack, that he shook him by the hand, and desired him to proceed with his song. This being performed, and the reckoning discharged, the two friends adjourned to the other room, where the lieutenant was informed of the manner in which the young gentleman had made his elopement from college, as well as of the other particulars of his present situation, as far as they had fallen within the sphere of his comprehension.

While they sat thus conferring together, Peregrine having taken his leave of his mistress for the night, came home, and was not a little surprised, when Hatchway entering his chamber in his sea attitude, thrust out his hand by way of salutation. His old pupil received him as usual, with great cordiality, and expressed his astonishment at meeting him in that place; but when he understood the cause and intention of his arrival, he started with concern; and his visage glowing with indignation, told him he was old enough to be judge of his own conduct, and when he should see it convenient, would return of himself; but those who thought he was to be compelled to his duty, would find themselves egregiously mistaken.

The lieutenant assured him, that for his own part he had no intention to offer him the least violence; but, at the same time, he represented to him the danger of incensing the commodore, who was already almost distracted on account of his absence: and in short, conveyed his arguments, which were equally obvious and valid, in such expressions of friendship and respect, that Peregrine yielded to his remonstrances, and promised to accompany him next day to Winchester.

Hatchway, overjoyed at the success of his negociation, went immediately to the hostler and bespoke a post-chaise for Mr. Pickle and his man, with whom he afterwards indulged himself in a double cann of rumbo, and when the night was pretty far advanced, left the lover to his repose, or rather to the thorns of his own meditation; for he slept not one moment, being incessantly tortured with the prospect of parting from his divine Emilia, who had now acquired the most absolute empire over his soul. One minute he proposed to depart early in the morning, without seeing this enchantress, in whose bewitching presence he durst not trust his own resolution. Then the thoughts of leaving her in such an abrupt and disrespectful manner, interposed in favour of his love and honour. This war of sentiments kept him all night upon the rack, and it was time to rise before he had determined to visit his charmer, and candidly impart the motives that induced him to leave her.

He accordingly repaired to her mother's house with a heavy heart, being attended to the gate by Hatchway, who did not choose to leave him alone; and being admitted, found Emilia just risen, and in his opinion, more beautiful than ever.

Alarmed at his early visit, and the gloom that overspread his countenance, she stood in silent expectation of hearing some melancholy tidings; and it was not till after a considerable pause, that he collected resolution enough to tell her he was come to take his leave. Though she strove to conceal her sorrow, nature was not to be suppressed; every feature of her countenance saddened in a moment, and it was not without the utmost difficulty that she kept her lovely eyes from overflowing. He saw the situation of her thoughts, and in order to alleviate her concern, assured her he should find means to see her again in a very few weeks; mean while he communicated his reasons for departing, in which she readily acquiesced; and having mutually consoled each other, their transports of grief subsided, and before Mrs. Gauntlet came down stairs they were in a condition to behave with great decency and resignation.

This good lady expressed her concern when she learnt his resolution, saying, she hoped his occasions and inclinations would permit him to favour them with his agreeable company another time.

The lieutenant, who began to be uneasy at Peregrine's stay, knocked at the door, and being introduced by his friend, had the honour of breakfasting with the ladies; on which occasion his heart received such a rude shock from the charms of Emilia, that he afterwards made a merit with his friend of having constrained himself so far, as to forbear commencing his professed rival.

At length they bad adieu to their kind entertainers, and in less than an hour setting out from the inn, arrived about two o'clock in Winchester, where Mr. Jolter was overwhelmed with joy at their appearance.

The nature of this adventure being unknown to all except those who could be depended upon, every body who inquired about the cause of Peregrine's absence, was told that he had been with a relation in the country, and the master condescended to overlook his indiscretion; so that Hatchway seeing every thing settled to the satisfaction of his friend, returned to the garrison, and gave the commodore an account of his expedition.

The old gentleman was very much startled when he heard there was a lady in the case, and very emphatically observed, that a man had better be sucked into the gulph of Florida than once get into the indraught of woman; because in one case, he may with good pilotage bring out his vessel safe between the Bahamas and the Indian shore; but in the other there is no outlet at all, and it is in vain to strive against the current; so that of course he must be embayed, and run chuck upon a lee-shore. He resolved, therefore, to lay the state of the case before Mr. Gamaliel Pickle, and concert such measures with him as should be thought likeliest to detach his son from the pursuit of an idle amour, which could not fail of interfering in a dangerous manner with the plan of his education.

In the mean time, Perry's ideas were totally engrossed by his amiable mistress, who, whether he slept or waked, was still present in his imagination, which produced the following stanzas in her praise.

I

Adieu, ye streams that smoothly flow,
Ye vernal airs that softly blow,
Ye plains by blooming spring array'd,
Ye birds that warble thro' the shade.

II

Unhurt from you my soul could fly,
Nor drop one tear, nor heave one sigh,
But forc'd from Celia's charms to part,
All joy deserts my drooping heart.

III

O! fairer than the rosy morn,
When flowers the dewy fields adorn;
Unsullied as the genial ray,
That warms the balmy breeze of May.

IV

Thy charms divinely bright appear,
And add new splendor to the year;
Improve the day with fresh delight,
And gild with joy the dreary night![1]

This juvenile production was inclosed in a very tender billet to Emilia, and committed to the charge of Pipes, who was ordered to set out for Mrs. Gauntlet's habitation with a present of venison, and a compliment to the ladies; and directed to take some opportunity of delivering the letter to miss, without the knowledge of her mamma.

CHAPTER XXII

His Messenger meets with a Misfortune,
to which he applies a very extraordinary Expedient
that is attended with strange Consequences

As a stage coach passed within two miles of the village where she lived, Tom bargained with the driver for a seat on the box, and accordingly departed on this message, though he was but indifferently qualified for commissions of such a nature: having received particular injunctions about the letter, he resolved to make that the chief object of his care, and very sagaciously conveyed it between his stocking and the sole of his foot, where he thought it would be perfectly secure from all injury and accident. Here it remained until he arrived at the inn where he had formerly lodged, when after having refreshed himself with a draught of beer, he pulled off his stocking, and found the poor billet sullied with dust, and torn into a thousand tatters by the motion of his foot in walking the last two miles of his journey. Thunderstruck at this phænomenon, he uttered a long and loud *whew!* which was succeeded by an exclamation of 'Damn my old shoes! a bite by G—!' then he rested his elbows on the table, and his forehead upon his two fists, and in that attitude deliberated with himself upon the means of remedying this misfortune.

As he was not distracted by a vast number of ideas, he soon concluded that his best expedient would be to employ the clerk of the parish, who he knew was a great scholar, to write another epistle according to the directions he should give him; and never dreaming that the mangled original would in the least facilitate this scheme, he very wisely committed it to the flames, that it might never rise up in judgment against him.

Having taken this wise step, he went in quest of his scribe, to whom he communicated his business, and promised a full-pot by way of gratification. The clerk, who was also school-master, proud of an opportunity to distinguish his talents, readily undertook the task; and repairing with his employer to the inn, in less than a quarter of an hour produced a morsel of eloquence so much to the satisfaction of Pipes, that he squeezed his hand by way of acknowledgment, and doubled his allowance of beer, which being discussed, our courier betook himself to the house of Mrs. Gauntlet with the haunch of venison and this succedaneous[1] letter, and delivered his message to the mother, who received it with great respect, and many kind inquiries about the health and welfare of his master, attempting to tip the messenger a crown, which he absolutely refused to accept, in consequence of Mr. Pickle's repeated caution. While the old gentlewoman turned to a servant, in order to give directions about the disposal of this present, Pipes looked upon this as a favourable occasion to transact his business with Emilia, and therefore, shutting one eye, with a jirk of his thumb towards his left shoulder, and a most significant twist of his countenance, he beckoned the young lady into another room, as if he had been fraught with something of consequence, which he wanted to impart. She understood the hint howsoever strangely communicated, and by stepping to one side of the room, gave him an opportunity of slipping the epistle into her hand, which he gently squeezed at the same time in token of regard; then throwing a side-glance at the mother, whose back was turned, clapped his finger to one side of his nose, thereby recommending secrecy and discretion.

Emilia conveying the letter into her bosom, could not help smiling at Tom's politeness and dexterity; but lest her mamma should detect him in the execution of his pantomime, she broke off this intercourse of signs, by asking aloud when he proposed to set out on his return to Winchester; and when he answered 'Tomorrow morning,' Mrs. Gauntlet recommended him to the hospitality of her own footman, desiring him to make much of Mr. Pipes below, where he was kept to supper, and very cordially entertained. Our young heroine, impatient to read her lover's billet, which made her heart throb with rapturous expectation, retired to her chamber as soon as possible, with a view of perusing the contents, which were these.

Divine empress of my soul!

If the refulgent flames of your beauty had not evaporated the particles of my transported brain, and scorched my intellects into a cinder of stolidity, perhaps the resplendency of my passion might shine illustrious through the sable curtain of my ink, and in sublimity transcend the galaxy itself, though wafted on the pinions of a grey goose quill! But ah! celestial enchantress! the negromancy of thy tyrannical charms hath fettered my faculties with adamantine chains, which unless thy compassion shall melt, I must eternally remain in the tartarean gulph of dismal despair. Vouchsafe therefore, O thou brightest luminary of this terrestrial sphere! to warm as well as shine; and let the genial rays of thy benevolence melt the icy emanations of thy disdain, which hath frozen up the spirits of, angelic prehemidence! thy most egregious admirer and superlative slave

PEREGRINE PICKLE

Never was astonishment more perplexing than that of Emilia, when she read this curious composition, which she repeated verbatim three times before she would credit the evidence of her own senses. She began to fear in good earnest that love had produced a disorder in her lover's understanding; but after a thousand conjectures by which she attempted to account for this extraordinary fustian of stile, she concluded that it was the effect of mere levity, calculated to ridicule the passion he had formerly professed. Irritated by this supposition, she resolved to baulk his triumph with affected indifference, and in the mean time endeavour to expel him from that place which he possessed within her heart. And indeed, such a victory over her inclinations might have been obtained without great difficulty; for she enjoyed an easiness of temper that could accommodate itself to the emergencies of her fate; and her vivacity by amusing her imagination, preserved her from the keener sensations of sorrow. Thus determined and disposed, she did not send any sort of answer, or the least token of remembrance by Pipes, who was suffered to depart with a general compliment from the mother, and arrived at Winchester the next day.

Peregrine's eyes sparkled when he saw his messenger come in, and he stretched out his hand in full confidence of receiving some particular mark of his Emilia's affection; but how was he confounded, when he felt his hope so cruelly disappointed! In an instant his countenance fell. He stood for some time silent and abashed, then thrice repeated the interrogation of 'What! not one word from Emilia?' And dubious of his courier's discretion, inquired minutely into all the particulars of his reception. He asked if he had seen the young lady, if she was in good health, if he had found an opportunity of delivering his letter, and how she looked when he put it into her hand? Pipes answered, that he had never seen her in better health or higher spirits; that he had managed matters so as not only to present the billet unperceived, but also to ask her commands in private before he took his leave, when she told him that the letter required no reply. This last circumstance he considered as a manifest mark of disrespect, and gnawed his lips with resentment. Upon further reflexion, however, he supposed that she could not conveniently write by the messenger, and would undoubtedly favour him by the post. This consideration consoled him for the present, and he waited impatiently for the fruits of his hope; but after he had seen eight days elapsed without reaping the satisfaction with which he had flattered himself, his temper forsook him, he raved against the whole sex, and was seized with a fit of sullen chagrin; but his pride in a little time came to his assistance, and rescued him from the horrors of the melancholy fiend. He resolved to retort her own neglect upon his ungrateful mistress, his countenance gradually resumed its former serenity; and though by this time he was pretty well cured of his foppery, he appeared again at public diversions with an air of gaiety and unconcern, that Emilia might have a chance of hearing how much, in all likelihood, he disregarded her disdain.

There are never wanting certain officious persons, who take pleasure in promoting intelligence of this sort. His behaviour soon reached the ears of Miss Gauntlet, and confirmed her in the opinion she had conceived from his letter; so that she fortified herself in her former sentiments, and bore his indifference with great philosophy. Thus a correspondence which had commenced with all the tenderness and sincerity of love, and every promise of duration, was interrupted in its infancy by a misunderstanding occasioned by the simplicity of Pipes, who never once reflected upon the consequences of his deceit.

Though their mutual passion was by these means suppressed for the present, it was not altogether extinguished, but glowed in secret, though even to themselves unknown, until an occasion which afterwards offered, blew up the latent flame, and love resumed his empire in their breasts.

While they moved, as it were, without the sphere of each other's attraction, the commodore fearing that Perry was in danger of involving himself in some pernicious engagement, resolved by advice of Mr. Jolter and his friend the parish priest, to recal him from the place where he had contracted such imprudent connexions, and send him to the university, where his education might be compleated, and his fancy weaned from all puerile amusements.

This plan had been proposed to his own father, who, as hath been already observed, stood always neuter in every thing that concerned his eldest son; and as for Mrs. Pickle, she had never heard his name mentioned since his departure with any degree of temper or tranquillity, except when her husband informed her that he was in a fair way of being ruined by this indiscreet amour. It was then she began to applaud her own foresight, which had discerned the mark of reprobation in that vicious boy, and launched out in comparisons between him and Gammy, who, she observed, was a child of uncommon parts and solidity, and with the blessing of God, would be a comfort to his parents, and an ornament to the family.

Should I affirm that this favourite whom she commended so much, was in every respect the reverse of what she described; that he was a boy of mean capacity, and though remarkably distorted in his body, much more crooked in his disposition; and that she had persuaded her husband to espouse her opinion, though it was contrary to common sense, as well as to his own perception; I am afraid the reader will think I represent a monster that never existed in nature, and be apt to condemn the œconomy of my invention; nevertheless, there is nothing more true than every circumstance of what I have advanced; and I wish the picture, singular as it is, may not be thought to resemble more than one original.

CHAPTER XXIII

Peregrine is summoned to attend his Uncle,
is more and more hated by his own Mother;
appeals to his Father, whose Condescension is
defeated by the Dominion of his Wife

BUT waving these reflections, let us return to Peregrine, who
received a summons to attend his uncle, and in a few days arrived
with Mr. Jolter and Pipes at the garrison, which he filled with joy
and satisfaction. The alteration, which, during his absence, had
happened in his person, was very favourable to his appearance,
which from that of a comely boy, was converted into that of a most
engaging youth. He was already taller than a middle-sized man,
his shape ascertained, his sinews well knit, his mien greatly improved, and his whole figure as elegant and graceful, as if it had
been cast in the same mould with the Apollo of Belvidere.

Such an outside could not fail of prepossessing people in his
favour. The commodore, notwithstanding the advantageous reports he had heard, found his expectation exceeded in the person
of Peregrine, and signified his approbation in the most sanguine
terms. Mrs. Trunnion was struck with his genteel address, and
received him with uncommon marks of complacency and affection;
he was caressed by all the people in the neighbourhood, who, while
they admired his accomplishments, could not help pitying his
infatuated mother, who was deprived of that unutterable delight
which any other parent would have enjoyed in the contemplation
of such an amiable son.

Divers efforts were made by some well-disposed people, to
conquer, if possible, this monstrous prejudice; but their endeavours, instead of curing, served only to inflame the distemper,
and she never could be prevailed upon to indulge him in the least
mark of maternal regard. On the contrary, her original disgust
degenerated into such inveteracy of hatred, that she left no stone
unturned to alienate the commodore's affection for this her innocent child, and even practised the most malicious defamation to
accomplish her purpose. Every day did she abuse her husband's
ear with some forged instance of Peregrine's ingratitude to his
uncle, well knowing that it would reach the commodore's knowledge at night.

Chapter XXIII

Accordingly Mr. Pickle used to tell him at the club, that his hopeful favourite had ridiculed him in such a company, and aspersed his spouse upon another occasion; and thus retail the little scandalous issue of his own wife's invention. Luckily for Peregrine, the commodore paid no great regard to the authority of his informer, because he knew from what canal his intelligence flowed; besides, the youth had a staunch friend in Mr. Hatchway, who never failed to vindicate him when he was thus unjustly accused, and always found argument enough to confute the assertions of his enemies. But, though Trunnion had been dubious of the young gentleman's principles, and deaf to the remonstrances of the lieutenant, Perry was provided with a bulwark strong enough to defend him from all such assaults. This was no other than his aunt, whose regard for him was perceived to increase in the same proportion as his own mother's diminished; and indeed, the augmentation of the one was, in all probability, owing to the decrease of the other; for the two ladies, with great civility, performed all the duties of good neighbourhood, and hated each other most piously in their hearts.

Mrs. Pickle having been disobliged at the splendor of her sister's new equipage, had ever since that time, in the course of her visiting, endeavoured to make people merry with satirical jokes on that poor lady's infirmities; and Mrs. Trunnion seized the very first opportunity of making reprisals, by inveighing against her unnatural behaviour to her own child; so that Peregrine, as on the one hand he was abhorred, so on the other was he caressed in consequence of this contention; and I firmly believe that the most effectual method of destroying his interest at the garrison, would have been the shew of countenancing him at his father's house: but, whether this conjecture be reasonable or chimerical, certain it is the experiment was never tried, and therefore Mr. Peregrine ran no risk of being disgraced. The commodore, who assumed, and justly too, the whole merit of his education, was now as proud of the youth's improvements, as if he had actually been his own offspring; and sometimes his affection rose to such a pitch of enthusiasm, that he verily believed him to be the issue of his own loins. Notwithstanding this favourable predicament in which our hero stood with his aunt and her husband, he could not help feeling the injury he suffered from the caprice of his mother; and though the gaiety of his disposition hindered him from afflicting himself with reflexions of any gloomy cast, he did not fail to forsee that if any sudden accident should deprive him of the commodore, he would in all likelihood find himself in a very disagreeable situation. Prompted by this consideration, he one evening accompanied his uncle to the club, and was introduced to his father, before that worthy gentleman had the least inkling of his arrival.

Mr. Gamaliel was never so disconcerted as at this rencounter. His own disposition would not suffer him to do any thing that might create the least disturbance, or interrupt his evening's enjoyment; and so strongly was he impressed with the terror of his wife, that he durst not yield to the tranquillity of his temper: and, as I have already observed, his inclination was perfectly neutral. Thus distracted between different motives, when Perry was presented to him, he sat silent and absorpt, as if he did not or would not perceive the application; and when he was urged to declare himself by the youth, who pathetically begged to know how he had incurred his displeasure, he answered in a peevish strain, 'Why, good now, child, what would you have me to do? your mother can't abide you.' 'If my mother is so unkind, I will not call it unnatural, (said Peregrine, the tears of indignation starting from his eyes) as to banish me from her presence and affection, without the least cause assigned; I hope you will not be so unjust as to espouse her barbarous prejudice.' Before Mr. Pickle had time to reply to this expostulation, for which he was not at all prepared, the commodore interposed, and enforced his favourite's remonstrance, by telling Mr. Gamaliel that he was ashamed to see any man drive in such a miserable manner under his wife's petticoat. 'As for my own part, (said he, raising his voice, and assuming a look of importance and command) before I would suffer myself to be steered all weathers by any woman in Christendom, d'ye see, I'd raise such a hurricane about her ears that'——Here he was interrupted by Mr. Hatchway, who thrusting his head towards the door, in the attitude of one that listens, cried 'Ahey! there's your spouse come to pay us a visit.' Trunnion's features that instant adopted a new disposition: fear and confusion took possession of his countenance; his voice from a tone of vociferation sunk into a whisper of 'Sure you must be mistaken, Jack;' and in great perplexity he wiped off the sweat which had started on his forehead at this false alarm. The lieutenant having thus punished him for the rhodomontade he had uttered, told him with an arch sneer, that he was deceived by the sound of the outward door creaking upon its hinges, which he mistook for Mrs. Trunnion's voice, and desired him to proceed with his admonitions to Mr. Pickle. It is not to be denied that this arrogance was a little unseasonable in the commodore, who was in all respects as effectually subdued to the dominion of his wife, as the person whose submission he then ventured to condemn; with this difference of disposition: Trunnion's subjection was like that of a bear, chequered with fits of surliness and rage; whereas Pickle bore the yoke like an ox, without repining. No wonder then that this indolence, this sluggishness, this stagnation of temper, rendered Gamaliel incapable of withstanding the arguments and importunity of his friends, to which he at length surrendered, acquiesced in the justice of their observations, and taking his son by the hand, promised to favour him for the future with his love and fatherly protection.

But this laudable resolution did not last; Mrs. Pickle still dubious of his constancy, and jealous of his communication with the commodore, never failed to interrogate him every night about the conversation that happened at the club; and regulate her exhortations according to the intelligence she received. He was no sooner, therefore, safely conveyed to bed, (that academy in which all notable wives communicate their lectures) when her catechism began; and she in a moment perceived something reluctant and equivocal in her husband's answers. Aroused at this discovery, she employed her influence and skill with such success, that he disclosed every circumstance of what had happened; and after having sustained a most severe rebuke for his simplicity and indiscretion, humbled himself so far as to promise that he would next day annul the condescensions he had made, and for ever renounce the ungracious object of her disgust. This undertaking was punctually performed in a letter to the commodore, which she herself dictated in these words.

SIR,

Whereas my good-nature being last night imposed upon, I was persuaded to countenance and promise I know not what to that vicious youth, whose parent I have the misfortune to be; I desire you will take notice that I revoke all such countenance and promises, and shall never look upon that man as my friend, who will henceforth in such a cause solicit,

Sir, yours, &c.
GAM. PICKLE

III

CHAPTER XXIV

Trunnion is enraged at the Conduct of Pickle.
Peregrine resents the Injustice of his Mother,
to whom he explains his Sentiments in a Letter.
Is entered at the University of Oxford, where he
signalizes himself as a Youth of an
enterprising Genius

UNSPEAKABLE were the transports of rage to which Trunnion was incensed by this absurd renunciation: he tore the letter with his gums, (teeth he had none) spit with furious grimaces, in token of the contempt he entertained for the author, whom he not only damned as a lousy, scabby, nasty, scurvy, sculking, lubberly noodle, but resolved to challenge to single combat with fire and sword; but he was dissuaded from this violent measure, and appeased by the intervention and advice of the lieutenant and Mr. Jolter, who represented the message as the effect of the poor man's infirmity, for which he was rather an object of pity than of resentment; and turned the stream of his indignation against the wife, whom he reviled accordingly. Nor did Peregrine himself bear with patience this injurious declaration, the nature of which he no sooner understood from Hatchway, than equally shocked and exasperated, he retired to his apartment, and in the first emotions of his ire, produced the following epistle, which was immediately conveyed to his mother.

MADAM,

Had nature formed me a bugbear to the sight, and inspired me with a soul as vicious as my body was detestable, perhaps I might have enjoyed particular marks of your affection and applause; seeing you have persecuted me with such unnatural aversion, for no other visible reason than that of my differing so widely in shape as well as disposition, from that deformed urchin who is the object of your tenderness and care. If those be the terms on which alone I can obtain your favour, I pray God you may never cease to hate,

Madam,

Your most injured son

PEREGRINE PICKLE

This letter, which nothing but his passion and inexperience could excuse, had such an effect upon his mother, as may be easily conceived. She was enraged to a degree of frenzy against the writer; though at the same time she considered the whole as the production of Mrs. Trunnion's particular pique, and represented it to her husband as an insult, that he was bound in honour to resent, by breaking off all correspondence with the commodore and his family. This was a bitter pill to Gamaliel, who, through a long course of years, was so habituated to Trunnion's company, that he could as easily have parted with a limb, as have relinquished the club all at once. He therefore ventured to represent his own incapacity to follow her advice, and begged that he might at least be allowed to drop the connexion gradually; protesting that he would do his endeavour to give her all manner of satisfaction.

Mean while preparations were made for Peregrine's departure to the university, and in a few weeks he set out in the seventeenth year of his age, accompanied by the same attendants who lived with him at Winchester, after his uncle had laid strong injunctions upon him to avoid the company of modest women,[1] to mind his learning, to let him hear of his welfare as often as he could spare time to write, and had settled his appointments at the rate of five hundred a year, including his governor's salary, which was one fifth part of the sum. The heart of our young gentleman dilated at the prospect of the figure he should make with such an handsome annuity, the management of which was left to his own discretion; and he amused his imagination with the most agreeable reveries during his journey to Oxford, which he performed in two days. Here being introduced to the head of the college, to whom he had been recommended, accommodated with genteel apartments, entered as gentleman commoner in the books, and provided with a judicious tutor, instead of returning to the study of Greek and Latin, in which he thought himself already sufficiently instructed; he renewed his acquaintance with some of his old school-fellows, whom he found in the same situation, and was by them initiated in all the fashionable diversions of the place.

It was not long before he made himself remarkable for his spirit and humour, which were so acceptable to the bucks of the university, that he was admitted as a member of their corporation, and in a very little time became the most conspicuous personage of the whole fraternity; not that he valued himself upon his ability in smoaking the greatest number of pipes, and drinking the largest quantity of ale; these were qualifications of too gross a nature to captivate his refined ambition. He piqued himself on his talent for raillery, his genius and taste, his personal accomplishments, and his success at intrigue; nor were his excursions confined to the small villages in the neighbourhood, which are commonly visited once a week by the students for the sake of carnal recreation. He kept his own horses, traversed the whole country in parties of pleasure, attended all the races within fifty miles of Oxford, and made frequent jaunts to London, where he used to lie incognito during the best part of many a term.

The rules of the university were too severe to be observed by a youth of his vivacity; and therefore he became acquainted with the proctor, by times. But all the checks he received were insufficient to moderate his career; he frequented taverns and coffee-houses, committed midnight frolics in the streets, insulted all the sober and pacific class of his fellow-students; the tutors themselves were not sacred from his ridicule; he laughed at the magistrate, and neglected every particular of college-discipline.

In vain did they attempt to restrain his irregularities by the imposition of fines; he was liberal to profusion, and therefore paid without reluctance. Thrice did he scale the windows of a tradesman, with whose daughter he had an affair of gallantry, as often was he obliged to seek his safety by a precipitate leap; and one night would, in all probability, have fallen a sacrifice to an ambuscade that was laid by the father, had not his trusty squire Pipes interposed in his behalf, and manfully rescued him from the clubs of his enemies.

In the midst of these excesses, Mr. Jolter finding his admonitions neglected, and his influence utterly destroyed, attempted to wean his pupil from his extravagant courses, by engaging his attention in some more laudable pursuit. With this view he introduced him into a club of politicians, who received him with great demonstrations of regard, accommodated themselves more than he could have expected to his jovial disposition, and while they revolved schemes for the reformation of the state, drank with such devotion to the accomplishment of their plans, that before parting the cares of their patriotism were quite overwhelmed.

Peregrine, though he could not approve of their doctrine, resolved to attach himself for some time to their company; because he perceived ample subject for his ridicule, in the characters of these wrong-headed enthusiasts. It was a constant practice with them, in their midnight consistories, to swallow such plentiful draughts of inspiration, that their mysteries commonly ended like

those of the Bacchanalian Orgia; and they were seldom capable of
maintaining that solemnity of decorum which by the nature of
their functions most of them were obliged to profess. Now as
Peregrine's satirical disposition was never more gratified than when
he had an opportunity of exposing grave characters in ridiculous
attitudes, he laid a mischievous snare for his new confederates,
which took effect in this manner. In one of their nocturnal deliberations, he promoted such a spirit of good fellowship, by the agreeable
sallies of his wit, which were purposely levelled against their
political adversaries, that by ten o'clock they were all ready to join
in the most extravagant proposal that could be made. They had
already broke their glasses in consequence of his suggestion, drank
healths out of their shoes, caps, and the bottoms of the candlesticks
that stood before them, sometimes standing with one foot on a
chair, and the knee bent on the edge of the table; and when they
could no longer stand in that posture, setting their bare posteriors
on the cold floor, they huzza'd, hollowed, danced and sung, and
in short were elevated to such a pitch of intoxication, that when
Peregrine proposed that they should burn their perriwigs, the hint
was immediately approved, and they executed the frolick as one
man; their shoes and caps underwent the same fate by the same
instigation, and in this trim he led them forth into the street, where
they resolved to compel every body they should find to subscribe
to their political creed, and pronounce the Shiboleth of their party.
In the atchievement of this enterprize, they met with more opposition than they expected; they were encountered with arguments
which they could not well withstand; the noses of some, and eyes
of others, in a very little time bore the marks of obstinate disputation; and their conductor having at length engaged the whole body
in a fray with another squadron which was pretty much in the same
condition, he very fairly gave them the slip, and slyly retreated to
his apartment, foreseeing that his companions would soon be
favoured with the notice of their superiors. Nor was he deceived
in his prognostic; the proctor going his round, chanced to fall in
with this tumultuous uproar, and interposing his authority, found
means to quiet the disturbance, and, after having taken cognizance
of their names, dismissed the rioters to their respective chambers,
not a little scandalized at the behaviour of some among them,
whose business and duty it was to set far other examples to the
youth under their care and direction.

About midnight Pipes, who had orders to attend at a distance,
and keep an eye upon Jolter, brought home that unfortunate

governor upon his back (Peregrine having beforehand secured his admittance into the college) and among other bruises, he was found to have received a couple of contusions on his face, which next morning appeared in a black circle that surrounded each eye. This was a mortifying circumstance to a man of his character and deportment, especially as he had received a message from the proctor, who desired to see him forthwith. With great humility and contrition he begged the advice of his pupil, who being used to amuse himself with painting, assured Mr. Jolter, that he would cover those signs of disgrace with a slight coat of flesh-colour, so dextrously, that it would be almost impossible to distinguish the artificial from the natural skin. The rueful governor, rather than expose such opprobrious tokens to the observation and censure of the magistrate, submitted to the expedient; and although his counsellor had over-rated his own skill, was persuaded to confide in the disguise, and actually attended the proctor, with such a staring addition to the natural ghastliness of his features, that his visage bore a very apt resemblance to some of those ferocious countenances that hang over the doors of certain taverns and alehouses, under the denomination of the Saracen's head.

Such a remarkable alteration of phisiognomy could not escape the notice of the most undiscerning beholder, much less the penetrating eye of this severe judge, already whetted with what he had seen overnight. He was therefore upbraided with his ridiculous and shallow artifice, and, together with the companions of his debauch, underwent such a cutting reprimand for the scandalous irregularity of his conduct, that all of them remained crest-fallen, and were ashamed, for many weeks, to appear in the publick execution of their duty.

Peregrine was too vain of his finesse, to conceal the part he acted in this comedy, with the particulars of which he regaled his companions, and thereby intailed upon himself the hate and resentment of the community, whose maxims and practices he had disclosed; for he was considered as a spy, who had intruded himself into their society with a view of betraying it; or, at best, an apostate and renegado from the faith and principles which he had professed.

CHAPTER XXV

He is insulted by his Tutor, whom he lampoons;
makes considerable Progress in polite Literature;
and in an Excursion to Windsor meets with Emilia
by Accident, and is very coldly received

AMONG those who suffered by his craft and infidelity was Mr. Jumble his own tutor, who could not at all digest the mortifying affront he had received, and was resolved to be revenged on the insulting author. With this view he watched the conduct of Mr. Pickle with the utmost rancour of vigilance, and let slip no opportunity of treating him with disrespect, which he knew the disposition of his pupil could less brook than any other severity it was in his power to exercise.

Peregrine had been several mornings absent from chapel; and as Mr. Jumble never failed to question him in a very peremptory stile about his non-attendance, he invented some very plausible excuses; but, at length, his ingenuity was exhausted; he received a very galling rebuke for his profligacy of morals, and that he might feel it the more sensibly, was ordered, by way of exercise, to compose a paraphrase in English verse, upon these two lines in Virgil,

Vane ligur, frustraque animis elate superbis,
Necquicquam, patrias, tentasti lubricus, artes.[1]

The imposition of this invidious theme had all the desired effect upon Peregrine, who not only considered it as a piece of unmannerly abuse levelled against his own conduct, but also as a retrospective insult on the memory of his grandfather, who (as he had been informed) was in his life-time more noted for his cunning than candour in trade.

Exasperated at this instance of the pedant's audacity, he had well nigh (in his first transports) taken corporal satisfaction on the spot; but foreseeing the troublesome consequences that would attend such a flagrant outrage against the laws of the university, he checked his indignation, and resolved to revenge the injury in a more cool and contemptuous manner. Thus determined, he set on foot an inquiry into the particulars of Jumble's parentage and education, and learnt that the father of this insolent tutor was a bricklayer, and that his mother sold pies, and that the son, at different periods of his youth, had amused himself in both occupations, before he converted his views to the study of learning. Fraught with this intelligence, he composed the following ballad in doggerel rhymes, and next day presented it as a gloss upon the text which the tutor had chosen.

I

Come, listen ye students of ev'ry degree,
I sing of a wit and a tutor *perdie*,
A statesman profound, a critick immense,
In short, a meer jumble of learning and sense;
And yet of his talents, tho' laudably vain,
His own family arts he could never attain.

II

His father intending his fortune to build,
In his youth would have taught him the trowel to wield,
But the mortar of discipline never would stick,
For his skull was secur'd by a facing of brick,
And with all his endeavours of patience and pain,
The skill of his sire he could never attain.

III

His mother an housewife neat, artful and wise,
Renown'd for her delicate biscuit and pies,
Soon alter'd his studies, by flatt'ring his taste,
From the raising of walls to the rearing of paste;
But all her instructions were fruitless and vain,
The pye-making myst'ry he ne'er could attain.

IV

Yet true to his race, in his labours was seen
A jumble of both their professions, I ween;
For, obliged to his own understanding to trust,
His pies seem'd of brick, and his houses of crust.
Then, good Mr. Tutor, pray be not so vain,
Since your family arts you could never attain.[1]

This impudent production was the most effectual vengeance he could have taken on his tutor, who had all the supercilious arrogance and ridiculous pride of a low-born pedant. Instead of overlooking this petulant piece of satire with that temper and decency of disdain that became a person of his gravity and station, he no sooner cast his eye over the performance, than the blood rushed into his countenance, which immediately after exhibited a ghastly pale colour, and with a quivering lip he told his pupil that he was an impertinent jackanapes, and he would take care that he should be expelled from the university, for having presumed to write and deliver such a licentious and scurrilous libel. Peregrine answered with great resolution, that when the provocation he had received should be known, he was persuaded that he should be acquitted by the opinion of all impartial people; and that he was ready to submit the whole to the decision of the master.

This arbitration he proposed, because he knew the master and Jumble were at variance; and for that reason the tutor durst not venture to put the cause on such an issue. Nay, when this reference was mentioned, Jumble, who was naturally jealous, suspected that Peregrine had a promise of protection before he undertook to commit such an outrageous insult; and this notion had such an effect upon him, that he resolved to devour his vexation, and wait for a more proper opportunity of gratifying his hate. Mean while copies of the ballad were distributed among the students, who sung it under the very nose of Mr. Jumble, to the tune of a *Cobler there was, &c.*[1] and the triumph of our hero was compleat. Neither was his whole time devoted to the riotous extravagancies of youth. He enjoyed many lucid intervals, during which he contracted a more intimate acquaintance with the classicks, applied himself to the reading of history, improved his taste for painting and musick, in which he made some progress; and above all things, cultivated the study of natural philosophy. It was generally after a course of close attention to some of these arts and sciences, that his disposition broke out into those irregularities and wild sallies of a luxuriant imagination, for which he became so remarkable; and he was perhaps the only young man in Oxford, who at the same time maintained an intimate and friendly intercourse with the most unthinking, as well as with the most sedate students at the university.

It is not to be supposed that a young man of Peregrine's vanity, inexperience and profusion, could suit his expence to his allowance, liberal as it was; for he was not one of those fortunate people who are born œconomists, and knew not the art of with-holding his purse when he saw his companion in difficulty: thus naturally generous and expensive, he squandered away his money, and made a most splendid appearance upon the receipt of his quarterly appointment; but long before the third month was elapsed, his finances were consumed, and as he could not stoop to ask an extraordinary supply, was too proud to borrow, and too haughty to run in debt with tradesmen, he devoted those periods of poverty to the prosecution of his studies, and shone forth again at the revolution of quarter day.

In one of these irruptions he and some of his companions went to Windsor, in order to see the royal apartments in the castle, whither they repaired in the afternoon, and as Peregrine stood contemplating the picture of Hercules and Omphale, one of his fellow-students whispered in his ear, 'Z—ds! Pickle, there are two fine girls.' He turned instantly about, and in one of them recognized his almost forgotten Emilia: her appearance acted upon his imagination like a spark of fire that falls among gun-powder; that passion which had lain dormant for the space of two years flashed up in a moment, and he was seized with an universal trepidation. She perceived and partook of his emotion; for their souls, like unisons, vibrated with the same impulse. However, she called her pride and resentment to her aid, and found resolution enough to retire from such a dangerous scene. Alarmed at her retreat, he recollected all his assurance, and impelled by love which he could no longer resist, followed her into the next room, where in the most disconcerted manner he accosted her with 'Your humble servant, Miss Gauntlet.' To which salutation she replied, with an affectation of indifference that did not, however, conceal her agitation, 'Your servant, Sir;' and immediately extending her finger towards the picture of Duns Scotus, which is fixed over one of the doors, asked her companion in a strange sort of giggling tone, if she did not think he looked like a conjurer. Peregrine nettled into spirits by this reception, answered for the other lady, 'that it was an easy matter to be a conjurer in those times, when the simplicity of the age assisted his divination; but were he, or Merlin himself to rise from the dead now, when such deceit and dissimulation prevail, they would not be able to earn their bread by the profession.' '—O! Sir, (said she, turning full upon him) without doubt they would adopt new maxims; 'tis no disparagement in this enlightened age for one to alter one's opinion.' 'No, sure, Madam, (replied the youth with some precipitation) provided the change be for the better;' 'and should it happen otherwise, (retorted the nymph with a flirt of her fan) inconstancy will never want countenance from the practice of mankind.' 'True, Madam, (resumed our hero, fixing his eyes upon her) examples of levity are every where to be met with.'

'O Lord, Sir, (cried Emilia, tossing her head) you'll scarce ever find a fop without it.' By this time his companion seeing him engaged with one of the ladies, entered into conversation with the other; and in order to favour his friend's gallantry, conducted her into the next apartment, on pretence of entertaining her with the sight of a remarkable piece of painting.

Peregrine laying hold on this opportunity of being alone with the object of his love, assumed a most seducing tenderness of look, and heaving a profound sigh, asked if she had utterly discarded him from her remembrance. Reddening at this pathetic question, which recalled the memory of the imagined slight he had put upon her, she answered in great confusion, 'Sir, I believe I once had the pleasure of seeing you at a ball in Winchester.' 'Miss Emilia, (said he, very gravely) will you be so candid as to tell me what mis-behaviour of mine you are pleased to punish, by restricting your remembrance to that single occasion?' 'Mr. Pickle, (she replied in the same tone) it is neither my province nor inclination to judge your conduct; and therefore you misapply your question when you ask such an explanation of me.' 'At least, (resumed our lover) give me the melancholy satisfaction to know for what offence of my committing you refused to take the least notice of that letter which I had the honour to write from Winchester by your own express permission.' 'Your letter, (said Miss with great vivacity) neither required, nor in my opinion, deserved an answer; and to be free with you, Mr. Pickle, it was but a shallow artifice to rid your-self of a correspondence you had deigned to sollicit.' Peregrine confounded at this repartee, replied that howsoever he might have failed in point of elegance or discretion, he was sure he had not been deficient in expressions of respect and devotion for those charms which it was his pride to adore: 'As for the verses, (said he) I own they were unworthy of the theme, but I flattered myself that they would have merited your acceptance, though not your approbation, and been considered not so much as the proof of my genius, as the genuine effusion of my love.' 'Verses? (cried Emilia with an air of astonishment) what verses? I really don't understand you.' The young gentleman was thunderstruck at this exclamation, to which, after a long pause, he answered, 'I begin to suspect, and heartily wish it may appear that we have misunderstood each other from the beginning. Pray, Miss Gauntlet, did not you find a copy of verses inclosed in that unfortunate letter?' 'Truly, Sir, (said the lady) I am not so much of a connoiseur as to distinguish whether that facetious production which you merrily stile an unfortunate letter was composed in verse or prose; but, methinks, the jest is a little too stale to be brought upon the carpet again.' So saying, she tripped away to her companion, and left her lover in a most tumultuous suspence. He now perceived that her neglect of his addresses when he was at Winchester, must have been owing to some mystery which he could not comprehend; and she began to suspect and to hope that the letter which she received was spurious, though she could not conceive how that could possibly happen, as it had been delivered to her by the hands of his own servant.

However, she resolved to leave the task of unravelling the affair to him who, she knew, would infallibly exert himself for his own as well as her satisfaction. She was not deceived in her opinion; he went up to her again at the staircase, and as they were unprovided with a male attendant, insisted upon squiring the ladies to their lodgings. Emilia saw his drift, which was no other than to know where she lived; and though she approved of his finesse, thought it was incumbent upon her for the support of her own dignity to decline his civility: she therefore thanked him for his polite offer, but would by no means consent to his giving himself such unnecessary trouble, especially as they had a very little way to walk. He was not repulsed by this refusal, the nature of which he perfectly understood; nor was she sorry to see him persevere in his determination; he therefore accompanied them in their return, and made divers efforts to speak with Emilia in particular: but she had a spice of the coquette in her disposition, and being determined to whet his impatience, artfully baffled all his endeavours, by keeping her companion continually engaged in the conversation, which turned upon the venerable appearance and imperial situation of the place. Thus tantalized, he lounged with them to the door of the house in which they lodged, when his mistress perceiving by the countenance of her comrade, that she was on the point of desiring him to walk in, checked her intention with a frown, then turning to Mr. Pickle, dropped him a very formal curt'sey, seized the other young lady by the arm, and saying 'Come, cousin Sophy,' vanished in a moment.

CHAPTER XXVI

After sundry unsuccessful Efforts, he finds Means to
come to an Explanation with his Mistress;
and a Reconciliation ensues

PEREGRINE, disconcerted at their sudden disappearance, stood
for some minutes gaping in the street, before he could get the
better of his surprize; and then deliberated with himself whether
he should demand immediate admittance to his mistress, or choose
some other method of application. Piqued at her abrupt behaviour,
though pleased with her spirit, he set his invention to work, in
order to contrive some means of seeing her; and in a fit of musing
arrived at the inn, where he found his companions whom he had
left at the Castle-gate. They had already made inquiry about the
ladies, in consequence of which, he learnt that Miss Sophy was
daughter of a gentleman in town to whom his mistress was related;
that an intimate friendship subsisted between the two young ladies;
that Emilia had lived about a month with her cousin, and appeared
at the last assembly, where she was universally admired; and that
several young gentlemen of fortune had since that time teized her
with addresses.

Our hero's ambition was flattered, and his passion inflamed with
this intelligence; and he swore within himself that he would not
quit the spot until he should have obtained an indisputed victory
over all his rivals.

That same evening he composed a most eloquent epistle, in
which he earnestly intreated that she would favour him with an
opportunity of vindicating his conduct; but she would neither
receive his billet nor see his messenger. Baulked in this effort, he
inclosed it in a new cover directed by another hand, and ordered
Pipes to ride next morning to London, on purpose to deliver it at
the post-office; that coming by such conveyance, she might have
no suspicion of the author, and open it before she should be aware
of the deceit.

Three days he waited patiently for the effect of this stratagem,
and in the afternoon of the fourth, ventured to hazard a formal
visit, in quality of an old acquaintance. But here too he failed in
his attempt; she was indisposed and could not see company. These
obstacles served only to increase his eagerness; he still adhered to

his former resolution; and his companions understanding his determination, left him next day to his own inventions. Thus relinquished to his own ideas, he doubled his assiduity, and practised every method his imagination could suggest, in order to promote his plan.

Pipes was stationed all day long within sight of her door, that he might be able to give his master an account of her motions; but she never went abroad except to visit in the neighbourhood, and was always housed before Peregrine could be apprized of her appearance. He went to church with a view of attracting her notice, and humbled his deportment before her; but she was so mischievously devout as to look at nothing but her book, so that he was not favoured with one glance of regard. He frequented the coffee-house, and attempted to contract an acquaintance with Miss Sophy's father, who, he hoped, would invite him to his house; but this expectation was also defeated. That prudent gentleman looked upon him as one of those forward fortune-hunters who go about the country seeking whom they may devour, and warily discouraged all his advances. Chagrined by so many unsuccessful endeavours, he began to despair of accomplishing his aim, and as the last suggestion of his art, paid off his lodging, took horse at noon, and departed, in all appearance, for the place from whence he had come. He rode, however, but a few miles, and in the dusk of the evening returned unseen, alighted at another inn, ordered Pipes to stay within doors, and keeping himself incognito, employed another person as a centinel upon Emilia.

It was not long before he reaped the fruits of his ingenuity. Next day in the afternoon he was informed by his spy, that the two young ladies were gone to walk in the park, whither he followed them on the instant, fully determined to come to an explanation with his mistress, even in presence of her friend, who might possibly be prevailed upon to interest herself in his behalf.

When he saw them at such a distance that they could not return to town before he should have an opportunity of putting his resolution in practice, he mended his pace, and found means to appear before them so suddenly, that Emilia could not help expressing her surprize in a scream. Our lover putting on a mein of humility and mortification, begged to know if her resentment was implacable; and asked why she had so cruelly refused to grant him the common privilege that every criminal enjoyed. 'Dear Miss Sophy, (said he, addressing himself to her companion) give me leave to implore your intercession with your cousin; I am sure you have humanity enough to espouse my cause, did you but know the justice of it; and I flatter myself, that by your kind interposition, I may be able to rectify that fatal misunderstanding which hath made me wretched.' 'Sir, (said Sophy) you appear like a gentleman, and I doubt not but your behaviour has been always suitable to your appearance; but you must excuse me from undertaking any such office in behalf of a person whom I have not the honour to know.' 'Madam, (answered Peregrine) I hope Miss Emy will justify my pretensions to that character, notwithstanding the mystery of her displeasure, which upon my honour I cannot for my soul explain.' 'Lord! Mr. Pickle, (said Emilia, who had by this time recollected herself) I never questioned your gallantry and taste, but I am resolved that you shall never have cause to exercise your talents at my expence; so that you teize yourself and me to no purpose: come, Sophy, let us walk home again.' 'Good God! madam, (cried the lover with great emotion) why will you distract me with such barbarous indifference? Stay, dear Emilia! I conjure you on my knees to stay and hear me: by all that is sacred! I was not to blame, you must have been imposed upon by some villain who envied my good fortune, and took some treacherous method to ruin my love.'

Miss Sophy, who possessed a large stock of good nature, and to whom her cousin had communicated the cause of her reserve, seeing the young gentleman so much affected with that disdain which she knew to be feigned, laid hold on Emilia's sleeve, saying with a smile, 'Not quite so fast, Emily; I begin to perceive that this is a love-quarrel, and therefore there may be hopes of a reconciliation; for I suppose both parties are open to conviction.' 'For my own part, (cried Peregrine with great eagerness) I appeal to Miss Sophy's decision. But why do I say appeal? Tho' I am conscious of having committed no offence, I am ready to submit to any penance, let it be never so rigorous, that my fair enslaver herself shall impose, provided it will intitle me to her favour and forgiveness at last.' Emily well nigh overcome by this declaration, told him that as she taxed him with no guilt, she expected no attonement; and pressed her companion to return into town. But Sophy, who was too indulgent to her friend's real inclination to comply with her request, observed that the gentleman seemed so reasonable in his concessions, she began to think her cousin was in the wrong, and felt herself disposed to act as umpire in the dispute.

Overjoyed at this condescension, Mr. Pickle thanked her in the most rapturous terms, and in the transport of his expectation, kissed the hand of his kind mediatrix; a circumstance which had a remarkable effect on the countenance of Emilia, who did not seem to relish the warmth of his acknowledgement.

After many supplications on one hand, and pressing remonstrances on the other, she yielded at length, and turning to her lover, while her face was overspread with blushes, 'Well, Sir, (said she) supposing I were to put the difference on that issue, how could you excuse the ridiculous letter which you sent to me from Winchester.' This expostulation introduced a discussion of the whole affair, in which all the circumstances were canvassed; and Emilia still affirmed with great heat, that the letter must have been calculated to affront her; for she could not suppose the author was so weak as to design it for any other purpose.

Peregrine, who still retained in his memory the substance of this unlucky epistle, as well as the verses which were inclosed, could recollect no particular expression which could have justly given the least umbrage; and therefore in the agonies of perplexity, begged that the whole might be submitted to the judgment of Miss Sophy; and faithfully promised to stand to her award.

In short, this proposal was with seeming reluctance embraced by Emilia, and an appointment made to meet next day in the same place, whither both parties were desired to come provided with their credentials, according to which definitive sentence would be pronounced.

Our lover having succeeded thus far, overwhelmed Sophy with acknowledgments on account of her generous mediation, and in the course of their walk, which Emilia was now in no hurry to conclude, whispered a great many tender protestations in the ear of his mistress, who, nevertheless, continued to act upon the reserve, until her doubts should be more fully resolved.

Mr. Pickle having found means to amuse them in the fields till the twilight, was obliged to wish them good even, after having obtained a solemn repetition of their promise to meet him at the appointed time and place; and then retreated to his apartment, where he spent the whole night in various conjectures on the subject of this letter, the gordian knot of which he could by no means untie.

One while he imagined that some wag had played a trick upon his messenger, in consequence of which Emilia had received a supposititious letter; but upon further reflection, he could not conceive the practicability of any such deceit. Then he began to doubt the sincerity of his mistress, who, perhaps, had only made that an handle for discarding him, at the request of some favoured rival; but his own integrity forbad him to harbour this mean suspicion; and therefore he was again involved in the labyrinth of perplexity. Next day he waited on the rack of impatience for the hour of five in the afternoon, which no sooner struck, than he ordered Pipes to attend him, in case there should be occasion for his evidence; and repaired to the place of rendezvous, where he had not tarried five minutes before the ladies appeared. Mutual compliments being passed, and the attendant stationed at a convenient distance, Peregrine persuaded them to sit down upon the grass, under the shade of a spreading oak, that they might be more at their ease; while he stretched himself at their feet, and desired that the paper on which his doom depended might be examined. It was accordingly put into the hand of his fair arbitress, who read it immediately with an audible voice. The first two words of it were no sooner pronounced, than he started with great emotion, and raised himself upon his hand and knee, in which posture he listened to the rest of the sentence; and then sprung upon his feet in the utmost astonishment, and glowing with resentment at the same time, exclaimed 'Hell and the devil! what's all that? Sure you make a jest of me, madam.' 'Pray, Sir, (said Sophy) give me the hearing for a few moments, and then urge what you shall think proper in your own defence.' Having thus cautioned him, she proceeded; but before she had finished one half of the performance, her gravity forsook her, and she was seized with a violent fit of laughter, in which neither of the lovers could help joining, notwithstanding the resentment which at that instant prevailed in the breasts of both. The judge, however, in a little time, resumed her solemnity, and having read the remaining part of this curious epistle, all three continued staring at each other alternately for the space of half a minute, and then broke forth at the same instant in another paroxism of mirth. From this unanimous convulsion, one would have thought that both parties were extremely well pleased with the joke; yet this was by no means the case.

Emilia imagined that notwithstanding his affected surprize, her lover in spite of himself had renewed the laugh at her expence, and in so doing, applauded his own unmannerly ridicule. This supposition could not fail of raising and reviving her indignation, while Peregrine highly resented the indignity with which he supposed himself treated, in their attempting to make him the dupe of such a gross and ludicrous artifice. This being the situation of their thoughts, their mirth was succeeded by a mutual gloominess of aspect, and the judge addressing herself to Mr. Pickle, asked if he had any thing to offer why sentence should not be pronounced. 'Madam, (answered the culprit) I am sorry to find myself so low in the opinion of your cousin, as to be thought capable of being deceived by such a shallow contrivance.' 'Nay, Sir, (said Emily) the contrivance is your own, and I cannot help admiring your confidence in imputing it to me.' 'Upon my honour, Miss Emily, (resumed our hero) you wrong my understanding as well as my love, in accusing me of having written such a silly impertinent performance: the very appearance and address of it is so unlike the letter which I did myself the honour to write, that I dare say my man, even at this distance of time, will remember the difference.' So saying, he extended his voice, and beckoned to Pipes, who immediately drew near. His mistress seemed to object to the evidence, by observing that to be sure Mr. Pipes had his cue; when Peregrine begging she would spare him the mortification of considering him in such a dishonourable light, desired his valet to examine the outside of the letter, and recollect if it was the same which he had delivered to Miss Gauntlet about two years ago. Pipes having taken a superficial view of it, pulled up his breeches, saying, 'Mayhap it is, but we have made so many trips, and been in so many creeks and corners since that time, that I can't pretend to be certain; for I neither keep journal nor logbook of our proceedings.' Emilia commended him for his candour, at the same time darting a sarcastic look at his master, as if she thought he had tampered with his servant's integrity in vain; and Peregrine began to rave and curse his fate for having subjected him to such mean suspicion, attesting heaven and earth in the most earnest manner, that far from having composed and conveyed that stupid production, he had never seen it before, nor been privy to the least circumstance of the plan.

Pipes, now for the first time, perceived the mischief which he had occasioned, and moved with the transports of his master, for whom he had a most inviolable attachment, frankly declared he was ready to make oath that Mr. Pickle had no hand in the letter which he delivered. All three were amazed at this confession, the meaning of which they could not comprehend; and Peregrine after some pause, leaped upon Pipes, and seizing him by the throat, exclaimed in an extasy of rage, 'Rascal! tell me this instant what became of the letter I intrusted to your care.' The patient valet, half strangled as he was, squirted a collection of tobacco juice out of one corner of his mouth, and with great deliberation replied, 'Why burnt it, you wouldn't have me give the young woman a thing that shook all in the wind in tatters, would you?' The ladies interposed in behalf of the distressed squire, from whom, by dint of questions which he had neither art nor inclination to evade, they extorted an explanation of the whole affair.

Such ridiculous simplicity and innocence of intention appeared in the composition of his expedient, that even the remembrance of all the chagrin which it had produced, could not rouse their indignation, or enable them to resist a third eruption of laughter which they forthwith underwent.

Pipes was dismissed with many menacing injunctions, to beware of such conduct for the future; Emilia stood with a confusion of joy and tenderness in her countenance; Peregrine's eyes kindled into rapture, and when Miss Sophy pronounced the sentence of reconciliation, advanced to his mistress, saying, 'Truth is mighty, and will prevail;' then clasping her in his arms, very impudently ravished a kiss, which she had not power to refuse. Nay, such was the impulse of his joy, that he took the same freedom with the lips of Sophy, calling her his kind mediatrix and guardian angel, and behaved with such extravagance of transport, as plainly evinced the fervour and sincerity of his love.

I shall not pretend to repeat the tender protestations that were uttered on one side, or describe the bewitching glances of approbation with which they were received on the other; suffice it to say, that the endearing intimacy of their former connexion was instantly renewed, and Sophy, who congratulated them upon the happy termination of their quarrel, favoured with their mutual confidence. In consequence of this happy pacification, they deliberated upon the means of seeing each other often; and as he could not without some previous introduction visit her openly at the house of her relation, they agreed to meet every afternoon in the park till the next assembly, at which he would solicit her as a partner, and she be unengaged, in expectation of his request. By this connexion he would be intitled to visit her next day, and thus an avowed correspondence would of course commence. This plan was actually put in execution, and attended with a circumstance which had well nigh produced some mischievous consequence, had not Peregrine's good fortune been superior to his discretion.

CHAPTER XXVII

He atchieves an Adventure at the Assembly, and quarrels with his Governor

AT the assembly, were no fewer than three gentlemen of fortune, who rivalled our lover in his passion for Emilia, and who had severally begged the honour of dancing with her upon that occasion. She had excused herself to each, on pretence of a slight indisposition that she foresaw would detain her from the ball, and desired they would provide themselves with other partners. Obliged to admit her excuse, they accordingly followed her advice; and after they had engaged themselves beyond the power of retracting, had the mortification to see her there unclaimed.

They in their turns made up to her, and expressed their surprize and concern at finding her in the assembly unprovided, after she had declined their invitation; but she told them that her cold had forsaken her since she had the pleasure of seeing them, and that she would rely upon accident for a partner. Just as she pronounced these words to the last of the three, Peregrine advanced as an utter stranger, bowed with great respect, told her he understood she was disengaged, and would think himself highly honoured in being accepted as her partner for the night; and had the good fortune to succeed in his application.

As they were by far the handsomest and best accomplished couple in the room, they could not fail of attracting the notice and admiration of the spectators, which inflamed the jealousy of his three competitors, who immediately entered into a conspiracy against this gaudy stranger, whom as their rival, they resolved to affront in publick. Pursuant to the plan which they projected for this purpose, the first country-dance was no sooner concluded, than one of them with his partner took the place of Peregrine and his mistress, contrary to the regulations of the ball. Our lover imputing this behaviour to inadvertency, informed the gentleman of his mistake, and civilly desired he would rectify his error. The other told him, in an imperious tone, that he wanted none of his advice, and bad him mind his own affairs. Peregrine answered with some warmth, and insisted upon his right; a dispute commenced, high words ensued, in the course of which, our impetuous youth hearing himself reviled with the appellation of scoundrel, pulled off his antagonist's periwig, and flung it in his face. The ladies immediately shriek'd, the gentlemen interposed, Emilia was seized with a fit of trembling, and conducted to her seat by her youthful admirer, who begged pardon for having discomposed her, and vindicated what he had done, by representing the necessity he was under to resent the provocation he had received.

Though she could not help owning the justice of his plea, she was not the less concerned at the dangerous situation in which he had involved himself, and in the utmost consternation and anxiety, insisted upon going directly home: he could not resist her importunities, and her cousin being determined to accompany her, he escorted them to their lodgings, where he wished them good night, after having, in order to quiet their apprehensions, protested that if his opponent was satisfied, he should never take any step towards the prosecution of the quarrel. Mean while the assembly-room became a scene of tumult and uproar; the person who conceived himself injured, seeing Peregrine retire, struggled with his companions who with-held him, in order to pursue and take satisfaction of our hero, whom he loaded with terms of abuse, and challenged to single combat.

The director of the ball held a consultation with all the subscribers who were present, and it was determined by a majority of votes, that the two gentlemen who had occasioned the disturbance, should be desired to withdraw. This resolution being signified to one of the parties then present, he made some difficulty of complying, but was persuaded to submit by his two confederates, who accompanied him to the street-door, where he was met by Peregrine on his return to the assembly.

This choleric gentleman, who was a country squire, no sooner saw his rival, than he began to brandish his cudgel in a menacing posture, when our adventurous youth stepping back with one foot, laid his hand upon the hilt of his sword, which he drew half way out of the scabbard. This attitude, and the sight of the blade which glittened by moonlight in his face, checked in some sort, the ardour of his assailant, who desired he would lay aside his toaster, and take a bout with him at equal arms. Peregrine, who was an expert cudgel-player, accepted the invitation, and exchanging weapons with Pipes who stood behind him, put himself in a posture of defence, and received the attack of his adversary, who struck at random without either skill or œconomy. Pickle could have beaten the cudgel out of his hand at the first blow, but as in that case he would have been obliged in honour to give immediate quarter, he resolved to discipline his antagonist without endeavouring to disable him until he should be heartily satisfied with the vengeance he had taken. With this view he returned the salute, and raised such a clatter about the squire's pate, that one who had heard without seeing the application, would have mistaken the sound for that of a salt-box, in the hand of a dext'rous Merry Andrew, belonging to one of the booths at Bartholomew Fair. Neither was this salutation confined to his head; his shoulders, arms, thighs, ancles and ribs, were visited with amazing rapidity, while Tom Pipes sounded the charge through his fist. Peregrine tired with this exercise, which had almost bereft his enemy of sensation, at last struck the decisive blow, in consequence of which, the squire's weapon flew out of his grasp, and he allowed our hero to be the better man. Satisfied with this acknowledgment, the victor walked up stairs with such elevation of spirits and insolence of mein, that no body chose to intimate the resolution which had been taken in his absence, and having amused himself for some time in beholding the country dances, he retreated to his lodging, where he indulged himself all night in the contemplation of his own success.

Next day in the forenoon he went to visit his partner, and the gentleman at whose house she lived, having been informed of his family and condition, received him with great courtesy, as the acquaintance of his cousin Gauntlet, and invited him to dinner that same day.

Emilia was remarkably well pleased, when she understood the issue of his adventure, which began to make some noise in town, even though it deprived her of a wealthy admirer; for the squire having consulted an attorney about the nature of the dispute, in hopes of being able to prosecute Peregrine for an assault, and finding little encouragement to go to law, resolved to pocket the insult and injury he had undergone, and to discontinue his addresses to her who was the cause of both.

Our lover being told by his mistress that she proposed to stay a fortnight longer at Windsor, determined to enjoy her company all that time, and then to give her a convoy to the house of her mother, whom he longed to see. In consequence of this plan, he every day contrived some fresh party of pleasure for the ladies, to whom he had by this time free access; and intangled himself so much in the snares of love, that he seemed quite enchanted by Emilia's charms, which were now indeed almost irresistible. While he thus heedlessly roved in the flowery paths of pleasure, his governor at Oxford alarmed at the unusual duration of his absence, went to the young gentlemen who had accompanied him in his excursion, and very earnestly intreated them to tell him what they knew concerning his pupil; they accordingly gave him an account of the rencounter that happened between Peregrine and Miss Emily Gauntlet in the castle, and mentioned circumstances sufficient to convince him that his charge was very dangerously engaged.

Far from having an authority over Peregrine, Mr. Jolter durst not even disoblige him, and therefore, instead of writing to the commodore, he took horse immediately, and that same night reached Windsor, where he found his stray sheep very much surprised at his unexpected arrival.

The governor desiring to have some serious conversation with him, they shut themselves up in an apartment, when Jolter with great solemnity, communicated the cause of his journey, which was no other than his concern for his pupil's welfare; and very gravely undertook to prove by mathematical demonstration, that this intrigue, if further pursued, would tend to the young gentleman's ruin and disgrace. This singular proposition raised the curiosity of Peregrine, who promised to yield all manner of attention, and desired him to begin without further preamble.

The governor, encouraged by this appearance of candour, expressed his satisfaction in finding him so open to conviction, and told him he would proceed upon geometrical principles. Then hemming thrice, observed, that no mathematical inquiries could be carried on, except upon certain *data*, or concessions to truths, that were self-evident; and therefore he must crave his assent to a few axioms, which he was sure Mr. Pickle would see no reason to dispute. 'In the first place then (said he) you will grant, I hope, that youth and discretion are with respect to each other as two parallel lines, which though infinitely produced, remain still equi-distant, and will never coincide: then you must allow that passion acts upon the human mind, in a ratio compounded of the acuteness of sense, and constitutional heat: and thirdly, you will not deny that the angle of remorse is equal to that of precipitation. These *postulata* being admitted, (added he, taking paper, pen and ink, and drawing a parallelogram) let youth be represented by the right line a, b, and discretion by another right line c, d, parallel to the former. Compleat the parallelogram, a, b, c, d, and let the point of intersection, b, represent perdition. Let passion, represented under the letter c, have a motion in the direction c, a. At the same time, let another motion be communicated to it, in the direction c, d, it will proceed in the diagonal c, b, and describe it in the same time that it would have described the side c, a, by the first motion, or the side *c, d,* by the second. To understand the demonstration of this corollary, we must premise this obvious principle, that when a body is acted upon by a motion or power parallel to a right line given in position, this power, or motion, has no effect to cause the body to approach towards that line, or recede from it, but to move in a line parallel to a right line only; as appears from the second law of motion: therefore *c, a,* being parallel to *d, b,*'——

His pupil having listened to him thus far, could contain himself no longer, but interrupted the investigation with a loud laugh, and told him that his *postulata* put him in mind of a certain learned and ingenious gentleman, who undertook to disprove the existence of natural evil, and asked no other *datum* on which to found his demonstration, but an acknowledgment that *every thing that is, is right.*[1] 'You may therefore (said he, in a peremptory tone) spare yourself the trouble of torturing your invention; for, after all, I am pretty certain that I shall want capacity to comprehend the discussion of your lemma, and consequently be obliged to refuse my assent to your deduction.'

Mr. Jolter was disconcerted at this declaration, and so much offended at Peregrine's disrespect, that he could not help expressing his displeasure, by telling him flatly, that he was too violent and headstrong to be reclaimed by reason and gentle means; that he (the tutor) must be obliged in the discharge of his duty and conscience, to inform the commodore of his nephew's imprudence; that if the laws of this realm were effectual, they would take cognizance of the gipsy who had led him astray; and observed, by way of contrast, that if such a preposterous intrigue had happened in France, she would have been clapt up in a convent two years ago.

Our lover's eyes kindled with indignation, when he heard his mistress treated with such irreverence; he could scarce refrain from inflicting manual chastisement on the blasphemer, whom he reproached in his wrath as an arrogant pedant, without either delicacy or sense, and cautioned him against using any such impertinent freedoms with his affairs for the future, on pain of incurring more severe effects of his resentment.

Mr. Jolter, who entertained very high notions of that veneration to which he thought himself intitled by his character and qualifications, had not bore without repining, his want of influence and authority over his pupil, against whom he cherished a particular grudge, ever since the adventure of the painted eye; and therefore, on this occasion, his politic forbearance had been overcome by the accumulated motives of his disgust. Indeed he would have resigned his charge with disdain, had not he been encouraged to persevere, by the hopes of a good living which Trunnion had in his gift, or known how to dispose of himself for the present to better advantage.

CHAPTER XXVIII

He receives a Letter from his Aunt,
breaks with the Commodore,
and disobliges the Lieutenant, who,
nevertheless, undertakes his Cause

MEAN while he quitted the youth in high dudgeon, and that same evening dispatched a letter for Mrs. Trunnion, which was dictated by the first transports of his passion, and of course replete with severe animadversions on the misconduct of his pupil.

In consequence of this complaint, it was not long before Peregrine received an epistle from his aunt, wherein she commemorated all the circumstances of the commodore's benevolence towards him, when he was helpless and forlorn, deserted and abandoned by his own parents, upbraided him for his misbehaviour and neglect of his tutor's advice, and insisted upon his breaking off all intercourse with that girl who had seduced his youth, as he valued the continuance of her affection and her husband's regard.

As our lover's own ideas of generosity were extremely refined, he was shocked at the indelicate insinuations of Mrs. Trunnion, and felt all the pangs of an ingenuous mind, that labours under obligations to a person whom it contemns; far from obeying her injunction, or humbling himself by a submissive answer to her reprehension, his resentment buoyed him up above every selfish consideration; he resolved to attach himself to Emilia, if possible, more than ever; and although he was tempted to punish the officiousness of Jolter, by recriminating upon his life and conversation, he generously withstood the impulse of his passion, because he knew that his governor had no other dependance than the good opinion of the commodore. He could not, however, digest in silence the severe expostulations of his aunt; to which he replied by the following letter, addressed to her husband.

Sir,

Tho' my temper could never stoop to offer, nor, I believe, your disposition deign to receive that gross incense which the illiberal only expect, and none but the base-minded condescend to pay; my sentiments have always done justice to your generosity, and my intention scrupulously adhered to the dictates of my duty. Conscious of this integrity of heart, I cannot but severely feel your lady's unkind (I will not call it ungenerous) recapitulation of the favours I have received; and as I take it for granted, that you knew and approved of her letter, I must beg leave to assure you, that far from being swayed by menaces and reproach, I am determined to embrace the most abject extremity of fortune, rather than submit to such dishonourable compulsion. When I am treated in a more delicate and respectful manner, I hope I shall behave as becomes,

Sir,

Your obliged

P. Pickle

The commodore, who did not understand those nice distinctions of behaviour, and dreaded the consequence of Peregrine's amour, against which he was strangely prepossessed, was exasperated at the insolence and obstinacy of this adopted son; to whose epistle he wrote the following answer, which was transmitted by the hands of Hatchway, who had orders to bring the delinquent along with him to the garrison.

Heark ye, child,

You need not bring your fine speeches to bear upon me. You only expend your ammunition to no purpose. Your aunt told you nothing but truth; for it is always fair and honest to be above board, d'ye see. I am informed as how you are in chace of a painted galley, which will decoy you upon the flats of destruction, unless you keep a better look-out and a surer reckoning than you have hitherto done; and I have sent Jack Hatchway to see how the land lies, and warn you of your danger: if so be as you will put about ship, and let him steer you into this harbour, you shall meet with a safe birth and friendly reception; but if you refuse to alter your course, you cannot expect any further assistance from yours, as you behave,

Hawser Trunnion

Peregrine was equally piqued and disconcerted at the receit of this letter, which was quite different from what he had expected, and declared in a resolute tone to the lieutenant, who brought it, that he might return as soon as he pleased; for he was determined to consult his own inclination, and remain for some time longer where he was.

Hatchway endeavoured to persuade him by all the arguments which his sagacity and friendship could supply, to shew a little more deference for the desire of the old man, who was by this time rendered fretful and peevish by the gout, which now hindered him from enjoying himself as usual, and who might, in his passion, take some step very much to the detriment of the young gentleman, whom he had hitherto considered as his own son. Among other remonstrances, Jack observed that mayhap Peregrine had got under Emilia's hatches, and did not choose to set her adrift; and if that was the case, he himself would take charge of the vessel, and see her cargo safely delivered; for he had a respect for the young woman, and his needle pointed towards matrimony; and as, in all probability, she could not be much the worse for the wear, he would make shift to scud thro' life with her under an easy sail.

Our lover was deaf to all his admonitions, and having thanked him for this last instance of his complaisance, repeated his resolution of adhering to his first purpose. Hatchway having profited so little by mild exhortations, assumed a more peremptory aspect, and plainly told him he neither could nor would go home without him; so he had best make immediate preparation for the voyage.

Peregrine made no other reply to this declaration than by a contemptuous smile, and rose from his seat in order to retire; upon which the lieutenant started up, and posting himself by the door, protested with some menacing gestures, that he would not suffer him to run a-head neither. The other, incensed at his presumption in attempting to detain him by force, tripped up his wooden leg, and laid him on his back in a moment; then walked deliberately towards the park, in order to indulge his reflection, which at that time teemed with disagreeable thoughts. He had not proceeded two hundred steps, when he heard something blowing and stamping behind him; and looking back, perceived the lieutenant at his heels, with rage and indignation in his countenance. This exasperated seaman, impatient of the affront he had received, and forgetting all the circumstances of their former intimacy, advanced with great eagerness to his old friend, saying, 'Look ye, brother, you're a saucy boy, and if you was at sea, I would have your arse brought to the David[1] for your disobedience; but as we are on shore, you and I must crack a pistol at one another; here is a brace, you shall take which you please.'

Peregrine, upon recollection, was sorry for having been laid under the necessity of disobliging honest Jack, and very frankly asked his pardon for what he had done. But this condescension was misinterpreted by the other, who refused any other satisfaction but that which an officer ought to claim; and, with some irreverent expressions, asked if Perry was afraid of his bacon. The youth, inflamed at this unjust insinuation, darted a ferocious look at the challenger, told him he had paid but too much regard to his infirmities, and bad him walk forward to the park, where he would soon convince him of his error, if he thought his concession proceeded from fear.

About this time, they were overtaken by Pipes, who having heard the lieutenant's fall, and seen him pocket his pistols, suspected that there was a quarrel in the case, and followed him with a view of protecting his master. Peregrine seeing him arrive, and guessing his intention, assumed an air of serenity, and pretending that he had left his handkerchief at the inn, ordered his man to go thither and fetch it to him in the park, where he would find them at his return. This command was twice repeated before Tom would take any other notice of the message, except by shaking his head: but being urged with many threats and curses to obedience, he gave them to understand that he knew their drift too well to trust them by themselves. 'As for you, lieutenant Hatchway, (said he) I have been your ship-mate, and know you to be a sailor, that's enough; and as for master, I know him to be as good a man as ever stept betwixt stem and stern, whereby, if you have any thing to say to him, I am your man, as the saying is. Here's my sapling, and I don't value your crackers of a rope's end.' This oration, the longest that ever Pipes was known to make, he concluded with a flourish of his cudgel, and enforced with such determined refusals to leave them, that they found it impossible to bring the cause to mortal arbitrement at that time, and strolled about the park in profound silence; during which, Hatchway's indignation subsiding, he all of a sudden thrust out his hand as an advance to reconciliation, which being cordially shaken by Peregrine, a general pacification ensued; and was followed by a consultation about the means of extricating the youth from his present perplexity. Had his disposition been like that of most other young men, it would have been no difficult task to overcome his difficulties; but such was the obstinacy of his pride, that he deemed himself bound in honour to resent the letters he had received; and, instead of submitting to the pleasure of the commodore, expected an acknowledgment from him, without which he would listen to no terms of accommodation. 'Had

I been his own son (said he) I should have bore his reproof, and sued for forgiveness; but knowing myself to be on the footing of an orphan who depends entirely upon his benevolence, I am jealous of every thing that can be construed into disrespect, and insist upon being treated with the most punctual regard. I shall now make application to my father, who is obliged to provide for me by the ties of nature, as well as the laws of the land; and if he shall refuse to do me justice, I can never want employment while men are required for his majesty's service.'

The lieutenant, alarmed at this intimation, begged he would take no new step, until he should hear from him; and that very evening set out for the garison, where he gave Trunnion an account of the miscarriage of his negotiation, told him how highly Peregrine was offended at the letter, communicated the young gentleman's sentiments and resolution; and finally assured him, that unless he should think proper to ask pardon for the offence he had committed, he would, in all appearance, never more behold the face of his godson.

The old commodore was utterly confounded at this piece of intelligence; he had expected all the humility of obedience and contrition from the young man; and instead of that, received nothing but the most indignant opposition, and even found himself in the predicament of an offender, obliged to make atonement, or forfeit all correspondence with his favourite. These insolent conditions at first threw him into an agony of wrath, and he vented execrations with such rapidity, that he left himself no time to breathe, and had almost been suffocated with his choler. He inveighed bitterly against the ingratitude of Peregrine, whom he mentioned with many opprobrious epithets, and swore that he ought to be keel-hauled for his presumption; but when he began to reflect more coolly upon the spirit of the young gentleman, which had already manifested itself on many occasions, and listened to the suggestions of Hatchway, whom he had always considered as an oracle in his way, his resentment abated, and he determined to take Perry into favour again; this placability being not a little facilitated by Jack's narrative of our hero's intrepid behaviour at the assembly, as well as in the contest with him in the park. But still this plaguy amour occurred like a bugbear to his imagination; for he held it as an infallible maxim, that woman was an eternal source of misery to man. Indeed this apothegm he seldom repeated since his marriage, except in the company of a very few intimates, to whose secrecy and discretion he could trust. Finding Jack himself at a non-plus in the affair of Emilia, he consulted Mrs. Trunnion, who was equally surprised and offended, when she understood that her letter did not produce the desired effect; and after having imputed the youth's obstinacy to his uncle's unseasonable indulgence, had recourse to the advice of the parson, who, still with an eye to his friend's advantage, counselled them to send the young gentleman on his travels, in the course of which he would, in all probability, forget the amusements of his greener years. The proposal was judicious, and immediately approved, when Trunnion going into his closet, after divers efforts, produced the following billet, with which Jack departed for Windsor that same afternoon.

My good lad,

If I gave offence in my last letter, I'm sorry for it, d'ye see; I thought it was the likeliest way to bring you up; but, in time to come, you shall have a larger swing of cable. When you can spare time, I shall be glad if you will make a short trip, and see your aunt, and him who is

Your loving godfather,
and humble servant,
HAWSER TRUNNION

P.S. If you want money, you may draw upon me payable at sight.

CHAPTER XXIX

*He becomes Melancholy and Despondent ; is favoured with
a condescending Letter from his Uncle, reconciles himself
to his Governor, and sets out with Emilia and her Friend
for Mrs. Gauntlet's House*

PEREGRINE, fortified as he was with pride and indignation, did not fail to feel the smarting suggestions of his present situation: after having lived so long in an affluent and imperious manner, he could ill brook the thoughts of submitting to the mortifying exigencies of life; all the gaudy schemes of pomp and pleasure, which his luxuriant imagination had formed, began to dissolve; a train of melancholy ideas took possession of his thoughts, and the prospect of losing Emilia was not the least part of his affliction. Though he endeavoured to suppress the chagrin that preyed upon his heart, he could not conceal the disturbance of his mind from the penetration of that amiable young lady, who sympathized with him in her heart, though she could not give her tongue the liberty of asking the cause of his disorder; for, notwithstanding all the ardour of his addresses, he never could obtain from her the declaration of a mutual flame; because, tho' he had hitherto treated her with the utmost reverence of respect, he had never once mentioned the final aim of his passion; and however honourable she supposed it to be, she had discernment enough to foresee, that vanity or interest co-operating with the levity of youth, might one day deprive her of her lover, and she was too proud to give him any handle of exulting at her expence; so that, although he was received by her with the most distinguished civility, and even an intimacy of friendship, all his sollicitations could never extort from her an acknowledgment of love; on the contrary, being of a gay disposition, she sometimes coquetted with other admirers, that his attention thus whetted might never abate, and that he might see she had other resources, in case he should flagg in his affection.

This being the prudential plan on which she acted, it cannot be supposed that she would condescend to inquire into the state of his thoughts, when she saw him thus affected; but she, nevertheless, imposed that task on her cousin and confidante, who, as they walked together in the park, observed that he seemed to be out of humour. When this is the case, such a question generally increases the disease; at least it had that effect upon Peregrine, who replied somewhat peevishly, 'I assure you, Madam, you never was more mistaken in your observations.' 'I think so too, (said Emilia) for I never saw Mr. Pickle in higher spirits.' This ironical encomium compleated his confusion; he affected to smile, but it was a smile of anguish, and in his heart cursed the vivacity of both. He could not for his soul recollect himself, so as to utter one connected sentence; and the suspicion that they observed every circumstance of his behaviour, threw such a damp on his spirits, that he was quite overwhelmed with shame and resentment, when Sophy casting her eyes towards the gate, said, 'Yonder is your servant, Mr. Pickle, with another man who seems to have a wooden leg.' Peregrine started at this intelligence, and immediately underwent sundry changes of complexion, knowing that his fate, in a great measure, depended upon the information he would receive from his friend.

Hatchway advancing to the company, after a brace of sea-bows to the ladies, took the youth aside, and put the commodore's letter into his hand, which threw him into such an agitation, that he could scarce pronounce, 'Ladies, will you give me leave?' And when, in consequence of their permission, he attempted to open the billet, he fumbled with such manifest disorder, that his mistress, who watched his motions, began to think there was something very interesting in the message; and so much was she affected with his concern, that she was fain to turn her head another way, and wipe the tears from her lovely eyes.

Mean while, Peregrine no sooner read the first sentence, than his countenance, which before was overcast with a deep gloom, began to be lighted up, and every feature unbending by degrees, he recovered his serenity; and having perused the letter, his eyes sparkling with joy and gratitude, he hugged the lieutenant in his arms, and presented him to the ladies as one of his best friends. Jack met with a most gracious reception, and shook Emilia by the hand, telling her, with the familiar appellation of *old acquaintance*, that he did not care how soon he was master of such another clean-going frigate as herself.

The whole company partook of this favourable change that evidently appeared in our lover's recollection, and enlivened his conversation with such an uncommon flow of sprightliness and good humour, as even made an impression on the iron countenance of Pipes himself, who actually smiled with satisfaction as he walked behind them.

The evening being pretty far advanced, they directed their course homeward; and while the valet attended Hatchway to the inn, Peregrine escorted the ladies to their lodgings, where he owned the justness of Sophy's remark, in saying he was out of humour, and told them he had been extremely chagrined at a difference which happened between him and his uncle, to whom (by the letter which they had seen him receive) he now found himself happily reconciled.

Having received their congratulations, and declined staying to sup with them, on account of the longing desire he had to converse with his friend Jack, he took his leave, and repaired to the inn, where Hatchway informed him of every thing that had happened in the garison upon his representations; and far from being dis-gusted, he was perfectly well pleased with the prospect of going abroad, which flattered his vanity and ambition, gratified his thirst after knowledge, and indulged that turn for observation, for which he had been remarkable from his most tender years: neither did he believe a short absence would tend to the prejudice of his love, but, on the contrary, inhance the value of his heart, because he should return better accomplished, and consequently a more welcome offering to his mistress. Elevated with these sentiments, his heart dilated with joy, and the sluices of his natural benevolence being opened by this happy turn of his affairs, he sent his compliments to Mr. Jolter, to whom he had not spoken during a whole week, and desired he would favour Mr. Hatchway and him with his company at supper.

The governor was not weak enough to decline this invitation, in consequence of which he forthwith appeared, and was cordially welcomed by the relenting pupil, who expressed his sorrow for the misunderstanding which had prevailed between them, and assured him, that for the future he would avoid giving him any just cause of complaint. Jolter, who did not want affections, was melted by this acknowledgment, which he could not have expected, and earnestly protested, that his chief study had always been, and ever should be, to promote Mr. Pickle's interest and happiness.

The best part of the night being spent in the circulation of a chearful glass, the company broke up; and next morning Peregrine went out, with a view of making his mistress acquainted with his uncle's intention of sending him out of the kingdom for his improvement, and of saying every thing which he thought necessary for the interest of his love. He found her at breakfast with her cousin; and as he was very full of the subject of his visit, had scarce fixed himself in his seat, when he brought it upon the carpet, by asking with a smile, if the ladies had any commands for Paris? Emilia at this question began to stare, and her confidante desired to know who was going thither? He no sooner gave them to understand, that he himself intended in a short time to visit that capital, than his mistress, with great precipitation, wished him a good journey, and affected to talk with indifference about the pleasures he would enjoy in France: but when he seriously assured Sophy, who asked if he was in earnest, that his uncle actually insisted upon his making a short tour, than the tears gushed in poor Emilia's eyes, and she was at great pains to conceal her concern, by observing that the tea was so scalding hot, as to make her eyes water. This pretext was too thin to impose upon her lover, or even deceive the observation of her friend Sophy, who after breakfast took an opportunity of quitting the room.

Thus left by themselves, Peregrine imparted to her what he had learnt of the commodore's intention, without, however, mentioning a syllable of his being offended at their correspondence;

and accompanied his information with such fervent vows of eternal constancy, and solemn promises of a speedy return, that Emily's heart, which had been invaded by a suspicion, that this scheme of travelling was the effect of her lover's inconstancy, began to be more at ease; and she could not help signifying her approbation of his design.

This affair being amicably compromised, he asked how soon she proposed to set out for her mother's house; and understanding that her departure was fixed for next day but one, and that her cousin Sophy intended to accompany her in her father's chariot, he repeated his intention of attending her, and in the mean time dismissed his governor and the lieutenant to the garison, with his compliments to his aunt and the commodore, and a faithful promise of his being with them in six days at farthest.

These previous measures being taken, he, attended by Pipes, set out with the ladies; and they had also a convoy for twelve miles from Sophy's father, who, at parting, recommended them piously to the care of Peregrine, with whom, by this time, he was perfectly well acquainted.

CHAPTER XXX

They meet with a dreadful Alarm on the Road,
arrive at their Journey's End.
Peregrine is introduced to Emily's Brother;
these two young Gentlemen misunderstand each other.
Pickle departs for the Garison

As they travelled at an easy rate, they had performed something more than one half of their journey, when they were benighted near an inn, at which they resolved to lodge; the accommodation was very good, they supped together with great mirth and enjoyment, and it was not till after he had been warned by the yawns of the ladies, that he conducted them to their apartment; and wishing them good night, retired to his own, and went to rest.

The house was crowded with country people who had been at a neighbouring fair, and now regaled themselves with ale and tobacco in the yard; so that their consideration, which at any time was but slender, being now overwhelmed by this debauch, they staggered in to their respective kennels, and left a lighted candle sticking to one of the wooden pillars that supported the gallery. The flame in a little time laid hold on the wood, which was as dry as tinder, and the whole gallery was on fire, when Peregrine suddenly waked, and found himself almost suffocated. He sprung up in an instant, slipped on his breeches, and throwing open the door of his chamber, saw the whole entry in a blaze.

Heavens! what were the emotions of his soul, when he beheld the volumes of flame and smoke rolling towards the room where his dear Emilia lay! Regardless of his own danger, he darted himself through the thickest of the gloom, when knocking hard, and calling at the same time to the ladies, with the most anxious intreaty to be admitted; the door was opened by Emilia in her shift, who asked with the utmost trepidation, what was the matter? He made no reply, but snatching her up in his arms, like another Æneas, bore her through the flames to a place of safety; where leaving her, before she could recollect herself, or pronounce one word, but 'Alas! my cousin Sophy!' he flew back to the rescue of that young lady, and found her already delivered by Pipes, who having been alarmed by the smell of fire, had got up, rushed immediately to the chamber where he knew these companions lodged, and (Emily being saved by her lover) brought off Miss Sophy, with the loss of his own shock-head of hair, which was singed off in his retreat.

By this time the whole inn was alarmed, every lodger, as well as servant, exerted himself, in order to stop the progress of this calamity; and there being a well replenished horsepond in the yard, in less than an hour the fire was totally extinguished, without having done any other damage than that of consuming about two yards of the wooden gallery.

All this time our young gentleman closely attended his fair charges, each of whom had swooned with apprehension; but as their constitutions were good, and their spirits not easily dissipated, when upon reflection they found themselves and their company safe, and that the flames were happily quenched, the tumult of their fears subsided, they put on their cloaths, recovered their good humour, and began to rally each other on the trim in which they had been secured. Sophy observed, that now Mr. Pickle had an indisputable claim to her cousin's affection; and therefore she ought to lay aside all affected reserve for the future, and frankly avow the sentiments of her heart. Emily retorted the argument, putting her in mind, that by the same claim Mr. Pipes was intitled to the like return from her. Her friend admitted the force of the conclusion, provided she could not find means of satisfying her deliverer in another shape; and turning to the valet, who happened to be present, asked if his heart was not otherwise engaged? Tom, who did not conceive the meaning of the question, stood silent according to custom; and the interrogation being repeated, answered with a grin, 'Heart-whole as a biscuit, I'll assure you, Mistress.' 'What! (said Emilia) have you never been in love, Thomas?' 'Yes, forsooth, (replied the valet, without hesitation) sometimes of a morning.' Peregrine could not help laughing, and his mistress looked a little disconcerted at this blunt repartee; while Sophy, slipping a purse into his hand, told him there was something to purchase a periwig. Tom having consulted his master's eyes, refused the present, saying, 'No, thank ye as much as if I did.' And though she insisted upon his putting it in his pocket, as a small testimony of her gratitude, he could not be prevailed upon to avail himself of her generosity; but following her to the other end of the room, thrust it into her sleeve without ceremony, exclaiming, 'I'll be damned to hell if I do.' Peregrine having checked him for his boorish behaviour, sent him out of the room, and begged that Miss Sophy would not endeavour to debauch the morals of his servant, who rough and uncultivated as he was, had sense enough to perceive that he had no pretension to any such acknowledgment. But she argued with great vehemence, that she should never be able to make an acknowledgment adequate to the service he had done her, and that she should never be perfectly easy in her own mind, until she found some opportunity of manifesting the sense she had of the obligation: 'I do not pretend (said she) to reward Mr. Pipes; but I shall be absolutely unhappy, unless I am allowed to give him some token of my regard.'

Peregrine thus earnestly sollicited, desired that since she was bent upon displaying her generosity, she would not bestow upon him any pecuniary gratification, but honour him with some trinket, as a mark of consideration; because he himself had such a particular value for the fellow, on account of his attachment and fidelity, that he should be sorry to see him treated on the footing of a common mercenary domestick.

There was not one jewel in the possession of this grateful young lady, that she would not have gladly given as a recompence, or badge of distinction, to her rescuer; but his master pitched upon a seal-ring of no great value that hung at her watch; and Pipes being called in, had permission to accept that testimony of Miss Sophy's favour. Tom received it accordingly with sundry scrapes, and having kissed it with great devotion, put it on his little finger, and strutted off, extremely proud of his acquisition.

Emilia, with a most enchanting sweetness of aspect, told her lover, that he had instructed her how to behave towards him; and taking a diamond ring from her finger, desired he would wear it for her sake. He received the pledge as became him, and presented another in exchange, which she at first refused, alledging that it would destroy the intent of her acknowledgment; but Peregrine assured her, he had accepted her jewel, not as a proof of her gratitude, but as the mark of her love; and that if she refused a mutual token, he should look upon himself as the object of her disdain. Her eyes kindled, and her cheeks glowed with resentment at this impudent intimation, which she considered as an unseasonable insult; and the young gentleman perceiving her emotion, stood corrected for his temerity, and asked pardon for the liberty of his remonstrance, which he hoped she would ascribe to the prevalence of that principle alone, which he had always taken pride in avowing.

Sophy seeing him disconcerted, interposed in his behalf, and chid her cousin for having practised such unnecessary affectation; upon which Emilia, softened into compliance, held out her finger as a signal of her condescension. Peregrine put on the ring with great eagerness, mumbled her soft white hand in an extasy, which would not allow him to confine his embraces to that limb, but urged him to seize her by the waist, and snatch a delicious kiss from her love-pouting lips; nor would he leave her a butt to the ridicule of Sophy, on whose mouth he instantly committed a rape of the same nature; so that the two friends, countenanced by each other, reprehended him with such gentleness of rebuke, that he was almost tempted to repeat the offence.

The morning being now lighted up, and the servants of the inn on foot, he ordered some chocolate for breakfast, and at the desire of the ladies sent Pipes to see the horses fed, and the chariot prepared, while he went to the bar, and discharged the bill.

These measures being taken, they set out about five o'clock, and having refreshed themselves and their cattle at another inn on the road, during the heat of the day, they proceeded in the afternoon; and, without meeting with any other accident, safely arrived at the place of their destination, where Mrs. Gauntlet expressed her joy at seeing her old friend Mr. Pickle, whom, however, she kindly reproached for the long discontinuance of his regard. Without explaining the cause of that interruption, he protested that his love and esteem had never been discontinued, and that for the future he should omit no occasion of testifying how much he had her friendship at heart. She then made him acquainted with her son, who at that time was in the house, being excused from his duty by furlow.

This young man, whose name was Godfrey, was about the age of twenty, of a middling size, vigorous make, remarkably well shaped, and the scars of the small pox, of which he bore a good number, added a peculiar manliness to the air of his countenance. His capacity was good, and his disposition naturally frank and easy; but he had been a soldier from his infancy, and his education was altogether in the military stile. He looked upon taste and letters as meer pedantry, beneath the consideration of a gentleman, and every civil station of life as mean, when compared with the profession of arms. He had made great progress in the gymnastic sciences of dancing, fencing and riding, played perfectly well on the German flute, and above all things valued himself upon a scrupulous observance of all the points of honour.

Had Peregrine and he considered themselves upon equal footing, in all probability they would have immediately entered into a league of intimacy and friendship; but this sufficient soldier looked upon his sister's admirer as a young student raw from the university, and utterly ignorant of mankind, while squire Pickle beheld Godfrey in the light of a needy volunteer, greatly inferior to himself in fortune, as well as every other accomplishment. This mutual misunderstanding could not fail of producing animosities. The very next day after Peregrine's arrival, some sharp repartees passed between them in presence of the ladies, before whom each endeavoured to assert his own superiority. In these contests our hero never failed of obtaining the victory, because his genius was more acute, and his talents better cultivated than those of his antagonist, who therefore took umbrage at his success, became jealous of his reputation, and began to treat him with marks of scorn and disrespect.

His sister saw, and dreading the consequence of his ferocity, not only took him to task in private for his impolite behaviour, but also intreated her lover to make allowances for the roughness of her brother's education. He kindly assured her, that whatever pains it might cost him to vanquish his own impetuous temper, he would for her sake endure all the mortifications to which her brother's arrogance might expose him; and after having stayed with her two days, and enjoyed several private interviews, during which he acted the part of a most passionate lover, he took his leave of Mrs.

Gauntlet over-night, and told the young ladies he would call early next morning, to bid them farewel. He did not neglect this piece of duty, and found the two friends and breakfast already prepared in the parlour. All three being extremely affected with the thoughts of parting, a most pathetic silence for some time prevailed, till Peregrine put an end to it, by lamenting his fate, in being obliged to exile himself so long from the dear object of his most interesting wish; and begged with the most earnest supplications, that she would now, in consideration of the cruel absence he must suffer, give him the consolation which she had hitherto refused, namely, that of knowing he possessed a place within her heart. The confidante seconded his request, representing that it was now no time to disguise her sentiments, when her lover was about to leave the kingdom, and might be in danger of contracting other connexions, unless he was confirmed in his constancy, by knowing how far he could depend upon her love; and in short, she was plied with such irresistible importunities, that she answered in the utmost confusion, 'Tho' I have avoided literal acknowledgments, methinks the circumstances of my behaviour might have convinced' Mr. Pickle, that I do not regard him as a common acquaintance.' 'My charming Emily! (cried the impatient lover, throwing himself at her feet) why will you deal out my happiness in such scanty portions? Why will you thus mince the declaration which would overwhelm me with pleasure, and chear my lonely reflection, while I sigh amid the solitude of separation?' His fair mistress, melted by this image, replied, with the tears gushing from her eyes, 'I'm afraid I shall feel that separation more severely than you imagine.' Transported at this flattering confession, he pressed her to his breast, and while her head reclined upon his neck, mingled his tears with hers in great abundance, and breathed the most tender vows of eternal fidelity. The gentle heart of Sophy could not bear this scene unmoved, she wept with sympathy, and encouraged the lovers to resign themselves to the will of fate, and support their spirits with the hope of meeting again on happier terms. Finally, after mutual promises, exhortations and endearments, Peregrine took his leave, his heart being so full, that he could scarce pronounce the word '*Adieu!*' and mounting his horse at the door, set out with Pipes for the garison.

CHAPTER XXXI

Peregrine is overtaken by Mr. Gauntlet, with whom
he fights a Duel, and contracts an intimate Friendship.
He arrives at the Garison, and finds his Mother as
implacable as ever. He is insulted by his Brother Gam,
whose Preceptor he disciplines with a Horse-whip

IN order to expel the melancholy images that took possession of his
fancy, at parting from his mistress, he called in the flattering ideas
of those pleasures he expected to enjoy in France; and before he had
rode ten miles, his imagination was effectually amused.

While he thus prosecuted his travels by anticipation, and indulged himself in all the insolence of hope, at the turning of a lane
he was all of a sudden overtaken by Emilia's brother on horseback,
who told him he was riding the same way, and should be glad of his
company.

This young gentleman, whether prompted by personal pique, or
actuated with zeal for the honour of his family, had followed our
hero, with a view of obliging him to explain the nature of his
attachment to his sister. Peregrine returned his compliment with
such disdainful civility, as gave him room to believe that he
suspected his errand; and therefore, without further preamble, he
declared his business in these words: 'Mr. Pickle, you have carried
on a correspondence with my sister for some time, and I should be
glad to know the nature of it?' To this question our lover replied,
'Sir, I should be glad to know what title you have to demand that
satisfaction?' 'Sir, (answered the other) I demand it in the capacity
of a brother, jealous of his own honour, as well as of his sister's
reputation; and if your intentions are honourable, you will not
refuse it.' 'Sir, (said Peregrine) I am not at present disposed to
appeal to your opinion for the rectitude of my intentions; and
I think you assume a little too much importance, in pretending
to judge my conduct.' 'Sir, (replied the soldier) I pretend to judge
the conduct of every man who interferes with my concerns, and
even to chastise him, if I think he acts amiss.' 'Chastise! (cried the
youth, with indignation in his looks) sure you dare not apply that
term to me?' 'You are mistaken, (said Godfrey) I dare do any thing
that becomes the character of a gentleman.' 'Gentleman, God wot!
(replied the other, looking contemptuously at his equipage, which

was none of the most superb) a very pretty gentleman, truly!' The
soldier's wrath was inflamed by this ironical repetition, the contempt of which his conscious poverty made him feel; and he called
his antagonist presumptuous boy, insolent upstart, with other
epithets, which Perry retorted with great bitterness: and a formal
challenge having passed between them, they alighted at the first
inn, and walked into the next field, in order to decide their quarrel
by the sword. Having pitched upon the spot, helped to pull off each
other's boots, and laid aside their coats and waistcoats, Mr. Gauntlet told his opponent, that he himself was looked upon in the army
as an expert swordsman, and that if Mr. Pickle had not made that
science his particular study, they should be upon a more equal
footing in using pistols. Peregrine was too much incensed to thank
him for his plain dealing, and too confident of his own skill to relish
the other's proposal, which he accordingly rejected; and drawing
his sword, observed, that were he to treat Mr. Gauntlet according
to his deserts, he would order his man to punish his audacity with
an horse-whip. Exasperated at this expression, which he considered
as an indelible affront, he made no reply, but attacked his adversary
with equal ferocity and address. The youth parried his first and
second thrust, but received the third in the outside of his sword
arm. Though the wound was superficial, he was transported with
rage at sight of his own blood, and returned the assault with such
fury and precipitation, that Gauntlet, loath to take advantage of his
unguarded heat, stood upon the defensive; and in the second longe,
Peregrine's weapon entering a kind of net-work in the shell of
Godfrey's sword, the blade snapped in two, and left him at the
mercy of the soldier, who, far from making an insolent use of the
victory he had gained, put up his Toledo with great deliberation,
like a man who had been used to that kind of rencounters, observed
that such a blade as Peregrine's was not to be trusted with a man's
life, and advising the owner to treat a gentleman in distress with
more respect for the future, slipped on his boots, and with sullen
dignity of demeanour stalked back to the inn.

Though Pickle was extremely mortified at his miscarriage in this
adventure, he was also struck with the behaviour of his antagonist,
which affected him the more, as he understood that Godfrey's *fiertè*
had proceeded from the jealous sensibility of a gentleman declined
into the vale of misfortune. Gauntlet's valour and moderation
induced him to put a favourable construction on all those circumstances of that young soldier's conduct, which before had given him
disgust; and though in any other case he would have industriously

avoided the least appearance of submission, he followed his conqueror to the inn, with a view of thanking him for his generous forbearance, and of solliciting his friendship and correspondence.

Godfrey had his foot in the stirrup to mount, when Peregrine coming up to him, desired he would defer his departure for a quarter of an hour, and favour him with a little private conversation. The soldier, who mistook the meaning of the request, immediately quitted his horse, and followed Pickle into a chamber, where he expected to find a brace of pistols loaded on the table; but he was very agreeably deceived, when our hero, in the most respectful terms, acknowledged his noble deportment in the field, owned that till then he had misunderstood his character, and begged that he would honour him with his intimacy and correspondence.

Gauntlet, who had seen undoubted proofs of Peregrine's courage, which had considerably raised him in his esteem, and had sense enough to perceive that this concession was not owing to any sordid or sinister motive, embraced his offer with demonstrations of infinite satisfaction; and when he understood the terms on which Mr. Pickle was with his sister, proffered his service in his turn, either as agent, mediator, or confidant: nay, to give this new friend a convincing proof of his sincerity, he disclosed to him a passion which he had for some time entertained for his cousin Miss Sophy, though he durst not reveal his sentiments to her father, lest he should be offended at his presumption, and withdraw his protection from the family.

Peregrine's generous heart was wrung with anguish, when he understood that this young gentleman, who was the only son of a distinguished officer, had carried arms for the space of five years, without being able to obtain a subaltern's commission, though he had always behaved with remarkable regularity and spirit, and acquired the friendship and esteem of all the officers under whom he had served.

He would, at that time, with the utmost pleasure, have shared his finances with him; but as he would not run the risk of offending the young soldier's delicacy of honour, by a premature exertion of his liberality, he resolved to insinuate himself into an intimacy with him, before he would venture to take such freedoms; and with that view pressed Mr. Gauntlet to accompany him to the garison, where he did not doubt of having influence enough to make him a welcome guest. Godfrey thanked him very courteously for his invitation, which he said he could not immediately accept, but promised if he would favour him with a letter, and fix the time at which he proposed to set out for France, he would endeavour to visit him at the commodore's habitation, and from thence give him a convoy to Dover. This new treaty being settled, and a dossil of lint with a snip of plaister applied to our adventurer's wound, he parted from the brother of his dear Emilia, to whom and his friend Sophy he sent his kindest wishes; and having lodged one night upon the road, arrived next day in the afternoon at the garison, where he found all his friends in good health, and overjoyed at his return.

The commodore, who was by this time turned of seventy, and altogether crippled by the gout, seldom went abroad; and as his conversation was not very entertaining, had but little company within doors; so that his spirits must have quite stagnated, had not they been kept in motion by the conversation of Hatchway, and received at different times an wholesome fillip from the discipline of his spouse, who, by the force of pride, religion and Coniac, had erected a most terrible tyranny in the house. There was such a quick circulation of domesticks in the family, that every suit of livery had been worn by figures of all dimensions: Trunnion himself had long before this time yielded to the torrent of her arbitrary sway; though not without divers obstinate efforts to maintain his liberty; and now, that he was disabled by his infirmities, when he used to hear his empress singing the loud Orthyan song[1] among the servants below, he would often in whispers communicate to the lieutenant, hints of what he would do if so be he was not deprived of the use of his precious limbs. Hatchway was the only person whom the temper of Mrs. Trunnion respected, either because she dreaded his ridicule, or looked upon his person with the eyes of affection. This being the situation of things in the garison, it is not to be doubted that the old gentleman highly enjoyed the presence of Peregrine, who found means to ingratiate himself so effectually with his aunt, that while he remained at home, she seemed to have exchanged the disposition of a tygress, for that of a gentle kid; but he found his own mother as implacable, and his father as much hen-pecked as ever.

Gamaliel, who now very seldom enjoyed the conversation of his old friend the commodore, had some time ago entered into an amicable society, consisting of the barber, apothecary, attorney and exciseman of the parish, among whom he used to spend the evening at Tunley's, and listen to their disputes upon philosophy and politicks, with great comfort and edification, while his sovereign lady domineered at home as usual, visited with great pomp in the neighbourhood, and employed her chief care in the education of her darling son Gam, who was now in the fifteenth year of his age, and so remarkable for his perverse disposition, that in spite of his mother's influence and authority, he was not only hated, but also despised both at home and abroad. She had put him under the tuition of the curate who lived in the family, and was obliged to attend him in all his exercises and excursions. This governor was a low bred fellow, who had neither experience nor ingenuity, but possessed a large fund of adulation and servile complaisance, by which he had gained the good graces of Mrs. Pickle, and presided over all her deliberations in the same manner as his superior managed those of Mrs. Trunnion.

He had one day rode out to take the air with his pupil, who, as I have already observed, was odious to the poor people, for having killed their dogs and broken their inclosures, and on account of his hump, distinguished by the title of my lord; when in a narrow lane they chanced to meet Peregrine on horseback.

The young squire no sooner perceived his elder brother, for whom he had been instructed to entertain the most inveterate grudge, than he resolved to insult him *en passant*, and actually rode against him full gallop. Our hero guessing his aim, fixed himself in his stirrups, and by a dexterous management of the reins, avoided the shock in such a manner, as that their legs only should encounter, by which means my lord was tilted out of his saddle, and in a twinkling laid sprawling in the dirt. The governor enraged at the disgrace of his charge, advanced with great insolence and fury, and struck at Peregrine with his whip. Nothing could be more agreeable to our young gentleman than this assault, which furnished him with an opportunity of chastising an officious wretch, whose petulance and malice he had longed to punish. He therefore, spurring up his horse towards his antagonist, overthrew him in the middle of a hedge; and before he had time to recollect himself from the confusion of the fall, alighted in a trice, and exercised his horse-whip with such agility about the curate's face and ears, that he was fain to prostrate himself before his enraged conqueror, and implore his forbearance in the most abject terms. While Peregrine was thus employed, his brother Gam had made shift to rise, and attack him in the rear; for which reason, when the tutor was quelled, the victor faced about, snatched the weapon out of his hand, and having broken it to pieces, remounted his horse, and rode off, without deigning to honour him with any other notice.

The condition in which they returned produced infinite clamour against the conqueror, who was represented as a ruffian who had lain in ambush to make away with his brother, in whose defence the curate was said to have received those cruel stripes, that hindered him from appearing for three whole weeks in the performance of his duty at church.

Complaints were made to the commodore, who having inquired into the circumstances of the affair, approved of what his nephew had done; adding, with many oaths, that, provided Peregrine had been out of the scrape, he wished Crookback had broke his neck in the fall.

CHAPTER XXXII

He projects a Plan of Revenge, which is executed against the Curate

OUR hero, exasperated at the villainy of the curate, in the treacherous misrepresentation he had made of this rencounter, determined to practise upon him a method of revenge, which should be not only effectual, but also unattended with any bad consequence to himself. For this purpose he and Hatchway, to whom he imparted his plan, went to the alehouse one evening, and called for an empty room, knowing there was no other but that which they had chosen for the scene of action. This apartment was a sort of a parlour that fronted the kitchen, with a window towards the yard; where, after they had sat some time, the lieutenant found means to amuse the landlord in discourse, while Peregrine stepping out into the yard, by the talent of mimickry, which he possessed in a surprising degree, counterfeited a dialogue between the curate and Tunley's wife; which reaching the ears of the publican, for whose hearing it was calculated, inflamed his naturally jealous disposition to such a degree, that he could not conceal his emotion, but made an hundred efforts to quit the room; while the lieutenant, smoking his pipe with great gravity, as if he neither heard what passed, nor took notice of the landlord's disorder, detained him on the spot by a succession of questions which he could not refuse to answer; though he stood sweating with agony all the time, stretching his neck every instant towards the window thro' which the voices were conveyed, scratching his head, and exhibiting sundry other symptoms of impatience and agitation. At length, the supposed conversation came to such a pitch of amorous complaisance, that the husband, quite frantic with his imaginary disgrace, rushed out at the door, crying, 'Coming, Sir.' But, as he was obliged to make a circuit round one half of the house, Peregrine had got in by the window, before Tunley arrived in the yard.

According to the feigned intelligence he had received, he ran directly to the barn, in expectation of making some very extraordinary discovery; and having employed some minutes in rummaging the straw to no purpose, returned in a state of distraction to the kitchen, just as his wife chanced to enter at the other door. The circumstance of her appearance confirmed him in the opinion, that the deed was done; but as the disease of being hen-peck'd was epidemic in the parish, he durst not express the least hint of his uneasiness to her, but resolved to take vengeance on the libidinous priest, who, he imagined, had corrupted the chastity of his spouse.

The two confederates, in order to be certified that their scheme had taken effect, as well as to blow up the flame which they had kindled, called for Tunley, in whose countenance they could easily discern his confusion; and Peregrine desiring him to sit down and drink a glass with them, began to interrogate him about his family, and among other things, asked him how long he had been married to that handsome wife? This question, which was put with an arch significance of look, alarmed the publican, who began to fear that Pickle had overheard his dishonour; and this suspicion was not at all removed, when the lieutenant, with a sly regard, pronounced, 'Tunley, wan't you noosed by the curate?' 'Yes, I was,' (replied the landlord, with an eagerness and perplexity of tone, as if he thought the lieutenant knew, that *thereby hangs a tale*;)[1] and Hatchway supported this suspicion, by answering, 'Nay, as for that matter, the curate may be a very sufficient man in his way.' This transition from his wife to the curate, convinced him that his shame was known to his guests; and in the transport of his indignation, he pronounced with great emphasis, 'A sufficient man! Odds heart! I believe they are all wolves in sheep's cloathing. I wish to God I could see the day, master, when there shall not be a priest, an exciseman, or a custom-house officer in this kingdom. As for that fellow of a curate, if I do catch him——It don't signify talking—— But, by the Lord!——Gentlemen, my service to you.'

The associates being satisfied by these abrupt insinuations, that they had so far succeeded in their aim, waited with impatience two or three days, in expectation of hearing that Tunley had fallen upon some method of being revenged for this imaginary wrong; but finding that either his invention was too shallow, or his inclination too languid to gratify their desire of his own accord, they determined to bring the affair to such a crisis, that he should not be able to withstand the opportunity of executing his vengeance. With this view, they one evening hired a boy to run to Mr. Pickle's house, and tell the curate, that Mrs. Tunley being taken suddenly ill, her husband desired he would come immediately, and pray with her. Mean while, they had taken possession of a room in the house; and Hatchway engaging the landlord in conversation, Peregrine in his return from the yard observed, as if by accident, that the parson was gone into the kitchen, in order, as he supposed, to catechise Tunley's wife.

The publican started at this intelligence, and under pretence of serving another company in the next room, went out to the barn, and arming himself with a flail, repaired to a lane thro' which the curate was under a necessity of passing in his way home. There he lay in ambush, with fell intent; and when the supposed author of his shame arrived, greeted him in the dark with such a salutation, as forced him to stagger backward three paces at least. If the second application had taken effect, in all probability that spot would have been the boundary of the parson's mortal peregrination; but, luckily for him, his antagonist was not expert in the management of his weapon, which, by a twist of the thong that connected the legs, instead of pitching upon the head of the astonished curate, descended in an oblique direction on his own pate, with such a swing, that the skull actually rung like an apothecary's mortar, and ten thousand lights seemed to dance before his eyes. The curate recollecting himself during the respite he obtained from this accident, and believing his aggressor to be some thief who lurked in that place for prey, resolved to make a running fight, until he should arrive within cry of his habitation. With this design he raised up his cudgel for the defence of his head, and betaking himself to his heels, began to roar for help with the lungs of a Stentor. Tunley throwing away the flail, which he durst no longer trust with the execution of his revenge, pursued the fugitive with all the speed he could exert; and the other, either unnerv'd by fear, or stumbling over a stone, was overtaken before he had run an hundred paces. He no sooner felt the wind of the publican's fist that whistled round his ears, than he fell flat upon the earth at full length, and the cudgel flew from his unclasping hand; when Tunley springing like a tyger upon his back, rained such a shower of blows upon his carcase, that he imagined himself under the discipline of ten pair of fists at least; yet the imaginary cuckold, not satisfied with annoying the priest in this manner, laid hold on one of his ears with his teeth, and bit so unmercifully, that the curate was found almost intranced with pain by two labourers, at whose approach the assailant retreated unperceived.

The lieutenant had posted himself at the window, in order to see the landlord at his first return; and no sooner perceived him enter the yard, than he called him into the apartment, impatient to learn the effects of their stratagem. Tunley obeyed the summons, and appeared before his guests in all the violence of rage, disorder and fatigue; his nostrils were dilated more than one half beyond their natural capacity, his eyes rolled, his teeth chattered, he snored in breathing as if he had been oppressed by the nightmare, and streams of sweat flowed down each side of his forehead.

Peregrine affecting to start at the approach of such an uncouth figure, asked if he had been wrestling with a spirit; upon which he answered with great vehemence, 'Spirit! No, no, master, I have had a roll and tumble with the flesh. A dog! I'll teach him to come a caterwauling about my doors.' Guessing from this reply, that his aim was accomplished, and curious to know the particulars of the rencounter, 'Well then, (said the youth) I hope you have prevailed against the flesh, Tunley.' 'Yes, yes, (answered the publican) I have cooled his capissens, as the saying is; I have played such a tune about his ears, that I'll be bound he shan't long for musick this month. A goatish ram-fac'd rascal! Why, he's a perfect parish bull, as I hope to live.'

Hatchway observing that he seemed to have made a stout battle, desired he would sit down and recover wind; and after he had swallowed a brace of bumpers, his vanity prompted him to expatiate upon his own exploit in such a manner, that the confederates, without seeming to know the curate was his antagonist, became acquainted with every circumstance of the ambuscade.

Tunley had scarce got the better of his agitation, when his wife entering the room, told them by way of news, that some waggish body had sent Mr. Sackbut the curate to pray with her. This name inflamed the husband's choler anew, and forgetting all his complaisance for his spouse, he replied with a rancorous grin, 'Add rabbit him! I doubt not but you found his admonitions deadly comfortable!' The landlady, looking at her vassal with a sovereign aspect, 'What crotchets (said she) have you got in your fool's head, I trow? I know no business you have to sit here like a gentleman with your arms akimbo, when there's another company in the house to be served.' The submissive husband took the hint, and without further expostulation, sneaked out of the room.

Next day it was reported, that Mr. Sackbut had been way-laid, and almost murdered by robbers, and an advertisement pasted upon the church-door, offering a reward to any person that should discover the assassin; but he reaped no satisfaction from this expedient, and was confined to his chamber a whole fortnight, by the bruises he had received.

CHAPTER XXXIII

Mr. Sackbut and his Pupil conspire against Peregrine,
who being apprized of their Design by his Sister,
takes Measures for counterworking their Scheme,
which is executed by Mistake upon Mr. Gauntlet.
This young Soldier meets with a cordial Reception from
the Commodore, who generously decoys him into
his own Interest

WHEN he considered the circumstances of the ambuscade, he could not persuade himself that he had been assaulted by a common thief, because it was not to be supposed that a robber would have amused himself in pummeling rather than in rifling his prey; he therefore ascribed his misfortune to the secret enmity of some person who had a design upon his life; and upon mature deliberation, fixed his suspicion upon Peregrine, who was the only man on earth from whom he thought he deserved such treatment. He communicated this conjecture to his pupil, who readily adopted his opinion, and advised him strenuously to revenge the wrong by a like contrivance, without seeking to make a narrower inquiry, lest his enemy should be thereby put upon his guard.

This proposal being relished, they in concert revolved the means of retorting the ambush with interest, and actually laid such a villainous plan for attacking our hero in the dark, that, had it been executed according to their intention, the young gentleman's scheme of travelling would have been effectually marred. But their machinations were overheard by Miss Pickle, who was now in the seventeenth year of her age, and, in spite of the prejudice of education, entertained in secret a most sisterly affection for her brother Perry, though she had never spoke to him, and was deterred by the precepts, vigilance and menaces of her mother, from attempting any means of meeting him in private. She was not, however, insensible to his praise, which was loudly sounded forth in the neighbourhood, and never failed of going to church, and every other place, where she thought she might have an opportunity of seeing this amiable brother. With these sentiments it cannot be supposed that she would hear the conspiracy without emotion. She was shocked at the treacherous barbarity of Gam, and shuddered at the prospect of the danger to which Peregrine would be exposed from their malice. She durst not communicate this plot to her mother, because she was afraid that lady's unaccountable aversion for her first-born would hinder her from interposing in his behalf, and consequently render her a sort of accomplice in the guilt of his assassins. She therefore resolved to warn Peregrine of the conspiracy, an account of which she transmitted to him in an affectionate letter, by means of a young gentleman in that neighbourhood, who made his addresses to her at that time, and who, at her request, offered his service to our hero, in defeating the projects of his adversaries.

Peregrine was startled when he read the particulars of their scheme, which was no other than an intention to sally upon him when he should be altogether unprovided against such an attack, cut off his ears, and otherwise mutilate him in such a manner, that he should have no cause to be vain of his person for the future.

Incensed as he was against the brutal disposition of his own father's son, he could not help being moved at the integrity and tenderness of his sister, of whose inclinations towards him he had been hitherto kept in ignorance. He thanked the gentleman for his honourable dealing, and expressed a desire of being better acquainted with his virtues; told him, that now he was cautioned, he hoped there would be no necessity for giving him any further trouble, and wrote by him a letter of acknowledgment to his sister, for whom he expressed the utmost love and regard, beseeching her to favour him with an interview before his departure, that he might indulge his fraternal fondness, and be blessed with the company and countenance of one at least belonging to his own family.

Having imparted this discovery to his friend Hatchway, they came to a resolution of countermining the plan of their enemies; and as they did not choose to expose themselves to the insinuations of slander, which would have exerted itself at their expence, had they, even in defending themselves, employed any harsh means of retaliation, they invented a method of disappointing and disgracing their foes, and immediately set Pipes at work to forward the preparations.

Miss Pickle having described the spot which the assassins had pitched upon for the scene of their vengeance, our triumvirate intended to have placed a centinel among the corn, who should come and give them intelligence when the ambuscade was laid; and in consequence of that information, they would steal softly towards the place, attended by three or four of the domesticks, and draw a large net over the conspirators, who being intangled in the toil, should be disarmed, fettered, heartily scourged, and suspended between two trees in the snare, as a spectacle to all passengers that should chance to travel that way.

The plan being thus digested, and the commodore made acquainted with the whole affair, the spy was sent upon duty, and every body within doors prepared to go forth upon the first notice. One whole evening did they spend in the most impatient expectation, but on the second their scout crept into the garison, and assured them that he had perceived three men skulking behind the hedge, on the road that led to the publick house from which Peregrine and the lieutenant used every night to return about that hour. Upon this intelligence the confederates set out immediately with all their implements, and approaching the scene with as little noise as possible, they heard the sound of blows; and though the night was dark, perceived a sort of tumultuous conflict on the very spot which the conspirators had possessed. Surprised at this occurrence, the meaning of which he could not comprehend, Peregrine ordered his myrmidons to halt and reconnoitre; and immediately his ears were saluted with an exclamation of 'You shan't 'scape me, rascal.' The voice being quite familiar to him, he all at once divined the cause of that confusion which they observed; and running up to the assistance of the exclaimer, found a fellow on his knees begging his life of Mr. Gauntlet, who stood over him with a naked hanger in his hand.

Pickle instantly made himself known to his friend, who told him, that having left his horse at Tunley's, he was in his way to the garison set upon by three ruffians, one of whom, being the very individual person now in his power, had come behind him, and struck with a bludgeon at his head, which however he missed, and the instrument descended on his left shoulder; that upon drawing his hanger, and laying about him in the dark, the other two fled, leaving their companion, whom he had disabled, in the lurch.

Peregrine congratulated him upon his safety, and having ordered Pipes to secure the prisoner, conducted Mr. Gauntlet to the garison, where he met with a very hearty reception from the commodore, to whom he was introduced as his nephew's intimate friend; not but that, in all likelihood, he would have abated somewhat of his hospitality, had he known that he was the brother of Perry's mistress; but her name the old gentleman had never thought of asking, when he inquired into the particulars of his godson's amour.

The captive being examined, in presence of Trunnion and all his adherents, touching the ambuscade, owned, that being in the service of Gam Pickle, he had been prevailed upon by the sollicitations of his master and the curate, to accompany them in their expedition, and undertake the part which he had acted against the stranger, whom he and his employers mistook for Peregrine. In consideration of this frank acknowledgment, and a severe wound he had received in his right arm, they resolved to inflict no other punishment on this malefactor, than to detain him all night in the garison, and next morning carry him before a justice of the peace, to whom he repeated all that he had said overnight, and with his own hand subscribed his confession, copies of which were handed about the neighbourhood, to the unspeakable confusion and disgrace of the curate and his promising pupil.

Mean while, Trunnion treated the young soldier with uncommon marks of respect, being prepossessed in his favour by this adventure, which he had so gallantly atchieved, as well as by the encomiums that Peregrine bestowed upon his valour and generosity. He liked his countenance, which was bold and hardy, admired his Herculean limbs, and delighted in asking questions concerning the service he had seen.

The day after his arrival, while the conversation turned on this last subject, the commodore, taking the pipe out of his mouth, 'I'll tell you what, brother, (said he) five and forty years ago, when I was third lieutenant of the Warwick man of war, there was a very stout young fellow on board, a subaltern officer of marines; his name was not unlike your own, d'ye see, being Guntlet, with a G. I remember he and I could not abide one another at first, because, d'ye see, I was a sailor and he a land-man, till we fell in with a Frenchman, whom we engaged for eight glasses, and at length boarded and took. I was the first man that stood on the enemy's deck, and should have come scurvily off, d'ye see, if Guntlet had not jumped to my assistance; but we soon cleared ship, and drove them to close quarters, so that they were obliged to strike; and from that day Guntlet and I were sworn brothers as long as he remained on board. He was exchanged into a marching regiment, and what became of him afterwards, Lord in heaven knows; but this I'll say of him, whether he be dead or alive, he feared no man that ever wore a head, and was, moreover, a very hearty messmate.'

The stranger's breast glowed at this eulogium, which was no sooner pronounced, than he eagerly asked, if the French ship was not the Diligence? The commodore replied with a stare, 'The very same, my lad.' 'Then (said Gauntlet) the person of whom you are pleased to make such honourable mention was my own father.' 'The devil he was! (cried Trunnion, shaking him by the hand) I am rejoiced to see a son of Ned Gauntlet in my house.'

This discovery introduced a thousand questions, in the course of which, the old gentleman learnt the situation of his friend's family, and discharged innumerable execrations upon the ingratitude and injustice of the ministry, which had failed to provide for the son of such a brave soldier. Nor was his friendship confined to such ineffectual expressions; he that same evening signified to Peregrine a desire of doing something for his friend; and this inclination was so much praised, encouraged and promoted by his godson, and even supported by his counsellor Hatchway, that our hero was empowered to present him with a sum of money sufficient to purchase a commission.

Though nothing could be more agreeable to Pickle than this permission, he was afraid that Godfrey's scrupulous disposition would hinder him from subjecting himself to any such obligation; and therefore proposed that he should be decoyed into his own interest by a feigned story, in consequence of which he would be prevailed upon to accept of the money, as a debt which the commodore had contracted of his father at sea. Trunnion made wry faces at this expedient, the necessity of which he could not conceive, without calling in question the common sense of Gauntlet, as he took it for granted, that such offers as those were not to be rejected on any consideration whatever. Besides, he could not digest an artifice, by which he himself must own that he had lived so many years, without manifesting the least intention of doing justice to his creditor. All these objections, however, were removed by the zeal and rhetoric of Peregrine, who represented that it would be impossible to befriend him on any other terms; that his silence hitherto would be imputed to his want of information touching the circumstances and condition of his friend; and that his remembring and insisting upon discharging the obligation, after such an interval of time, when the whole affair was in oblivion, would be the greatest compliment he could pay to his own honour and integrity.

Thus persuaded, he took an opportunity of Gauntlet's being alone with him to broach the affair, telling the young man, that his father had advanced a sum of money for him, when they sailed together, on account of the mess, as well as to stop the mouth of a clamorous creditor at Portsmouth; and that the said sum, with interest, amounted to about four hundred pounds, which he would now, with great thankfulness, repay.

Godfrey was amazed at this declaration, and after a considerable pause replied, that he had never heard his parents mention any such debt; that no memorandum or voucher of it was found among his father's papers; and that, in all probability, it must have been discharged long ago, although the commodore, in such a long course of time and hurry of occupation, might have forgot the repayment: he therefore desired to be excused from accepting what in his own conscience he believed was not his due; and complimented the old gentleman upon his being so scrupulously just and honourable.

The soldier's refusal, which was matter of astonishment to Trunnion, increased his inclination to assist him; and, on pretence of acquitting his own character, he urged his beneficence with such obstinacy, that Gauntlet, afraid of disobliging him, was in a manner compelled to receive a draught for the money, for which he subscribed an ample discharge, and immediately transmitted the order to his mother, whom at the same time he informed of the circumstances by which they had so unexpectedly gained this accession of fortune.

Such a piece of news could not fail of being agreeable to Mrs. Gauntlet, who by the first post wrote a polite letter of acknowledgment to the commodore, another to her own son, importing, that she had already sent the draught to a friend in London, with directions to deposit it in the hands of a certain banker, for the purchase of the first ensigncy to be sold; and she took the liberty of sending a third to Peregrine, couched in very affectionate terms, with a kind postscript, signed by Miss Sophy and his charming Emily.

This affair being transacted to the satisfaction of all concerned, preparations were set on foot for the departure of our hero, on whom his uncle settled an annuity of eight hundred pounds, being little less than one half of his whole income. By this time indeed the old gentleman could easily afford to alienate such a part of his fortune, because he entertained little or no company, kept few servants, was remarkably plain and frugal in his house-keeping; and Mrs. Trunnion being now some years on the wrong side of fifty, her infirmities began to increase; and tho' her pride had suffered no diminution, her vanity was altogether subdued by her avarice.

A Swiss valet de chambre, who had already made the tour of Europe, was hired for the care of Peregrine's own person; and Pipes being ignorant of the French language, as well as otherwise unfit for the office of a fashionable attendant, it was resolved that he should remain in garison; and his place was immediately supplied by a Parisian lacquey engaged at London for that purpose. Pipes did not seem to relish this disposition of things; and though he made no verbal objections to it, looked remarkably sour at his successor upon his first arrival; but this sullen fit seemed gradually to wear off; and long before his master's departure, he had recovered his natural tranquillity and unconcern.

CHAPTER XXXIV

The two young Gentlemen display their Talents
for Gallantry, in the Course of which they are
involved in a ludicrous Circumstance of Distress,
and afterwards take Vengeance on the Author
of their Mishap

MEAN while our hero and his new friend, together with honest Jack Hatchway, made daily excursions into the country, visited the gentlemen in the neighbourhood, and frequently accompanied them to the chace; all three being exceedingly caressed on account of their talents, which could accommodate themselves with great facility to the tempers and turns of their entertainers. The lieutenant was a droll in his way, Peregrine possessed a great fund of sprightliness and good humour, and Godfrey, among his other qualifications already recited, sung a most excellent song; so that the company of this triumvirate was courted in all parties, whether male or female; and if the hearts of our young gentlemen had not been pre-engaged, they would have met with opportunities in abundance of displaying their address in the art of love; not but that they gave a loose to their gallantry without much interesting their affections, and amused themselves with little intrigues, which, in the opinion of a man of pleasure, do not affect his fidelity to the acknowledged sovereign of his soul.[1]

Had they used those advantages which their skill and accomplishments gave them over the warm unpractised minds of the young ladies to whom they had access, almost every family in the county, might have had cause to rue their acquaintance; but our adventurers, wild and licentious as they were, governed their actions by certain notions of honour, which they never presumed to infringe, and therefore, no domestic tragedies took rise from their behaviour.

Among the lower class of people, they did not act with the same virtuous moderation, but laid close siege to every buxom country damsel that fell in their way; imagining that their dalliance with such Dulcineas could produce no fatal effects; and that it would be in their power to attone for any damage these inamoratas might sustain.

In the prosecution of these amours, Gauntlet could not help discovering a particular biass towards married women, and when questioned by his friend, defended his singularity of taste, by observing that such connections, if discreetly managed, are attended by none of those bad consequences which commonly pursue an amorous correspondence with single persons; because the wedded dame's fortune is already made, and her husband stands as a buttress before her reputation.

Though Peregrine could not approve of this maxim which the soldier had adopted in the course of a military education, he could not avoid engaging as a second and confidant to his friend, in an intrigue which he carried on with a farmer's wife in the neighbourhood. Godfrey had practised all his arts in attempting to overcome the chastity of this woman, who was an hale rosy wench, lately married; and at length succeeded so far in his addresses, that she promised to admit him one night when her husband would be absent on business, which called him once a fortnight to the next market town.

He communicated his good fortune to Perry, desiring that he would accompany him to the place, in case of accident; and our young gentleman having undertaken the office of standing centinel over his friend, while he should enjoy his conquest, they set out at the time appointed, and arriving at the door, the gallant made the signal which had been agreed upon, and was let in accordingly, after having assured his confidant that he would be with him again in two hours at farthest.

Thus left to his own meditations, our hero began his patrole, beguiling the time with the most amusing fancies of a glowing imagination, and enjoying by anticipation all the pleasures attending affluence and youth, till at length his reverie was interrupted by a plump shower that compelled him to seek for shelter in a sort of shed, the door of which stood open to his view. Thither therefore he betook himself, and groping about as he entered in the dark, chanced to lay hold on a bushy beard, to his infinite surprize and consternation. Before he had time to form any conjecture concerning this strange object of his touch, he received a sudden shock upon his forehead that felled him to the ground in an instant, and as he lay, underwent the trampling of a huge body that rushed over him into the field. In this attitude he remained extended for the space of several minutes, before he recovered the use of sensation which he had lost, and then he perceived the blood trickling down from his temples in a double stream. The cause of this misfortune was still a mystery to him, and he made shift to rise, cursing his fate for having sustained such visible marks of disgrace in the exercise of such a ridiculous office; when strolling about with his handkerchief applied to his hurts, he discerned on the farther side of a tree a pair of large eyes glancing like two coals of fire. He immediately unsheathed his hanger, in the belief that now he had found the author of his mischance; and springing forward on his adversary, aimed a furious stroke that entered the body of the tree, in which his weapon stuck so fast, that he could not disengage it without some difficulty; while the object of his wrath made a precipitate retreat, and by an exclamation, gave him to know that his assailant was no other than an he-goat.

Mad as he was with indignation and shame, he could not help laughing at the ludicrous adventure, and had just set his invention at work to find some plausible excuse which he might make to the world, for the patches he knew he must wear on his face, when a window of the first story flying open, he saw something white descend with astonishing velocity, and running to the spot, found his friend Godfrey naked to the shirt. Confounded at his condition, he began to inquire into the reason of his precipitation, but received no answer until he had followed the fugitive to a place where they could not be overheard. There he understood that the soldier had been decoyed into the snare by the connivance of the husband, by whose direction he had (without all doubt) been admitted not only into the house, but even into his wife's own bed, where the jilt had left him undressed, on pretence of fastening the doors, but in reality with a view of giving the hint to the farmer, who armed with a pitchfork and supported by his man, entered the room before he was aware, secured his sword and cloaths, and obliged him to take refuge in a closet, from the window of which he had thrown himself, in order to avoid the resentment of the boor, and the disgrace as well as expence of being taken in that situation.

Peregrine was tempted to laugh at the ridiculous issue of this adventure, but restrained himself in consideration of his friend's temper and condition, neither of which were at that time proper objects of mirth; and stripping off his own coat, accommodated Godfrey's naked shoulders; then after mature deliberation, they determined to leave the spoil in the hands of the enemy, because they foresaw it would be altogether impracticable to retrieve it, as well as hazardous both to their persons and reputation, to make any attempt towards the recovery of what was lost; the two friends, therefore, made their retreat in this trim to the garison, and the farmer remained in possession of all the soldier's cloaths, sword and ready money, to the amount of ten pounds. But here the disaster did not end, the malicious peasant propagated the whole story in the neighbourhood, and an advertisement was pasted on the church door, for the perusal of the whole parish, giving a description of the goods, signifying the place where they were found, and offering to restore them to any person who should prove himself the right owner. This was a mortifying joke to Gauntlet, who was ashamed to shew himself for a whole week; nor was Peregrine exempted from a share of the disgrace, to which he was exposed by the marks on his forehead, that confined him also to the house, and subjected him to the ridicule of the commodore, who having heard the story, rallied the two adventurers, observing that it was well Gauntlet's mast had not gone along with his rigging; and asking if the cuckold's horns had run foul of Peregrine's bows. Mrs. Trunnion, who chanced to be present, very demurely checked her husband for his profane scoffing, and in a severe lecture, rebuked the young men for their profligate courses, which, if they were not relinquished in time, would bring their bodies into trouble in this life, and their souls into perdition in that which is to come. While these fellow-sufferers were obliged to keep within doors, they held frequent consultations with the lieutenant, concerning some means of revenge, which the soldier was bent upon taking; because he could not forgive the double dealing of his mistress, who, he thought, might have declined his solicitations, without inveigling him into such a disgraceful situation. After much deliberation, they resolved to wait patiently, and watch for the husband's absence, when by a stratagem they had concerted, they would endeavour to obtain admittance, and punish the wife's perfidy, by fixing her as a monument, with her posteriors thrust out at a window, for the contemplation of her spouse when he should return in the morning.

The plan being laid, Peregrine found means to make himself acquainted with the farmer's voice and manner of speaking, which he overheard one night at Tunley's; and likewise to procure information of the day upon which he always went to a certain market, in order to dispose of his wheat, at such a distance, that he seldom failed of being abroad all night. According to this intelligence, the confederates attended by Pipes, set out one evening about nine o'clock for the house of the delinquent, where the lieutenant and Tom being placed at different avenues to prevent interruption, the two young gentlemen approached the door which was locked, and Peregrine in the rustic tone of the farmer demanded entrance; the wife never doubting that her husband was returned, in consequence of having met with a speedier sale than usual, sent her maid to let him in, and the door was no sooner opened, than our adventurers rushed into the house. The mistress was struck dumb with consternation, mistaking them for robbers, because they wore vizors, and were otherwise disguised; while the servant wench, terrified with the same apprehension, fell upon her knees, and begged they would spare her life and take all she had. Gauntlet taking the wife by the hand, led her trembling into that very chamber which had been the scene of his misfortune, where pulling off his mask, he upbraided her with the treachery she had practised upon him, and intimated the intention of his present visit. The lady asked pardon for what she had done with such submission, and deprecated his wrath so pathetically, that his heart relented, and he proposed terms of accommodation, which with some seeming reluctance she embraced, and he forthwith enjoyed a more agreeable revenge than that which he in his ire had projected.

Mean while Peregrine guessing the good fortune of his friend, and allured by the attractions of the maid, who was a cleanly florid girl, employed his address to such effectual purpose, that she yielded to his efforts; and he was as happy as such a conquest could make him.

The soldier and his companion having thus obtained all the satisfaction they required, and settled a correspondence which they did not afterwards neglect, retired in peace, applauding themselves on their success, and found their two centinels on their posts, whom they amused with a feigned story of having been so much moved by the tears and supplications of the criminal, that they desisted from their scheme of exposing her, and only inflicted the punishment of flagellation, which, they said, she had undergone.

Pipes was not well pleased when he found himself disappointed in the expectation of seeing her in the attitude to which she had been in council decreed; and Hatchway, though he pretended to acquiesce in their account, saw through the pretence, and ascribed their long stay to the true motive.

CHAPTER XXXV

Peregrine has an Interview with his Sister Julia.
Is interrupted and attacked by his Mother,
and relieved by his Friend Gauntlet.
Julia is settled in the Garison, and Trunnion
affronted by his old Friend Gamaliel Pickle

TWO days after this atchievement was so happily accomplished, our hero received an intimation from his sister, that she should be overjoyed to meet him next day, at five o'clock in the afternoon, at the house of her nurse, who lived in a cottage hard by her father's habitation, she being debarred from all opportunity of seeing him in any other place by the severity of her mother, who suspected her inclination.

He accordingly obeyed the summons, and went at the time appointed to the place of rendezvous, where he met this affectionate young lady, who when he entered the room, ran towards him with all the eagerness of transport; flung her arms about his neck, and shed a flood of tears in his bosom before she could utter one word, except a repetition of 'My dear, dear brother!' He embraced her with all the piety of fraternal tenderness, wept over her in his turn, assured her that this was one of the happiest moments of his life, and kindly thanked her for having resisted the example, and disobeyed the injunctions of his mother's unnatural aversion.

Chapter XXXV

He was ravished to find by her conversation, that she possessed a great share of sensibility and prudent reflexion; for she lamented the infatuation of her parents with the most filial regret, and expressed such abhorrence and concern at the villainous disposition of her younger brother, as a humane sister may be supposed to have entertained. He made her acquainted with all the circumstances of his own fortune, and as he supposed she spent her time very disagreeably at home, among characters which must be shockingly interesting, professed a desire of moving her into some other sphere, where she could live with more tranquillity and satisfaction.

She objected to this proposal as an expedient that would infallibly subject her to the implacable resentment of her mother, whose favour and affection she at present enjoyed but in a very inconsiderable degree; and they had canvassed divers schemes of corresponding for the future when the voice of Mrs. Pickle was heard at the door.

Miss Julia (that was the young lady's name) finding herself betrayed, was seized with a violent agitation of fear, and Peregrine scarce had time to encourage her with a promise of protection, before the door of the apartment being flung open, this irreconcileable parent rushed in, and with a furious aspect flew directly at her trembling daughter, when the son interposing, received the first discharge of her fury.

Her eyes gleamed with all the rage of indignation, which choked up her utterance, and seemed to convulse her whole frame; she twisted her left hand in his hair, and with the other buffeted him about the face, till the blood gushed from his nostrils and mouth; while he defended his sister from the cruelty of Gam, who assaulted her from another quarter, seeing his brother engaged. This attack lasted several minutes with great violence, till at length Peregrine finding himself in danger of being overpowered, if he should remain any longer on the defensive, laid his brother on his back; and before he could get up again, disentangled his mother's hand from his own hair, and having pushed her gently out of the room, bolted the door on the inside; then turning to Gam, threw him out at the window, among a parcel of hogs that fed under it. By this time, Julia was almost quite distracted with terror; she knew she had offended beyond all hope of forgiveness, and from that moment considered herself as an exile from her father's house; in vain did her brother strive to console her with fresh protestations of love and protection, she counted herself extremely miserable in being obliged to endure the eternal resentment of a parent with whom she had hitherto lived, and dreaded the censure of the world, which from her mother's misrepresentation she was sensible would condemn her unheard. That she might not however neglect any means in her power of averting this storm, she resolved to appease, if possible, her mother's wrath with humiliation, and even appeal to the influence of her father, weak as it was, before she would despair of being forgiven. But the good lady spared her this unnecessary application, by telling her through the key-hole, that she must never expect to come within her father's door again; for from that hour she renounced her as unworthy of her affection and regard. Julia weeping bitterly, endeavoured to soften the rigour of this sentence, by the most submissive and reasonable remonstrances; but as in her vindication she of necessity espoused her elder brother's cause, her endeavours instead of soothing, served only to exasperate her mother to an higher pitch of indignation, which discharged itself in invectives against Peregrine, whom she reviled with the epithets of a worthless abandoned reprobate.

The youth hearing these unjust aspersions, trembled with resentment through every limb, assuring the upbraider that he considered her as an object of compassion; 'for without all doubt, (said he) your diabolic rancour must be severely punished by the thorns of your own conscience, which this very instant taxes you with the malice and falsehood of your reproaches. As for my sister, I bless God that you have not been able to infect her with your unnatural prejudice, which because she is too just, too virtuous, too humane to imbibe, you reject her as an alien to your blood, and turn her out unprovided into a barbarous world. But even there your vitious purpose shall be defeated; that same providence that screened me from the cruelty of your hate shall extend its protection to her, until I shall find it convenient to assert by law that right of maintenance which nature, it seems, hath bestowed upon us in vain. In the mean time, you will enjoy the satisfaction of paying an undivided attention to that darling son, whose amiable qualities have so long engaged and engrossed your love and esteem.'

This freedom of expostulation exalted his mother's ire to meer frenzy; she cursed him with the bitterest imprecations, and raved like a Bedlamite at the door, which she attempted to burst open. Her efforts were seconded by her favourite son, who denounced vengeance against Peregrine, made furious assaults against the lock, which resisted all their applications, until our hero espying his friend Gauntlet and Pipes stepping over a style that stood about a furlong from the window, called them to his assistance; and giving them to understand how he was besieged, desired they would keep off his mother, that he might the more easily secure his sister Julia's retreat. The young soldier entered accordingly, and posting himself between Mrs. Pickle and the door, gave the signal to his friend, who lifting up his sister in his arms, carried her safe without the clutches of this she-dragon, while Pipes with his cudgel kept young master at bay.

The mother being thus deprived of her prey, sprung upon Gauntlet like a lioness robbed of her whelps, and he must have suffered sorely in the flesh, had he not prevented her mischievous intent by seizing both her wrists, and so keeping her at due distance. In attempting to disengage herself from his grasp, she struggled with such exertion, and suffered such agony of passion at the same time, that she actually fell into a severe fit, during which she was put to bed, and the confederates retired without further molestation.

In the mean time, Peregrine was not a little perplexed about the disposal of his sister whom he had rescued. He could not endure the thoughts of saddling the commodore with a new expence; and he was afraid of undertaking the charge of Julia, without his benefactor's advice and direction: for the present, however, he carried her to the house of a gentleman in the neighbourhood, whose lady was her godmother, where she was received with great tenderness and condolance; and he proposed to inquire for some creditable house, where she might be genteelly boarded in his absence, resolving to maintain her from the savings of his own allowance, which he thought might very well bear such deduction. But this intention was frustrated by the publication of the whole affair, which was divulged next day, and soon reached the ears of Trunnion, who chid his godson for having concealed the adventure; and, with the approbation of his wife, ordered him to bring Julia forthwith to the garison. The young gentleman, with tears of gratitude in his eyes, explained his design of maintaining her at his own expence, and earnestly begged that he might not be deprived of that satisfaction. But his uncle was deaf to all his intreaties, and insisted upon her living in the garison, though for no other reason than that of being company to her aunt, who, he observed, was lost for want of conversation.

Julia was accordingly brought home, and settled under the tuition of Mrs. Trunnion, who, whatever face she might put on the matter, could have dispensed with the society of her niece; though she was not without hope of gratifying her pique at Mrs. Pickle, by the intelligence she would receive from the daughter, of that lady's œconomy and domestic behaviour. The mother herself seemed conscious of this advantage which her sister-in-law had now gained over her, being as much chagrined at the news of Julia's reception at the garison, as if she had heard of her own husband's death. She even tortured her invention to propagate calumnies against the reputation of her own daughter, whom she slandered in all companies; she exclaimed against the commodore as an old ruffian who spirited up a rebellion among her children, and imputed the hospitality of his wife, in countenancing them, to nothing else but her inveterate enmity to their mother, whom they had disobliged. She now insisted, in the most peremptory terms, upon her husband's renouncing all commerce with the old lad of the castle and his adherents; and Mr. Gamaliel having by this time contracted other friendships, readily submitted to her will, and even refused to communicate with the commodore one night, when they happened to meet by accident at the public house.

CHAPTER XXXVI

The Commodore sends a Challenge to Gamaliel,
and is imposed upon by a waggish Invention of
the Lieutenant, Peregrine and Gauntlet

THIS affront Trunnion could by no means digest: he advised with the lieutenant upon the subject; and the result of their consultation was a defiance which the old commander sent to Pickle, demanding that he would meet him at such a place on horseback with a brace of pistols, and give satisfaction for the slight he had put upon him.

Nothing could have afforded more pleasure to Jack, than the acceptance of this challenge, which he delivered verbally to Mr. Gamaliel, who was called out from the club at Tunley's for that purpose. The nature of this message had an instantaneous effect upon the constitution of the pacific Pickle, whose bowels yearned with apprehension, and underwent such violent agitation on the spot, that one would have thought the operation proceeded from some severe joke of the apothecary which he had swallowed in his beer.

The messenger despairing of a satisfactory answer, left him in this woeful condition; and being loath to lose any opportunity of raising the laugh against the commodore, went immediately and communicated the whole affair to the young gentlemen, intreating them, for the love of God, to concert some means of bringing old Hannibal into the field. The two friends relished the proposal, and after some deliberation, it was resolved that Hatchway should tell Trunnion his invitation was accepted by Gamaliel, who would meet him at the place appointed, with his second, to-morrow in the twilight, because if either should fall, the other would have the better chance for escaping in the dark; that Godfrey should personate old Pickle's friend, and Peregrine represent his own father, while the lieutenant should take care in loading the pistols to keep out the shot, so as that no damage might be done in the rencounter.

These circumstances being adjusted, the lieutenant returned to his principal with a most thundering reply from his antagonist, whose courageous behaviour, though it could not intimidate, did not fail to astonish the commodore, who ascribed it to the spirit of his wife, which had inspired him. Trunnion that instant desired his counsellor to prepare his cartridge-box, and order the quietest horse in the stable to be kept ready saddled for the occasion; his eye seemed to lighten with alacrity and pleasure at the prospect of smelling gun-powder once more before his death; and when Jack advised him to make his will, in case of accident, he rejected his counsel with disdain, saying, 'What! dost think that Hawser Trunnion, who has stood the fire of so many floating batteries, runs any risk from the lousy pops of a landman? Thou shalt see, thou shalt see how I will make him lower his top-sails.' Next day Peregrine and the soldier provided themselves with horses at the public house, from whence, at the destined hour, they rode to the field of battle, each of them being muffled in a great coat, which, with the dimness of the light, effectually shielded them from the knowledge of the one-eyed commander, who having taken horse, on pretence of enjoying the fresh air, soon appeared with Hatchway in his rear. When they came within sight of each other, the seconds advanced, in order to divide the ground, and regulate the measures of the combat; when it was determined by mutual consent, that two pistols should be discharged on each side, and that if neither should prove decisive, recourse must be had to the broad-swords, in order to ascertain the victory. These articles being settled, the opponents rode forward to their respective stations, when Peregrine cocking his pistol, and presenting, counterfeited his father's voice, and bad Trunnion take care of his remaining eye. The commodore took his advice, being unwilling to hazard his day-light, and very deliberately opposed the patched side of his face to the muzzle of his antagonist's piece, desiring him to do his duty without further jaw. The young man accordingly fired, and the distance being small, the wad of his pistol took place with a smart stroke on the forehead of Trunnion, who mistaking it for the ball, which he thought was lodged in his brain, spurred up his steed in a state of desperation towards his antagonist, and holding his piece within two yards of his body, let it off, without any regard to the laws of battle. Surprised and enraged to see it had made no impression, he hollowed in a terrible tone, 'O! damn ye, you have got your netting stuffed, I see;' and advancing, discharged his second pistol so near his godson's head, that had he not been defended by his great coat, the powder must have scorched his face. Having thus thrown away his fire, he remained at the mercy of Peregrine, who clapping the piece he had in reserve to his head, commanded him to beg his life, and ask pardon for his presumption. The commodore made no reply to this imperious injunction, but dropping his pistol, and unsheathing his broad-sword with a jirk, attacked our hero with such incredible agility, that if he had not made shift to ward off the stroke with his piece, the adventure, in all likelihood, would have turned out a very tragical joke. Peregrine finding it would be in vain for him to think of drawing his weapon, and standing on the defensive against this furious aggressor, very fairly clapt spurs to his nag, and sought his safety in flight. Trunnion pursued him with infinite eagerness, and his steed being the better of the two, would have overtaken the fugitive to his peril, had he not been unfortunately encountered by the boughs of a tree that happened to stand on his blind side, and incommoded him so much, that he was fain to quit his sword, and lay hold on the mane, in order to maintain his seat. Perry perceiving his disaster, wheeled about, and now finding leisure to produce his weapon, returned upon his disarmed foe, and brandishing his Ferrara, threatened to make him shorter by the head, if he would not immediately crave quarter, and yield. There was nothing farther from the intention of the old gentleman than such submission, which he flatly refused to pay, alledging that he had already compelled his enemy to clap on all his sails, and that his own present misfortune was owing to accident, all one as if a ship should be attacked, after she had been obliged to heave her guns over-board in a storm.

Before Peregrine had time to answer this remonstrance, the lieutenant interposed, and taking cognizance of the case, established a truce, until he and the other second should discuss and decide upon the merits of the cause. They accordingly retired to a small distance, and after having conferred a few minutes, Hatchway returned, and pronounced the commodore vanquished by the chance of war.

Never was rage more transporting than that which took possession of old Hannibal, when he heard the sentence; it was some time before he could utter aught, except the reproachful expression, *You lie!* which he repeated more than twenty times, in a sort of delirious insensibility; and when he recovered the further use of speech, abused the arbitrators with such bitter invectives, renouncing their sentence, and appealing to another trial, that the confederates began to repent of having carried the joke so far; and Peregrine, in order to appease his choler, owned himself overcome.

This acknowledgement calmed the tumult of his wrath, though he could not for some days forgive the lieutenant; and the two young gentlemen rode back to Tunley's, while Hatchway, taking the commodore's horse by the bridle, reconducted him to his mansion, growling all the way at Jack for his unjust and unfriendly decree; though he could not help observing, as how he had made his words good, in making his adversary strike his top-sails: 'And yet (said he) before God! I think the fellow's head is made of a wool-pack; for my shot rebounded from his face like a wad of spun-yarn from the walls of a ship. But if so be that son of a bitch of a tree hadn't come athwart my weather-bow, d'ye see, I'll be damned if I hadn't snapt his main-yard in the slings, and mayhap let out his bulge-water into the bargain.' He seemed particularly vain of this exploit, which dwelt upon his imagination, and was cherished as the child of his old age; for though he could not with decency rehearse it to the young men and his wife at supper, he gave shrewd hints of his own manhood, even at these years, and attested Hatchway as a voucher for his mettle, while the triumvirate, diverted by his vanity, enjoyed in secret the success of their imposition.

177

CHAPTER XXXVII

Peregrine takes leave of his Aunt and Sister, sets out
from the Garison, parts with his Uncle and
Hatchway on the Road, and with his Governor
arrives in safety at Dover

THIS, however, was the last effort of invention which they practised upon him; and every thing being now prepared for the departure of his godson, that hopeful youth in two days took leave of
all his friends in the neighbourhood, was closeted two whole hours
with his aunt, who inriched him with many pious advices, recapitulated all the benefits which, through her means, had been
conferred upon him since his infancy, cautioned him against the
temptations of lewd women, who bring many a man to a morsel of
bread, laid strict injunctions upon him, to live in the fear of the
Lord and the true protestant faith, to eschew quarrels and contention, to treat Mr. Jolter with reverence and regard, and above all
things to abstain from the beastly sin of drunkenness, which
exposeth a man to the scorn and contempt of his fellow-creatures,
and by divesting him of reason and reflection, renders him fit for
all manner of vice and debauchery. She recommended to him
œconomy and the care of his health, bad him remember the honour
of his family, and in all the circumstances of his behaviour, assured
him, that he might always depend upon the friendship and
generosity of the commodore; and finally, presenting him with her
own picture set in gold, and an hundred guineas from her privy
purse, embraced him affectionately, and wished him all manner
of happiness and prosperity.

Being thus kindly dismissed by Mrs. Trunnion, he locked
himself up with his sister Julia, whom he admonished to cultivate her aunt with the most complaisant and respectful attention,
without stooping to any circumstance of submission that she
should judge unworthy of her practice; he protested, that his
chief study should be to make her amends for the privilege she
had forfeited by her affection for him; intreated her to enter
into no engagement without his knowledge and approbation, put
into her hand the purse which he had received from his aunt,
to defray her pocket expences in his absence, and parted from
her, not without tears, after she had for some minutes hung

178

about his neck, kissing him and weeping in the most pathetic silence.

Having performed these duties of affection and consanguinity overnight, he went to bed, and was by his own direction, called at four o'clock in the morning, when he found the post-chaise, coach and riding-horses ready at the gate, his friends Gauntlet and Hatchway on foot, the commodore himself almost dressed, and every servant in the garison assembled in the yard, to wish him a good journey. Our hero shook each of these humble friends by the hand, tipping them at the same time with marks of his bounty; and was very much surprized when he could not perceive his old attendant Pipes among the number. When he expressed his wonder at this disrespectful omission of Tom, some of those present ran to his chamber, in order to give him a call, but his hammock and room were both deserted, and they soon returned with an account of his having eloped. Peregrine was disturbed at this information, believing that the fellow had taken some desperate course, in consequence of his being dismissed from his service, and began to wish that he had indulged his inclination, by retaining him still about his person. However, as there was now no other remedy, he recommended him strenuously to the particular favour and distinction of his uncle and Hatchway, in case he should appear again; and as he went out at the gate, was saluted with three chears by all the domestics in the family. The commodore, Gauntlet, lieutenant, Peregrine and Jolter went into the coach together, that they might enjoy each other's conversation as much as possible, resolving to breakfast at an inn upon the road, where Trunnion and Hatchway intended to bid our adventurer farewel; the valet de chambre got into the post-chaise, the French lacquey rode one horse and led another, one of the valets of the garison mounted at the back of the coach; and thus the cavalcade set out on the road to Dover. As the commodore could not bear the fatigue of jolting, they travelled at an easy pace during the first stage; so that the old gentleman had an opportunity of communicating his exhortations to his godson, with regard to his conduct abroad; he advised him, now that he was going into foreign parts, to be upon his guard against the fair weather of the French politesse, which was no more to be trusted than a whirlpool at sea. He observed that many young men had gone to Paris with good cargoes of sense, and returned with a great deal of canvas, and no ballast at all, whereby they became crank all the days of their lives, and sometimes carried their keels above water. He desired Mr. Jolter to keep his pupil out of the clutches of those sharking priests who lie in wait to make converts of all young strangers, and in a particular manner cautioned the youth against carnal conversation with the Parisian dames, who, he understood, were no better than gaudy fire-ships ready primed with death and destruction.

Peregrine listened with great respect, thanking him for his kind admonitions, which he faithfully promised to observe. They halted and breakfasted at the end of the stage, where Jolter provided himself with a horse, and the commodore settled the method of corresponding with his nephew; and the minute of parting being arrived, the old commander wrung his godson by the hand, saying, 'I wish thee a prosperous voyage and good cheer, my lad; my timbers are now a little crazy, d'ye see; and God knows if I shall keep afloat till such time as I see thee again; but, howsomever, hap what will, thou wilt find thyself in a condition to keep in the line with the best of thy fellows.' He then reminded Gauntlet of his promise to call at the garison in his return from Dover, and imparted something in a whisper to the governor, while Jack Hatchway unable to speak, pulled his hat over his eyes, and squeezing Peregrine by the hand, gave him an iron pistol of curious workmanship, as a memorial of his friendship. Our youth, who was not unmoved on this occasion, received the pledge, which he acknowledged with the present of a silver tobacco-box, that he had bought for that purpose; and the two lads of the castle getting into the coach, were driven homewards, in a state of silent dejection.

Godfrey and Peregrine seated themselves in the post-chaise, and Jolter, the valet de chambre and lacquey bestriding their beasts, they proceeded for the place of their destination, at which they arrived in safety that same night, and bespoke a passage in the pacquet-boat which was to sail next day.

CHAPTER XXXVIII

He adjusts the Method of his Correspondence with Gauntlet ;
meets by Accident with an Italian Charlatan,
and a certain Apothecary,[1] who proves to be a noted Character

THERE the two friends adjusted the articles of their future correspondence, and Peregrine having written a letter to his mistress,
wherein he renewed his former vows of eternal fidelity, it was
intrusted to the care of her brother, while Mr. Jolter, at the desire
of his pupil, provided an elegant supper, and some excellent
Burgundy, that they might spend this eve of his departure with the
greater enjoyment.

Things being thus disposed, and a servant employed in laying the cloth, their ears were of a sudden invaded by a strange
tumultuous noise in the next room, occasioned by the overthrow
of tables, chairs and glasses, with odd unintelligible exclamations
in broken French, and a jargon of threats in the Welsh dialect. Our
young gentlemen ran immediately into the apartment from whence
this clamour seemed to proceed, and found a thin meagre swarthy
figure gasping in all the agony of fear, under the hands of a squat,
thick, hard-featured man, who collared him with great demonstrations of wrath, saying, 'If you was as mighty a magician as Owen
Glendower, or the witch of Entor, look you, ay, or as Paul Beor[2]
himself, I will make pold, by the assistance of Got, and in his
Majesty's naam, to seize and secure, and confine and confront you,
until such time as you suffer and endure and undergo the pains
and penalties of the law, for your diabolical practices. Shentlemens,
(added he, turning to our adventurers) I take you to witness that
I protest and assert and avow that this person is as pig a necromancer as you would desire to behold; and I supplicate and
beseech and intreat of you, that he may be prought pefore his
petters, and compelled to give an account of his compact and commerce with the imps of darkness, look you; for as I am a christian
soul, and hope for joyful resurrection, I have this plessed evening
seen him perform such things as could not be done without the aid
and instruction and connivance of the Tevil.'

Gauntlet seemed to enter into the sentiments of this Welch
reformer, and actually laid hold on the delinquent's shoulder,
crying, 'Damn the rascal! I'll lay any wager that he's a jesuit; for

none of his order travel without a familiar.' But Peregrine, who looked upon the affair in another point of view, interposed in behalf of the stranger, whom he freed from his aggressors, observing that there was no occasion to use violence, and asked in French what he had done to incur the censure of the informer. The poor foreigner, more dead than alive, answered that he was an Italian charlatan, who had practised with some reputation in Padua, until he had the misfortune to attract the notice of the Inquisition, by exhibiting certain wonderful performances by his skill in natural knowledge, which that tribunal considered as the effects of sorcery, and persecuted him accordingly; so that he had been fain to make a precipitate retreat into France, where not finding his account in his talents, he was now arrived in England, with a view of practising his art in London; and that in consequence of a specimen which he had given to a company below, the choleric gentleman had followed him up stairs to his own apartment, and assaulted him in that inhospitable manner. He therefore earnestly begged that our hero would take him under his protection; and if he entertained the least suspicion of his employing preternatural means in the operations of his art, he would freely communicate all the secrets in his possession.

The youth dispelled his apprehension, by assuring him that he was in no danger of suffering for his art in England, where, if ever he should be questioned by the zeal of superstitious individuals, he had nothing to do but appeal to the next justice of the peace, who would immediately acquit him of the charge, and punish his accusers for their impertinence and indiscretion.

He then told Gauntlet and the Welshman, that the stranger had a good action against them for an assault, by virtue of an act of parliament, which makes it criminal for any person to accuse another of sorcery and witchcraft, these idle notions being now justly exploded by all sensible men. Mr. Jolter, who had by this time joined the company, could not help signifying his dissent from this opinion of his pupil, which he endeavoured to invalidate by the authority of scripture, quotations from the fathers, and the confession of many wretches who suffered death for having carried on correspondence with evil spirits, together with the evidence of Satan's Invisible World, and Moreton's history of witchcraft.[1]

The soldier corroborated these testimonies by facts that had happened within the sphere of his own knowledge, and in particular mentioned the case of an old woman of the parish in which he was born, who used to transform herself into the shapes of sundry animals, and was at last killed by small-shot, in the character of an hare. The Welchman thus supported, expressed his surprize at hearing that the legislature had shewn such tenderness for criminals of so dark a hue; and offered to prove by undeniable instances, that there was not a mountain in Wales, which had not been in his memory the scene of necromancy and witchcraft; 'Wherefore, (said he) I am assuredly more than apove astonished and confounded and concerned, that the parliament of Great Pritain should in their great wisdoms and their prudence, and their penetration, give countenance and encouragement, look you, to the works of darkness and the empire of Pelzepup; ofer and apove the evidence of holy writ, and those writers who have been quoted by that aggurate and learned shentleman, we are informed by profane history, of the pribbles and pranks of the old serpent, in the bortents and oragles of antiquity; as you will find in that most excellent historian Bolypius, and Titus Lifius; ay, and moreofer, in the commentaries of Julius Cæsar himself, who, as the ole 'orld knows, was a most famous, and a most faliant, and a most wise, and a most prudent, and a most fortunate cheiftan, and a most renowned orator; ay, and a most elegant writer to boot.'

Peregrine did not think proper to enter the lists of dispute with three such obstinate antagonists; but contented himself with saying, that he believed it would be no difficult matter to impugn the arguments they had advanced; though he did not find himself at all disposed to undertake the task, which must of course break in upon the evening's entertainment. He therefore invited the Italian to supper, and asked the same favour of his accuser, who seemed to have something curious and characteristic in his manner and disposition, resolving to make himself an eye-witness of those surprising feats, which had given offence to the choleric Briton. This scrupulous gentleman thanked our hero for his courtesy, but declined communicating with the stranger, until his character should be further explained; upon which his inviter, after some conversation with the charlatan, assured him that he would himself undertake for the innocence of his art; and then he was prevailed upon to favour them with his company.

In the course of the conversation, Peregrine learnt that the Welchman was a surgeon of Canterbury, who had been called in to a consultation at Dover, and understanding that his name was Morgan, took the liberty of asking if he was not the person so respectfully mentioned in the Adventures of Roderick Random. Mr. Morgan assumed a look of gravity and importance at this interrogation, and screwing up his mouth, answered, 'Mr. Rantum, my goot sir, I believe upon my conscience and salfation, is my very goot frient and wellwisher; and he and I have been companions and messmates and fellow-sufferers, look you; but nevertheless, for all that, peradventure, he hath not pehaved with so much complaisance and affability and respect, as I might have expected from him; pecause he hath revealed and tivulged and buplished our private affairs, without my knowledge and privity and consent; but as God is my safiour, I think he had no evil intention in his pelly; and though there be certain persons, look you, who, as I am told, take upon them to laugh at his descriptions of my person, deportment and conversation, I do affirm and maintain, and insist with my heart, and my plood and my soul, that those persons are no petter than ignorant asses, and that they know not how to discern and distinguish and define true ridicule, or as Aristotle calls it, the το γελοῖον,[1] no more, look you, than a herd of mountain goats; for I will make pold to observe, and I hope this goot company will be of the same opinion, that there is nothing said of me in that performance, which is unworthy of a christian and a shentleman.'

Our young gentleman and his friends acquiesced in the justness of his observation, and Peregrine particularly assured him, that from reading the book, he had conceived the utmost regard and veneration for his character; and that he thought himself extremely fortunate in having this opportunity of enjoying his conversation. Morgan, not a little proud of such advances from a person of Peregrine's appearance, returned the compliment with a profusion of civility, and in the warmth of acknowledgement, expressed a desire of seeing him and his company at his house in Canterbury: 'I will not pretend, or presume, kind sir, (said he) to entertain you according to your merits and deserts; but you shall be as welcome to my poor cottage, and my wife and family, as the Prince of Wales himself; and it shall go hard, if one way or other, I do not find ways and means of making you confess that there is some goot fellowship in an ancient Priton: for though I am no petter than a simple apothecary, I have as goot plood circulating in my veins, as any he in the county; and I can describe and delineate and demonstrate my pedigree to the satisfaction of the 'ole 'orld; and moreofer, by Got's goot providence and assistance, I can afford to treat my friend with a joint of goot mutton, and a pottle of excellent wine, and no tradesman can peard me with a bill.' He was congratulated on his happy situation, and assured that our youth would visit him on his return from France, provided he should take Canterbury in his route;

and as Peregrine manifested an inclination of being acquainted with the state of his affairs, he very complaisantly satisfied his curiosity, by giving him to know that his spouse had left off breeding, after having blessed him with two boys and a girl, who were still alive and well; that he lived in good esteem with his neighbours, and by his practice, which was considerably extended immediately after the publication of Roderick Random, had saved some thousand pounds, and begun to think of retiring among his own relations in Glamorganshire, where he had already pitched upon a spot for his residence, though his wife had made objections to this proposal, and opposed the execution of it with such obstinacy, that he had been at infinite pains in asserting his own prerogative, by convincing her both from reason and example, that he was king and priest in his own family, and that she owed the most implicit submission to his will: he likewise informed the company, that he had lately seen his friend Roderick, who had come from London on purpose to visit him, after having gained his lawsuit with Mr. Topehall, who was obliged to pay Narcissa's fortune;[1] that Mr. Random, in all appearance, led a very happy life in the conversation of his father and bed-fellow, by whom he enjoyed a son and daughter; and that Morgan had received in a present from him, a piece of very fine linnen of his wife's own making, several kits of salmon, and two casks of pickled pork, the most delicate he had ever tasted; together with a barrel of excellent herrings for salmagundy, which he knew to be his favourite dish.

This topic of conversation being discussed, the Italian was desired to exhibit a specimen of his art, and in a few minutes conducted the company into the next room, where to their great astonishment and affright, they beheld a thousand serpents winding along the cieling. Morgan struck with this phænomenon, which he had not seen before, began to utter exorcisms with great devotion, Mr. Jolter ran terrified out of the room, Gauntlet drew his hanger, and Peregrine himself was disconcerted. The operator perceiving their confusion, desired them to retire, and calling them back in an instant, there was not a viper to be seen. He raised their admiration by sundry other performances, and the Welchman's former opinion and abhorrence of his character began to recur, when in consideration of the civility with which he had been treated, this Italian imparted to them all the methods by which he had acted such wonders, that were no other than the effects of natural causes curiously combined; so that Morgan became a convert to his skill, asked pardon for the suspicion he had entertained, and invited the stranger to pass a few days with him at Canterbury. The scruples of Godfrey and Jolter were removed at the same time, and Peregrine testified his satisfaction by an handsome gratuity which he bestowed upon their entertainer.

The evening being spent in this sociable manner, every man retired to his respective chamber, and next morning they breakfasted together, when Morgan declared he would stay till he should see our hero fairly embarked, that he might have the pleasure of Mr. Gauntlet's company to his own habitation; mean while, by the skipper's advice, the servants were ordered to carry a store of wine and provision on board in case of accident; and as the packet-boat could not sail before one o'clock, the company walked up hill to visit the castle, where they saw the sword of Julius Cæsar and Queen Elizabeth's pocket pistol, repeated Shakespear's description,[1] while they surveyed the chalky cliffs on each side, and cast their eyes towards the city of Calais, that was obscured by a thick cloud which did not much regale their eyesight, because it seemed to portend foul weather.

Having viewed every thing remarkable in this place, they returned to the pier, where after the compliments of parting, and an affectionate embrace between the two young gentlemen, Peregrine and his governor stept on board, the sails were hoisted, and they went to sea with a fair wind, while Godfrey, Morgan and the conjurer walked back to the inn, from whence they set out for Canterbury before dinner.

CHAPTER XXXIX

He embarks for France ; is overtaken by a Storm ;
is surprised with the Appearance of Pipes ; lands at Calais,
and has an Affair with the Officers of the Custom-house

SCARCE had the vessel proceeded two leagues on the passage, when the wind shifting, blew directly in their teeth; so that they were obliged to haul upon a wind, and alter their course; and the sea running pretty high at the same time, our hero, who was below in his cabbin, began to be squeamish, and in consequence of the skipper's advice, went upon deck for the comfort of his stomach; while the governor, experienced in these disasters, slipt into bed, where he lay at his ease, amusing himself with a treatise on the Cycloid, with algebraical demonstrations, which never failed to engage his imagination in the most agreeable manner.

In the mean time, the wind increased to a very hard gale, the vessel pitched with great violence, the sea washed over the decks, the master was alarmed, the crew were confounded, the passengers were overwhelmed with sickness and fear, and universal distraction ensued. In the midst of this uproar, Peregrine holding fast by the taffril, and looking ruefully ahead, the countenance of Pipes presented itself to his astonished view, rising as it were from the hold of the ship. At first he imagined it was a fear-formed shadow of his own brain; though he did not long remain in this error, but plainly perceived that it was no other than the real person of Thomas, who jumping on the quarter-deck, took charge of the helm, and dictated to the sailors with as much authority as if he had been commander of the ship. The skipper looked upon him as an angel sent to his assistance, and the crew soon discovering him to be a thoroughbred seaman, notwithstanding his livery-frock, obeyed his orders with such alacrity that in a little time the confusion vanished, and every necessary step taken to weather the gale.

Our young gentleman immediately conceived the meaning of Tom's appearance on board, and when the tumult was a little subsided, went up and encouraged him to exert himself for the preservation of the ship, promising to take him again into his service, from which he should never be dismissed, except by his own desire. This assurance had a surprising effect upon Pipes, who, though he made no manner of reply, thrust the helm into the master's hand, saying, 'Here, you old bum-boat woman, take hold of the tiller, and keep her thus, boy, thus;' and skipped about the vessel, trimming the sails, and managing the ropes with such agility and skill, that every body on deck stood amazed at his dexterity.

Mr. Jolter was far from being unconcerned at the uncommon motion of the vessel, the singing of the wind, and the uproar which he heard above him; he looked towards the cabbin-door with the most wishful expectation, in hope of seeing some person who could give some account of the weather, and what was doing upon deck; but not a soul appeared, and he was too well acquainted with the disposition of his own bowels to alter his own attitude in the least. When he had lain a good while in all the agony of suspence, the boy tumbled headlong into his apartment with such noisy ruin, that he believed the mast had gone by the board, and starting

upright in his bed, asked with all the symptoms of horror, what was
the cause of that disturbance? The boy, half stunned by his fall,
answered in a dolorous tone, 'I'm come to put up the dead-lights.'
At the mention of dead-lights, the meaning of which he did not
understand, the poor governor's heart died within him; he
shivered with despair, and his recollection forsaking him, he fell
upon his knees in the bed, and fixing his eyes upon the book which
was in his hand, began to pronounce aloud, with great fervor,
'The time of a compleat oscillation in the cycloid, is to the time in
which a body would fall through the axis of the cycloid DV, as the
circumference of a circle to its diameter—' He would in all likelihood have proceeded with the demonstration of this proposition,
had he not been seized with such a qualm as compelled him to drop
the book, and accommodate himself to the emergency of his
distemper; he therefore stretched himself at full length, and putting
up ejaculations to heaven, began to prepare himself for his latter
end, when all of a sudden the noise above was intermitted; and as
he could not conceive the cause of this tremendous silence, he
imagined that either the men were washed overboard, or that
despairing of safety, they had ceased to oppose the tempest. While
he was harrowed by this miserable incertainty, which, however, was
not altogether unenlightened by some scattered rays of hope, the
master entered the cabbin, and he asked with a voice half extinguished by fear, how matters went upon deck? The skipper, with
a large bottle of brandy applied to his mouth, answered in a hollow
tone, 'All's over now, master.' Upon which Mr. Jolter, giving
himself over for lost, exclaimed with the utmost horror, 'Lord have
mercy upon us! Christ have mercy upon us!' and repeated this
supplication as it were mechanically, until the master undeceived
him, by explaining the meaning of what he had said, and assuring
him that the squall was over.

Such a sudden transition from fear to joy, occasioned a violent
agitation both in his mind and body; and it was a full quarter of an
hour before he recovered the right use of his organs. By this time
the weather cleared up, the wind began to blow again from the
right corner, and the spires of Calais appeared at the distance of five
leagues; so that the countenances of all on board were lighted up
with joyous expectation; and Peregrine venturing to go down into
the cabbin, comforted his governor with an account of the happy
turn of their affairs.

Jolter, transported with the thought of a speedy landing, began
to launch out in praise of that country for which they were bound.

He observed, that France was the land of politeness and hospitality, which were conspicuous in the behaviour of all ranks and
degrees, from the peer to the peasant; that a gentleman and a
foreigner, far from being insulted and imposed upon by the lower
class of people, as in England, was treated with the utmost reverence, candour and respect; that their fields were fertile, their
climate pure and healthy, their farmers rich and industrious, and
the subjects in general the happiest of men. He would have
prosecuted this favourite theme still farther, had not his pupil been
obliged to run upon deck, in consequence of certain warnings he
received from his stomach.

The skipper seeing his condition, very honestly reminded him of
the cold ham and fowls, with a basket of wine, which he had ordered
to be sent on board, and asked if he would have the cloth laid
below. He could not have chosen a more seasonable opportunity of
manifesting his own disinterestedness. Peregrine made wry faces
at the mention of food, bidding him, for Christ's sake, talk no more
on that subject. He then descended into the cabbin, and put the
same question to Mr. Jolter, who, he knew, entertained the same
abhorrence for his proposal; and meeting with the like reception
from him, went between decks, and repeated his courteous proffer
to the valet de chambre and lacquey, who lay sprawling in all the
pangs of a double evacuation, and rejected his civility with the most
horrible loathing. Thus baffled in all his kind endeavours, he
ordered his boy to secure the provision in one of his own lockers,
according to the custom of the ship;[1] and he would have enjoyed
a pretty comfortable booty, had not Pipes interposed, and divided
the store among the sailors, who, he thought, were most deserving
of such indulgence; so that the skipper had the mortification of
seeing his plan miscarry by his own precipitate conduct; for, had
he held his tongue, no body would have dreamt of asking for the
provision, and he would have possessed his prize in peace.

It being low water when they arrived on the French coast, the
vessel could not enter the harbour, and they were obliged to bring
to, and wait for a boat, which in less than half an hour came along-
side from the shore. Mr. Jolter now came upon deck, and snuffing
up the French air with symptoms of infinite satisfaction, asked of
the boatmen, with the friendly appellation of *Mes enfans*, what they
must have for transporting them and their baggage to the pier.
But how was he disconcerted, when those polite, candid, reasonable
watermen, demanded a Louis d'or for that service! Peregrine, with
a sarcastic sneer, observed, that he already began to perceive the

justice of his encomiums on the French; and the disappointed governor could say nothing in his own vindication, but that they were debauched by their intercourse with the inhabitants of Dover. His pupil, however, was so much offended at their extortion, that he absolutely refused to employ them, even when they abated one half in their demand, and swore he would stay on board till the packet should be able to enter the harbour, rather than encourage such imposition.[1]

The master, who in all probability had some sort of fellow-feeling with the boatmen, in vain represented, that he could not with safety lie to, or anchor upon a lee-shore; our hero having consulted Pipes, answered, that he had hired his vessel to transport him to Calais, and that he would oblige him to perform what he had undertaken.

The skipper, very much mortified at this peremptory reply, which was not over and above agreeable to Mr. Jolter, dismissed the boat, notwithstanding the sollicitations and condescension of the watermen, who promised to submit to the generosity of their employer; and running a little farther in-shore, came to an anchor, and waited till there was water enough to float them over the bar. Then they stood in to the harbour, and our gentleman, with his attendants and baggage, were landed on the pier by the sailors, whom he liberally rewarded for their trouble.

He was immediately plied by a great number of porters, who, like so many hungry wolves, laid hold on his luggage, and began to carry it off piece-meal, without his order or direction. Incensed at this officious insolence, he commanded them to desist, with many oaths and opprobrious terms that his anger suggested; and perceiving that one of them did not seem to pay any regard to what he said, but marched off with his burthen, he snatched a cudgel out of his lacquey's hand, and overtaking the fellow in a twinkling, brought him to the ground with one blow. He was instantly surrounded by the whole congregation of this *canaille*, who resented the injury which their brother had sustained, and would have taken immediate satisfaction of the aggressor, had not Pipes, seeing his master involved, brought the whole crew to his assistance, and exerted himself so manfully, that the enemy were obliged to retreat with many marks of defeat, and menaces of interesting the commandant in their quarrel. Jolter, who knew and dreaded the power of the French governor, began to shake with apprehension, when he heard their repeated threats; but they durst not apply to this magistrate, who, upon a fair representation of the case, would have

punished them severely for their rapacious and insolent behaviour;
and Peregrine, without farther molestation, availed himself of his
own attendants, who shouldered his baggage, and followed him to
the gate, where they were stopt by the centinels, until their names
should be registered.

Mr. Jolter, who had undergone this examination before, resolved
to profit by his experience, and cunningly represented his pupil as
a young English lord. This intimation, supported by the appearance
of his equipage, was no sooner communicated to the officer, than he
turned out the guard, and ordered his soldiers to rest upon their
arms, while his lordship passed in great state to the *Lion d'Argent*,
where he took up his lodging for the night, resolving to set out for
Paris next morning in a post-chaise.

The governor triumphed greatly in this piece of complaisance
and respect with which they had been honoured, and resumed his
beloved topic of discourse, in applauding the method and subordination of the French government, which was better calculated
for maintaining order, and protecting the people, than any constitution upon earth; and of their courteous attention to strangers,
there needed no other proof than the compliment which had been
paid to them, together with the governor's connivance at Peregrine's employing his own servants in carrying the baggage to the
inn, contrary to the privilege of the inhabitants.

While he expatiated with a remarkable degree of self-indulgence
on this subject, the valet de chambre coming into the room, interrupted his harangue, by telling his master, that their trunks and
portmanteaus must be carried to the custom-house, in order to be
searched, and sealed with lead, which must remain untouched until
their arrival at Paris.

Peregrine made no objection to this practice, which was in itself
reasonable enough; but when he understood that the gate was
besieged by another multitude of porters, who insisted upon their
right of carrying the goods, and also of fixing their own price, he
absolutely refused to comply with their demand; and chastising
some of the most clamorous among them with his foot, told them,
that if their custom-house officers had a mind to examine his
baggage, they might come to the inn for that purpose. The valet
de chambre was abashed at this boldness of his master's behaviour,
which the lacquey, shrugging up his shoulders, observed was *bien
a l'Angloise*; while the governor represented it as an indignity to
the whole nation, and endeavoured to persuade his pupil to comply
with the custom of the place. But Peregrine's natural haughtiness

of disposition hindered him from giving ear to Jolter's wholesome advice; and in less than half an hour they perceived a file of musqueteers marching up to the gate. At sight of this detachment the tutor trembled, the valet grew pale, and the lacquey crossed himself; but our hero, without exhibiting any other symptoms than those of indignation, met them on the threshold, and with a ferocious air demanded their business. The corporal who commanded the file answered with great deliberation, that he had orders to convey his baggage to the custom-house; and seeing the trunks standing in the entry, placed his men between them and the owner, while the porters that followed, took them up, and proceeded to the Douane without opposition.

Pickle was not mad enough to dispute the authority of this message; but, in order to gall, and specify his contempt for those who brought it, he called aloud to his valet, desiring him, in French, to accompany his things, and see that none of his linen and effects should be stolen by the searchers. The corporal, mortified at this satirical insinuation, darted a look of resentment at the author, as if he had been interested for the glory of his nation; and told him, that he could perceive he was a stranger in France, or else he would have saved himself the trouble of such a needless precaution. Indeed this expression had no sooner escaped our young gentleman, than he was ashamed of his own petulance; for nothing was farther from his principles than the least encouragement of ungenerous suspicion.[1]

CHAPTER XL

He makes a fruitless Attempt in Gallantry ;
departs for Boulogne, where he spends the Evening
with certain English Exiles

HAVING thus yielded to the hand of power, he inquired if there was any other English company in the house; and understanding that a gentleman and lady lodged in the next apartment, and had bespoke a post-chaise for Paris, he ordered Pipes to ingratiate himself with their footman, and, if possible, learn their names and condition, while he and Mr. Jolter, attended by the lacquey, took a turn round the ramparts, and viewed the particulars of the fortification.

Tom was so very successful in his inquiry, that when his master returned, he was able to give him a very satisfactory account of his fellow-lodgers, in consequence of having treated his brother with a bottle of wine. The people in question were a gentleman and his lady, lately arrived from England, in their way to Paris. The husband was a man of good fortune, who had been a libertine in his youth, and a professed declaimer against matrimony. He neither wanted sense nor experience, and piqued himself in particular upon his art in avoiding the snares of the female sex, in which he pretended to be deeply versed. But, notwithstanding all his caution and skill, he had lately fallen a sacrifice to the attractions of an oyster-wench, who had found means to decoy him into the bands of wedlock; and, in order to evade the compliments and congratulations of his friends and acquaintance, he had come so far on a tour to Paris, where he intended to initiate his spouse in the beaumonde; though in the mean time he chose to live upon the reserve, because her natural talents had as yet received but little cultivation; and he had not the most implicit confidence in her virtue and discretion, which, it seems, had like to have yielded to the addresses of an officer at Canterbury, who had made shift to insinuate himself into her acquaintance and favour.

Peregrine's curiosity being inflamed by this information, he lounged about the yard, in hopes of seeing the Dulcinea who had captivated the old batchelor, and at length observing her at a window, took the liberty of bowing to her with great respect. She returned the compliment with a curt'sie, and appeared so decent in her dress and manner, that unless he had been previously informed of her former life and conversation, he never would have dreamt that her education was different from that of other ladies of fashion; so easy it is to acquire that external deportment on which people of condition value themselves so much. Not but that Mr. Pickle pretended to distinguish a certain vulgar audacity in her countenance, which in a lady of birth and fortune would have passed for an agreeable vivacity that enlivens the aspect, and gives a poignancy to every feature: but, as she possessed a pair of fine eyes and a clear complexion, overspread with the glow of health, which never fails of recommending the owner, he could not help gazing at her with desire, and forming the design of making a conquest of her heart. With this view, he sent his compliments to her husband, whose name was Hornbeck, with an intimation, that he proposed to set out next day for Paris, and as he understood that he was resolved upon the same journey, he should be extremely glad of his company on the road, if he was not better engaged. Hornbeck, who in all probability did not chuse to accommodate his wife with a squire of our hero's appearance, sent a civil answer to his message, professing infinite mortification at his being unable to embrace the favour of his kind offer, by reason of the indisposition of his wife, who, he was afraid, would not be in a condition for some days to bear the fatigue of travelling. This rebuff, which Peregrine ascribed to the husband's jealousy, stifled his project in embrio; he ordered his French servant to take a place for himself in the Diligence, where all his luggage was stowed, except a small trunk with some linen and other necessaries that was fixed upon the post-chaise which they hired of the landlord; and early next morning he and Mr. Jolter departed from Calais, attended by his valet de chambre and Pipes on horseback. They proceeded without any accident as far as Boulogne, where they breakfasted and visited old father Graham,[1] a Scottish gentleman of the governor's acquaintance, who had lived as a capuchin in that place for the space of threescore years, and during that period conformed to all the austerities of the order, with the most rigorous exactness; being equally remarkable for the frankness of his conversation, the humanity of his disposition, and the simplicity of his manners. From Boulogne they took their departure about noon, and as they proposed to sleep that night at Abbe Ville, commanded the postilion to drive with extraordinary speed; and perhaps it was well for his cattle that the axle-tree gave way, and the chaise of course overturned before they had travelled one third part of the stage.

This accident compelled them to return to the place from whence they had set out, and as they could not procure another convenience, they found themselves under the necessity of staying till their chaise could be refitted. Understanding that this operation would detain them a whole day, our young gentleman had recourse to his patience, and demanded to know what they could have for dinner; the garçon, or waiter thus questioned, vanished in a moment, and immediately they were surprized with the appearance of a strange figure, which from the extravagance of its dress and gesticulation, Peregrine mistook for a madman of the growth of France. This phantome (which by the bye, happened to be no other than the cook) was a tall, long-legged, meagre, swarthy fellow, that stooped very much; his cheek-bones were remarkably raised, his nose bent into the shape and size of a powder-horn, and the sockets of his eyes as raw round the edges, as if the skin had

been pared off; on his head he wore an handkerchief which had once
been white, and now served to cover the upper part of a black
periwig, to which was attached a bag, at least a foot square, with
a solitaire and rose that stuck up on each side to his ear; so that he
looked like a criminal in the pillory; his back was accommodated
with a linnen waistcoat, his hands adorned with long ruffles of the
same piece, his middle was girded by an apron tucked up, that it
might not conceal his white silk stockings rolled; and at his entrance
he brandished a bloody weapon full three feet in length. Peregrine,
when he first saw him approach in this menacing attitude, put
himself upon his guard, but being informed of his quality, perused
his list, and having bespoke three or four things for dinner, walked
out with Mr. Jolter to view both towns, which they had not leisure
to consider minutely before. In their return from the harbour they
met with four or five gentlemen, all of whom seemed to look with
an air of dejection, and perceiving our hero and his governor to be
English by their dress, bowed with great respect as they passed.
Pickle, who was naturally compassionate, felt an emotion of
sympathy; and seeing a person, who by his habit he judged to be
one of their servants, accosted him in English, and asked who the
gentlemen were. The lacquey gave him to understand that they
were his own countrymen, exiled from their native homes, in consequence of their adherence to an unfortunate and ruined cause;[1]
and that they were gone to the sea-side, according to their daily
practice, in order to indulge their longing eyes, with a prospect of
the white cliffs of Albion, which they must never more approach.

Though our young gentleman differed widely from them in point
of political principles, he was not one of those enthusiasts who look
upon every schism from the established articles of faith, as damnable,
and exclude the sceptick from every benefit of humanity and
christian forgiveness: he could easily comprehend how a man of
the most unblemished morals might, by the prejudice of education,
or indispensible attachments, be ingaged in such a blame-worthy
and pernicious undertaking; and thought that they had already
suffered severely for their imprudence. He was affected with the
account of their diurnal pilgrimage to the sea-side, which he considered as a pathetic proof of their affliction, and invested Mr.
Jolter with the agreeable office of going to them with a compliment
in his name, and begging the honour of drinking a glass with them
in the evening. They accepted the proposal with great satisfaction
and respectful acknowledgement, and in the afternoon waited upon
the kind inviter, who treated them with coffee, and would have

detained them to supper; but they intreated the favour of his company at the house which they frequented, so earnestly, that he yielded to their solicitations, and with his governor was conducted by them to the place, where they had provided an elegant repast, and regaled them with some of the best claret in France.

It was easy for them to perceive that their principal guest was no favourer of their state maxims, and therefore they industriously avoided every subject of conversation which could give the least offence; not but that they lamented their own situation, which cut them off from all their dearest connexions, and doomed them to perpetual banishment from their families and friends: but they did not even by the most distant hint, impeach the justice of that sentence by which they were condemned; although one among them, who seemed to be about the age of thirty, wept bitterly over his misfortune, which had involved a beloved wife and three children in misery and distress; and in the impatience of his grief, cursed his own fate with frantic imprecations.[1] His companions, with a view of beguiling his sorrow, and manifesting their own hospitality at the same time, changed the topic of discourse, and circulated the bumpers with great assiduity; so that all their cares were overwhelmed and forgotten, several French drinking catches were sung, and mirth and good fellowship prevailed.

In the midst of this elevation, which commonly unlocks the most hidden sentiment, and dispels every consideration of caution and constraint, one of the entertainers being more intoxicated than his fellows, proposed a toast, to which Peregrine with some warmth excepted, as an unmannerly insult. The other maintained his proposition with indecent heat, and the dispute beginning to grow very serious, the company interposed, and gave judgment against their friend, who was so keenly reproached and rebuked for his impolite behaviour, by the gentleman whose sensibility hath been mentioned, that he retired in high dudgeon, threatening to relinquish their society, and branding them with the appellation of apostates from the common cause. Mortified at the behaviour of their companion, those that remained were earnest in their apologies to their guests, whom they besought to forgive his intemperance; assuring them with great confidence, that he would upon the recovery of his reflection, wait upon them in person, and ask pardon for the umbrage he had given. Pickle was satisfied with their remonstrances, resumed his good humour, and the night being pretty far advanced, resisted all their importunities with which he was intreated to see another bottle go round, and was escorted to his own lodgings, more than half seas over. Next morning about eight o'clock, he was waked by his valet de chambre, who told him that two of the gentlemen with whom he had spent the evening were in the house, and desired the favour of being admitted into his chamber. He could not conceive the meaning of this extraordinary visit, and ordering his man to shew them into his apartment, beheld the person who had affronted him enter with the gentleman who had reprehended his rudeness.

He who had given the offence, after having made an apology for disturbing Mr. Pickle, told him that his friend there present had been with him early that morning, and proposed the alternative of either fighting with him immediately, or coming to beg pardon for his unmannerly deportment over night; that though he had courage enough to face any man in the field in a righteous cause, he was not so brutal as to disobey the dictates of his own duty and reflection, in consequence of which, and not out of any regard to the other's menaces, which he despised, he had now taken the liberty of interrupting his repose, that he might as soon as possible, atone for the injury he had done him, which he protested was the effect of intoxication alone, and begged his forgiveness accordingly. Our hero accepted of this acknowledgment very graciously, thanked the other gentleman for the gallant part he had acted in his behalf; and perceiving that his companion was a little irritated at his officious interposition, effected a reconciliation, by convincing him that what he had done was for the honour of the company. He then kept them to breakfast, expressed a desire of seeing their situation altered for the better, and the chaise being repaired, took his leave of his entertainers, who came to wish him a good journey, and with his attendants left Boulogne for the second time.

CHAPTER XLI

Proceeds for the Capital. Takes up his Lodging at Bernay,
where he is overtaken by Mr. Hornbeck,
whose Head he longs to fortify

DURING this day's expedition, Mr. Jolter took an opportunity of imparting to his pupil the remarks he had made upon the industry of the French, as an undeniable proof of which he bad him cast his eyes around, and observe with what care every spot of ground was cultivated; and from the fertility of that province, which is reckoned the poorest in France, conceive the wealth and affluence of the nation in general. Peregrine amazed as well as disgusted at this infatuation, answered that what he ascribed to industry, was the effect of meer wretchedness; the miserable peasants being obliged to plough up every inch of ground to satisfy their oppressive land-lords, while they themselves and their cattle looked like so many images of famine; that their extreme poverty was evident from the face of the country, on which there was not one inclosure to be seen, or any other object, except scanty crops of barley and oats, which could never reward the toil of the husbandman; that their habita-tions were no better than paultry huts; that in twenty miles of extent, not one gentleman's house appeared; that nothing was more abject and forlorn than the attire of their country people; and lastly, that the equipage of their travelling chaises was infinitely inferior to that of a dung-cart in England; and that the postilion who then drove their carriage, had neither stockings to his legs, nor a shirt to his back.

The governor finding his charge so intractable, resolved to leave him in the mist of his own ignorance and prejudice, and reserve his observations for those who would pay more deference to his opinion; and indeed this resolution he had often made, and as often broke, in the transports of his zeal, that frequently hurried him out of the plan of conduct which in his cooler moments he had laid down. They halted for a refreshment at Montreuil, and about eight in the evening arrived at a village called Bernay, where while they waited for fresh horses, they were informed by the landlord, that the gates of Abbe Ville were shut every night punctually at nine o'clock; so that it would be impossible for them to get admittance; and that there was not another place of entertainment on the road where they could pass the night; he therefore, as a friend, advised them to stay at his house, where they would find the best of accommodation, and proceed upon their journey by times in the morning.

Mr. Jolter, though he had travelled on that road before, could not recollect whether or not mine host spoke truth; but his remon-strance being very plausible, our hero determined to follow his advice, and being conducted into an apartment, asked what they could have for supper. The landlord mentioned every thing that was eatable in the house, and the whole being ingrossed for the use of him and his attendants, he amused himself till such time as it

could be dressed, in conversing with the daughter,[1] who was a
sprightly damsel about the age of seventeen; and in strolling about
the house, which stands in a very rural situation. While he thus
loitered away the time that hung heavy on his hands, another chaise
arrived at the inn, and upon inquiry he found that the new comers
were Mr. Hornbeck and his lady. The landlord, conscious of his
inability to entertain this second company, came and begged with
great humiliation that Mr. Pickle would spare them some part of
the victuals he had bespoke; but he refused to part with so much as
the wing of a partridge, though at the same time he sent his compliments to the strangers, and giving them to understand how ill the
house was provided for their reception, invited them to partake of
his supper. Mr. Hornbeck, who was not deficient in point of
politeness, and extremely well disposed for a relishing meal, which
he had reason to expect from the savoury steam that issued from
the kitchen, could not resist this second instance of our young
gentleman's civility, which he acknowledged by a message, importing that he and his wife would do themselves the pleasure of
profiting by his courteous offer. Peregrine's cheeks glowed when
he found himself on the eve of being acquainted with Mrs. Hornbeck, of whose heart he had already made a conquest in imagination; and he forthwith set his invention at work, to contrive some
means of defeating her husband's vigilance.

When supper was ready, he in person gave notice to his guests,
and leading the lady into his apartment, seated her in an elbow chair
at the upper end of the table, squeezing her hand and darting a most
insidious glance at the same time. This abrupt behaviour he practised on the presumption, that a lady of her breeding was not to be
addressed with the tedious forms that must be observed in one's
advances to a person of birth and genteel education; and in all
probability his calculation was just, for Mrs. Hornbeck gave no
signs of discontent at this sort of treatment, but on the contrary,
seemed to consider it as a proof of the young gentleman's regard;
and though she did not venture to open her mouth three times
during the whole repast, she shewed herself particularly well
satisfied with her entertainer, by sundry sly and significant looks,
while her husband's eyes were directed another way, and divers
loud peals of laughter, signifying her approbation of the sallies
which he uttered in the course of their conversation. Her spouse
began to be very uneasy at the frank demeanour of his yoke-fellow,
whom he endeavoured to check in her vivacity, by assuming a
severity of aspect; but whether she obeyed the dictates of her own

disposition, which, perhaps, was merry and unreserved, or wanted to punish Mr. Hornbeck for his jealousy of temper; certain it is, her gaiety increased to such a degree, that her husband was grievously alarmed and incensed at her conduct, and resolved to make her sensible of his displeasure, by treading in secret upon her toes. He was, however, so disconcerted by his indignation, that he mistook his mark, and applied the sharp heel of his shoe to the side of Mr. Jolter's foot, comprehending his little toe that was studded with an angry corn, which he invaded with such a sudden jerk, that the governor, unable to endure the torture in silence, started up, and dancing on the floor, roared hideously with repeated bellowings, to the unspeakable enjoyment of Peregrine and the lady, who laughed themselves almost into convulsions at the joke. Hornbeck, confounded at the mistake he had committed, begged pardon of the injured tutor with great contrition, protesting that the blow he had so unfortunately received, was intended for an ugly cur, which he thought had posted himself under the table. It was lucky for him that there was actually a dog in the room, to justify this excuse, which Jolter admitted with the tears running over his cheeks, and the œconomy of the table was re-composed.

As soon, however, as the strangers could with decency withdraw, this suspicious husband took his leave of the youth, on pretence of being fatigued with his journey, after having, by way of compliment, proposed that they should travel together next day; and Peregrine handed the lady to her chamber, where he wished her good night with another warm squeeze, which she returned. This favourable hint made his heart bound with a transport of joy; he lay in wait for an opportunity of declaring himself, and seeing the husband go down into the yard with a candle, he glided softly into his apartment, and found her almost undressed. Impelled by the impetuosity of his passion, which was still more inflamed by her present luscious appearance, and encouraged by the approbation she had already expressed, he ran towards her with eagerness, crying, 'Zounds! madam, your charms are irresistible!' and without further ceremony would have clasped her in his arms, had not she begged him for the love of God to retire, for should Mr. Hornbeck return and find him there, she would be undone for ever. He was not so blinded by his passion but that he saw the reasonableness of her fear, and as he could not pretend to crown his wishes at that interview, he avowed himself her lover, assured her that he would exhaust his whole invention in finding a proper opportunity for throwing himself at her feet; and in the mean time he ravished sundry small favours, which she in the hurry of her fright could not with-hold from his impudence of address. Having thus happily settled the preliminaries, he withdrew to his own chamber, and spent the whole night in contriving stratagems to elude the jealous caution of his fellow-traveller.

CHAPTER XLII

They set out in Company, breakfast at Abbe Ville,
dine at Amiens, and about Eleven O'clock arrive at
Chantilly, where Peregrine executes a Plan
which he had concerted upon Hornbeck

THE whole company by agreement rose and departed before day, and breakfasted at Abbe Ville, where they became acquainted with the finesse of their Bernay landlord, who had imposed upon them, in affirming that they would not have been admitted after the gates were shut. From thence they proceeded to Amiens, where they dined and were pestered by begging friars; and the roads being deep, it was eleven o'clock at night before they reached Chantilly, where they found supper already dressed, in consequence of having dispatched the valet de chambre before them on horseback.

The constitution of Hornbeck being very much impaired by a life of irregularity, he found himself so fatigued with this day's journey, which amounted to upwards of an hundred miles, that when he sat down at table, he could scarce sit upright; and in less than three minutes began to nod in his chair. Peregrine, who had foreseen and provided for this occasion, advised him to exhilarate his spirits with a glass of wine; and the proposal being embraced, tipt his valet de chambre the wink, who, according to the instructions he had received qualified the Burgundy with thirty drops of laudanum, which this unfortunate husband swallowed in one glass. The dose co-operating with his former drowsiness, lulled him so fast asleep, as it were instantaneously, that it was found necessary to convey him to his own chamber, where his footman undressed and put him to bed. Nor was Jolter (naturally of a sluggish disposition) able to resist his propensity to sleep, without suffering divers dreadful yawns, which encouraged his pupil to administer the same dose to him, which had operated so successfully upon the other

Argus. This cordial had not such a gentle effect upon the rugged organs of Jolter as upon the more delicate nerves of Hornbeck; but discovered itself in certain involuntary startings, and convulsive motions in the muscles of his face; and when his nature at length yielded to the power of this medicine, he sounded the trumpet so loud through his nostrils, that our adventurer was afraid the noise would awake his other patient, and consequently prevent the accomplishment of his aim. The governor was therefore committed to the care of Pipes, who lugged him into the next room, and having stripped off his cloaths, tumbled him into his nest, while the two lovers remained at full liberty to indulge their mutual passion.

Peregrine, in the impatience of his inclination, would have finished the fate of Hornbeck immediately; but his inamorata disapproved of his intention, and represented that their being together by themselves for any length of time, would be observed by her servant, who was kept as a spy upon her actions; so that they had recourse to another scheme, which was executed in this manner: He conducted her into her own apartment, in presence of her footman, who lighted them thither, and wishing her good rest, returned to his own chamber, where he waited till every thing was quiet in the house; and then stealing softly to her door, which had been left open for his admission in the dark, he found the husband still secure in the embraces of sleep, and the lady in a loose gown, ready to seal his happiness. He seized opportunity by the forelock, and bearing her in his arms to the place from whence he came, she was revenged upon the cuckold for the uneasy life he had made her lead, and our hero enjoyed the luscious fruits of his conquest.[1]

Their guilty raptures, however, were not without allay. The opium which had been given to Jolter, together with the wine he had drank, produced such a perturbation in his fancy, that he was visited with horrible dreams, and among other miserable situations, imagined himself in danger of perishing in the flames, which he thought had taken hold on his apartment. This vision made such an impression upon his faculties, that he alarmed the whole house with the repeated cries of *Fire! Fire!* and even leaped out of his bed, though he still remained fast asleep. The lovers were very disagreeably disturbed by this dreadful exclamation, and Mrs. Hornbeck running in great confusion to the door, had the mortification to see the footman with a light in his hand, enter her husband's chamber, in order to give them notice of this accident. She knew that she would be instantly missed, and could easily divine the consequence, unless her invention could immediately trump up some plausible excuse for her absence.

Women are naturally fruitful of expedients in cases of such emergency; she employed but a few seconds in recollection, and rushing directly towards the apartment of the governor, who still continued to hollow in the same note, exclaimed in a screaming tone, 'Lord have mercy upon us! where! where!' By this time, all the servants were assembled in strange attire; Peregrine slipt on his breeches, burst into Jolter's room, and seeing him stalking in his shirt with his eyes shut, bestowed such a slap upon his buttocks, as in a moment dissolved his dream, and restored him to the use of his senses. He was astonished and ashamed at being discovered in such an indecent attitude; and taking refuge under the cloaths, asked pardon of all present for the disturbance he had occasioned; solliciting with great humility the forgiveness of the lady, who, to a miracle, counterfeited the utmost agitation of terror and surprize. Mean while, Hornbeck being awakened by the repeated efforts of his man, no sooner understood that his wife was missing, than all the chimeras of jealousy taking possession of his imagination, he started up in a sort of frenzy, and snatching his sword, flew straight to Peregrine's chamber, where, though he found not that which he looked for, he unluckily perceived upon the bed an under-petticoat, which his wife had forgot in the hurry of her retreat. This discovery added fuel to the flame of his resentment. He seized the fatal proof of his dishonour, and meeting his spouse in her return to bed, presented it to her view, saying, with a most expressive countenance, 'Madam, you have dropped your under-petticoat in the next room.' Mrs. Hornbeck, who inherited from nature a most admirable presence of mind, looked earnestly at the object in question, and with incredible serenity of countenance, affirmed that the petticoat must belong to the house, for she had none such in her possession. Peregrine, who walked behind her, hearing this asseveration, immediately interposed, and pulling Hornbeck by the sleeve into his chamber, 'Gadszooks! (said he) what business had you with that petticoat? Can't you let a young fellow enjoy a little amour with an innkeeper's daughter, without exposing his infirmities to your wife? Pshaw! that's so malicious, because you have quitted these adventures yourself, to spoil the sport of other people.' The poor husband was so confounded at the effrontery of his wife, and this cavalier declaration of the young man, that his faith began to waver; he distrusted his own conscious diffidence of temper, which that he might not expose, he expressed no doubts of Peregrine's veracity, but asking pardon for the mistake he had committed, retired with a grim look, not yet satisfied with the behaviour of his ingenious helpmate, but on the contrary determined to inquire more minutely into the circumstances of this adventure; which turned out so little to his satisfaction, that he ordered his servant to get every thing ready for his departure by break of day; and when our adventurer rose next morning, he found that his fellow-travellers were gone above three hours, though they had agreed to stay all the forenoon, with a view of seeing the prince of Conde's palace, and to proceed all together for Paris in the afternoon.

Peregrine was a little chagrined, when he understood that he was so suddenly deprived of this almost untasted morsel; and Jolter could not conceive the meaning of their abrupt and uncivil disappearance, which after many profound conjectures, he accounted for, by supposing that Hornbeck was some sharper who had run away with an heiress, whom he found it necessary to conceal from the inquiry of her friends.

The pupil, who was well assured of the true motive, allowed his governor to enjoy the triumph of his own penetration, and consoled himself with the hope of seeing his Dulcinea again at some of the public places in Paris, which he proposed to frequent. Thus comforted, he visited the magnificent stables and palace of Chantilly, and immediately after dinner set out for Paris, where they arrived in the evening, and hired apartments at an hotel in the Fauxbourg St. Germaine, not far from the playhouse.

CHAPTER XLIII

He is involved in an Adventure at Paris,
and taken Prisoner by the City-guard.
Becomes acquainted with a French Nobleman,
who introduces him into the beau monde

THEY were no sooner settled in these lodgings, than our hero wrote to his uncle an account of their safe arrival, and sent another letter to his friend Gauntlet, with a very tender billet inclosed for his dear Emilia, to whom he repeated all his former vows of constancy and love.

The next care that ingrossed him was that of bespeaking several suits of cloaths suitable to the French mode, and in the mean time he never appeared abroad, except in the English coffee-house, where he soon became acquainted with some of his own country-men, who were at Paris on the same footing with himself. The third evening after his journey, he was engaged in a party of those young sparks, at the house of a noted Traiteur,[1] whose wife was remarkably handsome, and otherwise extremely well qualified for alluring customers to her house. To this lady our young gentleman was introduced as a stranger fresh from England; and he was charmed with her personal accomplishments, as well as with the freedom and gaiety of her conversation: having sat with them about an hour, she got up in order to retire, but being earnestly intreated to favour them with her company at supper, she promised to gratify their desire, and told them, without any ceremony or circumlocu-tion, that she would only step into the next room to make water, and return in an instant. This frank declaration sounded so oddly in the ears of Peregrine, that he concluded he might, without offence, take any sort of liberty with a woman who could thus behave so wide of decency and decorum; and on this supposition, he followed her cavalierly to her closet, where he addressed her in such palpable terms, as he thought her character intitled him to use. She was surprised at his confidence, which she began to rally as a specimen of English plain dealing, while she very deliberately executed in his presence the intent of her withdrawing; and he still more encouraged by this deportment, urged his suit with such impetuosity, that the fair Burgeoise was compelled to cry aloud in defence of her own virtue.[2] Her husband ran immediately to her assistance, and finding her in a very alarming situation, flew upon her ravisher with such fury, that he was fain to quit his prey, and turn against the exasperated Traiteur, whom he punished without mercy for his impudent intrusion. The lady seeing her yoke-fellow treated with so little respect, espoused his cause, and fixing her nails in his antagonist's face, scarified all one side of his nose. The noise of this encounter brought all the servants of the house to the rescue of their master, and Peregrine's company arriving at the same time, a general battle ensued, in which the French were totally routed, the wife being insulted, and the husband kicked down stairs.

The publican enraged at the indignity which had been offered to him and his family, went out into the street, and implored the pro-tection of the guet or city-guard, which having heard his complaint, fixed their bayonets and surrounded the door, to the number of twelve or fourteen. The young gentlemen flushed with their success, and considering the soldiers as so many London watchmen, whom they had often put to flight, drew their swords, and sallied out, with Peregrine at their head. Whether the guard respected them as foreigners, or inexperienced youths intoxicated with liquor, they opened to right and left, and gave them room to pass, without opposition. This complaisance, which was the effect of compassion, being misinterpreted by the English leader, he out of meer wantonness attempted to trip up the heels of the soldier that stood next him, but failed in the execution, and received a blow on his breast with the butt end of a fusil, that made him stagger several paces backward. Incensed at this audacious application, the whole company charged the detachment sword in hand, and after an obstinate engagement, in which divers wounds were given and received, every soul of them was taken, and conveyed to the main-guard, where the commanding officer being made acquainted with the circumstances of the quarrel, in consideration of their youth and national ferocity, for which the French make large allowances, set them all at liberty, after having gently rebuked them for the irregularity and insolence of their conduct: so that all our hero acquired by his gallantry and courage, was a number of scandalous marks upon his visage, that confined him a whole week to his chamber. It was impossible to conceal this disaster from Mr. Jolter, who having got intelligence of the particulars, did not fail to remonstrate against the rashness of the adventure, which, he observed, must have been fatal to them, had their enemies been other than Frenchmen, who of all nations under the sun, most rigorously observe the laws of hospitality.

As the governor's acquaintance lay chiefly among Irish and English priests, and a set of low people, who live by making themselves necessary to strangers, either in teaching the French language, or executing small commissions with which they are intrusted, he was not the most proper person in the world for regulating the taste of a young gentleman who travelled for improvement, in expectation of making a figure one day in his own country; and being conscious of his own incapacity, he contented himself with the office of a steward, and kept a faithful account of all the money that was disbursed in the course of their family expence: not but that he was acquainted with all the places which are visited by strangers on their first arrival at Paris; and knew to a liard what was commonly given to the Swiss of each remarkable hotel; though, with respect to the curious painting and statuary that every where abound in that metropolis, he was more ignorant than the domestic that attends for a livre a day.

In short, Mr. Jolter could give a very good account of the stages on the road, and save the expence of Antonini's detail of the curiosities in Paris;[1] he was a connoisseur in ordinaries, from twelve to five and thirty livres, knew all the rates of a Fiacre and Remise, could dispute with a Tailleur or Traiteur upon the articles of his bill, and scold the servants in tolerable French. But the laws, customs and genius of the people, the characters of individuals, and scenes of polished life, were subjects which he had neither opportunities to observe, inclination to consider, or discernment to distinguish. All his maxims were the suggestions of pedantry and prejudice; so that his perception was obscured, his judgment biassed, his address aukward, and his conversation absurd and unentertaining: yet such as I have represented this tutor, is the greatest part of those animals who lead raw boys about the world, under the denomination of travelling governors. Peregrine, therefore, being perfectly well acquainted with the extent of Mr. Jolter's abilities, never dreamt of consulting him in the disposition of his conduct, but parcelled out his time according to the dictates of his own reflection, and the information and direction of his companions, who had lived longer in France, and consequently were better acquainted with the pleasures of the place.

As soon as he was in a condition to appear a la Françoise, he hired a genteel chariot by the month, made the tour of the Luxembourg gallery, Palais Royal, all the remarkable hotels, churches and celebrated places in Paris; visited St. Cloud, Marli, Versailles, Trianon, St. Germain, and Fountainbleau;[2] enjoyed the opera, masquerades, Italian and French comedy; and seldom failed of appearing in the public walks, in hopes of meeting with Mrs. Hornbeck, or some adventure suited to his romantic disposition. He never doubted that his person would attract the notice of some distinguished inamorata, and was vain enough to believe that few female hearts were able to resist the artillery of his accomplishments, if once he had an opportunity of planting it to advantage. He presented himself, however, at all the *Spectacles* for many weeks, without reaping the fruits of his expectation; and began to entertain a very indifferent idea of the French discernment, which had overlooked him so long, when one day in his way to the opera, his chariot was stopped by an *embarras* in the street, occasioned by two peasants, who having driven their carts against each other, quarrelled, and went to loggerheads on the spot. Such a rencounter is so uncommon in France, that the people shut up their shops, and from their windows threw cold water upon the combatants, with a view of putting an end to the battle, which was maintained with great fury and very little skill, until one of them receiving an accidental fall, the other took the advantage of this misfortune, and fastening upon him as he lay, began to thump the pavement with his head. Our hero's equipage being detained close by the field of this contention, Pipes could not bear to see the laws of boxing so scandalously transgressed, and leaping from his station, pulled the offender from his antagonist, whom he raised up, and in the English language, encouraged to a second essay, instructing him at the same time, by clenching his fists according to art, and putting himself in a proper attitude. Thus confirmed, the enraged carman sprung upon his foe, and in all appearance would have effectually revenged the injury he had sustained, if he had not been prevented by the interposition of a lacquey belonging to a nobleman, whose coach was obliged to halt in consequence of the dispute. This footman, who was distinguished by a cane, descending from his post, without the least ceremony or expostulation, began to employ his weapon upon the head and shoulders of the peasant who had been patronized by Pipes; upon which Thomas, resenting such ungenerous behaviour, bestowed such a stomacher upon the officious intermeddler, as discomposed the whole œconomy of his entrails, and obliged him to discharge the interjection 'ah!' with demonstrations of great anguish and amazement. The other two footmen who stood behind the coach, seeing their fellow-servant so insolently assaulted, flew to his assistance, and rained a most disagreeable shower upon the head of his aggressor, who had no means of diversion or defence. Peregrine, though he did not approve of Tom's conduct, could not bear to see him so roughly handled, especially as he thought his own honour concerned in the fray, and therefore quitting his machine, came to the rescue of his attendant, and charged his adversaries sword in hand. Two of them no sooner perceived this reinforcement, than they betook themselves to flight; and Pipes having twisted the cane out of the hands of the third, belaboured him so unmercifully, that our hero thought proper to interpose his authority in his behalf. The common people stood aghast at this unprecedented boldness of Pickle, who understanding that the person whose servants he had disciplined, was a general and prince of the blood, went up to the coach, and asked pardon for what he had done, imputing his own behaviour to his ignorance of the other's quality. The old nobleman accepted of his apology with great politeness, thanking him for the trouble he had taken to reform the manners of his domesticks; and guessing from our youth's appearance that he was some stranger of condition, very courteously invited him into the coach, on the supposition that they were both bound for the opera. Pickle gladly embraced this opportunity of becoming acquainted with a person of such rank, and ordering his own chariot to follow, accompanied the count to his *loge*, where he conversed with him during the whole entertainment.

He soon perceived that Peregrine was not deficient in spirit or sense, and seemed particularly pleased with his engaging manner and easy deportment, qualifications for which the English nation is by no means remarkable in France, and therefore the more conspicuous and agreeable in the character of our hero, whom the nobleman carried home that same evening, and introduced to his lady, and several persons of fashion who supped at his house. Peregrine was quite captivated by their affable behaviour and the vivacity of their discourse; and after having been honoured with particular marks of consideration, took his leave, fully determined to cultivate such a valuable acquaintance.

His vanity suggested, that now the time was come when he should profit by his talents among the fair sex, on whom he resolved to employ his utmost art and address. With this view he assiduously engaged in all parties to which he had access, by means of his noble friend, who let slip no opportunity of gratifying his ambition. He for some time shared in all his amusements, and was entertained in many of the best families of France; but he did not long enjoy that elevation of hope which had flattered his imagination. He soon perceived that it would be impossible to maintain the honourable connexions he had made, without engaging every day at quadrille, or in other words, losing his money; for every person of rank, whether male or female, was a professed gamester, who knew and practised all the finesse of the art, of which he was intirely ignorant. Besides, he began to find himself a meer novice in French gallantry, which is supported by an amazing volubility of tongue, an obsequious and incredible attention to trifles, a surprising faculty of laughing out of pure complaisance, and a nothingness of conversation, which he could never attain. In short, our hero, who among his own countrymen would have passed for a sprightly entertaining fellow, was considered in the brilliant assemblies of France as a youth of a very phlegmatic disposition. No wonder then that his pride was mortified at his own want of importance, which he did not fail to ascribe to their defect in point of judgment and taste: he conceived a disgust at the mercenary conduct, as well as the shallow intellects of the ladies; and after he had spent some months, and a round sum of money, in fruitless attendance and addresses, he fairly quitted the pursuit, and consoled himself with the conversation of a merry *Fille de joye*, whose good graces he acquired by an allowance of twenty Louis per month; and that he might the more easily afford this expence, dismissed his chariot and French lacquey at the same time.

He then entered himself in a noted academy, in order to finish his exercises, and contracted an acquaintance with a few sensible people, whom he distinguished at the coffee-house and ordinary to which he resorted, and who contributed not a little to the improvement of his knowledge and taste; for, prejudice apart, it must be owned that France abounds with men of consummate honour, profound sagacity, and the most liberal education. From the conversation of such, he obtained a distinct idea of their government and constitution; and though he could not help admiring the excellent order and œconomy of their police, the result of all his inquiries was self-congratulation on his title to the privileges of a British subject. Indeed this invaluable birthright was rendered conspicuous by such flagrant occurrences, which fell every day almost under his observation, that nothing but the grossest prejudice could dispute its existence.

CHAPTER XLIV

*Acquires a distinct Idea of the French Government ;
quarrels with a Mousquetaire, whom he afterwards fights
and vanquishes, after having punished him for
interfering in his amorous Recreations*

AMONG many other instances of the same nature, I believe it will not be amiss to exhibit a few specimens of their administration, which happened during his abode at Paris, that those who have not the opportunity of observing for themselves, or are in danger of being influenced by misrepresentation, may compare their own condition with that of their neighbours, and do justice to the constitution under which they live.

A lady of distinguished character having been lampooned by some obscure scribler, who could not be discovered, the ministry, in consequence of her complaint, ordered no fewer than five and twenty abbés to be apprehended and sent to the Bastile, on the maxim of Herod, when he commanded the innocents to be murdered, hoping that the principal object of his cruelty would not escape in the general calamity; and the friends of those unhappy prisoners durst not even complain of the unjust persecution, but shrugged up their shoulders, and in silence deplored their misfortune, uncertain whether or not they should ever set eyes on them again.

About the same time, a gentleman of family, who had been oppressed by a certain powerful duke that lived in the neighbourhood, found means to be introduced to the king, who receiving his petition very graciously, asked in what regiment he served; and when the memorialist answered, that he had not the honour of being in the service, returned the paper unopened, and refused to hear one circumstance of his complaint; so that, far from being redressed, he remained more than ever exposed to the tyranny of his oppressors: nay, so notorious is the discouragement of all those who presume to live independent of court-favour and connexions, that one of the gentlemen, whose friendship Peregrine cultivated, frankly owned he was in possession of a most romantic place in one of the provinces, and deeply enamoured of a country life; and yet he durst not reside upon his own estate, lest by slackening in his attendance upon the great, who honoured him with their protection, he should fall a prey to some rapacious intendant.

As for the common people, they are so much inured to the scourge and insolence of power, that every shabby subaltern, every beggarly cadet of the noblesse, every low retainer to the court, insults and injures them with impunity. A certain Ecuyer,[1] or horse-dealer, belonging to the king, being one day under the hands of a barber, who by accident cut the head of a pimple on his face, he started up, and drawing his sword, wounded him desperately in the shoulder. The poor tradesman, hurt as he was, made an effort to retire, and was followed by this barbarous assassin, who not contented with the vengeance he had taken, plunged his sword a second time into his body, and killed him on the spot. Having performed this inhuman exploit, he dressed himself with great deliberation, and going to Versailles, immediately obtained a pardon for what he had done; triumphing in his brutality with such insolence, that the very next time he had occasion to be shaved, he sat with his sword ready drawn, in order to repeat the murder, in case the barber should commit the same mistake. Yet so tamed are those poor people to subjection, that when Peregrine mentioned this assassination to his own trimmer, with expressions of horror and detestation, the infatuated wretch replied, that without all doubt it was a misfortune, but it proceeded from the gentleman's passion; and observed, by way of encomium on the government, that such vivacity is never punished in France.

A few days after this outrage was committed, our youth, who was a professed enemy to all oppression, being in one of the first loges at the comedy, was eye-witness of an adventure which filled him with indignation: a tall, ferocious fellow in the parterre, without the least provocation, but prompted by the meer wantonness of pride, took hold of the hat of a very decent young man who happened to stand before him, and twirled it round upon his head. The party thus offended turned to his aggressor, and civilly asked the reason of such treatment; but he received no answer; and when he looked the other way, the insult was repeated: upon which he expressed his resentment as became a man of spirit, and desired the offender to walk out with him. No sooner did he thus signify his intention, than his adversary, swelling with rage, cocked his hat fiercely in his face, and fixing his hands in his sides, pronounced with the most imperious tone, 'Heark ye, Mr. Round Periwig, you must know that I am a mousquetaire.' Scarce had this awful word escaped from his lips, when the blood forsook the lips of the poor challenger, who with the most abject submission begged pardon for his presumption, and with difficulty obtained it, on condition that he should immediately quit the place. Having thus exercised his authority, he turned to one of his companions, and with an air of disdainful ridicule, told him he was like to have had an affair with a Bourgeois; adding, by way of heightening the irony, 'Egad! I believe he's a physician.'

Our hero was so much shocked and irritated at this licentious behaviour, that he could not suppress his resentment, which he manifested, by saying to this Hector, 'Sir, a physician may be a man of honour.' To this remonstrance, which was delivered with a very significant countenance, the mousquetaire made no other reply, but that of ecchoing his assertion with a loud laugh, in which he was joined by his confederates; and Peregrine glowing with resentment, called him a *Fanfaron*, and withdrew, in expectation of being followed into the street. The other understood the hint, and a rencounter must have ensued, had not the officer of the guard, who overheard what passed, prevented their meeting, by putting the mousquetaire immediately under arrest. Our young gentleman waited at the door of the parterre, until he was informed of this interposition, and then went home very much chagrined at his disappointment; for he was an utter stranger to fear and diffidence on these occasions, and had set his heart upon chastising the insolence of this bully, who had treated him with such disrespect.

This adventure was not so private but that it reached the ears of Mr. Jolter, by the canal of some English gentlemen who were present when it happened; and the governor, who entertained a most dreadful idea of the mousquetaires, being alarmed at a quarrel, the consequence of which might be fatal to his charge, waited on the British embassador, and begged he would take Peregrine under his immediate protection. His excellency having heard the circumstances of the dispute, sent one of his gentlemen to invite the youth to dinner; and after having assured him that he might depend upon his countenance and regard, represented the rashness and impetuosity of his conduct so much to his conviction, that he promised to act more circumspectly for the future, and drop all thoughts of the mousquetaire from that moment.

A few days after he had taken this laudable resolution, Pipes, who had carried a billet to his mistress, informed him, that he had perceived a laced hat lying upon a marble slab in her apartment; and that when she came out of her own chamber to receive the letter, she appeared in manifest disorder.

From these hints of intelligence, our young gentleman suspected, or rather made no doubt of her infidelity; and being by this time well nigh cloyed with possession, was not sorry to find that she had given him cause to renounce her correspondence. That he might therefore detect her in the very breach of duty, and at the same time punish the gallant who had the presumption to invade his territories, he concerted with himself a plan, which was executed in this manner: During his next interview with his Dulcinea, far from discovering the least sign of jealousy or discontent, he affected the appearance of extraordinary fondness; and after having spent the afternoon with the shew of uncommon satisfaction, told her he was engaged in a party for Fountainbleau, and would set out from Paris that same evening; so that he should not have the pleasure of seeing her again for some days.

The lady, who was very well versed in the arts of her occupation, pretended to receive this piece of news with great affliction, and conjured him with such marks of real tenderness, to return as soon as possible to her longing arms, that he went away almost convinced of her sincerity. Determined, however, to prosecute his scheme, he actually departed from Paris with two or three gentlemen of his acquaintance, who had hired a Remise for a jaunt to Versailles; and having accompanied them as far as the village of Passé, returned in the dusk of the evening on foot.

He waited impatiently till midnight, and then arming himself with a pair of pocket-pistols, and attended by trusty Tom with a cudgel in his hand, repaired to the lodgings of his suspected inamorata; and having given Pipes his cue, knocked gently at the door, which was no sooner opened by the lacquey than he bolted in, before the fellow could recollect himself from the confusion occasioned by his unexpected appearance; and leaving Tom to guard the door, ordered the trembling valet to light him up stairs into his lady's apartment. The first object that presented itself to his view, when he entered the anti-chamber, was a sword upon the table, which he immediately seized, exclaiming in a loud and menacing voice, that his mistress was false, and then in bed with another gallant, whom he would instantly put to death. This declaration, confirmed by many terrible oaths, he calculated for the hearing of his rival, who understanding his sanguinary purpose, started up in great trepidation, and naked as he was, dropt from the balcony into the street, while Peregrine thundered at the door for admittance; and guessing his design, gave him an opportunity of making this precipitate retreat. Pipes, who stood centinel at the door, observing the fugitive descend, attacked him with his cudgel, and sweating him from one end of the street to the other, at last committed him to the guet, by whom he was conveyed to the officer on duty in a most disgraceful and deplorable condition.

Mean while, Peregrine having burst open the chamber-door, found the lady in the utmost dread and consternation, and the spoils of her favourite scattered about the room: but his resentment was doubly gratified, when he learnt upon inquiry, that the person who had been so disagreeably interrupted, was no other than that individual mousquetaire with whom he had quarreled at the comedy. He upbraided the nymph with her perfidy and ingratitude, and telling her that she must not expect the continuance of his regard, or the appointments which she had hitherto enjoyed from his bounty, went home to his own lodgings, overjoyed at the issue of the adventure.

The soldier, exasperated at the disgrace he had undergone, as well as at the outragious insult of the English valet, whom he believed his master had tutored for that purpose, no sooner extricated himself from the opprobrious situation he had incurred, than breathing vengeance against the author of the affront, he came to Peregrine's apartment, and demanded satisfaction upon the ramparts next morning before sun-rise. Our hero assured him, he would not fail to pay his respects to him at the time and place appointed; and foreseeing that he might be prevented from keeping this engagement by the officious care of his governor, who saw the mousquetaire come in, he told Mr. Jolter, that the Frenchman had visited him in consequence of an order he had received from his superiors, to make an apology for his rude behaviour to him in the playhouse, and that they had parted very good friends. This assurance, together with Pickle's tranquil and unconcerned behaviour thro' the day, quieted the terrors which had begun to take possession of his tutor's imagination; so that the youth had an opportunity of giving him the slip at night, when he betook himself to the lodgings of a friend, whom he engaged as his second, and with whom he immediately took the field, in order to avoid the search which Jolter, upon missing him, might set on foot.

This was a necessary precaution; for as he did not appear at supper, and Pipes, who usually attended him in his excursions, could give no account of his motions, the governor was dreadfully alarmed at his absence, and ordered his man to run in quest of his master to all the places which he used to frequent, while he himself went to the commissaire, and communicating his suspicions, was accommodated with a party of the horse-guards, who patroled round all the *environs* of the city, with a view of preventing the rencounter. Pipes might have directed them to the lady, by whose information they could have learnt the name and lodgings of the mousquetaire, who being apprehended, the duel would not have happened; but he did not choose to run the risk of disobliging his master, by intermeddling in the affair, and was, moreover, very desirous that the Frenchman should be humbled; for he never doubted that Peregrine was more than a match for any two men in France. In this confidence, therefore, he sought his master with great diligence, not with a view of disappointing his intention, but in order to attend him to the battle, that he might stand by him, and see justice done.

While this inquiry was carried on, our hero and his companion concealed themselves among some weeds that grew on the edge of the parapet, a few yards from the spot where he had agreed to meet the mousquetaire; and scarce had the morning rendered objects distinguishable, when they perceived their men advancing boldly to the place. Peregrine seeing them approach, sprung forward to the ground, that he might have the glory of anticipating his antagonist; and swords being drawn, all four were engaged in a twinkling. Pickle's eagerness had well nigh cost him his life; for, without minding his footing, he flew directly to his opposite, and stumbling over a stone, was wounded on one side of his head before he could recover his attitude. Far from being dispirited at this check, it served only to animate him the more; being endowed with uncommon agility, he retrieved his posture in a moment, and having parried a second thrust, returned the longe with such incredible speed, that the soldier had not time to resume his guard, but was immediately run through the bend of his right arm; and the sword dropping out of his hand, our hero's victory was compleat.

Having dispatched his own business, and received the acknowledgment of his adversary, who with a look of infinite mortification observed, that his was the fortune of the day, he ran to part the seconds, just as the weapon was twisted out of his companion's hand: upon which he took his place; and, in all likelihood, an obstinate dispute would have ensued, had they not been interrupted by the guard, at sight of whom the two Frenchmen scampered off, while our young gentleman and his friend allowed themselves to be taken prisoners by the detachment which had been sent out for that purpose, and were carried before the magistrate, who having sharply reprimanded them for presuming to act in contempt of the laws, set them at liberty, in consideration of their being strangers, cautioning them at the same time to beware of such exploits for the future.

When Peregrine returned to his own lodgings, Pipes seeing the blood trickling down upon his master's neckcloth and solitaire, gave evident tokens of surprize and concern, not for the consequences of the wound, which he did not suppose dangerous, but for the glory of Old England, which he was afraid had suffered in the engagement; for, he could not help saying, with an air of chagrin, as he followed the youth into his chamber, 'I do suppose as how you gave that lubberly Frenchman as good as he brought.'

CHAPTER XLV

Mr. Jolter threatens to leave him on Account of his Misconduct, which he promises to rectify; but his Resolution is defeated by the Impetuosity of his Passions. He meets accidentally with Mrs. Hornbeck, who elopes with him from her Husband, but is restored by the Interposition of the British Embassador

THOUGH Mr. Jolter was extremely well pleased at the safety of his pupil, he could not forgive him for the terror and anxiety he had undergone on his account; and roundly told him, that notwithstanding the inclination and attachment he had to his person, he would immediately depart for England, if ever he should hear of his being involved in such another adventure; for it could not be expected that he would sacrifice his own quiet, to an unrequited regard for one who seemed determined to keep him in continual uneasiness and apprehension.

To this declaration Pickle made answer, that Mr. Jolter, by this time, ought to be convinced of the attention he had always paid to his ease and satisfaction; since he well knew, that he had ever looked upon him in the light of a friend rather than as a counsellor or tutor, and desired his company in France with a view of promoting his interest, and not for any emolument he could expect from his instruction. This being the case, he was at liberty to consult his own inclinations with regard to going or staying; though he could not help owning himself obliged by the concern he expressed for his safety, and would endeavour, for his own sake, to avoid giving him any cause of disturbance in time to come.

No man was more capable of moralizing upon Peregrine's misconduct than himself; his reflections were extremely just and sagacious, and attended with no other disadvantage, but that of occurring too late. He projected a thousand salutary schemes of deportment, but, like other projectors, he never had interest enough with the ministry of his passions to bring any one of them to bear. He had, in the hey-day of his gallantry, received a letter from his friend Gauntlet, with a kind postscript from his charming Emilia; but it arrived at a very unseasonable juncture, when his imagination was engrossed by conquests that more agreeably flattered his ambition; so that he could not find leisure and

217

inclination, from that day, to honour the correspondence which he himself had sollicited; and his vanity had, by this time, disapproved of the engagement he had contracted in the rawness and inexperience of youth; suggesting, that he was born to make such an important figure in life, as ought to raise his ideas above the consideration of any such middling connections, and fix his attention upon objects of the most sublime attraction. These dictates of ridiculous pride had almost effaced the remembrance of his amiable mistress, or at least so far warped his morals and integrity, that he actually began to conceive hopes of her altogether unworthy of his own character and her deserts.

Mean while, being destitute of a toy for the dalliance of his idle hours, he employed several spies, and almost every day made a tour of the public places in person, with a view of procuring intelligence of Mr. Hornbeck, with whose wife he longed to have another interview; and in this course of expectation had he exercised himself a whole fortnight, when chancing to be at the hospital of the invalids with a gentleman lately arrived from England, he no sooner entered the church than he perceived this lady, attended by her spouse, who at sight of our hero changed colour, and looked another way, in order to discourage any communication between them. But the young man, who was not so easily repulsed, advanced with great assurance to his fellow-traveller, and taking him by the hand, expressed his satisfaction at this unexpected meeting; and kindly upbraiding him for his precipitate retreat from Chantilly, before Hornbeck could make any reply, he went up to his wife, whom he complimented in the same manner, assuring her with some significant glances, he was extremely mortified, that she had put it out of his power to pay his respects to her, on his first arrival at Paris; and then turning to her husband, who thought proper to keep close to him in this conference, begged to know where he could have the honour of waiting upon him; observing at the same time, that he himself lived *a l'academie de Palfrenier*.

Mr. Hornbeck, without making an apology for his elopement on the road, thanked Mr. Pickle for his complaisance in a very cool and disobliging manner; saying, that as he intended to shift his lodgings in a day or two, he could not expect the pleasure of seeing him, until he should be settled, when he would call at the academy, and conduct him to his new habitation.

Pickle, who was not unacquainted with the sentiments of this jealous gentleman, did not put much confidence in his promise, and therefore made divers efforts to enjoy a little private conversation

with his wife; but he was baffled in all his attempts by the indefatigable vigilance of her keeper, and reaped no other immediate
pleasure from this accidental meeting, than that of a kind squeeze
while he handed her into the coach. However, as he had been
witness to some instances of her invention, and was no stranger to
the favourable disposition of her heart, he entertained some faint
hopes of profiting by her understanding, and was not deceived in
his expectation; for the very next forenoon a Savoyard called at
the academy, and put the following billet in his hand:

Coind Sur,

Heaving the playsure of meating with you at the ofspital of anvil-
heads, I take this lubbertea of latin you know, that I lotch at the
hottail de May cong dangle rouy Doghouseten, with two postis at the
gait, naytheir of um vary hole, ware I shall be at the windore, if in
kais you will be so good as to pass that way at sicks a cloak in the
heavening, when Mr. Hornbeck goes to the *Calfhay de Contea*.
Prey for the loaf of Geesus keep this from the nolegs of my hussban,
ells he will make me leed a hell upon urth. Being all from, deer Sur,

                    Your most umbell sarvan wile
                    DEBORAH HORNBECK

Our young gentleman was ravished at the receit of this elegant
epistle, which was directed, *A Monsʳ Monsʳ Pickhell, a la Gad-
damme de Paul Freny*, and did not fail to obey the summons at the
hour of assignation; when the lady, true to her appointment,
beckoned him up stairs, and he had the good fortune to be admitted
unseen.

After the first transports of their mutual joy at meeting, she told
him, that her husband had been very surly and cross ever since the
adventure at Chantilly, which he had not yet digested; that he had
laid severe injunctions upon her to avoid all commerce with Pickle,
and even threatened to shut her up in a convent for life, if ever she
should discover the least inclination to renew that acquaintance;
that she had been cooped up in her chamber since her arrival at
Paris, without being permitted to see the place, or indeed any
company, except that of her landlady, whose language she did not
understand; so that her spirit being broke, and her health impaired,
he was prevailed upon some days ago to indulge her in a few airings,
during which she had seen the gardens of the Luxembourg, the
Thuilleries and Palais Royal, though at those times when there was
no company in the walks; and that it was in one of those excursions

she had the happiness of meeting with him. Finally, she gave him to understand, that rather than continue longer in such confinement with the man whom she could not love, she would instantly give him the slip, and put herself under the protection of her lover.

Rash and unthinking as this declaration might be, the young gentleman was so much of a gallant, that he would not baulk the lady's inclinations, and too infatuated by his passion to foresee the consequences of such a dangerous step; he therefore, without hesitation, embraced the proposal, and the coast being clear, they sallied into the street, where Peregrine calling a Fiacre, ordered the coachman to drive them to a tavern: but knowing it would not be in his power to conceal her from the search of the lieutenant de police, if she should remain within the walls of Paris, he hired a Remise, and carried her that same evening to Villejuif, about four leagues from town, where he stayed with her all night; and having boarded her on a genteel pension, and settled the œconomy of his future visits, returned next day to his own lodgings.

While he thus enjoyed his success, her husband endured the tortures of the damned. When he returned from the coffee-house, and understood that his wife had eloped, without being perceived by any person in the family, he began to rave and foam at the mouth with rage and jealousy, and in the fury of distraction, accused the landlady of being an accomplice in her escape, threatening to complain of her to the commissaire. The woman could not conceive how Mrs. Hornbeck, who she knew was an utter stranger to the French language, and kept no sort of company, could elude the caution of her husband, and find any refuge in a place where she had no acquaintance, and began to suspect the lodger's emotion was no other than an affected passion to conceal his own practices upon his wife, who had perhaps fallen a sacrifice to his jealous disposition. She therefore spared him the trouble of putting his menaces in execution, by going to the magistrate without any further deliberation, and giving an account of what she knew concerning this mysterious affair, with certain insinuations against Hornbeck's character, which she represented as peevish and capricious to the last degree.

While she thus anticipated the purpose of the plaintiff, her information was interrupted by the arrival of the party himself, who exhibited his complaint with such evident marks of perturbation, anger and impatience, that the commissaire could easily perceive that he had no share in the disappearance of his wife; and directed him to the lieutenant de police, whose province it is to take cognizance of such occurrences. This gentleman, who presides over the city of Paris, having heard the particulars of Hornbeck's misfortune, asked if he suspected any individual person as the seducer of his yoke-fellow; and when he mentioned Peregrine as the object of his suspicion, granted a warrant and a detachment of soldiers, to search for and retrieve the fugitive.

The husband conducted them immediately to the academy where our hero lodged, and having rummaged the whole place, to the astonishment of Mr. Jolter, without finding either his wife or the supposed ravisher, accompanied them to all the public houses in the Fauxbourg; which having examined also without success, he returned to the magistrate in a state of despair, and obtained a promise of his making such an effectual inquiry, that in three days he should have an account of her, provided she was alive, and within the walls of Paris.

Our adventurer, who had foreseen all this disturbance, was not at all surprized when his governor told him what had happened; and being conjured to restore the woman to the right owner, with many pathetic remonstrances touching the heinous sin of adultery, the distraction of the unfortunate husband, and the danger of incurring the resentment of an arbitrary government, which, upon application being made, would not fail of espousing the cause of the injured; he denied, with great effrontery, that he had the least concern in the matter, pretended to resent the deportment of Hornbeck, whom he threatened to chastise for his scandalous suspicion, and expressed his displeasure at the credulity of Jolter, who seemed to doubt the veracity of his asseveration.

Notwithstanding this confident behaviour, Jolter could not help entertaining doubts of his sincerity; and visiting the disconsolate swain, begged he would, for the honour of his country, as well as for the sake of his own reputation, discontinue his addresses to the lieutenant de police, and apply to the British Embassador, who by dint of friendly admonitions, would certainly prevail upon Mr. Pickle to do him all the justice in his power, if he was really the author of the injury he had sustained. The governor urged this advice with the appearance of so much sympathy and concern, promising to co-operate with all his influence in his behalf, that Hornbeck embraced the proposal, communicated his purpose to the magistrate, who commended the resolution as the most decent and desirable expedient he could use, and then waited upon his excellency, who readily espoused his cause, and sending for the young gentleman that same evening, read him such a lecture in

private, as extorted a confession of the whole affair; not that he
assailed him with sour and supercilious maxims, or severe rebuke,
because he had penetration enough to discern, that Peregrine's
disposition was impregnable to all such attacks; but he first of all
rallied him upon his intriguing genius, then, in an humorous
manner, described the distraction of the poor cuckold, who he
owned was justly punished for the absurdity of his conduct; and
lastly, upon the supposition, that it would be no great effort in
Pickle to part with such a conquest, especially after it was for some
time possessed, represented the necessity and expediency of
restoring her, not only out of regard to his own character, and that
of his nation, but also with a view to his ease, which would in a little
time be very much invaded by such an incumbrance, that in all
probability would involve him in a thousand difficulties and disgusts. Besides, he assured him, that he was already, by order of the
lieutenant de police, surrounded with spies, who would watch all
his motions, and immediately discover the retreat in which he had
deposited his prize. These arguments, and the frank familiar
manner in which they were delivered, but above all, the last consideration, induced the young gentleman to disclose the whole of
his proceedings to the Embassador, and promise to be governed by
his direction, provided the lady should not suffer for the step she
had taken, but be received by her husband with due reverence and
respect. These stipulations being agreed to, he undertook to produce her in eight and forty hours; and taking coach immediately,
drove to the place of her residence, where he spent a whole day and
a night in convincing her of the impossibility of their enjoying each
other in that manner; and returning to Paris, delivered her into the
hands of the Embassador, who having assured her, that she might
depend upon his friendship and protection, in case she should find
herself aggrieved by the jealous temper of Mr. Hornbeck, restored
her to her legitimate lord, whom he counselled to exempt her from
that restraint which, in all probability, had been the cause of her
elopement, and endeavour to conciliate her affection by tender and
respectful usage.

The husband behaved with great humility and compliance,
protesting that his chief study should be to contrive parties for her
pleasure and satisfaction. But no sooner did he regain possession
of his stray-sheep, than he locked her up more closely than ever;
and after having revolved various schemes for her reformation,
determined to board her in a convent, under the inspection of a
prudent abbess, who should superintend her morals, and recal her

to the paths of virtue, which she had forsaken. With this view he consulted an English priest of his acquaintance, who advised him to settle her in a monastery at Lisle, that she might be as far as possible from the machinations of her lover; and gave him a letter of recommendation to the superior of a certain convent in that place, for which Mr. Hornbeck set out in a few days with his troublesome charge.

CHAPTER XLVI

Peregrine resolves to return to England,
is diverted with the odd Characters of Two of his
Countrymen, with whom he contracts an Acquaintance
in the Apartments of the Palais Royal

IN the mean time, our hero received a letter from his aunt, importing that the commodore was in a very declining way, and longed much to see him at the garison; and at the same time he heard from his sister, who gave him to understand that the young gentleman who had for some time made his addresses to her, was become very pressing in his solicitations; so that she wanted to know in what manner she should answer his repeated intreaties. These two considerations determined the young gentleman to return to his native country, a resolution that was far from being disagreeable to Jolter, who knew that the incumbent on a living which was in the gift of Trunnion, was extremely old, and that it would be his interest to be upon the spot at the said incumbent's decease.

Peregrine, who had resided about fifteen months in France, thought he was now sufficiently qualified for eclipsing most of his cotemporaries in England, and therefore prepared for his departure with infinite alacrity, being moreover inflamed with the most ardent desire of revisiting his friends, and renewing his connections, particularly with Emilia, whose heart, he by this time, thought he was able to reduce on his own terms.

As he proposed to make the tour of Flanders and Holland in his return to England, he resolved to stay in Paris a week or two after his affairs were settled, in hopes of finding some agreeable companion disposed for the same journey, and in order to refresh his memory, made a second circuit round all the places in that capital, where any curious production of art is to be seen. In the course of this second examination he chanced to enter the Palais Royal, just as two gentlemen alighted from a Fiacre at the gate, and all three being admitted at the same time, he soon perceived that the strangers were of his own country. One of them was a young man, in whose air and countenance appeared all the uncouth gravity and supercilious self-conceit of a physician piping hot from his studies,[1] while the other, to whom his companion spoke by the appellation of Mr. Pallet,[2] displayed at first sight a strange composition of levity and assurance. Indeed their characters, dress and address were strongly contrasted; the doctor wore a suit of black, and a huge tye-wig, neither suitable to his own age, nor the fashion of the country where he then lived; whereas the other, though seemingly turned of fifty, strutted in a gay summer dress of the Parisian cut, with a bag to his own grey hair, and a red feather in his hat, which he carried under his arm. As these figures seemed to promise something entertaining, Pickle entered into conversation with them immediately, and soon discovered that the old gentleman was a painter from London, who had stole a fortnight from his occupation, in order to visit the remarkable paintings of France and Flanders; and that the doctor had taken the opportunity of accompanying him in his tour. Being extremely talkative, he not only communicated these particulars to our hero in a very few minutes after their meeting, but also took occasion to whisper in his ear, that his fellow traveller was a man of vast learning, and beyond all doubt, the greatest poet of the age. As for himself, he was under no necessity of making his own elogium; for he soon gave such specimens of his taste and talents, as left Pickle no room to doubt of his capacity.

While they stood considering the pictures in one of the first apartments, which are by no means the most masterly compositions, the Swiss, who sets up for a connoisseur, looking at a certain piece, pronounced the word *magnifique!* with a note of admiration; upon which Mr. Pallet, who was not at all a critick in the French language, replied with great vivacity, '*Manufac*, you mean, and a very indifferent piece of manufacture it is; pray gentleman take notice, there is no keeping in those heads upon the back ground, nor no relief in the principal figure: then you'll observe the shadings are harsh to the last degree; and come a little closer this way— don't you perceive that the fore-shortening of that arm is monstrous —agad, sir! there is an absolute fracture in the limb—doctor, you understand anatomy, don't you think that muscle evidently misplaced? Heark ye, Mr. what d'ye call um, (turning to the attendant) what is the name of the dauber who painted that miserable performance?' The Swiss imagining that he was all this time expressing his satisfaction, sanctioned his supposed commendation, by exclaiming *sans prix*. 'Right, (cried Pallet) I could not recollect his name, though his manner is quite familiar to me. We have a few pieces in England, done by that same sangpree; but there they are in no estimation; we have more taste among us, than to relish the productions of such a miserable gout. Isn't he an ignorant coxcomb, doctor?' The physician ashamed of his companion's blunder, thought it was necessary for the honour of his own character, to take notice of it before the stranger, and therefore answered his question, by repeating this line from Horace,

Mutato nomine, de te fabula narratur.[1]

The painter, who was rather more ignorant of Latin that of French, taking it for granted that this quotation of his friend, conveyed an assent to his opinion, 'Very true, (said he) a most sensible observation! mute aye toe numbing he, (what is't?) Deity, fable honour hate her. It is indeed a most mute benumbing piece; and the fable shews that the painter was very little honoured by the deity.'[2] Peregrine was astonished at this surprising perversion of the words and meaning of a Latin line, which, at first, he could not help thinking was a premeditated joke; but upon second thoughts, he saw no reason to doubt that it was the extemporaneous effect of sheer pertness and ignorance, at which he broke out into an immoderate fit of laughter. Pallet believing that the gentleman's mirth was occasioned by his arch animadversion upon the work of sangpree, underwent the same emotion in a much louder strain, and endeavoured to heighten the jest, by more observations of the same nature, while the doctor confounded at his impudence and want of knowledge, reprimanded him in these words of Homer,

Σίγα, μή τις ἄλλος Ἀχαιῶν τοῦτον ἀκούσῃ μῦθον.[3]

This rebuke, the reader will easily perceive, was not calculated for the meridian of his friend's intellects, but uttered with a view of raising his own character in the opinion of Mr. Pickle, who retorted this parade of learning in three verses from the same author, being part of the speech of Polydamas to Hector, importing that it is impossible for one man to excel in every thing.[4] The self-sufficient physician, who did not expect such a repartee from a youth of Peregrine's appearance, looked upon his reply as a fair challenge, and instantly rehearsed forty or fifty lines of the Iliad in a breath; and observing that the stranger made no effort to match this effusion, interpreted his silence into submission; then, in order to ascertain his victory, insulted him with divers fragments of authors, whom his supposed competitor did not even know by name; while Mr. Pallet stared with admiration at the profound scholarship of his companion. Our young gentleman, far from repining at this superiority, laughed within himself at the ridiculous ambition of the pedantic doctor, who must have been at infinite pains in conning these detached pieces, with a view of retailing them in company for the credit of his genius and knowledge. He rated him in his own mind as a meer index-hunter, who held the eel of science by the tail, and foresaw an infinite fund of diversion in his solemnity and pride, if properly extracted by means of his fellow-traveller's vanity and assurance. Prompted by these considerations, he resolved to cultivate their acquaintance, and, if possible, amuse himself at their expence in his journey through Flanders, understanding that they were determined upon the same route. In this view he treated them with extraordinary attention, and seemed to pay particular deference to the remarks of the painter, who with great intrepidity pronounced judgment upon every picture in the palace, or in other words, exposed his own nakedness, in every sentence that proceeded from his mouth.

When they came to consider the murder of the innocents by Le Brun, the Swiss observed that it was *un beau morçeau*, and Mr. Pallet replied, 'Yes, yes, one may see with half an eye, that it can be the production of no other; for Bomorso's stile, both in colouring and drapery, is altogether peculiar; then his design is tame, and his expression antic and unnatural. Doctor, you have seen my judgment of Solomon, I think I may without presumption—but, I don't choose to make comparisons, I leave that odious task to other people, and let my works speak for themselves. France, to be sure, is rich in the arts, but what is the reason? the king encourages men of genius with honour and rewards: whereas, in England, we are obliged to stand upon our own feet, and combat the envy and malice of our brethren; agad! I have a good mind to come and settle here in Paris; I should like to have an apartment in the Louvre, with a snug pension of so many thousand livres.' In this manner did Pallet proceed with an eternal rotation of tongue, floundering from one mistake to another, until it was the turn of Poussin's seven sacraments to be examined. Here again the Swiss out of the abundance of his zeal, expressed his admiration, by

saying, these pieces were *impayable*; when the painter turning to
him with an air of exultation, 'Pardon me, friend, there you happen
to be mistaken, these are none of *impayable*'s, but done by Nicholas
Pouseen. I have seen prints of them in England, so that none of
your tricks upon travellers, Mr. Swish or Swash, or what's your
name.' He was very much elated by this imaginary triumph of his
understanding, which animated him to persevere in his curious
observations upon all the other pieces of that celebrated collection;
but perceiving that the doctor manifested no signs of pleasure and
satisfaction, but rather beheld them with a silent air of disdain, he
could not digest his indifference, and asked with a waggish sneer, if
ever he had seen such a number of master-pieces before? The
physician eying him with a look of compassion mingled with
contempt, observed that there was nothing there which deserved
the attention of any person acquainted with the ideas of the
ancients; and that the author of the finest piece now in being, was
unworthy to clean the brushes of one of those great masters, who
are celebrated by the Greek and Roman writers. 'O lud! O lud!
(exclaimed the painter, with a loud laugh) you have fairly brought
yourself into a dilemma at last, dear doctor; for it is well known
that your ancient Greek and Roman artists knew nothing at all of
the matter, in comparison with our modern masters; for this good
reason, because they had but three or four colours, and knew not
how to paint with oil: besides, which of all your old fusty Grecians
would you put upon a footing with the divine Raphael, the most
excellent Michael Angelo, Bona Roti, the graceful Guido, the
bewitching Titian, and above all others, the sublime Rubens, the'
————He would have proceeded with a long catalogue of names
which he had got by heart for the purpose, without retaining the
least idea of their several qualifications, had not he been interrupted
by his friend, whose indignation being kindled by the irreverence
with which he mentioned the Greeks; he called him blasphemer,
Goth, Bæotian, and in his turn, asked with great vehemence, which
of those puny moderns could match with Panænus of Athens, and
his brother Phidias, Polycletus of Sicyon, Polygnotus the Thrasian,
Parrhasius of Ephesus, sirnamed Ἀβροδίαιτος,[1] and Apelles the
prince of painters? He challenged him to shew any portrait of these
days that could vye with the Helen of Zeuxis the Heraclean, or any
composition equal to the sacrifice of Iphigenia, by Timanthes the
Sicyonian; not to mention the twelve gods of Asclepiadorus the
Athenian, for which Mnason, tyrant of Elatea, gave him about
three hundred pounds a piece, or Homer's hell by Nicias, who

refused sixty talents, amounting to upwards of eleven thousand pounds, and generously made a present of it to his own country. He desired him to produce a collection equal to that in the temple of Delphos, mentioned in the Ἰῶν of Euripides;[1] where Hercules and his companion Iolaus are represented in the act of killing the Lernæan hydra, with golden sickles Χρυσέαις ἅρπαις, where Bellerophon appears upon his winged steed, vanquishing the fire-breathing chimera τὰν πυριπνέουσαν; and the war of the giants is described. Here Jupiter stands wielding the red hot thunderbolts. Κεραυνὸν ἀμφίπυρον, there Pallas dreadful to the view Γοργωπόν, brandisheth her spear against the huge Enceladus; and Bacchus with slender ivy rods, defeats and slays the γᾶς τέκνον, or mighty son of earth. The painter was astonished and confounded at this rhapsody of names and instances, which was uttered with surprising eagerness and rapidity; suspecting at first that the whole was the creation of his own brain; but when Pickle, with a view of flattering the doctor's self-conceit, espoused his side of the question, and confirmed the truth of every thing he advanced, Mr. Pallet changed his opinion, and in emphatic silence adored the immensity of his friend's understanding. In short, Peregrine easily perceived that they were false enthusiasts, without the smallest pretensions to taste and sensibility; and pretended to be in raptures with they knew not what; the one thinking it was incumbent upon him to express transports on seeing the works of those who had been most eminent in his profession, whether they did or did not really raise his admiration; and the other as a scholar deeming it his duty to magnify the ancients above all competition, with an affected fervour, which the knowledge of their excellencies never inspired. Indeed our young gentleman so successfully accommodated himself to the disposition of each, that long before their review was finished, he was become a particular favourite with both.

From the Palais Royal he accompanied them to the cloisters of the Carthusians, where they considered the history of St. Bruno, by Le Sueur, whose name being utterly unknown to the painter, he gave judgment against the whole composition, as pitiful and paultry; though in the opinion of all good judges, it is a most masterly performance.

Having satisfied their curiosity in this place, Peregrine sollicited them to favour him with their company at dinner; but whether out of caution against the insinuations of one whose character they did not know, or by reason of a prior engagement, they declined his invitation on pretence of having an appointment at a certain ordinary, though they expressed a desire of being farther acquainted with him; and Mr. Pallet took the freedom of asking his name, which he not only declared, but promised, as they were strangers in Paris, to wait upon them next day in the forenoon, in order to conduct them to the hotel de Tholouse, and the houses of several other noblemen, remarkable for painting or curious furniture. They thankfully embraced his proposal, and that same day made inquiry among the English gentlemen, about the character of our hero, which they found so much to their satisfaction, that upon their second meeting, they courted his good graces without reserve; and as they had heard of his intended departure, begged earnestly to have the honour of accompanying him through the Low Countries. He assured them that nothing could be more agreeable to him, than the prospect of having such fellow-travellers; and they immediately appointed a day for setting out on that tour.

CHAPTER XLVII

He introduces his new Friends to Mr. Jolter,
with whom the Doctor enters into a Dispute upon
Government, which had well nigh terminated in open War

MEAN while, he not only made them acquainted with every thing worth seeing in town, but attended them in their excursions to all the king's houses within a day's journey of Paris; and in the course of these parties, treated them with an elegant dinner at his own apartments, where a dispute arose between the doctor and Mr. Jolter, which had well nigh terminated in an irreconcileable animosity. These gentlemen, with an equal share of pride, pedantry and saturnine disposition, were by the accidents of education and company, diametrically opposite in political maxims; the one, as we have already observed, being a bigotted high churchman, and the other a rank republican. It was an article of the governor's creed, that the people could not be happy, nor the earth yield its fruits in abundance, under a restricted clergy and limited government: whereas, in the doctor's opinion, it was an eternal truth, that no constitution was so perfect as the democracy, and that no country could flourish, but under the administration of the mob. These considerations being premised, no wonder that they happened to disagree in the freedom of an unreserved conversation, especially as their entertainer took all opportunities of encouraging and inflaming the contention. The first source of their difference was an unlucky remark of the painter, who observed that the partridge of which he was then eating, had the finest relish of any he had ever tasted. His friend owned that the birds were the best of the kind he had seen in France; but affirmed that they were neither so plump nor delicious as those that were caught in England. The governor considering this observation as the effect of prejudice and inexperience, said with a sarcastical smile, 'I believe, sir, you are very well disposed to find every thing here inferior to the productions of your own country.' 'True, sir, (answered the physician with a certain solemnity of aspect) and not without good reason I hope.' 'And pray, (resumed the tutor) why may not the partridges of France be as good as those of England?' 'For a very plain reason, (replied the other) because they are not so well fed. The iron hand of oppression is extended to all animals within the French dominions, even to the beasts of the field and the fowls of the air. *Kunessin ownoisi te pasi.*'[1] 'Egad! (cried the painter) that is a truth not to be controverted: for my own part, I am none of your tit-bits, one would think, but yet there's a freshness in the English complexion, a *ginseekeye*,[2] I think you call it, so inviting to a hungry Frenchman, that I have caught several in the very act of viewing me with an eye of extreme appetite, as I passed; and as for their curs, or rather their wolves, (for by jingo they are more liker the one than t'other) whenever I set eyes on one of 'em, Aha! your humble servant Mr. son of a bitch, I am upon my guard in an instant. The doctor can testify that their very horses, or more properly their live carrion that drew our chaise, used to reach back their long necks and smell at us, as a couple of delicious morsels.' This sally of Mr. Pallet, which was received with a general laugh of approbation, would, in all probability, have stifled the dispute in embrio, had not Mr. Jolter with a self-applauding simper, ironically complimented the strangers on their talking like true Englishmen. The doctor affronted at the insinuation, told him with some warmth, that he was mistaken in his conjecture, his affections and ideas being confined to no particular country; for he considered himself as a citizen of the world. He owned himself more attached to England than to any other kingdom, but this preference was the effect of reflexion, and not of prejudice; because the British constitution approached nearer than any other, to that perfection of government, the democracy of Athens, which he hoped one day to see revived: he mentioned the death of Charles the first, and the expulsion of his son, with raptures of applause, inveighed with great acrimony against the kingly name; and in order to sanction his opinion, repeated forty or fifty lines from one of the Philippicks of Demosthenes. Jolter hearing him speak so disrespectfully of the higher powers, glowed with indignation. He said his doctrines were detestable and destructive of all right, order and society; that monarchy was of divine institution, therefore indefeasible by any human power; and of consequence those events in the English history, which he had so liberally commended, were no other than flagrant instances of sacrilege, perfidy, and sedition; that the democracy of Athens was a most absurd constitution, productive of anarchy and mischief, which must always happen when the government of a nation depends upon the caprice of the ignorant hare-brained vulgar: that it was in the power of the most profligate member of the common-wealth, provided he was endowed with eloquence, to ruin the most deserving, by a desperate exertion of his talents upon the populace, who had been often persuaded to act in the most ungrateful and imprudent manner, against the greatest patriots that their country had produced: and finally, he averred, that the liberal arts and sciences had never flourished so much in a republick, as under the encouragement and protection of absolute power; witness the Augustan age, and the reign of Lewis the fourteenth: nor was it to be supposed that genius and merit could ever be so amply recompensed by the individuals, or distracted councils of a common-wealth, as by the generosity and magnificence of one, who had the whole treasures at his own command.

Peregrine, who was pleased to find the contest grow warm, observed that there seemed to be a good deal of truth in what Mr. Jolter advanced; and the painter, whose opinion began to waver, looked with a face of expectation at his friend, who modelling his features into an expression of exulting disdain, asked of his antagonist, if he did not think that very power of rewarding merit, enabled an absolute prince to indulge himself in the most arbitrary licence over the lives and fortunes of his people? Before the governor had time to answer this question, Pallet broke forth into an exclamation of 'By the Lord! that is certainly fact, egad! that was a home thrust, doctor.' When Mr. Jolter chastising this shallow intruder with a contempt'ous look, affirmed that though supreme power furnished a good prince with the means of exerting his virtues, it would not support a tyrant in the exercise of cruelty and oppression; because in all nations, the genius of the people must be consulted by their governors, and the burthen proportioned to the shoulders on which it is laid. 'Else, what follows?' said the physician. 'The consequence is plain, (replied the governor) insurrection, revolt, and his own destruction: for it is not to be supposed that the subjects of any nation would be so abject and pusilanimous, as to neglect the means which heaven hath put in their power for their own preservation.' 'Gadzooks! you're in the right, sir, (cried Pallet) that I grant you must be confessed: doctor, I'm afraid we have got into the wrong box.' This son of Pæan, however, far from being of his friend's opinion, observed with an air of triumph, that he would not only demonstrate the sophistry of the gentleman's last allegation, by argument and facts, but even confute him with his own words. Jolter's eyes kindling at this presumptuous declaration, he told his antagonist, while his lip quivered with resentment, that if his arguments were no better than his breeding, he was sure he would make very few converts to his opinion; and the doctor, with all the insolence of triumph, advised him to beware of disputes for the future, until he should have made himself more master of his subject.

Peregrine both wished and hoped to see the disputants proceed to arguments of more weight and conviction; and the painter dreading the same issue, interposed with the usual exclamation of 'For God's sake, gentlemen!' when the governor rose from table in great dudgeon, and left the room, muttering some ejaculation, of which the word 'coxcomb' only could be distinctly heard. The physician being thus left master of the field of battle, was complimented on his victory by Peregrine, and so elevated by his success, that he declaimed a full hour on the absurdity of Jolter's proposition, and the beauty of the democratic administration; canvassed the whole scheme of Plato's republic, with many quotations from that ideal author; touching the $\tau\grave{o}$ $\kappa\alpha\lambda\acute{o}\nu$:[1] from thence he made a transition to the moral sense of Shaftsbury,[2] and concluded his harangue with the greatest part of that frothy writer's rhapsody, which he repeated with all the violence of enthusiastic agitation; to the unspeakable satisfaction of his entertainer, and the unutterable admiration of Pallet, who looked upon him as something supernatural and divine. So intoxicated was this vain young man with the ironical praises of Pickle, that he forthwith shook off all reserve, and having professed a friendship for our hero, whose taste and learning he did not fail to extol, intimated in plain terms, that he was the only person in these latter ages, who professed that sublime genius, that portion of the divinity or $\tau\iota$ $\theta\epsilon\hat{\iota}o\nu$,[3] which immortalized the Grecian poets; that as Pythagoras affirmed the spirit of Euphorbus had transmigrated into his body, he, the doctor, was strangely possessed with the opinion that he himself was inspired by the soul of Pindar; because, making allowance for the difference of languages, in which they wrote, there was a surprising affinity between his own works and those of that celebrated Theban; and as a confirmation of this truth, he immediately produced a sample of each, which though in spirit and versification, as different as the Odes of Horace and our present laureat,[1] Peregrine did not scruple to pronounce altogether congenial; notwithstanding the violence he by this sentence offered to his own conscience, and a certain alarm of his pride, that was weak enough to be disturbed by the physician's ridiculous vanity and presumption, which not contented with displaying his importance in the world of taste and polite literature, manifested itself in arrogating certain material discoveries in the province of physick, which could not fail to advance him to the highest pinnacle of that profession, considering the recommendation of his other talents, together with a liberal fortune which he inherited from his father.

CHAPTER XLVIII

The Doctor prepares an Entertainment
in the Manner of the Ancients,[2] which is
attended with divers ridiculous Circumstances

IN a word, our young gentleman, by his insinuating behaviour, obtained the full confidence of the doctor, who invited him to an entertainment, which he intended to prepare in the manner of the ancients. Pickle, struck with this idea, eagerly embraced the proposal, which he honoured with many encomiums, as a plan in all respects worthy of his genius and apprehension; and the day was appointed at some distance of time, that the treater might have leisure to compose certain pickles and confections which were not to be found among the culinary preparations of these degenerate days.

With a view of rendering the physician's taste more conspicuous, and extracting from it the more diversion, Peregrine proposed that some foreigners should partake of the banquet; and the task being left to his care and discretion, he actually bespoke the company of a French marquis, an Italian count and a German baron, whom he knew to be egregious coxcombs, and therefore more likely to enhance the joy of the entertainment.

Accordingly, the hour being arrived, he conducted them to the hotel where the physician lodged, after having regaled their expectations with an elegant meal in the genuine old Roman taste; and they were received by Mr. Pallet, who did the honours of the house, while his friend superintended the rotisseur below. By this communicative painter, the guests understood that the doctor had met with numerous difficulties in the execution of his design; that no fewer than five cooks had been dismissed, because they could not prevail upon their own consciences to obey his directions in things that were contrary to the present practice of their art; and that although he had at last engaged a person, by an extraordinary premium, to comply with his orders, the fellow was so astonished, mortified and incensed at the commands he had received, that his hair stood on end, and he begged on his knees, to be released from the agreement he had made: but finding that his employer insisted upon the performance of his contract, and threatened to introduce him to the commissaire, if he should flinch from the bargain, he had, in the discharge of his office, wept, sung, cursed and capered for two whole hours without intermission; so that his brain seemed to have received a rude shock, and, in all probability, he would never be his own man again.[1]

While the company listened to this odd information, by which they were prepossessed with strange notions of the dinner, their ears were invaded by a piteous voice that exclaimed in French, 'For the love of God! dear Sir! for the passion of Jesus Christ! spare me the mortification of the honey and oil!' But this pathetic supplication having no effect upon the physician, who in all likelihood poured in, with his own hand, the sauce against which the cook had objected, the same voice was heard to utter a sort of yell, which was followed by a string of execrations in the French language, that gradually died away, as if the swearer had been forcibly conveyed into a more distant apartment.[2] Their ears still vibrated with the sound, when the doctor entering, was by Peregrine made acquainted with the strangers, to whom he, in the transports of his wrath, could not help of complaining of the want of complaisance he had found in the Parisian vulgar, by which his plan had been almost entirely ruined and set aside. The French marquis, who thought the honour of his nation was concerned at this declaration, professed his sorrow for what had happened, so contrary to the established character of the people, and undertook to see the delinquents severely punished, provided he could be informed of their names or places of abode. The mutual compliments that passed on this occasion were scarce finished, when a servant coming into the room, announced dinner; and the entertainer led the way into another apartment, where they found a long table, or rather two boards joined together, and furnished with a variety of dishes, the steams of which had such evident effect upon the nerves of the company, that the marquis made frightful grimaces, under pretence of taking snuff; the Italian's eyes watered, the German's visage underwent violent distortion of features; our hero found means to exclude the odour from his sense of smelling, by breathing only through his mouth; and the poor painter running into another room, plugged his nostrils with tobacco. The doctor himself, who was the only person then present whose organs were not discomposed, pointing to a couple of couches placed on each side of the table, told his guests, that he was sorry he could not procure the exact *triclinia*[1] of the ancients, which were somewhat different from these conveniences, and desired they would have the goodness to repose themselves without ceremony, each in his respective couchette, while he and his friend Mr. Pallet would place themselves upright at the ends, that they might have the pleasure of serving those that lay along. This disposition, of which the strangers had no previous idea, disconcerted and perplexed them in a most ridiculous manner; the marquis and baron stood bowing to each other, on pretence of disputing the lower seat, but in reality with a view of profiting by the example of one another, for neither of them understood the manner in which they were to loll; and Peregrine, who enjoyed their confusion, handed the count to the other side, where, with the most mischievous politeness, he insisted upon his taking possession of the upper place.

In this disagreeable and ludicrous suspence they continued acting a pantomime of gesticulations, until the doctor earnestly intreated them to wave all compliment and form, lest the dinner should be spoiled before the ceremonial could be adjusted. Thus conjured, Peregrine took the lower couch on the left-hand side, laying himself gently down, with his face towards the table. The marquis, in imitation of this pattern (though he would have much rather fasted three days than run the risk of discomposing his dress by such an attitude) stretched himself upon the opposite place, reclining upon his elbow in a most painful and aukward situation, with his head raised above the end of the couch, that the œconomy of his hair might not suffer by the projection of his body. The Italian being a thin, limber creature, planted himself next to Pickle, without sustaining any misfortune, but that of his stocking being torn by a ragged nail of the seat as he raised his legs on a level with the rest of his limbs. But the baron, who was neither so wieldy nor supple in his joints as his companions, flounced himself down with such precipitation, that his feet suddenly tilting up, came in furious contact with the head of the marquis, and demolished every curl in a twinkling, while his own skull, at the same instant, descended upon the side of his couch with such violence, that his periwig was struck off, and the whole room filled with pulvilio.[1]

The drollery of distress that attended this disaster entirely vanquished the affected gravity of our young gentleman, who was obliged to suppress his laughter by cramming his handkerchief in his mouth; for the bare-headed German asked pardon with such ridiculous confusion, and the marquis admitted his apology with such rueful complaisance, as were sufficient to awake the mirth of a quietist, whose insensibility was not utterly extinguished.

This misfortune being repaired as well as the circumstances of the occasion would permit, and every one settled according to the arrangement already described, the doctor graciously undertook to give some account of the dishes as they occurred, that the company might be directed in their choice; and with an air of infinite satisfaction thus began: 'This here, gentlemen, is a boiled goose, served up in a sauce composed of pepper, lovage, coriander, mint, rue, anchovies and oil; I wish for your sakes, gentlemen, it was one of the geese of Ferrara, so much celebrated among the ancients for the magnitude of their livers, one of which is said to have weighed upwards of two pounds: with this food, exquisite as it was, did the tyrant Heliogabalus[2] regale his hounds. But I beg pardon, I had almost forgot the soup, which I hear is so necessary an article at all tables in France. At each end there are dishes of the salacacabia of the Romans, one is made of parsley, pennyroyal, cheese, pinetops, honey, vinegar, brine, eggs, cucumbers, onions and hen-livers; the other is much the same as the soup-maigre of this country. Then there is a loin of veal boiled with fennel and caraway-seed, on a pottage composed of pickle, oil, honey and flour, and a curious hachis of the lights, liver and blood of an hare, together with a dish of roasted pigeons. Monsieur le baron, shall I help you to a plate of this soup?' The German, who did not at all disapprove of the ingredients, assented to the proposal, and seemed to relish the composition; while the marquis, being asked by the painter which of the sillykickabys he chose, was in consequence of his desire accommodated with a portion of the soup maigre; and the count, in lieu of spoon-meat, of which he said he was no great admirer, supplied himself with a pigeon, therein conforming to the choice of our young gentleman, whose example he determined to follow through the whole course of the entertainment.

The Frenchman having swallowed the first spoonful, made a full pause, his throat swelled, as if an egg had stuck in his gullet, his eyes rolled, and his mouth underwent a series of involuntary contractions and dilatations. Pallet, who looked stedfastly at this connoisseur, with a view of consulting his taste, before he himself would venture upon the soup, began to be disturbed at these emotions, and observed with some concern, that the poor gentleman seemed to be going into a fit; when Peregrine assured him that these were symptoms of extasy, and for further confirmation, asked the marquis how he found the soup. It was with infinite difficulty that his complaisance could so far master his disgust, as to enable him to answer, 'Altogether excellent, upon my honour!' And the painter being certified of his approbation, lifted the spoon to his mouth without scruple; but, far from justifying the elogium of his taster, when this precious composition diffused itself upon his palate, he seemed to be deprived of all sense and motion, and sat like the leaden statue of some river god, with the liquor flowing out at both sides of his mouth.

The doctor, alarmed at this indecent phænomenon, earnestly inquired into the cause of it; and when Pallet recovered his recollection, and swore that he would rather swallow porridge made of burning brimstone, than such an infernal mess as that which he had tasted, the physician, in his own vindication, assured the company, that, except the usual ingredients, he had mixed nothing in the soup but some sal armoniac instead of the ancient nitrum, which could not now be procured; and appealed to the marquis, whether such a succedaneum was not an improvement on the whole. The unfortunate petit maitre, driven to the extremity of his condescension, acknowledged it to be a masterly refinement; and deeming himself obliged, in point of honour, to evince his sentiments by his practice, forced a few more mouthfuls of this disagreeable potion down his throat, till his stomach was so much offended, that he was compelled to start up of a sudden, and in the hurry of his elevation overturned his plate into the bosom of the baron. The emergency of his occasions would not permit him to stay and make apologies for this abrupt behaviour, so that he flew into another apartment, where Pickle found him puking, and crossing himself with great devotion; and a chair, at his desire, being brought to the door, he slipt into it more dead than alive, conjuring his friend Pickle to make his peace with the company, and in particular excuse him to the baron, on account of the violent fit of illness with which he had been seized. It was not without reason that he employed a mediator; for when our hero returned to the dining-room, the German got up, and was under the hands of his own lacquey, who wiped the grease from a rich embroidered waistcoat, while he, almost frantic with his misfortune, stamped upon the ground, and in High Dutch cursed the unlucky banquet, and the impertinent entertainer, who all this time, with great deliberation, consoled him for the disaster, by assuring him, that the damage might be repaired with some oil of turpentine and an hot iron. Peregrine, who could scarce refrain from laughing in his face, appeased his indignation, by telling him how much the whole company, and especially the marquis, was mortified at the accident; and the unhappy salacacabia being removed, the places were filled with two pies, one of dormice liquored with syrup of white poppies, which the doctor had substituted in the room of toasted poppy-seed, formerly eaten with honey, as a desert; and the other composed of an hock of pork baked in honey.

Pallet hearing the first of these dishes described, lifted up his hands and eyes, and with signs of loathing and amazement pronounced, 'A pye made of dormice and syrup of poppies; Christ in heaven! what beastly fellows these Romans were!' His friend checked him for his irreverent exclamation with a severe look, and recommended the veal, of which he himself chearfully ate, with such encomiums to the company, that the baron resolved to imitate his example, after having called for a bumper of Burgundy, which the physician, for his sake, wished to have been the true wine of Falernum. The painter seeing nothing else upon the table which he would venture to touch, made a merit of necessity, and had recourse to the veal also; although he could not help saying, that he would not give one slice of the roast beef of old England for all the dainties of a Roman emperor's table. But all the doctor's invitations and assurances could not prevail upon his guests to honour the hachis and the goose; and that course was succeeded by another, in which he told them were divers of those dishes, which among the antients had obtained the appellation of *politeles*, or magnificent. 'That which smoaks in the middle (said he) is a sow's stomach, filled with a composition of minced pork, hog's brains, eggs, pepper, cloves, garlick, anniseed, rue, ginger, oil, wine and pickle. On the right hand side are the teats and belly of a sow, just farrowed, fried with sweet wine, oil, flour, lovage and pepper. On the left is a fricassee of snails, fed, or rather purged with milk. At that end next Mr. Pallet are fritters of pompions, lovage, origanum and oil; and here are a couple of pullets, roasted and stuffed in the manner of Apicius.'[1]

The painter, who had by wry faces, testify'd his abhorrence of the sow's stomach, which he compared to a bagpipe, and the snails which had undergone purgation, no sooner heard him mention the roasted pullets, than he eagerly sollicited a wing of the fowl; upon which the doctor desired he would take the trouble of cutting them up, and accordingly sent them round, while Mr. Pallet tucked the table-cloth under his chin, and brandished his knife and fork with singular address: but scarce were they set down before him, when the tears ran down his cheeks, and he called aloud, in manifest disorder, 'Z—ds! this is the essence of a whole bed of garlic!' That he might not, however, disappoint or disgrace the entertainer, he applied his instruments to one of the birds, and when he opened up the cavity, was assaulted by such an irruption of intolerable smells, that without staying to disengage himself from the cloth, he sprung away, with an exclamation of, 'Lord Jesus!' and involved the whole table in havock, ruin and confusion.

Before Pickle could accomplish his escape, he was sauced with the syrup of the dormouse pye, which went to pieces in the general wreck; and as for the Italian count, he was overwhelmed by the sow's stomach, which bursting in the fall, discharged its contents upon his leg and thigh, and scalded him so miserably, that he shrieked with anguish, and grinned with a most ghastly and horrible aspect.

The baron, who sat secure without the vortex of this tumult, was not at all displeased at seeing his companions involved in such a calamity as that which he had already shared; but the doctor was confounded with shame and vexation. After having prescribed an application of oil to the count's leg, he expressed his sorrow for the misadventure, which he openly ascribed to want of taste and prudence in the painter, who did not think proper to return, and make an apology in person; and protested, that there was nothing in the fowls which could give offence to a sensible nose, the stuffing being a mixture of pepper, lovage and assa fœtida, and the sauce consisting of wine and herring-pickle, which he had used instead of the celebrated garum of the Romans; that famous pickle having been prepared sometimes of the scombri, which were a sort of tunny fish, and sometimes of the silurus, or shad-fish: nay, he observed that there was a third kind, called garum hæmation, made of the guts, gills and blood of the thynnus.

The physician, finding it would be impracticable to re-establish the order of the banquet, by presenting again the dishes which had been discomposed, ordered every thing to be removed, a clean cloth to be laid, and the desert to be brought in.

Mean while, he regretted his incapacity to give them a specimen of the alieus, or fish meals of the ancients, such as the jus diabaton, the conger-eel, which in Galen's opinion is hard of digestion, the cornuta, or gurnard, described by Pliny in his Natural History, who says, the horns of many of them were a foot and a half in length; the mullet and lamprey, that were in the highest estimation of old, of which last Julius Cæsar borrowed six thousand for one triumphal supper. He observed, that the manner of dressing them was described by Horace, in the account he gives of the entertainment to which Mæcenas was invited by the epicure Nasiedenus:

Affertur squillas inter Murena natantes, &c.[1]

And told them, that they were commonly eaten with the rhus syriacum, a certain anodyne and astringent seed, which qualified the purgative nature of the fish. Finally, this learned physician gave them to understand, that though this was reckoned a luxurious dish in the zenith of the Roman taste, it was by no means comparable, in point of expence, to some preparations in vogue about the time of that absurd voluptuary Heliogabalus, who ordered the brains of six hundred ostriches to be compounded in one mess.

By this time the desert appeared, and the company were not a little rejoiced to see plain olives in salt and water: but what the master of the feast valued himself upon, was a sort of jelly, which he affirmed to be preferable to the hypotrimma of Hesychius,[2] being a mixture of vinegar, pickle and honey, boiled to a proper consistence, and candied assa fœtida, which he asserted, in contradiction to Humelbergius and Lister,[3] was no other than the laser syriacum, so precious, as to be sold among the ancients to the weight of a silver penny. The gentlemen took his word for the excellency of this gum, but contented themselves with the olives, which gave such an agreeable relish to the wine, that they seemed very well disposed to console themselves for the disgraces they had endured; and Pickle, unwilling to lose the least circumstance of entertainment that could be enjoyed in their company, went in quest of the painter, who remained in his penitentials in another apartment, and could not be persuaded to re-enter the banqueting-room, until Peregrine undertook to procure his pardon from those whom he had injured. Having assured him of this indulgence, our young gentleman led him in like a criminal, bowing on all hands with an air of humility and contrition; and particularly addressing himself to the count, to whom he swore in English, as God was his saviour, he had no intent to affront man, woman, or child; but was fain to make the best of his way, that he might not give the honourable company cause of offence, by obeying the dictates of nature in their presence.

When Pickle interpreted this apology to the Italian, Pallet was forgiven in very polite terms, and even received into favour by his friend the doctor, in consequence of our hero's intercession: so that all the guests forgot their chagrin, and paid their respects so piously to the bottle, that in a short time the Champaigne produced very evident effects in the behaviour of all present.

CHAPTER XLIX

The Italian Marquis and German Baron are
disgraced ; the Painter is persuaded to accompany
Pickle to a Masquerade in Woman's Apparel ;
is engaged in a troublesome Adventure,
and with his Companion conveyed to the Bastile

THE painter, at the request of Pickle, who had a design upon the count's sense of hearing, favoured the company with the song of *Bumper Squire Jones*,[1] which yielded infinite satisfaction to the baron; but affected the delicate ears of the Italian in such a manner, that his features expressed astonishment and disquiet; and by his sudden and repeated journeys to the door, it plainly appeared, that he was in the same predicament with those who, as Shakespear observes, when the bagpipe sings in the nose, cannot contain their urine for affection.[2]

With a view, therefore, of vindicating music from such a barbarous taste, Mr. Pallet had no sooner performed his task, than the count honoured his friends with some favourite airs of his own country, which he warbled with infinite grace and expression, though they had not energy sufficient to engage the attention of the

German, who fell fast asleep upon his couch, and snored so loud, as to interrupt, and totally annul this ravishing entertainment; so that they were fain to have recourse again to the glass, which made such innovation upon the brain of the physician, that he sung divers odes of Anacreon to a tune of his own composing, and held forth upon the music and recitative of the ancients with great erudition; while Pallet, having found means to make the Italian acquainted with the nature of his profession, harangued upon painting with wonderful volubility, in a language which (it was well for his own credit) the stranger did not understand.

At length the doctor was seized with such a qualm, that he begged Peregrine to lead him to his chamber;[1] and the count, tired with the eternal babble of the painter, reeled towards the sleeping baron, whom he viewed with rapture, repeating from the *Il Pastor Fido* of Guarini,

> *Come assetato infermo*
> *Che bramò lungamenté*
> *Il vietato licor—*
> *—Tal' Io! gran tempo infermo,*
> *E d'amorosa sete arso, e consunto.* [2]

Then boldly ravished a kiss, and began to tickle him under the ribs, with such expressions of tenderness, as scandalized the virtuous painter, who, conscious of his own attractions, was alarmed for his person, and staggered in great hurry and discomposure into the next room, where he put himself under the protection of our hero, to whom he imparted his suspicion of the count's morals, by describing the indecency of his deportment.

Peregrine, who entertained a just detestation for all such abominable practices, was incensed at this information; and stepping to the door of the dining-room where the two strangers were left together, saw with his own eyes enough to convince him, that Pallet's complaint was not without foundation, and that the baron was not averse to the addresses of the count. Our young gentleman's indignation had well nigh prompted him to rush in, and take immediate vengeance on the offenders; but, considering that such a precipitate step might be attended with troublesome consequences to himself, he resisted the impulse of his wrath, and tasked his invention with some method of inflicting upon them a disgrace suited to the grossness of their ideas. After having revolved sundry schemes of punishment, and even consulted Mr. Pipes, who being present at the discovery, undertook to sew them up in bags, with a reasonable quantity of ballast in each, and throw them over the Pont Neuf into the river; his imagination could not supply him with an expedient to his liking, and he was at a loss how to behave, when the landlady of the house, whom he knew to be a dame of remarkable vivacity, chancing to pass, furnished him with a hint, of which he immediately took the advantage, by begging she would do him the favour to step into the next room, and tell the gentlemen, that he would be with them as soon as the doctor could be put to bed.

The lady very graciously undertook the office, and entering the apartment, was so much offended and enraged at the mutual endearments of the two lovers, that instead of delivering the message with which she had been entrusted, she set the trumpet of reproach to her mouth, and seizing the baron's cane, which she found upon the side-table, belaboured them both with such eagerness of animosity, that they found themselves obliged to make a very disorderly retreat, and were actually driven down stairs, in a most disgraceful condition, by this exasperated virago, who loaded them with just invectives all the way, publishing their shame, not only to those of her own family, but likewise to the populace, who began to crowd about the door, and in all probability would have espoused her revenge, had not their lacqueys, who were in waiting, conveyed the delinquents into the Remise, and carried them off with great expedition.

Peregrine was so delighted with the manner of the chastisement they had undergone, that he embraced the mistress of the hotel with transport, for the spirit she had exerted; and being rendered frolicksome with the wine he had drank, proposed that he and Pallet should go to a masquerade, which he recollected was to be given that night. The painter did not want curiosity and inclination to accompany him, but expressed his apprehension of losing him in the ball; an accident which could not fail to be very disagreeable, as he was an utter stranger to the language and the town. To obviate this objection, the landlady, who was of their council, advised him to appear in a woman's dress, which would lay his companion under the necessity of attending him with more care, as he could not with decency detach himself from the lady whom he should introduce: besides, such a supposed connexion would hinder the ladies of pleasure from accosting, and employing their seducing arts upon a person already engaged.

Our young gentleman, foreseeing abundance of diversion in the execution of this project, seconded the proposal with such importunity and address, that the painter allowed himself to be habited in a suit belonging to the landlady, who also procured for him a mask and domino, while Pickle provided himself with a Spanish dress. In this disguise, which they put on about eleven o'clock, did they, attended by Pipes, set out in a Fiacre for the ball-room, into which Pickle led this supposititious female, to the astonishment of the whole company, who had never seen such an uncouth figure in the appearance of a woman.

After they had taken a view of all the remarkable masques, and the painter had been treated with a glass of liqueur, his mischievous companion gave him the slip, and vanishing in an instant, returned with another mask and a domino over his habit, that he might enjoy Pallet's perplexity, and be at hand to protect him from insult.

The poor painter having lost his guide, was almost distracted with anxiety, and stalked about the room, in quest of him, with such huge strides and oddity of gesture, that he was followed by a whole multitude, who gazed at him as a preternatural phæno-menon. This attendance increased his uneasiness to such a degree, that he could not help uttering a soliloquy aloud, in which he cursed his fate for having depended upon the promise of such a wag; and swore, that if once he was clear of this scrape, he would not bring himself into such a premunire again for the whole kingdom of France.

Divers petit maitres understanding the masque was a foreigner, who in all probability could not speak French, made up to him in their turns, in order to display their wit and address, and teized him with several arch questions; to which he made no other answer than, 'No *parly Francy*. Damn your chattering! Go about your business, can't ye ?'[1] But, what most of all contributed to his torture and mortification, was a pressing call from nature, in consequence of the Champaign he had so liberally swallowed in the afternoon. In the character of a woman, he neither knew whither to retire, nor, had he known, durst he run the risk of being discovered, in such a situation, by the individuals of that sex; and if he should use the privilege of a man, in his present appearance, he foresaw that he must subject himself to the ridicule of the whole company; so that he was obliged to suffer the most racking pangs of retention, and coursed round and round the whole place, casting many a woeful look among the crowd in search of Pickle, against whom he uttered innumerable execrations. At length, however, he was compelled to yield to the urgent dictates of necessity, and following several gentlemen into a small adjoining room furnished for the occasion,

discharged the source of his vexation in presence of them all, crying
in his own excuse, 'By your leave, by your leave. Egad! necessity
has no law.' The circumstances of this operation were so extraordinary and ridiculous, that some of those who were witnesses of
it, held up their hands in token of amazement; while others ran into
the ball-room, and called their companions to see such an unheard-
of spectacle.

Among the masques that, upon this intimation, came to see the
painter's attitude, was a person of great quality, who being a little
acquainted with the English language, waited till Pallet turned
about; and going up to him, 'Madam, (said he) I give you joy of
your happy pisse. It me seem, dat your vatere com vidout grand
pain.' 'Yes, thank God, Monsieur, (replied the painter) I never
was troubled with the stone.' 'Oho! (resumed the masque) so much
de bettre. You love to ave de stone vidout trouble, if I not mistake.'
'Gadzooks! my dear, you have nicked it to an hair! That is the very
case, as I hope to be saved,' cried Pallet, bursting into a violent fit of
laughter; which divesting the Frenchman of all ceremony and
reserve, he began to be very free with the supposed lady, and
attempted to plunge his hand into her bosom: but the painter was
too modest to suffer such indecent treatment; and when the gallant
repeated his efforts in a manner still more indelicate, lent him such
a box on the ear, as made the lights dance before him, and created
such a suspicion of Pallet's sex, that the nobleman swore he was
either a male or hermaphrodite, and insisted upon a scrutiny, for
the sake of his own honour, with such obstinacy of resentment,
that the fictitious nymph was in imminent danger, not only of
being exposed, but also of undergoing severe chastisement, for
having made so free with the prince's ear; when Peregrine, who
saw and over-heard every thing that passed, thought it was high
time to interpose; and accordingly, asserted his pretensions to the
insulted lady, who was overjoyed at this proof of his protection.

The affronted gallant persevered in demanding to know who she
was, and our hero as strenuously refused to give him that satisfaction: so that high words ensued; and the prince threatening to
punish his insolence, the young gentleman, who was not supposed
to know his quality, pointed to the place where his own sword used
to hang, and snapping his fingers in his face, laid hold on the
painter's arm, and led him to another part of the room, leaving his
antagonist to the meditations of his own revenge.

Pallet having chid his conductor for his barbarous desertion,
made him acquainted with the difficulty in which he had been

involved, and flatly telling him, he would not put it in his power to give him the slip again, held fast by his arm during the remaining part of the entertainment, to the no small diversion of the company, whose attention was altogether engrossed in the contemplation of such an aukward, ungainly stalking apparition. At last, Pickle being tired of exhibiting this rareeshew, complied with the repeated desires of his companion, and handed her into the coach; which he himself had no sooner entered, than they were surrounded by a file of musqueteers, commanded by an exempt, who ordering the coach-door to be opened, took his place with great deliberation, while one of his detachment mounted the box, in order to direct the driver.

Peregrine at once conceived the meaning of this arrest, and it was well for him that he had no weapon wherewith to stand upon his defence; for such was the impetuosity and rashness of his temper, that had he been armed, he would have run all risks rather than surrender himself to any odds whatever; but Pallet imagining that the officer was some gentleman who had mistaken their carriage for his own, desired his friend to undeceive the stranger; and when he was informed of the real state of their condition, his knees began to shake, his teeth to chatter, and he uttered a most doleful lamentation, importing his fear of being carried to some hideous dungeon of the Bastile, where he should spend the rest of his days in misery and horror, and never see the light of God's sun, nor the face of a friend; but perish in a foreign land, far removed from his family and connexions. Pickle damned him for his pusilanimity, and the Exempt hearing a lady bemoan herself so piteously, expressed his mortification at being the instrument of giving her such pain, and endeavoured to console them, by representing the lenity of the French government, and the singular generosity of the prince, by whose order they were apprehended.

Peregrine, whose discretion seemed to forsake him on all such occasions, exclaimed with great bitterness against the arbitrary administration of France, and inveighed with many expressions of contempt, against the character of the offended prince, whose resentment, far from being noble, he said, was pitiful, ungenerous and unjust. To this remonstrance the officer made no reply, but shrugged up his shoulders in silent astonishment at the *hardiesse* of the prisoner, and the Fiacre was just on the point of setting out, when they heard the noise of a scuffle at the back of the coach, and the voice of Tom Pipes, pronouncing 'I'll be damn'd if I do.' This trusty attendant had been desired by one of the guard to descend from his station in the rear, but as he resolved to share his master's fate, he took no notice of their intreaties, until they were seconded by force; and that he endeavoured to repel with his heel, which he applied with such energy to the jaws of the soldier who first came in contact with him, that they emitted a crashing sound like a dried walnut between the grinders of a templar in the pit. Exasperated at this outrage, the other saluted Tom's posteriors with his bayonet, which incommoded him so much, that he could no longer keep his post, but leaping upon the ground, gave his antagonist a chuck under the chin, that laid him upon his back, and then skipping over him with infinite agility, absconded among the crowd of coaches, till he saw the guard mount before and behind upon his master's Fiacre, which no sooner set forward than he followed at a small distance, to reconnoitre the place where Peregrine should be confined.

After having proceeded slowly through many windings and turnings to a part of Paris, in which Pipes was an utter stranger, the coach stopped at a great gate, with a wicket in the middle, which being opened at the approach of the carriage, the prisoners were admitted, and the guard returning with the Fiacre, Tom determined to watch in that place all night, that in the morning he might make such observations, as might be conducive to the enlargement of his master.

CHAPTER L

By the Fidelity of Pipes, Jolter is informed of his
Pupil's Fate. Confers with the Physician.
Applies to the Embassador, who with great
Difficulty obtains the Discharge of the Prisoners,
on certain Conditions

THIS plan he executed notwithstanding the pain of his wound, and the questions of the city guard both horse and foot, to which he could make no other answer than '*Anglois, Anglois*;' and as soon as it was light, taking an accurate survey of the castle (for such it seemed to be) into which Peregrine and Pallet had been conveyed, together with its situation in respect to the river, he went home to the lodgings, and waking Mr. Jolter, gave him an account of the adventure. The governor wrung his hands in the utmost grief and consternation, when he heard this unfortunate piece of news; he did not doubt that his pupil was imprisoned in the Bastile for life; and in the anguish of his apprehension, cursed the day on which he had undertaken to superintend the conduct of such an imprudent young man, who had by reiterated insults provoked the vengeance of such a mild forbearing administration. That he might not, however, neglect any means in his power to extricate him from his present misfortune, he dispatched Thomas to the doctor, with an account of his companion's fate, that they might join their interest in behalf of the captives; and the physician being informed of what had happened, immediately dressed himself and repaired to Jolter, whom he accosted in these words: 'Now, sir, I hope you are convinced of your error, in asserting that oppression can never be the effect of arbitrary power. Such a calamity as this could never have happened under the Athenian democracy: nay, even when the tyrant Pisistratus got possession of that common-wealth, he durst not venture to rule with such absolute and unjust dominion. You shall see now that Mr. Pickle and my friend Pallet will fall a sacrifice to the tyranny of lawless power; and in my opinion, we shall be accessory to the ruin of this poor enslaved people, if we bestir ourselves in demanding, or imploring the release of our unhappy countrymen; as we may thereby prevent the commission of a flagrant crime, which would fill up the vengeance of heaven against the perpetrators, and perhaps be the means of restoring a whole nation to the unspeakable fruition of freedom. For my own part, I should rejoice to see the blood of my father spilt in such a glorious cause, provided such a victim would furnish me with the opportunity of dissolving the chains of slavery, and vindicating that liberty which is the birth-right of man. Then would my name be immortalized among the patriot heroes of antiquity, and my memory like that of Harmodius and Aristogiton,[1] be honoured by statues erected at the public expence.' This rhapsody, which was delivered with great emphasis and agitation, gave so much offence to Jolter, that without speaking one word, he retired in great wrath to his own chamber, and the republican returned to his lodging, in full hope of his prognostic being verified in the death and destruction of Peregrine and the painter, which must give rise to some renowned revolution, wherein he himself would act a principal part. But the governor, whose imagination was not quite so warm and prolifick, went directly to the Embassador, whom he informed of his pupil's situation, and besought to interpose with the French ministry, that he and the other British subject might obtain their liberty.

Chapter L

His excellency asked if Jolter could guess at the cause of his imprisonment, that he might be the better prepared to vindicate or excuse his conduct; but neither he nor Pipes could give the smallest hint of intelligence on that subject; though he furnished himself from Tom's own mouth with a circumstantial account of the manner in which his master had been arrested, as well as of his own behaviour, and the disaster he had received on that occasion. His Lordship never doubted that Pickle had brought this calamity upon himself by some unlucky prank he had played at the masquerade; especially when he understood that the young gentleman had drank freely in the afternoon, and been so whimsical as to go thither with a man in woman's apparel; and he that same day waited on the French minister, in full confidence of obtaining his discharge; but met with more difficulty than he expected, the court of France being extremely punctilious in every thing that concerns a prince of the blood: the ambassador was, therefore, obliged to talk in very high terms, and though the present circumstances of the French politicks would not allow them to fall out with the British administration for trifles, all the favour he could procure, was a promise that Pickle should be set at liberty, provided he would ask pardon of the prince to whom he had given offence. His excellency thought this was but a reasonable condescension, supposing Peregrine to have been in the wrong; and Jolter was admitted to him, in order to communicate and reinforce his Lordship's advice, which was that he should comply with the terms proposed. The governor, who did not enter this gloomy fortress without fear and trembling, found his pupil in a dismal apartment void of all furniture, but a stool and truckle-bed; the moment he was admitted, he perceived the youth whistling with great unconcern, and working with his pencil at the bare wall, on which he had delineated a ludicrous figure labelled with the name of the nobleman whom he had affronted, and an English mastiff with his leg lifted up, in the attitude of making water in his shoe. He had been even so presumptuous as to explain the device with satirical inscriptions in the French language, which when Jolter perused, his hair stood on end with affright. The very turnkey was confounded and overawed by the boldness of his behaviour, which he had never seen matched by any inhabitant of that place; and actually joined his friend in persuading him to submit to the easy demand of the minister. But our hero, far from embracing the counsel of this advocate, handed him to the door with great ceremony, and dismissed him with a kick on the breech; and to all the supplications, and even tears of Jolter, made no other reply, than that he would stoop to no condescension, because he had committed no crime; but would leave his case to the cognizance and exertion of the British court, whose duty it was to see justice done to its own subjects: he desired, however, that Pallet, who was confined in another place, might avail himself of his own disposition, which was sufficiently plyable. But when the governor desired to see his fellow-prisoner, the turnkey gave him to understand that he had received no orders relating to the lady, and therefore could not admit him into her apartment; though he was complaisant enough to tell him, that she seemed very much mortified at her confinement, and at certain times behaved as if her brain was not a little disordered. Jolter thus baffled in all his endeavours, quitted the Bastile with a heavy heart, and reported his fruitless negociation to the Embassador, who could not help breaking forth into some acrimonious expressions against the obstinacy and insolence of the young man, who, he said, deserved to suffer for his folly. Nevertheless, he did not desist from his representations to the French ministry, which he found so unyielding, that he was obliged to threaten in plain terms, to make it a national concern; and not only write to his court for instructions, but even advise the council to make reprisals, and send some French gentleman in London to the Tower.

This intimation had an effect upon the ministry at Versailles, who rather than run the risk of incensing a people whom it was neither their interest nor inclination to disoblige, consented to discharge the offenders, on condition that they should leave Paris in three days after their enlargement. This proposal was readily agreed to by Peregrine, who was now a little more tractable, and heartily tired of being cooped up in such an uncomfortable abode, for the space of three long days, without any sort of communication or entertainment, but that which his own imagination suggested.

CHAPTER LI

Peregrine makes himself merry at the Expence
of the Painter, who curses his Landlady,
and breaks with the Doctor

As he could easily conceive the situation of his companion in adversity, he was unwilling to leave the place, until he had reaped some diversion from his distress, and with that view repaired to the dungeon of the afflicted painter, to which he had by this time free access. When he entered, the first object that presented itself to his eye, was so uncommonly ridiculous, that he could scarce preserve that gravity of countenance which he had affected in order to execute the joke he had planned. The forlorn Pallet sat upright in his bed in a dishabille that was altogether extraordinary. He had laid aside his monstrous hoop, together with his stays, gown and petticoat, wrapped his lappets about his head by way of a night-cap, and wore his domino as a loose morning dress; his grizzled locks hung down about his lack-lustre eyes and tawny neck, in all the disorder of negligence; his grey beard bristled about half an inch, through the remains of the paint with which his visage had been bedaubed, and every feature of his face was lengthened to the most ridiculous expression of grief and dismay. Seeing Peregrine come in, he started up in a sort of frantic extasy, and running towards him with open arms, no sooner perceived the woeful appearance into which our hero had modelled his physiognomy, than he stopped short all of a sudden, and the joy which had begun to take possession of his heart, was in a moment dispelled by the most rueful presages; so that he stood in a most ludicrous posture of dejection, like a malefactor at the Old Baily, when sentence is about to be pronounced. Pickle taking him by the hand, heaved a profound sigh, and after having protested that he was extremely mortified at being pitched upon as the messenger of bad news, told him with an air of sympathy and infinite concern, that the French court having discovered his sex, had resolved, in consideration of the outrageous indignity he offered in public to a prince of the blood, to detain him in the Bastile a prisoner for life; and that this sentence was a mitigation obtained by the importunities of the British Embassador; the punishment ordained by law being no other than breaking alive upon the wheel. These tidings aggravated the horrors of the painter to such a degree, that he roared aloud, and skipped about the room, in all the extravagance of distraction; taking God and man to witness that he would rather suffer immediate death, than endure one year's imprisonment in such a hideous place; and cursing the hour of his birth, and the moment on which he departed from his own country. 'For my own part, (said his tormentor in an hypocritical tone) I was obliged to swallow the bitter pill of making submissions to the prince, who, as I had not presumed to strike him, received acknowledgments, in consequence of which I shall be this day set at liberty; and there is even one expedient left for the recovery of your freedom. It is, I own, a disagreeable remedy, but one had better undergo a little mortification, than be for ever wretched. Besides, upon second thoughts, I begin to imagine that you will not for such a trifle sacrifice yourself to the unceasing horrors of a solitary dungeon; especially as your condescension will in all probability be attended with advantages which you could not otherwise enjoy.' Pallet interrupting him with great eagerness, begged for the love of God that he would no longer keep him in the torture of suspence, but mention that same remedy, which he was resolved to swallow, let it be never so unpalatable.

Peregrine having thus played upon his passions of fear and hope, answered, that as the offence was committed in the habit of a woman, which was a disguise unworthy of the other sex;[1] the French court was of opinion that the delinquent should for ever forfeit the privileges and characteristic of a man, which he had so shamefully deposited, or in other words, be deprived of his virility; so that there was an alternative at his own option, by which he had it in his power to regain immediate freedom.' 'What! (cried the painter in despair) part with my manhood, and become a singer? Gadzooks! and the devil and all that, I'll rather lie still where I am, and let myself be devoured by vermin.' Then thrusting out his throat, 'Here is my wind-pipe, (said he) be so good, my dear friend, as to give it a slice or two; if you don't, I shall one of these days be found dangling in my garters. What an unfortunate rascal I am! What a blockhead, and a beast, and a fool was I to trust myself among such a barbarous ruffian race! Lord forgive you, Mr. Pickle, for having been the immediate cause of my disaster; if you had stood by me from the beginning, according to your promise, and directed me to a proper place, where I could have made water without being exposed, I should not have been teized by that cox-comb who has brought me to this pass. And why did I put on this damn'd unlucky dress? Lard curse that chattering Jezabel of a landlady, who advised such a preposterous disguise! a disguise which hath not only brought me to this pass, but also rendered me abominable to myself, and frightful to others; for, when I this morning signified to the turnkey, that I wanted to be shaved, he looked at my beard with astonishment, and crossing himself, muttered his paternoster, believing me (I suppose) to be a witch, or something worse. And heaven confound that loathsome banquet of the ancients, which provoked me to drink too freely, that I might wash away the taste of that accursed sillikicaby.'

Our young gentleman, having heard his lamentation to an end, excused himself for his conduct, by representing, that he could not possibly foresee the disagreeable consequences that attended it; and in the mean time, strenuously counselled him to submit to the terms of his enlargement. He observed, that he was now arrived at that time of life, when the lusts of the flesh should be entirely mortified within him, and his greatest concern ought to be the health of his soul, to which nothing could more effectually contribute than the amputation which was proposed: that his body, as well as his mind, would profit by the change, because he would have no dangerous appetite to gratify, and no carnal thoughts to divert him from the duties of his profession; and his voice, which was naturally sweet, would improve to such a degree, that he would captivate the ears of all the people of fashion and taste, and in a little time he celebrated under the appellation of the English Senesino.[1]

These arguments did not fail to make impression upon the painter, who, nevertheless, started three objections to his compliance; namely, the disgrace of the punishment, the pain of the operation, and the dread of his wife. Pickle undertook to obviate these difficulties, by assuring him, that the sentence would be executed so privately, as never to transpire; that the excision (as he had learnt from Motecelli)[2] was not so painful as the drawing of a tooth, and that his wife could not be so unconscionable, after so many years of cohabitation, as to take exceptions to an expedient, by which she would not only enjoy the conversation of her husband, but even the fruits of those talents which the knife would so remarkably refine.

Pallet shook his head at this last remonstrance, as if he thought it would not be altogether convincing to his spouse; but yielded to the proposal, provided her consent could be obtained. Just as he signified this condescension, the gaoler entered, and addressing himself to the supposed lady, expressed his satisfaction in having the honour to tell her, that she was no longer a prisoner. As the painter did not understand one word of what he said, Peregrine undertook the office of interpreter, and made his friend believe, the gaoler's speech was no other than an intimation, that the ministry had sent a surgeon to execute what was proposed, and that the instruments and dressings were prepared in the next room. Alarmed and terrified at this sudden appointment, he flew to the other end of the room, and snatching up an earthen chamber-pot, which was the only offensive weapon in the place, put himself in a posture of defiance, and with many oaths threatened to try the temper of the barber's skull, if he should presume to set his nose within the apartment.

The gaoler, who little expected such a reception, concluded that the poor gentlewoman had actually lost her wits, and retreated with precipitation, leaving the door open as he went out. Upon which Pickle, gathering up the particulars of his dress with great dispatch, crammed them into Pallet's arms, and taking notice that now the coast was clear, exhorted him to follow his footsteps to the gate, where a hackney-coach stood for his reception. There being no time for hesitation, the painter took his advice, and without quitting the utensil, which in his hurry he forgot to lay down, sallied out in the rear of our hero, with all that wildness of terror and impatience which may be reasonably supposed to take possession of a man who flies from castration or perpetual imprisonment. Such was the tumult of his agitation, that his faculty of thinking was for the present utterly overwhelmed, and he saw no object but his conductor, whom he followed by a sort of instinctive impulse, without regarding the keepers and centinels, who, as he passed with his cloaths under one arm, and his chamber-pot brandished above his head, were confounded, and even dismayed at the strange apparition.

During the whole course of this irruption, he ceased not to cry with great vociferation, 'Drive, coachman, drive in the name of God!' And the carriage had proceeded the length of a whole street, before he manifested the least sign of reflection, but stared like the Gorgon's head, with his mouth wide open, and each particular hair crawling and twining like an animated serpent. At length, however, he began to recover the use of his senses, and asked if Peregrine thought him now out of all danger of being retaken. This unrelenting wag, not yet satisfied with the affliction he had imposed upon the sufferer, answered with an air of doubt and concern, that he hoped they would not be overtaken, and prayed to God they might not be retarded by an *Embaras.* Pallet fervently joined in this supplication, and they advanced a few yards further, when the noise of a coach at full speed behind them, invaded their ears; and Pickle having looked out at the window, withdrew his head in seeming confusion, and exclaimed, 'Lord have mercy upon us! I wish that may not be a guard sent after us. Methinks I saw the muzzle of a fusil sticking out of the coach.' The painter hearing these tidings, that instant thrust himself half out at the window, with his helmet still in his hand, bellowing to the coachman as loud as he could roar, 'Drive, damn ye drive! to the gates of Jericho and ends of the earth! Drive, you raggamuffin, you rapscallion, you hell-hound! drive us to the pit of hell, rather than we should be taken, and lose the treasures of virility.'

Such a phantom could not pass, without attracting the curiosity of the people, who ran to their doors and windows, in order to behold this object of admiration. With the same view that coach, which was supposed to be in pursuit of him, stopt just as the windows of each happened to be opposite; and Pallet looking behind, and seeing three men standing upon the foot-board armed with canes, which his fear converted into fusils, never doubted that his friend's suspicion was just; but, shaking his jordan at the imaginary guard, swore he would sooner die than part with his precious ware. The owner of the coach, who was a nobleman of the first quality, mistook him for some unhappy woman deprived of her senses; and ordering his coachman to proceed, convinced the fugitive, to his infinite joy, that this was no more than a false alarm. He was not, for all that, freed from anxiety and trepidation; but our young gentleman, fearing his brain would not bear a repetition of the same joke, permitted him to gain his own lodgings, without further molestation.

His landlady meeting him on the stair, was so affected at his appearance, that she screamed aloud, and betook herself to flight; while he, cursing her with great bitterness, rushed into the apartment of the doctor, who, instead of receiving him with cordial embraces, and congratulating him upon his deliverance, gave evident tokens of umbrage and discontent; and even plainly told him, he hoped to have heard that he and Mr. Pickle had acted the glorious part of Cato; an event which would have laid the foundation of such noble struggles, as could not fail to end in happiness and freedom; and that he had already made some progress in an ode that would have immortalized their names, and inspired the flame of liberty in every honest breast.

'There (said he) I would have proved, that great talents, and high sentiments of liberty, do reciprocally produce and assist each other; and illustrated my assertions with such notes and quotations from the Greek writers, as would have opened the eyes of the most blind and unthinking, and touched the most callous and obdurate heart. *O fool! to think the man, whose ample mind must grasp whatever yonder stars survey*——[1] Pray, Mr. Pallet, what is your opinion of that image of the mind's grasping the whole universe? For my own part, I can't help thinking it the most happy conception that ever entered my imagination.'

The painter, who was not such a flaming enthusiast in the cause of liberty, could not brook the doctor's reflexions, which he thought savoured a little too much of indifference and deficiency in point of private friendship; and therefore seized the present opportunity of mortifying his pride, by observing, that the image was, without all doubt, very grand and magnificent; but that he had been obliged for the idea to Mr. Bayes in *The Rehearsal*, who values himself upon the same figure, conveyed in these words, *But all these clouds, when by the eye of reason grasp'd, &c.*[2] Upon any other occasion, the painter would have triumphed greatly in this detection; but such was the flutter and confusion of his spirits, under the apprehension of being retaken, that without further communication, he retreated to his own room, in order to resume his own dress, which he hoped would alter his appearance in such a manner, as to baffle all search and examination; while the physician remained ashamed and abashed, to find himself convicted of plagiarism by a person of such contemptible talents. He was offended at this proof of his memory, and so much enraged at his presumption in exhibiting it, that he could never forgive his want of reverence, and took every opportunity of exposing his ignorance and folly in the sequel. Indeed, the ties of private affection were too weak to engage the heart of this republican, whose zeal for the community had entirely swallowed up his concern for individuals. He looked upon particular friendship as a passion unworthy of his ample soul, and was a professed admirer of L. Manlius, Junius Brutus, and those later patriots of the same name, who shut their ears against the cries of nature, and resisted all the dictates of gratitude and humanity.

CHAPTER LII

Pallet conceives an hearty Contempt for his
Fellow-traveller, and attaches himself to Pickle, who,
nevertheless, persecutes him with his mischievous Talent,
upon the Road to Flanders

IN the mean time, his companion having employed divers pails full of water, in clearing himself from the squalor of a jail, submitted his face to the barber, tinged his eye-brows with a sable hue, and being dressed in his own cloaths, ventured to visit Peregrine, who was still under the hands of his valet de chambre, and who gave him to understand, that his escape had been connived at, and that the condition of their deliverance was their departure from Paris in three days.

The painter was transported with joy, when he learnt that he ran no risque of being retaken; and far from repining at the terms of his enlargement, would have willingly set out on his return to England that same afternoon; for the Bastile had made such an impression upon him, that he started at the sound of every coach, and turned pale at sight of a French soldier. In the fullness of his heart, he complained of the doctor's indifference, and related what had passed at their meeting with evident marks of resentment and disrespect; which were not at all diminished, when Jolter informed him of the physician's behaviour, when he sent for him, to confer about the means of abridging their confinement. Pickle himself was incensed at his want of bowels, and perceiving how much he had sunk in the opinion of his fellow-traveller, resolved to encourage these sentiments of disgust, and occasionally foment the division to a downright quarrel, which he foresaw would produce some diversion, and perhaps expose the poet's character in such a light, as would effectually punish him for his arrogance and barbarity. With this view, he levelled several satirical jokes at the doctor's pedantry and want of taste, which had appeared so conspicuous in the quotations he had got by heart, from ancient authors, in his affected disdain of the best pictures in the world; which, had he been endowed with the least share of discernment, he could not have beheld with such insensibility; and lastly, in his ridiculous banquet, which none but an egregious coxcomb, devoid of all elegance and sense, would have prepared, or presented to rational beings. In a word, our young gentleman played the artillery of his wit against him with such success, that the painter seemed to wake from a dream, and went home with the most hearty contempt for the person he had formerly adored.

Instead of using the privilege of a friend, to enter his apartment without ceremony, he sent in his servant with a message, importing, that he intended to set out from Paris next day, in company with Mr. Pickle, and desiring to know whether or not he was, or would be prepared for the journey. The doctor, struck with the manner as well as the matter of this intimation, went immediately to Pallet's room, and demanded to know the cause of such a sudden determination, without his privity or concurrence; and when he understood the necessity of their affairs, rather than travel by himself, he ordered his baggage to be packed up, and signified his readiness to conform to the emergency of the case; though he was not at all pleased with the cavalier behaviour of Pallet, to whom he threw out some hints of his own importance, and the immensity of his condescension, in favouring him with such marks of regard. But by this time these insinuations had lost their effect upon the painter, who told him with an arch sneer, that he did not at all question his learning and abilities, and particularly his skill in cookery, which he should never forget while his palate retained its function; but nevertheless advised him, for the sake of the degenerate eaters of these days, to spare a little of his sal armoniac in the next sillykickaby he should prepare; and bate somewhat of the devil's dung, which he had so plentifully crammed into the roasted fowls, unless he had a mind to convert his guests into patients, with a view of licking himself whole for the expence of the entertainment.

The physician, nettled at these sarcasms, eyed him with a look of indignation and disdain, and being unwilling to express himself in English, lest in the course of the altercation Pallet should be so much irritated as to depart without him, he vented his anger in Greek, pronouncing with great rancour, Ἀκριτόμυθε, λιγύς περ ἐὼν ἀγορητής, Ἴσχεο, μηδ᾽ ἔθελ᾽ οἶος ἐριζέμεναι βασιλεῦσιν.[1] The painter, though by the sound he supposed this quotation to be Greek, complimented his friend upon his knowledge in the Welch language, and found means to rally him quite out of temper; so that he retired to his own chamber in the utmost wrath and mortification, and left his antagonist exulting o'er the victory he had won.

While these things passed between these originals, Peregrine waited upon the Embassador, whom he thanked for his kind interposition, acknowledging the indiscretion of his own conduct with such appearance of conviction, and promises of reformation, that his Excellency freely forgave him for all the trouble he had been put to on his account, fortified him with sensible advices, and assuring him of his continual favour and friendship, gave him at parting, letters of introduction to several persons of quality belonging to the British court.

Thus distinguished, our young gentleman took leave of all his French acquaintance, and spent the evening with some of those who had enjoyed the greatest share of his intimacy and confidence; while Jolter superintended his domestic concerns, and with infinite joy bespoke a post-chaise and horses, in order to convey him from a place where he lived in continual apprehension of suffering by the dangerous disposition of his pupil. Every thing being adjusted according to their plan, they and their fellow-travellers next day dined together, and about four in the afternoon took their departure in two chaises, escorted by the valet de chambre, Pipes and the doctor's lacquey on horseback, well furnished with arms and ammunition, in case of being attacked by robbers on the road.

It was about eleven o'clock at night when they arrived at Senlis, which was the place at which they proposed to lodge, and where they were obliged to knock up the people of the inn, before they could have their supper prepared. All the provision in the house was but barely sufficient to furnish one indifferent meal; however, the painter consoled himself for the quantity with the quality of the dishes, one of which was a fricassee of rabbit, a preparation that he valued above all the dainties that ever smoaked upon the table of the sumptuous Heliogabalus.

He had no sooner expressed himself to this effect, than our hero, who was almost incessantly laying traps for diversion at his neighbour's expence, laid hold on the declaration; and recollecting the story of Scipio and the muleteer in Gil Blas,[1] resolved to perpetrate a joke upon the stomach of Pallet, which seemed particularly well disposed to an hearty supper. He accordingly digested his plan; and the company being seated at table, affected to gaze with peculiar eagerness at the painter, who had helped himself to a large portion of the fricassee, and began to swallow it with infinite relish. Pallet, notwithstanding the keenness of his appetite, could not help taking notice of Pickle's demeanour; and making a short pause in the exercise of his grinders, 'You are surprized (said he) to see me make so much dispatch; but I was extremely hungry, and this is one of the best fricassees I ever tasted: the French are very expert in these dishes, that I must allow; and upon my conscience, I would never desire to eat a more delicate rabbit than this that lies upon my plate.'

Peregrine made no other reply to this encomium, than the repetition of the word 'rabbit!' with a note of admiration, and such a significant shake of the head, as effectually alarmed the other, who instantly suspended the action of his jaws, and with the morsel half chewed in his mouth, stared round him with a certain stolidity of apprehension, which is easier conceived than described, until his eyes encountered the countenance of Thomas Pipes, who being instructed, and posted opposite to him for the occasion, exhibited an arch grin, that compleated the painter's disorder. Afraid of swallowing his mouthful, and ashamed to dispose of it any other way, he sat some time in a most distressed state of suspence; and being questioned by Mr. Jolter touching his calamity, made a violent effort of the muscles of his gullet, which with difficulty performed their office; and then, with great confusion and concern, asked if Mr. Pickle suspected the rabbit's identity. The young gentleman assuming a mysterious air, pretended ignorance of the matter, observing, that he was apt to suspect all dishes of that kind, since he had been informed of the tricks which were commonly played at inns in France, Italy and Spain, and recounted that passage in Gil Blas, which we have hinted at above; saying, he did not pretend to be a connoisseur in animals, but the legs of the creature which composed that fricassee did not, in his opinion, resemble those of the rabbits he had usually seen. This observation had an evident effect upon the features of the painter, who with certain signs of loathing and astonishment, exclaimed, 'Lord Jesus!' and appealed to Pipes for a discovery of the truth, by asking if he knew any thing of the affair. Tom very gravely replied, that he did suppose the food was wholesome enough, for he had seen the skin and feet of a special ram-cat, new flea'd, hanging upon the door of a small pantry adjoining to the kitchen.

Before this sentence was uttered, Pallet's belly seemed to move in contact with his back-bone, his colour changed, no part but the whites of his eyes were to be seen, he dropped his lower jaw, and fixing his hands in his sides, reached with such convulsive agonies, as amazed and disconcerted the whole company; and what augmented his disorder, was the tenacious retention of his stomach, which absolutely refused to part with its contents, notwithstanding all the energy of his abhorrence, which threw him into a cold sweat, and almost into a swoon.

Pickle, alarmed at his condition, assured him it was a genuine rabbit, and that he had tutored Pipes to say otherwise for the joke's sake. But this confession he considered as a friendly artifice of Pickle's compassion, and therefore it had little effect upon his constitution. By the assistance, however, of a large bumper of brandy, his spirits were recruited, and his recollection so far recovered, that he was able to declare, with divers contorsions of face, that the dish had a particular rankness of taste, which he had imputed partly to the nature of the French coney, and partly to the composition of their sauces; then he inveighed against the infamous practices of French publicans, attributing such imposition to their oppressive government, which kept them so necessitous, that they were tempted to exercise all manner of knavery upon their unwary guests.

Jolter, who could not find in his heart to let slip any opportunity of speaking in favour of the French, told him that he was a very great stranger to their police, else he would know, that if upon information to the magistrate, it should appear that any traveller, native or foreigner, has been imposed upon, or ill-treated by a publican, the offender would be immediately obliged to shut up his house, and if his behaviour had been notorious, he himself would be sent to the gallies, without the least hesitation; 'and as for the dish which hath been made the occasion of your present disorder, (said he) I will take upon me to affirm, it was prepared of a genuine rabbit, which was skinned in my presence; and in confirmation of what I assert, though such fricassees are not the favourites of my taste, I will eat a part of this without scruple.' So saying, he swallowed several mouthfuls of the questioned coney, and Pallet seemed to eye it again with inclination; nay, he even resumed his knife and fork, and being just on the point of applying them, was seized with another qualm of apprehension, that broke out in an exclamation of, 'After all, Mr. Jolter, if it should be a real ram-cat— Lord have mercy upon me! here is one of the claws.' With these words he presented the tip of a toe, of which Pipes had snipt off five or six from a duck that was roasted, and purposely scattered them in the fricassee: and the governor could not behold this testimonial without symptoms of uneasiness and remorse; so that he and the painter sat silenced and abashed, and made faces at each other, while the physician, who hated them both, exulted over their affliction, bidding them be of good chear, and proceed with their meal; for he was ready to demonstrate, that the flesh of a cat was as nourishing and delicious as veal or mutton, provided they could prove, that the said cat was not of the boar-kind, and had fed chiefly on vegetable diet, or even confined its carnivorous appetite to rats and mice, which he affirmed to be dainties of exquisite taste and flavour. He said, it was a vulgar mistake to think that all flesh-devouring creatures were unfit to be eaten; witness the consumption of swine and ducks, animals that delight in carnage, as well as fish, that prey upon each other, and feed on bait and carrion; together with the demand for bear, of which the best hams in the world are made. He then observed, that the Negroes on the coast of Guinea, who are a healthy and vigorous people, prefer cats and dogs to all other fare; and mentioned from history several sieges, during which the inhabitants, who were blocked up, lived upon these animals, and had recourse even to human flesh, which, to his certain knowledge, was in all respects preferable to pork; for, in the course of his studies, he had, for the experiment's sake, eaten a steak cut from the buttock of a person who had been hanged.

This dissertation, far from composing, increased the disquiet in the stomachs of the governor and painter, who hearing the last illustration, turned their eyes upon the orator, at the same instant, with looks of horror and disgust; and the one muttering the term *Cannibal*, and the other pronouncing the word *abomination*, they rose from table in a great hurry, and running towards another apartment, justled with such violence in the passage, that both were overturned by the shock, which also contributed to the effect of their nausea, that mutually defiled them as they lay.

CHAPTER LIII

Nor is the Physician sacred from his Ridicule.
They reach Arras, where our Adventurer engages in Play
with two French Officers, who next Morning give the
Landlord an interesting Proof of their Importance

THOUGH Pickle enjoyed their disaster, he was resolved to practise some invention upon the doctor, that he might not triumph in his revenge with impunity; and thus determined, when Pallet had overcome the malady of his own imagination, he imparted to him a plan of reprizal, which agreeably flattered his resentment, and was executed in this manner: as the painter and physician lay in separate beds in the same chamber, the former watched, till by the other's snoring he was certified of his being fast asleep; then moving softly to the door, where Pipes stood ready furnished for the purpose, took a tea-kettle full of warm water, and cautiously conveying the spout under the cloaths of the doctor's bed, poured in the liquor, imperceptibly, to the quantity of half a gallon, and then retired to rest.

Peregrine having undertaken to rouze his fellow-travellers in the morning, entered the doctor's apartment with the dawn, and waked them both with the same hollow. The painter immediately sprung out of bed; but the physician, finding himself drenched from head to foot, was equally astonished and ashamed, never doubting that he had unfortunately bedewed himself in his sleep. This mistake he thought so inconsistent with the dignity of his character, that he durst not venture to disclose his condition, especially as he well knew how eagerly the company would seize such an occasion of making merry at his expence; and it would be impracticable to conceal it from their knowledge, if he should be obliged to get up in their presence: he therefore lay still in the utmost perplexity and tribulation, while his two companions, guessing his thoughts, and rejoicing at his anxiety, sat down by his bedside, and exhorted him to rise. He told them, that having sweated profusely all night, he could not, with any regard to his health, get up, until he should be shifted, and the pores of his skin regularly closed; and in the mean time, desired they would take the trouble of seeing the horses put to the chaises, and the reckoning adjusted; assuring them, he should be ready to attend them before their business could be dispatched. Our young gentleman gave him to understand, that Mr. Jolter had charged himself with the payment of the bill, and the servants were now employed about the carriages, so that he had not a moment to lose; he therefore rung the bell for his footman, and bade him bring a clean shirt for his master with all possible speed.

Ere the fellow returned, it was broad day; and a message came from the governor, importing that the horses were yoked. The doctor's confusion increased, he was tortured by the looks, and baited by the importunities of his company; and moreover, suffered the uncomfortable situation of being steeped, as he imagined, in his own brine. At length Peregrine, impatient of his delay, took the privilege of a comrade, and accusing the republican of sloth, pulled off the bed-cloaths at one snatch, and displayed him at full length, in this opprobrious condition.

The painter seeing him thus exposed, lifted up his hands, and in affected astonishment, 'Lord watch over us! (cried he) the doctor is a dead man; sure the whole sap of his body is run out, or have you spilt a whole dish of sillykickaby in the bed? for it smells cursedly strong of sal armoniac.' Peregrine, in order to compleat the physician's overthrow, shut up his nostrils with his finger and thumb, and asked in a snuffling tone, if he was subject to that infirmity.

Unspeakable were the shame and vexation of the modern Pindar on this occasion; he was at the same time tormented with all the pangs which mortified vanity can feel, and agitated by all the furies of resentment against the persons who had detected his disgrace, and who having thus insulted him in his distress, quitted the room with a loud laugh, leaving him to the thorny reflections of his own pride. Nor could the painter, who was not at all to be praised for his moderation, abstain from certain ill-natured allusions to his calamity, which by these means reached the ears of the governor, from whom (of all men) he desired to keep it concealed; so that he remained sullen and dejected during the whole journey:[1] not but that he attempted to recover his importance, by haranguing upon the Roman highways, when Mr. Jolter desired the company to take notice of the fine pavement upon which they travelled from Paris into Flanders; but Pallet, who thought he had now gained the ascendency over the physician, exerted himself in maintaining the superiority he had acquired, by venting various sarcasms upon his self-conceit and affectation of learning, and even uttering puns and conundrums upon the remarks which the republican retailed. When he talked of the Flaminian Way, the painter questioned if it was a better pavement than the Fleminian way on which they travelled: and the doctor having observed, that this road was made for the convenience of drawing the French artillery into Flanders, which was often the seat of war; his competitor in wit replied with infinite vivacity, 'There are more great guns than the French king knows of drawn along this causeway, doctor.'

Encouraged by the success of these efforts, which tickled the imagination of Jolter, and drew smiles (as he imagined) of approbation from our hero, he sported in many other æquivoques of the same nature; and at dinner told the physician, that he was like the root of the tongue, as being cursedly down in the mouth.

By this time, such was the animosity subsisting between these quondam friends, that they never conversed together, except with a view of exposing each other to the ridicule or contempt of their fellow-travellers. The doctor was at great pains to point out the folly and ignorance of Pallet in private to Peregrine, who was often conjured in the same manner by the painter, to take notice of the physician's want of manners and taste. Pickle pretended to acquiesce in the truth of their mutual severity, which indeed was extremely just, and by malicious insinuations blew up their contention, with a view of bringing it to open hostility. But, both seemed so averse to deeds of mortal purpose, that for a long time his arts were baffled, and he could not spirit them up to any pitch of resentment higher than scurrilous repartee.

Before they reached Arras, the city-gates were shut, so that they were obliged to take up their lodging at an indifferent house in the suburbs, where they found a couple of French officers, who had also rode post from Paris, so far on their way to Lisle. These gentlemen were about the age of thirty, and their deportment distinguished by such an air of insolence, as disgusted our hero, who, nevertheless, accosted them politely in the yard, and proposed that they should sup together. They thanked him for the honour of his invitation, which, however, they declined, upon pretence of having ordered something for themselves; but promised to wait upon him and his company immediately after their repast.

This they accordingly performed; and after having drank a few glasses of Burgundy, one of them asked, if the young gentleman would, for pastime, take an hand at quadrille. Peregrine easily divined the meaning of this proposal, which was made with no other view than that of fleecing him and his fellow-travellers; for he well knew to what shifts a subaltern in the French service is reduced, in order to maintain the appearance of a gentleman, and had reason to believe that most of them were sharpers from their youth: but, as he depended a good deal upon his own penetration and address, he gratified the stranger's desire; and a party was instantly formed of the painter, the physician, the proposer and himself, the other officer having professed himself utterly ignorant of the game; yet, in the course of the play, he took his station at the back of Pickle's chair, which was opposite to his friend, on pretence of amusing himself with seeing his manner of conducting the cards. The youth was not such a novice but that he perceived the design of this palpable piece of behaviour, which, notwithstanding, he overlook'd for the present, with a view of flattering their hopes in the beginning, that they might be the more effectually punished, by their disappointment in the end.

The game was scarce begun, when by the reflection of a glass he discerned the officer at his back, making signs to his companion, who, by these pre-concerted gestures, was perfectly informed of the contents of Peregrine's hand, and of consequence fortunate in the course of play.

Thus they were allowed to enjoy the fruits of their dexterity, until their money amounted to some Louis; when our young gentleman, thinking it high time to do himself justice, signified in very polite terms to the gentleman who stood behind him, that he could never play with ease and deliberation when he was overlooked by any bystander, and begg'd that he would have the goodness to be seated.

As this was a remonstrance which the stranger could not with any shew of breeding resist, he asked pardon, and retired to the chair of the physician, who frankly told him, that it was not the fashion of his country for one to submit his hand to the perusal of a spectator; and when, in consequence of this rebuff, he wanted to quarter himself upon the painter, he was refused by a wave of the hand, and a shake of the head, with an exclamation of, *Pardonnez moi!* which was repeated with such emphasis, as discomposed his effrontery, and he found himself obliged to sit down in a state of mortification.

The odds being thus removed, fortune proceeded in her usual channel; and though the Frenchman, deprived of his ally, endeavoured to practise divers strokes of finesse, the rest of the company observed him with such vigilance and caution, as baffled all his attempts, and in a very little time he was compelled to part with his winning: but having engaged in the match with an intention of taking all advantages, whether fair or unfair, that his superior skill should give him over the Englishman, the money was not refunded without a thousand disputes, in the course of which he essayed to intimidate his antagonist with high words, which were retorted by our hero with such interest, as convinced him that he had mistaken his man, and persuaded him to make his retreat in quiet. Indeed, it was not without cause that they repined at the bad success of their enterprize; because, in all likelihood, they had nothing to depend upon for the present but their own industry, and knew not how to defray their expences on the road, except by some acquisition of this kind.

Next morning they rose at day-break, and resolving to anticipate their fellow-lodgers, bespoke post-horses as soon as they could be admitted into the city; so that when our company appeared, their beasts were ready in the yard; and they only waited to discuss the bill, which they had ordered to be made out. The landlord of the inn presented his carte with fear and trembling to one of those ferocious cavaliers, who no sooner cast his eye upon the sum total, than he discharged a volley of dreadful oaths, and asked if the king's officers were to be treated in that manner. The poor publican protested with great humility, that he had the utmost respect for his majesty, and every thing that belonged to him; and that, far from consulting his own interest, all that he desired was, to be barely indemnified for the expence of their lodging.

This condescension seemed to have no other effect than that of encouraging their arrogance. They swore his extortion should be explained to the commandant of the town, who would, by making him a public example, teach other inn-keepers how to behave towards men of honour; and threatened with such confidence of indignation, that the wretched landlord, dreading the consequence of their wrath, implored pardon in the most abject manner, begging with many supplications, that he might have the pleasure of lodging them at his own charge. This was a favour which he with great difficulty obtained; they chid him severely for his imposition, exhorted him to have more regard for his own conscience, as well as for the convenience of his guests; and cautioning him in particular touching his behaviour to the gentlemen of the army, mounted their horses, and rode off in great state, leaving him very thankful for having so successfully appeased the choler of two officers, who wanted either inclination or ability to pay their bill: for experience had taught him to be apprehensive of all such travellers, who commonly lay the landlord under contribution, by way of atonement for the extravagance of his demands, even after he has professed his willingness to entertain them on their own terms.

CHAPTER LIV

Peregrine moralizes upon their Behaviour, which is
condemned by the Doctor, and defended by the Governor.
They arrive in Safety at Lisle, dine at an Ordinary,
visit the Citadel. The Physician quarrels with a
North-Briton, who is put in Arrest

THESE honourable adventurers being gone, Peregrine, who was present during the transaction, informed himself of the particulars from the mouth of the inn-keeper himself, who took God and the saints to witness, that he should have been a loser by their custom, even if the bill had been paid; because he was on his guard against their objections, and had charged every article at an under price: but such was the authority of officers in France, that he durst not dispute the least circumstance of their will; for had the case come under the cognizance of the magistrate, he must in course have suffered by the maxims of their government, which never fail to abet the oppression of the army; and besides, run the risque of incurring their future resentment, which would be sufficient to ruin him from top to bottom.

Our hero boiled with indignation at this instance of injustice and arbitrary power; and turning to his governor, asked if this too was a proof of the happiness enjoyed by the French people. Jolter replied, that every human constitution must in some things be imperfect; and owned, that in this kingdom gentlemen were more countenanced than the vulgar, because it was to be presumed, that their own sentiments of honour and superior qualifications, would entitle them to this preheminence, which had also a retrospective view to the merit of their ancestors, in consideration of which they were at first ennobled: but he affirmed, that the inn-keeper had misrepresented the magistracy, which in France never failed to punish flagrant outrages and abuse, without respect of persons.

The painter approved of the wisdom of the French government, in bridling the insolence of the mob, by which, he assured them, he had often suffered in his own person; having been often bespattered by hackney-coachmen, justled by draymen and porters, and reviled in the most opprobrious terms by the watermen of London, where he had once lost his bag, and a considerable quantity of hair, which had been cut off by some rascal in his passage through Ludgate, during the lord mayor's procession. On the other hand, the doctor with great warmth alledged, that those officers ought to suffer death, or banishment at least, for having plundered the people in this manner, which was so impudent and barefaced, as plainly to prove they were certain of escaping with impunity, and that they were old offenders in the same degree of delinquency. He said, that the greatest man in Athens would have been condemned to perpetual exile, and seen his estate confiscated for public use, had he dared in such a licentious manner to violate the rights of a fellow-citizen: and as for the little affronts to which a man may be subject, from the petulance of the multitude, he looked upon them as glorious indications of liberty, which ought not to be repressed, and would at any time rejoice to find himself overthrown in a kennel by the insolence of a son of freedom, even though the fall should cost him a limb: adding, by way of illustration, that the greatest pleasure he ever enjoyed, was in seeing a dustman wilfully overturn a gentleman's coach, in which two ladies were bruised, even to the danger of their lives. Pallet, shocked at the extravagance of this declaration, 'If that be the case, (said he) I wish you may see every bone in your body broke, by the first carman you meet in the streets of London.'

This argument being discussed, and the reckoning discharged without any deduction, although the landlord, in stating the articles, had an eye to the loss he had sustained by his own country-men, they departed from Arras, and arrived in safety at Lisle, about two o'clock in the afternoon.

They had scarce taken possession of their lodgings, in a large hotel on the Grande Place, when the inn-keeper gave them to understand, that he kept an ordinary below, which was frequented by several English gentlemen who resided in town, and that dinner was then upon the table. Peregrine, who seized all opportunities of observing new characters, persuaded his company to dine in public; and they were accordingly conducted to the place, where they found a mixture of Scotch and Dutch officers, who had come from Holland to learn their exercises at the academy, and some gentlemen in the French service, who were upon garison-duty in the citadel. Among these last was a person about the age of fifty, of a remarkably genteel air and polite address, dignified with a Maltese cross, and distinguished by the particular veneration of all those who knew him. When he understood that Pickle and his friends were travellers, he accosted the youth in English, which he spoke tolerably well; and as they were strangers, offered to attend them in the afternoon to all the places worth seeing in Lisle. Our hero thanked him for his excess of politeness, which (he said) was peculiar to the French nation; and struck with his engaging appearance, industriously courted his conversation, in the course of which he learnt, that this chevalier was a man of good sense and great experience, that he was perfectly well acquainted with the greatest part of Europe, had lived some years in England, and was no stranger to the constitution and genius of that people.

Having dined, and drank to the healths of the English and French kings, two Fiacres were called, in one of which the knight, with one of his companions, the governor and Peregrine seated themselves, the other being occupied by the physician, Pallet, and two Scottish officers, who proposed to accompany them in their circuit. The

first place they visited was the citadel, round the ramparts of which
they walked, under the conduct of the knight, who explained with
great accuracy the intention of every particular fortification belonging to that seemingly impregnable fortress; and when they had
satisfied their curiosity, took coach again, in order to view the
arsenal, which stands in another quarter of the town: but, just as
Pickle's carriage had crossed the Promenade, he heard his own
name bawled aloud by the painter; and ordering the Fiacre to stop,
saw Pallet with one half of his body thrust out at the window of the
other coach, crying with a terrified look, 'Mr. Pickle, Mr. Pickle,
for the love of God! halt, and prevent bloodshed, else here will
be carnage and cutting of throats.' Peregrine, surprized at this
exclamation, immediately alighted, and advancing to the other
vehicle, found one of their military companions standing upon the
ground, at the further side of the coach, with his sword drawn, and
fury in his countenance; and the physician, with a quivering lip
and haggard aspect, struggling with the other, who had interposed
in the quarrel, and detained him in his place.

Our young gentleman, upon inquiry, found that this animosity
had sprung from a dispute that happened upon the ramparts,
touching the strength of the fortification, which the doctor, according to custom, undervalued, because it was a modern work; saying,
that by the help of the military engines used among the ancients,
and a few thousands of pioneers, he would engage to take it in less
than ten days after he should sit down before it. The North-Briton,
who was as great a pedant as the physician, having studied fortification, and made himself master of Cæsar's Commentaries and
Polybius, with the observations of Folard,[1] affirmed, that all the
methods of besieging practised by the ancients, would be utterly
ineffectual against such a plan as that of the citadel of Lisle; and
began to compare the Vineæ, Aggeres, Arietes, Scorpiones and
Catapultæ of the Romans,[2] with the trenches, mines, batteries and
mortars used in the present art of war. The republican, finding
himself attacked upon what he thought his strong side, summoned
all his learning to his aid; and describing the famous siege of
Platæa, happened to misquote a passage of Thucydides, in which
he was corrected by the other, who having been educated for the
church, was also a connoisseur in the Greek language. The doctor,
incensed at being detected in such a blunder, in presence of Pallet,
who (he knew) would promulgate his shame, told the officer, with
great arrogance, that his objection was frivolous, and that he must
not pretend to dispute on these matters with one who had considered

them with the utmost accuracy and care. His antagonist, piqued at this supercilious insinuation, replied with great heat, that for ought he knew, the doctor might be a very expert apothecary, but that in the art of war, and knowledge in the Greek tongue, he was no other than an ignorant pretender. This asseveration produced an answer full of virulence, including a national reflection upon the soldier's country; and the contention rose to mutual abuse, when it was suppressed by the admonitions of the other two, who begged they would not expose themselves in a strange place, but behave themselves like fellow-subjects and friends. They accordingly ceased reviling each other, and the affair was seemingly forgot; but, after they had resumed their places in the coach, the painter unfortunately asked the meaning of the word Tortoise,[1] which he had heard them mention among the Roman implements of war. This question was answered by the physician, who described the nature of this expedient so little to the satisfaction of the officer, that he contradicted him flatly, in the midst of his explanation; a circumstance which provoked the republican to such a degree, that in the temerity of his passion, he uttered the epithet *impertinent scoundrel*; which was no sooner pronounced than the Caledonian made manual application to his nose, and leaping out of the coach, stood waiting for him on the plain; while he the (physician) made feeble efforts to join him, being easily retained by the other soldier; and Pallet, dreading the consequence in which he himself might be involved, bellowed aloud for prevention.

Our hero endeavoured to quiet the commotion, by representing to the Scot, that he had already taken satisfaction for the injury he had received; and telling the doctor, that he had deserved the chastisement which was inflicted upon him: but the officer (encouraged perhaps by the confusion of his antagonist) insisted upon his asking pardon for what he had said; and the doctor, believing himself under the protection of his friend Pickle, far from agreeing to such concession, breathed nothing but defiance and revenge: so that the chevalier, in order to prevent mischief, put the soldier under arrest, and sent him to his lodgings, under the care of the other French gentleman and his own companion; they being also accompanied by Mr. Jolter, who having formerly seen all the curiosities of Lisle, willingly surrendered his place to the physician.

CHAPTER LV

Pickle engages with a Knight of Malta,
in a Conversation upon the English Stage,
which is followed by a Dissertation on the Theatres
of the Ancients, by the Doctor

THE rest of the company proceeded to the arsenal, which having viewed, together with some remarkable churches, they, in their return, went to the comedy, and saw the Cid of Corneille tolerably well represented. In consequence of this entertainment, the discourse at supper turned upon dramatic performances; and all the objections of Mons. de Scudery to the piece they had seen acted, together with the decision of the French academy,[1] were canvassed and discussed. The knight was a man of letters and taste, and particularly well acquainted with the state of the English stage; so that when the painter boldly pronounced sentence against the French manner of acting, on the strength of having frequented a Covent-Garden club of criticks, and been often admitted by virtue of an order, into the pit; a comparison immediately ensued, not between the authors, but the actors of both nations, to whom the chevalier and Peregrine were no strangers. Our hero, like a good Englishman, made no scruple of giving the preference to the performers of his own country, who, he alledged, obeyed the genuine impulses of nature, in exhibiting the passions of the human mind; and entered so warmly into the spirit of their several parts, that they often fancied themselves the very heroes they represented. Whereas, the action of the Parisian players, even in their most interesting characters, was generally such an extravagance in voice and gesture, as is no where to be observed but on the stage. To illustrate this assertion, he availed himself of his talent, and mimicked the manner and voice of all the principal performers, male and female, belonging to the French comedy; to the admiration of the chevalier, who having complimented him upon this surprising modulation, begged leave to dissent in some particulars from the opinion he had avowed. 'That you have good actors in England, (said he) it would be unjust and absurd in me to deny; your theatre is adorned by one woman,[2] whose sensibility and sweetness of voice is such as I have never observed on any other stage; she has, besides, an elegance of person and expression of

272

features, that wonderfully adapt her for the most engaging characters of your best plays; and I must freely own that I have been as
highly delighted, and as deeply affected, by a Monimia and Belvidera at London, as ever I was by a Cornelia and Cleopatra at Paris.[1]
You can, moreover, boast of several comic actors who are perfect
masters of buffoonery and grimace; though, to be free with you,
I think, in these qualifications you are excelled by the players of
Amsterdam: neither are you destitute of those, who, with a good
deal of cultivation, might acquire some degree of excellence in the
representation of tragic characters: but I shall never cease to
wonder that the English, who are certainly a sensible and discerning people, should be so much infatuated, as to applaud and caress
with the most extravagant approbation, not to say adoration and
regard, one or two graciosos, who, I will be bold to say, would
scarce be able to earn their bread by their talents, on any other
theatre under the sun. I have seen one of these,[2] in the celebrated
part of Richard the third, which, I believe, is not a character of
ridicule, sollicit and triumph in the laugh of the audience, during
the best part of a scene in which the author has represented that
prince as an object of abhorrence. I have observed the same person
in the character of Hamlet, shake his fist with all the demonstrations
of wrath at his mistress, for no evident cause, and behave like
a ruffian to his own mother. Shocked at such want of dignity and
decorum in a prince, who seemed the favourite of the people, I
condemned the genius that produced him, but, upon a second
perusal of the play, transferred my censure to the actor, who, in
my opinion, had egregiously mistaken the meaning of the poet.
At a juncture, when his whole soul ought to be alarmed with terror
and amazement, and all his attention engrossed by the dreadful
object in view, I mean that of his friend whom he had murthered;
he expresses no passion but that of indignation against a drinking
glass, which he violently dashes in pieces on the floor, as if he had
perceived a spider in his wine; nay, while his eyes are fixed upon
the ground, he starts at the image of a dagger which he pretends
to see above his head, as if the pavement was a looking-glass that
represented it by reflexion: and at one time, I saw him walk a-cross
the stage, and lend an inferior character a box on the ear, after he
had with great wrath pronounced "Take thou that," or some
equivalent exclamation, at the other end of the scene. He represents
the grief of an hero, by the tears and manner of a whining school-
boy, and perverts the genteel deportment of a gentleman, into the
idle buffoonery of a miserable tobacconist; his whole art is no

other than a succession of frantic vociferation, such as I have heard in the cells of Bedlam, a slowness, hesitation and oppression of speech, as if he was troubled with an asthma, convulsive startings, and a ductility of features, suited to the most extravagant transitions. In a word, he is blessed with a distinct voice, and a great share of vivacity; but in point of feeling, judgment, and grace, is, in my opinion, altogether defective. Not to mention his impropriety in dress, which is so absurd, that he acts the part of a youthful prince, in the habit of an undertaker, and exhibits the gay, fashionable Lothario,[1] in the appearance of a mountebank. I beg pardon for treating this darling of the English with so little ceremony; and to convince you of my candour, frankly confess, that notwithstanding all I have said, he is qualified to make a considerable figure in the low characters of humour, which are so much relished by a London audience, if he could be prevailed upon to abate of that monstrous burlesque, which is an outrage against nature and common sense. As for his competitor in fame,[2] with an equal share of capacity, he is inferior to him in personal agility, sprightliness and voice. His utterance is a continual sing song, like the chanting of vespers, and his action resembles that of heaving ballast into the hold of a ship. In his outward deportment, he seems to have confounded the ideas of dignity and insolence of mien, acts the crafty, cool, designing Crookback, as a loud, shallow, blustering Hector; in the character of the mild patriot Brutus, loses all temper and decorum; nay, so ridiculous is the behaviour of him and Cassius at their interview, that setting foot to foot, and grinning at each other, with the aspect of two coblers enraged, they thrust their left sides together, with repeated shocks, that the hilts of their swords may clash for the entertainment of the audience; as if they were a couple of Merry Andrews, endeavouring to raise the laugh of the vulgar, on some scaffold at Bartholomew Fair. The despair of a great man who falls a sacrifice to the infernal practices of a subtle traitor, that enjoyed his confidence, this English Æsopus represents, by beating his own forehead, and bellowing like a bull; and indeed, in almost all his most interesting scenes, performs such strange shakings of the head, and other antic gesticulations, that when I first saw him act, I imagined the poor man laboured under that paralytical disorder, which is known by the name of St. Vitus's dance. In short, he seems to be a stranger to the more refined sensations of the soul, consequently his expression is of the vulgar kind, and he must often sink under the idea of the poet; so that he has recourse to such violence of affected agitation, as imposes upon the undiscerning spectator, but to the eye of taste, evinces him a meer player of that class whom your admired Shakespear justly compares to nature's journeymen tearing a passion to rags.[1] Yet this man, in spite of all these absurdities, is an admirable Falstaff, exhibits the character of the eighth Henry to the life, is reasonably applauded in the Plain Dealer, excels in the part of Sir John Brute,[2] and would be equal to many humorous situations in low comedy, which his pride will not allow him to undertake. I should not have been so severe upon these rivals, had not I seen them extolled by their partizans, with the most ridiculous and fulsome manifestation of praise, even in those very circumstances wherein (as I have observed) they chiefly failed.'

Pickle, not a little piqued to hear the qualifications of the two most celebrated actors in England treated with such freedom and disrespect, answered with some asperity, that the chevalier was a true critick, more industrious in observing the blemishes than in acknowledging the excellence of those who fell under his examination. It was not to be supposed that one actor could shine equally in all characters; and though his observations were undoubtedly very judicious, he himself could not help wondering that some of them had always escaped his notice, though he had been an assiduous frequenter of the playhouse. 'The two players in question, (said he) have, in your own opinion, a considerable share of merit in the characters of comic life; and as to the manners of the great personages in tragedy, and the operation of the grand passions of the soul, I apprehend, they may be variously represented, according to the various complexion and cultivation of different men. A Spaniard, for example, though impelled by the same passion, will express it very differently from a Frenchman; and what is looked upon as graceful vivacity and address by the one, would be considered as impertinence and foppery by the other: nay, so opposite is your common deportment from that of some other nations, that one of your own countrymen, in the relation of his travels, observes that the Persians even of this age, when they see any man perform unnecessary gestures, say he is either a fool or a Frenchman. The standard of demeanour being thus unsettled, a Turk, a Moor, an Indian, or inhabitant of any country, whose customs and dress are widely different from ours, may in his sentiments, possess all the dignity of the human heart, and be inspired by the noblest passion that animates the soul, and yet excite the laughter rather than the respect of an European spectator.

'When I first beheld your famous Parisian stage-heroine,[3] in one of her principal parts, her attitudes seemed so violent, and she tossed her arms around with such extravagance, that she put me in mind of a windmill under the agitation of a hard gale; while her voice and features exhibited the lively representation of an English scold. The action of your favourite male-performer[1] was, in my opinion, equally unnatural; he appeared with the affected airs of a dancing-master; at the most pathetic junctures of his fate, he lifted up his hands above his head, like a tumbler going to vault, and spoke as if his throat had been obstructed by an hair-brush; yet, when I compared their manners with those of the people before whom they performed, and made allowance for that exaggeration which obtains on all theatres, I was insensibly reconciled to their method of performance, and could distinguish abundance of merit beneath that oddity of appearance.'

The chevalier perceiving Peregrine a little irritated at what he had said, asked pardon for the liberty he had taken, in censuring the English players, assuring him that he had an infinite veneration for the British learning, genius and taste, which were so justly distinguished in the world of letters; and that notwithstanding the severity of his criticism, he thought the theatre of London much better supplied with actors than that of Paris. The young gentleman thanked him for his polite condescension, at which Pallet exulted, saying with a shake of the head, 'I believe so too, Monsieur;' and the physician, impatient of the dispute in which he had bore no share, observed with a supercilious air, that the modern stage was altogether beneath the notice of one who had an idea of ancient magnificence and execution; that plays ought to be exhibited at the expence of the state, as those of Sophocles were by the Athenians, and that proper judges should be appointed for receiving or rejecting all such performances as are offered to the public.

He then described the theatre at Rome, which contained eighty thousand spectators, gave them a learned disquisition into the nature of the Persona, or mask, worn by the Roman actors, which, he said, was a machine that covered the whole head, furnished on the inside with a brazen concavity, that, by reverberating the sound as it issued from the mouth, raised the voice, so as to render it audible to such an extended audience. He explained the difference between the Saltator and Declamator, one of whom acted, while the other rehearsed the part; and from thence took occasion to mention the perfection of their pantomimes, who were so amazingly distinct in the exercise of their art, that a certain prince of Pontus being at the court of Nero, and seeing one of them represent a story, begged him of the emperor, in order to employ him as an interpreter among barbarous nations, whose language he did not understand. Nay, divers cynic philosophers, who had condemned this entertainment unseen, when they chanced to be eye-witnesses of their admirable dexterity, expressed their sorrow for having so long debarred themselves of such rational enjoyment.

He dissented, however, from the opinion of Peregrine, who, as a proof of their excellence, had advanced, that some of the English actors fancied themselves the very thing they represented, and recounted a story from Lucian,[1] of a certain celebrated pantomime, who in acting the part of Ajax in his frenzy, was transported into a real fit of delirium, during which he tore to pieces the cloaths of that actor who stalked before him, beating the stage with iron shoes, in order to increase the noise, snatched an instrument from one of the musicians, and broke it over the head of him who represented Ulysses; and running to the consular bench, mistook a couple of senators for the sheep which were to be slain. The audience applauded him to the skies; but so conscious was the mimic of his own extravagance, when he recovered the use of his reason, that he actually fell sick with mortification; and being afterwards desired to re-act the piece, flatly refused to appear in any such character, saying, that the shortest follies were the best, and that it was sufficient for him to have been a madman once in his life.

CHAPTER LVI

An Adventure happens to Pipes, in Consequence of
which he is dismissed from Peregrine's Service.
The whole Company set out for Ghent in the Diligence.
Our Hero is captivated by a Lady in that Carriage;
interests her spiritual Director in his Behalf

THE doctor being fairly engaged on the subject of the ancients, would have proceeded the Lord knows how far, without hesitation, had not he been interrupted by the arrival of Mr. Jolter, who in great confusion told them, that Pipes having affronted a soldier, was then surrounded in the street, and would certainly be put to death, if some person of authority did not immediately interpose in his behalf.

Peregrine no sooner learn'd the danger of his trusty squire, than snatching up his sword, he ran down stairs, and was followed by the Chevalier, intreating him to leave the affair to his management. Within ten yards of the door they found Tom with his back to a wall, defending himself manfully with a mopstick against the assault of three or four soldiers, who at sight of the Maltese cross desisted from the attack, and were taken into custody by order of the knight. One of the aggressors being an Irishman, begged to be heard with great importunity, before he should be sent to the guard; and by the mediation of Pickle, was accordingly brought into the Hotel, with his companions, all three bearing upon their heads and faces evident marks of their adversary's prowess and dexterity. The spokesman being confronted with Pipes, informed the company, that having by accident met with Mr. Pipes, whom he considered as his countryman, though fortune had disposed of them in different services, he invited him to drink a glass of wine; and accordingly carried him to a Cabaret, where he introduced him to his comrades; but in the course of the conversation, which turned upon the power and greatness of the kings of France and England, Mr. Pipes had been pleased to treat his Most Christian Majesty with great disrespect; and when he (the entertainer) expostulated with him in a friendly manner about his impolite behaviour, observing, that he being in the French service, would be under the necessity of resenting his abuse, if he did not put a stop to it before the other gentlemen of the cloth should comprehend his meaning, he had set them all three at defiance, dishonoured him in particular with the opprobrious epithet of *rebel to his native king and country*, and even drank (in broken French) to the perdition of Lewis and all his adherents! that compelled by this outragious conduct, he, as the person who had recommended him to their society, had, in vindication of his own character, demanded satisfaction of the delinquent, who on pretence of fetching a sword, had gone to his lodging, from whence he all of a sudden sallied upon them with the mopstick, which he employed in the annoyance of them all without distinction, so that they were obliged to draw in their own defence.

Pipes being questioned by his master, with regard to the truth of this account, owned that every circumstance was justly represented; saying, he did not value their cheese-toasters a pinch of oakum; and that if the gentlemen had not shot in betwixt them, he would have trimmed them to such a tune, that they should not have had a whole yard to square. Peregrine reprimanded him sharply for his unmannerly behaviour, and insisted upon his asking pardon of those he had injured, upon the spot. But no consideration was efficacious enough to produce such concession; to this command he was both deaf and dumb, and the repeated threats of his master had no more effect than if they had been addressed to a marble statue. At length, our hero incensed at his obstinacy, started up, and would have chastised him with manual operation, had not he been prevented by the Chevalier, who found means to moderate his indignation so far, that he contented himself with dismissing the offender from his service; and after having obtained the discharge of the prisoners, gave them a Louis to drink, by way of recompence for the disgrace and damage they had sustained.

The Knight perceiving our young gentleman very much ruffled at this accident, and reflecting upon the extraordinary deportment and appearance of his valet, whose hair had by this time adopted a grizzled hue, imagined he was some favourite domestic, who had grown grey in the service of his master's family, and that, of consequence, he was uneasy at the sacrifice he had made. Swayed by this conjecture, he earnestly sollicited in his behalf; but all he could obtain, was a promise of re-admitting him into favour on the terms already proposed, or at least on condition that he should make his acknowledgment to the Chevalier, for his want of reverence and respect for the French monarch.

Upon this condescension, the culprit was called up stairs, and made acquainted with the mitigation of his fate; upon which he said, he would down on his marrow-bones to his own master, but would be damn'd before he would ask pardon of e'er a Frenchman in Christendom. Pickle, exasperated at this blunt declaration, ordered him out of his presence, and charged him never to appear before his face again; while the officer in vain employed all his influence and address to appease his resentment, and about midnight took his leave, with marks of mortification at his want of success.

Next day the company agreed to travel through Flanders in the Diligence, by the advice of Peregrine, who was not without hope of meeting with some adventure or amusement in that carriage; and Jolter took care to secure places for them all, it being resolved that the valet de chambre and the doctor's man should attend the vehicle on horseback; and as for the forlorn Pipes, he was left to reap the fruits of his own stubborn disposition, notwithstanding the united efforts of the whole triumvirate, who endeavoured to procure his pardon.

Every previous measure being thus taken, they set out from Lisle about six in the morning, and found themselves in the company of a female adventurer, a very handsome young lady, a Capuchin, and a Rotterdam Jew. Our young gentleman being the first of this society that entered, surveyed the strangers with an attentive eye, and seated himself immediately behind the beautiful unknown, who at once attracted his attention. Pallet seeing another lady unengaged, in imitation of his friend, took possession of her neighbourhood; the physician paired with the priest, and Jolter sat down by the Jew.

The machine had not proceeded many furlongs, when Pickle accosting the fair incognita, congratulated himself upon his happiness, in being the fellow-traveller of so charming a lady. She, without the least reserve or affectation, thanked him for his compliment, and replied with a sprightly air, that now they were embarked in one common bottom, they must club their endeavours to make one another as happy as the nature of their situation would permit them to be. Encouraged by this frank intimation, and captivated by her fine black eyes and easy behaviour, he attached himself to her from that moment; and in a little time the conversation became so particular, that the Capuchin thought proper to interfere in the discourse, in such a manner as gave the youth to understand, that he was there on purpose to superintend her conduct. He was doubly rejoiced at this discovery, in consequence of which he hoped to profit in his addresses, not only by the young lady's restraint, that never fails to operate in behalf of the lover, but also by the corruptibility of her guardian, whom he did not doubt of rendering propitious to his cause. Flushed with these expectations, he behaved with uncommon complacency to the father, who was charmed with the affability of his carriage, and on the faith of his generosity abated of his vigilance so much, that our hero carried on his suit without further molestation; while the painter, in signs and loud bursts of laughter, conversed with his Dulcinea, who was perfectly well versed in these simple expressions of satisfaction, and had already found means to make a dangerous invasion upon his heart.

Nor were the governor and physician unemployed, while their friends interested themselves in this agreeable manner. Jolter no sooner perceived the Hollander was a Jew, than he entered into an investigation of the Hebrew tongue, in which he was a connoisseur; and the doctor at the same time attacked the Mendicant on the ridiculous maxims of his order, together with the impositions of priest-craft in general, which (he observed) prevail so much among those who profess the Roman Catholic religion.

Thus coupled, each committee enjoyed their own conversation

apart, without any danger of encroachment; and all were so intent upon their several topics, that they scarce allowed themselves a small interval in viewing the desolation of Menin, as they passed through that ruined frontier. About twelve o'clock they arrived at Courtray, where the horses are always changed, and the company halt an hour for refreshment. Here Peregrine handed his charmer into an apartment, where she was joined by the other lady; and on pretence of seeing some of the churches in town, put himself under the direction of the Capuchin, from whom he learn'd, that the young lady was wife to a French gentleman, to whom she had been married about a year, and that she was now on her journey to visit her mother, who lived in Brussels, and who at that time laboured under a lingering distemper, which, in all probability, would soon put a period to her life. He then launched out in praise of her daughter's virtue and conjugal affection; and lastly told him, that he was her father confessor, and pitched upon to be her conductor through Flanders, by her husband, who, as well as his wife, placed the utmost confidence in his prudence and integrity.

Pickle easily comprehended the meaning of this insinuation, and took the hint accordingly. He tickled the priest's vanity with extraordinary encomiums upon the disinterested principles of his order, which were detached from all worldly pursuits, and altogether devoted to the eternal salvation of mankind. He applauded their patience, humility and learning, and lavished a world of praise upon their talent in preaching, which (he said) had more than once operated so powerfully upon him, that had he not been restrained by certain considerations which he could not possibly wave, he should have embraced their tenets, and begg'd admission into their fraternity; but, as the circumstances of his fate would not permit him to take such a salutary measure for the present, he intreated the good father to accept a small token of his love and respect, for the benefit of that convent to which he belonged. So saying, he pulled out a purse of ten guineas, which the Capuchin observing, turned his head another way, and lifting up his arm, displayed a pocket almost as high as his collar-bone, in which he deposited the money.

This proof of affection for the order produced a sudden and surprising effect upon the friar. In the transport of his zeal he wrung this semi-convert's hand, showered a thousand benedictions upon his head, and exhorted him, with the tears flowing from his eyes, to perfect the great work which the finger of God had begun in his heart; and as an instance of his concern for the welfare of his precious soul, the holy brother promised to recommend him strenuously to the pious admonitions of the young woman under his care, who was a perfect saint upon earth, and endued with the peculiar gift of mollifying the hearts of obdurate sinners. 'O father! (cried the hypocritical projector, who by this time perceived that his money was not thrown away) if I could be favoured but for one half hour with the private instructions of that inspired devotee, my mind presages, that I should be a stray'd sheep brought back into the fold, and that I should find easy entrance at the gates of heaven! There is something supernatural in her aspect; I gaze upon her with the most pious fervor, and my whole soul is agitated with tumults of hope and despair!' Having pronounced this rhapsody with transport half natural and half affected, the priest assured him, that these were operations of the spirit, which must not be repressed; and comforted him with the hope of enjoying the blessed interview which he desired, protesting, that as far as his influence extended, his wish should be that very evening indulged. The gracious pupil thanked him for his benevolent concern, which he swore should not be squandered upon an ungrateful object; and the rest of the company interrupting the conversation, they returned in a body to the inn, where they dined all together; and the ladies were persuaded to be our hero's guests.

As the subjects on which they had been engaged before dinner were not exhausted, each brace resumed their former theme, when they were replaced in the Diligence. The painter's mistress finished her conquest, by exerting her skill in the art of ogling, accompanied by frequent bewitching sighs, and some tender French songs that she sung with such pathetic expression, as quite melted the resolution of Pallet, and utterly subdued his affection: and he, to convince her of the importance of her victory, gave a specimen of his own talents, by entertaining her with that celebrated English ditty, the burthen of which begins with, *The pigs they lie with their arses bare.*

CHAPTER LVII

He makes some Progress in her Affections;
is interrupted by a Dispute between Jolter and a Jew;
appeases the Wrath of the Capuchin, who procures for him
an Interview with his fair Enslaver,
in which he finds himself deceived

PEREGRINE, mean while, employed all his insinuation and address in practising upon the heart of the Capuchin's fair charge. He had long ago declared his passion, not in the superficial manner of a French gallant, but with all the ardor of an enthusiast. He had languished, vow'd, flattered, kiss'd her hand by stealth, and had no reason to complain of his reception. Though by a man of a less sanguine disposition, her particular complaisance would have been deemed equivocal, and perhaps nothing more than the effect of French breeding and constitutional vivacity; he gave his own qualifications credit for the whole, and with these sentiments carried on the attack with such unabating vigour, that she was actually prevailed upon to accept a ring, which he presented as a token of his esteem; and every thing proceeded in a most prosperous train, when they were disturbed by the governor and Israelite, who in the heat of disputation raised their voices, and poured forth such effusions of gutturals, as set our lover's teeth on edge. As they spoke in a language unknown to every one in the carriage but themselves, and looked at each other with mutual animosity and rancour, Peregrine desired to know the cause of their contention. Upon which, Jolter exclaimed in a furious tone, 'This learned Levite, forsooth, has the impudence to tell me, that I don't understand Hebrew; and affirms, that the word *Benoni* signifies *child of joy*; whereas I can prove, and indeed have already said enough to convince any reasonable man, that in the Septuagint it is rightly translated into *son of my sorrow*.' Having thus explained himself to his pupil, he turned to the priest, with intention to appeal to his determination; but the Jew pulled him by the sleeve with great eagerness, saying, 'For the love of God be quiet, the Capuchin will discover who we are!' Jolter, offended at this conjunction, ecchoed 'Who we are!' with great emphasis; and repeating *nos poma natamus*,[1] asked ironically, to which of the Tribes the Jew thought he belonged? The Levite, affronted at his comparing him to a ball

283

of horse-dung, replied with a most significant grin, 'To the tribe of Issachar.'[1] And his antagonist, taking the advantage of his unwillingness to be known by the friar, and prompted by revenge for the freedom he had used, answered in the French language, that the judgment of God was still manifest upon their whole race, not only in their being in the state of exiles from their native land, but also in the spite of their hearts and pravity of their dispositions, which demonstrate them to be the genuine offspring of those who crucified the Saviour of the world.

His expectation was, however, defeated; the priest himself was too deeply engaged, to attend to the debates of other people. The physician, in the pride and insolence of his learning, had undertaken to display the absurdity of the Christian faith; having already (as he thought) confuted the Capuchin, touching the points of belief in which the Roman Catholics differ from the rest of the world. But, not contented with the imagined victory he had gained, he began to strike at the fundamentals of religion; and the father, with incredible forbearance, suffered him to make very free with the doctrine of the Trinity: but, when he levelled the shafts of his ridicule at the immaculate conception of the Blessed Virgin, the good man's patience forsook him, his eyes seemed to kindle with indignation, he trembled in every joint, and uttered with a loud voice, 'You are an abominable——I will not call thee heretic, for thou art worse (if possible) than a Jew; you deserve to be inclosed in a furnace seven times heated, and I have a good mind to lodge an information against you with the governor of Ghent, that you may be apprehended and punished as an impious blasphemer.'

This menace operated like a charm upon all present. The doctor was confounded, the governor dismayed, the Levite's teeth chattered, the painter was astonished at the general confusion, the cause of which he could not comprehend; and Pickle himself, not a little alarmed, was obliged to use all his interest and assiduity in appeasing this son of the church, who at length, in consideration of the friendship he professed for the young gentleman, consented to forgive what had passed, but absolutely refused to sit in contact with such a profane wretch, whom he looked upon as a fiend of darkness, sent by the enemy of mankind to poison the minds of weak people; so that, after having crossed himself, and muttered certain exorcisms, he insisted upon the doctor's changing places with the Jew, who approached the offended ecclesiastic in an agony of fear.

Matters being thus compromised, the conversation flowed in

a more general channel; and without the intervention of any other accident, or bone of contention, the carriage arrived at the city of Ghent about seven in the evening; and supper being bespoke for the whole company, our adventurer and his friends went out to take a superficial view of the place, leaving his new mistress to the pious exhortations of her confessor, whom (as we have already observed) he had secured in his interest. This zealous mediator spoke so warmly in his commendation, and interested her conscience so much in the affair, that she could not refuse her helping hand to the great work of his conversion, and promised to grant the interview he desired.

This agreeable piece of intelligence, which the Capuchin communicated to Peregrine at his return, elevated his spirits to such a degree, that he shone at supper with uncommon brilliance, in a thousand sallies of wit and pleasantry, to the admiration and delight of all present, especially of his fair Fleming, who seemed quite captivated by his person and behaviour.

The evening being thus spent to the satisfaction of all parties, the company broke up, and retired to their several apartments, when our lover, to his unspeakable mortification, learnt that the two ladies were obliged to lie in the same room, all the other chambers of the inn being preoccupied. When he imparted this difficulty to the priest, that charitable father, who was very fruitful in expedients, assured him, that his spiritual concerns should not be obstructed by such a slender impediment; and accordingly availed himself of his prerogative, by going into his daughter's chamber when she was almost undressed, and leading her into his own, on pretence of administring salutary food for her soul. Having brought the two votaries together, he prayed for success to the operations of grace, and left them to their mutual meditations, after having conjured them in the most solemn manner to let no impure sentiments, or temptations of the flesh, interfere with the hallowed design of their meeting.

The reverend intercessor being gone, and the door fastened on the inside, the pseudo-convert, transported with his passion, threw himself at his Amanda's feet; and begging she would spare him the tedious form of addresses, which the nature of their interview would not permit him to observe, began with all the impetuosity of love to profit by the occasion. But, whether she was displeased at the intrepidity and assurance of his behaviour, thinking herself intitled to more courtship and respect, or was really better fortified with chastity than he or his procurer had supposed her to be; certain it is, she expressed resentment and surprize at his boldness and presumption, and upbraided him with having imposed upon the charity of the friar. The young gentleman was really as much astonished at this rebuff, as she pretended to be at his declaration, and earnestly intreated her to consider how precious the moments were, and for once sacrifice superfluous ceremony, to the happiness of one who adored her with such a flame, as could not fail to consume his vitals, if she would not deign to bless him with her favour. Yet, notwithstanding all his tears, vows and supplications, his personal accomplishments and the tempting opportunity, all that he could obtain, was an acknowledgment of his having made an impression upon her heart, which she hoped the dictates of her duty would enable her to erase. This confession he considered as a delicate consent; and obeying the impulse of his love, snatched her up in his arms, with intention of seizing that which she declined to give; when this French Lucretia, unable to defend her virtue any other way, screamed aloud; and the Capuchin, setting his shoulder to the door, burst it open, and entered in an affected extasy of amazement. He lifted up his hands and eyes, and pretended to be thunderstruck at the discovery he had made; then, in broken exclamations, professed his horror at the wicked intention of our hero, who had covered such a damnable scheme with the mask of religion. In short, he performed his cue with such dexterity, that the lady believing him in earnest, begg'd he would forgive the stranger, on account of his youth and education, which had been tainted by the errors of heresy; and he was on these considerations content to accept the submission of our hero, who, far from renouncing his expectations, notwithstanding this mortifying repulse, confided so much in his own talents, and the confession which his mistress had made, that he resolved to make another effort, to which nothing could have prompted him but the utmost turbulence of unruly desire.

CHAPTER LVIII

*He makes another Effort towards the Accomplishment
of his Wish, which is postponed by a strange Accident*

HE directed his valet de chambre, who was a thorough-paced
pimp, to kindle some straw in the yard, and then pass by the door
of her apartment, crying with a loud voice that the house was on
fire. This alarm brought both ladies out of their chamber in a
moment, and Peregrine taking the advantage of their running to
the street door, entered the room and concealed himself under
a large table that stood in an unobserved corner. The nymphs, as
soon as they understood the cause of his Mercury's supposed
affright, returned to their apartment, and having said their prayers,
undressed themselves and went to bed. This scene, which fell
under the observation of Pickle, did not at all contribute to the
cooling of his concupiscence, but on the contrary, inflamed him
to such a degree, that he could scarce restrain his impatience, until
by her snoring, he concluded the fellow-lodger of his Amanda was
asleep. This welcome note no sooner saluted his ears, than he crept
to his charmer's bedside, and placing himself on his knees, gently
laid hold on her white hand, and pressed it to his lips. She had just
begun to close her eyes, and enjoy the agreeable oppression of
slumber, when she was roused by this rape, at which she started,
pronouncing in a tone of surprize and dismay, 'My God! who's
that?' The lover, with the most insinuating humility, besought
her to hear him; vowing that his intention in approaching her thus,
was not to violate the laws of decency, or that indelible esteem
which she had engraven on his heart; but to manifest his sorrow
and contrition for the umbrage he had given, to pour forth the
overflowings of his soul, and tell her that he neither could nor would
survive her displeasure. These and many more pathetic protestations, accompanied with sighs and tears, and other expressions of
genuine grief, which our hero had at command, could not fail to
melt the tender heart of the amiable Fleming, already prepossessed
in favour of his qualifications. She sympathized so much with his
affliction, as to weep in her turn, when she represented the impossibility of her rewarding his passion; and he seizing the favourable
moment, reinforced his sollicitations with such irresistible transports, that her resolution gave way, she began to breathe quick and
deep, expressed her fear of being overheard by the other lady, and

with an ejaculation of 'O heavens! I'm undone:' suffered herself, after a faint struggle, to be overpowered by her admirer, who made a lodgment upon the covered way of her bed, under the curtain of the counterscarp; and in all probability, would have in a few moments made himself master of the place; when her honour was secured for the present, by a strange sort of knocking upon the wainscot, at the other end of the room, hard by the bed in which the female adventurer lay.[1] Surprised at this circumstance which interrupted our assailant's operations, the lady begged him for heaven's sake to retreat, else her reputation would be ruined for ever: but when he represented to her, that her character would run a much greater risk, if he should be detected in withdrawing, she consented with great trepidation to his stay, and they listened in silence to the sequel of the noise that alarmed them. This was no other than an expedient of the painter, to awaken his Dulcinea, with whom he had made an assignation, or at least interchanged such signals as he thought amounted to a firm appointment. His nymph being disturbed in her first sleep, immediately understood the sound, and true to the agreement, rose, and unbolting the door as softly as possible, gave him admittance, leaving it open for his more commodious retreat.

While this happy gallant was employed in disengaging himself from the dishabille in which he had entered, the Capuchin suspecting that Peregrine would make another attempt upon his charge, had crept silently to the apartment, in order to reconnoitre, lest the adventure should be atchieved without his knowledge; a circumstance that would deprive him of the profits he might expect from his privity and concurrence. Finding the door unlatched, his suspicion was confirmed, and he made no scruple of creeping into the chamber on all-fours; so that the painter having stript himself to the shirt, in groping about for his Dulcinea's bed, chanced to lay his hand upon the shaven crown of the father's head, which by a circular motion, the priest began to turn round in his grasp, like a ball in a socket, to the surprize and consternation of poor Pallet, who having neither penetration to comprehend the case, nor resolution to withdraw his fingers from this strange object of his touch, stood sweating in the dark, and vented ejaculations with great devotion, till the friar tired with this exercise, and the painful posture in which he stooped, raised himself gradually upon his feet, heaving up at the same time the hand of the painter, whose terror and amazement increased to such a degree at this unaccountable elevation, that his faculties began to fail; and his palm in the confusion of his fright sliding over the priest's forehead, one of his fingers happened to slip into his mouth, and was immediately secured between the Capuchin's teeth, with as firm a fixure, as if it had been screwed in a blacksmith's vice. The painter was so much disordered by this sudden snap, which tortured him to the bone, that forgetting all other considerations, he roared aloud, 'Murder! fire! a trap, a trap! help, christians, for the love of God help!' Our hero confounded by these exclamations, which he knew would soon fill the room with spectators, and incensed at his own mortifying disappointment, was obliged to quit the untasted banquet, and approaching the cause of his misfortune, just as his tormentor had thought proper to release his finger, discharged such a hearty slap between his shoulders, as brought him to the ground with hideous bellowing, then retiring unperceived, to his own chamber, was one of the first who returned with a light, on pretence of having been alarmed with his cries. The Capuchin had taken the same precaution, and followed Peregrine into the room, pronouncing *Benedicite*, and crossing himself with many marks of astonishment; and the physician and Jolter appearing at the same time, the unfortunate painter was found lying naked on the floor, in all the agony of horror and dismay, blowing upon his left hand, that hung dangling from the elbow, like a boy who had burnt his fingers, in attempting to snatch roasted chesnuts from the fire. The circumstance of his being found in that apartment, and the attitude of his affliction, which was extremely ridiculous, provoked the doctor to a smile, and produced a small relaxation in the severity of the governor's countenance; while Pickle, testifying surprize and concern, lifted him from the ground, and enquired into the cause of his present situation. Having, after some recollection, and fruitless endeavours to speak, recovered the use of his tongue, he told them that the house was certainly haunted by evil spirits, by which he had been conveyed (he knew not how) into that apartment, and afflicted with all the tortures of hell; that one of them had made itself sensible to his feeling, in the shape of a round ball of smooth flesh, that turned round under his hand, like an astronomer's globe, and then rising up to a surprising height, was converted into a machine that laid hold on his finger, by a snap, and having pinned him to the spot, he continued for some moments in unspeakable agony, till at last the engine seemed to melt away from his finger, and he received a sudden thwack upon his shoulders, as if discharged by the arm of a giant, which overthrew him in an instant upon the floor. The priest hearing this strange account, pulled out of one of his pouches a piece of consecrated candle, which he lighted immediately, and muttered certain mysterious conjurations. Jolter, imagining that Pallet was drunk, shook his head, saying, he believed the spirit was no where but in his own brain. The physician, for once, condescended to be a wag, and looking towards one of the beds, observed, that in his opinion, the painter had been misled by the flesh, and not by the spirit. The fair Fleming lay in silent astonishment and affright; and her fellow-lodger, in order to acquit herself of all suspicion, exclaimed with incredible volubility, against the author of this uproar, who (she did not doubt) had concealed himself in the apartment, with a view of perpetrating some wicked attempt upon her precious virtue, and was punished and prevented by the immediate interposition of heaven. At her desire, therefore, and the earnest sollicitation of the other lady, he was conducted to his own bed, and the chamber being evacuated, they locked their door, fully resolved to admit no more visitants for that night: while Peregrine, mad with seeing the delicious morsel, snatched (as it were) from his very lip, stalked through the passage, like a ghost, in hopes of finding some opportunity of re-entering, till the day beginning to break, he was obliged to retire, cursing the ideotical conduct of the painter, which had so unluckily interfered with his delight.

CHAPTER LIX

*They depart from Ghent. Our Hero engages in a
political Dispute with his Mistress, whom he offends,
and pacifies with Submission. He practises an Expedient
to detain the Carriage at Alost, and confirms
the Priest in his Interest*

NEXT day, about one o'clock, after having seen every thing remarkable in town, and been present at the execution of two youths, who were hanged for ravishing a whore, they took their departure from Ghent, in the same carriage which had brought them thither; and the conversation turning upon the punishment they had seen inflicted, the Flemish beauty expressed great sympathy and compassion for the unhappy sufferers, who (as she had been informed) had fallen victims to the malice of the accuser. Her sentiments were espoused by all the company, except the French lady of pleasure, who, thinking the credit of the sisterhood concerned in the affair, bitterly inveighed against the profligacy of the age, and particularly the base and villainous attempts of man, upon the chastity of the weaker sex; saying, with a look of indignation directed to the painter, that for her own part, she should never be able to manifest the acknowledgment she owed to providence, for having protected her, last night, from the wicked aims of unbridled lust. This observation introduced a series of jokes, at the expence of Pallet, who hung his ears, and sat with a silent air of dejection, fearing that through the malevolence of the physician, his adventure might reach the ears of his wife. Indeed, though we have made shift to explain the whole transaction to the reader, it was an inextricable mystery to every individual in the diligence; because the part which was acted by the Capuchin, was known to himself alone; and even he was utterly ignorant of Pickle's being concerned in the affair; so that the greatest share of the painter's sufferings were supposed to be the exaggerations of his own extravagant imagination.

In the midst of their discourse on this extraordinary subject, the driver told them, that they were now on the very spot where a detachment of the allied army had been intercepted and cut off by the French; and stopping the vehicle, entertained them with a local description of the battle of Melle. Upon this occasion, the Flemish lady, who since her marriage had become a keen partizan for the French, gave a minute detail of all the circumstances, as they had been represented to her by her husband's brother, who was in the action; and this account, which sunk the number of the French to sixteen, and raised that of the allies to twenty thousand men, was so disagreeable to truth, as well as to the laudable partiality of Peregrine, that he ventured to contradict her assertions, and a fierce dispute commenced, that not only regarded the present question, but also comprehended all the battles in which the duke of Marlborough had commanded against Lewis the fourteenth. In the course of these debates, she divested that great general of all the glory he had acquired, by affirming, that every victory he gained, was purposely lost by the French generals, in order to bring the schemes of madam de Maintenon into discredit;[1] and as a particular instance, alledged that while the citadel of Lisle was besieged, Lewis said, in presence of the Dauphin, that if the allies should be obliged to raise the siege, he would immediately declare his marriage with that lady; upon which, the son sent private orders to marshal Boufflers to surrender the place. This strange allegation was supported by the asseverations of the priest and the courtezan, and admitted as truth by the governor, who pretended to have heard it from good authority: while the doctor sat neutral, as one who thought it scandalous to know the history of such modern events; and the Israelite, being a true Dutchman, listed himself under the banners of our hero, who in attempting to demonstrate the absurdity and improbability of what they had advanced, raised such a hue and cry against himself, and being insensibly heated in the altercation, irritated his Amanda to such a degree, that her charming eyes kindled with fury, and he saw great reason to think, that if he did not fall upon some method to deprecate her wrath, she would in a twinkling sacrifice all her esteem for him, to her own zeal for the glory of the French nation. Swayed by this apprehension, his ardour cooled by degrees, and he insensibly detached himself from the argument, leaving the whole care of supporting it on the Jew, who finding himself deserted, was fain to yield at discretion; so that the French remained masters of the field, and their young heroine resumed her good humour. And let the circumstances of this contention warn the reader, against all disputes with female politicians; unless he is desirous of incuring their animosity and implacable resentment; for, in matters of state, they are all, to a woman, enthusiasts, who believe that all those who differ from them in opinion, are in a state of reprobation; and, far from laying any stress upon probability, in the articles of their faith, like believers of another class, disdainfully reject the evidence of reason, and trust to the revelation of their own fancy.[1]

Our hero having therefore prudently submited to the superior intelligence of his fair enslaver, began to be harrassed with the fears of losing her for ever, upon their arrival at Brussels, and set his invention at work, to contrive some means of indemnifying himself for his assiduities, presents, and the disappointment he had already undergone, before they should reach that city: on pretence of enjoying a freer air, he mounted the box, and employed his elocution and generosity with such success, that the driver undertook to disable the Diligence from proceeding beyond the town of Alost for that day; and in consequence of his promise, gently overturned it, when they were about a mile short of that baiting place. He had taken his measures so discreetly, that this accident was attended with no other inconvenience than a fit of fear, that took possession of the ladies, and the necessity to which they were reduced, by the declaration of the coachman, who, upon examining the carriage, assured the company that the axle-tree had given way,

and advised them to walk forward to the inn, while he would jog
after them at a slow pace, and do his endeavour that the damage
should be immediately repaired. Peregrine pretended to be very
much concerned at what had happened, and even cursed the driver
for his inadvertency, expressing infinite impatience to be at
Brussels, and wishing that this misfortune might not detain them
another night upon the road; but when his under-strapper, according to his instructions, came afterwards to the inn, and gave them
to understand, that the workman he had employed, could not possibly refit the machine in less than six hours, the crafty youth
affected to lose all temper, stormed at his emissary, whom he
reviled in the most opprobious terms, and threatened to cane for his
misconduct. The fellow protested, with great humility, that their
being overturned was owing to the failure of the axle-tree, and not
to his want of care or dexterity in driving; though rather than be
thought the cause of incommoding him, he would inquire for a
post-chaise, in which he might depart for Brussels immediately.
This expedient Pickle rejected, unless the whole company could be
accommodated in the same manner; and he had been previously
informed by the driver, that the town could not furnish more than
one vehicle of that sort. His governor, who was quite ignorant of
his scheme, represented that one night would soon be passed,
and exhorted him to bear this small disappointment with a good
grace, especially as the house seemed to be well provided for their
entertainment, and the company so much disposed to be sociable.
The Capuchin, who had found his account in cultivating the
acquaintance of the young stranger, was not ill-pleased at this
event, which might, by protracting the term of their intercourse,
yield him some opportunity of profiting still further by his liberality:
he therefore joined Mr. Jolter in his admonitions, congratulating
himself upon the prospect of enjoying his conversation a little
longer than he had expected; and our young gentleman received a
compliment to the same purpose from the Hebrew, who had that
day exercised his gallantry upon the French coquette, and was not
without hope of reaping the fruits of his attention, his rival, the
painter, being quite disgraced and dejected by the adventure of
last night. As for the doctor, he was too much engrossed in the
contemplation of his own importance, to interest himself in the
affair, or its consequences, further than by observing, that the
European powers ought to establish public games, like those that
were celebrated of old in Greece; in which case, every state would
be supplied with such dextrous charioteers, as could drive a machine

at full speed, within a hair's breadth of a precipice, without any danger of its being overthrown. Peregrine could not help yielding to their remonstrances, and united complaisance, for which he thanked them in very polite terms, and his passion seeming to subside, proposed that they should amuse themselves in walking round the ramparts, with a view of enjoying some private conversation with his admired Fleming, who had this whole day behaved with remarkable reserve. The proposal being embraced, he (as usual) handed her into the street, and took all opportunities of promoting his suit; but they were attended so closely by her father confessor, that he foresaw it would be impracticable to accomplish his aim, without the connivance of that ecclesiastick, which he was obliged to purchase with another purse, that he offered, and was accepted as a charitable atonement for his criminal behaviour during the interview which the friar had procured for the good of his soul. This benefaction was no sooner made, than the pious mendicant edged off by little and little, till he joined the rest of the company, leaving his generous patron at full liberty to prosecute his purpose. It is not to be doubted that our adventurer made a good use of this occasion: he practised a thousand flowers of rhetoric, and actually exhausted his whole address, in persuading her to have compassion upon his misery, and indulge him with another private audience, without which he should run distracted, and be guilty of extravagancies, which, in the humanity of her disposition, she would weep to see. But, instead of complying with his request, she chid him severely for his presumption, in persecuting her with his vicious addresses; and assured him, that although she had secured a chamber for herself in this place, because she had no ambition to be better acquainted with the other lady, he would be in the wrong to disturb her with another nocturnal visit; for she was determined to deny him admittance. The lover was comforted by this hint, which he understood in the true acceptation, and his passion being inflamed by the obstacles he had met with in this intrigue, his heart beat high with the prospect of possession. These raptures of expectation produced an inquietude, which disabled him from bearing that share of the conversation for which he used to be distinguished. His behaviour at supper was a vicissitude of startings, and reveries; and the Capuchin imputing this disorder to a second repulse from his charge, began to be invaded with the apprehension of being obliged to refund, and in a whisper forbad our hero to despair.

CHAPTER LX

The French Coquet entraps the Heart of the Jew,
against whom Pallet enters into a Conspiracy;
by which Peregrine is again disappointed,
and the Hebrew's Incontinence exposed

MEAN while the French syren, baulked in her design upon her
English cully, who was so easily disheartened, and hung his ears in
manifest despondence, rather than run the risque of making a
voyage that should be altogether unprofitable, resolved to practise
her charms upon the Dutch merchant; and had already made such
innovation upon his heart, that he cultivated her with peculiar
complacency, gazed upon her with a most libidinous stare, and
unbended his aspect into a grin that was truly Israelitish. The
painter saw, and was offended at this correspondence, which he
considered as an insult upon his misfortune, as well as an evident
preference of his rival; and, conscious of his own timidity, swallowed
an extraordinary glass, that his invention might be stimulated, and
his resolution raised to the contrivance and execution of some
scheme of revenge. The wine, however, failed in the expected
effect, and without inspiring him with the plan, served only to
quicken his desire of vengeance; so that he communicated his
purpose to his friend Peregrine, and begged the assistance of his
imagination; but our young gentleman was too intent upon his own
affair, to mind the concerns of any other person, and he declining
to be engaged in the project, Pallet had recourse to the genius of
Pickle's valet de chambre, who readily embarked in the undertaking, and invented a plan, which was executed accordingly.

The evening being pretty far advanced, and the company
separated into their respective apartments, Pickle repaired, in all
the impatience of youth and desire, to the chamber of his charmer,
and finding the door unbolted, entered in a transport of joy. By the
light of the moon, which shone through the window, he was conducted to her bed, which he approached in the utmost agitation,
and perceiving her to all appearance asleep, essayed to wake her
with a gentle kiss; but this method proved ineffectual, because she
was determined to save herself the confusion of being an accomplice in his guilt. He repeated the application, murmured a most
passionate salutation in her ear, and took such other gentle methods

of signifying his presence, as persuaded him that she was resolved to sleep, in spite of all his endeavours: flushed with this agreeable supposition, he locked the door, in order to prevent interruption, and stealing himself under the cloaths, set fortune at defiance, while he held the fair creature circled in his arms.

Nevertheless, near as he seemed to be to the happy accomplishment of his desire, his hope was again frustrated by a fearful noise, which in a moment waked his Amanda in a fright, and for the present engaged all his attention: his valet de chambre, whom Pallet had consulted as a confederate, in his revenge against the lady of pleasure and her Jewish gallant, had hired of certain Bohemians, who chanced to lodge at the inn, a jack-ass adorned with bells, which, when every body was retired to rest, and the Hebrew supposed to be bedded with his mistress, they led up-stairs into a long thoroughfare, from which the chambers were detached on each side; and the painter, perceiving the lady's door a-jar, according to his expectation, mounted this animal, with intention to ride into the room, and disturb the lovers in the midst of their mutual endearments; but the ass, true to his kind, finding himself bestrid by an unknown rider, instead of advancing, in obedience to his conductor, retreated backwards to the other end of the passage, in spite of all the efforts of the painter, who spurred, and kicked, and pummelled to no purpose. It was the noise of this contention between Pallet and the ass, which invaded the ears of Peregrine and his mistress, neither of whom could form the least rational conjecture about the cause of such strange disturbance, which increased as the animal approached their apartment; till, at length, the Bourrique's retrograde motion was obstructed by their door, which it burst open, in a twinkling, with one kick, and entered with such complication of sound, as terrified the lady almost into a fit, and threw her lover into an agony of perplexity and confusion. The painter, finding himself thus violently intruded into the bed-chamber of he knew not whom, and dreading the resentment of the possessor, who might discharge a pistol at him, as a robber who had broke into his apartment, was overwhelmed with consternation, and redoubled his exertion, to accomplish a speedy retreat, sweating all the time with fear, and putting up petitions to heaven for his safety; but his obstinate companion, regardless of his situation, instead of submitting to his conduct, began to turn round like a millstone, the united sound of his feet and bells producing a most surprising concert. The unfortunate rider, whirled about in this manner, would have quitted his seat, and left the beast to his own amusement, but the rotation was so rapid, that the terror of a severe fall hindered him from attempting to dismount, and in the desperation of his heart, he seized one of its ears, which he pinched so unmercifully, that the creature set up his throat, and brayed aloud. This hideous exclamation was no sooner heard by the fair Fleming, already chilled with panic, and prepared with superstition, than, believing herself visited by the devil, who was permitted to punish her for her infidelity to the marriage-bed, she uttered a fearful scream, and began to repeat her paternoster with a loud voice. Her lover, finding himself under the necessity of retiring, started up, and stung with the most violent pangs of rage and disappointment, ran directly to the spot from whence this diabolical noise seemed to proceed, and encountering the ass, discharged such a volley of blows at him and his rider, that the creature carried him off at a round trot, and they roared in unison all the way. Having thus cleared the room of such disagreeable company, he went back to his mistress, and assuring her, that this was only some foolish prank of Pallet, took his leave, with a promise of returning after the quiet of the inn should be re-established.

In the mean time the noise of the Bourrique, the cries of the painter, and the lady's scream, had alarmed the whole house; and the ass, in the precipitation of his retreat, seeing people with lights before him, took shelter in the apartment for which he was at first designed, just as the Levite, arroused at the uproar, had quitted his Dulcinea, and was attempting to recover his own chamber, unperceived; but, seeing himself opposed by such an animal, mounted by a tall, meagre, lanthorn-jawed figure, half naked, with a white night-cap upon his head, which added to the natural paleness of his complexion, the Jew was sorely troubled in mind, and believing it to be an apparition of Balaam and his ass, fled backward with a nimble pace, and crept under the bed, where he lay concealed. Mr. Jolter, and the priest, who were the foremost of those who had been arroused by the noise, were not unmoved when they saw such a spectacle rushing into this chamber, from whence the lady of pleasure began to shriek. The governor made a full halt, and the Capuchin discovered no inclination to proceed. They were (however) by the pressure of the crowd that followed them, thrust forward to the door, through which the vision entered; and there Jolter, with great ceremony, complimented his reverence with the pas, beseeching him to walk in. The mendicant was too courteous and humble to accept this preheminence, and a very earnest dispute ensued; during which the ass, in the course of his circuit, shewed

himself and rider, and in a trice decided the contest; for, struck with
this second glimpse, both, at one instant, sprung backward with
such force, as overturned their next men, who communicated the
impulse to those that stood behind them, and these again to others;
so that the whole passage was strewed with a long file of people,
that lay in a line, like the sequel and dependance of a pack of cards.
In the midst of this havock, our hero returned from his own room,
with an air of astonishment, asking the cause of this uproar, and
receiving such hints of intelligence as Jolter's consternation would
permit him to give, snatched the candle out of his hand, and
advanced into the haunted chamber without hesitation, being
followed by all present, who broke forth into a long and loud peal
of laughter, when they perceived the ludicrous source of their
disquiet. The painter himself made an effort to join their mirth,
but he had been so harrowed by fear, and smarted so much with the
pain of the discipline he had received from Pickle, that he could not,
with all his endeavour, vanquish the ruefulness of his countenance;
and his attempt served only to increase the aukwardness of his
situation, which was not at all mended by the behaviour of the
coquette, who, furious with her disappointment, slipped on a petticoat and bed-gown, and springing upon him, like another Hecuba,
with her nails, deprived all one side of his nose of the skin, and
would not have left him an eye to see thro', if some of the company
had not rescued him from her unmerciful talons. Provoked at this
outrage, as well as by her behaviour to him in the Diligence, he
publickly explained his intention in entering her chamber in this
equipage; and, missing the Hebrew among the spectators, assured
them, that he must have absconded somewhere in the apartment:
in consequence of this intimation, the room was immediately
searched, and the mortified Levite pulled by the heels from his
lurking-place; so that Pallet had the good fortune, at last, to transfer
the laugh from himself to his rival, and the French inamorata, who
accordingly underwent the ridicule of the whole audience.

CHAPTER LXI

Pallet, endeavouring to unravel the
Mystery of the Treatment he had received,
falls out of the Frying Pan into the Fire

NEVERTHELESS, Pallet was still confounded, and chagrined by
one consideration, which was no other than that of his having
been so roughly handled in the chamber, belonging (as he found
upon enquiry) to the handsome young lady, who was under the
Capuchin's direction. He recollected, that the door was fast locked,
when his beast burst it open, and he had no reason to believe that
any person followed him in his irruption: on the other hand, he
could not imagine, that such a gentle creature would either attempt
to commit, or be able to execute such a desperate assault as that
which his body had sustained; and her demeanor was so modest
and circumspect, that he durst not harbour the least suspicion of
her virtue.

These reflexions bewildered him in the labyrinth of thought: he
rummaged his whole imagination, endeavouring to account for
what had happened; and at length concluded, that either Peregrine,
or the devil, or both, must have been at the bottom of the whole
affair, and determined, for the satisfaction of his curiosity, to watch
our hero's motions, during the remaining part of the night, so
narrowly, that his conduct, mysterious as it was, should not be able
to elude his penetration.

With these sentiments he retired to his own room, after the ass
had been restored to the right owners, and the priest had visited
and confirmed his fair ward, who had been almost distracted with
fear; and silence no sooner prevailed again, than he crawled darkling towards her door, and huddled himself up in an obscure corner,
from whence he might observe the ingress or egress of any human
creature. He had not long remained in this posture, when, fatigued
with this adventure, and that of the preceding night, his faculties
were gradually overpowered with slumber, and falling fast asleep,
he began to snore like a whole congregation of presbyterians. The
Flemish beauty, hearing this discordant noise in the passage, began
to be afraid of some new alarm, and very prudently bolted her door;
so that when her lover wanted to repeat his visit, he was not only
surprised and incensed at this disagreeable serenade, the author

299

of which he did not know; but when, compelled by his passion, which was by this time wound to the highest pitch, he ventured to approach the entrance, he had the extreme mortification to find himself shut out; and he durst not knock, or signify his presence in any other manner, on account of the lady's reputation, which would have greatly suffered, had the snorer been waked by his endeavours. Had he known that the person who thus thwarted his views, was the painter, he would have taken some effectual step to remove him; but he could not conceive what should induce Pallet to take up his residence in that corner; nor could he use the assistance of a light, to distinguish him, because there was not a candle burning in the house; and besides, the sleeper might have opened his eyes in the very moment of his being detected by Peregrine, who would have incurred suspicion, by appearing, at such an hour, at that part of the inn, so remote from his own bed-chamber.[1]

It is impossible to describe the rage and vexation of our hero, while he continued thus tantalized upon the brink of bliss, after his desire had been exasperated by the circumstances of his two former disappointments. He ejaculated a thousand execrations against his own fortune, cursed all his fellow-travellers, without exception, vowed revenge against the painter, who had twice confounded his most interesting scheme, and was tempted to execute immediate vengeance upon the unknown cause of his present misadventure. In this agony of distraction did he sweat two whole hours in the passage, though not without some faint hope of being delivered from his tormentor, who (he imagined) upon waking, would undoubtedly shift his quarters, and leave the field free to his designs; but when he heard the cock repeat his salutation to the morn, which began to open on the rear of night, he could no longer restrain his indignation, but going to his own chamber, filled a basin with cold water, and, standing at some distance, discharged it full in the face of the gaping snorer, who, over and above the surprize occasioned by the application, was almost suffocated by the liquor that entered his mouth, and ran down into his wind-pipe. While he gasped like a person half drowned, without knowing the nature of his disaster, or remembring the situation in which he fell asleep, Peregrine retired to his own door, and, to his no small astonishment, from a long howl that invaded his ears, learnt that the patient was no other than Pallet, who had now, for the third time, baulked his good fortune.

Enraged at the complicated trespasses of this unfortunate

offender, he rushed from his apartment with a horse-whip, and encountering the painter in his flight, overturned him in the passage, and exercised the instrument of his wrath with great severity, on pretence of mistaking him for some presumptuous cur, which had disturbed the repose of the inn; nay, when he called aloud for mercy in a supplicating tone, and his chastiser could no longer pretend to treat him as a quadruped, such was the virulence of the young gentleman's indignation, that he could not help declaring his satisfaction, by telling Pallet he had richly deserved the punishment he had undergone, for his madness, folly and impertinence, in contriving and executing such idle schemes, as had no other tendency than that of plaguing his neighbours.

Pallet protested with great vehemence, that he was innocent as the child unborn of any intention to give umbrage to any person whatever, except the Israelite and his doxy, who he knew had incurred his displeasure. 'But, as God is my Saviour! (said he) I believe I am persecuted with witchcraft, and begin to think that damn'd priest is an agent of the devil; for he has been but two nights in our company, during which I have not closed an eye, but on the contrary have been tormented by all the fiends of hell.' Pickle peevishly replied, that his torments had been occasioned by his own foolish imagination; and asked how he came to howl in that corner. The painter, who did not think proper to own the truth, said, that he had been transported thither by some preternatural conveyance, and soused in water by an invisible hand: and the youth, in hope of profiting by his absence, advised him to retire immediately to his bed, and by sleep strive to comfort his brain, which seemed to be not a little disordered by the want of that refreshment. Pallet himself began to be very much of the same way of thinking, and in compliance with such wholesome counsel, betook himself to rest, muttering prayers all the way for the recovery of his understanding.

Pickle attended him to his chamber, and locking him up, put the key in his own pocket, that he might not have it in his power to interrupt him again: but in his return he was met by Mr. Jolter and the doctor, who had been a second time alarmed by the painter's cries, and come thither to inquire about this new adventure. Half frantic with such a series of disappointments, he cursed them in his heart for their unseasonable appearance; and when they questioned him about Pallet, told them he had found him stark staring mad, howling in a corner and wet to the skin, and conducted him to his room, where he was now abed. The physician hearing this circumstance, made a merit of his vanity, and under pretence of concern for the patient's welfare, desired he might have an opportunity of examining the symptoms of his disorder, without loss of time, alledging, that many diseases might have been stifled in the birth, which afterwards baffled all the endeavours of the medical art. The young gentleman accordingly delivered the key, and once more withdrew into his own chamber, with a view of seizing the first occasion that should present itself of renewing his application to his Amanda's door; while the doctor, in his way to Pallet's apartment, hinted to the governor his suspicion, that the patient laboured under that dreadful symptom called the hydrophobia, which he observed had sometimes appeared in persons who were not previously bit by a mad dog. This conjecture he founded upon the howl he uttered when he was soused with water, and began to recollect certain circumstances of the painter's behaviour for some days past, which now he could plainly perceive had prognosticated some such calamity. He then ascribed the distemper to the violent frights he had lately undergone, affirmed that the affair of the Bastile had made such a violent incroachment upon his understanding, that his manner of thinking and speaking was intirely altered; and by a theory of his own invention, explained the effects of fear upon a loose system of nerves, and demonstrated the modus in which the animal spirits operate upon the ideas and power of imagination.

This disquisition, which was communicated at the painter's door, might have lasted till breakfast, had not Jolter reminded him of his own maxim, *Venienti occurrite morbo*;[1] upon which he put the key to immediate use, and they walked softly towards the bed, where the patient lay extended at full length in the arms of slumber. The physician took notice of his breathing hard, and his mouth being open; and from these diagnostics declared, that the liquidum nervosum was intimately affected, and the saliva impregnated with the spiculated particles of the virus, howsoever contracted. This sentence was still farther confirmed by the state of his pulse, which being full and slow, indicated an oppressed circulation, from a loss of elasticity in the propelling arteries; and he proposed, that he should immediately suffer a second aspersion of water, which would not only contribute to the cure, but also certify them beyond all possibility of doubt, with regard to the state of the disease: for it would evidently appear, from the manner in which he would bear the application, whether or not his horror of water amounted to a confirmed hydrophobia. Mr. Jolter, in compliance with this proposal, began to empty a bottle of water, which he found in the room in a basin; when he was interrupted by the prescriber, who advised him to use the contents of the chamber-pot, which being impregnated with salt, would operate more effectually than the pure element. Thus directed, the governor lifted up the vessel, which was replete with medicine, and with one turn of his hands discharged the whole healing inundation upon the ill-omen'd patient, who waking in the utmost distraction of horror, yelled most hideously, just at the time when Peregrine had brought his mistress to a parley, and entertained hopes of being admitted into her chamber.

Terrified at this exclamation, she instantly broke off the treaty, beseeching him to retire from the door, that her honour might receive no injury from his being found in that place; and he had just enough of recollection left to see the necessity of obeying the order; in conformity to which he retreated, well nigh deprived of his senses, and almost persuaded, that so many unaccountable disappointments must have proceeded from some supernatural cause, of which the idiot Pallet was no more than the involuntary instrument.

Mean while, the doctor having ascertained the malady of the patient, whose cries, interrupted by frequent sobs and sighs, he interpreted into the barking of a dog; having no more salt-water at hand, resolved to renew the bath with such materials as chance would afford, and actually laid hold of the bottle and basin. But by this time, the painter had recovered the use of his senses so well, as to perceive his drift; and starting up, like a frantic Bedlamite, ran directly to his sword, swearing with many horrid imprecations, that he would murder them both immediately, if he should be hanged before dinner. They did not choose to wait the issue of his threat, but retired with such precipitation, that the physician had almost dislocated his shoulder, by running against one side of the entry; and Jolter having pulled the door after him, and turned the key, betook himself to flight, roaring aloud for assistance. His colleague seeing the door secured, valued himself upon his resolution, and exhorted him to return; declaring, that for his own part, he was more afraid of the madman's teeth than of his weapon, and admonishing the governor to re-enter, and execute what they had left undone; 'Go in (said he) without fear or apprehension, and if any accident shall happen to you, either from his slaver or his sword, I will assist you with my advice, which from this station

I can more coolly and distinctly administer, than I should be able to supply, if my ideas were disturbed, or my attention engaged in any personal concern.'

Jolter, who could make no objection to the justness of the conclusion, frankly owned, that he had no inclination to try the experiment; observing, that self preservation was the first law of nature; that his connexions with the unhappy lunatic were but slight, and that it could not be reasonably expected, that he would run such risks for his service, as were declined by one who had set out with him from England on the footing of a companion. This insinuation introduced a dispute upon the nature of benevolence and the moral sense, which (the republican argued) existed independent of any private consideration, and could never be affected by any contingent circumstance of time and fortune; while the other, who abhorred his principles, asserted the duties and excellence of private friendship, with infinite rancour of altercation.

During the hottest of the argument, they were joined by the Capuchin, who being astonished to see them thus virulently engaged at the door, and to hear the painter bellowing within the chamber, conjured them in the name of God to tell him the cause of that confusion, which had kept the whole house in continual alarm during the best part of the night, and seemed to be the immediate work of the devil and his angels. When the governor gave him to understand, that Pallet was visited with an evil spirit, he muttered a prayer of St. Antonio de Padua, and undertook to cure the painter, provided he could be secured so as that he might, without danger to himself, burn part of a certain relick under his nose, which he assured them was equal to the miraculous power of Eleazar's ring.[1] They expressed great curiosity to know what this treasure was; and the priest was prevailed upon to tell them in confidence, that it was a collection of the parings of the nails belonging to those two madmen whom Jesus purged of the legion of devils that afterwards entered the swine. So saying, he pulled from one of his pockets a small box, containing about an ounce of the parings of an horse's hoof; at sight of which, the governor could not help smiling, on account of the grossness of the imposition; and the doctor asked, with a supercilious smile, whether those maniacs whom Jesus cured, were of the sorrel complexion, or dapple grey; for, from the texture of these parings, he could prove, that the original owners were of the quadruped order, and even distinguish, that their feet had been fortified with shoes of iron.

The mendicant, who bore an inveterate grudge against this son of Æsculapius, ever since he had made so free with the catholic religion, replied with great bitterness, that he was a wretch with whom no Christian ought to communicate; that the vengeance of heaven would one day overtake him, on account of his profanity; and that his heart was shod with a metal much harder than iron, which he was afraid nothing but hell-fire would be able to melt.

It was now broad day, and all the servants of the inn were afoot. Peregrine, seeing it would be impossible to obtain any sort of indemnification for the time he had lost, and the perturbation of his spirits hindering him from enjoying repose, which was, more-over, obstructed by the noise of Pallet and his attendants, put on his cloaths at once, and in exceeding ill humour arrived at the spot where this triumvirate stood debating about the means of over-powering the furious painter, who still continued his song of oaths and execrations, and made sundry efforts to break open the door. Chagrin'd as our hero was, he could not help laughing when he heard how the patient had been treated; and his indignation changing into compassion, he called to him through the key-hole, desiring to know the reason of his distracted behaviour. Pallet no sooner recognized his voice, than lowering his own to a whimpering tone, 'My dear friend! (said he) I have at last detected the ruffians who have persecuted me so much. I caught them in the fact of suffocating me with cold water; and by the Lord! I will be revenged, or may I never live to finish my Cleopatra. For the love of God! open the door, and I will make that conceited pagan, that pre-tender to taste, that false devotee of the ancients, who poisons people with sillykickabies and devil's dung; I say, I will make him a monument of my wrath, and an example to all the cheats and impostors of the faculty: and as for that thick-headed insolent pedant his confederate, who emptied my own jordan upon me while I slept, he had better have been in his beloved Paris, botching schemes for his friend the pretender, than incurred the effects of my resentment. Gadsbodikins! I won't leave him a wind-pipe for the hangman to stop, at the end of another rebellion.'

Pickle told him, that his conduct had been so extravagant, as to confirm the whole company in the belief, that he was actually deprived of his senses; on which supposition, Mr. Jolter and the doctor had acted the part of friends, in doing that which they thought most conducive to his recovery; so that their concern merited his thankful acknowledgment, instead of his frantic menaces: and that for his own part, he would be the first to con-demn him, as one utterly bereft of his wits, and give orders for his being secured as a madman, unless he would immediately give a proof of his sanity, by laying aside his sword, composing his spirits, and thanking his injured friends for their care of his person.

This alternative quieted his transports in a moment; he was terrified at the apprehension of being treated like a Bedlamite, being dubious of the state of his own brain; and on the other hand, had conceived such an horror and antipathy for his tormentors, that, far from believing himself obliged by what they had done, he could not even think of them without the utmost rage and detestation. He therefore, in the most tranquil voice he could assume, protested, that he never was less out of his senses than at present, though he did not know how long he might retain them, if he should be considered in the light of a lunatic; and that, in order to prove his being *compos mentis*, he was willing to sacrifice the resentment he so justly harboured against those who by their malice had brought him to this pass: but, as he apprehended, it would be the greatest sign of madness he could exhibit, to thank them for the mischiefs they had brought upon him, he desired to be excused from making any such concession, and swore he would endure every thing, rather than be guilty of such mean absurdity.

Peregrine held a consultation upon this reply, when the governor and physician strenuously argued against any capitulation with a maniac, and proposed that some method might be taken to seize, fetter and convey him into a dark room, where he might be treated according to the rules of art. But the Capuchin understanding the circumstances of the case, undertook to restore him to his former state, without having recourse to such violent measures: and Pickle, who was a better judge of the affair than any person present, opened the door without further hesitation, and displayed the poor painter standing with a woeful countenance, shivering in his shirt, which was as wet as if he had been dragged through the Dender; a spectacle which gave such offence to the chaste eyes of the Hebrew's mistress, who was by this time one of the spectators, that she turned her head another way, and withdrew to her own room, exclaiming against the indecent practices of men.

Pallet, seeing the young gentleman enter, ran to him, and shaking him by the hand, called him his best friend, and said he had rescued him from those who had a design against his life. The priest would have produced his parings, and applied them to his nose; but was hindered by Pickle, who advised the patient to shift himself, and put on his cloaths: and this being done with great order and deliberation, Mr. Jolter, who, with the doctor, had kept at a wary distance, in expectation of seeing some strange effects of his distraction, began to believe that he had been guilty of a mistake, and accused the physician of having misled him by his false diagnostic. The doctor still insisted upon his former declaration, assuring him, that although Pallet enjoyed a short interval for the present, the delirium would soon recur, unless they would profit by this momentary calm, and order him to be blooded, blistered and purged with all imaginable dispatch.

The governor, however, notwithstanding this caution, advanced to the injured party, and begg'd pardon for the share he had in giving him such disturbance, declaring in the most solemn manner, that he had no other intention than that of contributing towards his welfare, and that his behaviour was the result of the physician's prescription, which he affirmed was absolutely necessary for the recovery of his health.

The painter, who had very little gall in his disposition, was satisfied with this apology; but his resentment, which was before divided, now glowed with double fire against his first fellow-traveller, whom he looked upon as the author of all the mischances he had undergone, and marked out for his vengeance accordingly. Yet the doors of reconciliation were not shut against the doctor, who with great justice might have transferred this load of offence from himself to Peregrine, who was, without doubt, the source of the painter's misfortune: but, in that case, he must have owned himself mistaken in his medical capacity; and he did not think the friendship of Pallet important enough to sway him to such condescension; so that he resolved to neglect him intirely, and gradually forget the former correspondence he had maintained with a person whom he deemed so unworthy of his notice.

CHAPTER LXII

Peregrine, almost distracted with his Disappointments,
conjures the fair Fleming to permit his Visits at Brussels.
She withdraws from his Pursuit

THINGS being thus adjusted, and all the company dressed, they went to breakfast about five in the morning, and in less than an hour after were seated in the Diligence, where a profound silence prevailed. Peregrine, who used to be the life of the society, being extremely pensive and melancholy on account of his mishap, the Israelite and his Dulcinea dejected in consequence of their disgrace, the poet absorpt in lofty meditation, the painter in schemes of revenge, while Jolter, rocked by the motion of the carriage, made himself amends for the want of rest he had sustained, and the Mendicant, with his fair charge, were infested by the cloudy aspect of our youth, in whose disappointment each of them, for different reasons, bore no inconsiderable share. This general languor and recess from all bodily exercise, disposed them all to receive the gentle yoke of slumber, and in half an hour after they had embarked, there was not one of them awake, except our hero and his mistress, unless the Capuchin was pleased to counterfeit sleep, in order to indulge our young gentleman with an opportunity of enjoying some private conversation with his beauteous ward.

Peregrine did not neglect the occasion; but, on the contrary, seized the first minute, and in gentle murmurs lamented his hard hap in being thus the sport of fortune. He assured her (and that with great sincerity) that all the cross accidents of his life had not cost him one half of the vexation and keenness of chagrin which he had suffered last night; and that now he was on the brink of parting from her, he should be overwhelmed with the blackest despair, if she would not extend her compassion so far as to give him an opportunity of sighing at her feet in Brussels, during the few days his affairs would permit him to spend in that city.

This young lady, with an air of mortification, expressed her sorrow for being the innocent cause of his anxiety; said, she hoped last night's adventure would be a salutary warning to both their souls; for she was persuaded, that her virtue was protected by the intervention of heaven; that whatever impression it might have made upon him, she was enabled by it to adhere to that duty from which her passion had begun to swerve, and beseeching him to forget her for his own peace, gave him to understand, that neither the plan she had laid down for her own conduct, nor the dictates of her honour, would allow her to receive his visits, or carry on any other correspondence with him, while she was restricted by the articles of her marriage-vow.

This explanation produced such a violent effect upon her admirer, that he was for some minutes deprived of the faculty of speech, which he no sooner recovered, than he gave vent to the most unbridled transports of passion. He taxed her with barbarity and indifference; told her that she had robbed him of his reason and internal peace; that he would follow her to the ends of the earth, and cease to live sooner than cease to love her; that he would sacrifice the innocent fool who had been the occasion of all this disquiet, and murder every man whom he considered as an obstruction to his views. In a word, his passions, which had continued so long in a state of the highest fermentation, together with the want of that repose which calms and quiets the perturbation of the spirits, had wrought him up to a pitch of real distraction: and while he uttered these delirious expressions, the tears ran down his cheeks, and he underwent such agitation, that the tender heart of the fair Fleming was affected with his condition; and, while her own face was bedewed with the streams of sympathy, she begged him for heaven's sake to be composed, and promised, for his satisfaction, to abate somewhat of the rigor of her purpose. Consoled by this kind declaration, he recollected himself, and taking out his pencil, gave her his address, when she had assured him, that he should hear from her in four and twenty hours at farthest, after their separation.

Thus soothed, he regained the empire of himself, and by degrees recovered his serenity. But this was not the case with his Amanda, who, from this sample of his disposition, dreaded the impetuosity of his youth, and was effectually deterred from entering into any engagements that might subject her peace and reputation to the rash effects of such a violent spirit. Though she was captivated by his person and accomplishments, she had reflection enough to foresee, that the longer she countenanced his passion, her own heart would be more and more irretrievably engaged, and the quiet of her life the more exposed to continual interruption. She therefore profited by these considerations, and a sense of religious honour, which helped her to withstand the suggestions of inclination; and resolved to amuse her lover with false hopes, until she should have it in her power to relinquish his conversation, without running any risk of suffering by the inconsiderate sallies of his love. It was with this view, that she desired he would not insist upon attending her to her mother's house, when the Diligence arrived at Brussels; and he, cajoled by her artifice, took a formal leave of her, together with the other strangers, fixing his habitation at the inn to which he and his fellow-travellers had been directed, in the impatient expectation of receiving a kind summons from her, within the limited time.

Mean while, in order to divert his imagination, he went to see the stadthouse, park and arsenal, took a superficial view of the famous bookseller's cabinet of curiosities, and spent the evening at the

Italian opera, which was at that time exhibited for the entertainment of Prince Charles of Lorrain,[1] then governor of the Low Countries. In short, the stated period was almost elapsed, when Peregrine was favoured with a letter to this purpose:

'SIR,

If you knew what violence I do my own heart, in declaring that I have withdrawn myself for ever from your addresses, you would surely applaud the sacrifice I make to virtue, and strive to imitate this example of self-denial. Yes, Sir, heaven hath lent me grace to struggle with my guilty passion, and henceforth to avoid the dangerous sight of him who inspired it. I therefore conjure you, by the regard you ought to have for the eternal welfare of us both, as well as by the esteem and affection you profess, to war with your unruly inclination, and desist from all attempts of frustrating the laudable resolution I have made. Seek not to invade the peace of one who loves you, to disturb the quiet of a family that never did you wrong, and alienate the thoughts of a weak woman from a deserving man, who, by the most sacred claim, is vested with the full possession of her heart.'

This billet, without either date or subscription, banished all remains of discretion from the mind of our hero, who ran instantly to the landlord, in all the extasy of madness, and demanded to see the messenger who brought the letter, on pain of putting his whole family to the sword. The innkeeper, terrified by his looks and menaces, fell upon his knees, protesting in the face of heaven, that he was utterly ignorant and innocent of any thing that could give him offence, and that the billet was brought by a person whom he did not know, and who retired immediately, saying, it required no answer. He then gave utterance to his fury, in a thousand imprecations and invectives against the writer, whom he dishonoured with the appellations of a coquette, a jilt, an adventurer, who, by means of a pimping priest, had defrauded him of his money. He denounced vengeance against the Mendicant, whom he swore he would castrate, if ever he should set eyes on him again: and the painter unluckily appearing during this paroxysm of rage, he seized him by the throat, saying he was ruined by his accursed folly; and in all likelihood poor Pallet would have been strangled, had not Jolter interposed in his behalf, beseeching his pupil to have mercy upon the sufferer, and with infinite anxiety desiring to know the cause of this violent assault. He received no answer, but a string of incoherent curses, and when the painter, with unspeakable astonishment, took God to witness, that he had done nothing to disoblige him, the governor began to think in sad earnest, that Peregrine's vivacity had at length risen to the transports of actual madness, and was himself almost distracted with this supposition. That he might the better judge what remedy ought to be applied, he used his whole influence, and practised all his eloquence upon the youth, in order to learn the immediate cause of his delirium. He employed the most pathetic intreaties, and even shed tears in the course of his supplication; so that Pickle (the first violence of the hurricane being blown over) was ashamed of his own imprudence, and retired to his chamber, in order to recollect his dissipated thoughts: there he shut himself up, and, for the second time, perusing the fatal epistle, began to waver in his opinion of the author's character and intention. He sometimes considered her as one of those nymphs who, under the mask of innocence and simplicity, practise upon the hearts and purses of unwary and unexperienced youths: this was the suggestion of his wrath, inflamed by disappointment; but, when he reflected upon the circumstances of her behaviour, and recalled her particular charms to his imagination, the severity of his censure gave way, and his heart declared in favour of her sincerity. Yet even this consideration aggravated the sense of his loss, and he was in danger of relapsing into his former distraction, when his passion was a little becalmed by the hope of seeing her again, either by accident, or in the course of a diligent and minute inquiry, which he forthwith resolved to set on foot. He had reason to believe, that her own heart would espouse his cause, in spite of her virtue's determination, and did not despair of meeting with the Capuchin, whose good offices he knew he could at any time command. Comforted with these reflexions, the tempest of his soul subsided, and in less than two hours he joined his company with an air of composure, and asked the painter's forgiveness for the freedom he had taken, the cause of which he promised hereafter to explain. Pallet was glad of being reconciled on any terms to one whose countenance supported him in æquilibrio with his antagonist the doctor; and Mr. Jolter was rejoiced beyond measure at his pupil's recovery.

CHAPTER LXIII

Peregrine meets with Mrs. Hornbeck, and is
consoled for his Loss. His Valet de Chambre is embroiled
with her Duenna, whom, however, he finds Means to appease

EVERY thing having thus resumed its natural channel, they dined together in great tranquillity; and in the afternoon, Peregrine, on pretence of staying at home to write letters, while his companions were at the coffee-house, ordered a coach to be called, and with his valet de chambre, who was the only person acquainted with the present state of his thoughts, set out for the Promenade, to which all the ladies of fashion resort in the evening, during the summer-season, in hopes of seeing his fugitive among the rest.

Having made a circuit round the walk, and narrowly observed every female in the place, he perceived at some distance the livery of Hornbeck upon a lacquey that stood at the back of a coach: upon which, he ordered his man to reconnoitre the said carriage, while he pulled up his glasses, that he might not be discovered, before he should have received some intelligence, by which he might conduct himself on this unexpected occasion, that already began to interfere with the purpose of his coming thither, though it could not dispute his attention with the idea of his charming Unknown.

His Mercury having made his observations, reported, that there was no body in the coach but Mrs. Hornbeck and an elderly woman, who had all the air of a duenna, and that the servant was not the same footman who had attended them in France. Encouraged by this information, our hero ordered himself to be driven close up to that side of their convenience on which his old mistress sat, and accosted her with the usual salutation. This lady no sooner beheld her gallant, than her cheeks reddened with a double glow; and she exclaimed, 'Dear brother, I'm overjoy'd to see you! Pray come into our coach.' He took the hint immediately, and complying with her request, embraced this new sister with great affection.

Perceiving that her attendant was very much surprised and alarmed at this unexpected meeting, she, in order to banish her suspicion, and at the same time give her lover his cue, told him that his brother (meaning her husband) was gone to the Spa for a few weeks, by the advice of physicians, on account of his ill state of health; and that, from his last letter, she had the pleasure to tell him, he was in a fair way of doing well. The young gentleman expressed his satisfaction at this piece of news, observing with an air of fraternal concern, that if his brother had not made too free with his constitution, his friends in England would have had no occasion to repine at his absence and want of health, by which he was banished from his own country and connexions. He then asked with an affectation of surprize, why she had not accompanied her spouse? and was given to understand, that his tenderness of affection would not suffer him to expose her to the fatigues of the journey, which lay among rocks that were almost inaccessible.

The duenna's doubts being eased by this preamble of conversation, he changed the subject to the pleasures of the place; and among other such questions, inquired if she had as yet visited Versailles? This is a public house situated upon the canal, at the distance of about two miles from town, and accommodated with tolerable gardens for the entertainment of company. When she replied in the negative, he proposed to accompany her thither immediately; but the governante, who had hitherto sat silent, objected to this proposal, telling them, in broken English, that as the lady was under her care, she could not answer to Mr. Hornbeck for allowing her to visit such a suspicious place. 'As for that matter, Madam, (said the confident gallant) give yourself no trouble, the consequences shall be at my peril; and I will undertake to insure you against my brother's resentment.' So saying, he directed the coachman to the place, and ordered his own to follow, under the auspices of his valet de chambre, while the old gentlewoman, over-ruled by his assurance, quietly submitted to his authority.

Being arrived at the place, he handed the ladies from the coach, and then, for the first time, observed that the duenna was lame, a circumstance of which he did not scruple to take the advantage; for they had scarce alighted, and drank a glass of wine, when he advised his sister to enjoy a walk in the garden: and although the attendant made shift to keep them almost always in view, they enjoyed a detached conversation, in which Peregrine learnt, that the true cause of her being left behind at Brussels, whilst her husband proceeded to Spa, was his dread of the company and familiarities of that place, to which his jealousy durst not expose her; and that she had lived three weeks in a convent at Lisle, from which she was delivered by his own free motion, because indeed he could no longer exist without her company; and lastly, our lover understood, that her governante was a mere dragon, who had been recommended to him by a Spanish merchant, whose wife she attended to her dying day: but she very much questioned whether or not her fidelity was proof enough against money and strong waters. Peregrine assured her the experiment should be tried before parting; and they agreed to pass the night at Versailles, provided his endeavours should succeed.

Having exercised themselves in this manner, until his duenna's spirits were pretty much exhausted, that she might be the better disposed to recruit them with a glass of liqueur, they returned to their apartment, and the cordial was recommended and received in a bumper: but as it did not produce such a visible alteration as the sanguine hopes of Pickle had made him expect, and the old gentlewoman observed that it began to be late, and that the gates would be shut in a little time, he filled up a parting glass, and pledged her in equal quantity. Her blood was too much chilled to be warmed even by this extraordinary dose, which made immediate innovation in the brain of our youth, who in the gaiety of his imagination overwhelmed this She-Argus with such profusion of gallantry, that she was more intoxicated with his expressions than with the spirits she had drank; and when in the course of toying he dropt a purse into her bosom, she seemed to forget how the night wore, and with the approbation of her charge, assented to his proposal of having something for supper.

This was a great point which our adventurer had gained, and yet he plainly perceived that the governante mistook his meaning, by giving herself credit for all the passion he had professed. As this error could be rectified by no other means than those of plying her with the bottle, until her distinguishing faculties should be overpowered, he promoted a quick circulation, and she did him justice, without any manifest signs of inebriation, so long, that his own eyes began to reel in the sockets; and he found, that before his scheme could be accomplished, he should be effectually unfitted for all the purposes of love. He therefore had recourse to his valet de chambre, who understood the hint as soon as it was given, and readily undertook to perform the part, of which his master had play'd the prelude. This affair being settled to his satisfaction, and the night at odds with morning, he took an opportunity of imparting to the ear of this aged Dulcinea a kind whisper, importing a promise of visiting her, when his sister should be retired to her own chamber, and an earnest desire of leaving her door unlocked.

This agreeable intimation being communicated, he conveyed a caution of the same nature to Mrs. Hornbeck, as he led her to her apartment; and darkness and silence no sooner prevailed in the house, than he and his trusty squire set out on their different voyages; and every thing would have succeeded according to their wish, had not the valet de chambre suffered himself to fall asleep at the side of his inamorata, and in the agitation of a violent dream, exclaimed in a voice so unlike to that of her supposed adorer, that she distinguished the difference at once; and waking him with a pinch and a loud shriek, threatened to prosecute him for a rape, and reviled him with all the epithets her rage and disappointment could suggest.

The Frenchman finding himself detected, behaved with great temper and address: he begg'd she would compose herself, on account of her own reputation, which was extremely dear to him; protested, that he had a most inviolable esteem for her person; and that if he had not already given convincing proofs of his passion, he was disposed to do every thing in his power for her satisfaction. These representations, mingled with some little practical expressions of tenderness, had weight with the duenna, who, upon recollection, comprehended the whole affair, and thought it would be her interest to bring matters to an accommodation. She therefore admitted the apologies of her bedfellow, provided he would promise to atone by marriage for the injury she had sustained; and in this particular he set her heart at ease by repeated vows, which he uttered with surprising volubility, though without any intention to perform the least tittle of their contents.

Peregrine, who had been alarmed by her exclamation, and run to the door with a view of interposing, according to the emergency of the case, over-hearing the affair thus compromised, returned to his mistress, who was highly entertained with an account of what had passed, foreseeing, that for the future she should be under no difficulty or restriction from the severity of her guard.

Hornbeck is informed of his Wife's Adventure with
Peregrine, for whom he prepares a Stratagem, which is
rendered ineffectual by the Information of Pipes.
The Husband is ducked for his Intention, and our Hero
apprehended by the Patrole

THERE was another person, however, still ungained; and that was
no other than her footman, whose secrecy our hero attempted to
secure in the morning by an handsome present, which he received
with many professions of gratitude and devotion to his service; yet
this complaisance was nothing but a cloak used to disguise the
design he harboured of making his master acquainted with the
whole transaction. Indeed this lacquey had been hired, not only as
a spy upon his mistress, but also as a check on the conduct of the
governante, with promise of ample reward, if ever he should discover any sinister or suspicious practices in the course of their
behaviour: and as for the footman whom they had brought from
England, he was retained in attendance upon the person of his
master, whose confidence he had lost, by advising him to gentle
methods of reclaiming his lady, when her irregularities had subjected her to his wrath.

The Flemish valet, in consequence of the office he had undertaken, wrote to Hornbeck by the first post, giving an exact detail
of the adventure at Versailles, with such a description of the pretended brother, as left the husband no room to think he could be
any other person than his first dishonourer; and exasperated him
to such a degree, that he resolved to lay an ambush for this invader,
and at once disqualify him from disturbing his repose, by maintaining further correspondence with his wife.

Mean while the lovers enjoyed themselves without restraint, and
Peregrine's plan of inquiry after his dear Unknown was for the
present postponed. His fellow-travellers were confounded at his
mysterious motions, which filled the heart of Jolter with anxiety
and terror. This careful conductor was fraught with such experience of his pupil's disposition, that he trembled with the apprehension of some sudden accident, and lived in continual alarm, like
a man that walks under the wall of a nodding tower. Nor did he
enjoy any alleviation of his fears, when upon telling the young

gentleman, that the rest of the company were desirous of departing for Antwerp, he answered, they were at liberty to consult their own inclinations; but for his own part, he was resolved to stay in Brussels a few days longer. By this declaration, the governor was confirmed in the opinion of his having some intrigue upon the anvil; and in the bitterness of his vexation, took the liberty of signifying his suspicion, and reminding him of the dangerous dilemmas to which he had been reduced by his former precipitation.

Peregrine took his caution in good part, and promised to behave with such circumspection, as would screen him from any troublesome consequences for the future: but, nevertheless, behaved that same evening in such a manner, as plainly shewed, that his prudence was nothing else than vain speculation. He had made an appointment to spend the night, as usual, with Mrs. Hornbeck; and about nine o'clock hastened to her lodgings, when he was accosted in the street by his old discarded friend Thomas Pipes, who, without any other preamble, told him, that for all he had turned him adrift, he did not choose to see him run full sail into his enemy's harbour, without giving him timely notice of the danger. 'I'll tell you what, (said he) mayhap you think I want to curry favour, that I may be taken in tow again; if you do, you have made a mistake in your reckoning. I am old enough to be laid up, and have wherewithal to keep my planks from the weather. But this here is the affair; I have known you since you were no higher than a marlinspike, and shouldn't care to see you deprived of your carriages at these years: whereby I am informed by Hornbeck's man, whom I this afternoon fell in with by chance, as how his master has got intelligence of your boarding his wife, and has steer'd privately into this port, with a large compliment of hands, in order, d'ye see, to secure you while you are under the hatches, and cut away your tackle, without fear or mercy. Now if so be as how you have a mind to give him a salt eel for his supper, here am I, without hope of fee or reward, ready to stand by you as long as my timbers will stick together; and if I expect any recompence, may I be bound to eat oakum and drink bilge-water for life.'

Startled at this information, Peregrine examined him upon the particulars of his discourse with the lacquey; and when he understood that Hornbeck's intelligence flowed from the canal of his Flemish footman, he believed every circumstance of Tom's report, thanked him for this warning, and after having reprimanded him for his misbehaviour at Lisle, assured him that it should be his own fault if ever they should part again. He then deliberated with himself whether or not he should retort the purpose upon his adversary; but, when he considered that Hornbeck was not the aggressor, and made that unhappy husband's case his own, he could not help acquitting his intention of revenge; though, in his opinion, it ought to have been executed in a more honourable manner; and therefore he determined to chastise him for his want of spirit. Nothing surely can be more insolent and unjust than this determination, which induced him to punish a person, for his want of courage to redress the injury which he himself had done to his reputation and peace; and yet this barbarity of decision is sanctioned by the opinion and practice of mankind.

With these sentiments he returned to the inn, and putting a pair of pistols in his pocket, ordered his valet de chambre and Pipes to follow him at a small distance, so as that they should be within call, in case of necessity, and posted himself within thirty yards of his Dulcinea's door. There he had not been above half an hour, when he perceived four men take up their station on the other side, with a view, as he guessed, to watch for his going in, that he might be taken unaware. But when they had tarried a considerable time in that corner, without reaping the fruits of their expectation, their leader, persuaded that the gallant had gained admittance by some secret means, approached the door with his followers, who, according to the instructions they had received, no sooner saw it opened, than they rushed in, leaving their employer in the street, where he thought his person would be least endangered. Our adventurer seeing him alone, advanced with speed, and clapping a pistol to his breast, commanded him to follow his footsteps, without noise, on pain of immediate death.

Terrified at this sudden apparition, Hornbeck obeyed in silence; and in a few minutes they arrived at the quay, where Pickle halting, gave him to understand, that he was no stranger to his villainous design; and told him, that if he conceived himself injured by any circumstance of his conduct, he would now give him an opportunity of resenting the wrong, in a manner becoming a man of honour. 'You have a sword about you, (said he) or if you don't choose to put the affair on that issue, here is a brace of pistols, take which you please.' Such an address could not fail to disconcert a man of his character. After some hesitation, he in a faultering accent denied that his design was to mutilate Mr. Pickle, but that he thought himself intitled to the benefit of the law, by which he would have obtained a divorce, if he could have procured evidence of his wife's infidelity; and with that view had employed people to take advantage of the information he had received. With regard to his alternative, he declined it intirely, because he could not see what satisfaction he should enjoy, in being shot through the head, or run through the lungs, by a person who had already wronged him in an irreparable manner; and lastly, his fear made him propose, that the affair should be left to the arbitration of two creditable men, altogether unconcerned in the dispute.

To these remonstrances, Peregrine replied, in the stile of a hot-headed young man, conscious of his own unjustifiable behaviour, that every gentleman ought to be a judge of his own honour; and therefore he would submit to the decision of no umpire whatsoever; that he would forgive his want of courage, which might be a natural infirmity, but his mean dissimulation he could not pardon; and that, as he was certified of the rascally intent of his ambuscade, by undoubted intelligence, he would treat him, not with a retaliation of his own treachery, but with such indignity as a scoundrel deserves to suffer; unless he would make one effort to maintain the character he assumed in life: so saying, he again presented his pistol, which being rejected as before, he called his two ministers, and ordered them to duck him in the canal.

This command was pronounced and executed almost in the same breath, to the unspeakable terror and disorder of the poor shivering patient, who, having undergone the immersion, ran about like a drowned rat, squeaking for assistance and revenge. His cries were overheard by the patrole, which, chancing to pass that way, took him under their protection, and, in consequence of his complaint and information, went in pursuit of our adventurer and his attendants, who were soon overtaken and surrounded. Rash and inconsiderate as the young gentleman was, he did not pretend to stand upon the defensive, against a file of musketeers, although Pipes had drawn his cutlass at their approach, but surrendered himself without opposition, and was conveyed to the main guard, where the commanding officer, engaged by his appearance and address, treated him with all imaginable respect, and hearing the particulars of his adventure, assured him, that the prince would consider the whole as a *Tour de jeunesse*, and order him to be released without delay.

Next morning, when this gentleman gave in his report, he made such a favourable representation of the prisoner, that our hero was on the point of being discharged; when Hornbeck preferred a complaint, accusing him of a purposed assassination, and praying that such punishment should be inflicted upon him, as his highness should think adequate to the nature of the crime. The prince, perplexed with this petition, in consequence of which he foresaw, that he must disoblige a British subject, sent for the plaintiff, of whom he had some knowledge, and in person exhorted him to drop the prosecution, which would only serve to propagate his own shame. But Hornbeck was too much incensed to listen to any proposal of that kind, and peremptorily demanded justice against the prisoner, whom he represented as an obscure adventurer, who had made repeated attempts upon his honour and his life. Prince Charles told him, that what he had advised was in the capacity of a friend, but, since he insisted upon his acting as a magistrate, the affair should be examined, and determined according to the dictates of justice and truth.

The petitioner being dismissed with this promise, the defendant was in his turn brought before the judge, whose prepossession in his favour, was in a great measure weakened by what his antagonist had said to the prejudice of his birth and reputation.

CHAPTER LXV

Peregrine is released. Jolter confounded at his
mysterious Conduct. A Contest happens between the
Poet and Painter, who are reconciled by the Mediation
of their fellow Travellers

OUR hero, understanding from some expressions which escaped the prince, that he was considered in the light of a sharper and assassin, begged that he might have the liberty of sending for some vouchers, that would probably vindicate his character from the malicious aspersions of his adversary; and this permission being granted, he wrote a letter to his governor, desiring that he would bring to him the letters of recommendation which he had received from the British embassador at Paris, and such other papers as he thought conducive to evince the importance of his situation.

The billet was given in charge to one of the subaltern officers on duty, who carried it to the inn, and demanded to speak with

Chapter LXV

Mr. Jolter. Pallet, who happened to be at the door, when this messenger arrived, and heard him enquire for the tutor, ran directly to that gentleman's apartment, and in manifest disorder told him, that a huge fellow of a soldier, with a monstrous pair of whiskers, and a fur-cap as big as a bushel, was asking for him at the door. The poor governor began to shake at this intimation, though he was not conscious of having committed any thing that could attract the attention of the state; and, when the officer appeared at his chamber-door, his confusion increased to such a degree, that his perception seemed to vanish, and the subaltern repeated the purport of his errand three times, before he could comprehend his meaning, or venture to receive the letter which he presented. At length, however, he summoned all his fortitude, and having perused the epistle, his terror sunk into anxiety; his ingenious fear immediately suggested, that Peregrine was confined in a dungeon, for some outrage he had committed; he ran with great agitation to a trunk, and taking out a bundle of papers, followed his conductor, being attended by the painter, to whom he had hinted his apprehension. When they passed through the guard, which was under arms, the hearts of both died within them; and when they came into the presence, there was such an expression of awful horror on the countenance of Jolter, that the prince, observing his dismay, was pleased to encourage him with an assurance, that he had nothing to fear. Thus comforted, he recollected himself so well as to understand his pupil, when he desired him to produce the Embassador's letters; some of which being open, were immediately read by his highness, who was personally acquainted with the writer, and knew several of the noblemen to whom they were addressed. These recommendations were so warm, and represented the young gentleman in such an advantageous light, that the prince, convinced of the injustice his character had suffered by the misrepresentation of Hornbeck, took our hero by the hand, asked pardon for the doubts he had entertained of his honour, declared him from that moment at liberty, ordered his domesticks to be enlarged, and offered him his countenance and protection, as long as he should remain in the Austrian Netherlands. At the same time, he cautioned him against indiscretion in the course of his gallantries; and took his word and honour, that he should drop all measures of resentment against the person of Hornbeck, during his residence in that place.

The delinquent, thus honourably acquitted, thanked the prince in the most respectful manner, for his generosity and candour, and retired with his two friends, who were amazed and bewildered in their thoughts, at what they had seen and heard, the whole adventure still remaining without the sphere of their comprehension, which was not at all enlarged by the unaccountable appearance of Pipes, who, with the valet de chambre, joined them at the castle-gate. Had Jolter been a man of a luxuriant imagination, his brain would undoubtedly have suffered in the investigation of his pupil's mysterious conduct, which he strove in vain to unravel; but his intellects were too solid to be affected by the miscarriage of his invention; and as Peregrine did not think proper to make him acquainted with the cause of his being apprehended, he contented himself with supposing, that there was a lady in the case.

The painter, whose imagination was of a more flimsy texture, formed a thousand chimerical conjectures, which he communicated to Pickle, in imperfect insinuations, hoping, by his answers and behaviour, to discover the truth; but the youth, in order to tantalize him, eluded all his enquiries, with such appearance of industry and art, as heightened his curiosity, while it disappointed his aim, and inflamed him to such a degree of impatience, that his wits began to be unsettled, and Peregrine was fain to recompose his brain, by telling him in confidence, that he had been arrested as a spy. This secret he found more intolerable than his former uncertainty; he ran from one apartment to another, like a goose in the agonies of egg-laying, with intention of disburdening this important load; but, Jolter being engaged with his pupil, and all the people of the house ignorant of the only language he could speak, he was compelled, with infinite reluctance, to address himself to the doctor, who was, at that time, shut up in his own chamber. Having knocked at the door, to no purpose, he peeped through the key-hole, and saw the physician sitting at a table, with a pen in one hand, and paper before him, his head reclined upon his other hand, and his eyes fixed upon the ceiling, as if he had been intranced. Pallet, concluding that he was under the power of some convulsion, endeavoured to force the door open, and the noise of his efforts recalled the doctor from his reverie. This poetical republican, being so disagreeably disturbed, started up in a passion, and opening the door, no sooner perceived who had interrupted him, than he flung it in his face with great fury, and cursed him for his impertinent intrusion, which had deprived him of the most delightful vision that ever regaled the human fancy. He imagined, (as he afterwards imparted to Peregrine) that as he enjoyed himself in walking through the flowery plain that borders on Parnassus, he was met by a venerable sage, whom, by a certain divine vivacity that lightened from his eyes, he instantly knew to be the immortal Pindar. He was immediately struck with reverence and awe, and prostrated himself before the apparition, which taking him by the hand, lifted him gently from the ground; and with words more sweet than the honey of the Hybla bees, told him, that of all the moderns, he alone was visited by that celestial impulse by which he himself had been inspired, when he produced his most applauded odes. So saying, he led him up the sacred hill, persuaded him to drink a copious draught of the waters of the Hippocrene, and then presented him to the harmonious nine, who crowned his temples with a laurel-wreath.

No wonder then, that he was enraged to find himself cut off from such sublime society. He raved in Greek against the invader, who was so big with his own purpose, that, unmindful of the disgrace he had sustained, and disregarding all the symptoms of the physician's displeasure, he applied his mouth to the door, and in eager tone, 'I'll hold you any wager (said he) that I guess the true cause of Mr. Pickle's imprisonment.' To this challenge he received no reply; and therefore repeated it, adding, 'I suppose you imagine he was taken up for fighting a duel, for affronting a nobleman, or lying with some man's wife, or some such matter; but, agad! you was never more mistaken in your life; and I'll lay my Cleopatra against your Homer's head, that in four and twenty hours you shan't light on the true reason.'

The favourite of the muses, exasperated at this vexatious per-severance of the painter, who he imagined had come thither to teize and insult him, 'I would (said he) sacrifice a cock to Æscula-pius, were I assured that any person had been taken up for ex-tirpating such a troublesome Goth as you are from the face of the earth; and as for your boasted Cleopatra, which you say was drawn from your own wife, I believe the copy has as much of the $\tau\grave{o}$ $\kappa\alpha\lambda\acute{o}\nu$ [1] as the original. But, were it mine, it should be hung up in the temple of Cloacina, as the picture of that goddess; for any other apartment would be disgraced by its appearance.' 'Hark ye, Sir, (replied Pallet, enraged in his turn at this contemptuous mention of his darling performance) you may make as free with my wife as you think proper; but 'ware my works, those are the children of my fancy, conceived by the glowing imagination, and formed by the art of my own hands: and you yourself are a Goth, and a Turk, and a Tartar, and an impudent pretending jackanapes, to treat with such disrespect a production which, in the opinions of all the con-noisseurs of the age, will, when finished, be a master-piece in its kind, and do honour to human genius and skill. So I say again and again, (and I care not though your friend Playtor heard me) that you have no more taste than a drayman's horse, and that those foolish notions of the ancients ought to be drubb'd out of you with a good cudgel, that you might learn to treat men of parts with more veneration. Perhaps you may not always be in the company of one who will hollow for assistance, when you are on the brink of being chastised for your insolence, as I did, when you brought upon yourself the resentment of that Scot, who, by the Lard! would have paid you both scot and lot, as Falstaf says,[1] if the French officer had not put him in arrest.'

The physician to this declamation, which was conveyed through the key-hole, answered, that he (the painter) was a fellow so infinitely below his consideration, that his conscience upbraided him with no action of his life, except that of choosing such a wretch for his companion and fellow-traveller. That he had viewed his character through the medium of good nature and compassion, which had prompted him to give Pallet an opportunity of acquiring some new ideas under his immediate instruction; but he had abused his goodness and condescension in such a flagrant manner, that he was now determined to discard him intirely from his acquaintance, and desired him, for the present, to take himself away, on pain of being kicked for his presumption.

Pallet was too much incensed to be intimidated by this threat, which he retorted with great virulence, defying him to come forth, that it might appear which of them was best skilled in that pedestrian exercise which he immediately began to practise against the door with such thundering application, as reached the ears of Pickle and his governor, who coming out into the passage, and seeing him thus employed, asked if he had forgot the chamber-pots of Alost,[2] that he ventured to behave in such a manner, as intitled him to a second prescription of the same nature.

The doctor understanding that there was company at hand, opened the door in a twinkling, and springing upon his antagonist, like a tyger, a fierce contention would have ensued, to the infinite satisfaction of our hero, had not Jolter, to the manifest peril of his own person, interposed, and partly by force, and partly by exhortations, put a stop to the engagement before it was fairly begun. After having demonstrated the indecency of such a vulgar rencounter betwixt two fellow-citizens in a foreign land, he begg'd to know the cause of their dissention, and offered his good offices towards an accommodation. Peregrine also, seeing the fray was finished, expressed himself to the same purpose; and the painter, for obvious reasons, declining an explanation, his antagonist told the youth what a mortifying interruption he had suffered by the impertinent intrusion of Pallet, and gave him a detail of the particulars of his vision, as above recited. The arbiter owned, the provocation was not to be endured, and decreed, that the offender should make some atonement for his transgression. Upon which the painter observed, that howsoever he might have been disposed to make acknowledgments, if the physician had signified his displeasure like a gentleman, the complainant had now forfeited all claim to any such concessions, by the vulgar manner in which he had reviled him and his productions; observing, that if he (the painter) had been inclined to retort his slanderous insinuations, the republican's own works would have afforded ample subject for his ridicule and censure.

After divers disputes and representations, peace was at length concluded, on condition, that for the future the doctor should never mention Cleopatra, unless he could say something in her praise; and that Pallet, in consideration of his having been the first aggressor, should make a sketch of the physician's vision, to be engraved and prefixed to the next edition of his odes.

CHAPTER LXVI

Peregrine renews his Inquiries about his lost Amanda,
in the Course of which he is engaged in an Intrigue with
a Nun, which produces strange Consequences[1]

THOUGH this treaty was concluded at the instances of Peregrine and his governor, it was impossible that a lasting friendship could subsist between the two parties, because they entertained for each other the most perfect contempt, which, in the course of their communication, could not fail to minister daily food for animosity and aversion.

Our adventurer's next care was to exercise all his diligence and invention to find his lost Amanda, who, now that he was detached from Mrs. Hornbeck, resumed the full possession of his thoughts. As she would never tell him her own name, or that of her mother, his inquiries were directed by a personal description only; and that, in such a populous city as Brussels, could tend but very little to his satisfaction. He not only ordered his valet de chambre to exert his whole address, in order to discover the place of her abode, but this dexterous minister, who was very well acquainted in that city, retained half a dozen of noted pimps for the same purpose, who were directed to employ their researches for a very handsome young lady, of the middle stature, with fine black eyes, and teeth as white as snow, a native of Brussels, though married to a French gentleman, and lately arrived from her husband's house on a visit to her mother, who was dangerously ill.

Thus instructed, they put themselves in motion, while the lover in person frequented the court, the opera, the churches, public walks, and every place where he thought there was the least probability of seeing her. The description his Mercury had given to the understrappers of gallantry, in a good measure suited several ladies in town, whom Peregrine found means to see, in consequence of the reports he had received; but he could not recognize his dear fellow-traveller among the number. At last one of his terriers gave the valet de chambre to understand, that at the grate of a certain nunnery, he had observed a beautiful young creature, who resembled the picture he had drawn, and that upon inquiry, he found she had not taken the veil; but her mother being lately dead, had entered as a pensionaire, until her family-affairs could be adjusted.

This piece of intelligence was no sooner communicated to our hero, than he flew in the utmost impatience to the nunnery, and, without allowing himself to believe that this boarder could be any other than the object of his pursuit, desired the portress to tell the young lady who was lately admitted, that one of her relations begg'd to speak with her at the grate. He had not waited five minutes, when this nymph appeared; and though he found his expectation disappointed, he was so struck with the charms of this new figure, that his heart throbbed when she approached; and after he had asked pardon for the liberty he had taken, and explained the nature of his mistake, he could not help telling her, that he thought himself fortunate in the misinformation he had received, since it was attended with the pleasure of seeing such an amiable young lady. To this compliment she replied with great spirit and good humour, that encouraged the youth to continue the conversation, during which he professed himself her admirer; and when, for the sake of decorum, he was obliged to take his leave, earnestly begg'd he might be allow'd to repeat his visit: and having obtained this permission, and the knowledge of her name, returned to his lodgings in full confidence of bringing this intrigue to a prosperous issue.

Nor had the young gentleman in this case overrated his own success: the lady happened to be of a very amorous complexion, and her passions being inflamed rather than mortified, by the restraint in which she lived, she was captivated by the person of Peregrine, and his insinuating address had confirmed his conquest. He did not fail to be at the grate next day, where he urged his suit with such irresistible recommendations, that she confessed a mutual flame, after having observed, that the circumstances of her situation would not permit her to protract that acknowledgment in the usual form. He received this confession with transport, as the effusion of an ingenuous mind, that soars above all the little arts and disguises of the sex; and intreated her to tell him when or where he should have the happiness of conversing with her, without the interposition of these invidious bars.

She gave him to understand, that as her friends had put her under the direction of a severe abbess, it would be impossible for her to go abroad without the connivance of the portress, and equally impracticable for him to gain admittance into the convent, without running a manifest risk of being discovered, and consequently punished with the utmost severity.

When a fair lady was in the case, our adventurer despised all danger, and spared no expence. Thus informed, he studied the disposition of the old sister who kept the keys; and in her appearance and conversation, distinguished the implacable rancour of a woman who had spent her youth in all the mortification of detested celibacy. She bore a most inveterate grudge to all her juniors, who still remained within the possibility of enjoying those pleasures from which she was eternally cut off, and observed all the young men who appeared at the grate with the most envious suspicion. Not even the power of all-persuading gold could tame the spite, or soften the vigilant asperity of this indomitable maiden.

Our lover tampered with her in vain; nay, she threatened to inform the abbess of his sacrilegious attempt, that he might, for the future, be excluded from the privilege of speaking to the nuns: and, for the first time, he found the art of corruption ineffectual. Baffled in this endeavour, he conferred with his mistress about some other means of procuring an unrestricted interview; and she, in the fertility of her invention, proposed, that he should make it his business to find some woman, who, by her acquaintance in the convent, would introduce him in a female dress, as a stranger desirous of seeing the œconomy of the house. The expedient was wonderfully relished by the gallant, who had immediate recourse to the assistance of his valet de chambre, by whom he was next day made acquainted with a certain good-natured gentlewoman, who, for an handsome consideration, undertook the task. From this good lady's wardrobe he was accordingly accommodated with a proper suit, which, on account of his stature, was pieced for the purpose: and his mistress being previously prepared with the knowledge of their intention, he set out in the afternoon with his conductress, who had interest enough to obtain his admission, on pretence of his being an English lady, just arrived from her own country, and curious to see the menage and accommodations of a nunnery. Though the alteration of his dress, and a pair of artificial eye-brows, screened him from the penetrating eye of the portress, there was something so remarkably singular in his make, stature, countenance and mien, that the sisters gazed upon him as a prodigy; and he could hear them, as he passed, asking of each other, with expressions of astonishment, if all the women in England made such a strange appearance.

Having visited the cells and chapel, his charmer officiously offered her service in conducting the stranger to the garden; and after having attended them in walking several turns, invited them to repose in a small arbour, that stood at one corner, in the middle of a tuft of trees, which rendered it impervious to the view. The old gentlewoman understanding the hint, accompanied the lovers to the entrance of this grove, where she left them, on pretence of being still unwearied with the exercise of her legs; and their mutual raptures in this stolen interview began to rise to a very interesting pitch, when they were alarmed by the rustling of the leaves behind them; and turning their eyes towards the place, perceived they were discovered by a nun, who, either by accident or design, had concealed herself in the thicket, until, scandalized by their behaviour, she thought it high time to signify her presence.

It is not to be doubted that our hero and his mistress were grievously disconcerted on this occasion. The lady cried she was undone, and had almost fainted with fear, which was not at all without foundation, considering that not only her reputation, but even her life was at stake. Peregrine, though he could easily have made his escape over the garden-wall, had too much gallantry to leave his charmer and friend in such a dangerous dilemma; and therefore, with admirable presence of mind, advanced to the author of his perplexity, and without any ceremony or courtship, found means to make her a party in the secret, before she could recollect herself so far as to find fault with his proceeding.

This measure re-established the tranquillity of the scene: the two ladies embraced as sisters, and vowed eternal friendship on the spot; and the young gentleman having protested that he would share his affection between them, and practise the same method of visiting them in a few days, rejoined his directress, and returned in safety to his own lodgings, being but indifferently satisfied with the adventure of the day, by which he found himself obliged, either to forego all correspondence with the woman he loved, or carry on an intrigue with a person who was not at all to his liking; for the attractions of the nun were by no means inchanting.

He next day appeared at the grate in his own person, and intimated his sentiments on this subject to his mistress, who assured him, that notwithstanding her behaviour to the sister, in the emergency of yesterday, she would much rather be debarred of his company for ever, than enjoy it upon the terms which necessity had obliged him to propose. She said, the reflection on what had passed in the grove, had inspired her with such an unconquerable aversion for that accidental rival, that she could not think of her without hate and indignation. She wished she had run all risks, rather than submit to such detested partition; and vowed with great warmth, that let the consequence be what it would, she was determined to discover the whole affair to the abbess, if ever he should introduce himself again, in a manner which must subject him to the knowledge and claim of her competitor.

He applauded the delicacy of her sentiments, which he swore were exactly conformable to his own; and promised to desist from those visits that gave her umbrage, encouraging her to hope, that they would find some other means of settling an intercourse, in which she should ingross his undivided attention. Such a scheme was actually the subject of his thoughts at that time; and a youth of his fruitful imagination, assisted with the counsels of such a consummate politician as the valet de chambre, would undoubtedly have brought it to maturation, had not his aim been anticipated by an unforeseen accident, that flowed from the partial administration of his favour. The nun who had been indebted to chance for his addresses, was too conscious of her own inferior qualifications, to think she could dispute the heart of our hero with the young lady who was previously possessed of his affection; she knew, that her share of his good graces was altogether casual, and that the continuance of his assiduities must be the effect of policy and constrained complaisance; yet, even on these considerations, they were too agreeable to be given up; and therefore she resolved to guard her privilege with the most minute vigilance and caution. Jealousy was the natural consequence of these suggestions: the assignation in the garden, she knew, must have been preceded by some communication; and as there was no other opportunity of conversing with the male sex, except that of holding a conference through the grate, she went to the portress, with a view of obtaining some intelligence; and pumped the beldame so successfully, that she learnt how her rival had that very forenoon been favoured with a visit by a young gentleman, whom she supposed to be no other than their common gallant. Inflamed with this information, she taxed the young lady with double dealing; and scolded with such bitterness, that the other, already prejudiced against her pretensions, could no longer contain her resentment, which she uttered in contemptuous sneers against her personal attributes; and in the pride of her wrath declared, that she ought not to expect another interview with her lover in the grove; for he was already too much satiated with her charms to return to such a banquet, and had relinquished her to the chance of meeting with another charitable meal.

No tygress robbed of her young was ever exalted to an higher pitch of fury than this nun, when she found herself abandoned by her lover, and insulted in this mortifying explanation. She darted upon her antagonist, like a hawk upon a partridge, and with her nails disfigured that fair face which had defrauded her of her dearest expectation. Nor did the rival tamely bear the barbarity of her rage; what she wanted in strength she supplied with spirit, and twisting her hand in the hair of the aggressor, pulled her head with violence to the ground. The noise of this contention, increased by the cries of the combatants, whose tongues were more active than their hands, brought a croud of sisters to the spot; but so fiercely were they engaged, that they neither minded admonitions nor threats, nor paid the least regard to their own reputation; but on the contrary, as if they had not known that they were surrounded by numbers, who heard every word that proceeded from their mouths, they made no secret of the cause of their dispute, which, in the precipitancy of their wrath, they divulged with all its circumstances, to the amazement of the by-standers.

At length the lady abbess arrived, and what her authority could not accomplish, was effected by two lay-sisters, who being summoned for the purpose, separated the rivals, who were by this time quite exhausted with the fatigue of the battle. Had this mutual detection been made in any company of females, the secret would have hardly rested among those who heard it, much less in a convent, where so many old maidens happened to be present. One of these antiquated devotees accordingly imparted it to the superior, who having examined into the particulars, and found the information true, from the rash recrimination of the incensed parties on their trial, considered the affair as a very serious matter, which affected the good order and reputation of her convent, assembled all the sisters, and exhorted them to suppress the discovery, as a circumstance injurious to the character of the house; laid strict injunctions on the portress, to be very cautious for the future in the discharge of her office, delivered over the backsliding nun to a severe penance prescribed by her ghostly father, and that very day sent her boarder back to her relations, with a hint of what had happened, and an advice to dispose of her in some remote nunnery, where she would be less exposed to the machinations of her gallant.

Our lover, utterly ignorant of this unlucky fray and its consequence, was confounded when the wrinkled turnkey refused to admit him to the grate, telling him, that his impious contrivance had come to light; that the lewd young woman, for whose sake he had been guilty of such a flagrant crime, was banished from the convent; and that if ever he should make another attempt to disturb the tranquillity of their retreat, a formal complaint would be preferred against him to the civil magistrate.

Thunderstruck with this reception, he did not think proper to advance any thing in his own vindication, but retreated with all convenient dispatch, not ill pleased at the issue of an adventure which might have proved not only disagreeable, but dangerous in the highest degree. He at once conjectured, that the mutual jealousy of the ladies had betrayed the intrigue; and imagined, that now his charmer was delivered from the restrictions of a convent, she would be more accessible to his endeavours. On this supposition, he sent his couriers upon the scout; and as he knew her name, it was not long before he learnt, from their artful inquiries, that immediately after her dismission from one nunnery, she had been entered in another at Ghent, in consequence of the superior's advice, and in all likelihood would be compelled to take the veil by her guardians, who were remarkably zealous for the welfare of her soul.

CHAPTER LXVII

The Travellers depart for Antwerp, at which Place
the Painter gives a Loose to his Enthusiasm

OUR adventurer thus deprived of an agreeable correspondence, and baffled in all his efforts to retrieve the other object of his passion, yielded at length to the remonstrances of his governor and fellow-travellers, who, out of pure complaisance to him, had exceeded their intended stay by six days at least: and a couple of post-chaises, with three riding-horses, being hired, they departed from Brussels in the morning, dined at Mechlin, and arrived about eight in the evening at the venerable city of Antwerp. During this day's journey, Pallet was elevated to an uncommon flow of spirits, with the prospect of seeing the birth-place of Rubens, for whom he professed an enthusiastic admiration. He swore, that the pleasure he felt was equal to that of a Mussulman, on the last day of his pilgrimage to Mecca; and that he already considered himself a native of Antwerp, being so intimately acquainted with their so justly boasted citizen, from whom, at certain junctures, he could not help believing himself derived, because his own pencil adopted the manner of that great man with surprising facility, and his face wanted nothing but a pair of whiskers and a beard to exhibit the express image of the Fleming's countenance. He told them, he was so proud of this resemblance, that in order to render it more striking, he had at one time of his life resolved to keep his face sacred from the razor; and in that purpose had persevered, notwithstanding the continual reprehensions of Mrs. Pallet, who being then with child, said, his aspect was so hideous, that she dreaded a miscarriage every hour, until she threatened, in plain terms, to dispute the sanity of his intellects, and apply to the chancellor for a committee.

The doctor on his occasion observed, that a man who is not proof against the solicitations of a woman, can never expect to make a great figure in life; that painters and poets ought to cultivate no wives but the muses; or if they are, by the accidents of fortune, incumbered with families, they should carefully guard against that pernicious weakness, falsely honoured with the appellation of *natural affection*, and pay no manner of regard to the impertinent customs of the world. 'Granting that you had been for a short time deemed a lunatic, (said he) you might have acquitted yourself honourably of that imputation, by some performance that would have raised your character above all censure. Sophocles himself, that celebrated tragic poet, who for the sweetness of his versification, was stiled μέλιττα, or *the bee*, in his old age suffered the same accusation from his own children, who seeing him neglect his family affairs, and devote himself intirely to poetry, carried him before the magistrate, as a man whose intellects were so much impaired by the infirmities of age, that he was no longer fit to manage his domestic concerns; upon which the reverend bard produced his tragedy of Οἰδίπους ἐπι Κολωνῷ,[1] as a work he had just finished; which being perused, instead of being declared unsound of understanding, he was dismissed with admiration and applause. I wish your beard and whiskers had been sanctioned by the like authority; though I am afraid you would have been in the predicament of those disciples of a certain philosopher, who drank decoctions of cummin-seeds, that their faces might adopt the paleness of their master's complexion, hoping, that in being as wan, they would be as learned as their teacher.' The painter, stung with this sarcasm, replied, 'or like those Virtuosi, who by repeating Greek, eating sillikickaby, and pretending to see visions, think they equal the ancients in taste and genius.' The physician retorted, Pallet rejoined, and the altercation continued, until they entered the gates of Antwerp, when the admirer of Rubens broke forth into a rapturous exclamation, which put an end to the dispute, and attracted the notice of the inhabitants, many of whom, by shrugging up their shoulders, and pointing to their foreheads, gave shrewd indications, that they believed him a poor gentleman disordered in his brain.

They had no sooner alighted at the inn, than this pseudo-enthusiast proposed to visit the great church, in which he had been informed some of his master's pieces were to be seen; and was remarkably chagrined, when he understood that he could not be admitted till next day. He rose next morning by day-break, and disturbed his fellow-travellers in such a noisy and clamorous manner, that Peregrine determined to punish him with some new infliction, and while he put on his cloaths, actually formed the plan of promoting a duel between him and the doctor; in the management of which he promised himself store of entertainment, from the behaviour of both.

Being provided with one of those domestics who are always in waiting to offer their services to strangers on their first arrival, they were conducted to the house of a gentleman who had an excellent collection of pictures; and though the greatest part of them were painted by his favourite artist, Pallet condemned them all by the lump, because Pickle had told him beforehand, that there was not one performance of Rubens among the number.

The next place they visited, was what is called the academy of painting, furnished with a number of paultry pieces, in which our painter recognized the stile of Peter Paul, with many expressions of admiration, on the same sort of previous intelligence.

From this repository they went to the great church, and being led to the tomb of Rubens, the whimsical painter fell upon his knees, and worshipped, with such appearance of devotion, that the attendant, scandalized at his superstition, pulled him up, observing with great warmth, that the person buried in that place was no saint, but as great a sinner as himself: and that if he was spiritually disposed, there was a chapel of the Blessed Virgin, at the distance of three yards on the right hand, to which he might retire. He thought it was incumbent upon him to manifest some extraordinary inspiration, while he resided on the spot where Rubens was born; and therefore, his whole behaviour was an affectation of rapture, expressed in distracted exclamations, convulsive starts, and uncouth gesticulations. In the midst of this frantic behaviour, he saw an old Capuchin, with a white beard, mount the pulpit, and hold forth to the congregation with such violence of emphasis and gesture, as captivated his fancy; and bawling aloud, 'Zounds! what an excellent Paul preaching at Athens!' he pulled a pencil and small memorandum-book from his pocket, and began to take a sketch of the orator, with great eagerness and agitation, saying, 'Egad! friend Raphael, we shall see whether you or I have got the best knack at trumping up an Apostle.' This appearance of disrespect gave offence to the audience, which began to murmur against this heretic libertine; when one of the priests belonging to the choir, in order to prevent any ill consequence from their displeasure, came and told him in the French language, that such liberties were not permitted in their religion, and advised him to lay aside his implements, lest the people should take umbrage at his design, and be provoked to punish him as a profane scoffer at their worship.

The painter seeing himself addressed by a friar, who, while he spoke, bowed with great complaisance, imagined that he was a begging brother come to supplicate his charity; and his attention being quite ingrossed by the design he was making, he patted the priest's shaven crown with his hand, saying, *Oter tems, oter tems*;[1] and then resumed his pencil with great earnestness. The ecclesiastic perceiving that the stranger did not comprehend his meaning, pulled him by the sleeve, and explained himself in the Latin tongue: upon which, Pallet, provoked at his intrusion, cursed him aloud for an impudent beggarly son of a whore; and taking out a schelling, flung it upon the pavement, with manifest signs of indignation.

Some of the common people, enraged to see their religion contemned, and their priests insulted at the very altar, rose from their seats, and surrounding the astonished painter, one of the number snatched his book from his hand, and tore it into a thousand pieces. Frightened as he was, he could not help crying, 'Fire and faggots! all my favourite ideas are gone to wreck!' and was in danger of being very roughly handled by the croud, had not Peregrine stepped in, and assured them, that he was a poor unhappy gentleman, who laboured under a transport of the brain. Those who understood the French language communicated this information to the rest; so that he escaped without any other chastisement, than that of being obliged to retire. And as they could not see the famous descent from the cross till after the service was finished, they were conducted by their domestique to the house of a painter, where they found a beggar standing for his picture, and the artist actually employed in representing a huge louse that crawled upon his shoulder. Pallet was wonderfully pleased with this circumstance, which he said was altogether a new thought, and an excellent hint, of which he would make his advantage: and in the course of his survey of this Fleming's performances, perceiving a piece in which two flies were engaged upon the carcase of a dog half devoured, he ran to his brother brush, and swore he was worthy of being a fellow-citizen of the immortal Rubens. He then lamented, with many expressions of grief and resentment, that he had lost his common-place book, in which he had preserved a thousand conceptions of the same sort, formed by the accidental objects of his senses and imagination; and took an opportunity of telling his fellow-travellers, that in execution he had equalled, if not excelled, the two ancient painters who vied with each other in the representation of a curtain and a bunch of grapes; for he had exhibited the image of a certain object so like to nature, that the bare sight of it set a whole hogsty in an uproar.

When he had examined and applauded all the productions of this minute artist, they returned to the great church, and were entertained with the view of that celebrated master-piece of Rubens, in which he has introduced the portraits of himself and his whole family. The doors that conceal this capital performance were no sooner unfolded, than our enthusiast, debarred the use of speech, by a previous covenant with his friend Pickle, lifted up his hands and eyes, and putting himself in the attitude of Hamlet, when his father's ghost appears,[1] adored in silent extasy and awe. He even made a merit of necessity; and when they had withdrawn from the place, protested that his whole faculties were swallowed up in love and admiration. He now professed himself more than ever enamoured of the Flemish school, raved in extravagant encomiums, and proposed, that the whole company should pay homage to the memory of the divine Rubens, by repairing forthwith to the house in which he lived, and prostrating themselves on the floor of his painting room.

As there was nothing remarkable in the tenement, which had been rebuilt more than once since the death of that great man, Peregrine excused himself from complying with the proposal, on pretence of being fatigued with the circuit they had already performed. Jolter declined it for the same reason; and the question being put to the doctor, he refused his company with an air of disdain. Pallet, piqued at his contemptuous manner, asked if he would not go and see the habitation of Pindoor, provided he was in the city where that poet lived? And when the physician observed, that there was an infinite difference between the men; 'That I'll allow, (replied the painter) for the devil a poet ever lived in Greece or Troy, that was worthy to clean the pencils of our beloved Rubens.' The physician could not with any degree of temper and forbearance hear this outrageous blasphemy, for which, he said, Pallet's eyes ought to be picked out by owls: and the dispute rose, as usual, to such scurrilities of language and indecency of behaviour, that passengers began to take notice of their animosity; and Peregrine was obliged to interpose, for his own credit.

CHAPTER LXVIII

Peregrine artfully foments a Quarrel between Pallet
and the Physician, who fight a Duel on the Ramparts

THE painter betook himself to the house of the Flemish Raphael, and the rest of the company went back to their lodgings; where the young gentleman, taking the advantage of being alone with the physician, recapitulated all the affronts he had sustained from the painter's petulance, aggravating every circumstance of the disgrace, and advising him, in the capacity of a friend, to take care of his honour, which could not fail to suffer in the opinion of the world, if he allowed himself to be insulted with impunity, by one so much his inferior in every degree of consideration.

The physician assured him, that Pallet had hitherto escaped chastisement, by being deemed an object unworthy his resentment, and in consideration of the wretch's family, for which his compassion was interested; but, that repeated injuries would inflame the most benevolent disposition: and although he could find no precedent of duelling among the Greeks and Romans, whom he considered as the patterns of demeanour, Pallet should no longer avail himself of his veneration for the ancients, but be punished for the very next offence he should commit.

Having thus spirited up the doctor to a resolution from which he could not decently swerve, our adventurer acted the incendiary with the other party also; giving him to understand, that the physician treated his character with such contempt, and behaved to him with such insolence, as no gentleman ought to bear: that for his own part, he was every day put out of countenance by their mutual animosity, which appeared in nothing but vulgar expressions, more becoming shoe-boys and oyster-women than men of honour and education; and therefore he should be obliged, contrary to his inclination, to break off all correspondence with them both, if they would not fall upon some method to retrieve the dignity of their characters.

These representations would have had little effect upon the timidity of the painter, who was likewise too much of a Grecian to approve of single combat, in any other way than that of boxing, an exercise in which he was well skill'd, had not they been accompanied with an insinuation, that his antagonist was no Hector, and that he might humble him into any concession, without running the least personal risk. Animated by this assurance, our second Rubens set the trumpet of defiance to his mouth, swore that he valued not his life a rush, when his honour was concerned, and intreated Mr. Pickle to be the bearer of a challenge, which he would instantly commit to writing.

The mischievous fomentor highly applauded this manifestation of courage, by which he was at liberty to cultivate his friendship and society; but declined the office of carrying the billet, that his tenderness of Pallet's reputation might not be misinterpreted into an officious desire of promoting quarrels. At the same time he recommended Tom Pipes, not only as a very proper messenger on this occasion, but also as a trusty second in the field. The magnanimous painter took his advice, and retiring to his chamber, penn'd a challenge in these terms.

'SIR,

When I am heartily provoked, I fear not the devil himself; much less——I will not call you a pedantic coxcomb, nor an unmannerly fellow, because these are the hippythets of the wulgar: but, remember, such as you are, I neyther love you nor fear you; but, on the contrary, expect satisfaction for your audacious behaviour to me, on divers occasions; and will, this evening, in the twilight, meet you on the ramparts with sword and pistol, where the Lord have mercy on the soul of one of us; for your body shall find no favour with your incensed defier, till death,

LAYMAN PALLET.'

This resolute defiance, after having been submitted to the perusal, and honoured with the approbation of our youth, was committed to the charge of Pipes, who, according to his orders, delivered it in the afternoon; and brought for answer, that the physician would attend him at the appointed time and place. The challenger was evidently discomposed at the unexpected news of this acceptance, and ran about the house in great disorder, in quest of Peregrine, to beg his further advice and assistance; but, understanding that the youth was engaged in private with his adversary, he began to suspect some collusion, and cursed himself for his folly and precipitation. He even entertained some thoughts of retracting his invitation, and submitting to the triumph of his antagonist: but, before he would stoop to this opprobrious condescension, he resolved to try another expedient, which might be the means of saving both his character and person. In this hope he visited Mr. Jolter, and very gravely desired he would be so good as to undertake the office of his second, in a duel which he was to fight that evening with the physician.

The governor, instead of answering his expectation, in expressing fear and concern, and breaking forth into exclamations of, 'Good God! gentlemen, what d'ye mean? You shall not murther one another, while it is in my power to prevent your purpose. I will go directly to the governor of the place, who shall interpose his authority.' I say, instead of these and other friendly menaces of prevention, Jolter heard the proposal with the most phlegmatic tranquillity, and excused himself from accepting the honour he intended for him, on account of his character and situation, which would not permit him to be concerned in any such rencounters. Indeed this mortifying reception was owing to a previous hint from Peregrine, who dreading some sort of interruption from his governor, had made him acquainted with his design, and assured him, that the affair should not be brought to any dangerous issue.

Thus disappointed, the dejected challenger was overwhelmed with perplexity and dismay; and in the terrors of death or mutilation, resolved to deprecate the wrath of his enemy, and conform to any submission he should propose; when he was accidentally encountered by our adventurer, who with demonstrations of infinite satisfaction, told him in confidence, that his billet had thrown the doctor into an agony of consternation; and that his acceptance of his challenge was a meer effort of despair, calculated to confound the ferocity of the sender, and dispose him to listen to terms of accommodation: that he had imparted the letter to him with fear and trembling, on pretence of engaging him as a second, but in reality, with a view of obtaining his good offices in promoting a reconciliation; 'but, perceiving the situation of his mind, (added our hero) I thought it would be more for your honour to baffle his expectation; and therefore I readily undertook the task of attending him to the field, in full assurance, that he will there humble himself before you, even to prostration. In this security, you may go and prepare your arms, and bespeak the assistance of Pipes, who will squire you in the field, while I keep myself up, that our correspondence may not be suspected by the physician.' Pallet's spirits, that were sunk to dejection, rose at this encouragement to all the insolence of triumph; he again declared his contempt of danger, and his pistols being loaded and accommodated with new flints, by his trusty armour-bearer, he waited, without flinching, for the hour of battle.

On the first approach of twilight, somebody knocked at his door, and Pipes having opened it at his desire, he heard the voice of his antagonist pronounce, 'Tell Mr. Pallet, that I am going to the place of appointment.' The painter was not a little surprized at this anticipation, which so ill agreed with the information he had received from Pickle; and his concern beginning to recur, he fortified himself with a large bumper of brandy, which, however, did not overcome the anxiety of his thoughts. Nevertheless, he set out on the expedition with his second, betwixt whom and himself the following dialogue passed, in their way to the ramparts. 'Mr. Pipes, (said the painter, with disordered accent) methinks the doctor was in a pestilent hurry with that message of his.' 'Ey, ey, (answered Tom) I do suppose he longs to be foul of you.' 'What! (replied the other) d'ye think he thirsts after my blood?' 'To be sure a does,' (said Pipes, thrusting a large quid of tobacco in his cheek, with great deliberation.) 'If that be the case, (cried Pallet, beginning to shake) he is no better than a Cannibal, and no Christian ought to fight him on equal footing.' Tom observing his emotion, eyed him with a frown of indignation, saying, 'You an't afraid, are you?' 'God forbid! (replied the challenger, stammering with fear.) What should I be afraid of? The worst he can do, is to take my life, and then he'll be answerable both to God and man for the murder: Don't you think he will?' 'I think no such matter, (answered the second) if so be as how he puts a brace of bullets through your bows, and kills you fairly, it is no more murder than if I was to bring down a noddy from the main-top-sail-yard.' By this time, Pallet's teeth chattered with such violence, that he could scarce pronounce this reply, 'Mr. Thomas, you seem to make very light of a man's life; but I trust in the Almighty, I shall not be so easily brought down. Sure many a man has fought a duel, without losing his life. Do you imagine that I run such a hazard of falling by the hand of my adversary?' 'You may, or you may not, (said the unconcerned Pipes) just as it happens. What then? Death is a debt that every man owes, according to the song; and if you set foot to foot, I think one of you must go to pot.' 'Foot to foot! (exclaimed the terrified painter) that's downright butchery; and I'll be damn'd before I fight any man on earth in such a barbarous way. What! d'ye take me to be a savage beast?' This declaration he made while they ascended the ramparts; and his attendant perceiving the physician and his second at the distance of an hundred paces before them, gave him notice of their appearance, and advised him to make ready, and behave like a man. Pallet in vain endeavoured to conceal his pannic, which discovered itself in an universal trepidation of body, and the lamentable tone in which he answered this exhortation of Pipes; saying, 'I do behave like a man; but you would have me act the part of a brute. Are they coming this way?' When Tom told him that they had faced about, and admonished him to advance, the nerves of his arm refused their office, he could not hold out his pistol, and instead of going forward, retreated with an insensibility of motion; till Pipes, placing himself in the rear, set his own back to that of his principal, and swore he should not budge an inch farther in that direction.

Chapter LXVIII

While the valet thus tutored the painter, his master enjoyed the terrors of the physician, which were more ridiculous than those of Pallet, because he was more intent upon disguising them. His declaration to Pickle in the morning, would not suffer him to start any objections when he received the challenge; and finding that the young gentleman made no offer of mediating the affair, but rather congratulated him on the occasion, when he communicated the painter's billet, all his efforts consisted in oblique hints, and general reflections upon the absurdity of duelling, which was first introduced among civilized nations, by the barbarous Huns and Longobards. He likewise pretended to ridicule the use of fire-arms, which confounded all the distinctions of skill and address, and deprived a combatant of the opportunity of signalizing his personal prowess.

Pickle assented to the justness of his observations; but at the same time represented the necessity of complying with the customs of the world, (ridiculous as they were) on which a man's honour and reputation depend. So that, seeing no hopes of profiting by that artifice, the republican's agitation became more and more remarkable; and he proposed in plain terms, that they should contend in armour, like the combatants of ancient days; for it was but reasonable, that they should practise the manner of fighting, since they adopted the disposition of those iron times.

Nothing could have afforded more diversion to our hero, than the sight of two such duellists cased in iron; and he wished that he had promoted the quarrel in Brussels, where he could have hired the armour of Charles the fifth, and the valiant duke of Parma, for their accommodation: but, as there was no possibility of furnishing them cap-a-pee at Antwerp, he persuaded him to conform to the modern use of the sword, and meet the painter on his own terms; and suspecting that his fear would supply him with other excuses for declining the combat, he comforted him with some distant insinuations to the prejudice of his adversary's courage, which would in all probability, evaporate, before any mischief could happen.

Notwithstanding this encouragement, he could not suppress the reluctance with which he went to the field, and cast many a wishful look over his left shoulder, to see whether or not his adversary was at his heels; and when, by the advice of his second, he took possession of the ground, and turned about with his face to the enemy, it was not so dark, but that Peregrine could perceive the unusual paleness of his countenance, and the sweat standing in large drops upon his forehead; nay, there was a manifest disorder in his speech, when he regretted his want of the Pila and Parma,[1] with which he would have made a rattling noise, to astonish his foe, in springing forward, and singing the hymn to battle, in the manner of the ancients.

In the mean time, observing the hesitation of his antagonist, who, far from advancing, seemed to recoil, and even struggle with his second, he guessed the situation of the painter's thoughts; and collecting all the manhood that he possessed, seized the opportunity of profiting by his enemy's consternation; and striking his sword and pistol together, advanced in a sort of trot, raising a loud howl, in which he repeated, in lieu of the Spartan song, part of a strophe from one of Pindar's Pythia, beginning with "Ἐκ θεῶν γὰρ μαχαναὶ πᾶσαι βροτέαις ἀρεταῖς, &c.[2] This imitation of the Greeks had all the desired effect upon the painter, who seeing the physician running towards him, like a fury, with a pistol in his right hand, which was extended, and hearing the dreadful yell he uttered, and the outlandish words he pronounced, was seized with an universal palsy of his limbs, and would have dropp'd down upon the ground, had not Pipes supported and encouraged him to stand upon his defence. The doctor, contrary to his expectation, finding that he had not flinched from the spot, though he had now performed one half of his career, put in practice his last effort, by firing his pistol, the noise of which no sooner reached the ears of the affrighted painter, than he recommended his soul to God, and roared for mercy with great vociferation.

The republican, overjoyed at this exclamation, commanded him to yield, and surrender his arms, on pain of immediate death; upon which he threw away his pistols and sword, in spite of all the admonitions and even threats of his second, who left him to his fate, and went up to his master, stopping his nose with signs of loathing and abhorrence.

The victor having won the Spolia Opima,[3] granted him his life, on condition, that he would on his knees supplicate his pardon, acknowledge himself inferior to his conqueror in every virtue and qualification, and promise for the future to merit his favour by submission and respect. These insolent terms were readily embraced by the unfortunate challenger, who fairly owned, that he was not at all calculated for the purposes of war, and that henceforth he would contend with no weapon but his pencil. He begg'd with great humility, that Mr. Pickle would not think the worse of his morals for this defect of courage, which was a natural infirmity inherited from his father, and suspend his opinion of his talents, until he should have an opportunity of contemplating the charms of his Cleopatra, which would be finished in less than three months.

Our hero observed with an affected air of displeasure, that no man could be justly condemned for being subject to the impressions of fear; and therefore his cowardice might easily be forgiven: but, there was something so presumptuous, dishonest and disingenuous, in arrogating a quality to which he knew he had not the smallest pretension, that he could not forget his misbehaviour all at once, though he would condescend to communicate with him as formerly, in hopes of seeing a reformation in his conduct. Pallet protested, that there was no dissimulation in the case; for he was ignorant of his own weakness, until his resolution was put to the trial: he faithfully promised to demean himself, during the remaining part of the tour, with that conscious modesty and penitence which became a person in his condition; and, for the present, implored the assistance of Mr. Pipes, in desembarassing him from the disagreeable consequence of his fear.

CHAPTER LXIX

The Doctor exults in his Victory. They set out for
Rotterdam, where they are Entertained by two Dutch
Gentlemen in a Yacht, which is overturned in the Maes,
to the manifest Hazard of the Painter's Life.
They spend the Evening with their Entertainers,
and next Day visit a Cabinet of Curiosities

TOM was accordingly ordered to minister to his occasions; and the conqueror, elated with his success, which he in a great measure attributed to his manner of attack, and the hymn which he howled, told Peregrine, that he was now convinced of the truth of what Pindar sung in these words, Ὅσσα δὲ μὴ πεφίληκε Ζεύς, ἀτύζονται βοὰν Πιερίδων ἀΐοντα;[1] for he had no sooner begun to repeat the mellifluent strains of that divine poet, than the wretch his antagonist was confounded, and his nerves unstrung.

On their return to the inn, he expatiated on the prudence and tranquillity of his own behaviour, and ascribed the consternation of Pallet to the remembrance of some crime that lay heavy upon his conscience: for, in his opinion, a man of virtue and common sense could not possibly be afraid of death, which is not only the peaceful harbour that receives him shattered on the tempestuous sea of life, but also the eternal seal of his fame and glory, which it is no longer in his power to forfeit and forego. He lamented his fate, in being doomed to live in such degenerate days, when war is become a mercenary trade; and ardently wished, that the day would come, when he should have such an opportunity of signalizing his courage in the cause of liberty, as that of Marathon, where an handful of Athenians, fighting for their freedom, defeated the whole strength of the Persian empire. 'Would to heaven! (said he) my muse were blessed with an occasion to emulate that glorious testimony on the trophy in Cyprus, erected by Cimon, for two great victories gained on the same day over the Persians by sea and land; in which it is very remarkable, that the greatness of the occasion has raised the manner of expression above the usual simplicity and modesty of all other ancient inscriptions.'[1] He then repeated it with all the pomp of declamation, and signified his hope, that the French would one day invade us with such an army as that which Xerxes led into Greece, that it might be in his power to devote himself, like Leonidas, to the freedom of his country.

This memorable combat being thus determined, and every thing that was remarkable in Antwerp surveyed, they sent their baggage down the Scheld to Rotterdam, and set out for the same place in a post-waggon, which that same evening brought them in safety to the banks of the Maeze. They put up at an English house of entertainment, remarkable for the modesty and moderation of the landlord; and next morning the doctor went in person, to deliver letters of recommendation to two Dutch gentlemen, from one of his acquaintance at Paris. Neither of them happened to be at home when he called; so that he left a message at their lodgings, with his address; and in the afternoon they waited upon the company, and after many hospitable professions, one of the two invited them to spend the evening at his house.

Mean while, they had provided a pleasure-yacht, in which they proposed to treat them with an excursion upon the Maeze. This being almost the only diversion that place affords, our young gentleman relished the proposal; and notwithstanding the remonstrances of Mr. Jolter, who declined the voyage on account of the roughness of the weather, they went on board without hesitation, and found a collation prepared in the cabin. While they tacked to and fro in the river, under the impulse of a mackerel breeze, the physician expressed his satisfaction, and Pallet was ravished with

344

the entertainment. But the wind increasing, to the unspeakable joy of the Dutchmen, who had now an opportunity of shewing their dexterity in the management of the vessel, the guests found it inconvenient to stand upon deck, and impossible to sit below, on account of the clouds of tobacco-smoke which rolled from the pipes of their entertainers, in such volumes as annoyed them even to the hazard of suffocation. This fumigation, together with the extraordinary motion of the ship, began to affect the head and stomach of the painter, who begg'd earnestly to be set on shore: but the Dutch gentlemen, who had no idea of his sufferings, to which they had always been utter strangers, insisted, with surprising obstinacy of regard, upon his staying until he should see an instance of the skill of their mariners; and bringing him on deck, commanded the men to carry the vessel's lee-gunwale under water. This nicety of navigation they instantly performed, to the admiration of Pickle, the discomposure of the doctor, and terror of Pallet, who blessed himself from the courtesy of a Dutchman, and prayed to heaven for his deliverance.

While the Hollanders enjoyed the reputation of this feat, and the distress of the painter at the same time, the yacht was overtaken by a sudden squall, that overset her in a moment, and flung every man overboard into the Maeze, before they could have the least warning of their fate, much less, time to provide against the accident. Peregrine, who was an expert swimmer, reached the shore in safety; the physician, in the agonies of despair, laid fast hold on the trunk-breeches of one of the men, who dragged him to the other side; the entertainers landed at the bomb-keys, smoking their pipes all the way with great deliberation; and the poor painter must have gone to the bottom, had not he been encountered by the cable of a ship, that lay at anchor near the scene of their disaster. Though his senses had forsaken him, his hands fastened by instinct on this providential occurrence, which he held with such a convulsive grasp, that when a boat was sent out to bring him on shore, it was with the utmost difficulty that his fingers were disengaged. He was carried into a house, deprived of the use of speech, and bereft of all sensation; and being suspended by the heels, a vast quantity of water ran out of his mouth. This evacuation being made, he began to utter dreadful groans, which gradually increased to a continued roar; and after he had regained the use of his senses, underwent a delirium that lasted several hours. As for the treaters, they never dreamed of expressing the least concern to Pickle or the physician for what had happened, because it was an accident so common, as to pass without notice; but they were very much surprized to find, upon inquiry, that Pallet could not swim, it being as natural for a Dutchman, as a deal-board, to float upon the surface.[1]

Leaving the care of the vessel to the seamen, the company retired to their respective lodgings, in order to shift their cloaths; and in the evening our travellers were conducted to the house of their new friend, who, with a view of making his invitation the more agreeable, had assembled to the number of twenty or thirty Englishmen, of all ranks and degrees, from the merchant to the periwig-maker's prentice.

In the midst of this congregation stood a chafing-dish with live-coals, for the convenience of lighting their pipes, and every individual was accommodated with a spitting-box. There was not a mouth in the apartment unfurnished with a tube, so that they resembled a convocation of Chimeras breathing fire and smoke; and our gentlemen were fain to imitate their example in their own defence. It is not to be supposed that the conversation was either very sprightly or polite; the whole entertainment was of the Dutch cast, that is, frowzy and phlegmatic: and our adventurer, as he returned to his lodging, tortured with the head-ache, and disgusted with every circumstance of his treatment, cursed the hour in which the doctor had saddled them with such troublesome companions.

Next morning, by eight o'clock, these polite Hollanders returned the visit, and after breakfast, attended their English friends to the house of a person that possessed a very curious cabinet of curiosities, to which they had secured our company's admission. The owner of this collection was a cheesemonger, who received them in a woollen night-cap, with straps buttoned under his chin. As he understood no language but his own, he told them, by the canal of one of their conductors, that he did not make a practice of shewing his curiosities; but understanding that they were Englishmen, and recommended to his friends, he was content to submit them to their perusal. So saying, he led them up a dark stair, into a small room, decorated with a few paltry figures in plaister of Paris, two or three miserable landscapes, the skins of an otter, seal, and some fishes stuffed; and in one corner stood a glass-case, furnished with newts, frogs, lizzards and serpents, preserved in spirits; a human fœtus, a calf with two heads, and about two dozen of butterflies pinned upon paper.

The virtuoso having exhibited these particulars, eyed the strangers with a look solliciting admiration and applause; and as he could not perceive any symptom of either in their gestures or countenances, withdrew a curtain, and displayed a wainscot chest of drawers, in which, he gave them to understand, was something that would agreeably amuse the imagination. Our travellers, regaled with this notice, imagined that they would be entertained with the sight of some curious medals, or other productions of antiquity; but how were they disappointed, when they saw nothing but a variety of shells, disposed in whimsical figures, in each drawer! After he had detained them full two hours with a tedious commentary upon the shape, size and colour of each department, he, with a supercilious simper, desired that the English gentlemen would frankly and candidly declare, whether his cabinet, or that of mynheer Sloane,[1] at London, was the most valuable. When this request was signified in English to the company, the painter instantly exclaimed, 'By the Lard! they are not to be named of a day. And as for that matter, I would not give one corner of Saltero's coffee-house,[2] at Chelsea, for all the trash he hath shewn.' Peregrine, unwilling to mortify any person who had done his endeavour to please him, observed, that what they had seen was very curious and entertaining; but that no private collection in Europe was equal to that of Sir Hans Sloane, which, exclusive of presents, had cost an hundred thousand pounds. The two conductors were confounded at this asseveration, which being communicated to the cheese-monger, he shook his head with a significant grin; and tho' he did not choose to express his incredulity in words, gave our hero to understand, that he did not much depend upon his veracity.

From the house of this Dutch naturalist, they were dragged all round the city, by the painful civility of their attendants, who did not quit them till the evening was well advanced, and then not till after they had promised to be with them before ten o'clock next day, in order to conduct them to a country-house, situated in a pleasant village on the other side of the river.

Pickle was already so much fatigued with their hospitality, that, for the first time of his life, he suffered a dejection of spirits; and resolved, at any rate, to avoid the threatened persecution of to-morrow: with this view, he ordered his servants to pack up some cloaths and linnen in a portmanteau; and in the morning embarked, with his governor, in the Treckskuyt,[3] for the Hague, whither he pretended to be called by some urgent occasion, leaving his fellow-travellers to make his apology to their friends; and assuring them, that he would not proceed for Amsterdam, without their society. He arrived at the Hague in the forenoon, and dined at an ordinary frequented by officers and people of fashion; where being informed, that the princess would see company in the evening, he dressed himself in a rich suit of the Parisian cut, and went to court, without any introduction. A person of his appearance could not fail to attract the notice of such a small circle. The prince himself understanding he was an Englishman and a stranger, went up to him, without ceremony; and having welcomed him to the place, conversed with him, for some minutes, on the common topics of discourse.

CHAPTER LXX

They proceed to the Hague; from whence they depart
for Amsterdam, where they see a Dutch Tragedy.
Visit a Musick-house, in which Peregrine quarrels
with the Captain of a Man of War.
They pass through Haarlem, in their Way to Leyden.
Return to Rotterdam, where the Company separates, and
our Hero, with his Attendants, arrives in Safety at Harwich

BEING joined by their fellow-travellers, in the morning, they made a tour to all the remarkable places in this celebrated village; saw the Foundery, the Stadthouse, the Spinhuys,[1] Vauxhall, and Count Bentinck's gardens, and in the evening went to the French comedy, which was directed by a noted Harlequin, who had found means to flatter the Dutch taste so effectually, that they extolled him as the greatest actor that ever appeared in the province of Holland. This famous company[2] did not represent regular theatrical pieces, but only a sort of impromptus, in which this noted player always performed the greatest part of the entertainment. Among other sallies of wit that escaped him, there was one circumstance so remarkably adapted to the disposition and genius of his audience, that it were pity to pass it over in silence: A windmill being exhibited on the scene, Harlequin, after having surveyed it with curiosity and admiration, asks of one of the millers, the use of that machine; and being told, that it was a windmill, observes with some concern, that as there was not the least breath of wind, he could not have the pleasure of seeing it turn round. Urged by this consideration, he puts himself into the attitude of a person wrapt in profound meditation; and having continued a few seconds in this posture, runs to

348

the miller with great eagerness and joy, and telling him, that he had found an expedient to make his mill work, very fairly unbuttons his breeches, and presenting his posteriors to the sails of the machine, certain explosions are immediately heard, and the arms of the mill begin to turn round, to the infinite satisfaction of the spectators, who approve the joke with loud peals of applause.

Our travellers stayed a few days at the Hague, during which the young gentleman waited on the British embassador, to whom he was recommended by his Excellency at Paris, and lost about thirty guineas at billiards to a French adventurer, who decoyed him into the snare by keeping up his game; then they departed in a post-waggon for Amsterdam, being provided with letters of introduction to an English merchant residing in that city, under whose auspices they visited every thing worth seeing, and among other excursions went to see a Dutch tragedy acted; an entertainment which, of all others, had the strangest effect upon the organs of our hero: the dress of their chief personages was so antick, their manner so aukwardly absurd, and their language so ridiculously unfit for conveying the sentiments of love and honour, that Peregrine's nerves were diuretically affected with the complicated absurdity, and he was compelled to withdraw twenty times before the catastrophe of the piece.

The subject of this performance was the famous story of Scipio's continence and virtue, in restoring the fair captive to her lover. The young Roman hero was represented by a broad-fac'd Batavian, in a burgo-master's gown and a fur-cap, sitting smoking his pipe at a table furnished with a can of beer, a drinking-glass, and a plate of tobacco: the lady was such a person as Scipio might very well be supposed to give away, without any great effort of generosity; and indeed the Celtiberian prince seemed to be of that opinion; for, upon receiving her from the hand of the victor, he discovered none of those transports of gratitude and joy which Livy describes, in recounting this event.[1] The Dutch Scipio, however, was complaisant enough in his way; for he desired her to sit at his right hand, by the appellation of *Ya frow*, and with his own fingers filling a clean pipe, presented it to Mynheer Allucio the lover. The rest of the œconomy of the piece was in the same taste; which was so agreeable to the audience, that they seemed to have shaken off their natural phlegm, in order to applaud the performance.

From the play our company adjourned to the house of their friend, where they spent the evening; and the conversation turning upon poetry, a Dutchman who was present, and understood the

English language, having listened very attentively to the discourse, lifted up with both hands the greatest part of a Cheshire cheese that lay upon the table, saying, 'I do know vat is boetrie. Mine brotre be a great boet, and ave vrought a book as dick as all dat.' Pickle, diverted with this method of estimating an author according to the quantity of his works, inquired about the subjects of this bard's writings; but of these his brother could give no account, or other information, but that there was little market for the commodity, which hung heavy upon his hands, and induced him to wish he had applied himself to another trade.

The only remarkable scene in Amsterdam, which our company had not seen, was the Spuyl or musick-houses,[1] which, by the connivance of the magistrates, are maintained for the recreation of those who might attempt the chastity of creditable women, if they were not provided with such conveniences. To one of these night-houses did our travellers repair, under the conduct of the English merchant, and were introduced into such another place as the ever-memorable coffee-house of Moll King;[2] with this difference, that the company here were not so riotous as the Bucks of Covent-Garden, but formed themselves into a circle, within which some of the number danced to the musick of a scurvy organ and a few other instruments, that uttered tunes very suitable to the disposition of the hearers, while the whole apartment was shrouded with clouds of smoke impervious to the view. When our gentlemen entered, the floor was occupied by two females and their gallants, who, in the performance of their exercise, lifted their legs like so many oxen at plough; and the pipe of one of these hoppers happening to be exhausted in the midst of his sarabrand, he very deliberately drew forth his tobacco-box, filling and lighting it again, without any interruption to the dance. Peregrine being unchecked by the presence of his governor, who was too tender of his own reputation to attend them in this expedition, made up to a sprightly French girl that sat in seeming expectation of a customer, and prevailing upon her to be his partner, led her into the circle, and, in his turn, took the opportunity of dancing a minuet, to the admiration of all present. He intended to have exhibited another specimen of his ability in this art, when a captain of a Dutch man of war chancing to come in, and see a stranger engaged with the lady whom, it seems, he had bespoke for his bedfellow, he advanced, without any ceremony, and seizing her by the arm, pull'd her to the other side of the room. Our adventurer, who was not a man to put up with such a brutal affront, followed the ravisher with indignation in his eyes; and pushing him on one side, retook the subject of their contest, and led her back to the place from whence she had been dragged. The Dutchman, enraged at the youth's presumption, obeyed the first dictates of his choler, and lent his rival an hearty box on the ear; which was immediately repaid with interest, before our hero could recollect himself sufficiently to lay his hand upon his sword, and beckon the aggressor to the door.

Notwithstanding the confusion and disorder which this affair produced in the room, and the endeavours of Pickle's company, who interposed, in order to prevent bloodshed, the antagonists gained the street; and Peregrine drawing, was surprised to see the captain advance against him with a long knife, which he preferred to the sword that hung by his side. The youth, confounded at this preposterous behaviour, desired him, in the French tongue, to lay aside that vulgar implement, and approach like a gentleman: but the Hollander, who neither understood the proposal, nor would have complied with his demand had he been made acquainted with his meaning, rushed forward like a desperado, before his adversary could put himself on his guard; and if the young gentleman had not been endued with surprising agility, his nose would have fallen a sacrifice to the fury of the assailant. Finding himself in such imminent jeopardy, he jumped to one side, and the Dutchman passing him, in the force of his career, he with one nimble kick made such application to his enemy's heels, that he flew like lightening into the canal, where he had almost perished, by pitching upon one of the posts with which it was faced.

Peregrine having performed this exploit, did not stay for the captain's coming on shore, but retreated with all dispatch, by the advice of his conductor; and next day embarked, with his companions, in the Skuyt, for Haarlem, where they dined, and in the evening arrived at the antient city of Leyden, where they met with some English students, who treated them with great hospitality. Not but that the harmony of the conversation was that same night interrupted by a dispute that arose between one of those young gentlemen and the physician, about the cold and hot methods of prescription in the gout and rheumatism; and proceeded to such a degree of mutual reviling, that Pickle ashamed and incensed at his fellow-traveller's want of urbanity, espoused the other's cause, and openly rebuked him for his unmannerly petulance, which (he said) rendered him unfit for the purposes, and unworthy of the benefit of, society. This unexpected declaration overwhelmed the doctor with amazement and confusion; he was instantaneously

351

deprived of his speech, and during the remaining part of the partie, sat in silent mortification. In all probability he deliberated with himself, whether or not he should expostulate with the young gentleman on the freedom he had taken with his character in a company of strangers; but as he knew that he had not a Pallet to deal with, he very prudently suppressed that suggestion, and in secret chewed the cud of resentment.

After they had visited the physic garden, the university, the anatomical hall, and every other thing that was recommended to their view, they returned to Rotterdam, and held a consultation upon the method of transporting themselves to England. The doctor, whose grudge against Peregrine was rather inflamed than allayed by our hero's indifference and neglect, had tampered with the simplicity of the painter, who was proud of his advances towards a perfect reconciliation; and now took the opportunity of parting with our adventurer, by declaring that he and his friend Mr. Pallet were resolved to take their passage in a trading sloop, after he had heard Peregrine object against that tedious, disagreeable, and uncertain method of conveyance. Pickle immediately saw his intention; and, without using the least argument to dissuade them from their design, or expressing the smallest degree of concern at their separation, very coolly wished them a prosperous voyage, and ordered his baggage to be sent to Helvoetsluys, where he himself, and his retinue, went on board of the pacquet next day, and, by the favour of a fair wind, in eighteen hours arrived at Harwich.

CHAPTER LXXI

Peregrine delivers his Letters of Recommendation
at London, and returns to the Garison,
to the unspeakable Joy of the Commodore and
his whole Family

Now that our hero found himself on English ground, his heart dilated with the proud recollection of his own improvement since he left his native soil; he began to recognize the interesting ideas of his tender years; he enjoyed, by anticipation, the pleasure of seeing his friends in the garison, after an absence of eighteen months; and

the image of his charming Emily, which other less worthy considerations had depressed, resumed the full possession of his breast.
He remembered, with shame, that he had neglected the correspondence with her brother, which he himself had sollicited, and
in consequence of which he had received a letter from that young
gentleman while he lived at Paris. In spite of these conscientious
reflections, he was too self-sufficient to think he should find any
difficulty in obtaining forgiveness for these sins of omission; and
began to imagine, that his passion would be prejudicial to the
dignity of his situation, if it could not be gratified upon terms which
formerly his imagination durst not conceive.

Sorry am I, that the task I have undertaken, lays me under the
necessity of divulging this degeneracy in the sentiments of our
imperious youth, who was now in the heyday of his blood, flushed
with the consciousness of his own qualifications, vain of his fortune,
and elated on the wings of imaginary expectation. Tho' he was
deeply enamoured of miss Gauntlet, he was far from proposing her
heart as the ultimate aim of his gallantry, which (he did not doubt)
would triumph o'er the most illustrious females of the land, and
at once regale his appetite and ambition.

Mean while, being willing to make his appearance at the garison
equally surprising and agreeable, he cautioned Mr. Jolter against
writing to the commodore, who had not heard of them since their
departure from Paris, and hired a post-chaise and horses for
London. The governor going out to give orders about the carriage,
inadvertently left a paper book open upon the table; and his pupil
casting his eyes upon the page, chanced to read these words:
'Sept. 15. Arrived in safety, by the blessing of God, in this unhappy
kingdom of England. And thus concludes the journal of my last
peregrination.' Peregrine's curiosity being inflamed by this extraordinary conclusion, he turned to the beginning, and perused
several sheets of a diary, such as is commonly kept by that class of
people known by the denomination of travelling governors, for the
satisfaction of themselves and the parents or guardians of their
pupils, and for the edification and entertainment of their friends.

That the reader may have a clear idea of Mr. Jolter's performance,
we shall transcribe the transactions of one day, as he had recorded
them; and that abstract will be a sufficient specimen of the whole
plan and execution of the work.

'May 3. At eight o'clock set out from Boulogne in a post-chaise:
the morning hazy and cold. Fortified my stomach with a cordial.
Recommended ditto to Mr. P. as an antidote against the fog. Mem.

He refused it. The hither horse greased in the off-pastern of the hind-leg. Arrive at Samers. Mem. This last was a post and a half; i.e. three leagues, or nine English miles. The day clears up. A fine champain country, well stored with corn. The postilion says his prayers in passing by a wooden crucifix upon the road. Mem. The horses staled in a small brook that runs in a bottom, betwixt two hills. Arrive at Cormont. A common post. A dispute with my pupil, who is obstinate, and swayed by an unlucky prejudice. Proceed to Montreuil, where we dine on choice pigeons. A very moderate charge. No chamberpot in the room; owing to the negligence of the maid. This an ordinary post. Set out again for Nampont. Troubled with flatulencies and indigestion. Mr. P. is sullen, and seems to mistake an eructation for the breaking of wind backwards. From Nampont depart for Bernay, at which place we arrive in the evening, and propose to stay all night. N.B. The two last are double posts, and our cattle very willing, tho' not strong. Sup on a delicate ragout and excellent partridges, in company with Mr. H. and his spouse. Mem. The said H. trod upon my corn by mistake. Discharge the bill, which is not very reasonable. Dispute with Mr. P. about giving money to the servant: he insists upon my giving a twenty-four sol piece; which is too much by two thirds, in all conscience. N.B. She was a pert baggage, and did not deserve a liard.'

Our hero was so much disobliged with certain circumstances of this amusing and instructing journal, that, by way of punishing the author, he interlined these words betwixt two paragraphs, in a manner that exactly resembled the tutor's hand-writing; 'Mem. Had the pleasure of drinking myself into a sweet intoxication, by toasting our lawful king, and his royal family, among some worthy English fathers of the society of Jesus.'

Having taken this revenge, he set out for London, where he waited upon those noblemen to whom he had letters of recommendation from Paris; and was not only graciously received, but even loaded with caresses and proffers of service, because they understood he was a young gentleman of fortune, who, far from standing in need of their countenance or assistance, would make an useful and creditable addition to the number of their adherents. He had the honour of dining at their tables, in consequence of pressing invitations, and of spending several evenings with the ladies, to whom he was particularly agreeable, on account of his person, address, and bleeding freely at play.

Being thus initiated in the beau monde, he thought it was high time to pay his respects to his generous benefactor the commodore; and accordingly departed one morning, with his train, for the garison, at which he arrived in safety the same night. When he entered the gate, which was opened by a new servant that did not know him, he found his old friend Hatchway stalking in the yard, with a night-cap on his head, and a pipe in his mouth; and advancing to him, took him by the hand, before he had any intimation of his approach. The lieutenant, thus saluted by a stranger, stared at him in silent astonishment, till he recollected his features, which were no sooner known, than dashing the pipe upon the pavement, he exclaimed, 'Smite my cross-trees! th'art welcome to port;' and hugg'd him in his arms with great affection. He then, by a cordial squeeze, expressed his satisfaction at seeing his old ship-mate Tom, who applying his whistle to his mouth, the whole castle ecchoed with his performance.

The servants hearing the well-known sound, poured out in a tumult of joy; and understanding that their young master was returned, raised such a peal of acclamation, as astonished the commodore and his lady, and inspired Julia with such an interesting presage, that her heart began to throb with violence; and running out in the hurry and perturbation of her hope, she was so much overwhelmed at sight of her brother, that she actually fainted in his arms. But from this trance she soon awaked; and Peregrine having testified his pleasure and affection, went up stairs, and presented himself before his godfather and aunt. Mrs. Trunnion rose, and received him with a gracious embrace, blessing God for his happy return from a land of impiety and vice, in which she hoped his morals had not been corrupted, nor his principles of religion altered or impaired. The old gentleman being confined to his chair, was struck dumb with pleasure at his appearance; and having made divers ineffectual efforts to get up, at length discharged a volley of curses against his own limbs, and held out his hand to his godson, who kiss'd it with great respect.

After he had finished his apostrophe to the gout, which was the daily and hourly subject of his execrations, 'Well, my lad, (said he) I care not how soon I go to bottom, now I behold thee safe in harbour again: and yet, I tell a damn'd lie: I would I could keep afloat, until I should see a lusty boy of thy begetting. Odds my timbers! I love thee so well, that I believe thou art the spawn of my own body; though I can give no account of thy being put upon the stocks.' Then turning his eye upon Pipes, who by this time had penetrated into his apartment, and addressed him with the usual salutation of 'What cheer?' 'Ahey! (cried he) are you there, you herring-fac'd son of a sea-calf? What a slippery trick you played your old commander! But, come, you dog, there's my fist; I forgive you, for the love you bear to my godson. Go man your tackle, and hoist a cask of strong beer into the yard, knock out the bung, and put a pump in it, for the use of all my servants and neighbours: and d'ye hear, let the patereroes be fired, and the garison illuminated, as rejoicings for the safe arrival of your master. By the Lord! if I had the use of these damn'd shambling shanks, I would dance an hornpipe with the best of you.'

The next object of his attention was Mr. Jolter, who was honoured with particular marks of distinction, and the repeated promise of enjoying the living in his gift, as an acknowledgment of the care and discretion with which he had superintended the education and morals of our hero. The governor was so affected by the generosity of his patron, that the tears ran down his cheeks, while he expressed his gratitude, and the infinite satisfaction he felt, in contemplating the accomplishments of his pupil.

Mean while, Pipes did not neglect the orders he had received: the beer was produced, the gates were thrown open for the admission of all comers, the whole house was lighted up, and the patereroes discharged in repeated vollies. Such phænomena could not fail to attract the notice of the neighbourhood. The club at Tunley's were astonished at the report of the guns, which produced various conjectures among the members of that sagacious society. The landlord observed, that in all likelihood the commodore was visited by hobgoblins, and ordered the guns to be fired in token of distress, as he had acted twenty years before, when he was annoyed by the same grievance. The exciseman, with a waggish sneer, expressed his apprehension of Trunnion's death, in consequence of which, the patereroes might be discharged with an equivocal intent, either as signals of his lady's sorrow or rejoicing. The attorney signified a suspicion of Hatchway's being married to Miss Pickle, and that the firing and illumination were in honour of the nuptials: upon which Gamaliel discovered some faint signs of emotion, and taking the pipe from his mouth, gave it as his opinion, that his sister was brought to bed.

While they were thus bewildered in the maze of their own imaginations, a company of countrymen, who sat drinking in the kitchen, and whose legs were more ready than their invention, sallied out to know the meaning of these exhibitions; and understanding that there was a butt of strong beer abroach in the yard, to which they were invited by the servants, saved themselves the trouble and expence of returning to spend the evening at the public house, and listed themselves under the banner of Tom Pipes, who presided as director of this festival.

The news of Peregrine's return being communicated to the parish, the parson and three or four neighbouring gentlemen, who were well-wishers to our hero, immediately repaired to the garison, in order to pay their compliments on this happy event; and being detained to supper, an elegant entertainment was prepared by the direction of Miss July, who was an excellent housewife; and the commodore was so invigorated with joy, that he seemed to have renewed his age.

Among those who honoured the occasion with his presence was Mr. Clover, the young gentleman that made his addresses to Peregrine's sister; and his heart was so big with his passion, that while the rest of the company were ingrossed by their cups, he seized an opportunity of our hero's being detached from the conversation, and in the impatience of his love, conjured him to consent to his happiness; protesting, that he would comply with any terms of settlement that a man of his fortune could embrace, in favour of a young lady who was absolute mistress of his affection.

Our youth thanked him very politely for his favourable sentiments and honourable intention towards his sister, and told him, that at present he saw no reason to obstruct his desire; that he would consult Julia's own inclinations, and confer with him about the means of gratifying his wish: but, in the mean time, begg'd to be excused from discussing any point of such importance to them both, and reminding him of the jovial purpose on which they were happily met, promoted such a quick circulation of the bottle, that their mirth grew noisy and obstreperous: they broke forth into repeated peals of laughter, without any previous incitement, except that of claret. These explosions were succeeded by Bacchanalian songs, in which the old gentleman himself attempted to bear a share; the sedate governor snapped time with his fingers, and the parish-priest assisted in the chorus with a most expressive nakedness of countenance. Before midnight, they were almost all pinned to their chairs, as if they had been fixed by the power of inchantment; and what rendered the confinement still more unfortunate, every servant in the house was in the same situation; so that they were fain to take their repose as they sat, and nodded to each other like a congregation of anabaptists.

Next day, Peregrine communed with his sister on the subject of

357

her match with Mr. Clover, who (she told him) had offered to settle a jointure of four hundred pounds, and take her to wife, without any expectation of a dowry. She, moreover, gave him to understand, that in his absence she had received several messages from her mother, commanding her to return to her father's house; but that she had refused to obey these orders, by the advice and injunction of her aunt and the commodore, which were indeed seconded by her own inclination; because she had all the reason in the world to believe, that her mother only wanted an opportunity of treating her with severity and rancour: for the resentment of that lady had been carried to such indecent lengths, that seeing her daughter at church one day, she rose up before the parson entered, and reviled her with great bitterness, in the face of the whole congregation.

CHAPTER LXXII

Sees his Sister happily married. Visits Emilia,
who receives him according to his Deserts

HER brother being of opinion, that Mr. Clover's proposal was not to be neglected, especially as Julia's heart was engaged in his favour, communicated the affair to his uncle, who, with the approbation of Mrs. Trunnion, declared himself well satisfied with the young man's addresses, and desired that they might be buckled with all expedition, without the knowledge or concurrence of her parents, to whom (on account of their unnatural barbarity) she was not bound to pay the least regard. Though our adventurer entertained the same sentiments of the matter, and the lover dreading some obstruction, earnestly begg'd the immediate condescension of his mistress, she could not be prevailed upon to take such a material step, without having first solicited the permission of her father, resolved, nevertheless, to comply with the dictates of her own heart, should his objections be frivolous or unjust.

Urged by this determination, her admirer waited upon Mr. Gamaliel at the public house, and with the appearance of great deference and respect, made him acquainted with his affection for his daughter, communicated the particulars of his fortune, with the terms of settlement he was ready to make; and in conclusion told him, that he would marry her without a portion. This last offer seemed to have some weight with the father, who received it with civility, and promised, in a day or two, to favour him with a final answer to his demand. He, accordingly, that same evening consulted his wife, who being exasperated at the prospect of her daughter's independency, argued with the most virulent expostulation against the match, as an impudent scheme of her own planning, with a view of insulting her parents, towards whom she had already been guilty of the most vicious disobedience. In short, she used such remonstrances, as not only averted this weak husband's inclination from the proposal which he had relished before, but even instigated him to apply for a warrant to apprehend his daughter, on the supposition that she was about to bestow herself in marriage, without his privity or consent.

The justice of peace to whom this application was made, though he could not refuse the order, yet, being no stranger to the malevolence of the mother, which, together with Gamaliel's simplicity, was notorious in the county, he sent an intimation of what had happened to the garison; upon which, a couple of centinels were placed on the gate, and at the pressing solicitation of the lover, as well as the desire of the commodore, her brother and aunt, Julia was wedded without further delay; the ceremony being performed by Mr. Jolter, because the parish-priest prudently declined any occasion of giving offence, and the curate was too much in the interest of their enemies, to be employed in that office.

This domestic concern being settled to the satisfaction of our hero, he escorted her next day to the house of her husband, who immediately wrote a letter to her father, declaring his reasons for having thus superseded his authority; and Mrs. Pickle's mortification was unspeakable.

That the new-married couple might be guarded against all insult, our young gentleman and his friend Hatchway, with their adherents, lodged in Mr. Clover's house for some weeks; during which, they visited their acquaintance in the neighbourhood, according to custom; and when the tranquillity of their family was perfectly established, and the contract of marriage executed in the presence of the old commodore and his lady, who gave her niece five hundred pounds to purchase jewels and cloaths, Mr. Peregrine could no longer restrain his impatience to see his dear Emily; and told his uncle, that next day he proposed to ride across the country, in order to visit his friend Gauntlet, from whom he had not heard for a long time.

The old gentleman, looking stedfastly in his face, 'Ah! damn your cunning! (said he) I find the anchor holds fast: I did suppose

o 359

as how you would have slipt your cable, and changed your birth; but, I see, when a young fellow is once brought up by a pretty wench, he may man his capstans and viol-block,[1] if he wool; but he'll as soon heave up the Pike of Teneriff, as bring his anchor aweigh! Odds heartlikins! had I known the young woman was Ned Gauntlet's daughter, I shou'dn't have thrown out signal for leaving off chace.'

Our adventurer was not a little surprized to hear the commodore talk in this stile; and immediately conjectured, that his friend Godfrey had informed him of the whole affair. Instead of listening to this approbation of his flame, with those transports of joy which he would have felt, had he retained his former sentiments, he was chagrined at Trunnion's declaration, and offended at the presumption of the young soldier, in pretending to disclose the secret with which he had intrusted him. Reddening with these reflections, he assured the commodore, that he never had serious thoughts of matrimony: so that, if any person had told him he was under any engagement of that kind, he had abused his ear; for, he protested, that he would never contract such attachments, without his knowledge and express permission.

Trunnion commended him for his prudent resolution, and observed, that though no person mentioned to him what promises had passed betwixt him and his sweetheart, it was very plain that he had made love to her; and therefore, it was to be supposed, that his intentions were honourable: for, he could not believe he was such a rogue in his heart, as to endeavour to debauch the daughter of a brave officer, who had served his country with credit and reputation. Notwithstanding this remonstrance, which Pickle imputed to the commodore's ignorance of the world, he set out for the habitation of Mrs. Gauntlet, with the unjustifiable sentiments of a man of pleasure, who sacrifices every consideration to the desire of his ruling appetite; and as Winchester lay in his way, resolved to visit some of his friends who lived in that place. It was in the house of one of these, that he was informed of Emilia's being then in town with her mother; upon which, he excused himself from staying to drink tea, and immediately repaired to their lodgings, according to the direction he had received.

When he arrived at the door, instead of undergoing that perturbation of spirits, which a lover, in his interesting situation, might be supposed to feel, he suffered no emotion but that of vanity and pride, favoured with an opportunity of self-gratification, and entered his Emilia's apartment with the air of a conceited petit maitre, rather than that of the respectful admirer, when he visits the object of his passion, after an absence of seventeen months.

The young lady having been very much disobliged at his mortifying neglect of her brother's letter, had summoned all her own pride and resolution to her aid; and by means of a happy disposition, so far overcame her chagrin at his indifference, that she was able to behave in his presence with apparent tranquillity and ease. She was even pleased to find, he had by accident chosen a time for his visit, when she was surrounded by two or three young gentlemen, who professed themselves her admirers. Our gallant was no sooner anounced, than she collected all her coquettry, put on the gayest air she could assume, and contrived to giggle just as he appeared at the room-door. The compliments of salutation being performed, she welcomed him to England in a careless manner, asked the news of Paris, and, before he could make any reply, desired one of the other gentlemen to proceed with the sequel of that comical adventure, in the relation of which he had been interrupted.

Peregrine smiled within himself at this behaviour, which (without all doubt he believed) she had affected to punish him for his unkind silence, while he was abroad; being fully persuaded, that her heart was absolutely at his devotion. On this supposition, he practised his Parisian improvements on the art of conversation, and uttered a thousand prettinesses in the way of compliment, with such incredible rotation of tongue, that his rivals were struck dumb with astonishment; and Emilia fretted out of all temper, at seeing herself deprived of the prerogative of the sex. He persisted, however, in this surprising loquacity, until the rest of the company thought proper to withdraw, and then contracted his discourse into the focus of love, which now put on a very different appearance from that which it had formerly worn. Instead of that awful veneration which her presence used to inspire, that chastity of sentiment and delicacy of expression, he now gazed upon her with the eyes of a libertine, he glowed with the impatience of desire, talked in a strain that barely kept within the bounds of decency, and attempted to snatch such favours as she, in the tenderness of mutual acknowledgement, had once vouchsafed to bestow.

Grieved and offended as she was, at this palpable alteration in his carriage, she disdained to remind him of his former deportment, and with dissembled good humour, rallied him on the progress he had made in gallantry and address: but, far from submitting to the liberties he would have taken, she kept her person sacred from his touch, and would not even suffer him to ravish a kiss of her fair hand: so that he reaped no other advantage from the exercise of his talents, during this interview, which lasted a whole hour, than that of knowing he had over-rated his own importance; and that Emily's heart was not a garison likely to surrender at discretion.

At length, his addresses were interrupted by the arrival of the mother, who had gone abroad to visit by herself; and the conversation becoming more general, he understood, that Godfrey was at London, soliciting for a lieutenancy that had fallen vacant in the regiment to which he belonged; and that Miss Sophy was at home with her father.

Though our adventurer had not met with all the success he expected in his first visit, he did not despair of reducing the fortress, believing that in time there would be a mutiny in his favour; and accordingly, carried on the siege for several days, without profiting by his perseverance; till at length, having attended the ladies to their own house in the country, he began to look upon this adventure as time mispent, and resolved to discontinue his attack, in hopes of meeting with a more favourable occasion; being, in the mean time, ambitious of displaying, in an higher sphere, those qualifications which his vanity told him, were at present misapplied.

CHAPTER LXXIII

*He attends his Uncle with great Affection, during a
Fit of Illness. Sets out again for London ; meets with his
Friend Godfrey, who is prevailed upon to accompany him
to Bath ; on the Road to which Place, they chance to dine
with a Person, who entertains them with a curious
Account of a certain Company of Adventurers*

THUS determined, he took leave of Emilia and her mother, on pretence of going to London upon some urgent business, and returned to the garison, leaving the good old lady very much concerned, and the daughter incensed at his behaviour, which was the more unexpected, because Godfrey had told them, that the commodore approved of his nephew's passion.

Our adventurer found his uncle so ill of the gout, which, for the first time, had taken possession of his stomach, that his life was in

imminent danger, and the whole family in disorder: he therefore
took the reins of government in his own hands, sent for all the
physicians in the neighbourhood, and attended him in person with
the most affectionate care, during the whole fit, which lasted a fortnight, and then retired before the strength of his constitution.

When the old gentleman recovered his health, he was so penetrated with Peregrine's behaviour, that he actually would have
made over to him his whole fortune, and depended upon him for
his own subsistence, had not our youth opposed the execution of the
deed with all his influence and might, and even persuaded him to
make a will, in which his friend Hatchway, and all his other
adherents, were liberally remembered, and his aunt provided for,
on her own terms. This material point being settled, he, with his
uncle's permission, departed for London, after having seen the
family-affairs established under the direction and administration
of Mr. Jolter and the lieutenant: for, by this time, Mrs. Trunnion
was wholly occupied with her spiritual concerns.

On his first arrival at London, he sent a card to the lodgings of
Gauntlet, in consequence of a direction from his mother; and that
young gentleman waited on him next morning, though not with
that alacrity of countenance and warmth of friendship, which
might have been expected from the intimacy of their former connexion. Nor was Peregrine himself actuated by the same unreserved
affection for the soldier, which he had formerly entertained. Godfrey, over and above the offence he had taken at Pickle's omission,
in point of corresponding with him, had been informed, by a letter
from his mother, of the youth's cavalier behaviour to Emilia,
during his last residence at Winchester; and our young gentleman
(as we have already observed) was disgusted at the supposed discovery which the soldier had made, in his absence, to the commodore. They perceived their mutual umbrage at meeting, and
received each other with that civility of reserve, which commonly
happens between two persons, when their friendship is in the wane.

Gauntlet at once divined the cause of the other's displeasure;
and, in order to vindicate his own character, after the first compliments were passed, took the opportunity of inquiring after the
health of the commodore, to tell Peregrine, that while he tarried
at the garison, in his return from Dover, the subject of the conversation, one night, happening to turn on our hero's passion, the old
gentleman had expressed his concern about that affair; and, among
other observations, said, he supposed the object of his love was
some paultry hussy, whom he had picked up when he was a boy at

school. Upon which, Mr. Hatchway assured him, that she was a young woman of as good a family as any in the county; and after having prepossessed him in her favour, ventured (out of the zeal of his friendship) to tell who she was: wherefore, the discovery was not to be imputed to any other cause: and he hoped Mr. Pickle would acquit him of all share in the transaction.

Peregrine was very well pleased to be thus undeceived; his countenance immediately cleared up, the formality of his behaviour relaxed into his usual familiarity; he asked pardon for his unmannerly neglect of Godfrey's letter, which, he protested, was not owing to any disregard, or abatement of friendship, but to a hurry of youthful engagements, in consequence of which, he had procrastinated his answer from time to time, until he was ready to return in person.

The young soldier was contented with this apology; and as Pickle's intention, with respect to his sister, was still dubious and undeclared, he did not think it was incumbent upon him, as yet, to express any resentment on that score; but was wise enough to foresee, that the renewal of his intimacy with our young gentleman, might be the means of reviving that flame which had been dissipated by a variety of new ideas. With those sentiments he laid aside all reserve, and their communication immediately resumed its former channel. Peregrine made him acquainted with all the adventures in which he had been engaged since their parting; and he, with the same confidence, related the remarkable incidents of his own fate; among other things, giving him to understand, that upon obtaining a commission in the army, the father of his dear Sophy, without once inquiring about the occasion of his promotion, had not only favoured him with his countenance in a much greater degree than heretofore, but also contributed his interest, and even promised the assistance of his purse, in procuring for him a lieutenancy, which he was then soliciting with all his power; whereas, if he had not been enabled, by a most accidental piece of good fortune, to lift himself into the sphere of an officer, he had all the reason in the world to believe, that this gentleman, and all the rest of his wealthy relations, would have suffered him to languish in obscurity and distress; and, by turning his misfortune into reproach, made it a plea for their own want of generosity and friendship.

Peregrine, understanding this situation of his friend's affairs, would have accommodated him, upon the instant, with a sum to accelerate the passage of his commission through the offices; but,

being too well acquainted with his scrupulous disposition, to manifest his benevolence in that manner, he found means to introduce
himself to one of the gentlemen of the war-office, who was so well
satisfied with the arguments he used in behalf of his friend, that
Godfrey's business was transacted in a very few days, though he
himself knew nothing of his interest's being thus reinforced.

By this time, the season at Bath was begun; and our hero, panting
with the desire of distinguishing himself at that resort of the
fashionable world, communicated his design of going thither to his
friend Godfrey, whom he importuned to accompany him in the
excursion: and leave of absence from his regiment being obtained,
by the influence of Peregrine's new quality-friends, the two companions departed from London in a post-chaise, attended, as usual,
by the valet de chambre and Pipes, who were become almost as
necessary to our adventurer as any two of his own organs.

At the inn, when they alighted for dinner, Godfrey perceived a
person walking by himself in the yard, with a very pensive air, and
upon observing him more narrowly, recognized him to be a professed gamester, whom he had formerly known at Tunbridge. On
the strength of this acquaintance, he accosted the peripatetic, who
knew him immediately; and, in the fulness of his grief and vexation, told him, that he was now on his return from Bath, where he
had been stripp'd by a company of sharpers, who resented that he
should presume to trade upon his own bottom.

Peregrine, who was extremely curious in his inquiries, imagining
that he might learn some entertaining and useful anecdotes from
this artist, invited him to dinner, and was accordingly fully informed of all the political systems at the Bath. He understood,
that there was at London one great company of adventurers, who
employed agents, in all the different branches of imposition,
throughout the whole kingdom of England, allowing these
ministers a certain proportion of the profits accruing from their
industry and skill, and reserving the greatest share for the benefit
of the common stock, which was chargeable with the expence of
fitting out individuals in their various pursuits, as well as with the
loss sustained in the course of their adventures. Some, whose
persons and qualifications are by the company judged adequate to
the task, exert their talents in making love to ladies of fortune,
being accommodated with money and accoutrements for that
purpose, after having given their bonds payable to one or other of
the directors, on the day of marriage, for certain sums, proportioned
to the dowries they are to receive. Others, versed in the doctrine of

chances, and certain secret expedients, frequent all those places where games of hazard are allowed; and such as are masters in the arts of billiards, tennis and bowls, are continually lying in wait, in all the scenes of these diversions, for the ignorant and unwary. A fourth class attend horse-races, being skilled in those mysterious practices, by which the knowing-ones are taken in. Nor is this community unfurnished with those who lay wanton wives and old rich widows under contribution, and extort money, by prostituting themselves to the embraces of their own sex, and then threatening their admirers with prosecution. But their most important returns are made by that body of their undertakers who exercise their understandings in the innumerable stratagems of the card table, at which no sharper can be too infamous to be received, and even caressed by persons of the highest rank and distinction. Among other articles of intelligence, our young gentleman learn'd, that those agents, by whom their guest was broke, and expelled from Bath, had constituted a bank against all sporters, and monopolized the advantage in all sorts of play. He then told Gauntlet, that if he would put himself under his direction, he would return with them, and lay such a scheme, as would infallibly ruin the whole society at billiards, as he knew that Godfrey excelled them all in his knowledge of that game.

The soldier excused himself from engaging in any party of that kind; and after dinner the travellers parted; but, as the conversation between the two friends turned upon the information they had received, Peregrine projected a plan for punishing those villanous pests of society, who prey upon their fellow creatures; and it was put in execution by Gauntlet, in this manner.

CHAPTER LXXIV

Godfrey executes a Scheme at Bath, by which a whole Company of Sharpers is ruined

ON the evening after their arrival at Bath, Godfrey, who had kept himself up all day for that purpose, went in boots to the billiard table; and two gentlemen being at play, began to bet with so little appearance of judgment, that one of the adventurers then present was inflamed with the desire of profiting by his inexperience; and when the table was vacant, invited him to take a game for amusement.

The soldier, assuming the air of a self-conceited dupe, answered, that he did not choose to throw away his time for nothing, but, if he pleased, would piddle for a crown a game. This declaration was very agreeable to the other, who wanted to be further confirmed in the opinion he had conceived of the stranger, before he would play for any thing of consequence. The partie being accepted, Gauntlet put off his coat, and beginning with seeming eagerness, won the first game, because his antagonist kept up his play, with a view of encouraging him to wager a greater sum. The soldier purposely bit at the hook, the stakes were doubled, and he was again victorious, by the permission of his competitor. He now began to yawn; and observing, that it was not worth his while to proceed in such a childish manner, the other swore, in an affected passion, that he would play with him for twenty guineas. The proposal being embraced (thro' the connivance of Godfrey) the money was won by the sharper, who exerted his dexterity to the uttermost, fearing that otherwise his adversary would decline continuing the game.

Godfrey thus conquered, pretended to lose his temper, curs'd his own ill luck, swore that the table had a cast, and that the balls did not run true, changed his mast, and with great warmth challenged his enemy to double the sum. The gamester, with feigned reluctance, complied with his desire, and having got the first two hazards, offered to lay one hundred guineas to fifty on the game. The odds were taken; and Godfrey having allowed himself to be overcome, began to rage with great violence, broke the mast to pieces, threw the balls out at the window, and, in the fury of his indignation, defied his antagonist to meet him to-morrow, when he should be refreshed from the fatigue of travelling. This was a very welcome invitation to the gamester, who imagining that the soldier would turn out a most beneficial prize, assured him, that he would not fail to be there next forenoon, in order to give him his revenge.

Gauntlet went home to his lodgings, fully certified of his own superiority; and took his measures with Peregrine, touching the prosecution of their scheme; while his opponent made a report of his success to the brethren of the gang, who resolved to be present at the decision of the match, with the view of taking advantage of the stranger's passionate disposition.

Affairs being thus concerted on both sides, the players met, according to appointment, and the room was immediately filled with spectators, who either came thither by accident, curiosity, or design. The match was fixed for one hundred pounds a game, the principals chose their instruments, and laid aside their coats, and one of the knights of the order proffered to lay another hundred on the head of his associate. Godfrey took him up on the instant. A second worthy of the same class seeing him so eager, challenged him to treble the sum; and his proposal met with the same reception, to the astonishment of the company, whose expectation was raised to a very interesting pitch. The game was begun, and the soldier having lost the first hazard, the odds were offered by the confederacy, with great vociferation; but no body would run such a risk, in favour of a person who was utterly unknown. The sharper having gained the second also, the noise increased to a surprising clamour, not only of the gang, but likewise of almost all the spectators, who desired to lay two to one against the brother of Emilia.

Peregrine, who was present, perceiving the cupidity of the association sufficiently inflamed, all of a sudden opened his mouth, and answered their betts, to the amount of twelve hundred pounds; which were immediately deposited, on both sides, in money and notes: so that this was (perhaps) the most important game that ever was plaid at billiards. Gauntlet seeing the agreement settled, struck his antagonist's ball into the pocket, in a twinkling, tho' it was in one of those situations which are supposed to be against the striker. The betters were a little discomposed at this event, for which, however, they consoled themselves, by imputing the success to accident; but when, at the very next stroke, he sprung it over the table, their countenances underwent an instantaneous distraction of feature, and they waited, in the most dreadful suspense, for the next hazard, which being likewise taken, with infinite ease, by the soldier, the blood forsook their cheeks, and the interjection *Zounds!* pronounced with a look of consternation, and in a tone of despair, proceeded from every mouth, at the same instant of time. They were overwhelmed with horror and astonishment at seeing three hazards taken in as many strokes, from a person of their friend's dexterity; and shrewdly suspected, that the whole was a scheme preconcerted for their destruction: on this supposition they changed the note, and attempted to effect their own indemnification, by proposing to lay the odds in favour of Gauntlet; but so much was the opinion of the company altered by that young gentleman's success, that no body would venture to espouse the cause of his competitor, who chancing to improve his game by the addition of another lucky hit, diminished the concern, and revived the hopes of his adherents. But, this gleam of fortune, did not long continue:

Godfrey collected his whole art and capacity, and augmenting his score to number ten, indulged himself with a view of the whole fraternity. The visages of these professors had adopted different shades of complexion, at every hazard he had taken; from their natural colour they had shifted into a sallow hue; from thence into pale; from pale into yellow, which degenerated into a mahogony tint; and now they saw seventeen hundred pounds of their stock depending upon a single stroke, they stood like so many swarthy Moors, jaundiced with terror and vexation. The fire which naturally glowed in the cheeks and nose of the player, seemed utterly extinct, and his carbuncles exhibited a livid appearance, as if a gangrene had already made some progress in his face; his hand began to shake, and his whole frame was seized with such trepidation, that he was fain to swallow a bumper of brandy, in order to re-establish the tranquillity of his nerves. This expedient, however, did not produce the desired effect; for he aimed the ball at the lead with such discomposure, that it struck on the wrong side, and came off at an angle which directed it full in the middle hole. This fatal accident was attended with an universal groan, as if the whole universe had gone to wreck: and notwithstanding that tranquillity for which adventurers are so remarkable, this loss made such an impression upon them all, that each, in particular, manifested his chagrin, by the most violent emotions. One turned up his eyes to heaven, and bit his nether lip; another gnawed his fingers, while he stalked across the room; a third blasphemed with horrible imprecations; and he who played the partie, sneaked off, grinding his teeth together, with a look that baffles all description, and as he crossed the threshold, exclaiming, 'A damn'd bite, by G—d!'

The victors, after having insulted them, by asking if they were disposed for another chance, carried off their winning, with the appearance of great composure, though in their hearts they were transported with unspeakable joy; not so much on account of the booty they had gained, as in consideration of having so effectually destroyed such a nest of pernicious miscreants.

Peregrine believing, that now he had found an opportunity of serving his friend, without giving offence to the delicacy of his honour, told him, upon their arrival at their lodgings, that fortune had at length enabled him to become in a manner independent, or at least to make himself easy in his circumstances, by purchasing a company with the money he had won. So saying, he put his share of the success in Gauntlet's hand, as a sum that of right belonged to him, and promised to write in his behalf to a nobleman, who had interest enough to promote such a quick rise in the service.

Godfrey thanked him for his obliging intention, but absolutely refused, with great loftiness of demeanour, to appropriate to his own use any part of the money which Pickle had gained, and seemed affronted at the other's entertaining a sentiment so unworthy of his character. He would not even accept, in the way of loan, such an addition to his own stock, as would amount to the price of a company of foot; but expressed great confidence in the future exertion of that talent which had been blessed with such a prosperous beginning. Our hero finding him thus obstinately deaf to the voice of his own interest, resolved to govern himself in his next endeavours of friendship, by his experience of this ticklish punctilio; and in the mean time, gave a handsome benefaction to the hospital, out of these first fruits of his success in play, and reserved two hundred pounds for a set of diamond ear-rings and solitaire, which he intended for a present to Miss Emily.

CHAPTER LXXV

The two Friends eclipse all their Competitors in
Gallantry, and practise a pleasant Project of Revenge upon
the Physicians of the Place

THE fame of their exploit against the sharpers, was immediately diffused through all companies at the Bath; so that when our adventurers appeared in public, they were pointed out by an hundred extended fingers, and considered as consummate artists in all the different species of finesse, which they would not fail to practise with the first opportunity. Nor was this opinion of their characters any obstacle to their reception into the fashionable parties in the place; but, on the contrary, such a recommendation, which (as I have already hinted) never fails to operate for the advantage of the possessor.

This first adventure, therefore, served them as an introduction to the company at Bath, who were not a little surprized to find their expectations baffled by the conduct of the two companions; because, far from engaging deeply at play, they rather shunned all occasions of gaming, and directed their attention to gallantry, in which our hero shone unrivalled. His external qualifications, exclusive of any other merit, were strong enough to captivate the common run of the female sex; and these, reinforced with a sprightliness of conversation, and a most insinuating address, became irresistible, even by those who were fortified with pride, caution or indifference. But, among all the nymphs of this gay place, he did not meet with one object that disputed the empire of his heart with Emilia; and therefore he divided his attachment according to the suggestions of vanity and whim; so that, before he had resided a fortnight at the Bath, he had set all the ladies by the ears, and furnished all the hundred tongues of scandal with full employment. The splendor of his appearance excited the inquiries of envy, which, instead of discovering any circumstance to his prejudice, was cursed with the information of his being a young gentleman of a good family, and heir to an immense fortune.

The countenance of some of his quality-friends, who arrived at Bath, confirmed this piece of intelligence: upon which, his acquaintance was courted and cultivated with great assiduity; and he met with such advances from some of the fair sex, as rendered him extremely fortunate in his amours. Nor was his friend Godfrey a stranger to favours of the same kind; his accomplishments were exactly calculated for the meridian of female taste; and with certain individuals of that sex, his muscular frame, and the robust connection of his limbs, were more attractive than the delicate proportions of his companion. He accordingly reigned paramount among those inamoratas who were turned of thirty, without being under the necessity of proceeding by tedious addresses; and was thought to have co-operated with the waters, in removing the sterility of certain ladies, who had long undergone the reproach and disgust of their husbands: while Peregrine set up his throne among those who laboured under the disease of celibacy, from the pert miss of fifteen, who, with a fluttering heart, tosses her head, bridles up, and giggles involuntarily at sight of an handsome young man, to the staid maiden of twenty-eight, who with a demure aspect moralizes on the vanity of beauty, the folly of youth and simplicity of woman, and expatiates on friendship, benevolence and good sense, in the stile of a platonic philosopher.

In such a diversity of dispositions, his conquests were attended with all the heart-burnings, animosities and turmoils of jealousy and spite. The younger class took all opportunities of mortifying their seniors in public, by treating them with that indignity which (contrary to the general privilege of age) is by the consent and connivance of mankind, levelled against those who have the misfortune to come under the denomination of old maids; and these last retorted their hostilities in the private machinations of slander, supported by experience and subtilty of invention. Not one day passed, in which some new story did not circulate, to the prejudice of one or other of those rivals.

If our hero, in the long-room, chanced to quit one of the moralists, with whom he had been engaged in conversation, he was immediately accosted by a number of the opposite faction, who, with ironical smiles, upbraided him with cruelty to the poor lady he had left, exhorted him to have compassion on her sufferings, and turning their eyes towards the object of their intercession, broke forth into an universal peal of laughter. On the other hand, when Peregrine, in consequence of having danced with one of the minors over-night, visited her in the morning, the Platonists immediately laid hold on the occasion, tasked their imaginations, associated ideas, and in sage insinuations retailed a thousand circumstances of the interview, which never had any foundation in truth. They observed, that if girls are determined to behave with such indiscretion, they must lay their accounts with incurring the censure of the world; that she in question, was old enough to act more circumspectly; and wondered that her mother would permit any young fellow to approach the chamber, while her daughter was naked in bed. As for the servant's peeping through the key-hole, to be sure it was an unlucky accident; but people ought to be upon their guard against such curiosity, and give their domestics no cause to employ their penetration. These, and other such reflections, were occasionally whispered as secrets among those who were known to be communicative; so that, in a few hours, it became the general topic of discourse; and as it had been divulged under injunctions of secrecy, it was almost impossible to trace the scandal to its origin; because every person concerned, must have promulgated her own breach of trust, in discovering her author of the report.

Peregrine, instead of allaying, rather exasperated this contention, by an artful distribution of his attention among the competitors; well knowing, that should his regard be converged into one point, he would soon forfeit the pleasure he enjoyed, in seeing them at variance; for both parties would join against the common enemy, and his favourite would be persecuted by the whole coalition. He perceived, that among the secret agents of scandal, none were so busy as the physicians, a class of animals who live in this place, like so many ravens hovering about a carcase, and even ply for employment, like scullers at Hungerford-stairs. The greatest part of them have correspondents in London, who make it their business to inquire into the history, character, and distemper of every one that repairs to Bath, for the benefit of the waters; and if they cannot procure interest to recommend their medical friends to these patients, before they set out, they at least furnish them with a previous account of what they could collect, that their correspondents may use this intelligence for their own advantage. By these means, and the assistance of flattery and assurance, they often insinuate themselves into the acquaintance of strangers, and by consulting their dispositions, become necessary and subservient to their prevailing passions. By their connexion with apothecaries and nurses, they are informed of all the private occurrences in each family; and therefore, enabled to gratify the rancour of malice, amuse the spleen of peevish indisposition, and entertain the eagerness of impertinent curiosity.

In the course of these occupations, which frequently affected the reputation of our two adventurers, this whole body fell under the displeasure of our hero, who, after divers consultations with his friend, concerted a stratagem, which was practised upon the faculty in this manner. Among those who frequented the pump-room, was an old officer, whose temper, naturally impatient, was, by repeated attacks of the gout, which had almost deprived him of the use of his limbs, sublimated into a remarkable degree of virulence and perverseness: he imputed the inveteracy of his distemper to the malpractice of a surgeon who had administered to him, while he laboured under the consequences of an unfortunate amour; and this supposition had inspired him with an insurmountable antipathy to all the professors of the medical art, which was more and more confirmed by the information of a friend at London, who had told him, that it was a common practice among the physicians at Bath, to dissuade their patients from drinking the water, that the cure, and of consequence their attendance, might be the longer protracted.

Thus prepossessed, he had come to Bath, and, conformable to a few general instructions he had received, used the waters without any farther direction, taking all occasions of manifesting his hatred and contempt of the sons of Æsculapius, both by speech and gesticulations, and even by pursuing a regimen quite contrary to that which he knew they prescribed to others, who seemed to be exactly in his condition. But he did not find his account in this method, how successful soever it may have been in other cases. His complaints, instead of vanishing, were every day more and more enraged; and at length he was confined to his bed, where he lay blaspheming from morn to night, and from night to morn, though still more determined than ever to adhere to his former maxims.

In the midst of his torture, which was become the common joke of the town, being circulated through the industry of the physicians, who triumphed in his disaster; Peregrine, by means of Mr. Pipes, employed a country-fellow, who had come to market, to run with great haste, early one morning, to the lodgings of all the doctors in town, and desire them to attend the colonel with all imaginable dispatch. In consequence of this summons, the whole faculty put themselves in motion; and three of the foremost arriving at the same instant of time, far from complimenting one another with the door, each separately essayed to enter, and the whole triumvirate stuck in the passage. While they remained thus wedged together, they descried two of their brethren posting towards the same goal, with all the speed that God had enabled them to exert; upon which they came to a parley, and agreed to stand by one another. This covenant being made, they disentangled themselves, and inquiring about the patient, were told by the servant, that he had just fallen asleep.

Having received this intelligence, they took possession of his anti-chamber, and shut the door, while the rest of the tribe posted themselves on the outside, as they arrived; so that the whole passage was filled, from the top of the stair-case to the street-door; and the people of the house, together with the colonel's servant, struck dumb with astonishment. The three leaders of this learned gang had no sooner made their lodgment good, than they began to consult about the patient's malady, which every one of them pretended to have considered with great care and assiduity. The first who gave his opinion, said, the distemper was an obstinate Arthritis; the second affirmed, that it was no other than a confirmed pox; and the third swore it was an inveterate scurvy. This diversity of opinions was supported by a variety of quotations from medical authors, ancient as well as modern: but these were not of sufficient authority, or at least not explicit enough to decide the dispute; for there are many schisms in medicine, as well as in religion, and each sect can quote the fathers, in support of the tenets they profess. In short, the contention rose to such a pitch of clamour, as not only alarmed their brethren on the stair, but also waked the patient from the first nap he had enjoyed in the space of ten whole days.

Had it been simply waking, he would have been obliged to them for the noise that disturbed him; for, in that case, he would have been relieved from the tortures of hell-fire, to which, in his dream, he fancied himself exposed: but this dreadful vision had been the result of that impression which was made upon his brain, by the intolerable anguish of his joints; so that, when he waked, the pain, instead of being allayed, was rather aggravated by a greater acuteness of sensation; and the confused vociferation in the next room, invading his ears at the same time, he began to think his dream was realized; and, in the pangs of despair, applied himself to a bell that stood by his bed-side, which he rung with great violence and perseverance.

This alarm put an immediate stop to the disputation of the three doctors, who, upon this notice of his being awake, rushed into his chamber without ceremony; and each seizing an arm, the third made the like application to one of his temples. Before the patient could recollect himself from the amazement which had laid hold on him, at this unexpected irruption, the room was filled by the rest of the faculty, who followed the servant that entered, in obedience to his master's call; and the bed was, in a moment, surrounded by these gaunt ministers of death. The colonel, seeing himself beset with such an assemblage of solemn visages and figures, which he had always considered with the utmost detestation and abhorrence, was incensed to a most inexpressible degree of indignation; and so inspirited by his rage, that though his tongue denied its office, his other limbs performed their function; he disengaged himself from the triumvirate, who had taken possession of his body, sprung out of bed with incredible agility, and seizing one of his crutches, applied it so effectually to one of the three, just as he stooped to examine the patient's water, that his tye-periwig dropped into the pot, while he himself fell motionless on the floor.

This significant explanation disconcerted the whole fraternity; every man turned his face, as if it were by instinct, towards the door; and the retreat of the community being obstructed by the efforts of individuals, confusion and tumultuous uproar ensued: for the colonel, far from limiting his prowess to the first exploit, handled his weapon with astonishing vigour and dexterity, without respect of persons; so that few or none of them had escaped without marks of his displeasure, when his spirits failed, and he sunk down again, quite exhausted, on his bed. Favoured by this respite, the discomfited faculty collected their hats and wigs, which had fallen off in the fray; and perceiving the assailant too much enfeebled to renew the attack, set up their throats together, and loudly threatened to prosecute him severely for such an outrageous assault.

By this time, the landlord had interposed; and inquiring into the cause of the disturbance, was informed of what had happened by the complainants, who, at the same time, giving him to understand, that they had been severally summoned to attend the colonel that morning, he assured them, that they had been imposed upon by some wag; for his lodger had never dream'd of consulting any one of their profession.

Thunderstruck at this declaration, the general clamour instantaneously ceased; and each, in particular, at once comprehending the nature of the joke, they sneaked silently off with the loss they had sustained, in unutterable shame and mortification; while Peregrine and his friend, who took care to be passing that way by accident, made a full stop at sight of such an extraordinary efflux, and enjoyed the countenance and condition of every one as he appeared: nay, even made up to some of those who seemed most affected with their situation, and mischievously tormented them with questions touching this unusual congregation; then, in consequence of the information they received from the landlord and the colonel's valet, subjected the sufferers to the ridicule of all the company in town. As it would have been impossible for the authors of this farce to keep themselves concealed from the indefatigable inquiries of the physicians, they made no secret of their having directed the whole; though they took care to own it in such an ambiguous manner, as afforded no handle of prosecution.

CHAPTER LXXVI

They distress the Housekeepers of Bath, by another mischievous Contrivance. Peregrine humbles a noted Hector, and meets with a strange Character at the House of a certain Lady

THIS adventure was attended with another small tour, that involved almost all the inhabitants of Bath in a very ludicrous scene of distress. Our hero, among his other remarks, had observed, that in this place there was no such utensil as a jack, and that all the spits were turned by dogs, which never failed to appear, at the hour of employment, with surprising exactness and regularity: so that every family depended with great confidence upon their known punctuality, without taking the trouble to secure them beforehand.

Our companions therefore, by means of their understrappers, who employed several chairmen for the purpose, apprehended all these useful animals, on Saturday at night, and confined them in an outhouse, with a view of perplexing the people with regard to their Sunday's dinner. Nor were they disappointed in their expectations; the surloins being spitted at the usual time, the cook-maid appeared at every door almost at the same instant; and after having earnestly cast their eyes around, they began to run about the street, and whistle with great vehemence, ejaculating curses between whiles against the innocent curs, that were disabled from obeying the dictates of their duty. Frivolous as this circumstance may seem to be, it was here considered as a family-concern of some consequence; for the maids having communicated the affair to their respective mistresses, every house in a twinkling sent forth its master in a night-cap, slippers, and morning-gown, in order to find some remedy for this dreadful calamity; and a second concert of whistling was performed in vain. They even assembled in committees in the street, to deliberate on this unheard-of defection of the dogs; and having cudgelled their brains to no purpose, returned to their several homes, in manifest terror of losing a favourite meal.

Over and above this their distraction, which our young gentlemen in person enjoyed, they afterwards understood, that the affliction in many houses was increased, by the miscarriage of the shifts to which they were reduced on this occasion. One master of a family, through the perverseness of his servants, was obliged to undertake the office of turnspit in *propria persona*, to the destruction of his appetite, and the danger of his health; another being driven to the necessity of cutting the roast into steaks, fell sick of mortification, and had well nigh lost his wits; and a third having contrived to suspend the surloin before the fire, in order to be twirled about by the hand of an attendant, the pack-thread gave way towards the end of the operation, and the meat falling down, discharged the contents of the dripping-pan upon his leg, which was scalded in a miserable manner: and what added to their vexation, about one o'clock, when the disappointment was most severely felt, and the misfortune irretrievable, Peregrine ordered the prisoners to be discharged, and every kitchen was visited by

377

one of these quadrupeds, as if they had come on purpose to insult the distress they had occasioned. These, and a variety of other stratagems, practised upon the objects of ridicule, hatred and contempt, confirmed and augmented the reputation of our adventurers, who had, by this time, rendered themselves terrible to all sorts of delinquents of both sexes, from the brazen-fronted gamester and female libertine, to the stale maiden that deals in scandal and strong waters, and the puny flutterer, who seems to have resigned all pretensions to manhood.[1] Among those who never failed to reside at Bath, during the season, was a certain person, who, from the most abject misery, had by his industry and art at play, amassed about fifteen thousand pounds; and though his character was notorious, insinuated himself so far into the favour of what is called the best company, that very few private parties of pleasure took place, in which he was not principally concerned. He was of a gigantic stature, a most intrepid countenance; and his disposition, naturally over-bearing, had in the course of his adventures and success, acquired a most intolerable degree of insolence and vanity. By the ferocity of his features, and audacity of his behaviour, he had obtained a reputation for the most undaunted courage, which had been confirmed by divers adventures, in which he had humbled the most assuming heroes of his own fraternity; so that he now reigned chief Hector of the place, with unquestioned authority.

With this son of fortune was Peregrine one evening engaged at play, and so successful, that he could not help informing his friend of his good luck. Godfrey hearing the description of the loser, immediately recognized the person, whom he had known at Tunbridge; and assuring Pickle, that he was a sharper of the first water, cautioned him against any future connexion with such a dangerous companion, who (he affirmed) had suffered him to win a small sum, that he might be encouraged to lose a much greater, upon some other occasion.

Our young gentleman treasured up this advice; and though he did not scruple to give the gamester an opportunity of retrieving his loss, when he next day demanded his revenge, he absolutely refused to proceed, after he had refunded his winning. The other, who considered him as a hot-headed unthinking youth, endeavoured to inflame his pride to a continuance of the game, by treating his skill with scorn and contempt; and, among other sarcastic expressions, advising him to go to school again, before he pretended to engage with masters of the art. Our hero, incensed at his arrogance, replied with great warmth, that he knew himself sufficiently qualified for playing with men of honour, who deal upon the square, and hoped he should always deem it infamous, either to learn or practise the tricks of a professed gamester. 'Blood and thunder! meaning me, Sir? (cried this artist, raising his voice, and curling his visage into a most intimidating frown.) Zounds! I'll cut the throat of any scoundrel who has the presumption to suppose, that I don't play as honourably as e'er a nobleman in the kingdom: and I insist upon an explanation from you, Sir; or, by hell and brimstone! I shall expect other sort of satisfaction.' Peregrine (whose blood by this time boiled within him) answered without hesitation; 'Far from thinking your demand unreasonable, I will immediately explain myself without reserve, and tell you, that, upon unquestionable authority, I believe you to be an impudent rascal and common cheat.'

The Hector was so amazed and confounded at the freedom of this declaration, which he thought no man on earth would venture to make in his presence, that for some minutes he could not recollect himself; but, at length, whispered a challenge in the ear of our hero, which was accordingly accepted. When they arrived next morning upon the field, the gamester, arming his countenance with all its terrors, advanced with a sword of a monstrous length, and putting himself in a posture, called aloud in a most terrific voice, 'Draw, damn ye, draw; I will this instant send you to your fathers.' The youth was not slow in complying with his desire; his weapon was unsheathed in a moment, and he began the attack with such unexpected spirit and address, that his adversary, having made shift with great difficulty to parry the first pass, retreated a few paces, and demanded a parley, in which he endeavoured to persuade the young man, that to lay a man of his character under the necessity of chastising his insolence, was the most rash and inconsiderate step that he could possibly have taken; but, that he had compassion upon his youth, and was willing to spare him, if he would surrender his sword, and promise to ask pardon in public for the offence he had given. Pickle was so much exasperated at this unparalleled effrontery, that, without deigning to make the least reply, he flung his own hat in the proposer's face, and renewed the charge with such undaunted agility, that the gamester, finding himself in manifest hazard of his life, betook himself to his heels, and fled homewards with incredible speed, being closely pursued by Peregrine, who having sheathed his sword, pelted him with stones as he ran, and compelled him to go, that

379

same day, into banishment from Bath, where he had domineered
so long.

By this atchievement, which was the subject of astonishment to
all the company, who had looked upon the fugitive as a person of
heroic courage, our adventurer's reputation was rendered formidable in all its circumstances; although he thereby disobliged
a good many people of fashion, who had contracted an intimacy
of friendship with the exile, and who resented his disgrace, as if it
had been the misfortune of a worthy man. These generous patrons,
however, bore a very small proportion to those who were pleased
with the event of the duel; because, in the course of their residence
at Bath, they had either been insulted or defrauded by the challenger. Nor was this instance of our hero's courage unacceptable
to the ladies, few of whom could now resist the united force of
such accomplishments. Indeed, neither he nor his friend Godfrey
would have found much difficulty in picking up an agreeable companion for life; but Gauntlet's heart was pre-engaged to Sophy;
and Pickle, exclusive of his attachment to Emily, which was
stronger than he himself imagined, possessed such a share of
ambition, as could not be satisfied with the conquest of any female
he beheld at Bath.

His visits were, therefore, promiscuous, without any other view
than that of amusement; and though his pride was flattered by the
advances of the fair whom he had captivated, he never harboured
one thought of proceeding beyond the limits of common gallantry,
and carefully avoided all particular explanations. But, what above all
other enjoyments yielded him the most agreeable entertainment, was
the secret history of characters, which he learn'd from a very extraordinary person, with whom he became acquainted in this manner.

Being at the house of a certain lady, on a visiting-day, he was
struck with the appearance of an old man, who no sooner entered
the room than the mistress of the house very kindly desired one
of the wits present to roast the old put. This petit maitre, proud
of the employment, went up to the senior, who had something
extremely peculiar and significant in his countenance, and saluting
him with divers fashionable congés, accosted him in these words:
'Your servant, you old rascal. I hope to have the honour of seeing
you hang'd. I vow to Gad! you look extremely shocking, with these
gummy eyes, lanthorn jaws, and toothless chaps. What! you squint
at the ladies, you old rotten medlar? Yes, yes, we understand your
ogling; but you must content yourself with a cook-maid, sink me!
I see you want to sit. These wither'd shanks of yours tremble under

their burthen: but you must have a little patience, old Hirco; indeed you must. I intend to mortify you a little longer, curse me!'

The company was so tickled with this address, which was delivered with much grimace and gesticulation, that they burst out into a loud fit of laughter, which they fathered upon a monkey that was chained in the room; and when the peal was over, the wit renewed his attack, in these words: 'I suppose you are fool enough to think this mirth was occasioned by Pug: ay, there he is; you had best survey him; he is of your own family, switch me: but the laugh was at your expence; and you ought to thank heaven for making you so ridiculous.' While he uttered these ingenious ejaculations, the old gentleman bowed alternately to him and the monkey, that seemed to grin and chatter in imitation of the beau, and with an arch solemnity of visage, pronounced, 'Gentlemen, as I have not the honour to understand your compliments, they will be much better bestowed on each other.' So saying, he seated himself, and had the satisfaction to see the laugh returned upon the aggressor, who remained confounded and abashed, and in a few minutes left the room, muttering, as he retired, 'the old fellow grows scurrilous, stap my breath.'

While Peregrine wondered in silence at this extraordinary scene, the lady of the house perceiving his surprize, gave him to understand, that the ancient visitant was utterly bereft of the sense of hearing; that his name was Cadwallader Crabtree; his disposition altogether misanthropical; and that he was admitted into company on account of the entertainment he afforded by his sarcastic observations, and the pleasant mistakes to which he was subject from his infirmity. Nor did our hero wait a long time for an illustration of this odd character. Every sentence he spoke was replete with gall; nor did his satire consist in general reflections, but in a series of remarks, which had been made through the medium of a most whimsical peculiarity of opinion.

Among those who were present at this assembly was a young officer, who having by dint of interest obtained a seat in the lower house, thought it incumbent upon him to talk of affairs of state; and accordingly regaled the company with an account of a secret expedition which the French were busied in preparing; assuring them, that he had it from the mouth of the minister, to whom it had been transmitted by one of his agents abroad. In descanting upon the particulars of the armament, he observed, that they had twenty ships of the line, ready manned and victualled at Brest, which were destined for Toulon, where they would be joined by as many more;

and from thence proceed to the execution of their scheme, which he imparted as a secret not fit to be divulged.

This piece of intelligence being communicated to all the company, except Mr. Crabtree, who suffered by his loss of hearing, that cynic was soon after accosted by a lady, who, by means of an artificial alphabet, formed by a certain conjunction and disposition of the fingers, asked if he had heard any extraordinary news of late? Cadwallader, with his usual complaisance, replied, that he supposed she took him for a courier or spy, by teizing him eternally with that question. He then expatiated upon the foolish curiosity of mankind, which, he said, must either proceed from idleness or want of ideas; and repeated almost verbatim the officer's information, as a vague ridiculous report, invented by some ignorant coxcomb, who wanted to give himself airs of importance, and believed only by those who were utterly unacquainted with the politics and strength of the French nation.

In confirmation of what he had advanced, he endeavoured to demonstrate how impossible it must be for that people to fit out even the third part of such a navy, so soon after the losses they had sustained during the war; and confirmed his proof by asserting, that, to his certain knowledge, the harbours of Brest and Toulon could not at that time produce a squadron of eight ships of the line.

The member, who was an utter stranger to this misanthrope, hearing his own asseverations treated with such contempt, glowed with confusion and resentment, and raising his voice, began to defend his own veracity with great eagerness and trepidation, mingling with his arguments many blustering invectives against the insolence and ill manners of his supposed contradictor, who sat with the most mortifying composure of countenance, till the officer's patience was quite exhausted; and then, to the manifest increase of his vexation, he was informed, that his antagonist was so deaf, that, in all probability, the last trumpet would make no impression upon him, without a previous renovation of his organs.

CHAPTER LXXVII

He cultivates an Acquaintance with the Misanthrope,
who favours him with a short Sketch of his own History

PEREGRINE was extremely well pleased at this occasional rebuke,
which occurred so seasonably, that he could scarce believe it
accidental. He looked upon Cadwallader as the greatest curiosity
he had ever known, and cultivated the old man's acquaintance with
such insinuating address, that in less than a fortnight he obtained
his confidence; and as they one day walked into the fields together,
the Manhater disclos'd himself, in these words: 'Tho' the term of
our communication has been but short, you must have perceived,
that I treat you with uncommon marks of regard; which, I assure
you, is not owing to your personal accomplishments, nor the pains
you take to oblige me; for the first I overlook, and the last I see
through: but there is something in your disposition which indi-
cates a rooted contempt for the world, and I understand you have
made some successful efforts, in exposing one part of it to the
ridicule of the other. It is upon this assurance, that I offer you my
advice and assistance, in prosecuting other schemes of the same
nature; and to convince you that such an alliance is not to be
rejected, I will now give you a short sketch of my history, which
will be published after my death, in forty-seven volumes of my own
compiling.

I was born about forty miles from this place, of parents who
having a very old family-name to support, bestowed their whole
fortune on my elder brother; so that I inherited of my father little
else than a large share of choler, to which I am indebted for a great
many adventures that did not always end to my satisfaction. At the
age of eighteen I was sent up to town, with a recommendation to a
certain peer, who found means to amuse me with the promise of
a commission, for seven whole years; and 'tis odds but I should
have made my fortune by my perseverance, had not I been arrested,
and thrown into the Marshalsea by my landlord, on whose credit
I had subsisted three years, after my father had renounced me as
an idle vagabond. There I remained six months, among those
prisoners who have no other support than chance charity; and
contracted a very valuable acquaintance, which was of great service
to me in the future emergencies of my life.

I was no sooner discharged, in consequence of an act of parliament for the relief of insolvent debtors, than I went to the house of my creditor, whom I cudgelled without mercy; and that I might leave nothing undone of those things which I ought to have done, my next stage was to Westminster-hall, where I waited until my patron came forth from the house, and saluted him with a blow that laid him senseless on the pavement: but my retreat was not so fortunate as I could have wished, the chairmen and lacquies in waiting having surrounded and disarmed me in a trice, I was committed to Newgate, and loaded with chains; and a very sagacious gentleman, who was afterwards hanged, having sat in judgment upon my case, pronounced me guilty of a capital crime, and foretold my condemnation at the Old Baily. His prognostic, however, was disappointed; for no body appearing to prosecute me at the next sessions, I was discharged, by order of the court. It would be impossible for me to recount, in the compass of one day's conversation, all the particular exploits in which I bore a considerable share: suffice it to say, I have been, at different times, prisoner in all the jails within the bills of mortality. I have broke from every roundhouse on this side Temple-bar. No bailiff, in the days of my youth and desperation, durst execute a writ upon me without a dozen followers; and the justices themselves trembled when I was brought before them.

I was once maimed by a carman, with whom I quarrelled, because he ridiculed my leek on St. David's day; my skull was fractured by a butcher's cleaver, on the like occasion. I have been run thro' the body five times, and lost the tip of my left ear by a pistol bullet. In a rencounter of this kind, having left my antagonist for dead, I was wise enough to make my retreat into France; and a few days after my arrival at Paris entering into conversation with some officers on the subject of politics, a dispute arose, in which I lost my temper, and spoke so irreverently of the *Grand Monarque*, that next morning I was sent to the bastile, by virtue of a *Lettre de Cachet*. There I remained for some months, deprived of all intercourse with rational creatures; a circumstance for which I was not sorry, as I had the more time to project schemes of revenge against the tyrant who confined me, and the wretch who had betrayed my private conversation: but tired, at length, with these fruitless suggestions, I was fain to unbend the severity of my thoughts by a correspondence with some industrious spiders, who had hung my dungeon with their ingenious labours.

I considered their work with such attention, that I soon became an adept in the mystery of weaving, and furnished myself with as many useful observations and reflections on that art, as will compose a very curious treatise, which I intend to bequeath to the Royal Society, for the benefit of our woolen manufacture; and this with a view to perpetuate my own name, rather than befriend my country: for, thank heaven! I am weaned from all attachments of that kind, and look upon myself as one very little obliged to any society whatsoever. Although I presided with absolute power over this long-legg'd community, and distributed rewards and punishments to each, according to his deserts, I grew impatient of my situation; and my natural disposition, one day, prevailing, like a fire which had long been smothered, I wreaked the fury of my indignation upon my innocent subjects, and in a twinkling destroyed the whole race. While I was employed in this general massacre, the turnkey, who brought me food, opening the door, and perceiving my transport, shrugged up his shoulders, and leaving my allowance, went out, pronouncing, *Le pauvre diable! la tete lui tourne.* My passion no sooner subsided than I resolved to profit by this opinion of the jailor, and from that day counterfeited lunacy with such success, that in less than three months I was delivered from the bastile, and sent to the gallies, in which they thought my bodily vigour might be of service, although the faculties of my mind were decayed. Before I was chained to the oar, I received three hundred stripes by way of welcome, that I might thereby be rendered more tractable, notwithstanding I used all the arguments in my power to persuade them, I was only *mad north, north west, and when the wind was southerly, knew a hawk from a hand-saw.*[1]

In our second cruize we had the good fortune to be overtaken by a tempest, during which the slaves were unbound, that they might contribute the more to the preservation of the galley, and have a chance for their lives, in case of a shipwreck. We were no sooner at liberty, than making ourselves masters of the vessel, we robbed the officers, and ran her on shore among rocks on the coast of Portugal; from whence I hastened to Lisbon, with a view of obtaining my passage in some ship bound for England, where, by this time, I hoped my affair would be forgotten.

But before this scheme could be accomplished, my evil genius led me into company; and being intoxicated, I began to broach doctrines on the subject of religion, at which some of the partie were scandalized and incensed; and I was next day dragged out of bed by the officers of the inquisition, and conveyed to a cell in the prison belonging to that tribunal.

At my first examination my resentment was strong enough to support me under the torture, which I endured without flinching; but my resolution abated, and my zeal immediately cooled, when I understood from a fellow-prisoner, who groaned on the other side of the partition, that in a short time there would be an *Auto da Fe*; in consequence of which I would, in all probability, be doomed to the flames, if I would not renounce my heretical errors, and submit to such penance as the church should think fit to prescribe. This miserable wretch was convicted of Judaism, which he had privately practised, by connivance, for many years, until he had amassed a fortune sufficient to attract the regard of the church. To this he fell a sacrifice, and accordingly prepared himself for the stake; while I, not at all ambitious of the crown of martyrdom, resolved to temporize: so that, when I was brought to the question the second time, I made a solemn recantation; and, as I had no worldly fortune to obstruct my salvation, was received into the bosom of the church, and, by way of penance, enjoined to walk barefoot to Rome, in the habit of a pilgrim.

During my peregrination thro' Spain, I was detained as a spy, until I could procure credentials from the inquisition at Lisbon; and behaved with such resolution and reserve, that, after being released, I was deemed a proper person to be employed in quality of a secret intelligencer, at a certain court. This office I undertook, without hesitation; and being furnished with money and bills of credit, crossed the Pyrenees, with intention to revenge myself upon the Spaniard for the severities I had undergone, during my captivity.

Having therefore effectually disguised myself, by a change of dress, and a large patch on one eye, I hired an equipage, and appeared at Bologna, in quality of an itinerant physician; in which capacity I succeeded tolerably well, till my servants decamped in the night, with my baggage, and left me in the condition of Adam. In short, I have travelled over the greatest part of Europe, as a beggar, pilgrim, priest, soldier, gamester, and quack; and felt the extremes of indigence and opulence, with the inclemency of weather, in all its vicissitudes. I have learned that the characters of mankind are every where the same; that common sense and honesty bear an infinitely small proportion to folly and vice; and that life is at best a paultry province.[1]

After having suffered innumerable hardships, dangers, and disgraces, I returned to London, where I lived some years in a garret, and picked up a subsistence, such as it was, by vending purges in the streets, from the back of a pied horse; in which situation I used to harrangue the mob, in broken English, under pretence of being an High German doctor.

At last an uncle died, by whom I inherit an estate of three hundred pounds per annum, tho', in his life-time, he would not have parted with a six-pence, to save my soul and body from perdition.

I now appear in the world, not as a member of any community, or what is called a social creature; but meerly as a spectator, who entertains himself with the grimaces of a jack-pudding, and banquets his spleen in beholding his enemies at loggerheads. That I may enjoy this disposition, abstracted from all interruption, danger, and participation, I feign myself deaf; an expedient by which I not only avoid all disputes, and their consequences, but also become master of a thousand little secrets, which are every day whispered in my presence, without any suspicion of their being overheard. You saw how I handled that shallow politician at my lady Plausible's the other day. The same method I practise upon the crazed tory, the bigot whig, the sour supercilious pedant, the petulant critic, the blustering coward, the fawning tool, the pert pimp, sly sharper, and every other species of knaves and fools with which this kingdom abounds.

In consequence of my rank and character I obtain free admission to the ladies, among whom I have obtained the appellation of the Scandalous Chronicle; and as I am considered (while silent) in no other light than that of a footstool or elbow chair, they divest their conversation of all restraint before me, and gratify my sense of hearing with strange things, which (if I could prevail upon myself to give the world that satisfaction) would compose a curious piece of secret history, and exhibit a quite different idea of characters from what is commonly entertained.

By this time, young gentleman, you may perceive, that I have it in my power to be a valuable correspondent; and that it will be your interest to deserve my confidence.'

CHAPTER LXXVIII

A Treaty is concluded betwixt Cadwallader and our Hero ;
in Consequence of which divers pleasant Adventures occur,
until the young Gentleman is summoned to the Garison
on a very interesting Occasion[1]

HERE the Misanthrope left off speaking, desirous to know the
sentiments of our hero, who embraced the proffered alliance, in
a transport of joy and surprize; and the treaty was no sooner concluded than Mr. Crabtree began to perform articles, by imparting
to him a thousand delicious secrets, from the possession of which
he promised himself innumerable scenes of mirth and enjoyment.
By means of this associate, whom he considered as the ring of
Gyges,[2] he foresaw that he should be enabled to penetrate not only
into the chambers but even to the inmost thoughts of the female
sex; and, in order to ward off suspicion, they agreed to revile each
other in public, and meet at a certain private rendezvous, to communicate their mutual discoveries, and concert their future
operations. So precious did Peregrine esteem this treasure, that
he would not even make his friend Godfrey acquainted with his
good fortune, tho' the first use he made of it, was in behalf of that
young gentleman, whom he undeceived in two very interesting
particulars.

The soldier's addresses were, at that time, shared betwixt two
ladies, who received them in a very different manner. By one of them
he was caress'd with marks of particular regard, and by small favours
flattered with the expectation of supreme success; while the other
treated him with such severity and shyness, that he could never find
an opportunity or resolution to make an unrestricted declaration of
his flame. As every woman has a confidant, to whom she pours forth
her heart on these occasions, Mr. Crabtree happened to be present
when each of them disburthened herself of her sentiments with regard to her lover; and learned from their own confessions, that the
frank lady cajoled him for the sake of the money which he suffered
himself to lose at cards, though she had not the least intention to
extend her complaisance beyond the limits of exterior civilities;
while the prude was actually enamoured of his person, and through
a remnant of modesty avoided him for no other reason, but because
she knew herself incapable of resisting his sollicitations.

Mr. Gauntlet profited by this discovery, which was communicated to him through the canal of his friend, relinquished the mercenary coquet, and found means to vanquish the reserve of the other. Peregrine himself was, in like manner, set to rights, in certain opinions he had conceived of his own influence with particular ladies; and as no person ever offended him with impunity, he projected a scheme of vengeance against a remarkable inamorato, who to his assiduities preferred those of a brawny fellow, that, from the place of a private trooper in the horse-guards, had been preferred to the rank of a lieutenant, by the interest of a dowager lately deceased. With this favourite did the lady make an assignation, in the hearing of Cadwallader, who gave our hero to understand, that he was to be received by her woman, in the dark, at a parlour-door that opened into a small garden, the wall of which he could easily overleap, after the servants should be retired to rest.

Peregrine, fraught with this intelligence, resolved to anticipate his rival; and accordingly, by the ministration of his companion, engaged a couple of stout chairmen, who being posted on the spot, seized the lover in his endeavours to surmount the wall, and conveyed him to a place of confinement, on pretence of supposing his design was to rob the house. He was no sooner secured in this manner, than Pickle, being determined to prosecute the adventure, transported himself into the garden, and personating the lieutenant, went to the door, made the signal which had been agreed upon, was admitted by the attendant, conducted to her lady's apartment, that was darkened for her reception; and having enjoyed his revenge, with every circumstance of satisfaction, made his retreat before day, without being discovered, after having been gratified with a valuable ring, as a testimony of her ladyship's affection.

Mean while the disappointed captive finding himself involved in a troublesome affair, that must end either in his own disgrace, or in that of his mistress, whom he could not with honour expose, employed all his art in tampering with his detainers, who pretended to have detected him as they passed that way by accident, and who would not listen to the terms he proposed for his release until it was almost day; and then, by the permission of their employers, they set him at liberty, in consideration of five guineas, which he divided between them. From the time of his discharge he waited with the utmost impatience for the hour of breakfast, and when it approached hied him to the house of his Dulcinea, with a view of excusing himself for the breach of punctuality he was obliged to commit.

He was confounded at the air of satisfaction and complacency that manifested itself in the lady's appearance; but believing it was no other than affectation, to conceal her inward disquiet and chagrin, he assumed a most dejected look, and with many expressions of mortification recounted the cursed accident which had disabled him from reaping the delicious fruits of his expectation. The nymph, who was not at all subject to the vulgar symptoms of confusion, hearing this circumstantial detail, fixed her eyes upon the soldier's countenance, and regarding him attentively for some minutes; 'If this declaration (said she) be an effort of your delicacy, you may spare such ridiculous reserve for the future. When things are come to a certain pass, such ceremony is superfluous and disagreeable. But perhaps you remember your good fortune with regret, and actually wish you had met with that adventure you have been at such pains to feign, rather than have enjoyed so cheap a conquest. Indeed you was so impatient to be gone before morning, that you seemed rather tired of your stay, than sollicitous about my reputation.'

The trooper, amazed and alarmed at this unexpected address, swore with many vulgar execrations, that he could prove he was in custody from twelve till six o'clock in the morning; and that he began to perceive he had been finely flung by some rascal, who had visited her in his place. He even hinted a suspicion, that the whole affair had been transacted by her connivance; and became extremely rough and unmannerly in his expostulations: so that the lady, who had more of the tygress than of the lamb in her disposition, being exasperated at the freedom of his behaviour, ordered him down stairs, and (to use the common phrase) forbad him her house. He accordingly retired, not without many invectives and threats, which he bawled aloud in his march; while his incensed patroness, by this time sensible that she had been the dupe of some stratagem, remained in a state of unspeakable anxiety and mortification. Being blessed, however, with a great share of penetration, she forthwith set it at work; and, after some recollection, concluded that the substitute could be no other than Peregrine, who had either learned the circumstance of the assignation from her maid, or extracted them from the vanity and indiscretion of the gallant himself.

Now that she had an opportunity of being acquainted with all our young gentleman's qualifications, she did not repine at the *qui pro quo* which had been played upon her, and resolved to transfer her good graces to Peregrine, without reserve. With this view she favoured him with the most palpable advances and allusions, which he would not understand, but on the contrary, conveyed the ring to her in a letter, written in a counterfeited character, with a feigned name, importing, that as he had reason to believe the token was intended for another, he could not in conscience reserve it for his own use: and to crown her vexation, by his contrivance, every circumstance of the story was divulged, except the name of the person who had represented the lover.

While our adventurer thus enjoyed his disposition, he was summoned to the castle by an express from his friend Hatchway, representing that the commodore lay at the point of death; and in less than an hour after the receipt of this melancholy piece of news, he set out post for his uncle's habitation, having previously taken leave of his associate Crabtree, who promised to meet him in two months at London, and settled a correspondence with Gauntlet, who proposed to remain at Bath during the remaining part of the season.

CHAPTER LXXIX

Peregrine arrives at the Garison, where he receives the
last Admonitions of Commodore Trunnion,
who next Day resigns his Breath, and is buried according
to his own Directions. Some Gentlemen in the Country
make a fruitless Attempt to accommodate Matters
betwixt Mr. Gamaliel Pickle and his eldest Son

ABOUT four o'clock in the morning our hero arrived at the garison, where he found his generous uncle in extremity, supported in bed, by Julia on one side, and lieutenant Hatchway on the other; while Mr. Jolter administered spiritual consolation to his soul, and between whiles comforted Mrs. Trunnion, who, with her maid, sat by the fire, weeping with great decorum; the physician having just taken his last fee, and retired, after pronouncing the fatal prognostic, in which he anxiously wished he might not be mistaken.

Though the commodore's speech was interrupted by a violent hiccup, he still retained the use of his senses; and when Peregrine approached, stretched out his hand with manifest signs of satisfaction. The young gentleman, whose heart overflowed with gratitude and affection, could not behold such a spectacle, unmoved. He endeavoured to conceal his tenderness, which in the wildness of his youth, and in the pride of his disposition, he considered as a derogation from his manhood; but, in spite of all his endeavours, the tears gushed from his eyes, while he kissed the old man's hand; and he was so utterly disconcerted by his grief, that when he attempted to speak, his tongue denied its office: so that the commodore, perceiving his disorder, made a last effort of strength, and consoled him in these words: 'Swab the spray from your bowsprit, my good lad, and coil up your spirits. You must not let the top-lifts of your heart give way, because you see me ready to go down at these years; many a better man has foundered before he has made half my way; thof I trust, by the mercy of God, I shall be sure in port in a very few glasses,[1] and fast moored in a most blessed riding: for my good friend Jolter hath overhauled the journal of my sins; and by the observation he hath taken of the state of my soul, I hope I shall happily conclude my voyage, and be brought up in the latitude of heaven. Here has been a doctor that wanted to stow me chock-full of physic; but, when a man's hour is come, what signifies his taking his departure with a 'pothecary's shop in his hold? Those fellows come along side of dying men, like the messengers of the admiralty with sailing orders: but, I told him as how I could slip my cable without his direction or assistance, and so he hauled off in dudgeon. This cursed hiccup (damnation seize it) makes such a rippling in the current of my speech, that mayhap you don't understand what I say. Now, while the sucker of my wind-pump[2] will go, I would willingly mention a few things, which I hope you will set down in the log-book of your remembrance, when I am stiff, d'ye see. There's your aunt sitting whimpering by the fire. I desire you will keep her tight, warm, and easy in her old age; she's an honest heart in her own way, and thof she goes a little crank and humoursome, by being often overstowed with Nantz and religion, she has been a faithful ship-mate to me, and I dare say never turned in with another man, since we first embarked in the same bottom. Jack Hatchway, you know the trim of her as well as e'er a man in England, and I believe she has a kindness for you; whereby, if you two will grapple in the way of matrimony, when I am gone, I do suppose, that my godson, for love of me, will allow you to live in the garison all the days of your life.'

Peregrine assured him, he would with pleasure comply with any request he should make, in behalf of two persons whom he esteemed so much; and the lieutenant, with a waggish sneer, which even the gravity of the situation could not prevent, thanked them both for their good will, telling the commodore, he was obliged to him for his friendship, in seeking to promote him to the command of a vessel which he himself had wore out in the service: that notwithstanding, he should be content to take charge of her, tho' he could not help being shy of coming after such an able navigator.

Trunnion, exhausted as he was, smiled at this sally, and after some pause, resumed his admonitions in this manner: 'I need not talk of Pipes, because I know you will do for him, without my recommendation; the fellow has sailed with me in many a hard gale, and I'll warrant him as stout a seaman as ever set face to the weather: but I hope you will take care of the rest of my crew, and not disrate them after I am dead, in favour of new followers. As for that young woman, Ned Gauntlet's daughter, I am informed as how she is an excellent wench, and has a respect for you; whereby, if you run her on board in an unlawful way, I leave my curse upon you, and trust you will never prosper in the voyage of life: but, I believe you are more of an honest man, than to behave so much like a pirate. I beg of all love, you wool take care of your constitution, and beware of running foul of harlots, who are no better than so many mermaids, that sit upon rocks in the sea, and hang out a fair face for the destruction of passengers; thof I must say, for my own part, I never met with any of those sweet singers, and yet I have gone to sea for the space of thirty years. But, howsomever, steer your course clear of all such brimstone bitches; shun going to law as you would shun the devil, and look upon all attornies as devouring sharks, or ravenous fish of prey. As soon as the breath is out of my body, let minute guns be fired, till I am safe under ground: I would also be buried in the red jacket I had on, when I boarded and took the *Renummy.*[1] Let my pistols, cutlass, and pocket-compass be laid in the coffin along with me. Let me be carried to the grave by my own men, dressed in the black caps and white shirts which my barge's crew were wont to wear; and they must keep a good look-out, that none of your pilfering rapscallions may come and heave me up again, for the lucre of what they can get, until my carcase is belayed by a tomb-stone. As for the motto, or what you call it, I leave that to you and Mr. Jolter, who are scholars; but I do desire, that it may not be ingraved in the Greek or Latin lingos, and much less in the French, which I abominate, but in plain English, that when the angel comes to pipe *all hands* at the great day, he may know that I am a British man, and speak to me in my mother tongue. And now I have no more to say, but God in heaven have mercy upon my soul, and send you all fair weather, wheresoever you are bound.'

So saying, he regarded every individual around him with a look of complacency, and closing his eye, composed himself to rest, while the whole audience (Pipes himself not excepted) were melted with sorrow; and Mrs. Trunnion consented to quit the room, that she might not be exposed to the unspeakable anguish of seeing him expire.

His last moments, however, were not so near as they imagined; he began to dose, and enjoyed small intervals of ease, till next day in the afternoon; during which remissions, he was heard to pour forth many pious ejaculations, expressing his hope, that, for all the heavy cargo of his sins, he should be able to surmount the foothook-shrouds of despair,[1] and get aloft to the cross-trees of God's good favour. At last, his voice sunk so low, as not to be distinguished; and having lain about an hour, almost without any perceptible signs of life, he gave up the ghost, with a groan which anounced his decease.

Julia was no sooner certified of this melancholy event, than she ran to her aunt's chamber, weeping aloud; and immediately a very decent concert was performed by the good widow and her attendants. Peregrine and Hatchway retired till the corpse should be laid out; and Pipes having surveyed the body, with a face of rueful attention, 'Well fare thy soul! old Hawser Trunnion, (said he) man and boy I have known thee these five and thirty years, and sure a truer heart never broke biscuit. Many a hard gale hast thou weathered; but now thy spells are all over, and thy hull fairly laid up. A better commander I'd never desire to serve; and who knows but I may help to set up thy standing rigging in another world?'

All the servants of the house were affected with the loss of their old master, and the poor people in the neighbourhood assembled at the gate, and by repeated howlings expressed their sorrow for the death of their charitable benefactor. Peregrine, though he felt every thing which love and gratitude could inspire on this occasion, was not so much overwhelmed with affliction, as to be incapable of taking the management of the family into his own hands. He gave directions about the funeral with great discretion, after having paid the compliments of condolance to his aunt, whom he consoled with the assurance of his inviolable esteem and affection. He ordered suits of mourning to be made for every person in the garison, and invited all the neighbouring gentlemen to the burial, not even excepting his father and brother Gam, who did not, however, honour the ceremony with their presence; nor was his mother humane enough to visit her sister-in-law in her distress.

In the method of interment, the commodore's injunctions were obeyed to a tittle; and at the same time our hero made a donation of fifty pounds to the poor of the parish, as a benefaction which his uncle had forgot to bequeath.

Having performed these obsequies with the most pious punctuality, he examined the will, to which there was no addition since it had been first executed, adjusted the payment of all the legacies, and being sole executor, took an account of the estate to which he had succeeded, and which, after all deductions, amounted to thirty thousand pounds. The possession of such a fortune, of which he was absolute master, did not at all contribute to the humiliation of his spirit, but inspired him with new ideas of grandeur and magnificence, and elevated his hope to the highest pinnacle of expectation.

His domestic affairs being settled, he was visited by almost all the gentlemen of the county, who came to pay their compliments of congratulation, on his accession to the estate; and some of them offered their good offices towards a reconciliation betwixt his father and him, induced by the general detestation which was entertained for his brother Gam, who was by this time looked upon by his neighbours as a prodigy of insolence and malice. Our young squire thanked them for their kind proposal, which he accepted; and old Gamaliel, at their intreaties, seemed very well disposed to an accommodation: but, as he would not venture to declare himself, before he had consulted his wife, that favourable disposition was rendered altogether ineffectual, by the instigations of that implacable woman; and our hero resigned all expectation of being reunited to his father's house. His brother, as usual, took all opportunities of injuring his character, by false aspersions and stories misrepresented, in order to prejudice his reputation: nor was his sister Julia suffered to enjoy her good fortune in peace. Had he undergone such persecution from an alien to his blood, the world would have heard of his revenge; but, notwithstanding his indignation, he was too much tinctured by the prejudices of consanguinity, to lift his arm in judgment against the son of his own parents; and this consideration abridged the term of his residence at the garison, where he had proposed to stay for some months.

CHAPTER LXXX

The young Gentleman having settled his domestic Affairs,
arrives in London, and sets up a gay Equipage.
He meets with Emilia, and is introduced to her Uncle

HIS aunt, at the earnest solicitation of Julia and her husband, took up her quarters at the house of that affectionate kinswoman, who made it her chief study to comfort and cherish the disconsolate widow; and Jolter, in expectation of the living, which was not yet vacant, remained in garison, in quality of land-steward upon our hero's country-estate. As for the lieutenant, our young gentleman communed with him, in a serious manner, about the commodore's proposal of his taking Mrs. Trunnion to wife; and Jack, being quite tired of the solitary situation of a batchelor, which nothing but the company of his old commander could have enabled him to support so long, far from discovering aversion to the match, observed with an arch smile, that it was not the first time he had commanded a vessel in the absence of Captain Trunnion; and therefore, if the widow was willing, he would chearfully stand by her helm, and, as he hoped the duty would not be of long continuance, do his endeavour to steer her safe into the port, where the commodore might come on board, and take charge of her again.

In consequence of this declaration, it was determined that Mr. Hatchway should make his addresses to Mrs. Trunnion, as soon as decency would permit her to receive them; and Mr. Clover and his wife promised to exert their influence in his behalf. Mean while, Jack was desired to live at the castle as usual, and assured, that it should be put wholly in his possession, as soon as he should be able to accomplish this matrimonial scheme.

When Peregrine had settled all these points to his own satisfaction, he took leave of all his friends, and repairing to the great city, purchased a new chariot and horses, put Pipes and another lacquey into rich liveries, took elegant lodgings in Pall-mall, and made a most remarkable appearance among people of fashion. It was owing to this equipage, and the gaiety of his personal deportment, that common fame, which is always a common liar, represented him as a young gentleman who had just succeeded to an estate of five thousand pounds *per annum*, by the death of an uncle; that he was intitled to an equal fortune at the decease of his own father, exclusive of two considerable jointures, which would devolve upon him, at the demise of his mother and aunt. This report (false and ridiculous as it was) he could not find in his heart to contradict; not but that he was sorry to find himself so misrepresented: but his vanity would not allow him to take any step that might diminish his importance in the opinion of those who courted his acquaintance, on the supposition that his circumstances were actually as affluent as they were said to be. Nay, so much was he infatuated by this weakness, that he resolved to encourage the deception, by living up to the report; and accordingly, engaged in the most expensive parties of pleasure; believing, that before his present finances should be exhausted, his fortune would be effectually made, by the personal accomplishments he should have occasion to display to the beau monde, in the course of his extravagance. In a word, vanity and pride were the ruling foibles of our adventurer, who imagined himself sufficiently qualified to retrieve his fortune in various shapes, long before he could have any idea of want or difficulty. He thought he should have it in his power, at any time, to make prize of a rich heiress, or opulent widow; his ambition had already aspired to the heart of a young handsome duchess dowager, to whose acquaintance he had found means to be introduced: or, should matrimony chance to be unsuitable to his inclinations, he never doubted, that by the interest he might acquire among the nobility, he should be favoured with some lucrative post, that would amply recompense him for the liberality of his disposition. There are many young men, who entertain the same expectations, with half the reason he had to be so presumptuous.

In the midst of these chimerical calculations, his passion for Emilia did not subside; but, on the contrary, began to rage to such an inflammation of desire, that her idea interfered with every other reflection, and absolutely disabled him from prosecuting the other lofty schemes which his imagination had projected. He therefore laid down the honest resolution of visiting her in all the splendor of his situation, in order to practise upon her virtue with all his art and address, to the utmost extent of his influence and fortune. Nay, so effectually had his guilty passion absorb'd his principles of honour, conscience, humanity, and regard for the commodore's last words, that he was base enough to rejoice at the absence of his friend Godfrey, who being then with his regiment in Ireland, could not dive into his purpose, or take measures for frustrating his vicious design.

Fraught with these heroic sentiments, he determined to set out for Sussex in his chariot and six, attended by his valet de chambre and two footmen; and he was now as sensible, that in his last essay he had mistaken his cue, he determined to change his battery, and sap the fortress, by the most submissive, soft, and insinuating behaviour.

On the evening that preceded this purposed expedition, he went into one of the boxes at the play-house, as usual, to shew himself to the ladies; and in reconnoitring the company through a glass, (for no other reason, but because it was fashionable to be purblind) perceived his mistress very plainly dressed, in one of the seats above the stage, talking to another young woman of a very homely appearance. Though his heart beat the alarm with the utmost impatience at sight of his Emilia, he was for some minutes deterred from obeying the impulse of his love, by the presence of some ladies of fashion, who, he feared, would think the worse of him, should they see him make his compliments in public to a person of her figure. Nor would the violence of his inclination have so far pre-vailed over his pride, as to lead him thither, had not he recollected, that his quality-friends would look upon her as some handsome Abigail, with whom he had an affair of gallantry, and of con-sequence give him credit for the intrigue.

Encouraged by this suggestion, he complied with the dictates of love, and flew to the place where his charmer sat. His air and dress were so remarkable, that it was almost impossible he should have escaped the eyes of a curious observer, especially as he had chosen a time for coming in, when his entrance could not fail to attract the notice of the spectators; I mean, when the whole house was hushed in attention to the performance on the stage. Emilia, there-fore, had perceived him at his first approach; she found herself discovered by the direction of his glass, and guessing his intention by his abrupt retreat from the box, summoned all her fortitude to her aid, and prepared for his reception. He advanced to her with an air of eagerness and joy, tempered with modesty and respect, and expressed his satisfaction at seeing her, with a seeming reverence of regard. Though she was extremely well pleased at this un-expected behaviour, she suppressed the emotions of her heart, and answered his compliments with affected ease and unconcern, such as might denote the good humour of a person who meets by acci-dent with an indifferent acquaintance. After having certified himself of her own good health, he very kindly inquired about her mother and Miss Sophy, gave her to understand, that he had lately been favoured with a letter from Godfrey, and that he had actually

intended to set out next morning on a visit to Mrs. Gauntlet, which
(now that he was so happy as to meet with her) he would postpone,
until he should have the pleasure of attending her to the country.
After having thanked him for his polite intention, she told him,
that her mother was expected in town in a few days, and that she
herself had come to London some weeks ago, to give her attendance
upon her aunt, who had been dangerously ill, but was now pretty
well recovered.

Although the conversation of course turned upon general
topics, during the entertainment, he took all opportunities of
being particular with his eyes, through which he conveyed a
thousand tender protestations. She saw, and inwardly rejoiced
at the humility of his looks; but, far from rewarding it with one
approving glance, she industriously avoided this ocular intercourse,
and rather coquetted with a young gentleman that ogled her from
the opposite box. Peregrine's penetration easily detected her
sentiments, and he was nettled at her dissimulation, which served
to confirm him in his unwarrantable designs upon her person.
He persisted in his assiduities with indefatigable perseverance;
when the play was concluded, handed her and her companion
to an hackney-coach, and with difficulty was permitted to escort
them to the house of Emilia's uncle, to whom our hero was introduced by the young lady, as an intimate friend of her brother
Godfrey.

The old gentleman, who was no stranger to the nature of Peregrine's connexion with his sister's family, prevailed upon him to
stay to supper, and seemed particularly well pleased with his
conversation and deportment, which, by help of his natural
sagacity, he wonderfully adapted to the humour of his entertainer.
After supper, when the ladies were withdrawn, and the citizen
called for his pipe, our sly adventurer followed his example; and
though he abhorred the plant, smoaked with an air of infinite
satisfaction, and expatiated upon the virtues of tobacco, as if he
had been deeply concerned in the Virginia trade. In the progress of
the discourse, he consulted the merchant's disposition; and the
national debt coming upon the carpet, held forth upon the funds
like a professed broker. When the alderman complained of the
restrictions and discouragement of trade, his guest inveighed
against exorbitant duties, with the nature of which he seemed as
well acquainted as any commissioner of the customs; so that the
uncle was astonished at the extent of his knowledge, and expressed
his surprize, that a gay young gentleman, like him, should have

found either leisure or inclination to consider subjects so foreign to the fashionable amusements of youth.

Pickle laid hold on this opportunity to tell him, that he was descended from a race of merchants; and that, early in life, he had made it his business to instruct himself in the different branches of trade, which he not only studied as his family-profession, but also as the source of all our national riches and power. He then launched out in praise of commerce, and the promoters thereof; and, by way of contrast, employed all his ridicule, in drawing such ludicrous pictures of the manners and education of what is called high life, that the trader's sides were shaken by laughter, even to the danger of his life; and he looked upon our adventurer as a miracle of sobriety and good sense.

Having thus ingratiated himself with the uncle, Peregrine took his leave, and next day in the forenoon visited the niece in his chariot, after she had been admonished by her kinsman to behave with circumspection, and cautioned against neglecting or discouraging the addresses of such a valuable admirer.

CHAPTER LXXXI

He prosecutes his Design upon Emilia with great
Art and Perseverance

Our adventurer, having by his hypocrisy obtained free access to his mistress, began the siege, by professing the most sincere contrition for his former levity, and imploring her forgiveness with such earnest supplication, that, guarded as she was against his flattering arts, she began to believe his protestations, which were even accompanied with tears, and abated a good deal of that severity and distance she had proposed to maintain, during this interview. She would not, however, favour him with the least acknowledgment of a mutual passion, because, in the midst of his vows of eternal constancy and truth, he did not mention one syllable of wedlock, though he was now intirely master of his own conduct; and this consideration created a doubt, which fortified her against all his attacks: yet, what her discretion would have concealed, was discovered by her eyes, which, in spite of all her endeavours, breathed forth complacency and love. For, her inclination was flattered by her own self-sufficiency, which imputed her

admirer's silence, in that particular, to the hurry and perturbation
of his spirits, and persuaded her, that he could not possibly regard
her with any other than honourable intentions.

The insidious lover exulted in the tenderness of her looks, from
which he presaged a compleat victory: but, that he might not over-
shoot himself by his own precipitation, he would not run the risk of
declaring himself, until her heart should be so far entangled within
his snares, as that neither the suggestions of honour, prudence, or
pride should be able to disengage it. Armed with this resolution, he
restrained the impatience of his temper within the limits of the
most delicate deportment; and after having solicited and obtained
permission to attend her to the next opera, took her by the hand,
and pressing it to his lips in the most respectful manner, went away,
leaving her in a most whimsical state of suspence, checquered with
an interesting vicissitude of hope and fear.

On the appointed day, he appeared again about five o'clock in the
afternoon, and found her native charms so much improved by the
advantages of dress, that he was transported with admiration and
delight; and while he conducted her to the Hay-market, could
scarce bridle the impetuosity of his passion, so as to observe the
forbearing maxims he had adopted. When she entered the pit, he
had abundance of food for the gratification of his vanity; for, in a
moment, she eclipsed all the female part of the audience, each
individual allowing in her own heart, that the stranger was by far
the handsomest woman there present, except herself.

Here it was that our hero enjoyed a double triumph; he was vain
of this opportunity to enhance his reputation for gallantry among
the ladies of fashion, who knew him, and proud of an occasion to
display his quality-acquaintance to Emilia, that she might entertain
the greater idea of the conquest she had made, and pay the more
deference to his importance in the sequel of his addresses. That he
might profit as much as possible by this situation, he went up and
accosted every person in the pit, with whom he ever had the least
communication, whispered and laughed with an affected air of
familiarity, and even bowed at a distance to some of the nobility, on
the slender foundation of having stood near them at court, or
presented them with a pinch of Rapee[I] at White's chocolate-house.

This ridiculous ostentation, though now practised with a view of
promoting his design, was a weakness that, in some degree, infected
the whole of his behaviour; for nothing gave him so much joy in
conversation, as an opportunity of giving the company to understand, how well he was with persons of distinguished rank and

character: he would often (for example) observe, as it were occasionally, that the duke of G—— was one of the best natured men in the world, and illustrate his assertion by some instance of his affability, in which he himself was concerned: then, by an abrupt transition, he would repeat some repartee of lady T——, and mention a certain *bon mot* of the earl of C——, which was uttered in his hearing.[1]

Abundance of young men, in this manner, make free with the names, though they have never had access to the persons of the nobility: but, this was not the case with Peregrine, who, in consideration of his appearance and supposed fortune, together with the advantage of his introduction, was by this time freely admitted to the tables of the great.

In his return with Emilia from the opera, though he still maintained the most scrupulous decorum in his behaviour, he plied her with the most passionate expressions of love, squeezed her hand with great fervency, protested that his whole soul was ingrossed by her idea, and that he could not exist independent of her favour. Pleased as she was with his warm and pathetic addresses, together with the respectful manner of his making love, she yet had prudence and resolution sufficient to contain her tenderness, which was ready to run over; being fortified against his arts, by reflecting, that if his aim was honourable, it was now his business to declare it. On this consideration, she refused to make any serious reply to his earnest expostulations, but affected to receive them as the undetermined effusions of gallantry and good breeding.

This fictitious gaiety and good humour, though it baffled his hope of extorting from her an acknowledgment of which he might have taken immediate advantage, nevertheless encouraged him to observe, (as the chariot passed along the Strand) that the night was far advanced; that supper would certainly be over, before they could reach her uncle's house; and to propose, that he should wait upon her to some place, where they might be accommodated with a slight refreshment. She was offended at the freedom of this proposal, which, however, she treated as a joke, thanking him for his courteous offer, and assuring him, that when she should be disposed for a tavern-treat, he alone should have the opportunity of bestowing it.

Her kinsman being engaged with company abroad, and her aunt retired to rest, he had the good fortune to enjoy a *tête à tête* with her during a whole hour, which he employed with such consummate skill, that her caution was almost overcome. He not only assailed her with the artillery of sighs, vows, prayers and tears, but even pawned his honour in behalf of his love. He swore with many imprecations, that although her heart were surrendered to him at discretion, there was a principle within him, which would never allow him to injure such innocence and beauty; and the transports of his passion had, upon this occasion, so far overshot his purpose, that if she had demanded an explanation, while he was thus agitated, he would have engaged himself to her wish by such ties, as he could not possibly break, with any regard to his reputation. But, from such expostulation, she was deterred partly by pride, and partly by the dread of finding herself mistaken in such an interesting conjecture. She therefore enjoyed the present flattering appearance of her fate, was prevailed upon to accept the jewels which he had purchased with part of his winning at Bath, and with the most inchanting condescension submitted to a warm embrace, when he took his leave, after having obtained permission to visit her, as often as his inclination and convenience would permit.

In his return to his own lodgings, he was buoyed up with his success to an extravagance of hope, already congratulated himself upon his triumph over Emilia's virtue, and began to project future conquests among the most dignified characters of the female sex. But his attention was not at all dissipated by these vain reflections; he resolved to concentrate the whole exertion of his soul upon the execution of his present plan, desisted, in the mean time, from all other schemes of pleasure, interest and ambition, and took lodgings in the city, for the more commodious accomplishment of his purpose.

While our lover's imagination was thus agreeably regaled, his mistress did not enjoy her expectations, without the intervention of doubts and anxiety. His silence touching the final aim of his addresses was a mystery on which she was afraid of exercising her sagacity; and her uncle tormented her with inquiries into the circumstances of Peregrine's professions and deportment. Rather than give this relation the least cause of suspicion, which must have cut off all intercourse betwixt her and her admirer, she said every thing which she thought would satisfy his care and concern for her welfare; and in consequence of such representation, she enjoyed, without reserve, the company of our adventurer, who prosecuted his plan with surprising eagerness and perseverance.

CHAPTER LXXXII

He prevails upon Emilia to accompany him to a
Masquerade, makes a treacherous Attempt upon her Affection,
and meets with a deserved Repulse

SCARCE a night elapsed in which he did not conduct her to some
public entertainment; and when, by dint of his insidious carriage,
he thought himself in full possession of her confidence and affection, he lay in wait for an opportunity; and hearing her observe in
conversation, that she had never been at a masquerade, begged
leave to attend her to the next ball; at the same time, extending his
invitation to the young lady, in whose company he had found her
at the play, she being present when this subject of discourse was
introduced. He had flattered himself, that this gentlewoman would
decline the proposal, as she was a person seemingly of a demure
disposition, who had been born and bred in the city, where such
diversions are looked upon as scenes of lewdness and debauchery.
For once, however, he reckoned without his host; curiosity is as
prevalent in the city as at the court-end of the town: Emilia no
sooner signified her assent to his proposal, than her friend, with
an air of satisfaction, agreed to make one of the *partie*; and he was
obliged to thank her for that complaisance which laid him under
infinite mortification. He set his genius at work, to invent some
scheme for preventing her unseasonable intrusion. Had an opportunity offered, he would have acted as her physician, and administered a medicine that would have laid her under the necessity
of staying at home: but his acquaintance with her being too slight
to furnish him with the means of executing this expedient, he
devised another, which was practised with all imaginable success.
Understanding that her grandmother had left her a sum of money
independent of her parents, he conveyed a letter to her mother,
intimating, that her daughter, on pretence of going to the masquerade, intended to bestow herself in marriage to a certain person, and
that in a few days she would be informed of the circumstances
of the whole intrigue, provided she would keep this information
secret, and contrive some excuse for detaining the young lady at
home, without giving her cause to believe she was apprized of her
intention. This billet, subscribed, *Your well-wisher and unknown*
humble servant, had the desired effect upon the careful matron,

who, on the ball-day, feigned herself so extremely ill, that miss could not, with any decency, quit her mamma's apartment; and therefore sent her apology to Emilia in the afternoon, immediately after the arrival of Peregrine, who pretended to be very much afflicted with the disappointment, while his heart throbbed with a transport of joy.

About ten o'clock the lovers set out for the Hay-market, he being dressed in the habit of Pantaloon, and she in that of Columbine; and they had scarce entered the house, when the music struck up, the curtain was withdrawn, and the whole scene displayed at once, to the admiration of Emilia, whose expectation was infinitely surpassed by this exhibition. Our gallant having conducted her through all the different apartments, and described the œconomy of the place, led her into the circle, and, in their turn, they danced several minuets; then going to the sideboard, he prevailed upon her to eat some sweetmeets and drink a glass of Champagne; and, after a second review of the company, they engaged in country-dances, at which exercise they continued, until our adventurer concluded, that his partner's blood was sufficiently warmed for the prosecution of his design. On this supposition, which was built upon her declaring, that she was thirsty and fatigued, he persuaded her to take a little refreshment and repose; and for that purpose, handed her down stairs into the eating-room, where having seated her on the floor, he presented her with a glass of wine and water; and as she complained of being faint, enriched the draught with some drops of a certain elixir, which he recommended as a most excellent restorative, though it was no other than a stimulating tincture, which he had treacherously provided for the occasion. Having swallowed this potion, by which her spirits were manifestly exhilerated, she ate a slice of ham with the wing of a cold pullet, and concluded the meal with a glass of Burgundy, which she drank at the earnest intreaty of her admirer. These extraordinary cordials co-operating with the ferment of her blood, which was heated by violent motion, could not fail to affect the constitution of a delicate young creature, who was naturally sprightly and volatile. Her eyes began to sparkle with unusual fire and vivacity, a thousand brilliant sallies of wit escaped her, and every mask that accosted her, underwent some smarting repartee.

Peregrine, overjoyed at the success of his administration, proposed that they should resume their places at the country-dances, with a view to promote and assist the efficacy of his elixir; and when he thought her disposition was properly adapted for the theme, began to ply her with all the elocution of love. In order to elevate his own spirits to that pitch of resolution which his scheme required, he drank two whole bottles of Burgundy, which inflamed his passion to such a degree, that he found himself capable of undertaking and perpetrating any scheme for the gratification of his desire.

Emilia, warmed by so many concurring incentives, in favour of the man she loved, abated considerably of her wonted reserve, listened to his protestations with undissembled pleasure, and in the confidence of her satisfaction, even owned him absolute master of her affections. Ravished with this confession, he now deemed himself on the brink of reaping the delicious fruits of his art and assiduity; and the morning being already pretty far advanced, assented with rapture to the first proposal she made of retiring to her lodgings. The blinds of the chariot being pulled up, he took advantage of the favourable situation of her thoughts; and on pretence of being whimsical, in consequence of the wine he had swallowed, clasped her in his arms, and imprinted a thousand kisses on her pouting lips, a freedom which she pardoned as the privilege of intoxication. While he thus indulged himself with impunity, the carriage halted, and Pipes opening the door, his master handed her into the passage, before she perceived that it was not her uncle's house, at which they had alighted.

Alarmed at this discovery, she with some confusion desired to know his reason for conducting her to a strange place at these hours: but he made no reply, until he had led her into an apartment, when he gave her to understand, that as her uncle's family must be disturbed by her going thither so late in the night, and the streets near Temple-bar were infested by a multitude of robbers and cutthroats, he had ordered his coachman to halt at this house, which was kept by a relation of his, a mighty good sort of a gentlewoman, who was proud of an opportunity to accommodate a person for whom he was known to entertain such tenderness and esteem.

Emilia had too much penetration to be imposed upon by this plausible pretext: in spite of her partiality for Peregrine, which had never been inflamed to such a pitch of complacency before, she comprehended his whole plan in a twinkling; and though her blood boiled with indignation, thanked him, with an affected air of serenity, for his kind concern, and expressed her obligation to his cousin; but, at the same time, insisted upon going home, lest her absence should terrify her uncle and aunt, who she knew would not retire to rest, till her return.

He urged her, with a thousand remonstrances, to consult her own ease and safety, promising to send Pipes into the city, for the satisfaction of her relations: but finding her obstinately deaf to his intreaties, he assured her, that he would in a few minutes comply with her request; and, in the mean time, begg'd she would fortify herself against the cold with a cordial, which he poured out in her presence, and which (now that her suspicion was aroused) she refused to taste, notwithstanding all his importunities. He then fell upon his knees before her, and the tears gushing from his eyes, swore that his passion was wound up to such a pitch of impatience, that he could no longer live upon the unsubstantial food of expectation; and that, if she would not vouchsafe to crown his happiness, he would forthwith sacrifice himself to her disdain. Such an abrupt address, accompanied with all the symptoms of frantic agitation, could not fail to perplex and affright the gentle Emilia, who, after some recollection, replied with a resolute tone, that she could not see what reason he had to complain of her reserve, which she was not at liberty to lay intirely aside, until he should have avowed his intentions in form, and obtained the sanction of those whom it was her duty to obey. 'Divine creature! (cried he, seizing her hand, and pressing it to his lips) it is from you alone I hope for that condescension, which would overwhelm me with transports of celestial bliss. The sentiments of parents are sordid, silly, and confined; seek not then to subject my passion to such low restrictions as were calculated for the purposes of common life. My love is too delicate and refined, to wear those vulgar fetters, which serve only to destroy the merit of voluntary affection, and to upbraid a man incessantly with the articles of compulsion, under which he lies. My dear angel! spare me the mortification of being compelled to love you, and reign sole empress of my heart and fortune. I will not affront you so much as to talk of settlements; my all is at your disposal. In this pocket-book are notes to the amount of two thousand pounds; do me the pleasure to accept of them; to-morrow I will lay ten thousand more in your lap. In a word, you shall be mistress of my whole estate, and I shall think myself happy in living dependent on your bounty!'

Heavens! what were the emotions of the virtuous, the sensible, the delicate, the tender Emilia's heart, when she heard this insolent declaration from the mouth of a man, whom she had honoured with her affection and esteem! It was not simply horror, grief, or indignation that she felt, in consequence of this unworthy treatment, but the united pangs of all together, which produced a sort of hysteric laugh, while she told him, that she could not help admiring his generosity.

Deceived by this convulsion, and the ironical compliment that attended it, the lover thought he had already made great progress in his operations, and that it was now his business to storm the fort by a vigorous assault, that he might spare her the confusion of yielding without resistance. Possessed by this vain suggestion, he started up, and folding her in his arms, began to obey the furious dictates of his unruly and ungenerous desire; upon which, with an air of cool determination, she demanded a parley; and when, upon her repeated request, he granted it, addressed herself to him in these words, while her eyes gleamed with all the dignity of the most awful resentment. 'Sir, I scorn to upbraid you with a repetition of your former vows and protestations, nor will I recapitulate the little arts you have practised to ensnare my heart; because, though by dint of the most perfidious dissimulation, you have found means to deceive my opinion, your utmost efforts have never been able to lull the vigilance of my conduct, or to engage my affection beyond the power of discarding you without a tear, whenever my honour should demand such a sacrifice. Sir, you are unworthy of my concern or regret, and the sigh that now struggles from my breast, is the result of sorrow, for my own want of discernment. As for your present attempt upon my chastity, I despise your power, as I detest your intention. Though, under the mask of the most delicate respect, you have decoyed me from the immediate protection of my friends, and contrived other impious stratagems to ruin my peace and reputation, I confide too much in my own innocence, and the authority of the law, to admit one thought of fear, much less to sink under the horror of this shocking situation, into which I have been seduced. Sir, your behaviour on this occasion, is in all respects low and contemptible: for, ruffian as you are, you durst not harbour one thought of executing your execrable scheme, while you knew my brother was near enough to prevent, or revenge the insult; so that you must not only be a treacherous villain, but also a most despicable coward.' Having expressed herself in this manner, with a most majestic severity of aspect, she opened the door, and walked down stairs with surprising resolution, committed herself to the care of a watchman, who accommodated her with a hackney-chair, in which she was safely conveyed to her uncle's house.

Mean while, the lover was so confounded and over-awed, by these cutting reproaches, and her animated behaviour, that all his resolution forsook him, and he found himself not only incapable of obstructing her retreat, but even of uttering one syllable to deprecate her wrath, or extenuate the guilt of his own conduct. The nature of his disappointment, and the keen remorse that seized him, when he reflected upon the dishonourable predicament in which his character stood with Emilia, raised such perturbation in his mind, that his silence was succeeded by a violent fit of distraction, during which he raved like a Bedlamite, and acted a thousand extravagancies, which convinced the people of the house, (a certain bagnio) that he had actually lost his wits. Pipes, with great concern, adopted the same opinion; and, being assisted by the waiters, hindered him, by main force, from running out and pursuing the fair fugitive, whom, in his delirium, he alternately cursed and commended, with horrid imprecations, and lavish applause. His faithful valet, having waited two whole hours, in hope of seeing this gust of passion overblown, and perceiving that the paroxysm seemed rather to increase, very prudently sent for a physician of his master's acquaintance, who having considered the circumstances and symptoms of the disorder, directed, that he should be plentifully blooded, without loss of time, and prescribed a draught to compose the tumult of his spirits. These orders being punctually performed, he grew more calm and tractable, recovered his reflection so far, as to be ashamed of the extasy he had undergone, suffered himself quietly to be undressed, and put to bed, where the fatigue occasioned by his exercise at the masquerade, co-operated with the present dissipation of his spirits to lull him in a profound sleep, which greatly tended to the preservation of his intellects: not that he found himself in a state of perfect tranquillity, when he waked about noon; the remembrance of what had passed overwhelmed him with mortification. Emilia's invectives still sounded in his ears; and while he deeply resented her disdain, he could not help admiring her spirit, and in his heart did homage to her charms.

CHAPTER LXXXIII

He endeavours to reconcile himself to his Mistress,
and expostulates with the Uncle,
who forbids him the House

IN this state of division, he went home to his own lodgings in a
chair; and while he deliberated with himself, whether he should
relinquish the pursuit, and endeavour to banish her idea from his
breast, or go immediately and humble himself before his exasperated
mistress, and offer his hand, as an atonement for his crime, his servant put in his hand a packet, which had been delivered by a ticket-
porter at the door. He no sooner perceived that the superscription
was in Emilia's hand-writing, than he guessed the nature of the contents; and opening the seal with disordered eagerness, found the
jewels he had given to her, inclosed in a billet couched in these words.

'That I may have no cause to reproach myself with having
retained the least memorial of a wretch whom I equally despise and
abhor, I take this opportunity of restoring these ineffectual instruments of his infamous design upon the honour of   EMILIA'

His chagrin was so much galled and inflamed by the bitterness of
this contemptuous message, that he gnawed his fingers till the
blood ran over his nails, and even wept with vexation. Sometimes
he vowed revenge against her haughty virtue, and reviled himself
for his precipitate declaration, before his scheme was brought to
maturity; then he would consider her behaviour with reverence
and regard, and bow before the irresistible power of her attractions.
In short, his breast was torn by conflicting passions; love, shame,
and remorse contended with vanity, ambition, and revenge; and
the superiority was still doubtful, when headstrong desire interposed, and decided in favour of an attempt towards a reconciliation
with the offended fair.

Impelled by this motive, he set out in the afternoon for the house
of her uncle, not without hopes of that tender enjoyment, which
never fails to attend an accommodation betwixt two lovers of taste
and sensibility. Though the consciousness of his trespass encumbered him with an air of awkward confusion, he was too confident of his own qualifications and address to despair of forgiveness;
and by that time he arrived at the citizen's gate, he had conned
a very artful and pathetic harangue, which he proposed to utter in

his own behalf, laying the blame of his conduct on the impetuosity of his passion, incensed by the Burgundy, which he had too liberally drank: but he did not meet with an opportunity to avail himself of this preparation. Emilia, suspecting that he would take some step of this kind to retrieve her favour, had gone abroad on pretence of visiting, after having signified to her kinsman, her resolution to avoid the company of Peregrine, on account of some ambiguities which (she said) were last night remarkable in his demeanour, at the masquerade. She chose to insinuate her suspicions in these hints, rather than give an explicit detail of the young man's dis-honourable contrivance, which might have kindled the resentment of the family to some dangerous pitch of animosity and revenge.

Our adventurer, finding himself baffled in his expectation of seeing her, inquired for the old gentleman, with whom he thought he had influence enough to make his apology good, in case he should find him prepossessed by the young lady's information. But here too he was disappointed; the uncle had gone to dine in the country, and his wife was indisposed; so that he had no pretext for staying in the house, till the return of his charmer. Being, however, fruitful of expedients, he dismissed his chariot, and took possession of a room in a tavern, the windows of which fronted the merchant's gate; and there he proposed to watch until he should see her approach. This scheme he put in practice with indefatigable patience, though it was not attended with the expected success.

Emilia, whose caution was equally vigilant and commendable, foreseeing that she might be exposed to the fertility of his invention, came home by a private passage, and entered by a postern, which was altogether unknown to her admirer; and her uncle did not arrive, until it was so late, that he could not with any decency demand a conference.

Next morning, he did not fail to present himself at the door, and his mistress being denied by her own express direction, insisted upon seeing the master of the house, who received him with such coldness of civility, as plainly gave him to understand, that he was acquainted with the displeasure of his niece. He therefore, with an air of candour, told the citizen, he could easily perceive, by his behaviour, that he was the confidant of Miss Emily, of whom he was come to ask pardon for the offence he had given; and did not doubt, if he could be admitted to her presence, that he should be able to convince her, that he had not erred intentionally, or at least propose such reparation, as would effectually atone for his fault.

To this remonstrance the merchant, without any ceremony or

circumlocution, answered, that though he was ignorant of the nature of his offence, he was very certain, that it must have been something very flagrant, that could irritate his niece to such a degree, against a person for whom she had formerly a most particular regard. He owned, she had declared her intention to renounce his acquaintance for ever, and, doubtless, she had good reason for so doing; neither would he undertake to promote an accommodation, unless he would give him full power to treat on the score of matrimony, which he supposed would be the only means of evincing his own sincerity, and obtaining Emilia's forgiveness.

Peregrine's pride was kindled by this blunt declaration, which he could not help considering as the result of a scheme concerted betwixt the young lady and her uncle, in order to take the advantage of his heat. He therefore replied, with manifest signs of disgust, that he did not apprehend there was any occasion for a mediator to reconcile the difference betwixt Emilia and him; and that all he desired, was an opportunity of pleading in his own behalf.

The citizen frankly told him, that as his niece had expressed an earnest desire of avoiding his company, he would not put the least constraint upon her inclination; and in the mean time gave him to know, that he was particularly engaged.

Our hero glowing with indignation at this supercilious treatment; 'I was in the wrong (said he) to look for good manners, so far on this side of Temple-bar: but, you must give me leave to tell you, Sir, that unless I am favoured with an interview with Miss Gauntlet, I shall conclude, that you have actually laid a constraint upon her inclination, for some sinister purposes of your own.' 'Sir, (replied the old gentleman) you are welcome to make what conclusions shall seem good unto your own imagination; but, pray be so good as to allow me the privilege of being master in my own house.' So saying, he very complaisantly shewed him to the door; and our lover, being diffident of his own temper, as well as afraid of being used with greater indignity, in a place where his personal prowess would only serve to heighten his disgrace, quitted the house in a transport of rage which he could not wholly suppress, telling the landlord, that if his age did not protect him, he would have chastised him for his insolent behaviour.

CHAPTER LXXXIV

He projects a violent Scheme, in consequence of which
he is involved in a most fatiguing Adventure,
which greatly tends towards the Augmentation of his Chagrin

THUS debarred of personal communication with his mistress, he essayed to retrieve her good graces by the most submissive and pathetic letters, which he conveyed by divers artifices to her perusal; but reaping no manner of benefit from these endeavours, his passion acquired a degree of impatience, little inferior to downright frenzy; and he determined to run every risk of life, fortune, and reputation, rather than desist from his unjustifiable pursuit. Indeed his resentment was now as deeply concerned as his love, and each of these passions equally turbulent and loud in demanding gratification. He kept centinels continually in pay, to give him notice of her outgoings, in expectation of finding some opportunity to carry her off; but her circumspection entirely frustrated this design; for she suspected every thing of that sort from a disposition like his, and regulated her motions accordingly.

Baffled by her prudence and penetration, he altered his plan, and, on pretence of being called to his country-house by some affair of importance, he departed from London, and taking lodgings at a farmer's house, that stood near the road through which she must have necessarily passed, in her return to her mother, concealed himself from all intercourse, except with his valet de chambre and Pipes, who had orders to scour the country, and reconnoitre every horse, coach, or carriage, that should appear on that high way, with a view of intercepting his Amanda in her passage.

He had waited in this ambuscade a whole week, when his valet gave him notice, that he and his fellow-scout had discovered a chaise and six, driving at full speed towards them; upon which, they had flapped their hats over their eyes, so as that they might not be known, in case they should be seen, and concealed themselves behind a hedge, from whence they could perceive in the carriage, as it passed, a young man plainly dressed, with a lady in a mask, of the exact size, shape, and air of Emilia; and that Pipes followed them at a distance, while he rode back to communicate this piece of intelligence.

Peregrine would scarce allow him time to conclude his information; he ran down to the stable, where his horse was kept ready saddled for the purpose, and never doubting that the lady in question was his mistress, attended by one of her uncle's clerks, mounted immediately, and rode full gallop after the chaise, which (when he had proceeded about two miles) he understood from Pipes, had put up at a neighbouring inn. Though his inclination prompted him to enter her apartment without farther delay, he suffered himself to be dissuaded from taking such a precipitate step, by his privy counsellor, who observed, that it would be impracticable to execute his purpose of conveying her against her will from a public inn, that stood in the midst of a populous village, which would infallibly rise in her defence; and advised him to lie in wait for the chaise, in some remote and private part of the road, where they might accomplish their aim without difficulty or danger. In consequence of this admonition, our adventurer ordered Pipes to reconnoitre the inn, that she might not escape another way, while he and the valet, in order to avoid being seen, took a circuit by an unfrequented path, and placed themselves in ambush, on a spot which they chose for the scene of their atchievement. Here they tarried a full hour, without seeing the carriage, or hearing from their centinel; so that the youth, unable to exert his patience one moment longer, left the foreigner in his station, and rode back to his faithful lacquey, who assured him, that the travellers had not yet hove up their anchor, or proceeded on their voyage.

Notwithstanding this intimation, Pickle began to entertain such alarming suspicions, that he could not refrain from advancing to the gate, and inquiring for the company which had lately arrived in a chaise and six. The inn-keeper, who was not at all pleased with the behaviour of those passengers, did not think proper to observe the instructions he had received; on the contrary, he plainly told him, that the chaise did not halt, but only entered at one door, and went out at the other, with a view to deceive those who pursued it, as he guessed from the words of the gentleman, who had earnestly desired, that his route might be concealed from any person who should inquire about their motions. 'As for my own peart, measter, (continued this charitable publican) I believes as how they are no better than they should be, else they wouldn't be in such a deadly fear of being overtaken. Methinks, (said I) when I saw them in such a woundy pother to be gone, oddsheartikins! this must be some Lundon prentice running away with his measter's daughter, as sure as I'm a living soul. But, be he who will, sartain it is, a has nothing

414

of the gentleman about en; for, thof a axed such a favour, a never once put hand in pocket, or said, "Dog, will you drink?" Howsomever, that don't argufy in reverence of his being in a hurry; and a man may be sometimes a little too judgmatical in his conjunctures.' In all probability, this loquacious landlord would have served the travellers effectually, had Peregrine heard him to an end; but this impetuous youth, far from listening to the sequel of his observations, interrupted him in the beginning of his career, by asking eagerly, which road they followed; and having received the inn-keeper's directions, clapp'd spurs to his horse, commanding Pipes to make the valet acquainted with his course, that they might attend him with all imaginable dispatch.

By the publican's account of their conduct, his former opinion was fully confirmed; he plied his steed to the height of his mettle, and so much was his imagination ingrossed by the prospect of having Emilia in his power, that he did not perceive the road on which he travelled, was quite different from that which led to the habitation of Mrs. Gauntlet. The valet de chambre was an utter stranger to that part of the country; and as for Mr. Pipes, such considerations were altogether foreign to the œconomy of his reflection.

Ten long miles had our hero rode, when his eyes were blessed with the sight of the chaise ascending an hill, at the distance of a good league; upon which, he doubled his diligence in such a manner, that he gained upon the carriage every minute, and at length approached so near to it, that he could discern the lady and her conductor, with their heads thrust out at the windows, looking back, and speaking to the driver alternately, as if they earnestly besought him to augment the speed of his cattle.

Being thus, as it were, in sight of port, while he crossed the road, his horse happened to plunge into a cart-rut, with such violence, that he was thrown several yards over his head; and the beast's shoulder being slipt by the fall, he found himself disabled from plucking the fruit, which was almost within his reach; for he had left his servants at a considerable distance behind him; and although they had been at his back, and supplied him with another horse, they were so indifferently mounted, that he could not reasonably expect to overtake the flyers, who profited so much by this disaster, that the chaise vanished in a moment.

It may be easily conceived, how a young man of his disposition passed his time, in this tantalizing situation. He ejaculated with great fervency, but his prayers were not the effects of resignation. He ran back on foot with incredible speed, in order to meet his valet, whom he unhorsed in a twinkling; and taking his seat, began to exercise his whip and spurs, after having ordered the Swiss to follow him on the other gelding, and commit the lame hunter to the care of Pipes.

Matters being adjusted in this manner, our adventurer prosecuted the race with all his might; and having made some progress, was informed by a countryman, that the chaise had struck off into another road, and, according to his judgment, was by that time about three miles ahead; though, in all probability, the horses would not be able to hold out much longer, because they seemed to be quite spent when they passed his door. Encouraged by this intimation, Peregrine pushed on with great alacrity; though he could not regain sight of the desired object, till the clouds of night began to deepen, and even then he enjoyed nothing more than a transient glimpse; for the carriage was no sooner seen, than shrouded again from his view. These vexatious circumstances animated his endeavours, while they irritated his chagrin; and in short, he continued his pursuit till the night was far advanced, and himself so uncertain about the object of his care, that he entered a solitary inn, with a view of obtaining some intelligence, and to his infinite joy, perceived the chaise standing by itself, and the horses panting in the yard. In full confidence of his having arrived at last at the goal of all his wishes, he alighted instantaneously, and running up to the coachman, with a pistol in his hand, commanded him, in an imperious tone, to conduct him to the lady's chamber, on pain of death. The driver, affrighted at this menacing address, protested with great humility, that he did not know whither his fare had retired; for that he himself was paid and dismissed from this service, because he would not undertake to drive them all night cross the country, without stopping to refresh his horses: but he promised to go in quest of the waiter, who would shew him to their apartment. He was accordingly detached on that errand, while our hero stood centinel at the gate, till the arrival of his valet de chambre, who joining him by accident, before the coachman returned, relieved him in his watch; and then the young gentleman, exasperated at his messenger's delay, rushed with fury in his eyes from room to room, denouncing vengeance upon the whole family; but he did not meet with one living soul, until he entered the garret, where he found the landlord and his wife in bed. This chicken-hearted couple, by the light of a rush-candle that burned on the hearth, seeing a stranger burst into the chamber, in such a terrible attitude, were seized with consternation; and exalting their voices, in a most lamentable strain, begg'd for the passion of Christ, that he would spare their lives, and take all they had.

Peregrine, guessing from this exclamation, and the circumstance of their being abed, that they mistook him for a robber, and were ignorant of that which he wanted to know, dispelled their terror, by making them acquainted with the cause of his visit, and desired the husband to get up with all possible dispatch, in order to assist and attend him in his search.

Thus reinforced, he rummaged every corner of the inn, and at last finding the ostler in the stable, was by him informed, (to his unspeakable mortification) that the gentleman and lady who arrived in the chaise, had immediately hired post-horses for a certain village at the distance of fifteen miles, and departed without halting for the least refreshment. Our adventurer, mad with his disappointment, mounted his horse in an instant, and, with his attendant, took the same road, with full determination to die, rather than desist from the prosecution of his design. He had, by this time, rode upwards of thirty miles since three o'clock in the afternoon; so that the horses were almost quite jaded, and travelled this stage so slowly, that it was morning before they reached the place of their destination, where, far from finding the fugitives, he understood, that no such persons as he described had passed that way, and that, in all likelihood, they had taken a quite contrary direction, while, in order to mislead him in his pursuit, they had amused the ostler with a false route. This conjecture was strengthened, by his perceiving (now for the first time) that he had deviated a considerable way from the road, through which they must have journeyed, in order to arrive at the place of her mother's residence; and these suggestions utterly deprived him of the small remains of recollection, which he had hitherto retained. His eyes rolled about, witnessing rage and distraction; he foamed at the mouth, stamped upon the ground with great violence, uttered incoherent imprecations against himself and all mankind, and would have sallied forth again he knew not whither, upon the same horse, which he had already almost killed with fatigue, had not his confidant found means to quiet the tumult of his thoughts, and recal his reflection, by representing the condition of the poor animals, and advising him to hire fresh horses, and ride post across the country, to the village in the neighbourhood of Mrs. Gauntlet's habitation, where they should infallibly intercept the daughter, provided they could get the start of her upon the road.

Peregrine not only relished, but forthwith acted in conformity with this good counsel. His own horses were committed to the charge of the landlord, with directions for Pipes, in case he should come thither in quest of his master; and a couple of stout geldings being prepared, he and his valet took the road again, steering their course according to the motions of the post-boy, who undertook to be their guide. They had almost finished the first stage, when they descried a post-chaise just halting at the inn where they proposed to change horses; upon which, our adventurer, glowing with a most interesting presage, put his beast to the full speed, and approached near enough to distinguish, (as the travellers quitted the carriage) that he had at last come up with the very individual persons whom he had pursued so long.

Flushed with the discovery, he galloped into the yard so suddenly, that the lady and her conductor scarce had time to shut themselves up in a chamber, to which they retreated with great precipitation; so that the pursuer was now certain of having housed his prey. That he might, however, leave nothing to fortune, he placed himself upon the stair, by which they had ascended to the apartment, and sent up his compliments to the young lady, desiring the favour of being admitted to her presence, otherwise he should be obliged to wave all ceremony, and take that liberty which she would not give. The servant having conveyed this message through the keyhole, returned with an answer, importing, that she would adhere to the resolution she had taken, and perish rather than comply with his will. Our adventurer, without staying to make any rejoinder to this reply, ran up stairs, and thundering at the door for entrance, was given to understand by the nymph's attendant, that a blunderbuss was ready primed for his reception, and that he would do well to spare him the necessity of shedding blood, in defence of a person who had put herself under his protection. 'All the laws of the land (said he) cannot now untie the knots by which we are bound together; and therefore I will guard her as my own property; so that you had better desist from your fruitless attempt, and thereby consult your own safety: for, by the God that made me! I will discharge my piece upon you, as soon as you set your nose within the door; and your blood be upon your own head.' These menaces from a citizen's clerk, would have been sufficient motives for Pickle to storm the breach, although they had not been reinforced by that declaration, which informed him of Emilia's having bestowed herself in marriage upon such a contemptible rival. This sole consideration added wings to his impetuosity, and he applied his foot to the door with such irresistible force, as bursted it open in an instant, entering at the same time with a pistol ready cock'd in his hand. His antagonist, instead of firing his blunderbuss, when he saw him approach, started back, with evident signs of surprize and consternation, exclaiming, 'Lord Jesus! Sir, you are not the man! and, without doubt, are under some mistake with regard to us.'

Before Peregrine had time to answer this salutation, the lady hearing it, advanced to him, and pulling off a mask, discovered a face which he had never seen before. The Gorgon's head, according to the fables of antiquity, never had a more instantaneous or petrifying effect, than that which this countenance produced upon the astonished youth. His eyes were fixed upon this unknown object, as if they had been attracted by the power of inchantment, his feet seemed rivetted to the ground, and after having stood motionless for the space of a few minutes, he dropped down in an apoplexy of disappointment and despair. The Swiss, who had followed him, seeing his master in this condition, lifted him up, and laying him upon a bed in the next room, let him blood immediately, without hesitation, being always provided with a case of lancets, against all accidents on the road. To this foresight our hero, in all probability, was indebted for his life. By virtue of a very copious evacuation, he recovered the use of his senses; but the complication of fatigues, and violent transports which he had undergone, brewed up a dangerous fever in his blood; and a physician being called from the next market-town, several days elapsed before he would answer for his life.

CHAPTER LXXXV

Peregrine sends a Message to Mrs. Gauntlet,
who rejects his Proposal. He repairs to the Garison

AT length, however, his constitution overcame his disease, though not before it had in a great measure tamed the fury of his disposition, and brought him to a serious consideration of his conduct. In this humiliation of his spirits, he reflected with shame and remorse upon his treachery to the fair, the innocent Emilia; he remembered his former sentiments in her favour, as well as the injunctions of his dying uncle; he recollected his intimacy with her brother, against which he had so basely sinned; and revolving all the circumstances of her conduct, found it so commendable, spirited, and noble, that he deemed her an object of sufficient dignity to merit his honourable addresses, even though his duty had not been concerned in the decision: but, obligated as he was, to make reparation to a worthy family, which he had so grosly injured, he thought he could not manifest his reformation too soon; and, whenever he found himself able to hold the pen, wrote a letter to Mrs. Gauntlet, wherein he acknowledged, with many expressions of sorrow and contrition, that he had acted a part altogether unbecoming a man of honour, and should never enjoy the least tranquillity of mind, until he should have merited her forgiveness. He protested, that although his happiness intirely depended upon the determination of Emilia, he would even renounce all hope of being blessed with her favour, if she could point out any other method of making reparation to that amiable young lady, but by laying his heart and fortune at her feet, and submitting himself to her pleasure during the remaining part of his life. He conjured her, therefore, in the most pathetic manner, to pardon him, in consideration of his sincere repentance, and use her maternal influence with her daughter, so as that he might be permitted to wait upon her with a wedding-ring, as soon as his health would allow him to undertake the journey.

This explanation being dispatched by Pipes, who had, by this time, found his master, the young gentleman inquired about the couple whom he had so unfortunately pursued, and understood from his valet de chambre, who learn'd the story from their own mouths, that the lady was the only daughter of a rich Jew, and her attendant no other than his apprentice, who had converted her to christianity, and married her at the same time; that this secret having taken air, the old Israelite had contrived a scheme to separate them for ever; and they being apprized of his intention, had found means to elope from his house, with a view of sheltering themselves in France, until the affair could be made up: that seeing three men ride after them with such eagerness and speed, they never doubted that the pursuers were her father, accompanied by some friends or domestics, and on that supposition had fled with the utmost dispatch and trepidation, until they had found themselves happily undeceived, at that very instant, when they expected nothing but mischief and misfortune: and lastly, the Swiss gave him to understand, that after having professed some concern for his deplorable situation, and enjoyed a slight refreshment, they had taken their departure for Dover, and, in all likelihood, were safely arrived at Paris.

Chapter LXXXV

In four and twenty hours after Pipes was charged with his commission, he brought back an answer from the mother of Emilia, couched in these words.

'SIR,

I received the favour of yours, and am glad, for your own sake, that you have attained a due sense and conviction of your unkind and unchristian behaviour to poor Emy. I thank God, none of my children were ever so insulted before. Give me leave to tell you, Sir, my daughter was no upstart, without friends or education, but a young lady as well bred, and better born, than most private gentlewomen in the kingdom: and therefore, though you had no esteem for her person, you ought to have paid some regard to her family, which (no disparagement to you, Sir) is more honourable than your own. As for your proposal, Miss Gauntlet will not hear of it, being, that she thinks her honour will not allow her to listen to any terms of reconciliation; and she is not yet so destitute, as to embrace an offer to which she has the least objection. In the mean time, she is so much indisposed, that she cannot possibly see company; so I beg you will not take the trouble of making a fruitless journey to this place. Perhaps your future conduct may deserve her forgiveness; and really, as I am concerned for your happiness, which (you assure me) depends upon her condescension, I wish with all my heart it may; and am (notwithstanding all that has happened)

Your sincere well-wisher,
CECILIA GAUNTLET'

From this epistle, and the information of his messenger, our hero learn'd, that his mistress had actually profited by his wild-goose-chace, so as to make a safe retreat to her mother's house; and, though sorry to hear of her indisposition, he was also piqued at her implacability, as well as at some stately paragraphs of the letter, in which (he thought) the good lady had consulted her own vanity rather than her good sense. These motives of resentment helped him to bear his disappointment like a philosopher, especially as he had now quieted his conscience, in proffering to redress the injury he had done; and, moreover, found himself, with regard to his love, in a calm state of hope and resignation.

A seasonable fit of illness is an excellent medicine for the turbulence of passion. Such a reformation had the fever produced in the œconomy of his thoughts, that he moralized like an apostle, and projected several prudential schemes for his future conduct.

In the mean time, as soon as his health was sufficiently re-established, he took a trip to the garison, in order to visit his friends; and learn'd from Hatchway's own mouth, that he had broke the ice of courtship to his aunt, and that his addresses were now fairly afloat; though when he first declared himself to the widow, after she had been duly prepared for the occasion, by her niece and the rest of her friends, she had received his proposal with a becoming reserve, and piously wept at the remembrance of her husband, observing, that she should never meet with his fellow.

Peregrine promoted the lieutenant's suit with all his influence; and all Mrs. Trunnion's objections to the match being surmounted, it was determined, that the day of marriage should be put off for three months, that her reputation might not suffer by a precipitate engagement. His next care was to give orders for erecting a plain marble monument to the memory of his uncle, on which the follow-ing inscription, composed by the bridegroom, actually appeared in golden letters.

Here lies,
Foundered in a fathom and an half,
The Shell
Of

Hawser Trunnion, Esq;

Formerly commander of a squadron
In his Majesty's service,
Who broach'd to, at five P.M. Octr. X.
In the year of his age
Threescore and nineteen.

He kept his guns always loaded,
And his tackle ready manned,
And never shewed his poop to the enemy,
Except when he took her in tow;
But, his shot being expended,
His match burnt out,
And his upper works decayed,
He was sunk
By death's superior weight of metal.

Chapter LXXXV

Nevertheless,
He will be weighed again
At the Great Day,
His rigging refitted,
And his timbers repaired,
And, with one broad-side,
Make his adversary
Strike in his turn.

CHAPTER LXXXVI

He returns to London, and meets with Cadwallader,
who entertains him with a curious Dialogue

THE young gentleman having performed these last offices, in honour of his deceased benefactor, and presented Mr. Jolter to the long-expected living, which at this time happened to be vacant, returned to London, and resumed his former gaiety: not that he was able to shake Emilia from his thoughts, or even to remember her without violent emotions; for, as he recovered his vigour, his former impatience recurred, and therefore he resolved to plunge himself headlong into some intrigue, that might engage his passions, and amuse his imagination.

A man of his accomplishments could not fail to meet with a variety of subjects, on which his gallantry would have been properly exercised; and this abundance distracted his choice, which at any time was apt to be influenced by caprice and whim. I have already observed, that he had lifted his view, through a matrimonial perspective, as high as a lady of the first quality and distinction; and now, that he was refused by Miss Gauntlet, and enjoyed a little respite from the agonies of that flame which her charms had kindled in his heart, he renewed his assiduities to her grace; and, though he durst not yet risk an explanation, enjoyed the pleasure of seeing himself so well received in quality of a particular acquaintance, that he flattered himself with the belief of his having made some progress in her heart; and was confirmed in this conceited notion, by the assurances of her woman, whom, by liberal largesses, he retained in his interest, because she found means to persuade him, that she was in the confidence of her lady. But, notwithstanding this encouragement, and the sanguine suggestions of his own

423

vanity, he dreaded the thoughts of exposing himself to her ridicule and resentment, by a premature declaration, and determined to postpone his addresses, until he should be more certified of the probability of succeeding in his attempt.

While he remained in this hesitation and suspence, he was one morning very agreeably surprized with the appearance of his friend Crabtree, who, by the permission of Pipes, to whom he was well known, entered his chamber before he was awake, and, by a violent shake of the shoulder, disengaged him from the arms of sleep. The first compliments having mutually passed, Cadwallader gave him to understand, that he had arrived in town over-night in the stage-coach from Bath, and entertained him with such a ludicrous account of his fellow-travellers, that Peregrine, for the first time since their parting, indulged himself in mirth, even to the hazard of suffocation.[1]

This relation was confined to a curious dialogue that passed betwixt a woollen-draper and his wife, who were his only companions during the best part of the journey. The lady laboured under a Diabetes, in consequence of having used the waters injudiciously for another complaint; and, that she might not be an impediment to the carriage, by ordering it to halt, as often as she should have occasion to disembogue, she had provided herself with a leathern convenience, which her husband carried in the pocket of his great coat, conveying it privately to her, when she found herself necessitated to use it; and afterwards, taking the opportunity to empty it out at the window, when the Misanthrope's head chanced to be turned another way.

As this couple embarked with Crabtree, in the full persuasion of his being utterly bereft of the sense of hearing, they kept no sort of reserve in their conversation; and at last fairly quarrelled, on account of the good man's want of alertness, in handing the commodity, when his help-mate's occasions were so extremely pressing, that her flood-gates gave way, before she was prepared for the irruption. Smarting with this disagreeable circumstance, 'Odds plague! you nincompoop, (cried she) you have fumbled so long about the pot, that I have drenched myself all over. I wish to God you had received the stream in your mouth.' 'I thank you for your good-will, my dear, (answered the patient husband) you would promote me to the honour of being a pissing-post.' 'I'm sure, (retorted his yoke-fellow, snatching the utensil from his hand) you are fit for no other post; and, accordingly, suffer yourself to be piss'd upon by every body. Witness your pitiful behaviour at the

E. O. table,[1] when that officer bullied you out of twenty guineas, which you wan't obliged to pay.' 'There you happen to be wide of the matter, (said the draper) the whole company gave it against me, as a fair bett; besides, the captain threatened to cut my throat, and I did not choose to give him that trouble.' 'Cut your throat! (exclaimed the virago) I would a durst; you had a good action against him for putting you in fear of your life. But you are a poor tool, good for nothing but squandering away my money. If you had possessed spirit enough to follow my advice, you might have been a deputy of the ward, by this time. But, all your care is to sit among your companions of the garden, and sing bunting-songs, till you get drunk, leaving your trade at sixes and sevens, and your family to go to the dogs.'

The husband (pacific as he was) being nettled at these insinuations, frankly told her, that his affairs had never prospered, since she had persuaded him to swear a book-debt against a gentleman's executor, after he had been paid by the deceased. Upon which, her eyes lightened with fury, and she called him a mean-spirited sorry fellow, for upbraiding her, a weak woman, with what she had done for his own good. 'Sirrah, (said she) I suppose you would be base enough to turn evidence against me, if you thought you could get any thing by the information, though that was the only thing you ever did for your poor family. Who is to provide for my children, if their father don't?' 'And I wish from my heart their father would provide for them,' (said the husband, irritated by the epithets she had uttered.) 'An't you their father, Mr. Wiseacre, (cried the aggressor:) Ha'n't I brought you five as fine babes as any in the parish?' 'Yes, yes, (replied the other) you have brought me several very fine children, that must be allowed; but, whether or not they are of my begetting, is a question that I am not quite so clear about.' 'How, fellor! (replied the wife) do you doubt my vartue?' 'No, not I, (answered the shopkeeper) I have no doubts about the matter. It is a long time since surgeon C—— assured me, that he would suckle upon his thumb all the children I should ever beget; and I have other convincing reasons to support his opinion.'

These last words had scarce proceeded from his mouth, when his sweet-blooded spouse, leaving her duty and obedience on the left hand, and forgetting that she was subject to the eye of any unconcerned spectator, lifted up the machine she had just replenished, and made such application with it to the forehead of her husband, as pressed the two sides of it together, by which means, the contents were squirted out in a full stream, that played upon the visage of the astonished Misanthrope; and, not satisfied with the vengeance she had taken, she quitted her weapon, and assaulted him with tooth and nail, exclaiming all the time, 'Ah! you pitiful cuckoldy scrub, have you the impudence to own to my face, that you married a woman of my character, when you knew your own infirmities? You had a base design upon my fortune, you slave, although you was sensible that you could never deserve it. But, I'll be revenged of you, if there be a man to be had for love or money.'

Thus, far from attempting to clear herself from the imputation implied in her husband's words, she construed his declaration into an acknowledgment of the ill usage she had suffered; and while she trumpeted her own wrongs, with great vociferation, exercised her claws with such rancour and agility, that the poor draper was fain to roar aloud for assistance; and as Cadwallader had no inclination to interpose, he would, in all probability, have met with the fate of Orpheus, had not his cries reached the ears of the coachman, who descended from his box, and partly by threats, and partly by intreaties, put an end to her operations.

CHAPTER LXXXVII

Crabtree sounds the Duchess, and undeceives Pickle,
who, by an extraordinary Accident, becomes
acquainted with another Lady of Quality

CRABTREE having rehearsed this adventure, in such a peculiarity of manner, as added infinite ridicule to every circumstance, and repeated every scandalous report which had circulated at the Bath, after Peregrine's departure, was informed by the youth, that he harboured a design upon the person of such a duchess, and in all appearance had no reason to complain of his reception; but, that he would not venture to declare himself, until he should be more ascertained of her sentiments: and therefore, he begg'd leave to depend upon the intelligence of his friend Cadwallader, who, he knew, was admitted to her parties.

The Misanthrope, before he would promise his assistance, asked if his prospect verged towards matrimony? and our adventurer (who guessed the meaning of his question) replying in the negative, he undertook the office of reconnoitring her inclination, protesting at the same time, that he would never concern himself in any scheme, that did not tend to the disgrace and deception of all the sex. On these conditions, he espoused the interest of our hero, and a plan was immediately concerted, in consequence of which they met by accident at her grace's table; and Pickle having stayed all the fore-part of the evening, and sat out all the company, except the Misanthrope and a certain widow-lady, who was said to be in the secrets of my lady duchess, went away, on pretence of an indispensible engagement, that Crabtree might have a proper opportunity of making him the subject of conversation.

Accordingly, he had scarce quitted the apartment, when this Cynic attending him to the door, with a look of morose disdain, 'Were I an absolute prince, (said he) and that fellow one of my subjects, I would order him to be cloath'd in sack-cloth, and he should drive my asses to water, that his lofty spirit might be lowered to the level of his deserts. The pride of a peacock is downright self-denial, when compared with the vanity of that coxcomb, which was naturally arrogant, but is now rendered altogether intolerable, by the reputation he acquired at Bath, for kicking a bully, outwitting a club of raw sharpers, and divers other pranks, in the execution of which he was more lucky than wise. But nothing has contributed so much to the increase of his insolence and self-conceit, as the favour he found among the ladies. Ay, the ladies, Madam, I care not who knows it: the ladies, who (to their honour be it spoken) never fail to patronize foppery and folly, provided they solicit their encouragement. And yet, this dog was not on the footing of those hermaphroditical animals, who may be reckoned among the number of waiting-women, who air your shifts, comb your lap-dogs, examine your noses with magnifying glasses, in order to squeeze out the worms, clean your teeth-brushes, sweeten your handkerchiefs, and soften waste paper for your occasions. This fellow Pickle was entertained for more important purposes; his turn of duty never came till all those lapwings were gone to roost; then he scaled windows, leaped over garden-walls, and was let in by Mrs. Betty, in the dark. Nay, the magistrates of Bath complimented him with the freedom of the corporation, merely because, through his means, the waters had gained extraordinary credit; for every female of a tolerable appearance, that went thither on account of her sterility, got the better of her complaint, during his residence at the Bath: and now, the fellow thinks no woman can withstand his addresses. He had not been here three minutes, when I could perceive with half an eye, that he had marked out your grace for a conquest; I mean in an honourable way; though the rascal has impudence enough to attempt any thing.' So saying, he fixed his eyes upon the duchess, who (while her face glowed with indignation) turning to her confidant, expressed herself in these words. 'Upon my life! I believe there is actually some truth in what this old ruffian says; I have myself observed that young fellow eying me with a very particular stare.' 'It is not to be at all wondered at, (said her friend) that a youth of his complexion should be sensible to the charms of your grace; but I dare say, he would not presume to entertain any, but the most honourable and respectful sentiments.' 'Respectful sentiments! (cried my lady, with a look of ineffable disdain) if I thought the fellow had assurance enough to think of me in any shape, I protest I would forbid him my house. Upon my honour, such instances of audacity should induce persons of quality to keep your small gentry at a greater distance; for they are very apt to grow impudent, upon the least countenance or encouragement.'

Cadwallader, satisfied with this declaration, changed the subject of discourse, and next day communicated his discovery to his friend Pickle, who, upon this occasion, felt the most stinging sensations of mortifying pride, and resolved to quit his prospect with a good grace. Nor did the execution of this self-denying scheme cost him one moment's uneasiness; for his heart had never been interested in the pursuit, and his vanity triumphed in the thoughts of manifesting his indifference. Accordingly, the very next time he visited her grace, his behaviour was remarkably frank, sprightly, and disengaged; and the subject of love being artfully introduced by the widow, who had been directed to sound his inclinations, he rallied the passion with great ease and severity, and made no scruple of declaring himself heart-whole.

Though the duchess had resented his supposed affection, she was now offended at his insensibility, and even signified her disgust, by observing, that perhaps his attention to his own qualifications screened him from the impression of all other objects.

While he enjoyed this sarcasm, the meaning of which he could plainly discern, the company was joined by a certain virtuoso, who had gained free access to all the great families of the land, by his notable talent of gossipping and buffoonery. He was now in the seventy-fifth year of his age; his birth was so obscure, that he scarce knew his father's name, his education suitable to the dignity of his descent, his character publickly branded with homicide, profligacy, and breach of trust; yet this man, by the happy inheritance of impregnable effrontery, and a lucky prostitution of all principle, in rendering himself subservient to the appetites of the great, had attained to an independency of fortune, as well as to such a particular share of favour among the quality, that although he was well known to have pimped for three generations of the nobility, there was not a lady of fashion in the kingdom, who scrupled to admit him to her toilette, or even to be squired by him, in any public place of entertainment. Not but that this sage was occasionally useful to his fellow-creatures, by these connexions with people of fortune; for, he often undertook to solicite charity in behalf of distressed objects, with a view of embezzling one half of the benefactions. It was an errand of this kind that now brought him to the house of her grace.

After having sat a few minutes, he told the company, that he would favour them with a very proper opportunity to extend their benevolence, for the relief of a poor gentlewoman, who was reduced to the most abject misery, by the death of her husband, and just delivered of a couple of fine boys. They, moreover, understood from his information, that this object was daughter of a good family, who had renounced her, in consequence of her marrying an ensign without a fortune; and even obstructed his promotion with all their influence and power; a circumstance of barbarity, which had made such an impression upon his mind, as disordered his brain, and drove him to despair, in a fit of which he had made away with himself, leaving his wife then big with child, to all the horrors of indigence and grief.

Various were the criticisms on this pathetic picture, which the old man drew with great expression. My lady duchess concluded, that she must be a creature void of all feeling and reflection, who could survive such aggravated misery; therefore, did not deserve to be relieved, except in the character of a common beggar; and was generous enough to offer a recommendation, by which she would be admitted into an infirmary, to which her grace was a subscriber; at the same time, advising the sollicitor to send the twins to the Foundling-hospital, where they would be carefully nursed and brought up, so as to become useful members of the commonwealth. Another lady, with all due deference to the opinion of the duchess, was free enough to blame the generosity of her grace, which would only serve to encourage children in their disobedience to their parents, and might be the means not only of prolonging the distress of the wretched creature, but also of ruining the constitution of some young heir, perhaps the hope of a great family; for, she did suppose that madam, when her month should be up, and her brats disposed of, would spread her attractions to the public, (provided she could profit by her person) and, in the usual way, make a regular progress from St. James's to Drury-lane. She apprehended, for these reasons, that their compassion would be most effectually shewn, in leaving her to perish in her present necessity; and that the old gentleman would be unpardonable, should he persist in his endeavours to relieve her. A third member of this tender-hearted society, after having asked if the young woman was handsome? and been answered in the negative, allowed, that there was a great deal of reason in what had been said by the honourable person who had spoke last; nevertheless, she humbly conceived, her sentence would admit of some mitigation. 'Let the bantlings (said she) be sent to the hospital, according to the advice of her grace, and a small collection be made for the present support of the mother; and when her health is recovered, I will take her into my family, in quality of an upper-servant, or medium between me and my woman; for, upon my life! I can't endure to chide, or give directions to a creature, who is, in point of birth and education, but one degree above the vulgar.'

This proposal met with universal approbation. The duchess (to her immortal honour) began the contribution with a crown; so that the rest of the company were obliged to restrict their liberality to half the sum, that her grace might not be affronted; and the proposer demanding the poor woman's name and place of abode, the old mediator could not help giving her ladyship a verbal direction, though he was extremely mortified (on more accounts than one) to find such an issue to his solicitation.

Peregrine, who, *though humorous as winter, had a tear for pity, and an hand open as day, for melting charity,*[1] was shocked at the nature and result of this ungenerous consultation. He contributed his half-crown, however; and retiring from the company, betook himself to the lodgings of the forlorn lady in the straw, according to the direction he had heard. Upon inquiry, he understood, that she was then visited by some charitable gentlewoman, who had sent for a nurse, and waited the return of the messenger; and he sent up his respects, desiring he might be permitted to see her, on pretence of having been intimate with her late husband.

Though the poor woman had never heard of his name, she did not think proper to deny his request; and he was conducted to a paultry chamber in the third story, where he found this unhappy widow sitting up in a truckle-bed, and suckling one of her infants, with the most piteous expression of anguish in her features, which were naturally regular and sweet, while the other was fondled on the knee of a person, whose attention was so much ingrossed by her little charge, that for the present she could mind nothing else: and it was not till after the first compliments passed betwixt the hapless mother and our adventurer, that he perceived the stranger's countenance, which inspired him with the highest esteem and admiration. He beheld all the graces of elegance and beauty, breathing sentiment and beneficence, and softened into the most inchanting tenderness of weeping sympathy: and when he declared the cause of his visit, which was no other than the desire of befriending the distressed lady, to whom he presented a bank-note for twenty pounds, he was favoured with such a look of complacency by this amiable phantom, who might have been justly taken for an angel ministering to the necessities of mortals, that his whole soul was transported with love and veneration. Nor was this prepossession diminished by the information of the widow, who, after having manifested her gratitude in a flood of tears, told him, that the unknown object of his esteem was a person of honour, who having heard by accident of her deplorable situation, had immediately obeyed the dictates of her humanity, and come in person to relieve her distress; that she had not only generously supplied her with money for present sustenance, but also undertaken to provide a nurse for her babes, and even promised to favour her with protection, should she survive her present melancholy situation. To these articles of intelligence she added, that the name of her benefactress was the celebrated lady ———,[1] to whose character the youth was no stranger, though he had never seen her person before. The killing edge of her charms was a little blunted by the accidents of time and fortune; but no man of taste and imagination, whose nerves were not quite chilled with the frost of age, could, even at that time, look upon her with impunity: and as Peregrine saw her attractions heightened by the tender office in which she was engaged, he was smitten with her beauty, and so ravished with her compassion, that he could not suppress his emotions, but applauded her benevolence with all the warmth of enthusiasm.

Her ladyship received his compliments with great politeness and affability; and the occasion on which they met being equally interesting to both, an acquaintance commenced between them, and they concerted measures for the benefit of the widow and her two children, one of whom our hero bespoke for his own godson; for Pickle was not so obscure in the beau monde, but that his fame had reached the ears of this lady, who, therefore, did not discourage his advances towards her friendship and esteem.

All the particulars relating to their charge being adjusted, he attended her ladyship to her own house; and, by her conversation, had the pleasure of finding her understanding suitable to her other accomplishments. Nor had she any reason to think, that our hero's qualifications had been exaggerated by common report.

One of their adopted children died before it was baptized; so that their care concentered in the other, for whom they stood sponsors; and understanding that the old agent was become troublesome in his visits to the mother, to whom he now began to administer such counsel as shocked the delicacy of her virtue, they removed her into another lodging, where she would not be exposed to his machinations; and in less than a month, our hero learn'd from a nobleman of his acquaintance, that the hoary pandar had actually engaged to procure for him, this poor afflicted gentlewoman; and being frustrated in his intention, substituted in her room a nymph from the purlieus of Covent-garden, that made his lordship smart severely for the favours she bestowed.

Mean while, Peregrine cultivated his new acquaintance with all his art and assiduity, presuming, from the circumstance of her reputation and fate, as well as on the strength of his own merit, that, in time, he should be able to indulge that passion which had begun to glow within his breast.

As her ladyship had undergone a vast variety of fortune and adventure, which he had heard indistinctly related, with number-less errors and misrepresentations, he was no sooner intitled, by the familiarity of communication, to ask such a favour, than he earnestly intreated her to entertain him with the particulars of her story; and, by dint of importunity, she was at length prevailed upon (in a select partie) to gratify his curiosity in these words.

CHAPTER LXXXVIII

The Memoirs of a Lady of Quality[1]

By the circumstances of the story which I am going to relate, you will be convinced of my candour, while you are informed of my indiscretion; and be enabled, I hope, to perceive, that howsoever my head may have erred, my heart hath always been uncorrupted, and that I have been unhappy, *because I loved, and was a woman.*

I believe I need not observe, that I was the only child of a man of good fortune, who indulged me, in my infancy, with all the tenderness of paternal affection; and when I was six years old, sent me to a private school, where I stayed till my age was doubled, and became such a favourite, that I was (even in those early days) carried to all the places of public diversion, the court itself not excepted; an indulgence that flattered my love of pleasure, to which I was naturally addicted, and encouraged those ideas of vanity and ambition, which spring up so early in the human mind.

I was lively and good-natured, my imagination apt to run riot, my heart liberal and disinterested; though I was so obstinately attached to my own opinions, that I could not well brook contradiction; and in the whole of my disposition, resembled that of Henry the fifth, as described by Shakespear.[1]

In my thirteenth year I went to Bath, where I was first introduced into the world as a woman, having been intitled to that privilege by my person, which was remarkably tall for my years; and there my fancy was quite captivated by the variety of diversions in which I was continually engaged: not that the parties were altogether new to me, but because I now found myself considered as a person of consequence, and surrounded by a croud of admirers, who courted my acquaintance, and fed my vanity with praise and adulation. In short, whether or not I deserved their encomiums, I leave the world to judge; but my person was commended, and my talent in dancing met with universal applause. No wonder then, that every thing appeared joyous to a young creature, who was so void of experience and dissimulation, that she believed every body's heart as sincere as her own, and every object such as it appeared to be.

Among the swains who sighed, or pretended to sigh for me, were two that bore a pretty equal share of my favour; (it was too superficial to deserve the name of love.) One of these was a forward youth of sixteen, extremely handsome, lively, and impudent, who attended in quality of page upon the princess Amelia,[2] who spent that season at the Bath; the other was a Scotch nobleman turned of thirty, who was graced with a red ribbon, and danced particularly well, two qualifications of great weight with a girl of my age, whose heart was not deeply interested in the cause. Nevertheless, the page prevailed over this formidable rival; though our amour went no farther than a little flirting, and ceased intirely when I left the place.

433

Next year, however, I revisited this agreeable scene, and passed my time in the same circle of amusements; in which, indeed, each season at Bath is exactly resembled by that which succeeds, allowing for the difference of company, which is continually varying. There I met with the same incense, and again had my favourite, who was a North Briton, and captain of foot, near forty years of age, and a little lame, an impediment which I did not discover, until it was pointed out by some of my companions, who rallied me upon my choice. He was always chearful, and very amorous, had a good countenance and an excellent understanding, possessed a great deal of art, and would have persuaded me to marry him, had I not been restrained by the authority of my father, whose consent was not to be obtained in favour of a man of his fortune.

At the same time, many proposals of marriage were made to my parents; but, as they came from people whom I did not like, I rejected them all, being determined to refuse every man who did not make his addresses to myself in person, because I had no notion of marrying for any thing but love.

Among these formal proposers was a Scottish earl, whose pretensions were broke off by some difference about settlements; and the son of an English baron, with whom my father was in treaty, when he carried me to town, on a visit to a young lady, with whom I had been intimate from my infancy. She was just delivered of her first son, for whom we stood sponsors; so that this occasion detained us a whole month, during which, I went to a ball at court on the queen's birthday, and there, for the first time, felt what love and beauty were.

The second son of duke ————,[1] who had just returned from his travels, was dancing with the princess royal, when a young lady came and desired me to go and see a stranger, whom all the world admired: upon which, I followed her into the circle, and observed this object of admiration. He was dressed in a coat of white cloth, faced with blue sattin embroidered with silver, of the same piece with his waistcoat; his fine hair hung down his back in ringlets below his waist, and his hat was laced with silver, and garnished with a white feather; but his person beggared all description. He was tall and graceful, neither corpulent nor meagre, his limbs finely proportioned, his countenance open and majestic, his eyes full of sweetness and vivacity, his teeth regular, and his pouting lips of the complexion of the damask rose. In short, he was formed for love, and inspired it wherever he appeared; nor was he a niggard of his talents, but liberally returned it; at least what passed for such: for he had a flow of gallantry, for which many ladies of this land can vouch from their own experience: but he exclaimed against marriage, because he had, as yet, met with no woman, to whose charms he would surrender his liberty, though a princess of France, and a lady of the same rank in ———, were said to be, at that time, enamoured of his person.

I went home, totally ingrossed by his idea, flattering myself, that he had observed me with some attention; for I was young and new, and had the good fortune to attract the notice and approbation of the queen herself.

Next day, being at the opera, I was agreeably surprised with the appearance of this amiable stranger, who no sooner saw me enter, than he approached so near to the place where I sat, that I overheard what he said to his companions; and was so happy as to find myself the subject of his discourse, which abounded with rapturous expressions of love and admiration.

I could not listen to these transports without emotion; my colour changed, my heart throbbed with unusual violence, and mine eyes betrayed my inclinations in sundry favourable glances, which he seemed to interpret aright, though he could not then avail himself of his success, so far as to communicate his sentiments by speech, because we were strangers to each other.

I passed that night in the most anxious suspence, and several days elapsed, before I saw him again. At length, however, being at court on a ball-night, and determined against dancing, I perceived him among the croud, and, to my unspeakable joy, saw him advance with my lord P———,[1] who introduced him to my acquaintance. He soon found means to alter my resolution; and I condescended to be his partner all the evening; during which, he declared his passion in the most tender and persuasive terms that real love could dictate, or fruitful imagination invent.

I believed his protestations, because I wished them true, and was an unexperienced girl of fifteen. I complied with his earnest request of being permitted to visit me, and even invited him to breakfast next morning; so that you may imagine (I speak to those that feel) I did not, that night, enjoy much repose. Such was the hurry and flutter of my spirits, that I rose at six to receive him at ten. I dressed myself in a new pink sattin-gown and my best laced night-cloaths, and was so animated by the occasion, that if ever I deserved a compliment upon my looks, it was my due at this meeting.

The wished-for moment came, that brought my lover to my view: I was overwhelmed with joy, modesty, and fear of I knew not what. We sat down to breakfast, but did not eat. He renewed his addresses with irresistible eloquence, and pressed me to accept of his hand, without farther hesitation: but, to such a precipitate step, I objected, as a measure repugnant to decency, as well as to that duty which I owed to my father, whom I tenderly loved.

Though I withstood this premature proposal, I did not attempt to disguise the situation of my thoughts; and thus commenced a tender correspondence, which was maintained by letters while I remained in the country, and carried on (when I was in town) by private interviews, twice or thrice a week, at the house of my milliner, where such endearments passed as refined and happy lovers know, and others can only guess. Truth and innocence prevailed on my side, while his heart was fraught with sincerity and love. Such frequent intercourse created an intimacy which I began to think dangerous, and therefore yielded to his repeated desire, that we might be united for ever: nay, I resolved to avoid him, until the day should be fixed, and very innocently (though not very wisely) told him my reason for this determination, which was no other than a consciousness of my incapacity to refuse him any thing he should demand as a testimony of my love.

The time was accordingly appointed, at the distance of a few days, during which I intended to have implored my father's consent, though I had but faint hopes of obtaining it: but, he was by some means or other apprized of our design, before I could prevail upon myself to make him acquainted with our purpose. I had danced with my lover at the Ridotto[1] on the preceding evening, and there, perhaps, our eyes betrayed us. Certain it is, several of lord W——m's relations, who disapproved of the match, came up and rallied him on his passion; lord S——k[2] in particular, used this remarkable expression, 'Nephew, as much love as you please, but no matrimony.'

Next day, the priest being prepared, and the bridegroom waiting for me at the appointed place, in all the transports of impatient expectation, I was, without any previous warning, carried into the country by my father, who took no notice of the intelligence he had received, but decoyed me into the coach, on pretence of taking the air; and when we had proceeded as far as Turnham green, gave me to understand, that he would dine in that place.

There was no remedy: I was obliged to bear my disappointment, though with an aching heart, and followed him up stairs into an apartment, where he told me he was minutely informed of my matrimonial scheme. I did not attempt to disguise the truth, but assured him, while the tears gushed from my eyes, that my want of courage alone had hindered me from making him privy to my passion; though I owned, I should have married lord W——m, even though he had disapproved of my choice. I reminded him of the uneasy life I led at home, and frankly acknowledged, that I loved my admirer too well to live without him; though if he would favour me with his consent, I would defer my intention, and punctually observe any day he should fix for our nuptials. Mean while, I begged he would permit me to send a message to lord W——m, who was waiting in expectation of my coming, and might (without such notice) imagine I was playing the jilt. He granted this last request; in consequence of which, I sent a letter to my lover, who, when he received it, had almost fainted away, believing that I should be locked up in the country, and snatched for ever from his arms. Tortured with these apprehensions, he changed cloaths immediately, and taking horse, resolved to follow me whithersoever we should go.

After dinner, we proceeded as far as Brentford, where we lay, intending to be at my father's country-house next night; and my admirer putting up at the same inn, practised every expedient his invention could suggest, to procure an interview; but all his endeavours were unsuccessful, because I, who little dream'd of his being so near, had gone to bed upon our first arrival, overwhelmed with affliction and tears.

In the morning I threw myself at my father's feet, and conjured him by all the ties of paternal affection, to indulge me with an opportunity of seeing my admirer once more, before I should be conveyed from his wishes. The melancholy condition in which I preferred this supplication, melted the tender heart of my parent, who yielded to my solicitation, and carried me back to town, for that purpose.

Lord W——m, who had watched our motions, and arrived at his own lodgings, before we alighted at my father's house, obeyed my summons on the instant, and appeared before me like an angel. Our faculties were, for some minutes, suspended by a conflict of grief and joy. At length, I recovered the use of speech, and gave him to understand, that I was come to town, in order to take my leave of him, by the permission of my father, whom I had promised to attend into the country next day, before he would consent to my return; the chief cause and pretence of which, was my earnest desire to convince him, that I was not to blame for the disappointment he had suffered, and that I should see him again in a month, when the nuptial knot should be tied in spite of all opposition.

My lover, who was better acquainted with the world, had well nigh run distracted with this information. He swore he would not leave me, until I should promise to meet and marry him next day; or, if I refused to grant that request, he would immediately leave the kingdom, to which he would never more return; and before his departure, sacrifice lord H—B—, son to the duke of S. A——,[1] who was the only person upon earth who could have betrayed us to my father, because he alone was trusted with the secret of our intended marriage, and had actually undertaken to give me away; an office which he afterwards declined. Lord W——m also affirmed, that my father decoyed me into the country, with a view of cooping me up, and sequestering me intirely from his view and correspondence.

In vain I pleaded my father's well-known tenderness, and used all the arguments I could recollect to divert him from his revenge upon lord H——.[2] He was deaf to all my representations, and nothing, I found, would prevail upon him to suppress his resentment, but a positive promise to comply with his former desire. I told him, I would hazard every thing to make him happy; but could not, with any regard to my duty, take such a step, without the knowledge of my parent; or, if I were so inclined, it would be impracticable to elude his vigilance and suspicion. However, he employed such pathetic remonstrances, and retained such a powerful advocate within my own breast, that before we parted, I assured him, my whole power should be exerted for his satisfaction; and he signified his resolution of sitting up all night, in expectation of seeing me at his lodgings.

He had no sooner retired, than I went into the next room, and desired my father to fix a day for the marriage; in which case, I would chearfully wait upon him into the country; whereas, should he deny my request, on pretence of staying for the consent of my lover's relations, which was very uncertain, I would seize the first opportunity of marrying lord W——m, cost what it would. He consented to the match, but would not appoint a day for the ceremony, which he proposed to defer until all parties should be agreed; and such a favourable crisis, I feared, would never happen.

I therefore resolved within myself to gratify my lover's expectation, by eloping, if possible, that very night; though the execution of this plan was extremely difficult, because my father was upon the alarm, and my own maid, who was my bedfellow, altogether in his interest. Notwithstanding these considerations, I found means to engage one of the house-maids in my behalf, who bespoke an hackney-coach, to be kept in waiting all night; and to bed I went with my Abigail, whom (as I had not closed an eye) I waked about five in the morning, and sent to pack up some things for our intended journey.

While she was thus employed, I got up, and huddled on my cloaths, standing upon my pillow, lest my father, who lay in the chamber below, should hear me afoot, and suspect my design.

Having dressed myself with great dispatch and disorder, I flounced down stairs, stalking as heavily as I could tread, that he might mistake me for one of the servants; and my confederate opening the door, I sallied out into the street, though I knew not which way to turn, and, to my unspeakable mortification, neither coach nor chair appeared.

Having travelled on foot a good way, in hope of finding a con-venience; and being not only disappointed in that particular, but also bewildered in my peregrination, I began to be exceedingly alarmed with the apprehension of being met by some person who might know me; because, in that case, my design would un-doubtedly have been discovered, from every circumstance of my appearance at that time of day; for I had put on the very cloaths which I had pulled off over night, so that my dress was altogether odd and peculiar: my shoes were very fine, and over a large hoop I wore a pink sattin quilted petticoat trimmed with silver, which was partly covered by a white dimity night-gown, a full quarter of a yard too short: my handkerchief and apron were hurried on without pinning; my night-cap could not contain my hair, which hung about my ears in great disorder, and my countenance denoted a mixture of hope and fear, joy and shame.

In this dilemma, I made my addresses to that honourable mem-ber of society a shoe-black, whom I earnestly intreated to provide me with a coach or chair, promising to reward him liberally for his trouble: but he having the misfortune to be lame, was unable to keep up with my pace; so that, by his advice and direction, I went into the first public-house I found open, where I stayed some time, in the utmost consternation, among a crew of wretches whom I thought proper to bribe for their civility, not without the terror of being stripped. At length, however, my messenger returned with a chair, of which I took immediate possession; and fearing that, by this time, my family would be alarmed, and send directly to lord W——m's lodgings, I ordered myself to be carried thither backwards, that so I might pass undiscovered.

This stratagem succeeded according to my wish; I ran up stairs, in a state of trepidation, to my faithful lover, who called an hackney-coach, in which we went to church and were married.[1]

His fears were then all over, but mine recurred with double aggravation: I dreaded the sight of my father, and shared all the sorrow he suffered on account of my undutiful behaviour: for I loved him with such piety of affection, that I would have endured every other species of distress, rather than have given him the least uneasiness: but love (where he reigns in full empire) is altogether irresistible, surmounts every difficulty, and swallows up all other considerations. This was the case with me; and now the irrevocable step was taken, my first care was to avoid his sight. With this view, I begged that lord W——m would think of some remote place in the country, to which we might retire for the present; and he forthwith conducted me to an house on Blackheath, where we were very civilly received by a laughter-loving dame, who seemed to mistake me for one of her own sisterhood.

I no sooner perceived her opinion, than I desired lord W——m to undeceive her; upon which she was made acquainted with the predicament in which I stood, and shewed us into a private room, where I called for pen and paper, and wrote an apology to my father, for having acted contrary to his will, in so important a concern.

This task being performed, the bridegroom gave me to understand, that there was a necessity for our being bedded immediately, in order to render the marriage binding, lest my father should discover and part us before consummation. I pleaded hard for a respite till the evening, objecting to the indecency of going to bed before noon; but he found means to invalidate all my arguments, and to convince me, that it was now my duty to obey. Rather than hazard the imputation of being obstinate and refractory on the first day of my probation, I suffered myself to be led into a chamber, which was darkened by my express stipulation, that my shame and confusion might be the better concealed, and yielded to the privilege of a dear husband, who loved me to adoration.

About five o'clock in the afternoon we were called to dinner, which we had ordered to be ready at four; but such a paultry care had been forgot, amidst the transports of our mutual bliss. We got up, however, and when we came down stairs, I was ashamed to see the light of day, or meet the eyes of my beloved lord. I ate little, said less, was happy, though overwhelmed with confusion, underwent a thousand agitations, some of which were painful, but by far the greater part belonged to rapture and delight; we were imparadised in the gratification of our mutual wishes, and felt all that love can bestow, and sensibility enjoy.

In the twilight, we returned to lord W——m's lodgings in town, where I received a letter from my father, importing, that he would never see me again. But there was one circumstance in his manner of writing, from which I conceived an happy presage of his future indulgence. He had begun with his usual appellation of *Dear Fanny*, which, though it was expunged to make way for the word *Madam*, encouraged me to hope that his paternal fondness was not yet extinguished.

At supper, we were visited by lord W——m's youngest sister,[1] who laughed at us for our inconsiderate match, though, she owned, she envied our happiness, and offered me the use of her cloaths, until I could retrieve my own. She was a woman of a great deal of humour, plain but genteel, civil, friendly, and perfectly well-bred. She favoured us with her company till the night was pretty far advanced, and did not take her leave till we retired to our apartment.

As our lodgings were not spacious or magnificent, we resolved to see little company; but this resolution was frustrated by the numerous acquaintance of lord W——m, who let in half the town; so that I ran the gauntlet for a whole week among a set of wits, who always delight in teazing a young creature of any note, when she happens to make such a stolen match. Among those that visited us upon this occasion, was my lord's younger brother, who was at that time in keeping with a rich heiress of masculine memory, and took that opportunity of making a parade with his equipage, which was indeed very magnificent, but altogether disregarded by us, whose happiness consisted in the opulence of mutual love.

This ceremony of receiving visits being performed, we went to wait on his mother the duchess of H——,[2] who hearing I was an heiress, readily forgave her son for marrying without her knowledge and consent, and favoured us with a very cordial reception; insomuch that, for several months, we dined almost constantly at her table; and I must own, I always found her unaltered in her civility and affection, contrary to her general character, which was haughty and capricious. She was undoubtedly a woman of great spirit and understanding, but subject to an infirmity which very much impairs and disguises every other qualification.

In about three weeks after our marriage, I was so happy as to obtain the forgiveness of my father, to whose house we repaired, in order to pay our respects and submission. At sight of me he wept; nor did I behold his tears unmoved: my heart was over-charged with tenderness and sorrow, for having offended such an indulgent parent; so that I mingled my tears with his, while my dear husband, whose soul was of the softest and gentlest mould, melted with sympathy at the affecting scene.

Being thus reconciled to my father, we attended him into the country, where we were received by my mother, who was a sensible good woman, though not susceptible of love, and therefore less apt to excuse a weakness, to which she was an utter stranger. This was likewise the case with an uncle, from whom I had great expectations. He was a plain good-natured man, and treated us with great courtesy; though his notions, in point of love, were not exactly conformable to ours. Nevertheless, I was, and seemed to be so happy in my choice, that my family not only became satisfied with the match, but exceedingly fond of lord W———m.

After a short stay with them in the country, we returned to London, in order to be introduced at court, and then set out for the North, on a visit to my brother-in-law the duke of H———, who had, by a letter to lord W———m, invited us to his habitation. My father accordingly equipped us with horses and money; for our own finances were extremely slender, consisting only of a small pension allowed by his grace, upon whom the brothers were intirely dependent, the father having died suddenly, before suitable provision could be made for his younger children.

When I took my leave of my relations, bidding adieu to my paternal home, and found myself launching into a world of care and trouble, though the voyage on which I had embarked was altogether voluntary, and my companion the person on whom I doated to distraction, I could not help feeling some melancholy sensations, which, however, in a little time, gave way to a train of more agreeable ideas. I was visited in town by almost all the women of fashion, many of whom, I perceived, envied me the possession of a man who had made strange havock among their hearts, and some of them knew the value of his favour. One in particular endeavoured to cultivate my friendship with singular marks of regard; but I thought proper to discourage her advances, by keeping within the bounds of bare civility; and indeed, to none of them was I lavish of my complaisance; for I dedicated my whole time to the object of my affection, who engrossed my wishes to such a degree, that although I was never jealous (because I had no reason to be so) I envied the happiness of every woman whom he chanced at any time to hand into a coach.

The duchess of ———, who was newly married to the earl of P———,[1] a particular friend of lord W———m's, carried me to court, and presented me to the queen, who expressed her approbation of my person in very particular terms, and observed the satisfaction that appeared in my countenance with marks of admiration; desiring her ladies to take notice, how little happiness depended upon wealth, since there was more joy in my face than in all her court beside.

Such a declaration could not fail to overwhelm me with blushes, which her majesty seemed to behold with pleasure; for she frequently repeated the remark, and shewed me to all the foreigners of distinction, with many gracious expressions of favour. She wished lord W———m happiness instead of joy, and was pleased to promise, that she would provide for her pretty beggars: and poor enough we certainly were in every article but love. Nevertheless, we felt no necessities, but passed the summer in a variety of pleasures and parties, the greatest part of which were planned by lord W———m's sister and another lady, who was at that time mistress to the prime minister.[2] The first was a wit, but homely in her person; the other, a woman of great beauty and masculine understanding; and a particular friendship subsisted between them, though they were both lovers of power and admiration.

This lady, who sat at the helm, was extremely elegant as well as expensive in her diversions, in many of which we bore a share; particularly in her parties upon the water, which were contrived in all the magnificence of taste. In the course of these amusements, a trifling circumstance occurred, which I shall relate as an instance of that jealous sensibility which characterised lord W———'s disposition. A large company of ladies and gentlemen having agreed to dine at Vauxhall, and sup at Marblehall, where we proposed to conclude the evening with a dance, one barge being insufficient to contain the whole company, we were divided by lots; in consequence of which, my husband and I were parted. This separation was equally mortifying to us both, who, though married, were still lovers; and my chagrin was increased, when I perceived that I was doomed to sit by Sir W——— Y———,[3] a man of professed gallantry: for, although lord W———m had, before his marriage, made his addresses to every woman he saw, I knew very well he did not desire that any person should make love to his wife.

That I might not therefore give umbrage, by talking to this

gallant, I conversed with a Scotch nobleman, who, according to common report, had formerly sighed among my admirers: by these means, in seeking to avoid one error, I unwittingly plunged myself into a greater; and disobliged Lord W——m so much, that he could not conceal his displeasure; nay, so deeply was he offended at my conduct, that in the evening, when the ball began, he would scarce deign to take me by the hand in the course of dancing, and darted such unkind looks as pierced me to the very soul; and what augmented my concern, was my ignorance of the trespass I had committed. I was tortured with a thousand uneasy reflections; I began to fear that I had mistaken his temper, and given my heart to a man who was tired of possession; tho' I resolved to bear without complaining the misfortune I had entailed upon myself.

I seized the first opportunity of speaking to him, and thereby discovered the cause of his chagrin; but, as there was no time for expostulation, the misunderstanding continued on his side, with such evident marks of uneasiness, that every individual of the company made up to me, and inquired about the cause of his disorder; so that I was fain to amuse their concern, by saying that he had been ill the day before, and dancing did not agree with his constitution. So much was he incensed by this unhappy circumstance of my conduct, which was void of all intention to offend him, that he determined to be revenged of me, for my indiscretion, and at supper, chancing to sit between two very handsome ladies, (one of whom is lately dead, and the other, at present, my neighbour in the country) he affected an air of gaiety, and openly coquetted with them both.

This was not the only punishment he inflicted on his innocent wife. In the course of our entertainment, we engaged in some simple diversion, in consequence of which, the gentlemen were ordered to salute the ladies; when Lord W——m, in performing this command, unkindly neglected me in my turn; and I had occasion for all my discretion and pride, to conceal from the company the agonies I felt at this mark of indifference and disrespect. However, I obtained the victory over myself, and pretended to laugh at his husband-like behaviour, while the tears stood in my eyes, and my heart swelled even to bursting.

We broke up about five, after having spent the most tedious evening I had ever known; and this offended lover went to bed in a state of sullen silence and disgust. Whatever desire I had to come to an explanation, I thought myself so much aggrieved by his unreasonable prejudice, that I could not prevail upon myself to demand a conference, till after his first nap, when my pride giving way to my tenderness, I clasped him in my arms, though he pretended to discourage these advances of my love: I asked how he could be so unjust as to take umbrage at my civility to a man whom, he knew, I had refused for his sake. I chid him for his barbarous endeavours to awake my jealousy, and used such irresistible arguments in my own vindication, that he was convinced of my innocence, sealed my acquittal with a kind embrace, and we mutually enjoyed the soft transports of a fond reconciliation.

Never was passion more eager, delicate, or unreserved, than that which glowed within our breasts. Far from being cloyed with the possession of each other, our raptures seemed to increase with the term of our union. When we were parted, though but for a few hours, by the necessary avocations of life, we were unhappy during that brief separation, and met again, like lovers who knew no joy but in one another's presence. How many delicious evenings did we spend together, in our own little apartment, after we had ordered the candles to be taken away, that we might enjoy the agreeable reflection of the moon, in a fine summer's evening. Such a mild and solemn scene naturally disposes the mind to peace and benevolence; but when improved with the conversation of the man one loves, it fills the imagination with ideas of ineffable delight! For my own part, I can safely say, my heart was so wholly ingrossed by my husband, that I never took pleasure in any diversion, where he was not personally concerned; nor was I ever guilty of one thought repugnant to my duty and my love.

In the autumn we set out for the north, and were met on the road by the duke and twenty gentlemen, who conducted us to H———n,[1] where we lived in all imaginable splendor. His grace, at that time, maintained above an hundred servants, with a band of music, which always performed at dinner, kept open table, and was visited by a great deal of company. The œconomy of his house was superintended by his eldest sister, a beautiful young lady of an amiable temper, with whom I soon contracted an intimate friendship. She and the duke used to rally me upon my fondness for lord W———m, who was a sort of an humourist, and apt to be in a pet, in which case he would leave the company, and go to bed by seven o'clock in the evening. On these occasions I always disappeared, giving up every consideration to that of pleasing my husband, notwithstanding the ridicule of his relations, who taxed me with having spoiled him with too much indulgence. But how could I express too much tenderness and condescension for a man, who

445

doated upon me to such excess, that when business obliged him to leave me, he always snatched the first opportunity to return, and often rode through darkness, storms and tempests to my arms.

Having stayed about seven months in this place, I found myself in a fair way of being a mother; and that I might be near my own relations, in such an interesting situation, I and my dear companion departed from H———n, not without great reluctance; for I was fond of the Scots in general, who treated me with great hospitality and respect; and to this day, they pay me the compliment of saying, I was one of the best wives in that country, which is so justly celebrated for good women.

Lord W———m having attended me to my father's house, was obliged to return to Scotland, to support his interest in being elected member of parliament; so that he took his leave of me, with a full resolution of seeing me again, before the time of my lying-in; and all the comfort I enjoyed in his absence, was the perusal of his letters, which I punctually received, together with those of his sister, who, from time to time, favoured me with assurances of his constancy and devotion. Indeed these testimonials were necessary to one of my disposition; for I was none of those who could be contented with half an heart. I could not even spare one complacent look to any other woman, but expected the undivided homage of his love. Had I been disappointed in this expectation, I should (though a wife) have rebelled or died.

Mean while, my parents treated me with great tenderness, intending that lord W———m should be settled in a house of his own, and accommodated with my fortune; and his expectations from the queen were very sanguine, when I was taken ill, and delivered of a dead child: an event which affected me so much, that when I understood the extent of my misfortune, my heart throbbed with such violence, that my breast could scarce contain it; and my anxiety being aggravated by the absence of my lord, produced a dangerous fever, of which he was no sooner apprized by letter, than he came post from Scotland; but before his arrival, I was supposed to be in a fair way.

During this journey, he was tortured with all that terrible suspence which prevails in the minds of those who are in danger of losing that which is most dear to them; and when he entered the house, was so much overwhelmed with apprehension, that he durst not inquire about the state of my health.

As for my part, I never closed an eye from the time on which I expected his return; and when I heard his voice, threw open my curtains, and sat up in the bed to receive him, though at the hazard of my life. He ran towards me with all the eagerness of passion, and clasp'd me in his arms; he kneeled by my bed-side, kissed my hand a thousand times, and wept with transports of tenderness and joy. In short, this meeting was so pathetic, as to overcome my enfeebled constitution; and we were parted by those who were wiser than ourselves, and saw that nothing was so proper for us as a little repose.

But how shall I relate the deplorable transition from envied happiness to excess of misery, which I now sustained! My month was hardly up, when my dear husband was taken ill: perhaps the fatigue of body as well as mind, which he had undergone on my account, occasioned a fatal ferment in his blood, and his health fell a sacrifice to his love. Physicians were called from London; but alas! they brought no hopes of his recovery. By their advice, he was removed to town, for the convenience of being punctually attended. Every moment was too precious to be thrown away; he was therefore immediately put into the coach, though the day was far spent; and I, though exceedingly weak, accompanied him in the journey, which was performed by the light of flambeaus, and rendered unspeakably shocking, by the dismal apprehension of losing him every moment.

At length, however, we arrived at our lodgings in Pall-mall, where I lay by him on the floor, and attended the issue of his distemper, in all the agonies of horror and despair. In a little time his malady settled upon his brain, and in his delirium, he uttered such dreadful exclamations, as were sufficient to pierce the most savage heart. What effect then must they have had on mine, which was fraught with every sentiment of the most melting affection! It was not a common grief that took possession of my soul; I felt all the aggravation of the most acute distress. I sometimes ran down to the street in a fit of distraction: I sent for the doctors every minute: I wearied heaven with my prayers; even now my heart akes at the remembrance of what I suffered, and I cannot without trembling proceed with the woeful story.

After having lain insensible some days, he recovered the use of speech, and called upon my name, which he had a thousand times repeated, while he was bereft of reason. All hopes of his life were now relinquished, and I was led to his bed-side to receive his last adieu, being directed to summon all my fortitude, and suppress my sorrow, that he might not be disturbed by my agitation. I collected all my resolution to support me in this affecting scene: I saw my dear lord in extremity; the beauties of his youth were all decayed, yet his eyes, though languid, retained unspeakable sweetness and expression. He felt his end approaching, put forth his hand, and with a look full of complacency and benevolence, uttered such a tender tale——Good heaven! how had I deserved such accumulated affliction! the bare remembrance of which now melts me into tears. Human nature could not undergo my situation, without suffering an extasy of grief! I clasped him in my arms, and kissed him a thousand times, with the most violent emotions of woe: but I was torn from his embrace, and in a little time he was ravished for ever from my view.

On that fatal morning, which put a period to his life, I saw the duchess of L——[1] approach my bed, and, from her appearance, concluded that he was no more; yet I begg'd she would not confirm the unhappy presage, by announcing his death; and she accordingly preserved the most emphatic silence. I got up, and trod softly over his head, as if I had been afraid of interrupting his repose. Alas! he was no longer sensible of such disturbance. I was seized with a stupification of sorrow: I threw up the window, and looking around, thought the sun shone with the most dismal aspect; every thing was solitary, chearless, and replete with horror.

In this condition I was, by the direction of my friend, conveyed to her house, where my faculties were so overpowered by the load of anguish which oppressed me, that I know not what passed during the first days of my unhappy widowhood: this only I know, the kind duchess treated me with all imaginable care and compassion, and carried me to her country-house, where I stayed some months; during which, she endeavoured to comfort me with all the amusements she could invent, and laid me under such obligations, as shall never be erased from my remembrance: yet, notwithstanding all her care and concern, I was, by my excess of grief, plunged into a languishing distemper, for which my physicians advised me to drink the Bath waters.

In compliance with this prescription, I went thither towards the end of summer, and found some benefit by adhering to their directions; though I seldom went abroad, except when I visited my sister-in-law, who was there with the princess; and upon these occasions, I never failed to attract the notice of the company, who were struck with the appearance of such a young creature in weeds. Nor was I free from the persecution of professed admirers; but being dead to all joy, I was deaf to the voice of adulation.

About Christmas, I repaired to my father's house, where my

sorrows were revived by every object that recalled the idea of my dear lamented lord. But these melancholy reflections I was obliged to bear, because I had no other home or habitation, being left an unprovided widow, altogether dependant on the affection of my own family.

During this winter, divers overtures were made to my father, by people who demanded me in marriage; but my heart was not yet sufficiently weaned from my former passion, to admit the thoughts of another master. Among those that presented their proposals, was a certain young nobleman,[1] who upon the first news of lord W———m's death, came post from Paris, in order to declare his passion. He made his first appearance in a hired chariot and six, accompanied by a big fat fellow, whom (as I afterwards learn'd) he had engaged to sound his praises, with the promise of a thousand pounds, in lieu of which he paid him with forty. Whether it was with a view of screening himself from the cold, or of making a comfortable medium in case of being overturned, and falling under his weighty companion, I know not; but certain it is, the carriage was stuffed with hay, in such a manner, that when he arrived, the servants were at some pains in rummaging and removing it, before they could come at their master, or help him to alight. When he was lifted out of the chariot, he exhibited a very ludicrous figure to the view: he was a thin, meagre, shivering creature, of a low stature, with little black eyes, a long nose, sallow complexion, and pitted with the small pox, dressed in a coat of light brown frize, lined with pink-coloured shag, a monstrous solitaire and bag, and (if I remember aright) a pair of huge jack-boots. In a word, his whole appearance was so little calculated for inspiring love, that I had (on the strength of seeing him once before at Oxford) set him down as the last man on earth, whom I would chuse to wed; and I will venture to affirm, that he was, in every particular, the very reverse of my late husband.

As my father was not at home, he stayed but one evening, and left his errand with my mother, to whom he was as disagreeable as to myself; so that his proposal was absolutely rejected; and I heard no more of him during the space of three whole months, at the expiration of which, I went to town, where this mortifying figure presented itself again, and renewed his suit, offering such advantageous terms of settlement, that my father began to relish the match, and warmly recommended it to my consideration.

Lord W———m's relations advised me to embrace the opportunity of making myself independent; all my acquaintance plied me with arguments to the same purpose: I was uneasy at home, and indifferent to all mankind. I weighed the motives with the objections, and with reluctance yielded to the importunity of my friends.

In consequence of this determination, the little gentleman was permitted to visit me; and the manner of his address did not at all alter the opinion I had conceived of his character and understanding. I was even shocked at the prospect of marrying a man whom I could not love; and, in order to disburthen my own conscience, took an opportunity of telling him one evening, as we sat opposite to each other, that it was not in my power to command my affection, and therefore he could not expect the possession of my heart, lord W——m's indulgence having spoiled me for a wife. Nevertheless, I would endeavour to contract a friendship for him, which would intirely depend upon his own behaviour.

To this declaration he replied (to my great surprize) that he did not desire me to love him, my friendship was sufficient; and next day, repeated this strange instance of moderation in a letter, which I communicated to my sister, who laughed heartily at the contents, and persuaded me, that since I could love no man, he was the properest person to be my husband.

Accordingly, the wedding-cloaths and equipage being prepared, the day—*the fatal day was fixed!* on the morning of which, I went to the house of my brother-in-law duke H——, who loved me tenderly, and took my leave of the family; a family which I shall always remember with love, honour, and esteem. His grace received me in the most affectionate manner, saying at parting, 'Lady W——m, if he does not use you well, I will take you back again.'

The bridegroom and I met at Ox—— chapel,[1] where the ceremony was performed by the bishop of W———, in presence of his mother, my father, and another lady; and the nuptial knot being tied, we set out for my father's house in the country, and proceeded full twenty miles on our journey, before my lord opened his mouth; my thoughts having been all that time employed on something quite foreign to my present situation; for I was then but a giddy girl of eighteen. At length my father broke silence, and clapping his lordship on the shoulder, told him he was but a dull bridegroom; upon which, my lord gave him to understand, that he was out of spirits. This dejection continued all the day, notwithstanding the refreshment of a plentiful dinner, which he ate upon the road; and in the evening we arrived at the place of destination, where we were kindly received by my mother, though she had no liking to the match; and after supper, we retired to our apartment.

It was here that I had occasion to perceive the most disagreeable contrast between my present help-mate and my former lord: instead of flying to my arms with all the eagerness of love and rapture, this manly representative sat moping in a corner, like a criminal on execution-day, and owned he was ashamed to bed a woman, whose hand he had scarce ever touched.

I could not help being affected with this pusilanimous behaviour: I remembered lord W———m, while I surveyed the object before me, and made such a comparison as filled me with horror and disgust: nay, to such a degree did my aversion to this phantom prevail, that I began to sweat with anguish at the thought of being subjected to his pleasure: and when, after a long hesitation, he ventured to approach me, I trembled as if I had been exposed to the embraces of a rattlesnake. Nor did the efforts of his love diminish this antipathy; his attempts were like the pawings of an imp, sent from hell to teize and torment some guilty wretch, such as are exhibited in some dramatic performance, which I never see acted, without remembering my wedding-night. By such shadowy, unsubstantial, vexatious behaviour, was I tantalized, and robb'd of my repose; and early next morning I got up, with a most sovereign contempt for my bedfellow, who indulged himself in bed till eleven.

Having passed a few days in this place, I went home with him to his house at Twickenham; and soon after we were presented at court, when the queen was pleased to say to my lord's mother, she did not doubt that we should be an happy couple, for I had been a good wife to my former husband.

Whatever deficiencies I had to complain of in my new spouse, he was not wanting in point of liberality: I was presented with a very fine chariot studded with silver nails, and such a profusion of jewels as furnished a joke to some of my acquaintance, who observed that I was formerly queen of hearts, but now metamorphosed into the queen of diamonds.[1] This uncommon splendour attracted the eyes and envy of my competitors, who were the more implacable in their resentments, because, notwithstanding my marriage, I was as much as ever followed by the men of gallantry and pleasure, among whom it is a constant maxim, that a woman never with-holds her affections from her husband, without an intention to bestow them somewhere else. I never appeared without a train of admirers, and my house in the country was always crouded with gay young men of quality.

Among those who cultivated my good graces with the greatest skill and assiduity, were the earl C——,[1] and Mr. S——, brother to lord F——.[2] The former of whom, in the course of his addresses, treated me with an entertainment of surprising magnificence, disposed into a dinner, supper, and ball; to which I, at his desire, invited eleven ladies, whom he paired with the like number of his own sex: so that the whole company amounted to twenty-four. We were regaled with a most elegant dinner, in an apartment which was altogether superb, and served by gentlemen only, no livery-servant being permitted to come within the door. In the afternoon we embarked in two splendid barges, being attended by a band of musick, in a third; and enjoyed a delightful evening upon the river, till the twilight, when we returned, and began the ball, which was conducted with such order and taste, that mirth and good humour prevailed, and no dissatisfaction appeared, except in the countenance of one old maid, since married to a son of the duke of ——, who, tho' she would not refuse to partake of such an agreeable entertainment, was displeased that I should have the honour of inviting her. O baleful Envy! thou self-tormenting fiend! How do'st thou predominate in all assemblies, from the grand gala of a court to the meeting of simple peasants at their harvest-home! Nor is the prevalence of this sordid passion to be wondered at, if we consider the weakness, pride, and vanity of our sex. The presence of one favourite man shall poison the enjoyment of a whole company, and produce the most rancorous enmity betwixt the closest friends.

I danced with the master of the ball, who employed all the artillery of his eloquence in making love; yet I did not listen to his addresses, for he was not to my taste, tho' he possessed an agreeable person, and a good acquired understanding; but he was utterly ignorant of that gentle prevailing art which I afterwards experienced in Mr. S——, and which was the only method he could have successfully practised, in seducing a young woman like me, born with sentiments of honour, and trained up in the paths of religion and virtue. He was, indeed, absolutely master of those insinuating qualifications which few women of passion and sensibility can resist; and had a person every way adapted for profiting by these insidious talents.[3] He was well acquainted with the human heart, conscious of his own power and capacity, and exercised these endowments with unwearied perseverance. He was tall and thin, which was perfectly agreeable to my taste, with large blue eloquent eyes, good teeth, and a long head turned to gallantry. His behaviour was the standard of politeness, and all his advances were conducted with the most profound respect; which is the most effectual expedient a man can use against us, if he can find means to persuade us, that it proceeds from the excess and delicacy of his passion. It is no other than a silent compliment, by which our accomplishments are continually flattered, and pleases in proportion to the supposed understanding of him who pays it.

By these arts and advantages this consummate politician in love began by degrees to sap the foundations of my conjugal faith; he stole imperceptibly into my affection, and, by dint of opportunity, which he well knew how to improve, triumphed, at last, over all his rivals.

Nor was he the only person that disputed my heart with Earl C——, who was also rivaled by lord C— H—,[1] a Scotchman, who had been an intimate and relation of my former husband. This gentleman I would have preferred to most of his competitors, and I coqueted with him for some time: but this amour was interrupted by his going to Ireland; upon which occasion, understanding that he was but indifferently provided with money, I made him a present of a gold snuff-box, in which was inclosed a bank-note; a trifling mark of my esteem, which he afterwards justified by the most grateful, friendly, and genteel behaviour; and as we corresponded by letters, I frankly told him, that Mr. S— had stept in, and won the palm from all the rest of my admirers.

This new favourite's mother and sisters, who lived in the neighbourhood, were my constant companions; and, in consequence of this intimacy, he never let a day pass without paying his respects to me in person; nay, so ingenious was he in contriving the means of promoting his suit, that whether I rode or walked, went abroad or stayed at home, he was always of course one of the party: so that his design seemed to ingross his whole vigilance and attention. Thus he studied my disposition, and established himself in my good opinion, at the same time. He found my heart was susceptible of every tender impression, and saw that I was not free from the vanity of youth; he had already acquired my friendship and esteem, from which he knew there was a short and easy transition to love; and by his penetration choosing proper seasons for the theme, urged it with such pathetic vows and artful adulation, as well might captivate a young woman of my complexion and inexperience, and circumstanced as I was, with a husband whom I had such reason to despise.

Tho' he thus made an insensible progress in my heart, he did not find my virtue an easy conquest; and I myself was ignorant of the advantage he had gained, with regard to my inclinations, until I was convinced of his success by an alarm of jealousy which I one day felt, at seeing him engaged in conversation with another lady. I forthwith recognized this symptom of love, with which I had been formerly acquainted, and trembled at the discovery of my own weakness. I underwent a strange agitation and mixture of contrary sensations: I was pleased with the passion, yet ashamed of avowing it even to my own mind. The rights of a husband (tho' mine was but a nominal one) occurred to my reflexion, and virtue, modesty and honour forbad me to cherish the guilty flame.

While I encouraged these laudable scruples, and resolved to sacrifice my love to duty and reputation, my lord was almost every day employed in riding post to my father, with complaints of my conduct, which was hitherto irreproachable; tho' the greatest grievance which he pretended to have suffered, was my refusing to comply with his desire, when he intreated me to lie a whole hour every morning, with my neck uncovered, that by gazing he might quiet the perturbation of his spirits. From this request you may judge of the man, as well as of the regard I must entertain for his character and disposition.

During the whole summer I was besieged by my artful undoer, and in the autumn set out with my lord for Bath, where, by reason of the intimacy that subsisted between our families, we lived in the same house with my lover and his sister, who, with another agreeable young lady, accompanied us in this expedition. By this time Mr. S— had extorted from me a confession of a mutual flame, tho' I assured him that it should never induce me to give up the valuable possessions of an unspotted character, and a conscience void of offence. I offered him all the enjoyment he could reap from an unreserved intercourse of souls, abstracted from any sensual consideration; and he eagerly embraced the Platonic proposal, because he had sagacity enough to foresee the issue of such chimerical contracts, and knew me too well to think he could accomplish his purpose without seeming to acquiesce in my own terms, and cultivating my tenderness under the specious pretext.

In consequence of this agreement we took all opportunities of seeing each other in private; and these interviews were spent in mutual protestations of disinterested love. This correspondence, tho' dangerous, was (on my side) equally innocent and endearing; and many happy hours we pass'd, before my sentiments were discovered. At length my lover was taken ill, and then my passion burst out beyond the power of concealment; my grief and anxiety became so conspicuous in my countenance, and my behaviour was so indiscreet, that every body in the house perceived the situation of my thoughts, and blamed my conduct accordingly.

Certain it is I was extremely imprudent, tho' intentionally innocent. I have lain whole nights by my lord, who teized and tormented me for that which neither I could give nor he could take, and ruminated on the fatal consequence of this unhappy flame, until I was worked into a fever of disquiet. I saw there was no safety but in flight, and often determined to banish myself for ever from the sight of this dangerous intruder. But my resolution always failed at the approach of day, and my desire of seeing him as constantly recurred. So far was I from persisting in such commendable determinations, that, on the eve of our departure from Bath, I felt the keenest pangs of sorrow at our approaching separation; and as we could not enjoy our private interviews at my house in town, I promised to visit him at his own apartments, after he had sworn by all that's sacred, that he would take no sinister advantage of my condescension, by presuming upon the opportunities I should give.

He kept his word; for he saw I trusted to it with fear and trembling, and perceived that my apprehension was not affected, but the natural concern of a young creature, distracted between love and duty, whom, had he alarmed, he never would have seen within his doors again. Instead of pressing me with sollicitations in favour of his passion, he was more than ever respectful and complaisant; so that I found myself disengaged of all restraint, conducted the conversation, shortened and repeated my visits, at my own pleasure, till, at last, I became so accustomed to this communication, that his house was as familiar to me as my own.

Having in this manner secured himself in my confidence, he resumed the favourite topic of love, and warming my imagination by gradual advances on the subject, my heart began to pant; and when he saw me thus, he snatched the favourable occasion to practise all his eloquence and art. I could not resist his energy, nor even fly from the temptation that assailed me, until he had obtained a promise that he should, at our next meeting, reap the fruits of his tedious expectation. Upon this condition I was permitted to retire, and blessed heaven for my escape, fully determined to continue in the path of virtue I had hitherto trod, and stifle the criminal flame, by which my peace and reputation were endangered. But his

R   455

idea, which reigned within my heart, without controul, soon baffled all those prudent suggestions.

I saw him again; and he reminded me of my promise, which I endeavoured to evade with affected pleasantry; upon which he manifested the utmost displeasure and chagrin, shedding some crocodile tears, and upbraiding me with levity and indifference. He observed, that he had sollicited my favour for ten long months, without intermission, and imagined I had held out so long on virtuous motives only; but now he could plainly perceive that his want of success had been owing to my want of affection; and that all my professions were insincere: in a word, he persuaded me, that his remonstrances were just and reasonable. I could not see the affliction of a man I loved, when I knew it was in my power to remove it; and rather than forfeit his opinion of my sincerity and love, I consented to his wish. My heart now flutters at the remembrance of the dear, tho' fatal indiscretion; yet I reflect without remorse, and even remember it with pleasure.

If I could not avoid the censure of the world, I was resolved to bear it without repining; and sure the guilt (if there was any in my conduct) was but venial; for I considered myself as a person absolved of all matrimonial ties, by the insignificance of lord ——, who, tho' a nominal husband, was, in fact, a mere non entity. I therefore contracted a new engagement with my lover, to which I resolved to adhere with the most scrupulous fidelity, without the least intention of injuring my lord or his relations; for had our mutual passion produced any visible effects, I would immediately have renounced and abandoned my husband for ever, that the fruit of my love for Mr. S—— might not have inherited, to the detriment of the right heir. This was my determination, which I thought just, if not prudent; and for which I have incurred the imputation of folly, in the opinion of this wise and honest generation, by whose example and advice I have, since that time, been a little reformed in point of prudentials, tho' I still retain a strong tendency to return to my primitive way of thinking.

When I quitted Mr. S——, after the sacrifice I had made, and returned to my own bed, it may perhaps be supposed that I slept but little. True: I was kept awake by the joyful impatience of revisiting my lover. Indeed I neglected no opportunity of flying to his arms: when lord —— was in the country we enjoyed each other's company without interruption, but when he resided in town our correspondence was limited to stolen interviews, which were unspeakably delicious, as genuine love presided at the entertainment.

Such was my happiness, in the course of this tender communication, that to this day I remember it with pleasure, tho' it has cost me dear in the sequel, and was at that time enjoyed at a considerable expence; for I devoted myself so intirely to my lover, who was desirous of engrossing my time and thoughts, that my acquaintance, which was very numerous, justly accused me of neglect, and of consequence cooled in their friendships: but I was *all for love, or the world well lost*. And were the same opportunity to offer, I would act the same conduct over again.

Some there are who possibly may wonder how I could love twice with such violence of affection: but all such observers must be unacquainted with the human heart. Mine was naturally adapted for the tender passions, and had been so fortunate, so cherished, in its first impressions, that it felt with joy the same sensations revive, when influenced by the same engaging qualifications. Certain it is I loved the second time as well as the first, and better was impossible. I gave up my all for both: fortune and my father's favour for the one; reputation, friends, and fortune for the other. Yet, notwithstanding this intimate connexion, I did not relinquish the world all at once; on the contrary I still appeared at court, and attracted the notice and approbation of my royal patroness; I danced with the p— of W—;[1] a circumstance which so nearly affected Mr. S—, who was present, that, in order to manifest his resentment, he chose the ugliest woman in the ball for his partner; and I no sooner perceived his uneasiness than I gave over, with a view of appeasing his displeasure.

Without repeating particular circumstances, let it suffice to say, our mutual passion was a perfect copy of that which had subsisted between me and my dear lord W——m. It was jealous, melting and delicate, and checquered with little accidents, which serve to animate and maintain the flame, in its first ardency of rapture. When my lover was sick, I attended and nursed him with indefatigable tenderness and care; and during an indisposition which I caught in the performance of this agreeable office, he discharged the obligation with all the warmth of sympathy and love.

It was, however, judged necessary by the physicians, that I should use the Bath-waters for the recovery of my health; and I set out for that place, glad of a pretence to be absent from lord ——, with whom I lived on very unhappy terms. He had, about nine months after our marriage, desired that we might sleep in separate beds, and gave a very whimsical reason for this proposal. He said, the immensity of his love deprived him of the power of gratification,[2] and that some commerce with an object, to which his heart was not attached, might, by diminishing the transports of his spirits, recompose his nerves, and enable him to enjoy the fruits of his good fortune.

You may be sure I made no objections to this plan, which was immediately put in execution. He made his addresses to a nymph of Drury-lane, whose name (as he told me) was Mrs. Rock. She made shift to extract some money from her patient; but his infirmity was beyond the power of her art; though she made some mischief between us; and I communicated my suspicion to duke H————,[1] who intended to have expostulated with her upon the subject; but she got intimation of his design, and saved him the trouble, by a precipitate retreat.

After my return from the Bath, where Mr. S. and I had lived happily, until we were interrupted by the arrival of my husband, his lordship expressed an inclination to be my bedfellow again; but in this particular I desired to be excused: for though I would not be the first to propose the separation, which, though usual in other countries, is contrary to the custom of England, being unwilling to furnish the least handle for censure, as my character was still unblemished; yet, when the proposal came from himself, I thought myself intitled to refuse a re-union, to which I accordingly objected.

This opposition produced a quarrel, which rose to a state of perpetual animosity; so that we began to talk of parting. My lord relished the expedient, agreeing to add three hundred pounds a year to my pin-money, which (by the bye) was never paid; and I renounced all state and grandeur, to live in a small house that I hired at Casehorton, where I passed my time for two months, in the most agreeable retirement, with my dear lover, till I was disturbed by the intrusion of my lord, who molested me with visits and solicitations to return, pretending that he had changed his mind, and insisting upon my compliance with his desire.

I exhausted my invention in endeavours to evade his request; but he persecuted me without ceasing: so that I was fain to capitulate, on condition that we should immediately set out for France; and that he should not presume to approach my bed, till our arrival at Calais. We accordingly departed for that kingdom; and, far from infringing the last article of our treaty, his lordship did not insist upon his privilege, before we reached the capital of France.

Mean while, I began to feel the effect of my passion in a very interesting manner, and communicated my discovery to the dear author of it, who would not leave me in such an affecting situation, but took the first opportunity of following us to France.

In our road to Paris, we stopp'd to visit Chantilly, a magnificent Chateau belonging to the prince of Condé, and there met by accident with some English noblemen, to whom I was known. The prince and his sisters invited me very politely into the gallery where they sat. They complimented me on my person, and seemed to admire my dress, which was altogether new to them, being a blue English riding-habit trimmed with gold, and an hat with a feather. They were particularly well pleased with my hair, which hung down to my waist, and pressed me to stay a fortnight at their house; an invitation which I was very much mortified at being obliged to refuse, because my lord did not understand the French language. I was inchanted with the place and the company, the women being amiable and the men polite; nor were they strangers to my name and story; for Mr. S—— calling at the same place a few days after, they rallied him on my account.

When we arrived at Paris, the first thing I did was to metamorphose myself into a French woman. I cut off my hair, hid a very good complexion of my own with *Rouge*, reconciled myself to powder, which I had never used before, put on a robe with a large hoop, and went to the *Thuilleries*, full of spirits and joy; for at that time every thing conspired to make me happy: I had health, youth and beauty, love, vanity and affluence, and found myself surrounded with diversions, which were gay, new and agreeable. My appearance drew upon me the eyes of the whole company, who considered me as a stranger, but not a foreigner, so compleatly was I equipped in the fashion of the French; and when they understood who I was, they applauded my person with the most lavish encomiums, according to their known politeness.

After having made a circuit round all the public places of entertainment in Paris, I was introduced into company, by an English family residing in that city; and, among others, became acquainted with a French lady, whose charms were remarkably attractive. The duke of K——[1] was her admirer; but she lived in reputation with her mother and an agreeable sister, whose lover was the prince of C——,[2] (for almost every lady in France has her *Amant*.)

With this charming woman, whose name was Madam De la T——,[3] I often made parties of pleasure. The duke, Mr. S——, she and I, used to meet in the Bois de Boulogne, which is a pleasant wood at a small distance from Paris, whither the company repairs, in the summer-season, for the benefit of the air; and after having amused ourselves among the groves, embarked in his grace's equipage, which was extremely elegant, being a calash drawn by six fine long-tailed greys, adorned with ribbons in the French taste; and thus we were conducted to a little inchanted, or at least inchanting palace, possessed by the duke, at one end of the town. The lower apartment, appropriated to me, was furnished with yellow and silver, the bed surrounded with looking-glasses, and the door opened into a garden, laid out in a cradle-walk, and intervening parterres of roses and other flowers. Above stairs my female companion lodged, in a chamber furnished with chintz. We supped all together in the saloon, which, though small, was perfectly elegant. The company was always good-humoured, the conversation sprightly and joyous, and the scene, though often repeated, still delightful and entertaining.

At other times, Mr. S—— and I used to pass our evenings at the palace of the prince of C——, which his highness lent us for our accommodation. The apartments opened into the gardens of the Luxembourg, and were, in point of magnificence, suitable to the owner. Thither I used to repair in a flaming equipage, on pretence of visiting, and spent the best part of the night with him, who was dearer to me than all the princes in the world.

While I was happily engaged in these ravishing parties, my little lord was employed in efforts to recover his health by restoratives, and I know not what; for he still lamented the enfeebling effects of his passion, and complained, that he loved me more like an angel than a woman, though he strove to govern his affection according to the doctrines of the christian religion, as he regulated his life by the maxims of Charles the twelfth of Sweden. The meaning of this declaration I could never learn; and indeed, I have been often tempted to believe he had no meaning at all.

Be that as it will, I found my size visibly increasing, and my situation extremely uneasy, on account of the perpetual wrangling which prevailed betwixt us, in consequence of his desiring to sleep with me again, after we had parted beds for the second time: and, that I might be no longer exposed to such disagreeable persecution, I resolved to leave him, though at the hazard of my life.

Thus determined, I went to the British embassador in an hackney coach; and, in order to disguise my youth, which might have prepossessed him against my judgment, muffled myself up in a black hood, which (as he said) instead of lending an air of gravity to my countenance, added a wildness to my looks, which was far from being disagreeable. He had been a gallant man in his youth, and even then, though well stricken in years, was not insensible to the power of beauty. This disposition, perhaps, rendered him more favourable to my cause, though he at first advised me to return to my husband; but finding me obstinate, he undertook to serve me in my own way, and procure a protection from the French king, by virtue of which, I could live at Paris unmolested by my lord. Nevertheless, he advised me (if I was determined to leave him) to make the best of my way to England, and sue for a divorce.

I relished his opinion, and concealed myself about three days in Paris, during which I borrowed some linen; for, as it was impossible to convey any thing out of my own house without suspicion, I had neither cloaths for my accommodation, nor a servant to wait on me.

In this solitary condition I took the road to Flanders, after I had put my lord upon a wrong scent, by writing a letter to him, dated at Calais, and travelled through an unknown country, without any other attendant than the postilion, being subjected to this inconvenience by the laws of France, which are so severe in some particulars, that if any person had been apprehended with me, he would have suffered death, for going off with a man's wife; though any man might go to bed with the same woman, without fear of incurring any legal punishment.

I proceeded night and day without intermission, that I might the sooner reach Flanders, where I knew I should be safe; and as the nights were excessively cold, I was fain to wrap myself up in flannel, which I bought for the purpose, as I had no cloaths to keep me warm, and travelled in an open chaise. While we passed through dreary woods, quite remote from the habitations of men, I was not without apprehension of being stripped and murthered by the postilion; and, in all probability, owed my safety to the indigence of my appearance, which might also protect me in two miserable places where I was obliged to lie, before I got out of the territories of France: for, as I could not reach the great towns where I intended to lodge, I was under the necessity of putting up at little wretched hovels, where no provision was to be had, but sour brown bread and sourer cheese; and every thing seemed to denote the dens of despair and assassination.

I made shift, however, to subsist on this fare, uncomfortable as it was, confided in the meanness of my equipage for the security of my person; and at length arriving at Brussels, fixed my quarters in the Hotel de Flandre (so well known to the English since) where

I thought myself extremely happy in the accomplishment of my flight.

I had not been full two days in this place, when I was blessed with the sight of my lover; and having concerted measures for proceeding to England,[1] I hired a tall fine Liegeoise for a maid; and setting out for Ostend, we embarked in a vessel, in which Mr. S—— had bespoke our passage. Our voyage was short and prosperous, and the time most agreeably spent in the company of my dear partner, who was a most engaging man in all respects, as I dare say my lady O——[2] has since found him.

I assumed a fictitious name, took private lodgings in Poland-street, retained lawyers, and commenced a suit for separation against my lord. I communicated the reasons of my elopement to my father, who was shocked and surprised at my conduct, which he condemned with expressions of sorrow and resentment. But the step was taken; nor did I repent of what I had done, except on his account.

In the morning after my arrival at London, I waited upon the lord-chief-justice,[3] to whom I complained of the usage I had received from my lord, whose temper was teazing, tiresome, and intolerably capricious. His behaviour was a strange compound of madness and folly, seasoned with a small proportion of sense: no wonder then that I, who am hot and hasty, should be wretched, under the persecution of such a perverse humourist, who used to terrify me, and scold at me the whole night without intermission, and shake my pillow from time to time, that I might not sleep, while he tormented me with his disagreeable expostulations. I have been often frightened almost out of my senses, at seeing him convulsed by the most unreasonable passion; and chagrined to the highest degree of disgust, to find (by repeated observation) his disposition so preposterous, that his satisfaction and displeasure never depended upon the cause he had to be satisfied or disobliged; but, on the contrary, when he had most reason to be pleased, he was always most discontented, and very often in good humour, when he had reason enough for vexation.

While I lived in Poland-street, I was engaged with lawyers, and so often visited by my father, that I could not dedicate my whole time, as usual, to my lover; nor was it convenient that he should be seen in my company: he therefore took a small house at Camber-well, whither I went as often as I had an opportunity; and maintained the correspondence with such eagerness and industry, that although I was six months gone with child, I have often, by myself, set out for his habitation, in an hackney-coach, at eleven o'clock at night, and returned by six in the morning, that I might be in my own bed, when my father came to see me; for I concealed my amour, as well as the effects of it, from his knowledge, and frequently took water from the Bridge, that my motions might not be discovered. Nothing but the most passionate love could have supported my spirits under such vicissitudes of fatigue, or enabled my admirer to spend whole days by himself, in such a solitary retirement.

By this time, my lord was arrived in England, and employed in discovering the place of my retreat; so that I lived in continual alarm, and provided myself with a speaking-trumpet, which stood by my bed-side, to be used in calling for assistance, in case my pursuer should make an attack upon my lodgings.

This situation being extremely uncomfortable, I had no sooner begun my process against him, than I put myself intirely under the protection of Mr. S——, who conducted me to the house of a friend of his who lived in the country, where I was secure from the attempts of my husband.

The world had now given me up, and I had renounced the world with the most perfect resignation. I weighed in my own breast what I should lose in point of character, with what I suffered in my peace at home, and found, that my reputation was not to be preserved, except at the expence of my quiet, (for his lordship was not disposed to make me easy, had I been never so discreet.) I therefore determined to give up a few ceremonial visits, and empty professions, for the more substantial enjoyments of life.

We passed our time very agreeably, in various amusements, with this friend of Mr. S——, until the term of my reckoning was almost expired, then returned to London, and took lodgings in Southampton-street, where I began to make preparations for the approaching occasion. Here I proposed to live with the utmost circumspection. I disguised my name, saw nobody but my lawyer and lover, and never approached the window, lest I should be discovered by accident.

Notwithstanding these precautions, my French maid, whom I had sent for some of my cloaths, was dogged in her return, and next morning my lord took my lodgings by storm. Had he given the assault in his own person only, I make no doubt but he would have suffered a repulse, from the opposition of the Liegeoise, who made all the resistance in her power, but was obliged to give way to superior numbers.

I was at that time abed, and hearing an unusual noise below, rung my bell, in order to know the cause of such disturbance. I drew my curtain at the same time, and who should I see entering my chamber, but his lordship, attended by a constable, and the footman who had detected my retreat!

Such an unexpected visit could not fail to affect me with surprize and consternation: however, I summoned all my fortitude to my aid, and perceiving the fellows were about to open my window-shutters, desired their principal to order them down stairs. He readily complied with my request, and sitting down by my bed-side, told me with an air of triumph, that he had found me at last; and I frankly owned, that I was heartily sorry for his success. Instead of upbraiding me with my escape, he proceeded to enter-tain me with all the news in town, and gave me a minute detail of every thing which had happened to him since our parting; among other articles of intelligence, giving me to understand, that he had challenged Mr. S——, who had refused to fight him, and was in disgrace with the prince of W—— on that account.

But here his lordship did not strictly adhere to the naked truth: he had indeed, before our departure for the country, gone to my lover, and insisted upon having satisfaction in Hyde-park, two days from the date of his demand, and at three o'clock in the after-noon; S—— believing him in earnest, accepted the invitation; though he observed, that these affairs could not be discussed too soon, and wished the time of meeting might be at an earlier hour. But his lordship did not choose to alter the circumstances of his first proposal; and when he went away, said he should expect him at the appointed time and place, if it did not rain.

His antagonist gave me an account of the conversation, when I assured him the whole business would end in smoke. Accordingly, my lord sent him a letter on Monday, desiring that the assignation might be deferred till Thursday, that he might have time to settle his affairs, and pay S— an hundred pounds, which he had for-merly borrowed of him. When Thursday came, he was favoured with another epistle, importing, that the challenger had changed his mind, and would seek satisfaction at law. Thus ended that heroic exploit, which his lordship now boasted of with such arrogant misrepresentation.

Whilst he regaled me with these interesting particulars, I was contriving a scheme to frustrate the discovery he had made; so that I did not contradict his assertions, but told him, that if he would go down stairs, I would rise and come to breakfast. He consented to this proposal with great chearfulness; and I own, I was not a little surprized to find him, at this first interview, in as good humour, as if nothing had happened to interrupt the felicity of our matrimonial union.

It cost me some invention to conceal my condition from his notice, being now within a week of the expected crisis: but I knew I had to do with a man of no great penetration, and succeeded in my attempt accordingly. We breakfasted with great harmony, and I invited him to dinner, after having prevailed upon him to send away his myrmidons, whom, nevertheless, he ordered to return at eleven o'clock at night. We conversed together with great gaiety and mirth; and when I rallied him for visiting me in such a dishabille, he stood a-tiptoe to view himself in the glass; and owning I was in the right, said he would go and dress himself before dinner.

He accordingly went away, charging my maid to give him entrance at his return; and he was no sooner gone than I wrote to Mr. S——, giving him an account of what had happened; then, without having determined upon any certain plan, huddled on my cloaths, muffled myself up, and calling a chair, went to the next tavern, where I stayed no longer than was sufficient to change my vehicle; and, to the astonishment of the drawers, who could not conceive the meaning of my perturbation, proceeded to a shop in the neighbourhood, where I dismissed my second chair, and procured an hackney coach, in which I repaired to the lodgings of my lawyer, whom I could trust. Having made him acquainted with the circumstances of my distress, and consulted him about a proper place of retreat, after some recollection he directed me to a little house in a court, to which, by the assistance of my lover, my woman and cloaths were safely conveyed that same evening.

My lord, however, came to dinner, according to invitation, and did not seem at all alarmed when my maid told him I was gone, but stepped to my lawyer, to know if he thought I should return; and upon his answering in the affirmative, and advising his lordship to go back in the mean time, and eat the dinner I had provided, he very deliberately took his advice, made a very hearty meal, drank his bottle of wine, and, as I did not return, according to his expectation, withdrew, in order to consult his associates.

This motion of his furnished my woman with an opportunity of making her retreat; and when he returned at night, the coast was clear, and he found no body in the house but a porter, who had been left to take care of the furniture. He was so enraged at this disappointment, that he made a furious noise, which raised the whole neighbourhood, reinforced his crew with the authority of a justice of the peace, tarried in the street till three o'clock in the morning, discharged a lodging he had hired at a barber's shop, opposite to the house from which I had escaped, and retired with the comfortable reflexion of having done every thing which man could do to retrieve me.

The hurry of spirits, and surprize I had undergone in effecting this retreat, produced such a disorder in my constitution, that I began to fear I should be delivered before I could be provided with necessaries for the occasion. I signified my apprehension to Mr. S——, who with infinite care and concern endeavoured to find a more convenient place; and, after all his inquiries, was obliged to fix upon a paultry apartment in the city, tho' his tenderness was extremely shocked at the necessity of choosing it. However, there was no remedy, nor time to be lost: to this miserable habitation I was carried in an hackney coach; and, tho' extremely ill, bore my fate with spirit and resignation, in testimony of my sincere and indelible attachment to my lover, for whose ease and pleasure I could have suffered every inconvenience, and even sacrificed my life.

Immediately after I had taken possession of my wretched apartment, I was constrained by my indisposition to go to bed, and send for the necessary help; and in a few hours a living pledge of my love and indiscretion saw the light, tho' the terrors and fatigue I had undergone had affected this little innocent so severely, that it scarce discovered any visible signs of life.

My grief at this misfortune was inexpressible: I forthwith dispatched a message to the dear, the anxious father, who flew to my arms, and shared my sorrow, with all the gentleness of love and parental fondness; yet our fears were happily disappointed by the recovery of our infant daughter, who was committed to the charge of a nurse in the neighbourhood; so that I could every day be satisfied in my inquiries about her health. Thus I continued a whole fortnight, in a state of happiness and tranquillity, being blessed with the conversation and tender offices of my admirer, whose love and attention I wholly ingrossed. In a word, he gave up all business and amusement, and concentred all his care and assiduity in ministring to my ease and satisfaction. And sure I had no cause to regret what I had suffered on his account.

But this my agreeable situation was one day disturbed by a most alarming accident, by which my life was drawn into imminent danger. The room under my bed-chamber took fire; I immediately smelled it, and saw the people about me in the utmost perplexity and consternation, tho' they would not own the true cause of their confusion, lest my health should suffer in the fright. Nevertheless I was so calm in my inquiries, that they ventured to tell me my suspicion was but too just: upon which I gave such directions as I thought would secure me from catching cold, in case there should be a necessity for removing me; but the fire being happily extinguished, I escaped that ceremony, which might have cost me my life. Indeed it was surprising, that the agitation of my spirits did not produce some fatal effect upon my constitution; and I looked upon my deliverance as the protection of a particular providence.

Tho' I escaped the hazard of a sudden removal, I found it was high time to change my lodgings, because the neighbours rushing into the house, upon the alarm of fire, had discovered my situation, though they were ignorant of my name; and I did not think myself safe, in being the subject of their conjectures. Mr. S— therefore procured another apartment, with better accommodation, to which I was carried, as soon as my health would admit of my removal; and soon after my lord wrote to me, by the hands of my lawyer, earnestly intreating me to drop my prosecution, and come home. But I would not comply with his request; and nothing was farther from my intention than the desire of receiving any favours at his hands.

Thus repulsed, he set on foot a most accurate search for my person; in the course of which he is said to have detected several ladies and young girls, who had reasons for keeping themselves concealed; and had like to have been very severely handled for his impertinent curiosity. Being unsuccessful in all his attempts, he entered into treaty with one Sir R— H—, a person of a very indifferent character, who undertook to furnish him with an infallible expedient to discover the place of my abode, if he would gratify him with a bond for a thousand pounds; which being executed accordingly, this worthy knight advertised me and my maid in the public papers, offering one hundred pounds as a reward to any person who should disclose the place of our retirement.[1]

As soon as the paper fell into my hands I was again involved in perplexity; and being afraid of staying in town, resolved, with the concurrence of my lover, to accept of an invitation I had received from the duke of K—, who had by this time arrived in England, with that lady whom I have already mentioned, as one of our parties at Paris. Having visited my little infant, I next day set out for the duke's country-seat,[1] which is a most elegant *chateau*, and stands in a charming situation: Mr. S— followed in a few days; we met with a very cordial reception; his grace was civil and good-natured, lived nobly and loved pleasure; Madam la T—— was formed to please: there was always a great deal of good company in the house; so that we passed our time agreeably in playing at billiards and cards, hunting, walking, reading and conversation.

But my terms of happiness were generally of short duration. In the midst of all this felicity I was overtaken by a most severe affliction, in the death of my dear hapless infant, who had ingrossed a greater share of my tenderness than perhaps I even should have paid to the offspring of a legitimate contract, because the circumstance of her birth would have been an unsurmountable misfortune to her thro' the whole course of her life, and rendered her absolutely dependent on my love and protection.

While I still lamented the untimely fate of this fair blossom, lord —— came down, and demanded me as his wife; but the suit which I then maintained against him deprived him, for the present, of an husband's right; and therefore the duke would not deliver me into his hands.

In six months he repeated his visit and demand; and an agreement was patched up, in consequence of which I consented to live in the same house with him, on condition that he should never desire to sleep with me, or take any other measure to disturb my peace; otherwise I should be at liberty to leave him again, and intitled to the provision of a separate maintenance. To these articles I assented, by the advice of my lawyers, with a view of obtaining the payment of my pin-money, which I had never received since our parting, but subsisted on the sale of my jewels, which were very considerable, and had been presented to me with full power of alienation. As to my lover, he had no fortune to support me; and for that reason I was scrupulously cautious of augmenting his expence.

We had now enjoyed each other's company for three years, during which our mutual passion had suffered no abatement, nor had my happiness been mixed with any considerable allay, except that late stroke of providence which I have already mentioned, and the reflexion of the sorrow that my conduct had intailed upon my dear father, whom I loved beyond expression, and whom nothing could have compelled me to disoblige but a more powerful flame, that prevailed over every other consideration. As I was now forced to break off this inchanting correspondence, it is not to be doubted that our parting cost us the most acute sensations of grief and disappointment. However, there was no remedy: I tore myself from his arms, took my leave of the family, after having acknowledged my obligations to the duke, and set out for the place of rendezvous, where I was met by my lord, attended by a steward whom he had lately engaged, and who was one chief cause of our future separations. My lord having quitted his house in town, conducted me to his lodgings in Pall-Mall, and insisted upon sleeping with me the first night; but I refused to gratify his desire, on the authority of our agreement.

This dispute produced a quarrel, in consequence of which I attempted to leave the house; and he endeavouring to prevent my retreat, I fairly locked him in, ran down stairs, and calling a hackney coach, made the best of my way into the city, to my father's lodgings, where I lay, the family being in town, tho' he himself was in the country. I wrote to him immediately, and when he came to London, declared my intention of separating from my lord, with which, seeing me obstinate and determined, he at length acquiesced, and a formal separation accordingly ensued, which at that time I thought binding and immutable.

I was now sheltered under the wings of an indulgent father, who had taken me into favour again, on the supposition that my commerce with Mr. S— was absolutely at an end. Nevertheless, tho' we had separated, in all appearance, for ever, we had previously agreed to maintain our correspondence in private interviews, which should escape the notice of the world, with which I was again obliged to keep some measures.

Our parting at the duke of K—'s house in the country was attended with all the genuine marks of sincere and reciprocal affection, and I lived in the sweet hope of seeing him again, in all the transport of his former passion, when my lawyer, who received my letters, brought me a billet one night, just as I had gone to bed. Seeing the superscription of S—'s hand-writing, I opened it with all the impatience of an absent lover; but how shall I describe the astonishment and consternation with which I was seized, when I perused the contents! Instead of the most tender vows and protestations, this fatal epistle began with, *Madam, the best thing you can do is to return to your father*; or some cold and killing expression, to that effect.

Heaven and earth! what did I feel at this dire conjuncture! The light forsook my eyes, a cold sweat bedewed my limbs, and I was overwhelmed with such a torrent of sorrow and surprize, that every body present believed I would have died under the violent agitation. They endeavoured to support my spirits with repeated draughts of strong liquor, which had no sensible effect upon my constitution, tho' for eight whole years I had drank nothing stronger than water; and I must have infallibly perished in the first extasy of my grief, had it not made its way in a fit of tears and exclamation, in which I continued all night, to the amazement of the family, whom my condition had alarmed, and raised from their repose. My father was the only person who guessed the cause of my affliction; he said he was sure I had received some ill usage in a letter or message from that rascal S— (so he termed him in the bitterness of passion).

At mention of that name my agony redoubled to such a degree, that all who were present wept at sight of my deplorable condition. My poor father shed a flood of tears, and conjured me to tell him the cause of my disquiet: upon which, rather than confess the truth, I amused his concern, by pretending that my lover was ill. The whole family having stayed by me till I was a little more composed, left me to the care of my maid, who put me into bed about six in the morning; but I enjoyed no rest: I revolved every circumstance of my conduct, endeavouring to find out the cause of this fatal change in S—'s disposition; and as I could recollect nothing which could justly give offence, concluded that some malicious persons had abused his ears with stories to my prejudice.

With this conjecture I got up, and sent my lawyer to him with a letter, wherein I insisted upon seeing him, that I might have an opportunity of justifying myself in person; a task which would be easily performed, as I had never offended, but in loving too well. I waited with the most anxious impatience for the return of my messenger, who brought me an answer couched in the coldest terms of civility which indifference could dictate; acknowledging, however, that he had nothing to lay to my charge, but that it was for the good of us both we should part.—He ought to have reflected on that before, not after I had sacrificed my all for his love! I was well nigh distracted by this confirmation of his inconstancy; and I wonder to this day how I retained the use of reason, under such circumstances of horror and despair! My grief laid aside all decorum and restraint; I told my father that S— was dying, and that I would visit him with all expedition.

Startled at the proposal, this careful parent demonstrated the fatal consequence of such an unguarded step, reminded me of the difficulty with which he had prevailed upon my mother and uncle to forgive my former imprudence, observed that his intention was to carry me into the country next day, in order to effect a perfect reconciliation; but now I was on the brink of forfeiting all pretensions to their regard, by committing another fatal error, which could not possibly be retrieved; and that for his part, whatever pangs it might cost him, he was resolved to banish me from his sight for ever.

While he uttered this declaration the tears trickled down his cheeks, and he seemed overwhelmed with the keenest sorrow and mortification; so it may be easily conceived what were the impressions of my grief, reinforced with the affliction of a father whom I dearly loved, and the consciousness of being the cause of all his disquiet! I was struck dumb with remorse and woe; and when I recovered the use of speech, I told him how sensible I was of his great goodness and humanity, and owned how little I deserved his favour and affection; that the sense of my own unworthiness was one cause of my present distraction; for such was the condition of my fate, that I must either see S— or die. I said, tho' I could not expect his forgiveness, I was surely worthy of his compassion; that nothing but the most irresistible passion could have misled me at first from my duty, or tempted me to incur the least degree of his displeasure; that the same fatal influence still prevailed, and would, in all probability, continue to the grave, which was the only abode in which I hoped for peace.

While I expressed myself in this manner, my dear good father wept with the most tender sympathy, and saying I might do as I pleased, for he had done with me, quitted the room, leaving me to the cruel sensations of my own heart, which almost bursted with anguish, upbraiding me with a fault which I could not help committing.

I immediately hired a chariot and six, and would have set out by myself, had not my father's affection, which all my errors could not efface, provided an attendant. He saw me quite delirious and desperate; and therefore engaged a relation of my own to accompany and take care of me in this rash expedition.

During this journey, which lasted two days, I felt no remission of grief and anxiety, but underwent the most intolerable sorrow and suspense: at last we arrived at a little house called the Hut, on Salisbury plain, where, in the most frantic agitation, I wrote a letter to S—, describing the miserable condition to which I was reduced by his unkindness, and desiring to see him, with the most earnest sollicitations.

This billet I committed to the care of my attendant, and laid strong injunctions upon him to tell Mr. S——, my injuries were so great, and my despair so violent, that if he did not favour me with a visit, I would go to him, though at his sister's house, where he then was.

He received my message with great coldness, and told my friend, that if I would return to London, without insisting upon the interview I demanded, he would in a little time follow me to town, and every thing should be amicably adjusted. But when the messenger assured him, that I was too much transported with grief, to hear of such a proposal, he consented to meet me in the middle of Salisbury plain, that we might avoid all observation: and though I was little able to walk, I set out on foot for the place of assignation, my companion following at a small distance.

When I saw him leading his horse down the hill, I collected all my fortitude, and advanced to him with all the speed I could exert; but when I made an effort to speak, my tongue denied its office; and so lively was the expression of unutterable sorrow in my countenance, that his heart (hard as it was) melted at sight of my sufferings, which he well knew proceeded from the sincerity of my love. At length I recovered the use of speech, enough to tell him, that I was come to take my leave; and when I would have proceeded, my voice failed me again: but, after a considerable pause, I found means, with great difficulty, to let him know how sensible I was of my own incapacity to retrieve his lost affections; but that I was willing (if possible) to retain his esteem, of which, could I be assured, I would endeavour to compose myself; that I was determined to leave the kingdom, because I could not bear the sight of those places where we had been so happy in our mutual love; and that, till my departure, I hoped he would visit me sometimes, that I might, by degrees, wean myself from his company; for, I should not be able to survive the shock of being deprived of him all at once.

This address may seem very humble to an unconcerned observer; but love will tame the proudest disposition, as plainly appeared in my case; for I had naturally as much spirit, or more, than the generality of people have. Mr. S—— was so much confounded at the manner of my behaviour, that he scarce knew what answer to make; for (as he afterwards owned) he expected to hear himself upbraided; but he was not proof against my tenderness. After some hesitation, he said he never meant to forsake me intirely, that his affection was still unimpaired, and that he would follow me directly to London. I imposed upon myself, and believed what he said, because I could not bear to think of parting with him for ever, and returned to town in a more tranquil state of mind than that in which I had left my father, though my heart was far from being at ease; my fears being ingenious enough to foresee, that I should never be able to overcome his indifference.

I took lodgings in Mount-street, and my maid having disposed of herself in marriage, hired another, who supplied her place very much to my satisfaction; she was a good girl, had a particular attachment to me, and for many years, during which she lived in my service, was indefatigably assiduous in contributing to my ease, or rather, in alleviating my affliction: for, though S—— came up to town according to promise, and renewed a sort of correspondence with me for the space of five months, his complaisance would extend no farther; and he gave me to understand, that he had determined to go abroad with Mr. V——,[1] whom he accordingly accompanied in his envoyship to D——n.

I understood the real cause of this expedition, which, notwithstanding his oaths and protestations of unabated love and regard, I construed into a palpable mark of dislike and disrespect; nor could the repeated assurances I received from him in letters, mitigate the anguish and mortification that preyed upon my heart. I therefore gave up all hopes of recovering the happiness I had lost: I told him, on the eve of his departure, that he might exercise his gallantry a great while, before he would meet with my fellow, in point of sincerity and love; for I would rather have been a servant in his house, with the privilege of seeing him, than the queen of England, debarred of that pleasure.

When he took his leave, and went down stairs, I shrunk at every step he made, as if a new wound had been inflicted upon me; and when I heard the door shut behind him, my heart died within me. (I had the satisfaction to hear afterwards, he lamented the loss of me prodigiously, and that he had never been so happy since.) I sat down to write a letter, in which I forgave his indifference, because I knew the affections are altogether involuntary, and wished him all the happiness he deserved. I then walked up and down the room in the most restless anxiety, was put to bed by my maid, rose at six, mounted my horse, and rode forty miles, in order to fatigue myself, that I might, next night, enjoy some repose. This exercise I daily underwent for months together; and when it did not answer my purpose, I used to walk round Hyde-park in the evening, when the place was quite solitary, and unvisited by any other creature.

In the course of this melancholy perambulation, I was one day accosted by a very great man,[1] who, after the first salutation, asked whether or not my intercourse with S—— was at an end; and if I had any allowance from my husband? To the first of these questions I replied in the affirmative; and to the last answered, that my lord did not allow me a great deal; indeed I might have truly said, nothing at all: but I was too proud to own my indigence. He then expressed his wonder, how one like me, who had been used to splendor and affluence from my cradle, could make shift to live in my present narrow circumstances; and when I told him that I could make a very good shift, so I had peace, he seemed to lament my situation, and very kindly invited me to sup with his wife, at his house. I accepted the invitation, without any apprehension of the consequence; and when I went to the place, was introduced into an apartment, magnificently lighted up (I suppose) for my reception.

After I had stayed alone for some time in this mysterious situation, without seeing a living soul, my inviter appeared, and said, he hoped I would not take it amiss, that he and I were to sup by ourselves, as he had something to say, which could not be so properly communicated before company or servants. I then, for the first time, perceived his drift, to my no small surprize and indignation; and with evident marks of displeasure told him, I was sure he had nothing to propose that would be agreeable to my inclination, and that I would immediately leave the house. Upon which, he gave me to understand, that I could not possibly retire, because he had sent away my chair, and all his servants were disposed to obey his orders.

Incensed at this declaration, which I considered as an insult, I answered with an air of resolution, it was very well; I despised his contrivance, and was afraid of nobody. Seeing me thus alarmed, he assured me I had no reason to be afraid; that he had loved me long, and could find no other opportunity of declaring his passion. He said, the Q— had told him, that lord C——[2] had renewed his addresses to me; and as he understood from my own mouth, my correspondence with S—— was absolutely broke off, he thought himself as well intitled as another to my regard. In conclusion, he told me, that I might command his purse, and that he had power enough to bring me into the world again with *éclat*. To these advances I replied, that he was very much mistaken in his opinion of my character, if he imagined I was to be won by any temptations of fortune, and very frankly declared, that I would rather give myself to a footman, than sell myself to a prince.

Supper being served, we sat down together; but I would neither eat nor drink any thing, except a little bread and water; for I was an odd whimsical girl; and it came into my head, that he might, perhaps, have mixed something in the victuals or wine, which would alter my way of thinking. In short, finding himself baffled in all his endeavours, he permitted me, about twelve o'clock, to depart in peace, and gave up his suit, as a desperate cause.

This uncomfortable life did I lead for a whole twelvemonth, without feeling the least abatement of my melancholy; and finding myself worn to a skeleton, I resumed my former resolution of trying to profit by change of place, and actually went abroad with no other attendant but my woman, and the utmost indifference for life. My intention was to have gone to the South of France, where I thought I could have subsisted on the little I had left, which amounted to five hundred pounds, until the issue of my law-suit, by which I hoped to obtain some provision from my lord; and, without all doubt, my expectation would have been answered, had I put this my plan in execution: but being at Paris, from whence I purposed to set forward in a few days, I sent to Mr. K———,[1] who had been formerly intimate with my father, and shewn me many civilities during my first residence in France.

This gentleman favoured me with a visit, and when I made him acquainted with my scheme, dissuaded me from it, as an uncomfortable determination, and advised me to stay at Paris, where, with good œconomy, I could live as cheap as in any other place, and enjoy the conversation and countenance of my friends, among which number he declared himself one of the most faithful; assuring me, that I should be always welcome to his table, and want for nothing; and promising to recommend me as a lodger to a friend of his, with whom I would live in a frugal and decent manner; and that, as the woman was well known and esteemed by all the English company in Paris, it would be the most reputable step I could take, (considering my youth and situation) to lodge with a creditable person, who could answer for my conduct. Thus persuaded, I very simply followed his advice; I say simply, because, notwithstanding his representations, I soon found my money melt away, without any prospect of a fresh supply. In lieu of this, however, I passed my time very agreeably in several English, and some French families, where, in a little time, I became quite intimate, saw a great deal of company, and was treated with the utmost politeness and regard; yet, in the midst of these pleasures, many a melancholy sigh would rise at the remembrance of my beloved S———, whom for several years I could not recollect without emotion; but time, company, amusements, and change of place, in a great measure dissipated these ideas, and enabled me to bear my fate with patience and resignation.

On my last arrival at Paris, I was surrounded by a croud of professed admirers, who sighed and flattered in the usual forms; but, besides that my heart was not yet in a condition to contract new engagements, I was prepossessed against them all, by supposing that they presumed upon the knowledge of my indiscretion with S———; and therefore rejected their addresses with detestation and disdain: for, as I have already observed, I was not to be won, but by the appearance of esteem and the most respectful carriage; and though, by a false step, I had, in my own opinion, forfeited my title to the one, I was resolved to discourage the advances of any man who seemed deficient in the other.

In this manner, my lovers were, one by one, repulsed, almost as soon as they presented themselves, and I preserved the independance of my heart, until I became acquainted with a certain peer,[1] whom I often saw at the house of Mrs. P———, an English lady then resident at Paris. This young nobleman professed himself deeply enamoured of me, in a stile so different from that of my other admirers, that I heard his protestations without disgust; and though my inclinations were still free, could not find in my heart to discountenance his addresses, which were preferred with the most engaging modesty, disinterestedness and respect.

By these never-failing arts, he gradually conquered my indifference, and gained the preference in my esteem from lord C———y[2] and the prince of C———, who were at that time his rivals. But what contributed (more than any consideration) to his success, was his declaring openly, that he would marry me without hesitation, as soon as I could obtain a divorce from my present husband, which, in all probability, might have been easily procured; for before I left England, lord ——— had offered me five thousand pounds, if I would consent to such a mutual release, that he might be at liberty to espouse one Miss W——— of Kent,[3] to whom he then made love upon honourable terms: but I was fool enough to refuse his proposal, by the advice of S———: and whether or not his lordship finding it impracticable to wed his new mistress, began to make love upon another footing, I know not; but certain it is, the mother forbad him the house, a circumstance which he took so heinously ill, that he appealed to the world in a public advertisement, beginning with, *Whereas, for some time, I have passionately loved Miss* W———, *and upon my not complying with the mother's proposals, they have turned me out of doors; this is to justify, &c.*

This declaration, signed with his name, was actually printed in a number of detached advertisements, which he ordered to be distributed to the public; and afterwards, being convinced by some of his friends, that he had done a very silly thing, he recalled them at half a guinea apiece. A copy of one of them was sent to me at Paris; and I believe my father has now one of the originals in his possession. After this wise vindication of his conduct, he made an attempt to carry off the lady from church, by force of arms; but she was rescued by the neighbours, headed by her brother, who being an attorney, had like to have made his lordship smart severely for this exploit.

Mean while, my new admirer had made some progress in my heart; and my finances being exhausted, I was reduced to the alternative of returning to lord —— again, or accepting earl B——'s love. When my affairs were brought to that issue, I made no hesitation in my choice, putting myself under the protection of a man of honour, whom I esteemed, rather than suffer every sort of mortification, from a person who was the object of my abhorrence and contempt. From a mistaken pride, I chose to live in lord B——k's house,¹ rather than be maintained at his expence in any other place. We spent several months agreeably in balls and other diversions, visited lord B—k, who lived at the distance of a few leagues from Paris, and stayed some days at his house, where the entertainment was, in all respects, delightful, elegant, and refined. Their habitation was the rendezvous of the best company in France; and lady B——k maintained the same superiority in her own sex, for which her lord is so justly distinguished among the men.

About Christmas we set out for England, accompanied by a little North Briton,² who lived with lord B—— as his companion, and did not at all approve of our correspondence; whether out of real friendship for his patron, or apprehension that in time I might supersede his own influence with my lord, I shall not pretend to determine. Be that as it will, the frost was so severe, that we were detained ten days at Calais, before we could get out of the harbour; and during that time, I reflected seriously on what my new lover had proposed: as he was very young, and unacquainted with the world, I thought my story might have escaped him; and therefore determined to give him a faithful detail of the whole, that he might not have any thing to reproach me with in the sequel; besides, I did not think it honest to engage him to do more for me than he might afterwards, perhaps, think I was worth. Accordingly, I communicated to him every particular of my life; and the narration, far from altering his sentiments, rather confirmed his good opinion, by exhibiting an undoubted proof of my frankness and sincerity. In short, he behaved with such generosity, as made an absolute conquest of my heart: but my love was of a different kind from that which had formerly reigned within my breast, being founded upon the warmest gratitude and esteem, exclusive of any other consideration, though his person was very agreeable, and his address engaging.

When we arrived in England, I went directly to his country-seat, about twelve miles from London, where he soon joined me, and we lived some time in perfect retirement,[1] his relations being greatly alarmed with the apprehension that lord —— would bring an action against him; though he himself desired nothing more, and lived so easily under that expectation, that they soon laid aside their fears on his account.

We were visited by Mr. H—— B——,[2] a relation of my lord, and one Mr. R—— of the guards,[3] who, with the little Scotch gentleman and my lover, made an agreeable set, among whom I enjoyed hunting, and all manner of country diversions. As to Mr. H—— B——, if ever there was perfection in one man, it centered in him; or at least, he, of all the men I ever knew, approached nearest to that idea which I had conceived of a perfect character. He was both good and great, possessed an uncommon genius and the best of hearts. Mr. R— was a very sociable man, had a good person and cultivated understanding; and my lord was excessively good humoured; so that, with such companions, no place could be dull or insipid: for my own part, I conducted the family; and as I endeavoured to please and make every body happy, I had the good fortune to succeed. Mr. B— told me, that before he saw me, he heard I was a fool; but finding (as he was pleased to say) that I had been egregiously misrepresented, he courted my friendship, and a correspondence commenced between us: indeed, it was impossible for any person to know him, without entertaining the utmost esteem and veneration for his virtue.

After I had lived some time in this agreeable retreat, my husband began to make a bustle: he sent a message, demanding me from lord B——; then came in person, with his night-cap in his pocket, intending to have stayed all night, had he been asked, and attended by a relation, whom he assured that I was very fond of him, and detained by force from his arms.

478

Finding himself disappointed in his expectations, he commenced a law-suit against lord B——, though not for a divorce, as we desired, but with a view to reclaim me as his lawful wife. His lawyers, however, attempted to prove criminal conversation, in hopes of extorting money from my lover; but their endeavours were altogether fruitless; for no servant of lord B——'s or mine, could with justice say, we were ever seen to trespass against modesty and decorum; so that the plaintiff was nonsuited.

While this cause was depending, all my lover's friends expressed fear and concern for the issue, while he himself behaved with the utmost resolution, and gave me such convincing proofs of a strong and steady affection, as augmented my gratitude, and rivetted the ties of my love, which was unblemished, faithful and sincere.

Soon after this event, I was seized with a violent fit of illness, in which I was visited by my father, and attended by two physicians, one of whom despaired of my life, and took his leave accordingly; but Dr. S——,[1] who was the other, persisted in his attendance, and, in all human appearance, saved my life; a circumstance by which he acquired a great share of reputation: yet, notwithstanding all his assistance, I was confined to my bed for ten weeks; during which, lord B——'s grief was immoderate, his care and generosity unlimited. Whilst I lay in this extremity, Mr. S——, penetrated by my melancholy condition, which revived his tenderness, begg'd leave to be admitted to my presence; and lord B—— would have complied with his request, had I not been judged too weak to bear the shock of such an interview. My constitution, however, agreeably disappointed their fears; and the fever had no sooner left me, than I was removed to a hunting-seat belonging to my lover, from whence, after I had recovered my strength, we went to B—— Castle, where we kept open house: and while we remained at this place, lord B—— received a letter from lord ——, dated in November, challenging him to single combat in May, upon the frontiers of France and Flanders. This defiance was sent in consequence of what had passed betwixt them long before my indisposition, at a meeting in a certain tavern, where they quarrelled, and in the fray my lover threw his antagonist under the table. I counselled him to take no notice of this rhodomontade, which I knew was void of all intention of performance; and he was wise enough to follow my advice; resolved, however, should the message be repeated, to take the challenger at his word.

Having resided some time in this place, we returned to the other country-house which we had left, where lord B—— addicted himself so much to hunting, and other male diversions, that I began to think he neglected me, and apprized him of my suspicion; assuring him, at the same time, that I would leave him as soon as my opinion should be confirmed.

This declaration had no effect upon his behaviour, which became so remarkably cold, that even Mr. R——, who lived with us, imagined that his affection was palpably diminished. When I went to town, I was usually attended by his cousin, or this gentleman, or both, but seldom favoured with his company; nay, when I repaired to Bath, for the re-establishment of my health, he permitted me to go alone; so that I was quite persuaded of his indifference; and yet, I was mistaken in my opinion: but, I had been spoiled by the behaviour of my first husband, and Mr. S——, who never quitted me for the sake of any amusement, and often resisted the calls of the most urgent business, rather than part from me, tho' but for a few hours. I thought every man who loved me truly, would act in the same manner; and whether I am right or wrong in my conjectures, I leave wiser casuists to judge. Certain it is, such sacrifice and devotion is the most pleasing proof of an admirer's passions; and *Voyez moi plus souvent, & ne me donnez rien*, is one of my favourite maxims. A man may give money, because he is profuse; he may be violently fond, because he is of a sanguine constitution; but if he gives me his time, he gives me an unquestionable proof of my being in full possession of his heart.

My appearance at Bath, without the company of lord B——, occasioned a general surprize, and encouraged the men to pester me with addresses; every new admirer endeavouring to advance his suit, by demonstrating the unkind and disrespectful behaviour of his lordship. Indeed, this was the most effectual string they could touch: my pride and resentment were alarmed, and I was weak enough to listen to one man,[1] who had like to have insinuated himself into my inclinations. He was tall and large boned, with white hair, inclining to what is called sandy, and had the reputation of being handsome, tho' I think he scarce deserved that epithet. He possessed a large fortune, loved mischief, and stuck at nothing for the accomplishment of his designs; one of his chief pleasures, being that of setting any two lovers at variance. He employed his address upon me with great assiduity, and knew so well how to manage my resentment, that I was pleased with his manner, heard his vows without disgust, and, in a word, promised to deliberate with myself upon his proposals, and give him an account of my determination in writing.

Thus resolved, I went to lord B——, in Wiltshire, whither I was followed by this pretender to my heart, who visited us on the footing of an acquaintance; but when I reflected on what I had done, I condemned my own conduct, as indiscreet, though nothing decisive had passed between us, and began to hate him in proportion to the self-conviction I felt; perceiving that I had involved myself in a difficulty from which I should not be easily disengaged. For the present, however, I found means to postpone my declaration; he admitted my excuse, and I returned to London with lord B——, who was again summoned to the field by his former challenger.

H—d—n,[1] governor, counsellor, and steward to this little hero, came to lord B—— with a verbal message, importing, that his lordship had changed his mind about going to Flanders, but expected to meet him, on such a day and hour, in the burying-ground near Red-lion-square. Lord B—— accepted the challenge, and gave me an account of what had passed; but he had been anticipated by the messenger, who had already tried to alarm my fears, from the consideration of the consequence, that I might take some measures to prevent their meeting. But I perceived his drift, and told him plainly that lord —— had no intention to risque his person, tho' he endeavoured with all his might to persuade me, that his principal was desperate and determined. I knew my little husband too well, to think he would bring matters to any dangerous issue, and was apprehensive of nothing but foul play, from the villainy of H—n, with which I was equally well acquainted. Indeed I signified my doubts on that score to Mr. B——, who would have attended his kinsman to the field, had he not thought he might be liable to censure, if any thing should happen to lord B——, because he himself was heir at law: for that reason, he judiciously declined being personally concerned; and we pitched upon the earl of A—, his lordship's uncle,[2] who willingly undertook the office.

At the appointed time they went to the place of rendezvous, where they had not waited long when the challenger appeared, in a new pink satin waistcoat, which he had put on for the occasion, with his sword under his arm, and his steward by him, leaving, in an hackney coach, at some distance, a surgeon whom he had provided for the care of his person. Thus equipped, he advanced to his antagonist, and desired him to choose his ground; upon which lord B— told him, that if he must fall, it was not material which grave he should tumble over.

Our little hero finding him so jocose and determined, turned to lord A—, and desired to speak with him, that he might disburden his conscience before they should begin the work of death. They accordingly went aside; and he gave him to understand, that his motive for fighting was lord B—'s detaining his wife from him, by compulsion. The earl of A— assured him, he was egregiously mistaken in his conjecture; that his nephew used no force or undue influence, to keep me in his house; but it could not be expected that he would turn me out of doors.

This explanation was altogether satisfactory to lord —, who said he was far from being so unreasonable as to expect lord B— would commit such a breach of hospitality; and all he desired was, that his wife should be left to her own inclinations. Upon these articles peace was concluded, and they parted without bloodshed. At least these are the particulars of the story, as they were related by lord A——, with whom I laugh'd heartily at the adventure; for I never doubted that the challenger would find some expedient to prevent the duel, tho' I wondered how he mustered up resolution enough to carry it so far.

That he might not, however, give us any more trouble, we resolved to go and enjoy ourselves in France, whither I went by myself, in hopes of being soon joined by my lover, who was obliged to stay some time longer in England, to settle his affairs. He was so much affected at our parting (tho' but for a few weeks) that he was almost distracted; and this affliction renewed my tenderness for him, because it was an undoubted proof of his love. I wrote to him every post from France; and, as I had no secrets, desired him to take care of all the letters that should come to his house, directed to me, after my departure from England.

This was an unfortunate office for him, in the execution of which he chanced to open a letter from Sir T— A—,[1] with whom (as I have already observed) I had some correspondence at Bath. I had, according to my promise, given this gentleman a decisive answer, importing, that I was determined to remain in my present situation; but as lord B— was ignorant of my sentiments in that particular, and perceived from the letter that something extraordinary had passed between us, and that I was earnestly sollicited to leave him, he was seized with the utmost consternation and concern; and having previously obtained the king's leave to go abroad, set out that very night for France, leaving his affairs in the greatest confusion.

Sir T— A— hearing I was gone, without understanding the cause of my departure, took the same rout, and both arrived at

Dover next day. They heard of each other's motions: each bribed the master of a packet-boat to transport him with expedition; but that depending upon the wind, both reached Calais at the same time, tho' in different vessels. Sir T— sent his valet de chambre, post, with a letter, intreating me to accompany him into Italy, where he would make me mistress of his whole fortune, and to set out directly for that country, that he might not lose me by the arrival of lord B—, promising to join me on the road, if I would consent to make him happy. I sent his messenger back with an answer, wherein I expressed surprize at his proposals, after having signified my resolution to him before I left England; and he was scarce dismissed, when I received another letter from lord B—, beseeching me to meet him at Clermont, upon the road from Calais; and conjuring me to avoid the sight of his rival, should he get the start of him in travelling. This, however, was not likely to be the case, as lord B— rode post, and the other was, by his corpulence, obliged to travel in a chaise; yet, that I might not increase his anxiety, I left Paris immediately on the receit of his message, and met him at the appointed place, where he received me with all the agitation of joy and fear, and asked if I had ever encouraged Sir T—A— in his addresses. I very candidly told him the whole transaction, at which he was incensed; but his indignation was soon appeased, when I professed my penitence, and assured him, that I had totally rejected his rival. Not that I approve of my behaviour to Sir T— who (I own) was ill used in this affair; but surely it was more excusable to halt here, than proceed farther in my indiscretion.

My lover being satisfied with my declaration, we went together to Paris, being attended by the Scotchman whom I have already mentioned, tho' I believe he was not over and above well pleased to see matters thus amicably compromised. The furious knight followed us to the capital; insisted upon seeing me in person; told this North Briton, that I was actually engaged to him; wrote every hour, and railed at my perfidious conduct. I took no notice of these delirious transports, which were also disregarded by lord B—, till one night he was exasperated by the insinuations of Mr. C—,[1] who, I believe, inflamed his jealousy, by hinting a suspicion that I was really in love with his rival. What passed betwixt them I know not, but he sent for me from the opera, by a physician of Paris, who was a sort of go-between among us all, and who told me, that if I did not come home on the instant, a duel would be fought on my account.

I was very much shocked at this information; but by being used to alarms from the behaviour of lord —, I had acquired a pretty good share of resolution, and with great composure entered the room where lord B— was, with his companion, whom I immediately ordered to withdraw. I then gave his lordship to understand, that I was informed of what had passed, and thought myself so much injured by the person who had just quitted the apartment, that I would no longer live under the same roof with him.

Lord B— raved like a bedlamite, taxing me with want of candour and affection; but I easily justified my own integrity, and gave him such assurances of my love, that his jealousy subsided, and his spirits were recomposed. Nevertheless I insisted upon his dismissing Mr. C—, on pain of my leaving the house, as I could not help thinking he had used his endeavours to prejudice me in the opinion of my lord. If his conduct was the result of friendship for his patron, he certainly acted the part of an honest and trusty adherent. But I could not easily forgive him, because, a few weeks before, he had, by my interest, obtained a considerable addition to his allowance; and even after the steps he had taken to disoblige me, I was not so much his enemy but that I prevailed upon lord B— to double his salary, that his leaving the family might be no detriment to his fortune.

His lordship having complied with my demand, this gentleman, after having stayed three days in the house, to prepare for his departure, during which I would not suffer him to be admitted into my presence, made his retreat with a fine young girl who was my companion; and I have never seen him since that time.

Sir T— still continued furious, and would not take a denial, except from my own mouth; upon which, with the approbation of lord B—, I indulged him with an interview. He entered the apartment with a stern countenance, and told me I had us'd him ill. I pleaded guilty to the charge, and begg'd his pardon accordingly. I attempted to reason the case with him, but he would hear no arguments except his own, and even tried to intimidate me with threats; which provoked me to such a degree, that I defied his vengeance, telling him that I feared nothing but the reproach of my own conscience; that tho' I had acted a simple part, he durst not say there was any thing criminal in my conduct; and that, from his present frantic and unjust behaviour, I thought myself happy in having escaped him. He swore I was the most inflexible of all creatures, asked if nothing would move me? and when I answered, 'Nothing,' took his leave, and never afterwards persecuted me with his addresses; tho' I have heard he was vain and false enough to boast of favours, which, upon my honour, he never received, as he himself, at one time, owned to doctor Cantwell at Paris.[1]

While he underwent all this frenzy and distraction upon my account, he was loved with the same violence of passion by a certain Scotch lady of quality, who, when he followed me to France, pursued him thither with the same eagerness and expedition; and, far from being jealous of me as a rival, us'd to come to my house, implore my good offices with the object of her love, and laying herself on the floor at full length, before the fire, weep and cry like a person bereft of her senses. She bitterly complained, that he had never obliged her but once; and begg'd, with the most earnest supplications, that I would give her an opportunity of seeing him at my house. But I thought proper to avoid her company, as soon as I perceived her intention.

We continued at Paris for some time, during which I contracted an acquaintance with the sister of madam la T—. She was the supposed mistress of the prince of C—, endowed with a great share of understanding, and loved pleasure to excess, tho' she maintained her reputation on a respectable footing, by living with her husband and mother. This lady, perceiving that I had inspired her lover with a passion, which gave me uneasiness on her account, actually practised all her eloquence and art, in persuading me to listen to his love; for it was a maxim with her, to please him at any rate. I was shocked at her indelicate complaisance, and rejected the proposal, as repugnant to my present engagement, which I held as sacred as any nuptial tie, and much more binding than a forced or unnatural marriage.

Upon our return to England we lived in great harmony and peace; and nothing was wanting to my happiness, but the one thing to me most needful; I mean the inchanting tenderness and delightful enthusiasm of love. Lord B—'s heart (I believe) felt the soft impressions; and, for my own part, I loved him with the most faithful affection. It is not enough to say I wished him well; I had the most delicate, the most genuine esteem for his virtue, I had an intimate regard and anxiety for his interest, and felt for him as if he had been my own son: but still there was a vacancy in my heart; there was not that fervour, that transport, that ecstasy of passion which I had formerly known; my bosom was not filled with the little deity; I could not help recalling to my remembrance the fond, the ravishing moments I had passed with S—; and had I understood the conditions of life, those pleasures were happily exchanged for my present situation, because, if I was now deprived of those rapturous enjoyments, I was also exempted from the cares and anxiety that attended them; but I was generally extravagant in my notions of happiness, and therefore construed my present tranquillity into an insipid languor and stagnation of life.

While I remained in this inactivity of sentiment, lord —— having received a very considerable addition to his fortune, sent a message to me, promising, that if I would leave lord B—, he would make me a present of an house and furniture, where I should live at my ease, without being exposed to his visits, except when I should be disposed to receive them.¹ This proposal he made, in consequence of what I had always declared, namely, that if he had not reduced me to the necessity of putting myself under the protection of some person or other, by depriving me of any other means of subsistence, I should never have given the world the least cause to scandalize my reputation; and that I would withdraw myself from my present dependance, as soon as he should enable me to live by myself. I was therefore resolved to be as good as my word, and accepted his offer, on condition that I should be wholly at my own disposal, and that he should never enter my door but as a visitant or common friend.

These articles being sanctioned by his word and honour (the value of which I did not then know) an house was furnished according to my directions; and I signified my intention to lord B—, who consented to my removal, with this proviso, that I should continue to see him. I wrote also to his relation Mr. B—,² who, in his answer, observed, that it was too late to advise when I was actually determined. All my friends and acquaintance approved of the scheme, tho' it was one of the most unjustifiable steps I had ever taken, being a real act of ingratitude to my benefactor; which I soon did, and always shall regret and condemn. So little is the world qualified to judge of private affairs!

When the time of our parting drew near, lord B— became gloomy and discontented, and even intreated me to postpone my resolution; but I told him, that now every thing was prepared for my reception, I could not retract without incurring the imputation of folly and extravagance. On the very day of my departure Mr. B— endeavoured, with all the arguments he could suggest, to dissuade me from my purpose; and I made use of the same answer which had satisfied his friend. Finding me determined upon removing, he burst out into a flood of tears, exclaiming, 'By G—d, if lord B—— can bear it, I can't.' I was thunderstruck at this expression; for tho' I had been told that Mr. B— was in love with me, I gave no credit to the report, because he had never declared his passion, and this was the first hint of it that ever escaped him in my hearing. I was therefore so much amazed at the circumstance of this abrupt explanation, that I could make no answer; but having taken my leave, went away, ruminating on the unforeseen event.

Lord B— (as I was informed) spoke not a word that whole night, and took my leaving him so much to heart, that two years elapsed before he got the better of his grief. This intelligence I afterwards received from his own mouth, and asked his forgiveness for my unkind retreat, tho' I shall never be able to obtain my own. As for Mr. B—, he was overwhelmed with sorrow, and made such efforts to suppress his concern, as had well nigh cost him his life. Dr. S— was called to him in the middle of the night, and found him almost suffocated. He soon guessed the cause, when he understood that I had left the house: so that I myself was the only person concerned who was utterly ignorant of his affection; for I solemnly declare he never gave me the least reason to suspect it while I lived with his relation, because he had too much honour to entertain a thought of supplanting his friend, and too good an opinion of me to believe he should have succeeded in the attempt. Tho' my love for lord B— was not so tender and interesting as the passion I had felt for S——, my fidelity was inviolable, and I never harboured the most distant thought of any other person, till after I had resolved to leave him, when (I own) I afforded some small encouragement to the addresses of a new admirer, by telling him, that I should, in a little time, be my own mistress, tho' I was not now at my own disposal.

I enjoyed my new house as a little paradise: it was accommodated with all sorts of conveniences; every thing was new, and therefore pleasing, and the whole absolutely at my command. I had the company of a relation, a very good woman, with whom I lived in the most amicable manner; was visited by the best people in town (I mean those of the male sex, the ladies having long ago forsaken me;) I frequented all reputable places of publick entertainment, and had a concert at home once a week: so that my days rolled on in happiness and quiet, till all my sweets were imbittered by the vexatious behaviour of my husband, who began to importune me again to live with him; and by the increasing anxiety of lord B—, who (tho' I still admitted his visits) plainly perceived that I wanted to relinquish his correspondence. This discovery raised such tempests of jealousy and despair within his breast, that he kept me in continual alarms: he sent messages to me every hour, signed his letters with his own blood, raved like a man in an ecstasy of madness, railed at my ingratitude, and praised my conduct, by turns; offered to sacrifice every thing for my love, to leave the kingdom forthwith, and live with me for ever in any part of the world where I should choose to reside.

These were generous and tempting proposals; but I was beset with counsellors who were not totally disinterested, and who dissuaded me from embracing the proffers of my lover, on pretence that lord —— would be highly injured by my compliance. I listened to their advice, and hardened my heart against lord B—'s sorrow and solicitations. My behaviour on this occasion is altogether unaccountable; this was the only time that ever I was a slave to admonition. The condition of lord B— would have melted any heart but mine, and yet mine was one of the most sensible: he employed his cousin as an advocate with me, till that gentleman actually refused the office, telling him candidly, that his own inclinations were too much engaged, to permit him to perform the task with fidelity and truth. He accordingly resolved to avoid my presence, until my lord and I should come to some final determination, which was greatly retarded by the perseverance of his lordship, who would not resign his hopes even when I pretended that another man had engaged my heart, but said, that in time my affection might return.

Our correspondence, however, gradually wore off; upon which Mr. B— renewed his visits, and many agreeable and happy hours we passed together. Not that he, or any other person whom I now saw, succeeded to the privilege of a fortunate lover: I knew he loved me to madness; but I would not gratify his passion any other way than by the most profound esteem and veneration for his virtues, which were altogether amiable and sublime; and I would here draw his character minutely, but it wou'd take up too much time to set forth his merits; the only man living of my acquaintance who resembles him is lord F—,[1] of whom I shall speak in the sequel.

About this time, I underwent a very interesting change in the situation of my heart. I had sent a message to my old lover S——, desiring he would allow my picture, which was in his possession, to be copied; and he now transmitted it to me by my lawyer, whom he directed to ask, if I intended to be at the next masquerade. This curiosity had a strange effect upon my spirits; my heart fluttered at the question, and my imagination glowed with a thousand fond presages. I answered in the affirmative, and we met by accident at the ball. I could not behold him without emotion; when he accosted me, his well-known voice made my heart vibrate, like a musical chord, when its unison is struck. All the ideas of our past love, which the lapse of time and absence had enfeebled and lulled asleep, now awoke, and were re-inspired by his appearance; so that his artful excuses were easily admitted: I forgave him all that I had suffered on his account, because he was the natural lord of my affection; and our former correspondence was renewed.

I thought myself in a new world of bliss, in consequence of this reconciliation, the raptures of which continued unimpaired for the space of four months, during which time he was fonder of me, if possible, than before, repeated his promise of marriage, if we should ever have it in our power; assured me he had never been happy since he left me; that he believed no woman had ever loved like me: and indeed, to have a notion of my passion for that man, you must first have loved as I did: but, through a strange caprice, I broke off the correspondence, out of apprehension that he would forsake me again. From his past conduct, I dreaded what might happen; and the remembrance of what I had undergone by his inconstancy, filled my imagination with such horror, that I could not endure the shocking prospect, and prematurely plunged myself into the danger, rather than endure the terrors of expectation.[1] In consequence of this desertion, I received a letter from him, acknowledging that he was rightly served, but that it gave him inexpressible concern.

Mean while, lord —— continued to act in the character of a fiend, tormenting me with his nauseous importunities: he prevailed upon the duke of L——[2] to employ his influence in persuading me to live with him; assuring his grace, that I had actually promised to give him that proof of my obedience, and that I would come home the sooner for being pressed to compliance by a person of his rank and character. Induced by these representations, the duke honoured me with a visit; and in the course of his exhortations I understood how he had been thus misinformed: upon which I sent for lord ——, and in his presence convicted him of the falshood, by communicating to his grace the articles of our last agreement, which he did not think proper to deny; and the duke being undeceived, declared that he would not have given me the trouble of vindicating myself, had he not been misled by the insincerity of my lord.

Baffled in this attempt, he engaged Mr. H— V—,[3] and afterwards my own father, in the same task; and tho' I still adhered to my first resolution, persisted with such obstinacy in his endeavours to make me unhappy, that I determined to leave the kingdom; and accordingly, after I had spent the evening with him at Ranelagh, I went away about two o'clock in the morning, leaving my companion, with directions to restore to my lord his house, furniture, plate, and every thing he had given me since our last accommodation; so far was I, upon this occasion, or at any other time of my life, from embezzling any part of his fortune. My friend followed my instructions most punctually; and his lordship knows, and will acknowledge, the truth of this assertion.

Thus have I explained the true cause of my first expedition to Flanders, whither the world was good-natured enough to say I followed Mr. B—— and the whole army, which happened to be sent abroad that summer.[1] Before my departure I likewise transmitted to lord B— the dressing-plate, china, and a very considerable settlement, of which he had been generous enough to make me a present. This was an instance of my integrity, which I thought due to a man who had laid me under great obligations; and tho' I have lived to be refused a small sum both by him and S—, I do not repent of my disinterested behaviour; and all the revenge I harbour against the last of these lovers, is the desire of having it in my power to do him good.

I now found myself adrift in the world again, and very richly deserved the hardships of my condition, for my indiscretion in leaving lord B—, and in trusting to the word of lord ——, without some farther security; but I have dearly paid for my imprudence. The more I saw into the character of this man whom destiny hath appointed my scourge, the more was I determined to avoid his fellowship and communication; for he and I are, in point of disposition, as opposite as any two principles in nature. In the first place, he is one of the most unsocial beings that ever existed; when I was pleased and happy he was always out of temper, but if he could find means to overcast and cloud my mirth, tho' never so innocent, he then discovered the signs of uncommon satisfaction and content, because, by this disagreeable temper, he banished all company from his house. He is extremely weak of understanding, tho' he possesses a good share of low cunning, which has so egregiously imposed upon some people, that they have actually believed him a good-natured easy creature, and blamed me because I did not manage him to better purpose; but, upon further acquaintance, they have always found him obstinate as a mule, and capricious as a monkey. Not that he is utterly void of all commendable qualities: he is punctual in paying his debts, liberal when in good humour, and would be well bred, were he not subject to fits of absence, during which he is altogether unconversable; but he is proud, naturally suspicious, jealous, equally with and without cause, never made a friend, and is an utter stranger to the joys of intimacy; in short, he hangs like a damp upon society, and may be properly called *Kill-joy*, an epithet which he has justly acquired. He honours me with constant professions of love, but his conduct is so opposite to my sentiments of that passion, as to have been the prime source of all my misfortunes and affliction; and I have often wished myself the object of his hate, in hopes of profiting by a change in his behaviour.

Indeed, he has not been able to make me more unhappy than, I believe, he is in his own mind; for he is literally a self-tormentor, who never enjoyed one gleam of satisfaction, except at the expence of another's quiet; and yet with this (I had almost called it diabolical) quality, he expects that I should cherish him with all the tenderness of affection; and after he has been at pains to incur my aversion, punishes my disgust, by contriving schemes to mortify and perplex me, which have often succeeded so effectually, as to endanger my life and constitution; for I have been fretted and frighted into sundry fits of illness, and then I own I have experienced his care and concern.

Over and above the oddities I have mentioned, he is so unsteady in his œconomy, that he is always new modelling his affairs, and exhausting his fortune, by laying out ten pounds, in order to save a shilling; he inquires into the character of a servant after he has lived two years in his family, and is so ridiculously stocked with vanity and self-conceit, that notwithstanding my assurance before, and the whole series of my conduct since our marriage, which ought to have convinced him of my dislike, he is still persuaded, that at bottom, I must admire and be enamoured of his agreeable person and accomplishments, and that I would not fail to manifest my love, were I not spirited up against him by his own relations. Perhaps it might be to their interest to foment the misunderstanding betwixt us; but really, they give themselves no trouble about our affairs; and, so far as I know them, are a very good sort of people. On the whole, I think I may with justice pronounce my precious yoke-fellow a trifling, teazing, insufferable, inconsistent creature.

With the little money which remained of what I had received from his lordship, for housekeeping, I transported myself to Flanders, and arrived in Ghent, a few days after our troops were quartered in that city, which was so much crowded with these new visitants, that I should have found it impracticable to procure a lodging, had I not been accommodated by lord R— B—, the duke of A——'s youngest brother,[1] who very politely gave me up his own. Here I saw my friend Mr. B——, who was overjoyed at my arrival, though jealous of every man of his acquaintance; for he loved me with all the ardour of passion, and I regarded him with all the perfection of friendship, which, had he lived, in time might have produced love; but it never did. Notwithstanding his earnest solicitations to the contrary, I stayed but a week in Ghent, from whence I proceeded to Brussels, and fixed my abode in the Hotel de Flandre, among an agreeable set of gentlemen and ladies, with whom I spent my time very chearfully. There being a sort of court in this city, it was frequented by all the officers, who could obtain permission to go thither; and the place in general was gay and agreeable. I was introduced to the best families, and very happy in my acquaintance; for the ladies were polite, good tempered, and obliging, and treated me with the utmost hospitality and respect. Among others, I contracted a friendship with Madam la comtesse de C——, and her two daughters, who were very amiable young ladies; and became intimate with the princess C—— and countess W——, lady of the bed-chamber to the queen of Hungary, and a great favourite of the governor Monsieur D'H——, in whose house she lived with his wife, who was also a lady of a very engaging disposition.[2]

Soon after I had fixed my habitation in Brussels, the company at our Hotel was increased by three officers, who professed themselves my admirers, and came from Ghent, with a view of soliciting my love. This triumvirate consisted of the Scotch earl of ——, lord R— M—,[3] and another young officer: the first was a man of a very genteel figure and amorous complexion, danced well, and had a great deal of good humour, with a mixture of vanity and self-conceit. The second had a good face, though a clumsy person, and a very sweet disposition, very much adapted for the sentimental passion of love: and the third (Mr. W—— by name) was tall, thin, and well-bred, with a great stock of good nature and vivacity. These adventurers began their addresses in general acts of gallantry, that comprehended several of my female friends, with whom we used to engage in parties of pleasure, both in the city and the *environs*, which are extremely agreeable; and when they thought they had taken the preliminary steps of securing themselves in my good opinion and esteem, they agreed to go on without farther delay, and that lord —— should make the first attack upon my heart.

He accordingly laid siege to me, with such warmth and assiduity, that I believe he deceived himself, and began to think he was actually in love; though at bottom, he felt no impulse that deserved the sacred name. Though I discouraged him in the beginning, he persecuted me with his addresses; he always sat by me at dinner, and imparted a thousand trifles in continual whispers, which attracted the notice of the company so much, that I began to fear his behaviour would give rise to some report to my prejudice; and therefore avoided him with the utmost caution. Notwithstanding all my care, however, he found means one night, while my maid, who lay in my room, went down stairs, to get into my chamber after I was abed: upon which, I started up, and told him, that if he should approach me, I would alarm the house; for I never wanted courage and resolution. Perceiving my displeasure, he kneeled by the bedside, begg'd I would have pity on his sufferings, and swore I should have *carte blanche* to the utmost extent of his fortune. To these proposals I made no other reply, but that of protesting I would never speak to him again, if he did not quit my apartment that moment; upon which, he thought proper to withdraw; and I never afterwards gave him an opportunity of speaking to me on the same subject: so that, in a few weeks, he separated himself from our society; though the ladies of Brussels considered him as my lover, because, of all the other officers, he was their greatest favourite.

His lordship being thus repulsed, Mr. W—— took the field, and assailed my heart in a very different manner. He said, he knew not how to make love, but was a man of honour, would keep the secret, and so forth. To this cavalier address I answered, that I was not angry, as I otherwise should have been at his blunt declaration, because I found, by his own confession, he did not know what was due to the sex; and my unhappy situation in some shape excused him for a liberty, which he would not have dream'd of taking, had not my misfortunes encouraged his presumption. But I would deal with him in his own way; and far from assuming the prude, frankly assured him, that he was not at all to my taste, hoping he would consider my dislike as a sufficient reason to reject his love.

Lord R—— began to feel the symptoms of a genuine passion, which he carefully cherished in silence, being naturally diffident and bashful; but, by the very means he used to conceal it from my observation, I plainly discerned the situation of his heart, and was not at all displeased at the progress I had made in his inclinations. Mean while, he cultivated my acquaintance with great assiduity and respect, attended me in all my excursions, and particularly in an expedition to Antwerp, with two other gentlemen, where, in downright *gaietè de cœur*, we sat for our pictures, which were drawn in one piece; one of the partie being represented in the dress of an hussar, and another in that of a running footman. This incident I mention, because the performance, which is now in my possession, gave birth to a thousand groundless reports, that circulated in England at our expence.

It was immediately after this jaunt, that lord R—— began to disclose his passion; though he, at the same time, started such objections as seemed well nigh to extinguish his hopes, lamenting, that even if he should have the happiness to engage my affections, his fortune was too inconsiderable to support us against the efforts of lord ——, should he attempt to interrupt our felicity; and that he himself was obliged to follow the motions of the army. In short, he seemed to consider my felicity more than his own, and behaved with such delicacy, as gradually made an impression on my heart; so that when we parted, we agreed to renew our correspondence in England.

In the midst of these agreeable amusements, which I enjoyed in almost all the different towns of Flanders, I happened to be at Ghent one day, sitting among a good deal of company, in one of their Hotels, when a post-chaise stopped at the gate; upon which we went to the windows to satisfy our curiosity, when who should step out of the convenience, but my little insignificant lord. I no sooner announced him to the company, than all the gentlemen asked whether they should stay and protect me, or withdraw; and when I assured them, that their protection was not necessary, one and all of them retired; though lord R—— M—— went no farther than the parlour below, being determined to screen me against all violence and compulsion. I sent a message to my lord, desiring him to walk up into my apartment; but although his sole errand was to see and carry me off, he would not venture to accept of my invitation, till he had demanded me in form, from the governor of the place.

That gentleman being altogether a stranger to his person and character, referred him to the commanding officer of the English troops, who was a man of humour, and upon his lordship's application, pretended to doubt his identity; observing, that he had always heard lord —— represented as a jolly corpulent man. He gave him to understand, however, that even granting him to be the person, I was by no means subject to military law, unless he could prove, that I had ever inlisted in his majesty's service.

Thus disappointed in his endeavours, he returned to the inn, and, with much persuasion, trusted himself in my dining-room, after having stationed his attendant at the door, in case of accidents. When I asked, what had procured me the honour of this visit; he told me, his business and intention were to carry me home; and this declaration produced a conference, in which I argued the case with him; and matters were accommodated for the present, by my promising to be in England some time in September, on condition that he would permit me to live by myself, as before, and immediately order the arrears of my pin-money to be paid. He assented to every thing I proposed, returned in peace to his own country, and the deficiencies of my allowance were made good; while I returned to Brussels, where I stayed until my departure for England, which I regulated in such a manner as was consistent with my engagement.

I took lodgings in Pall-mall, and sending for my lord, convinced him of my punctuality, and put him in mind of his promise; when, to my utter astonishment and confusion, he owned, that his promise was no more than a decoy to bring me over, and that I must lay my account with living in his house, like a dutiful and obedient wife. I heard him with the indignation such treatment deserved, upbraided him with his perfidious dealing, which I told him would have determined me against cohabitation with him, had I not been already resolved: and being destitute of all resource, repaired to Bath, where I afterwards met with Mr. D—— and Mr. R——, two gentlemen who had been my fellow-passengers in the yacht from Flanders, and treated me with great friendship and politeness, without either talking or thinking of love.

With these gentlemen, who were as idle as myself, I went to the jubilee at Preston, which was no other than a great number of people assembled in a small town extremely ill accommodated, to partake of diversions that were bad imitations of plays, concerts, and masquerades. If the world should place to the account of my indiscretion, my travelling in this manner, with gentlemen to whom I had no particular attachment; let it also be considered, as an alleviation, that I always lived in terror of my lord, and consequently was often obliged to shift my quarters; so that my finances being extremely slender, I stood the more in need of assistance and protection. I was, besides, young, inconsiderate, and so simple, as to suppose the figure of an ugly man would always secure me from censure on his account: neither did I ever dream of any man's addresses, until he made an actual declaration of his love.

Upon my return to Bath, I was again harrassed by lord ——, who came thither accompanied by my father, whom I was very glad to see, though he importuned me to comply with my husband's desire, and for the future keep measures with the world. This remonstrance about living with my lord, which he constantly repeated, was the only instance of his unkindness which I ever felt. But all his admonitions were not of force sufficient to shake my resolution in that particular; though the debate continued so late, that I told his lordship, it was high time to retire, for I could not accommodate him with a bed. He then gave me to understand, that he would stay where he was; upon which my father took his leave, on pretence of looking out for a lodging to himself.

The little gentleman being now left *tête a tête* with me, began to discover some signs of apprehension in his looks; but mustering up all his resolution, he went to the door, called up three of his servants, whom he placed as centinels upon the stair, and flung himself in my elbow-chair, where he resigned himself to rest. Intending to go to bed, I thought it was but just and decent that I should screen myself from the intrusion of his footmen, and with that view bolted the door. Lord —— hearing himself locked in, started up in the utmost terror and consternation, kicked the door with his heel, and screamed aloud, as if he had been in the hands of an assassin. My father, who had not yet quitted the house, hearing these outcries, ran up stairs again, and coming through my bed-chamber, into the dining-room where we were, found me almost suffocated with laughter, and his heroic son-in-law staring like one who had lost his wits, with his hair standing on end.

When my father asked the meaning of his exclamations, he told him with all the symptoms of dismay, that I had lock'd him in, and he did not understand such usage: but I explained the whole mystery, by saying, I had bolted the door, because I did not like the company of his servants, and could not imagine the cause of his pannic, unless he thought I designed to ravish him; an insult, than which nothing was farther from my intention. My father himself could scarce refrain from laughing at his ridiculous fear; but seeing him in great confusion, took pity on his condition, and carried him off to his own lodgings, after I had given my word, that I would not attempt to escape, but give him audience next morning. I accordingly kept my promise, and found means to persuade them to leave me at my own discretion. Next day, I was rallied upon the stratagem I had contrived to frighten lord ——; and a thousand idle stories were told about this adventure, which happened literally as I have related it.

From Bath I betook myself to a small house near Lincoln, which

I hired of the d— of A——,[1] because a country life suited best with my income, which was no more than four hundred pounds a year, and that not well paid. I continued some months in this retirement, and saw no company, except lord R—— M——, who lived in the neighbourhood, and visited me twice; till finding myself indisposed, I was obliged to remove to London, and took lodgings in Maddox-street, where my garison was taken by storm, by my lord and his steward, reinforced by Mr. L—— V——,[2] (who, as my lord told me, had a subsidy of five and twenty pounds, before he would take the field) and a couple of hardy footmen. This formidable band rushed into my apartment, laid violent hands upon me, dragged me down stairs, without gloves or a cloak, and thrusting me into a coach that stood at the door, conveyed me to my lord's lodgings in Gloucester-street.

Upon this occasion, his lordship courageously drew his sword upon my woman, who attempted to defend me from his insults, and, in all probability, would have intimidated him from proceeding; for he looked pale and aghast, his knees knocked together, and he breathed thick and hard, with his nostrils dilated, as if he had seen a ghost. But he was encouraged by his mercenary associate, who, for the five and twenty pounds, stood by him in the day of trouble, and spirited him on to this gallant enterprize.

In consequence of this exploit, I was cooped up in a paultry apartment in Gloucester-street, where I was close beset by his lordship, and his worthy steward Mr. H——, with a set of servants that were the creatures of this fellow, of whom lord —— himself stood in awe; so that I could not help thinking myself in Newgate, among thieves and ruffians: and to such a degree did my terror prevail, that I actually believed I was in danger of being poisoned, and would not receive any sustenance, except from the hands of one harmless-looking fellow, a foreigner, who was my lord's valet de chambre. I will not pretend to say my fears were just; but such was my opinion of H—n, that I never doubted he would put me out of the way, if he thought my life interfered with his interest.

On the second day of my imprisonment, I was visited by the duke of L——, a friend of my lord, who found me sitting upon a trunk, in a poor little dining-room filled with lumber, and lighted with two bits of tallow-candle, which had been left over night. He perceived in my countenance a mixture of rage, indignation, terror and despair: he compassionated my sufferings, though he could not alleviate my distress, any other way than by interceding with my tyrant to mitigate my oppression. Nevertheless, I remained eleven

497

days in this comfortable situation: I was watched like a criminal all day, and one of the servants walked from one room to another all night, in the nature of a patrole; while my lord, who lay in the chamber above me, got out of bed, and tripp'd to the window, at the sound of every coach that chanced to pass through the street. H——n, who was consummate in the arts of a sycophant, began to court my favour, by condoling my affliction, and assuring me, that the only method by which I could regain my liberty, was a chearful compliance with the humour of my lord. I was fully convinced of the truth of this observation; and though my temper is altogether averse to dissimulation, attempted to affect an air of serenity and resignation. But this disguise, I found, would not answer my purpose; and therefore I had recourse to the assistance of my maid, who was permitted to attend me in my confinement. With her I frequently consulted about the means of accomplishing my escape; and, in consequence of our deliberations, she directed a coach and six to be ready at a certain part of the town, and to wait for me three days in the same place, in case I could not come before the expiration of that term.

This previous measure being taken according to my instructions, the next necessary step was to elude the vigilance of my guard: and in this manner did I effectuate my purpose. Being, by this time, indulged in the liberty of going out in the coach, for the benefit of the air, attended by two footmen, who had orders to watch all my motions, I made use of this privilege one forenoon, when lord —— expected some company to dinner, and bad the coachman drive to the lodgings of a man who wrote with his mouth, intending to give my spies the slip, on pretence of seeing this curiosity: but they were too alert in their duty to be thus outwitted, and followed me up stairs into the very apartment.

Disappointed in this hope, I revolved another scheme, which was attended with success: I bought some olives at an oil-shop; and telling the servants I would proceed to St. James's gate, and take a turn in the park, broke one of the bottles by the way, complained of the misfortune when I was set down, and desired that my coach might be cleaned before my return. While my attendants were employed in this office, I tripp'd across the parade to the horse-guards, and chanced to meet with an acquaintance in the park, who said, he saw by my countenance, that I was upon some expedition. I owned his supposition was just; but, as I had not time to relate particulars, I quickened my pace, and took possession of a hackney-coach, in which I proceeded to the vehicle which I had appointed to be in waiting.

Chapter LXXXVIII

While I thus compassed my escape, there was nothing but perplexity and confusion at home; dinner was delayed till six o'clock; my lord ran half over the town in quest of his equipage, which at last returned, with an account of my elopement. My maid was brought to the question, and grievously threatened; but (like all the women I ever had) remained unshaken in her fidelity. In the mean time, I travelled night and day towards my retreat in Lincoln-shire, of which his lordship had not, as yet, got the least intelligence; and as my coachman was but an unexperienced driver, I was obliged to make use of my own skill in that exercise, and direct his endeavours the whole way, without venturing to go to bed, or take the least repose, until I reached my own habitation, where I lived in peace and tranquillity for the space of six weeks, when I was alarmed by one of my lord's myrmidons, who came into the neighbourhood, blustering and swearing, that he would carry me off, either dead or alive.

It is not to be supposed that I was perfectly easy, when I was made acquainted with his purpose and declaration, as my whole family consisted of no more than a couple of women and one footman. However, I summoned up my courage, which had been often tried, and never forsook me in the day of danger; and sent him word, that if ever he should presume to approach my house, I would order him to be shot, without ceremony. The fellow did not choose to put me to the trial, and returned to town without his errand. But as the place of my abode was now discovered, I laid my account with having a visit from his employer: I therefore planted spies upon the road, with a promise of reward to him who should bring me the first intelligence of his lordship's approach.

Accordingly, I was one morning apprized of his coming; and mounting horse immediately, with my woman and valet, away we rode, in defiance of winter, and in two days got through the wilds of Lincolnshire and hundreds of Essex, crossed the river at Tilbury, breakfasted at Chatham, by the help of a guide and moon-light, arrived at Dover the same evening, and embarked for Calais, in which place I found myself next day at two o'clock in the afternoon; and being heartily tired with my journey, betook myself to rest. My maid, who was not able to travel with such expedition, followed me at an easier pace; and the footman was so astonished at my perseverance, that he could not help asking upon the road, if ever I was weary in my life. Certain it is, my spirits and resolution have enabled me to undergo fatigues that are almost incredible. From Calais I went to Brussels,[1] where I again set up my rest in private lodgings; was again perfectly well received by the fashionable people of that place; and, by the interest of my friends, obtained the queen of Hungary's protection against the persecution of my husband, while I should reside in the Austrian Netherlands.

Thus secured, I lived uncensured, conversing with the English company, with which this city was crouded, but spent the most agreeable part of my time with the countess of Calemberg, in whose house I generally dined and supped; and I also contracted an intimacy with the princess of Chemay, who was a great favourite with Madam D'Harrach, the governor's lady.

I had not been long in this happy situation, when I was disturbed by the arrival of lord ——, who demanded me of the governor; but finding me sheltered from his power, he set out for Vienna; and, in consequence of his representations, strengthened with the duke of N—'s[1] name, my protection was withdrawn. But, before this application, he had gone to the camp, and addressed himself to my lord Stair,[2] who was my particular friend, and ally by my first marriage, desiring he would compel me to return to his house. His lordship told him, that I was in no shape subject to his command; but invited him to dinner, with a view of diverting himself and company, at the expence of his guest. In the evening, he was plied with so many bumpers to my health, that he became intoxicated, and extremely obstreperous, insisted upon seeing lord Stair, after he was retired to rest, and quarrelled with lord D——, who being a tall, large, raw-boned Scotchman, could have swallowed him at one mouthful; but he thought he might venture to challenge him, in hopes of being put under arrest by the general: though he reckoned without his host; lord Stair knew his disposition, and, in order to punish his presumption, winked at the affair. The challenger, finding himself mistaken in his conjecture, got up early in the morning, and went off post for Vienna: and lord Stair desired a certain man of quality to make me a visit, and give me an account of his behaviour.

Being now deprived of my protection and pin-money, which my generous husband would no longer pay, I was reduced to great difficulty and distress. The duchess D'Aremberg, lord G——,[3] and many other persons of distinction, interceded in my behalf with his majesty, who was then abroad; but he refused to interpose between man and wife. The countess of Calemberg wrote a letter to my father, in which she represented my uncomfortable situation, and undertook to answer for my conduct, in case he would allow me a small annuity, on which I could live independant of lord ——, who, by all accounts, was a wretch with whom I could never enjoy the least happiness or quiet; otherwise, she would be the first to advise me to an accommodation. She gave him to understand, that her character was neither doubtful nor obscure; and that if my conduct there had not been irreproachable, she should not have taken me under her protection: that as I proposed to board in a convent, a small sum would answer my occasions; but, if that should be denied, I would actually go to service, or take some other desperate step, to avoid the man who was my bane and aversion.

To this kind remonstrance my father answered, that his fortune would not allow him to assist me; he had now a young family; and that I ought, at all events, to return to my husband. By this time, such was the extremity of my circumstances, that I was forced to pawn my cloaths, and every trifling trinket in my possession, and even to descend so far as to sollicit Mr. S— for a loan of fifty pounds, which he refused.

Thus was I deserted, in my distress, by two persons, to whom, in the season of my affluence, my purse had been always open. Nothing so effectually subdues a spirit unused to supplicate, as want: repulsed in this manner, I had recourse to lord B—, who was also (it seems) unable to relieve my necessities. This mortification I deserved at his hands, tho' he had once put it in my power to be above all such paultry demands; and I should not have been compelled to the disagreeable task of troubling my friends, had not I voluntarily resigned what he formerly gave me. As to the other gentleman to whom I addressed myself, on this occasion, I think he might have shewn more regard to my application, not only for the reasons already mentioned, but because he knew me too well to be ignorant of what I must have suffered, in condescending to make such a request.

Several officers, who guess'd my adversity, generously offered to supply me with money; but I could not bring myself to make use of their friendship, or even to own my distress, except to one person, of whom I borrowed a small sum. To crown my misfortunes, I was taken very ill, at a time when there was no other way of avoiding the clutches of my persecutor, but by a precipitate flight. In this emergency, I applied to a worthy gentleman of Brussels, a very good friend of mine, but no lover. I say no lover, because every man is supposed to act in that capacity who befriends a young woman in distress. This generous Fleming set out with me, in the night, from Brussels, and conducted me to the frontiers of France. Being very much indisposed both in mind and body when I was obliged to undertake this expedition, I should, in all probability, have sunk under the fatigue of travelling, had not my spirits been kept up by the conversation of my companion, who was a man of business and consequence, and undertook to manage my affairs in such a manner as would enable me to re-establish my residence in the place I had left. He was young and active, attended me with the utmost care and assiduity, and left nothing undone which he thought would contribute to my ease and satisfaction. I believe his friendship for me was a little tinctured with another passion; but he was married, and lived very well with his wife, who was also my friend; so that he knew I would never think of him in the light of a lover.

Upon our arrival at Valenciennes, he accommodated me with a little money (for a little was all I would take) and returned to his own city, after we had settled a correspondence by letters. I was detained a day or two in this place by my indisposition, which increased; but nevertheless proceeded to Paris, to make interest for a protection from the king of France, which that monarch graciously accorded me, in three days after my first application; and his minister sent orders to all the governors and intendants of the province towns, to protect me against the efforts of lord ———, in whatever place I should choose to reside.

Having returned my thanks at Versailles for this favour, and tarried a few days at Paris, which was a place altogether unsuitable to the low ebb of my fortune, I repaired to Lisle, where I intended to fix my habitation; and there my disorder recurred with such violence, that I was obliged to send for a physician, who seemed to have been a disciple of Sangrado; for he scarce left a drop of blood in my body, and yet I found myself never a whit the better. Indeed I was so much exhausted by these evacuations, and my constitution so much impaired by fatigue and perturbation of mind, that I had no other hope of recovering but that of reaching England, and putting myself under the direction of a physician on whose ability I could depend.

With this doubtful prospect, therefore, I determined to attempt a return to my native air, and actually departed from Lisle, in such a melancholy enfeebled condition, that I had almost fainted when I was put into the coach. But before I resolved upon this journey I was reduced to the utmost exigence of fortune; so that I could scarce afford to buy provisions, had it been in my power to eat, and should not have been able to defray my travelling expences, had I not been generously befriended by lord R— M— who (I am sure) would have done any thing for my ease and accommodation, tho' he has unjustly incurred the imputation of being parsimonious, and I had no reason to expect any such favour at his hands.

In this deplorable state of health I was conveyed to Calais, being all the way (as it were) in the arms of death, without having swallowed the least sustenance on the road; and so much was my indisposition augmented by the fatigue of the journey, that I swooned when I was brought into the inn, and had almost expired before I could receive the least assistance or advice: however, my spirits were a little revived by some bread and wine, which I took at the persuasion of a French surgeon, who chancing to pass by the door, was called up to my relief; and having sent my servant to Brussels to take care of my cloaths, embarked in the packet-boat, and by that time we arrived at Dover, was almost in extremity.

Here I found a return coach, in which I was carried to London, and was put to bed in the house at which we put up, more dead than alive. The people of the inn sent for an apothecary, who administred some cordial that recalled me to life; and when I recovered the use of speech, I told him who I was, and desired him to wait upon Dr. S—[1] and inform him of my situation. A young girl who was niece to the landlord's wife, seeing me unattended, made a tender of her service to me, and I accepted the offer, as well as of a lodging in the apothecary's house, to which I was conveyed as soon as my strength would admit of my removal; and there was visited by my physician, who was shocked to find me in such a dangerous condition: however, having considered my case, he perceived that my indisposition proceeded from the calamities I had undergone, and encouraged me with the hope of a speedy cure, provided I could be kept easy and undisturbed.

I was accordingly tended with all imaginable care; my lord's name being never mentioned in my hearing, because I considered him as the fatal source of all my misfortunes; and in a month I recovered my health, by the great skill and tenderness of my doctor, who now finding me strong enough to encounter fresh troubles, endeavoured to persuade me, that it would be my wisest step to return to my husband, whom, at that time, he had often occasion to see. But I rejected his proposal, commenced a new lawsuit for separation,[2] and took a small house in St. James's Square.

About this time, my woman returned from Brussels, but without my cloaths, which were detained on account of the money I owed in that place; and asking her dismission from my service, set up shop for herself. I had not lived many weeks in my new habitation, when my persecutor renewed his attempts to make himself master of my person; but I had learn'd from experience, to redouble my vigilance, and he was frustrated in all his endeavours. I was again happy in the conversation of my former acquaintance, and visited by a great number of gentlemen, mostly persons of probity and sense, who cultivated my friendship, without any other motive of attachment. Not that I was unsolicited on the article of love; that was a theme on which I never wanted orators; and could I have prevailed upon myself to profit by the advances that were made, I might have managed my opportunities, so as to have set fortune at defiance for the future. But I was none of those œconomists, who can sacrifice their hearts to interested considerations.

One evening, while I was conversing with three or four of my friends, my lawyer came in, and told me he had something of consequence to impart: upon which, all the gentlemen but one went away; and he gave me to understand, that my suit would immediately come to trial; and though he hoped the best, the issue was uncertain: that if it should be given against me, the decision would inspire my lord with fresh spirits to disturb my peace; and therefore it would be convenient for me to retire, until the affair should be brought to a determination.

I was very much disconcerted at this intelligence; and the gentleman who stayed perceiving my concern, asked what I intended to do, or if he could serve me in any shape, and desired to know whither I proposed to retreat. I affected to laugh, and answered, 'To a garret I believe.' To this over-strained raillery he replied, that if I should, his friendship and regard would find the way to my apartment; and I had no reason to doubt the sincerity of his declaration. We consulted about the measures I should take, and I determined to remove into the country, where I was soon favoured with a letter from him, wherein he expressed the infinite pleasure he had, in being able to assure me, that my suit had been successful, and that I might appear again with great safety.

Accordingly, I returned to town in his coach and six, which he had sent for my convenience, and the same evening went with him to the masquerade, where we passed the night very agreeably, his spirits, as well as mine, being elevated to a joyous pitch, by the happy event of my process. This gentleman was a person of great honour, worth and good nature; he loved me extremely, but did not care that I should know the extent of his passion: on the contrary, he endeavoured to persuade me, he had laid it down as a maxim, that no woman should ever have power enough over his heart, to give him the least pain or disquiet. In short, he had made a progress in my affection, and to his generosity was I indebted for my subsistence two whole years; during which, he was continually professing this philosophic indifference, while, at the same time, he was giving me daily assurances of his friendship and esteem, and treating me with incessant marks of the most passionate love: so that I concluded his intention was cold, though his temper was warm; and considering myself as an incumbrance upon his fortune, I redoubled my endeavours to obtain a separate maintenance from my lord, and removed from St. James's Square to lodgings at Kensington, where I had not long enjoyed myself in tranquillity, before it was interrupted by a very unexpected visit.

While I was busy one day dressing in my dining-room, I found his lordship at my elbow, before I was aware of his approach, although his coach was at the door, and the house already in the possession of his servants. He accosted me in the usual stile, as if we had parted the night before; and I answered him with an appearance of the same careless familiarity, desiring him to sit down, while I retreated to my chamber, lock'd the door, and fairly went to bed; being, perhaps, the first woman who went thither for protection from the insults of a man. Here then I immured myself with my faithful Abigail; and my lord finding me secured, knocked at the door, and through the key-hole begg'd to be admitted; assuring me, that all he wanted was a conference. I desired to be excused, though I believed his assurance; but I had no inclination to converse with him, because I knew from experience the nature of his conversation, which was so disagreeable and tormenting, that I would have exchanged it at any time for a good beating, and thought myself a gainer by the bargain. However, he persisted in his importunities to such a degree, that I assented to his proposal, on condition that the duke of L—— should be present at the interview; and he immediately sent a message to his grace, while I in peace ate my breakfast, conveyed in a basket, which was hoisted up to the window of my bed-chamber.

The duke was so kind as to come at my lord's request, and before I would open the door, gave me his word, that I should be protected from all violence and compulsion. Thus assured, they were permitted to enter; and my little gentleman sitting down by the bed-side, began to repeat the old hackneyed arguments he had formerly used, with the view of inducing me to live with him; and I, on my side, repeated my former objections, or pretended to listen to his representations, while my imagination was employed in contriving the means of effecting an escape, as the duke easily perceived by my countenance.

Finding all his remonstrances ineffectual, he quitted the chamber, and left his cause to the eloquence of his grace, who sat with me a whole half hour, without exerting himself much in behalf of his client, because he knew I was altogether obstinate, and determined on that score; but joked upon the behaviour of his lordship, who (though jealous of most people) had left him alone with me in my bed-chamber, observing, that he must either have great confidence in his virtue, or a very bad opinion of him otherwise. In short, I found means to defer the categorical answer till next day, and invited the duke and his lordship to dine with me to-morrow. My wise yoke-fellow seemed to doubt the sincerity of this invitation, and was very much disposed to keep possession of my house: but, by the persuasions of his grace, and the advice of H—n, who was his chief counsellor and back, he was prevailed upon to take my word, and for the present left me.

They were no sooner retired, than I rose with great expedition, pack'd up my cloaths, and took shelter in Essex for the first time. Next day, my lord and his noble friend came to dinner, according to appointment; and being informed of my escape by my woman, whom I had left in the house, his lordship discovered some signs of discontent, and insisted upon seeing my papers; upon which, my maid produced a parcel of bills which I owed to different people. Notwithstanding this disappointment, he sat down to what was provided for dinner, and with great deliberation ate up a leg of lamb, the best part of a fowl, and something else, which I do not now remember; and then very peaceably went away, giving my maid an opportunity of following me to the place of my retreat.

My intention was to have sought refuge, as formerly, in another country; but I was prevented from putting my design in execution by a fit of illness, during which I was visited by my physician and some of my own relations, particularly a distant cousin of mine, whom my lord had engaged in his interests, by promising to recompence her amply, if she could persuade me to comply with his desire. In this office she was assisted by the doctor, who was my friend, and a man of sense, for whom I have the most perfect esteem, though he and I have often differed in point of opinion. In a word, I was exposed to the incessant importunities of all my acquaintance, which, added to the desperate circumstances of my fortune, compelled me to embrace the terms that were offered, and I again returned to the domestic duties of a wife.

I was conducted to my lord's house by an old friend of mine, a gentleman turned of fifty, of admirable parts and understanding; he was a pleasing companion, chearful and humane, and had acquired a great share of my esteem and respect. In a word, his advice had great weight in my deliberations, because it seemed to be the result of experience and disinterested friendship. Without all doubt, he had an unfeigned concern for my welfare; but, being an admirable politician, his scheme was to make my interest coincide with his own inclinations; for I had unwittingly made an innovation upon his heart; and as he thought I should hardly favour his passion, while I was at liberty to converse with the rest of my admirers, he counselled me to surrender that freedom, well knowing that my lord would be easily persuaded to banish all his rivals from the house; in which case, he did not doubt of his being able to insinuate himself into my affections; because he laid it down as an eternal truth, that if any two persons of different sexes were obliged to live together in a desart, where they would be excluded from all other human intercourse, they would naturally and inevitably contract an inclination for each other.

How just this hypothesis may be, I leave to the determination of the curious; though, if I may be allowed to judge from my own disposition, a couple so situated would be apt to imbibe mutual disgusts, from the nature and necessity of their union; unless their association was at first the effect of reciprocal affection and esteem. Be this as it will, I honour the gentleman for his plan, which was ingeniously contrived, and artfully conducted: but I happened to have too much address for him in the sequel, cunning as he was, though at first I did not perceive his drift; and his lordship was much less likely to comprehend his meaning.

Immediately after this new accommodation, I was carried to a country house belonging to my lord, and was simple enough to venture myself (unattended by any servant on whose integrity I could depend) in the hands of his lordship and H——n, whose villainy I always dreaded; tho' at this time my apprehensions were considerably increased, by recollecting, that it was not his interest to let me live in the house, lest his conduct should be inquired into; and by remembering, that the very house to which we were going, had been twice burnt down in a very short space of time, not without suspicion of his having been the incendiary, on account of some box of writings, which was lost in the conflagration. True it is, this imputation was never made good; and perhaps he was altogether innocent of the charge, which nevertheless affected my spirits in such a manner, as rendered me the most miserable of all mortals; and in this terror did I remain, till my consternation was weakened by the arrival of Mr. Bal—, a good natured worthy man, whom my lord had invited to his house, and I thought would not see me ill used; and in a few weeks, we were joined by Dr. S— and his lady, who visited us according to their promise; and it was resolved that we should set out for Tunbridge, on a partie of pleasure, and at our return examine H——n's accounts.

This last part of our scheme was not at all relished by our worthy steward, who, therefore, determined to overturn our whole plan, and succeeded accordingly. My lord, all of a sudden, declared himself against the jaunt we had projected, and insisted upon my staying at home, without assigning any reason for this peremptory behaviour; his countenance became cloudy, and for the space of three days he did not open his mouth.

At last, he one night entered my bed-chamber, to which he now had free access, with his sword under his arm, and, if I remember aright, it was ready drawn. I could not help taking notice of this alarming circumstance, which shocked me the more, as it happened immediately after a gloomy fit of discontent. However, I seemed to overlook the incident, and dismissing my maid, went to bed; because I was ashamed to acknowledge, even to my own heart, any dread of a person whom I despised so much. However, the strength of my constitution was not equal to the fortitude of my mind: I was taken ill, and the servants were obliged to be called up; while my lord himself, terrified at my situation, ran up stairs to Mrs. S——, who was in bed, told her, with evident perturbation of spirits, that I was very much indisposed, and said, he believed I was frightened by his entering my chamber with his sword in hand.

This lady was so startled at his information, that she ran into my apartment half-naked, and as she went down stairs, asked what reason could induce him to have carried his sword with him? Upon which he gave her to understand, that his intention was to kill the bats. I believe and hope he had no other design than that of intimidating me, but when the affair happened, I was of a different opinion. Mrs. S— having put on her cloaths, sat up all night by my bed-side, and was so good as to assure me, that she would not leave me, until I should be safely delivered from the apprehensions that surrounded me in this house, to which she and the doctor had been the principal cause of my coming; for my lord had haunted and importuned them incessantly on this subject, protesting that he loved me with the most inviolable affection; and all he desired was, that I would sit at his table, manage his family, and share his fortune. By these professions, uttered with an air of honesty and goodnature, he had imposed himself upon them, for the best tempered creature upon earth; and they used all their influence with me to take him into favour. This hath been the case with a great many people, who had but a superficial knowledge of his disposition; but, in the course of their acquaintance, they have never failed to discern and acknowledge their mistake.

The doctor, on his return from Tunbridge, to which place he had made a trip by himself, found me ill a-bed, and the whole family in confusion: surprized and concerned at this disorder, he entered into expostulation with my lord, who owned, that the cause of his displeasure and disquiet was no other than jealousy: H— had informed him, that I had been seen to walk out with Mr. Bal— in a morning; and that our correspondence had been observed with many additional circumstances, which were absolutely false and groundless. This imputation was no sooner understood, than it was resolved that the accuser should be examined, in presence of us all. He accordingly appeared, exceedingly drunk, tho' it was morning, and repeated the articles of the charge, as an information he had received from a man who came from town to hang the bells, and was long ago returned to London.

This was an instance of his cunning and address, which did not forsake him even in his hours of intoxication. Had he fixed the calumny on any one of the servants, he would have been confronted and detected in his falshood. Nevertheless, tho' he could not be legally convicted, it plainly appeared that he was the author of this defamation, which incensed Mr. Bal— to such a degree, that he could scarce be with-held from punishing him on the spot, by manual chastisement. However, he was prevailed upon to abstain from such immediate vengeance, as a step unworthy of his character; and the affair was brought to this issue, that his lordship should either part with me or Mr. H—; for I was fully determined against living under the same roof with such an incendiary.

This alternative being proposed, my lord dismiss'd his steward, and we returned to town with the doctor and Mrs. S—; for I had imbibed such horror and aversion for this country seat (tho' one of the pleasantest in England) that I could not bear to live in it. We therefore removed to an house in Bond-street, where, according to the advice of my friends, I exerted my whole power and complaisance, in endeavours to keep my husband in good humour; but was so unsuccessful in my attempts, that if ever he was worse tempered, more capricious, or intolerable, at one time than at another, this was the season in which his ill-humour predominated to the most rancorous degree. I was scarce ever permitted to stir abroad, saw no-body at home but my old male-friend whom I have mentioned above, and the doctor with his lady, from whose conversation also I was at last excluded.

Nevertheless, I contrived to steal a meeting, now and then, with my late benefactor, for whom I entertained a great share of affection, exclusive of that gratitude which was due to his generosity. It was not his fault that I compromised matters with my lord; for he was as free of his purse as I was unwilling to use it. It would, therefore, have been unfriendly, unkind, and ungrateful in me (now that I was in affluence) to avoid all intercourse with a man who had supported me in adversity.—I think people cannot be too shy and scrupulous in receiving favours; but once they are conferred, they ought never to forget the obligation: and I was never more concerned at any incident of my life, than at hearing that this gentleman did not receive a letter, in which I acknowledged the last proof of his friendship and liberality which I had occasion to use, because I have since learned, that he suspected me of neglect.

But, to return to my situation in Bond-street, I bore it as well as I could for the space of three months, during which I lived in the midst of spies who were employed to watch my conduct; and underwent every mortification that malice, power, and folly could inflict. Nay, so ridiculous, so unreasonable was my tyrant in his spleen, that he declared he would even be jealous of Heydigger,[1] if there was no other man to incur his suspicion: he expected that I should spend my whole time with him, *tête à tête*; and when I sacrificed my enjoyment to these comfortable parties, he never failed to lay hold on some innocent expression of mine, which he made the foundation of a quarrel; and when I strove to avoid these disagreeable misinterpretations, by reading or writing, he incessantly teized and tormented me with the imputation of being peevish, sullen and reserved.

Harrassed by this insufferable behaviour, I communicated my case to Dr. S— and his lady, intimating that I neither could nor would expose myself any longer to such usage. The doctor exhorted me to bear my fate with patience, and Mrs. S— was silent on the subject; so that I still hesitated between staying and going, when the doctor being one night at supper, happened to have some words with my lord, who was so violently transported with passion, that I was actually afraid of going to bed with him; and next morning when he waked, there was such an expression of frantic wildness in his countenance, that I imagined he was actually distracted.

This alarming circumstance confirmed me in my resolution of decamping; and I accordingly moved my quarters to an house in Sackville-street, where I had lodged when I was a widow; and when I was settled, sent a message to the duke of L—, desiring he would make my lord acquainted with the place of my abode, my reasons for removing, and my intention to defend myself against all his attempts. The first night of this separation I went to bed by myself, with as much pleasure as a man could do in going to bed to his mistress, whom he had long solicited in vain. So rejoiced was I to be delivered from my obnoxious bedfellow!

I had not long changed my lodgings, which I did to Brook-street, and enjoyed the sweets of my escape, when I was importuned to return, by a new steward whom my lord had engaged in the room of H—n. This gentleman, who bore a very fair character, made such judicious representations, and behaved so candidly in the discharge of his function, that I agreed he should act as umpire in the difference between us; and once more a reconciliation was effected, tho' his lordship began to be dissatisfied even before the execution of our agreement, in consequence of which he attended me to Bath, whither I went for the benefit of my health, which was not a little impaired.

This accommodation had a surprising effect upon my lover, who, notwithstanding his repeated declarations, that no woman should ever gain such an ascendency over his heart, as to be able to give him pain, suffered all the agonies of disappointed love, when he now found himself deprived of the opportunities of seeing me, and behaved very differently from what he had imagined he should: his words and actions were desperate; one of his expressions to me was, 'It is like twisting my heart-strings, and tearing it out of my body.' And I should never have done it, had I thought he would have suffered; but I protest I believed him when he said otherwise so much, that it was the occasion of my giving him up; and it was now too late to retract.

In our expedition to the Bath I was accompanied by a very agreeable young lady, with whom I pass'd my time very happily, amid the diversions of the place, which screened me, in a good measure, from the vexatious society of my hopeful partner. From this place we repaired to his seat in the country, where we spent a few months, and thence returned again to our house in Bond-street. Here, while I was confined to my bed by illness, it was supposed my indisposition was no other than a private lying in, tho' I was under the roof with my lord, and attended by his servants.

While my distemper continued, my lord (to do him justice) behaved with all imaginable tenderness and care; and his concern on these occasions I have already mentioned, as a strange inconsistency in his disposition. If his actions were at all accountable, I should think he took pains to fret me into a fever first, in order to manifest his love and humanity afterwards. When I recovered my strength and spirits, I went abroad, saw company, and should have been easy, had he been contented; but as my satisfaction increased, his good humour decayed, and he banished, from his house, one by one, all the people whose conversation could have made my life agreeable.

I often expostulated with him upon this malignant behaviour, protesting my desire of living peaceably with him; and begging he would not lay me under the necessity of changing my measures. He was deaf to all my remonstrances, (tho' I warned him more than once of the event) persisted in his maxims of persecution; and, after repeated quarrels, I again left his house, fully determined to suffer all sorts of extremity, rather than subject myself to the tyranny of his disposition.

This year was productive of one fatal event, which I felt with the utmost sensibility of sorrow, and shall always remember with regret: I mean the death of Mr. B—,[1] with whom I had constantly maintained an intimate correspondence since the first commencement of our acquaintance. He was one of the most valuable men, and promised to be one of the brightest ornaments that this or any other age had produced. I enjoyed his friendship, without reserve; and such was the confidence he reposed in my integrity, from long experience of my truth, that he often said he would believe my bare assertion, even tho' it should contradict the evidence of his own senses. These being the terms upon which we lived, it is not to be supposed that I bore the loss of him without repining: indeed my grief was unspeakable; and tho' the edge of it be now smoothed by the lenient hand of time, I shall never cease to cherish his memory with the most tender remembrance.

During the last period of my living with my lord, I had agreed to the expediency of obtaining an act of parliament, which would enable him to pay his debts; on which occasion there was a necessity for cancelling a deed that subsisted between us, relating to a separate maintenance; to which, on certain provisos, I was intitled: and this was to be set aside, so far as it interfered with the above mentioned scheme, while the rest of it should remain in force. When this affair was about to be transacted, my lord very generously insisted upon my concurrence, in annulling the whole settlement; and when I refused to comply with this demand, because this was the sole resource I had against his ill usage, he would not proceed in the execution of his plan, tho' by dropping it he hurt no-body but himself; and accused me of having receded from my word, after I had drawn him into a considerable expence.

This imputation of breaking my word, which I defy the whole world to prove I ever did, incensed me the more, as I myself had proposed the scheme for his service, altho' I knew the accomplishment of it would endanger the validity of my own settlement; and my indignation was still more augmented by the behaviour of Mr. G—, who had always professed a regard for my interest, and upon my last accommodation with my lord, undertaken to effect a reconciliation between my father and me: but when he was questioned about the particulars of this difference, and desired to declare whether his lordship or I was to blame, he declined the office of arbitrator, refused to be explicit on the subject, and by certain shrewd hums and ha's signified his disapprobation of my conduct; and yet this very man, when I imparted to him, in confidence, my intention of making another retreat, and frankly asked his opinion of my design, seemed to acquiesce in the justice of it, in these remarkable words: 'Madam, if I thought, or had hopes of my lord's growing better, I would down on my knees, to desire you to stay; but as I have not, I say nothing.'

If he connived at my conduct in this particular, why should he disapprove of it, when all I asked was but common justice? But he was a dependent; and therefore I excuse his phlegmatic (not to call it unfriendly) behaviour. Indeed he could not be too cautious of giving offence to his lordship, who sometimes made him feel the effects of that wrath which other people had kindled; particularly, in consequence of a small adventure which happened about this very period of time.

A very agreeable, sprightly, good-natured young man, a near relation of my lord, happening to be at our house one evening, when there was a fire in the neighbourhood, we agreed to go and sup at a tavern, *en famille*; and having spent the evening with great mirth and good humour, this young gentleman, who was naturally facetious, in taking his leave, saluted us all round. My lord, who had before entertained some jealousy of his kinsman, was very much provoked by this trifling incident, but very prudently suppressed his displeasure till he returned to his own house, where his rage co-operating with the Champagne he had drank, inflamed him to such a degree of resolution, that he sprung upon the innocent G—n, and collared him with great fury, though he was altogether unconcerned in the cause of his indignation.

This extravagant and frantic behaviour, added to the other grievances under which I laboured, hastened my resolution of leaving him; and he to this day blames his relation, as the immediate cause of my escape, whereas he ought to place it to the account of his own madness and indiscretion. When I retired to Park-street, he cautioned all my tradesmen (not even excepting my baker) against giving me credit, assuring them that he would not pay any debts I should contract; and the difficulties to which I was reduced, in consequence of this charitable declaration, together with the reflection of what I had suffered, and might undergo, from the caprice and barbarity of his disposition, affected my health so much, that I was taken again ill, and my life thought in danger.

My constitution, however, got the better of my distemper, and I was ordered into the country by my physicians, for the benefit of the air; so that I found myself under the necessity of keeping two houses, when I was little able to support one, and set up my chariot, because I could not defray the expence of an hackney coach; for I had as much credit given me as I ask'd for, notwithstanding my lord's orders to the contrary.

Having recruited my spirits in the country, I returned to town, and was visited by my friends, who never forsook me in adversity, and in the summer removed to an house in Essex, where I lived a few months in great tranquillity, unmolested by my tyrant, who sometimes gave me a whole year's respite. Here I used to ride and drive by turns (as my humour dictated) with horses which were lent me; and I had the company of my lover, and another gentleman, who was a very agreeable companion, and of singular service to me in the sequel.

At last, my lord having received intelligence of the place of my abode, and his tormenting humour recurring, he set out for my habitation, and in the morning appeared in his coach and six, attended by Mr. G—n, and another person, whom he had engaged for the purpose, with several domesticks armed. I immediately shut up my doors at his approach, and refused him admittance, which he endeavoured to obtain by a succession of prayers and threats; but I was deaf to both, and resolved to hold out to the last.

Seeing me determined, he began his attack, and his servants

actually forced their way into the house; upon which I retreated up stairs, and fortified myself in an apartment, which the assailants stormed with such fury, that the door began to give way, and I retired into another room.

Whilst I remained in this post, Mr. G—n demanded a parley, in which he begg'd I would favour my lord with an interview, otherwise he knew not what would be the consequence. To this remonstrance I replied, that I was not disposed to comply with his request; and that though their design should be murder, I was not at all afraid of death. Upon this declaration they renewed their attacks, which they carried on with indifferent success till the afternoon, when my lord (as if he had been at play) sent a formal message to me, desiring that all hostilities should cease, till after both parties should have dined. At the same time, my own servants came for instructions: and I ordered them to let him have every thing which he should call for, as far as the house would afford.

He did not fail to make use of this permission; but, sitting down with his companions, ate up my dinner without hesitation, after he had paid me the compliment, of desiring to know what he should send up to my apartment. Far from having any stomach to partake of his meal, I sat solitary upon my bed, in a state of melancholy expectation, having fastened the door of the outward room for my security, while I kept my chamber open for the convenience of air, the weather being excessively hot.

His lordship having indulged his appetite, resumed his attempt, and all of a sudden I heard a noise in the next room; upon which I started up, and perceiving that he had got into my anti-chamber, by the help of a bench that stood under the window, I flung to the door of my room, which I locked with great expedition, and opening another that communicated with the stair-case, ran out of the house, through a croud of more than an hundred people, whom this fray had gathered together.

Being universally beloved in the neighbourhood, and respected by my lord's servants, I passed among them untouched, and took refuge in a neighbouring cottage; while his lordship bawled and roared for assistance, being afraid to come out as he had got in. Without waiting for his deliberations, I changed cloaths with the poor woman who had given me shelter, and in her blue apron and straw-hat sallied out into the fields, intending to seek protection at the house of a gentleman not far off, though I was utterly ignorant of the road that led to it. However, it was my good fortune to meet with a farmer, who undertook to conduct me to the place; otherwise

I should have missed my way, and, in all probability, lain in the fields; for, by this time, it was eight o'clock at night.

Under the direction of this guide, I traversed hedges and ditches, (for I would not venture to travel in the highway, lest I should fall into the hands of my pursuer) and after I had actually tumbled in the mire, and walked six or seven long miles, by the help of a good spirit, which never failed me on such occasions, I arrived at the place, and rung the bell at the garden-gate for admittance. Seeing my figure, which was very uncouth, together with my draggled condition, they denied me entrance; but when they understood who I was, immediately opened the door, and I was hospitably entertained, after having been the subject of mirth, on account of my dress and adventure.

Next day I returned, and took possession of my house again, where I resumed my former amusements, which I enjoyed in quiet, for the space of a whole month, waiting with resignation for the issue of my law-suit; when one afternoon, I was apprized of his lordship's approach, by one of my spies, whom I always employed to reconnoitre the road; and so fortunate was I in the choice of these scouts, that I never was betrayed by one of them, though they were often bribed for that purpose.

I no sooner received this intelligence, than I ordered my horse to be saddled, and mounting, rode out of sight immediately, directing my course a different way from the London road. I had not long proceeded in this tract, when my career was all of a sudden stopp'd by a five-bar gate, which, after some hesitation, I resolved to leap (my horse being an old hunter) if I should find myself pursued. However, with much difficulty I made shift to open it, and arrived in safety at the house of my very good friend Mr. G——, who being a justice of the peace, had promised me his protection, if it should be wanted.

Thus secured for the present, I sent out spies to bring information of his lordship's proceedings, and understood that he had taken possession of my house, turned my servants adrift, and made himself master of all my moveables, cloaths and papers. As for the papers, they were of no consequence, but of cloaths I had a good stock; and when I had reason to believe that he did not intend to relinquish his conquest, I thought it was high time for me to remove to a greater distance from his quarters. Accordingly, two days after my escape, I set out at eleven o'clock at night, in a chariot and four, which I borrowed of my friend, attended by a footman, who was a stout fellow and well armed, I myself being provided with a brace of good pistols, which I was fully determined to use, against any person who should presume to lay violent hands upon me, except my lord, for whom a less mortal weapon would have sufficed, such as a bodkin or a tinder-box. Nothing could be farther from my intention, than the desire of hurting any living creature, much less my husband; my design was only to defend myself from cruelty and oppression, which I knew, by fatal experience, would infallibly be my lot, should he get me into his power: and I thought I had as good a right to preserve my happiness, as that which every individual has to preserve his life, especially against a set of ruffians, who were engaged to rob me of it, for a little dirty lucre.

In the midst of our journey, the footman came up, and told me I was dogg'd; upon which I looked out, and seeing a man riding by the chariot-side, presented one of my pistols out at the window, and preserved that posture of defence, until he thought proper to retreat, and rid me of the fears that attended his company. I arrived in town, and changing my equipage, hired an open chaise, in which (though I was almost starved with cold) I travelled to Reading, which I reached by ten next morning; and from thence proceeded farther in the country, with a view of taking refuge with Mrs. C——, who was my particular friend. Here I should have found shelter, though my lord had been beforehand with me, and endeavoured to prepossess her against my conduct, had not the house been crouded with company, among whom I could not possibly have been concealed, especially from her brother, who was an intimate friend of my persecutor.

Things being thus situated, I enjoyed but a very short interview with her, in which her sorrow and perplexity on my account appeared with great expression in her countenance; and though it was not in her power to afford me the relief I expected, she, in the most genteel manner, sent after me a small sum of money, thinking that, considering the hurry in which I left my house, I might have occasion for it on the road. I was by this time benumbed with cold, fatigued with travelling, and almost fretted to death by my disappointment. However, this was no time to indulge despondence; since no body could, or would, assist me, I stood the more in need of my own resolution and presence of mind. After some deliberation, I steered my course back to London; and being unwilling to return by the same road in which I came, as well as impatient to be at the end of my journey, I chose the Bagshot way, and ventured to cross the heath by moon-light.

Here I was attacked by a foot-pad armed with a broad-sword,

who came up, and demanded my money. My stock amounted to twelve guineas; and I foresaw, that should I be stripp'd of the whole sum, I could not travel without discovering who I was, and, consequently, running the risk of being detected by my pursuer. On these considerations, I gave the fellow three guineas and some silver; with which he was so far from being satisfied, that he threatened to search me for more: but I ordered the coachman to proceed, and by good fortune escaped that ceremony; though I was under some apprehension of being overtaken with a pistol-bullet in my flight, and therefore held down my head in the chaise, in imitation of some great men, who are said to have ducked in the same manner, in the day of battle.

My fears happened to be disappointed: I lay at an inn upon the road, and next day arrived in town, in the utmost difficulty and distress; for I knew not where to fix my habitation, and was destitute of all means of support. In this dilemma, I applied to my lawyer, who recommended me to the house of a tradesman in Westminster, where I lodged and boarded, upon credit, with my faithful Abigail, (whom I shall distinguish by the name of Mrs. S——r) for the space of ten weeks, during which I saw nobody, and never once stirred abroad.

While I was thus harrassed out of all enjoyment of life, and reduced to the utmost indigence, by the cruelty of my persecutor, who had even stripp'd me of my wearing apparel, I made a conquest of lord D——, a nobleman who is now dead, and therefore I shall say little of his character, which is perfectly well known: this only will I observe, that, next to my own tyrant, he was the only person of whom I had the greatest abhorrence. Nevertheless, when these two came in competition, I preferred the offers of this new lover, which were very considerable; and as an asylum was the chief thing I wanted, agreed to follow him to his country-seat, whither I actually sent my cloaths, which I had purchased upon credit.

However, upon mature deliberation, I changed my mind, and signified my resolution in a letter, desiring at the same time, that my baggage might be sent back. In consequence of this message, I expected a visit from him, in all the rage of indignation and disappointment, and gave orders, that he should not be admitted into my house: yet, notwithstanding this precaution, he found means to procure entrance; and one of the first objects that I saw, next morning, in my bed-chamber, was my lover, armed with his horse-whip, against which (from the knowledge of the man) I did not think myself altogether secure; though I was not much alarmed, because I believed myself superior to him in point of bravery, should the worst come to the worst: but, contrary to my expectation, and his usual behaviour to our sex, he accosted me very politely, and began to expostulate upon the contents of my letter. I freely told him, that I had rashly assented to his proposal, for my own convenience only; that when I reflected on what I had done, I thought it ungenerous in me to live with him upon these terms; and that, as I did not like him, and could not dissemble, such a correspondence could never tend to the satisfaction of either. He allowed the inference was just, though he was very much chagrined at my previous proceeding: he relinquished his claim, restored my cloaths, and never afterwards upbraided me with my conduct in this affair; though he at one time owned, that he still loved me, and ever should, because I had used him ill; a declaration that strongly marks the peculiarity of his character. As for my own part, I own that my behaviour on this occasion, is no other way excusable, than on account of the miserable perplexity of my circumstances, which were often so calamitous, that I wonder I have not been compelled to take such steps, as would have rendered my conduct much more exceptionable than it really is.

At last, all my hopes were blasted by the issue of my suit, which was determined in favour of my lord. Even then I refused to yield; on the contrary, coming out of retirement, I took lodgings in Suffolk-street, and set my tyrant at defiance. But, being unwilling to trust my doors to the care of other people, I took an house in Conduit-street; and no sooner appeared in the world again, than I was surrounded by divers and sundry sorts of admirers. I believe I received the incense and addresses of all kinds under the sun, except that sort which was most to my liking, a man capable of contracting and inspiring a mutual attachment; but such a one is equally rare and inestimable: not but that I own myself greatly obliged to all those who cultivated my good graces, though they were very little beholden to me; for, where I did not really love, I could never profess that passion: that sort of dissimulation is a slavery that no honest nature will undergo. Except one worthy young man whom I sometimes saw, they were a strange medley of insignificant beings; one was insipid, another ridiculously affected, a third void of all education, a fourth altogether inconsistent; and in short, I found as many trifling characters among the men, as ever I observed in my own sex. Some of them I endeavoured to bring over to my maxims, while they attempted to make a proselyte of me; but, finding the task impracticable on both sides, we very wisely dropt each other.

At length, however, I was blessed with the acquaintance of one nobleman, who is, perhaps, the first character in England, in point of honour, integrity, wit, sense and benevolence: when I have thus distinguished him, I need scarce mention lord ———.[1] This great, this good man, possesses every accomplishment requisite to inspire admiration, love and esteem. With infinitely more merit than almost ever fell to one man's share, he manifests such diffidence of his own qualifications, as cannot fail to prepossess every company in his favour. He seems to observe nothing, yet sees every thing; his manner of telling a story, and making trifles elegant, is peculiar to himself; and though he has a thousand oddities, they serve only to make him more agreeable. After what I have said, it may be supposed that I was enamoured of his person: but this was not the case; love is altogether capricious and fanciful; yet I admire, honour, and esteem him to the highest degree; and when I observe, that his character resembled that of my dear departed friend Mr. B——; or rather, that Mr. B——, had he lived, would have resembled lord ———, I pay the highest compliment I can conceive both to the living and the dead.

In this nobleman's friendship and conversation I thought myself happy; though I was, as usual, exposed to the indefatigable efforts of my lord, who, one day, while I was favoured with the company of this generous friend, appeared at my door in his coach, attended by another gentleman, who demanded entrance, with an air of authority. A very honest footman, who had been long in my service, ran up stairs in the utmost consternation, and gave me an account of what had happened below. Upon which, I told him he had nothing to answer for, and ordered him to keep the door fast shut against all opposition: though I was so much affected with this unexpected assault, that lord ——— said, he was never more surprized and shocked in his life, than at the horror which appeared in my countenance, when I saw the coach stop at my door.

My little hero being refused admittance, went away, threatening to return speedily with a reinforcement; and during this interval, I provided myself with a soldier, whom I placed centinel at the door withinside, to guard me from the danger of such assaults for the future. My lord, true to his promise, marched back with his auxiliaries, reinforced with a constable, and repeated his demand of being admitted; and my soldier opening the sash, in order to answer him according to my directions, he no sooner perceived the red coat, than he was seized with such a pannic, that he instantly fled with great precipitation; and when he recounted the adventure,

like Falstaff in the play, multiplied my guard into a whole file of
musqueteers. He also made shift to discover the gentleman, who had
been so kind as to lend me one of his company, and complained of
him to the duke of N——, in hopes of seeing him broke for this mis-
demeanour; but in that expectation he was luckily disappointed.

Perceiving that in England I should never enjoy peace, but be
continually subject to those alarms and disquiets which had already
impaired my health and spirits, I resolved to repair again to
France, my best refuge and sure retreat from the persecution of my
tyrant. Yet, before I took this step, I endeavoured, by the advice
of my friends, to conceal myself near Windsor; but was in a little
time discovered by my lord, and hunted out of my lurking place,
accordingly. I then removed to Chelsea, where I suffered inconceivable uneasiness and agitation of mind, from the nature of
my situation, my tranquillity being thus incessantly invaded by a
man who could not be satisfied with me, and yet could not live
without me: so that, though I was very much indisposed, I set out
for France, by the way of the Hague, as the war had shut up all other
communication, having no other attendant but my woman S—r,
who, though she dreaded the sea, and was upon the brink of matrimony, would not quit me in such a calamitous condition, until I was
joined by my footman and other maid, whom I ordered to follow
me with the baggage. But, before my departure, I sent a message
to lord ——, demanding my cloaths, which he had seized in Essex;
and he refusing to deliver them, I was obliged to equip myself anew,
upon credit.

I was supplied with money for my journey by my good friend
L——; and after a short and pleasant passage, arrived at the
Hague, where I stayed two months, and parted with S——r, on
whom I settled an annuity of five and twenty pounds, payable out
of the provision which I had or might obtain from my husband.
The same allowance had I prevailed upon lord B——— to grant to
another maid, who attended me while I lived in his house.

I did not much relish the people in Holland, because they
seemed entirely devoted to self-interest, without any taste for
pleasure or politeness; a species of disposition that could not be
very agreeable to me, who always despised money, had an unbounded benevolence of heart, and loved pleasure beyond every
other consideration. When I say pleasure, I would not be understood to mean sensuality, which constitutes the supreme happiness
of those only, who are void of sentiment and imagination. Nevertheless, I received some civilities in this place; and among the rest,

the reputation of having for my lover the king of P———'s minister, who was young and airy, and visited me often; circumstances that were sufficient to lay me under the imputation of an amour, which I frequently incurred, without having given the least cause of suspicion.

Having taken leave of my Dutch friends, I departed from the Hague, in company with an Englishwoman, whom I had chose for that purpose, and arrived at Antwerp, with much difficulty and danger, the highway being infested with robbers. After having reposed myself a few days in this city, I hired a coach for myself, and set out, with my companion, for Brussels; but, before we reached Mechlin, our vehicle was attacked by two hussars, who, with their sabres drawn, obliged the coachman to drive into a wood near the road. I at first imagined they wanted to examine our passports, but was soon too well convinced of their design; and though very much shocked at the discovery, found resolution enough to suppress my concern, so that it should not aggravate the terrors of the young woman, who had almost died with apprehension. I even encouraged her to hope for the best; and addressing myself to the robbers in French, begg'd in the most suppliant manner, that they would spare our lives; upon which, one of them, who was a little fellow, assured me in the same language, that we had nothing to fear for our persons.

When we were conveyed in a state of dreadful suspense about three quarters of a mile into the wood, the ruffians came into the coach, and taking my keys, which I kept ready in my hand for them, opened three large trunks, that contained my baggage, and emptying them of every thing but my hoops and a few books, packed up their booty in a cloth; then robbing me of my money and jewels, even to my shoe-buckles and sleeve-buttons, took my footman's laced hat, and gave it, by way of gratification, to a peasant, who came from behind the bushes, and assisted them in packing.

This affair being dispatched, they ordered us to return to the road, by a different way from that in which we were carried into the wood; and mounting their horses, rode off with the plunder, though not before the little fellow, who was the least ferocious of the two, had come and shaken me by the hand, wishing us a good journey; a compliment which I heartily returned, being extremely well pleased at the retreat of two such companions, who had detained us a whole half hour; during which, notwithstanding the assurance I had received, I was in continual apprehension of seeing their operation conclude with the murder of us all; for I supposed they were of that gang, who had some time before murthered a French officer, and used a lady extremely ill, after having rifled her of all she had.

Having thus undergone pillage, and being reduced to the extremity of indigence in a foreign land, it is not to be supposed that my reflections were very comfortable; and yet, though I sustained the whole damage, I was the only person in the company who bore the accident with any resolution and presence of mind. My coachman and valet seemed quite petrified with fear; and it was not, till I had repeated my directions, that the former drove farther into the wood, and took the first turning to the right, in order to regain the road, according to the command of the robbers, which I did not choose to disobey.

This misfortune I suffered by the misinformation I received at Antwerp, where I would have provided myself with an escort, had I not been assured, that there was not the least occasion to put myself to such extraordinary expence: and indeed, the robbers took the only half hour in which they could have had an opportunity of plundering us; for we no sooner returned into the Highway, than we met with the French artillery coming from Brussels, which was a security to us, during the rest of our journey. We were afterwards informed at a small village, that there was actually a large gang of deserters, who harboured in that wood, from which they made excursions in the neighbourhood, and kept the peasants in continual alarms.

Having proceeded a little way, we were stopp'd by the artillery crossing a bridge; and as the train was very long, must have been detained till night, had not a soldier informed me, that if I would take the trouble to come out of my coach, and apply to the commandant, he would order them to halt, and allow me to pass. I took the man's advice, and was by him conducted, with much difficulty, through the croud to some officers, who seemed scarce to deserve the name; for, when I signified my request, they neither rose up, nor desired me to sit down; but lolling in their chairs, with one leg stretched out, asked, with an air of disrespectful raillery, where I was going; and when I answered, 'To Paris;' desired to know what I would do there.

I, who am naturally civil where I am civilly used, and saucy enough where I think myself treated with disregard, was very much piqued at their insolent and unmannerly behaviour, and began to reply to their impertinent questions, very abruptly; so that a very tart dialogue would have ensued, had not the conversation been interrupted by a tall, thin, genteel young French nobleman, an officer in the army, who chancing to come in, asked with great politeness, what I would please to have. I then repeated my desire, and produced my passports, by which he learn'd who I was. He immediately gave orders, that my coach should pass; and afterwards visited me at Paris, having obtained my permission, and taken my address at parting; while the others, understanding my name and quality, asked pardon for their impolite carriage, which they told me was owing to the representation of the soldier, who gave them to understand, that I was a strolling actress.

I could not help laughing heartily at this mistake, which might have proceeded from the circumstances of my appearance, my footman having been obliged to change hats with the peasant, and myself being without buckles in my shoes, and buttons in my riding-shirt, while my countenance still retained marks of the fear and confusion I had undergone. After all, perhaps the fellow was a droll, and wanted to entertain himself at my expence.

The day was so far consumed in these adventures, that I was obliged to take up my lodging at Mechlin, where I addressed myself to the intendant, giving him an account of the disaster I had met with, and desiring I might have credit at the inn, as our whole company could not raise the value of a six-pence. This gentleman, tho' a provincial, was polite in his way, and not only granted my request, but invited me to lodge at his own house. I accordingly gave him my company at supper, but did not choose to sleep in his quarters, because he appeared to be what the French call *un vieux debauchè*.

Next day, he sent a trumpet to the general, with a detail of my misfortune, in hopes of retrieving what I had lost; but, notwithstanding all possible search, I was fain to put up with my damage, which, in linen, laces, cloaths and baubles, amounted to upwards of seven hundred pounds: a loss which never deprived me of one moment's rest; for though I lodged at a miserable inn, and lay in a paultry bed, I slept as sound as if nothing extraordinary had happened, after I had written to London and Paris, directing that the payment of my bills of credit might be stopp'd. Indeed, I know but of two misfortunes in life, capable of depressing my spirits, namely, the loss of health and friends; all others may be prevented, or endured. The articles of that calamity, which I chiefly regretted, were a picture of lord W——m, and some inimitable letters from Mr. B——.

From Mechlin I proceeded to Brussels, where being known, I

got credit for some necessaries, and borrowed twenty guineas, to defray the expence of my journey to Paris. Having consulted with my friends, about the safest method of travelling through Flanders, I was persuaded to take places in the public Voiture; and accordingly departed, not without fears of finding one part of the country as much infested with robbers as another. Nor were these apprehensions assuaged by the conversation of my fellow-travellers, who being of the lower sort of people, that delight in exaggerating dangers, entertained me all the way, with an account of all the robberies and murders which had been committed on that road, with many additional circumstances of their own invention.

After having been two days exposed to this comfortable conversation, among very disagreeable company, which is certainly one of the most disagreeable situations in life, I arrived at Lisle, where, thinking the dangerous part of the journey was now past, I hired a post-chaise, and in two days more reached Paris, without any farther molestation.

Upon my arrival in this capital, I was immediately visited by my old acquaintances, who hearing my disaster, offered me their cloaths, and insisted upon my wearing them, until I could be otherwise provided. They likewise engaged me in parties, with a view of amusing my imagination, that I might not grow melancholy in reflecting upon my loss; and desired me to repeat the particulars of my story forty times over, expressing great surprize at our not being murthered, or ravished at least. As for this last species of outrage, the fear of it never once entered my head, otherwise I should have been more shocked and alarmed than I really was: but it seems this was the chief circumstance of my companion's apprehension; and I cannot help observing, that an homely woman is always more apt to entertain those fears, than one whose person exposes her to much more imminent danger. However, I now learned, that the risk I ran was much greater than I imagined it to be, those ruffians being familiarized to rape as well as murder.

Soon after my appearance in Paris, I was favoured with the addresses of several French lovers; but I never had any taste for foreigners, or indeed for any amusement of that kind, except such as were likely to be lasting, and settled upon a more agreeable footing than that of common gallantry. When I deviated from this principle, my conduct was the effect of compulsion, and therefore I was never easy under it, having been reduced to the alternative of two evils, the least of which I was obliged to choose, as a man leaps into the sea, in order to escape from a ship that is on fire.

Though I rejected their love, I did not refuse their company and conversation; and though my health was considerably impaired by the shock I received in my last adventure, which was considerably greater than I at first imagined, and affected my companion so much, that she did not recover her spirits, till she returned to England: I say, though I was for some time a valetudinarian, I enjoyed myself in great tranquillity for the space of ten months, during which I was visited by English, Scotch, and French, of all parties and persuasions; for pleasure is of no faction, and that was the chief object of my pursuit; neither was I so ambitious of being a politician, as to employ my time and thoughts upon subjects which I did not understand. I had admirers of all sides, and should have spent my time very much to my liking, had not I felt my funds sensibly diminish, without any prospect of their being repaired; for I had been obliged to lay out a great part of the sum allotted for my subsistence, in supplying my companion, my servant and myself with necessaries, in lieu of those which we had lost.

Having before mine eyes the uncomfortable prospect of wanting money in a strange place, I found myself under the necessity of returning to England, where I had more resources than I could possibly have among foreigners; and with that view wrote to lord ———'s agents, desiring that I might be enabled to discharge my obligations at Paris, by the payment of my pin-money. Thus a negotiation commenced, and his lordship promised to remit money for the clearance of my Paris debts, which amounted to four hundred pounds: but he would not advance one farthing more, though I gave him to understand, that while he protracted the agreement, I must inevitably be adding to my incumbrances, and that I should be as effectually detained by a debt of twenty pounds, as if I owed a thousand. Notwithstanding all my representations, he would not part with one shilling over the neat sum which I had at first stipulated; so that all my measures were rendered abortive, and I found it altogether impracticable to execute those resolutions I had formed in his favour.

Thus did he, for a meer trifle, embarrass the woman for whom he professes the most unlimited love, and whose principles he pretends to hold in the utmost veneration. Indeed his confidence in my integrity is not without foundation; for many wives, with one half of my provocation, would have ruined him to all intents and purposes; whereas, notwithstanding all the extraordinary expences, to which I have been exposed by his continual persecution, he never paid a shilling on my account, except one thousand pounds, exclusive of the small allowance which was my due. In a word, so much time elapsed before my lord could prevail upon himself to advance the bare four hundred, that I was involved in fresh difficulties, from which I found it impossible to extricate myself: and though I had occasion to write a letter to my benefactor lord ——, in which I expressed my acknowledgment for past favours, I could not venture to sollicit more; even when I was encouraged by a very obliging answer, wherein he declared, that the good qualities of my mind and heart, would bind him to me in friendship for ever.

While I ruminated on my uncomfortable situation, which would neither permit me to return to England, nor to stay much longer where I was, a young Englishman of immense fortune took Paris in his way from Italy, accompanied by a most agreeable Scotchman of very good sense and great vivacity. It was my good or ill fortune to become acquainted with these gentlemen, who having seen me at the opera, expressed a desire of being known to me, and accordingly favoured me with a visit one afternoon, when the brisk North Briton ingrossed the whole conversation; while the other seemed fearful and diffident even to a degree of bashfulness, through which, however, I could discern a delicate sensibility and uncommon understanding: there was in his person (which was very agreeable) as well as in his behaviour, a certain *naivetè* that was very pleasing; and at this first interview, we relished each other's company so well, that a sort of intimacy immediately commenced, and was carried on in a succession of parties of pleasure, in the course of which I found him fraught with all the tenderness and sentiment that render the heart susceptible of the most refined love; a disposition that immediately made me partial to him, while it subjected his own heart to all the violent impressions of a passion, which I little imagined our correspondence would have produced.

Nevertheless, I was far from being displeased with my conquest, because his person and qualifications, as well as his manner of address, were very much to my liking, and recommended him in a particular manner to my affection. Indeed, he made a greater progress in my heart than I myself suspected; for there was something congenial in our souls, which from our first meeting I believe had attracted us (unknown to ourselves) under the notions of friendship and regard, and now disclosed itself in the most passionate love.

I listened to his addresses, and we were truly happy. His attachment was the quintessence of tenderness and sincerity, while his generosity knew no bounds. Not contented with having paid twelve hundred pounds on my account, in the space of one fortnight, he would have loaded me with present after present, had not I absolutely refused to accept such expensive marks of his munificence. I was even mortified at those instances of his liberality, which my situation compelled me to receive, lest, being but little acquainted with my disposition, he should suspect me of being interested in my love, and judge my conduct by the malicious reports of common fame, which (he afterwards owned) had at first obtained such credit with him, that he believed our mutual attachment would not be of long duration. But, in this particular, he was soon undeceived: his heart, though naturally adapted for the melting passion, had hitherto escaped untouched by all the ladies of Italy and France; and therefore the first impressions were the more deeply fixed. As he was unpractised in the ways of common gallantry and deceit, the striking simplicity in his character was the more likely to engage the heart of one who knew the perfidy of the world, and despised all the farce and bombast of fashionable profession, which I had always considered as the phrase of vanity and ostentation, rather than the genuine language of love. Besides, gratitude had a considerable share in augmenting my affection, which manifested itself in such a warm, cordial, artless manner, as increased his esteem, and rivetted his attachment; for he could easily perceive, from the whole tenour of my conduct, that my breast was an utter stranger to craft and dissimulation: yet I was at first fearful of contracting any engagement with him, because, being younger than me, he might be the more apt to change, and the world might be malicious enough to suppose I had practised upon his inexperience; but, conscious of my own integrity, I set slander at defiance, trusting to my own behaviour, and his natural probity, for the continuance of his love. Though we did not live together in the same house, the greatest part of our time was spent in each other's company; we dined and supped at the same table, frequented public places, went upon parties to the country, and never parted, but for a few hours in the night, which we passed in the utmost impatience to meet again.

In this agreeable manner did the days roll on, when my felicity was interrupted by a fit of jealousy with which I happened to be seized. I had contracted an acquaintance with a young married lady, who, though her personal attractions were but slender, was, upon the whole, an agreeable, chearful, good-natured companion, with a little dash of the coquette in her composition. This woman being in very indigent circumstances, occasioned by some losses her husband had sustained, no sooner had an opportunity of seeing and conversing with my lover, than she formed the design of making a conquest of him. I should have forgiven her for this scheme, whatever pangs it might have cost me, had I believed it the effect of real passion; but I knew her too well, to suppose her heart was susceptible of love, and accordingly resented it. In the execution of her plan, she neglected nothing which she thought capable of engaging her attention. She took all opportunities of sitting near him at table, ogled him in the most palpable manner, directed her whole discourse to him, trod upon his toes; nay, I believe, squeezed his hand. My blood boiled at her, though my pride, for some time, enabled me to conceal my uneasiness; till at length her behaviour became so arrogant and gross, that I could no longer suppress my indignation, and one day told my lover, that I would immediately renounce his correspondence.

He was greatly alarmed at this unexpected declaration; and when he understood the cause of it, assured me, that for the future he would never exchange one word with her. Satisfied with this mark of his sincerity and regard, I released him from this promise, which he could not possibly keep, while she and I lived upon any terms; and we continued to visit each other as usual, though she still persisted in her endeavours to rival me in his affection, and contracted an intimacy with his companion, who seemed to entertain a passion for her, that she might have the more frequent opportunities of being among us; for she had no objection against favouring the addresses of both. One evening, I remember, we set out in my coach for the opera; and in the way, this inamorata was so busy with her feet, that I was incensed at her behaviour; and when we arrived at the place, refused to alight; but, setting them down, declared my intention of returning home immediately. She was so much pleased with this intimation, that she could not conceal the joy she felt at the thoughts of conversing with him, uninterrupted by my presence; an opportunity with which I had never favoured her before. This open exultation increased my anger and anxiety: I went home; but, being still tortured with the reflection of having left them together, adjusted myself in the glass, though I was too angry to take notice of my own figure, and without farther delay returned to the opera.

Having inquired for the box in which they sat, I took possession of one that fronted them, and reconnoitring them, without being perceived, had the satisfaction of seeing him removed to as great a distance from her as the place would permit, and his head turned another way. Composed by this examination, I joined them without further scruple, when my young gentleman expressed great joy at my appearance, and told me he was determined to have left the entertainment, and come in quest of me, had not I returned at that instant.

In our way homewards, my rival repeated her usual hints, and with her large hoop almost overshadowed my lover from my view: upon which my jealousy and wrath recurred with such violence, that I pulled the string, as a signal for the coachman to stop, with a view of getting out, and going home afoot; a step which would have afforded a new spectacle to the people of Paris. But I reflected, in a moment, upon the folly of such a resolution, and soon recollected myself, by calling my pride to my assistance. I determined, however, that she should act no more scenes of this kind in my presence, and that same night insisted upon my lover's dropping all intercourse and connexion with this tormentor. He very chearfully complied with my desire, and was even glad of an occasion to break off his acquaintance with a person about whom I had plagued him so much.

Thus was I freed from the persecution of one of those creatures, who, tho' of little consequence in themselves, are yet the pests of society, and find means to destroy that harmony which reigns between two lovers, by the intrusion of a loose appetite, void of all sensibility and discretion: having no feeling themselves, they cannot sympathize with that of other people, and do mischief out of meer wantonness.

My lover being obliged to go to England, had settled me in a genteel house in Paris, with a view of returning when his affairs should be adjusted; but when the time of his departure approached, he began to be uneasy at the prospect of separation, and, in order to alleviate his anxiety, desired me to accompany him to Calais, where we stayed together three or four days, during which the dread of parting became more and more intense: so that we determined upon my following him into England, by the first opportunity, where I should live altogether *incog*, that I might be concealed from the inquiries and attempts of my lord. Even after this resolution was fixed, we parted with all the agonies of lovers who despair of ever meeting again; and the wind blowing very high after he had imbarked, increased my fears. But by the return of the packet-boat, I was blessed with the report of his being safe arrived in England, and had the satisfaction of perusing his letters by every post.

My admirer being thus detached from me, my thoughts were intirely employed in concerting some private method of conveying myself to him. As I would not trust myself in the common packet, for fear of being discovered, after having revolved divers schemes, I determined to transport myself in one of the Dutch fishing-boats, tho' I knew the passage would be hazardous; but, in a case of such interesting concern, I overlooked all danger and inconvenience. Before I put this resolution in practice, I was so fortunate as to hear of a small English vessel that arrived at Calais with a prisoner of war, in which I embarked with my companion, and another lady, who lived with me for some time afterwards; and when we came on board, discovered that the ship was no other than a light collier, and that her whole company amounted to no more than three men. Nevertheless, tho' the sea was so rough, and the weather so unpromising, that no other boat would venture to put to sea, we set sail, and between two storms, in about three hours arrived in safety at Dover.

From hence my first companion went to her friends, in the stage-coach, while the other lady and I hired an open post-chaise (tho' it snowed very hard) and without any accident performed our journey to London, where I met with my lover, who flew to my arms in all the transports of impatient joy; and, doubtless, I deserved his affection, for the hardships, perils, and difficulties I had undergone to be with him; for I never scrupled to undertake any thing practicable, in order to demonstrate the sincerity of what I professed.

In consequence of our plan, I assumed a fictitious name, and never appeared in publick, being fully satisfied and happy in the company and conversation of the man I loved; and when he went into the country, contented myself with his correspondence, which he punctually maintained, in a series of letters equally sensible, sincere and affectionate.

Upon his return to town for the remainder of the season, he devoted the greatest part of his time to our mutual enjoyment; left me with reluctance, when he was called away by indispensible business, and the civility which was due to his acquaintance, and very seldom went to any place of publick entertainment, because I could not accompany and share with him in the diversion: nay, so much did I ingross his attention, that one evening, after he had been teized into an agreement of meeting some friends at a play, he went thither precisely at the appointed hour, and as they did not arrive punctually at the very minute, he returned to me immediately, as much rejoiced at his escape as if he had met with some signal deliverance. Nor was his constancy inferior to the ardour of his love: we went once together to a ball in the Haymarket, where, in the midst of a thousand fine women, whose charms were inhanced by the peculiarity of the dresses they wore, he remained unshaken, unseduced, preserving his attachment for me, in spite of all temptation.

In the summer he provided me with a house in the neighbourhood of his own; but the accommodations being bad, and that country affording no other place fit for my residence, he brought me home to his own seat, and by that step raised an universal clamour, tho' I saw no company, and led such a solitary life, that nothing but excessive love could have supported my spirits: not but that he gave me as much of his time as he could possibly spare from the necessary duties of paying and receiving visits, together with the avocations of hunting, and other country amusements, which I could not partake. Formerly, indeed, I used to hunt and shoot, but I had left off both; so that I was now reduced to the alternative of reading and walking by myself: but, *Love made up for all deficiencies to me, who think nothing else worth the living for !— Had I been blessed with a partner for life, who could have loved sincerely, and inspired me with a mutual flame, I would have asked no more of fate. Interest and ambition have no share in my composition ; love which is pleasure, or pleasure which is love, makes up the whole. A heart so disposed cannot be devoid of other good qualities ; it must be subject to the impressions of humanity and benevolence, and enemy to nothing but itself.* This you will give me leave to affirm, in justice to myself, as I have frankly owned my failings and misconduct.

Towards the end of summer my heart was a little alarmed by a report that prevailed, of my lover's being actually engaged in a treaty of marriage: however, I gave little credit to this rumour, till I was obliged to go to town about business, and there I heard the same information confidently affirmed. Tho' I still considered it as a vague surmise, I wrote to him an account of what I had heard; and in his answer, which is still in my possession, he assured me, with repeated vows and protestations, that the report was altogether false. Satisfied with this declaration, I returned to his house; and tho' the tale was incessantly thundered in my ears, still believed it void of all foundation, till my suspicion was awaked by a very inconsiderable circumstance.

One day, on his return from hunting, I perceived he had a very fine pair of Dresden ruffles on his shirt, which I could not suppose he would wear at such a rustic exercise; and therefore my fears immediately took the alarm. When I questioned him about this particular of his dress, his colour changed; and tho' he attempted to elude my suspicion, by imputing it to a mistake of his servant, I could not rest satisfied with this account of the matter, but inquired into the truth with such eagerness and penetration, that he could not deny he had been to make a visit; and, by degrees, I even extorted from him a confession, that he had engaged himself farther than he ought to have proceeded, without making me acquainted with his design, tho' he endeavoured to excuse his conduct, and pacify my displeasure, by saying that the affair would not be brought to bear for a great while, and perhaps might never come to a determination: but he was in great confusion, and indeed hardly knew what he said.

I would have quitted his house that moment, had not he, beforehand, obtained a promise that I would take no rash resolution of that kind, and put it out of my power to procure any method of conveyance by which I could make my retreat. I gave no vent to reproaches, and only upbraided him with his having permitted me to return in ignorance to the country, after I was once fairly gone: upon which he swore that he could not bear the thoughts of parting with me. This declaration was a mystery at that time, but I have been since so fully satisfied of his reasons for his conduct, that I heartily acquit him of all injustice to me.[1] And indeed, it is my sincere opinion, that if ever a young man deserved to be happy, he is certainly intitled to that privilege; and, if I may be allowed to judge, has an heart susceptible of the most refined enjoyment.

The violence of the grief and consternation which I suffered from this stroke, having a little subsided, I deliberated with myself about the measures I should take, and determined to leave his house some day when he should be abroad. I was encouraged in this resolution by the advice of our Scotch friend, who came about this time from London, on a visit to his fellow-traveller: we thought such an abrupt departure would be less shocking than to stay and take a formal leave of my lover, whose heart was of such a delicate frame, that after I told him I should one day withdraw myself, in his absence, he never came home from the chace, or any other avocation, without trembling with apprehension that I had escaped.

After he had been some time accustomed to these fears by my previous intimation, I at length decamped, in good earnest, tho' my heart aked upon the occasion, because I left him loving and beloved; for his affection was evident, notwithstanding the step he had taken, by the advice and importunity of all his relations, who laid a disagreeable restraint upon his inclinations, while they consulted his interest in every other particular.

While I halted in the next great town, until I could be supplied with fresh horses, I was visited by a gentleman who had been formerly intimate with my lover; but a breach had happened in their friendship, and he now came to complain of the treatment he had received. Perceiving that I was not in a humour to listen to his story, he shifted the conversation to my own, and observed, that I had been extremely ill used. I told him I was of a different opinion : that it was not only just, but expedient, that a young man of Mr. ———'s fortune should think of making some alliance to strengthen and support the interest of his family; and that I had nothing to accuse him of but his letting me remain so long in ignorance of his intention. He then gave me to understand, that I was still ignorant of a great part of the ill usage I had received, affirming, that while I lived in his house, he had amused himself with all the common women in that town, to some of whom this gentleman had personally introduced him.

At first, I could not believe this imputation; but he supported his assertions with so many convincing circumstances, that I could no longer doubt the truth of them; and I felt so much resentment, that my love vanished immediately into air. Instead of proceeding in my journey to London, I went back a considerable way, and sent a message, desiring to see him in a little house, about mid way between his own habitation and the town from whence I came. He obeyed my summons, and appeared at the place appointed, where I reproached him with great bitterness. He pleaded guilty to the charge, so far as acknowledging that he had corresponded with other women lately, in order to get the better of his affection for me, but the experiment had failed, and he found that he should be for ever miserable.

I did not look upon this candid confession as a sufficient atonement for his past dissimulation, and, in the sharpness of my revenge, demanded a settlement, which he peremptorily refused; so that, for the present, we held each other in the utmost contempt. Indeed, I afterwards despised myself for my condescension, which was owing to the advice of my companion, supported and inflamed by the spirit of resentment. Nevertheless, he begged that I would return to his house, or stay all night where I was; but I was deaf to his intreaties, and, after a great deal of ironical civility on my side, I took my leave, and went away; yet, before I set out, I looked back, and saw him on horseback, with such an air of simplicity and truth, as called up a profound sigh, notwithstanding all that had passed in our conversation.

Upon my arrival in London, I took lodgings in Leicester-Fields, and answered a letter which I had some months before received from my lord; telling him, that I would go home to him, without stipulating for any terms, to try what effect my confidence would have upon his generosity. He readily embraced the offer, and took an house in St. James's street, where I proposed to comply with his humour in every thing that was consistent with my own peace and tranquillity.

Mean while, my lover passed his time very disagreeably in the country, with his friend, of whom (it seems) he had conceived some jealousy, which was increased by a letter I wrote to that gentleman, till he was made acquainted with the contents, which he read over forty times; and then his passion breaking out with more violence than ever, he not only expressed his feeling, in an epistle which I immediately received, but when he came to town, suffered such agonies of despair as I had never seen before, except in lord B——. It was then in my power to have taken ample revenge upon him, as well as upon my insolent rival, who had insisted upon my leaving his house, in a very abrupt manner, tho' he absolutely refused to gratify her malice; for he was now disposed to do any thing for my satisfaction: but I knew his worth, and had too much regard for his reputation to advise him to act inconsistent with his honour.

About this time, many tender meetings and sorrowful partings happened between us, till the marriage-knot was tied, when he sent me a bank-note for a thousand pounds, by way of specimen (as he called it) of his friendship, and of what he would do for me, should I ever want his assistance. This mark of his generosity I received in a most tender billet, which I shall never part with, together with his picture set in diamonds.

I now employed my thoughts in keeping measures with my lord; we lay in the same apartment, and for the first four or five months I neither dined nor supped abroad, above twice; and then he knew where I was, and approved of my company. But all this complacency and circumspection had no effect upon his temper, which remained as capricious and dissatisfied as ever. Nay, to such a provoking degree did this unhappy humour prevail, that one day, in the presence of his lawyer, he harrangued upon my misconduct since our last re-union; and very freely

affirmed, that every step I had taken was diametrically opposite
to his will.

Conscious of the pains I had been at to please him, I was so
incensed at these unjust invectives, that starting up, I told him he
was a little dirty fellow; and would have left the house immediately, had not his lawyer, and others, who were in the next room,
interposed, and by dint of argument and importunity diverted me
from my purpose. By the bye, I have been informed by a person
of rank, that my lord discovered exactly the same disposition in his
father's life-time, and only changes the subject of his complaint
from the word *father* to that of *wife*. Indeed he takes all opportunities of plaguing my dear parent, as he has just sagacity enough to
know, that this is the most effectual way he can take to distress me.

After repeated trials, I have given up all hopes of making him
happy, or of finding myself easy in my situation; and live with him
at present to avoid a greater inconvenience. Not that his ill-nature
is all the grievance of which I complain: exclusive of the personal
disgust I entertain for him, his folly is of that species which disobliges rather than diverts, and his vanity and affectation altogether
intolerable; for he actually believes himself, or at least would impose himself upon mankind, as a pattern in gallantry and taste;
and, in point of business, a person of infinite sagacity and penetration: but the most ridiculous part of his character is his pretended
talent for politics, in which he so deeply concerns himself, that he
has dismissed many a good servant, because he suspected him of
having wrong connexions; a theme upon which he has often quarrelled with me, even almost to parting, accusing me of holding correspondence with the earls of B— and C—,[1] and Mr. H— V— tho' I
never had the least acquaintance with any of these gentlemen, except
the earl of C——, to whom I have not spoke for these ten years past.

In short, I have often been at a loss to know, whether he was
more mad or malicious in those fits of enthusiasm, wherein he
seemed transported with zeal for the commonwealth, and tormented me with his admonitions, out of all temper and patience.
At length, however, I contrived an expedient which freed me from
these troublesome expostulations, and silenced him effectually on
the score of politicks. This was no other than an open avowal of
being connected with all those people whom I have named. Indeed,
I knew him too well to believe there was any thing solid in his
intention or professions, even when he carried them so far as to
demand a private audience of the K—, in order to communicate
a scheme for suppressing the rebellion; and that being denied,

sollicited the duke of D——'s interest,[1] for permission to raise and
head a regiment of Kentish smugglers: nay, to such a pitch did
his loyalty soar, that he purchased a firelock of particular mechanism,
calculated for the safety of the bearer, in case he had been placed
centinel at his majesty's door; and kept his horses ready caparisoned,
with a view of attending his sovereign to the field. Notwithstanding
all these pompous preparations, had he been put to the proof, he
would have infallibly crept out of his engagements, thro' some
sneaking evasion, his imagination being very fertile in such saving
pretences. Yet he will talk sometimes so fervently, and even sensibly,
on the subject, that a stranger would mistake him for a man of
understanding, and determined zeal for the good of his country.

Since my last return to his house, that act of parliament passed,
by which he was enabled to pay his debts, and among the rest, a
thousand pounds of my contracting, the only burden of that kind
I ever intailed upon him, exclusive of my pin-money, which was
never regularly paid; nor would he have been subject to this, had
he not, by his persecution and pursuit, exposed me to an extraordinary expence. I have also had it in my power to reward some
of my faithful Abigails; in particular, to relieve from extreme distress that maid to whom (as I have already observed) lord B—
granted an annuity, which she had sold: so that she was reduced
to the most abject poverty, and I found her in a dismal hole, with
two infants, perishing for want; a spectacle which drew tears from
my eyes, and indeed could not but make a deep impression upon
an heart like mine, which the misery of my fellow-creatures never
failed to melt.

Nor did I, upon this occasion, forget the attachment and fidelity
of my other woman Mrs. S—, who hearing I was robbed in my
passage thro' Flanders, had generously relinquished the allowance
I had settled upon her at parting. The exercise of such acts of
humanity and benevolence, and the pleasure of seeing my dear and
tender parent often, in some measure alleviate the chagrin to which
I am subject, from the disagreeable disposition of my lord, who,
consistent with his former inconsistency, upon our last reconciliation chearfully agreed to a proposal I made of having concerts in
the house, and even approved of the scheme with marks of particular satisfaction: but before one half of the winter was expired,
he found means to banish all the company, beginning with lord
R— B—, who, as he walked up stairs one evening, was stopped
by a footman, who plainly told him he had orders to say to him in
particular, that his lordship was not at home: yet the very next day

perceiving that nobleman and me walking together in the park, he joined us with an air of alacrity, as if no such thing had happened, and even behaved to lord R—— with the most fawning complaisance. His deportment was equally absurd and impertinent to the rest of our friends, who forsook us gradually, being tired of maintaining any friendly communication with such a disagreeable composition of ignorance and arrogance. For my own part, I look upon him as utterly incorrigible; and as fate hath subjected me to his power, endeavour to make the bitter draught go down, by detaching myself, as much as possible, from the supposition that there is any such existence upon earth. Indeed, if I had not fatal experience of the contrary, I should be apt to believe that such a character is not to be found among the sons of men; because his conduct is altogether unaccountable by the known rules and maxims of life, and falls intirely under the poet's observation, when he says,

> *'Tis true, no meaning puzzles more than wit.*[1]

Her ladyship having thus concluded her story, to the entertainment of the company, and the admiration of Peregrine, who expressed his astonishment at the variety of adventure she had undergone, which was such as he thought sufficient to destroy the most hardy and robust constitution, and therefore infinitely more than enough to overwhelm one of her delicate frame; one of the gentlemen present, roundly taxed her with want of candour, in suppressing some circumstances of her life, which he thought essential in the consideration of her character.

She reddened at this peremptory charge, which had an evident effect upon the countenances of the whole audience, when the accuser proceeded to explain his imputation, by observing, that, in the course of her narration, she had omitted to mention a thousand acts of uncommon charity, of which he himself knew her to be guilty; that she had concealed a great many advantageous proposals of marriage, which she might have accepted, before she was engaged;[2] that she had not spoke one word of her first husband's debts, which, to his certain knowledge, she had paid out of her own privy purse, after her second marriage, and on that account received the thanks of lord W——'s elder brother, who, though he had undertaken to discharge them, delayed the execution of his purpose longer than she thought they should remain unpaid: and that, in relating her inducements for leaving Mr. S—, (whether out of forgetfulness, or from tenderness to a lover once so dear to her, he would not pretend to say) she had omitted a very cogent motive for her own conduct; for as he had first courted her favour in her rising fortune, and left her in its decline, she could not avoid reflecting, that, after this precipitate re-engagement, when the first transports of their meeting were over, he would again act the same conduct, as soon as her tranquillity should be disturbed by the persecution of her lord.

The company were agreeably undeceived by this explanation; which her ladyship acknowledged in very polite terms, as a compliment equally genteel and unexpected: and our hero, after having testified the sense he had of her complaisance and condescension, in regaling him with such a mark of her confidence and esteem, took his leave, and went home in a state of confusion and perplexity; for, from the circumstances of the tale he had heard, he plainly perceived, that her ladyship's heart was too delicate to receive such incense, as he, in the capacity of an admirer, could at present pay; because, though he had in some measure abridged the empire of Emilia in his own breast, it was not in his power to restrain it so effectually, but that it would interfere with any other sovereign whom his thoughts should adopt: and, unless lady —— could ingross his whole love, time and attention, he foresaw, that it would be impossible for him to support the passion which he might have the good fortune to inspire. He was, moreover, deterred from declaring his love, by the fate of her former admirers, who seemed to have been wound up to a degree of enthusiasm, that looked more like the effect of inchantment, than the inspiration of human attractions; an extasy of passion which he durst not venture to undergo; therefore resolved to combat with the impressions he had already received, and, if possible, cultivate her friendship without soliciting her affection: but, before he could fix upon this determination, he desired to know the predicament in which he stood in her opinion; and by the intelligence of Crabtree, obtained in the usual manner, understood that her sentiments of him were very favourable, though without the least tincture of love. He would have been transported with joy, had her thoughts of him been of a more tender texture; though his reason was better pleased with the information he received; in consequence of which, he mustered up the ideas of his first passion, and set them in opposition to those of this new and dangerous attachment; by which means, he kept the balance *in equilibrio*, and his bosom tolerably quiet.

CHAPTER LXXXIX

Peregrine amuses his Imagination,
by slight Incursions upon the Territory of Vice and Folly;
reforms a back-sliding Brother,
and sends a celebrated Sharper into Exile

HIS heart being thus, as it were, suspended between two objects that lessened the force of each other's attraction, he took this opportunity of enjoying some respite, and for the present detached his sentiments from both; resolving to indulge himself in the exercise of that practical satire, which was so agreeable and peculiar to his disposition. In this laudable determination he was confirmed by the repeated suggestions of his friend Cadwallader, who taxed him with letting his talents rust in indolence, and stimulated his natural vivacity, with a succession of fresh discoveries in the world of scandal.[1]

Thus reinforced, they took the field, and performed various exploits, to the mortification, astonishment and dismay of all those coxcombs, whether male or female, fierce or feeble, insolent or tame, that hang like tatters on the skirts of gallantry, and bring the fashion into disgrace. As I might trespass upon the patience of the reader, in giving a minute detail of each adventure of this kind which they atchieved, I shall content myself with relating two only, to which indeed all the rest bore some resemblance.

Peregrine's intelligencer, who (as we have already observed) was a privileged person in all parties, happened one morning to breakfast with a sort of a great man, who, with a large stock of timorous superstition and exterior piety, had at bottom a spice of carnality, which all his religion could not extinguish. Among the rest of his dependants, there was a certain favourite, who by the most assiduous attention to his humour, in a course of artful flattery and servile complaisance, had insinuated himself so far into his confidence and esteem, that he now acted in the capacity of his counsellor and director, both in his spiritual and temporal concerns.

This cunning parasite having discovered his patron's infirmity, began to be afraid, that in the instigations of the flesh, he might be tempted to employ some other agent for the gratification of his appetite: and foreseeing that any minister of this kind would infallibly prove a dangerous rival to him, in the good graces of his master, he resolved to anticipate the misfortune, and, with his other offices, monopolize the functions of a Mercury, for which his talents were perfectly well adapted. But this was not the whole of his task; he knew there were certain qualms and scruples of conscience to be removed, as well as other motives of shyness and distrust, which he durst not leave to the operation of his friend's own desires, lest he should choose some other confident; he therefore observed the different seasons of his constitution, and culled the proper opportunities of expressing a relaxation in his sentiments of chastity; which being gratefully received, he proceeded in the work of conversion, already half effected by his patron's own passions; and in conclusion, found a willing dame to quench this fire that scorched his vitals. He had overnight obtained her consent, and the particulars of their meeting were adjusted, in presence of Cadwallader, who gave his associate to understand that, with a view of keeping the rendezvous secret and mysterious, as well as of saving the lovers that mutual confusion which the light must have produced, the scene of their interview was laid in a summer-house, that stood at the end of his garden, to which the lady and her conductor would be admitted in the dark, through a back-door that should be left open for the purpose. Peregrine being made acquainted with these particulars, together with the hour of assignation, ordered Pipes to purchase a live calf, and carried it in a sack, about the twilight, to the back-garden-door, which our hero entered without hesitation, disposing himself and his attendants in a dark alcove immediately under the summer-house, where (without disengaging the animal from its covering) he besmeared its front with liquid phosphorus, and directed Tom to unveil, and present it to the company at their approach, while he himself absconded behind a pillar, from whence he could view the entertainment. They had continued a whole hour in this situation, when they perceived by starlight, three persons enter the postern, and advance towards the place where they lay; upon which, Pipes began to disentangle his charge, that he might be ready to play it off at the proper time; but, as he was not very expert in this business, the calf finding itself disengaged from its confinement, sprung all of a sudden out of his hands, and running directly forwards, encountered those that approached, and as it passed them, uttered a loud *Baa.*

The gallant, whose passions were exalted to a pitch of enthusiasm, as susceptible of religious horror as of love, seeing such an apparition, when he was at the point of indulging a criminal appetite, and hearing the dreadful cry, accompanied with the terrible word *damnation*, which Pipes, in his peculiar tone, exclaimed from the alcove, when the animal made its escape; he was seized with consternation and remorse, and falling upon his face, lay in all the agonies of terror, believing himself warned by a particular message from above. His trusty squire, who was not quite so visionary, recollecting himself from the surprize he had suffered at the first appearance of such a glaring phænomenon, which had also such an effect upon the lady, that she ran out into the fields, screaming all the way: I say, he no sooner recovered the faculty of reflection, which this accident had for some minutes taken away, than he observed his patron's prostration; and guessing the condition of his thoughts, resolved to profit by his sagacity. He accordingly laid himself gently down upon the cold walk, and lay very quietly, till the lover, having in a faultring voice called thrice upon his name, without being favoured with an answer, raised himself up, and coming to the spot, shook him by the arm; upon which he seemed to wake from his trance, and in a most penitent tone pronounced a very pious ejaculation, which confirmed the opinion of his principal, who asked him with fear and trembling, if he had heard the voice and seen the light. Being an excellent actor, he replied with all the marks of amazement, that he was struck blind with a gush of light, far exceeding that of the sun at noon, and his ears appalled with a voice, like the sound of many waters, denouncing damnation to those who obey the lusts of the flesh.

The converted lover, though he was not sensible of such extraordinary circumstances of visitation, implicitely believed every tittle of his account, imputing the difference of his own perception to the weakness of his organs, which were sooner disturbed than those of his purveyor. He therefore proposed, that they should adjourn to the chamber which had been destined for the scene of his transgression, and with sorrow and contrition ask pardon of heaven for his intended offence, acknowledging at the same time, the seasonable and salutary interposition of providence. This duty was accordingly performed, after they had searched in vain for the nymph, who (the squire seemed to think) was conveyed by some supernatural means from the garden; for he said, as he lay intranced upon the ground, he heard a rattling like the chariots of Aminadab, and the shrieks of the young woman gradually sinking in a distant cadence, as if she had been transported through the air.

As this pair of penitents walked up stairs to the summer-house, the patron, in an extasy of faith, pronounced, 'After this tremendous scene, who can be so incredulous, so dead to all conviction, as to doubt the miracle of the loaves and fishes, or the amazing circumstances that attended the conversion of St. Paul?' While they were employed in the exercise of their devotion, our hero and his attendant retired by the back-door, which opened into the fields; and while Pipes went in pursuit of his calf, which had taken shelter under the wall, his master proceeded forwards to the place from whence he had come, where he had agreed to meet Cadwallader, and communicate the success of his enterprize, with which he was perfectly well pleased. In crossing the field that lay betwixt him and that part of the town for which he was bound, he chanced to pass by a heap of wood, upon which he perceived a woman, tolerably well dressed, sitting, and holding a smelling-bottle to her nose. He immediately guessed her to be the lady whom he had interrupted in her assignation; and thinking it was incumbent upon him to make some atonement for the injury he had done, he accosted her with great politeness and respect, telling her, he presumed, from her being in such a solitary place, at such an hour, that she had met with some misfortune; and that, if she would put herself under his protection, he would defend her from any farther insult.

His conjecture was right; this was the individual inamorata who had fled from the garden, and who was so terrified at the vision, the meaning of which she could not comprehend, that she found herself unable to proceed farther homewards, and sat down on a log of wood, to enjoy a little pause of rest, and endeavour to recollect her dissipated spirits. She had not yet got the better of her apprehension, which was rather increased by the darkness of the night and the loneliness of the place; so that she, without scruple, embraced the offer of a person who behaved with such gentle address: and as she was enervated by fear, he carefully supported her in walking, with his arm round her waist, encouraging her all the way with assurances of safety, and expressing his curiosity to know the adventure, in consequence of which she had occasion for assistance. She spoke very little during her passage through the field, because, notwithstanding his professions and appearance, he was still a stranger; and therefore she could not be altogether easy, while she thought herself absolutely in his power: but, when they entered the town, and mingled with the concourse of people that pass and repass through all the streets of this metropolis, her diffidence intirely vanished, and her conversation became altogether unreserved.

The remembrance of what had discomposed her so much in the

garden, now afforded subject for her mirth; and when her conductor still repeated his desire of information, she could not help
laughing heartily, at the circumstances which his questions recalled.
Encouraged by this manifestation of good humour, he observed,
that as her spirits were exhausted by the fatigue and disquiet she
had undergone, it would be impossible for her to walk much
farther, and begg'd she would step with him into the next tavern,
where they might send for an hackney-coach or chair, in which
she would be conveyed to her own lodging. After much intreaty, she
consented to his proposal; and he had the pleasure to see, that she
was a very handsome young woman, about the age of eighteen.

The joy he felt at this discovery lightened in his eyes; nor was she
able to conceal a certain alacrity and satisfaction that appeared in
her countenance, when she obtained a distinct view of her protector's person. In short, she was prevailed upon to drink a glass of
wine; and Peregrine presuming upon his knowledge of her adventure, began to make love with great vehemence. At first, she
pretended to take offence at his presumption; but, perceiving from
certain insinuations which he artfully dropp'd, that he was better
acquainted with her character than she had imagined, her shyness
gradually wore off, and they soon came to a satisfactory explanation;
in the beginning of which, he frankly unravelled the whole mystery
of the apparition: a discovery which had almost proved fatal to her,
from the violence of mirth it produced; and she as candidly disclosed her own private history. She told him, that her lover's
honourable agent had formerly lived in the house of her mother,
who being a poor widow, supported her family by letting lodgings;
that he had, by the opportunities of familiarity and friendship,
employed his arts upon her, and actually debauched this girl, when
she was no more than fifteen years of age; that upon the remonstrances of her mother, who detected their correspondence, by
perceiving she was with child, he had quitted the house, with an
absolute refusal to provide for her; so that she was obliged to sue
him for the maintenance of the infant, and reduced to the necessity
of receiving gallants in private; though she had always managed her
occupation in such a manner, as to preserve her character un-
suspected in the neighbourhood: and lastly, that her first seducer
had lately renewed his correspondence, by dint of presents and
apologies, and procured her as a virgin for his patron, who had
promised to settle some small provision upon her for life.

Peregrine comforted her for her disappointment, by reciting
what he had overheard of the conversation that passed in the

garden, after she made her elopement; from whence he inferred, that her interest would suffer no prejudice from that interruption; because, in all probability, her intended lover's flesh would soon get the better of the spirit again, in spite of a thousand apparitions; in which case, he would again have recourse to her compliance; or, should his superstition prevail, he would look upon himself as in duty and conscience bound, to enable her, by a suitable settlement, to withstand such temptations for the future.

She seemed to concur with his opinion, and was perfectly satisfied with that expectation, while our hero was more and more engaged by her easy and agreeable deportment. Her conversation was that of a gay libertine, who had a good share of sense and imagination, which, with a natural vivacity, she employed in accommodating herself to the humour of her gallant: but his ears were not disgusted with the nauseous ribaldry and vulgar execrations which characterise the discourse of those nymphs, whose temporary endearments are solicited by the distinguishing youth of this refined age. In a word, this accidental meeting was productive of very agreeable consequences to both; and an intimacy of intercourse immediately commenced, the result of which was, her promising to reserve her favours for him alone, till farther notice, and to enter into no measures with the visionary, but such as he should know and approve.

Having passed the evening with this new acquaintance, and informed himself of the particulars necessary to be known, for the support of the correspondence they had established, he favoured her with some marks of his bounty, and repaired to the lodgings of his friend Crabtree, who was so much incensed at his breach of punctuality, that he ordered himself to be denied; and when the young gentleman forced his entrance into his chamber, *vi & armis*, would not open his mouth; but assuming the most grim contraction of his countenance, sat in sullen silence, till the circumstances of the adventure, which his associate knew how to relate to the greatest advantage, gradually unbended his features to an involuntary smile, which soon dilated into an unrestrained laugh, assuring Peregrine of his forgiveness and approbation: for though (as I have already observed) this Misanthrope had gained an absolute ascendency over the muscles of his face, and, when under the eye of the world, could laugh inwardly, without betraying the least symptom of mirth, this self-denial was not exerted without pains; and therefore he, in private, indemnified himself for the trouble he was at, in preserving that inflexible gravity in public.

Next day in the evening, our adventurer visited his fair Phillis, and understood that she had a message from the new convert, exhorting her to repentance and reformation, and promising to support her in her laudable endeavours, as soon as she should be disposed to begin the great work. At the same time, his trusty messenger had talked of his patron's conversion in the most ludicrous terms, accounted for the apparition, by affirming, that it was no other than a dog, with a paper-lanthorn hanging to his neck, equipped in that manner by some prentices for their diversion; that he had been thrown over the wall, with a view to frighten the servants of the family; and not liking his quarters, no sooner perceived the garden-door opened, than he naturally ran towards it, in order to make his escape. He likewise frankly owned, that he had, with a view to his own interest, encouraged his lord and master in his superstitious fears, and even counselled him to execute, in the course of his penitence, a plan which he had formerly laid, of commencing author, and espousing in print the cause of miracles, against the children of perverseness and incredulity: and in conclusion, this faithful adviser had made strong love on his own score, proposing to maintain a correspondence with her, for which she would be amply recompenced by the bounty of his patron, whom he undertook to deceive with a feigned account of her repentance.

The wench, having an aversion to the character of this parasite, whom she had too great reason to know, instead of embracing his proposal with chearfulness and alacrity, told him with an affected air of severity, that howsoever his heart might be hardened against the warnings of heaven, she had the internal comfort to find her own breast touched with a due sense of her unworthiness, and would, by the blessing of providence, imitate the salutary example of his good friend, to whom she intended to write an account of her inward workings, which she hoped were no other than the motions of the spirit.

Mr. Mercury hearing this unexpected declaration, which was delivered with a face of pious resolution, immediately availed himself of that hypocrisy, which he possessed to such a consummate degree; and after having protested with great earnestness, that what he had said, was uttered with a view to try whether or not she was intirely mortified to all the lusts of the flesh, he applauded her determination with the most lofty encomiums, and admonished her to perseverance, in an enthusiastic harangue; during which, the tears actually gushed from his eyes, and his looks adopted a sort of wildness and extatic stare, as if he had been really transported.

Though she saw through the disguise, she seemed convinced of his sincerity; as a confirmation of which, he gave her his purse, and took his leave, assuring her that she should never want, so long as she could retain grace enough to persist in the happy work she had so righteously begun. Peregrine approved of her behaviour, and having instructed her with regard to her future conduct, returned to his auxiliary and intelligencer, with whom he concerted another stratagem, to be practised upon a certain she-gamester of fashion, and a French adventurer, who, under the title of count, supported with invincible effrontery, and a large stock of finesse, had found means to introduce himself among the quality, from many of whom he had extracted large sums of money at play. Among those whom he laid under contribution, was this lady, who with all the inclination of a rank sharper, had fallen a sacrifice to his superior talents, and become his debtor for five hundred pounds, which she could not pay without the assistance of her husband, whom she did not think proper to inform of the loss. She had for some days evaded the demands of her creditor, by divers specious pretences, which, however, were soon exhausted; and he grew so disagreeably importunate, as to threaten an application to her lord, if she would not discharge the debt immediately.

The lady being a latitudinarian in her principles, and reduced to great perplexity by these menaces, could think of no other expedient to extricate herself, than that of practising upon the foreigner's heart, which she accordingly assailed with all the arts of coquetry, reinforced by a very agreeable person, to which she had been often indebted for sundry fortunate events. Nevertheless, in all probability she would have found the count impregnable, had not he, at this crisis, luckily met with such a flow of success, as elevated his fancy, and opened his heart to amorous impressions. In this state of exultation did he first perceive, or at least acknowledge the attractions of his debtor, to whom he, in a billet, declared his passion, and frankly proposed the alternative, which it was her sole aim to procure.

After the necessary scruples of decent reluctance, the affair was compromised, in the hearing of Cadwallader, who reported to his associate, that she had given the count an assignation at the house of a discreet matron, who, under the denomination of a milliner, kept commodious apartments for interviews of this kind.

Peregrine, who was not unknown to this priestess of love, no sooner received this intelligence, than he went and bespoke one of her chambers, contiguous to that which the foreigner had chosen for his accommodation; and some time before the hour of their appointment, took possession of it, accompanied by Crabtree, whom he had dressed in woman's apparel, because the Misanthrope would not run the risque of being observed *in propria persona*.

The lovers, true to their contract, met precisely at the hour; the lady having disguised herself in an ordinary dishabille, with a capuchin, the hood of which effectually concealed her countenance; and the door of their apartment being shut, the count found himself on the brink of enjoying his good fortune, when all of a sudden, Peregrine, placing himself at the door, pronounced aloud, in the very voice and manner of her lord, whom he personally knew, 'Stand firm upon your post, Mr. Constable, and take care that none shall pass, while I break open the door, and make sure of the delinquent; for now I think her ladyship is fairly caught.'

This exclamation produced an instantaneous effect in the chamber: the count, terrified at the prospect of immediate death or prosecution, ran directly to the window, and throwing up the sash, would have made his exit into the street, without ceremony; but my lady, who never doubted that her husband was at the door, had recourse to that presence of mind, which never forsook her upon such occasions; and seizing her gallant by the collar, exalted her voice, crying, 'Rape! Murder! Rape! Ah villain! do you attempt my virtue? Are these the laces you invited me to come and see? Ah, you beastly monster! Help, good people, help!'

The noise of these outcries, (in consequence of which Pickle immediately retreated to his den) alarmed the whole family. The landlady, whose reputation was at stake, ran up stairs, accompanied by two chairmen, who waited for my lady below; and the door being burst open by her directions, they found her ladyship in a violent agitation, holding fast by the count, who stood without his perriwig, shaking from head to foot, in all the agony of horror and dismay. My lady, finding herself delivered from the attempts of this ravisher, sunk down upon the couch in a swoon; and while the matron of the house administered to her nostrils, the chairmen secured the poor gallant, whose faculties were actually suppressed by the extasy of his fear.

The lady having a little recollected her spirits, and looking around, without perceiving her husband, concluded that he was satisfied of her innocence, by the artifice of her behaviour, and omitted to shew himself, that she might not be shocked at his appearance. On this supposition, she renewed her clamour against the count, whom she reviled with the epithets of perfidious wretch, and abominable ruffian; and expressed her doubts about the honesty of the house, to which (she said) he had decoyed her, on pretence of shewing some laces of a new pattern, that the milliner had received from abroad.

The landlady was no stranger to her person or character, and therefore had never doubted the truth of the count's information, when he made her privy to the nature of this interview; but her ladyship's present behaviour, (the true cause of which she did not know) intirely altered her opinion; and she now believed, that the count intended to have made her house the scene of a rape in good earnest. This suggestion divested her of all regard for her customer, against whom she exclaimed with great virulence, as a person who had endeavoured to intail the curse of infamy upon her house; and assured the plaintiff, that he had hired the apartment for a young lady, whom he pretended to have privately espoused, without the consent of her parents, from whose inquiries he had reasons to conceal the place of her abode.

The rueful foreigner, baited with their joint invectives, and more than half distracted with the terrors of an English jury, never dream'd of attempting to vindicate himself from the imputation he had incurred; because he imagined the whole affair was the result of a conspiracy against his life and fortune; but falling upon his knees before his accuser, in the most suppliant manner, implored her pardon, which he offered to acknowledge by a present of a thousand pounds. Had these terms been seasonably proposed, matters would soon have been brought to an accommodation; but she could not decently enter into a treaty with him, in presence of such witnesses; and besides, she believed herself still under the inspection of her husband. She therefore rejected his proffer with disdain, observing, that his guilt was of such a nature, as to preclude all hopes of forgiveness; and ordered the chairmen to take charge of his person, until he should be taken into custody by an officer properly authorized.

Having given these directions, at which the poor prisoner wrung his hands in horror and despair, she withdrew with the matron into another room, in expectation of being visited by her husband; and after having waited some time with manifest impatience, could not forbear asking if there were any other lodgers in the house: when the landlady replied in the negative, she began to sift her with a variety of questions, in the course of which she learn'd, that not a soul had entered the house after her own arrival; and then conjectured, that the voice she had mistaken for her husband's, must

549

have been part of a conversation that passed in the next house, from which she was separated by a thin party-wall.

This discovery mortified her in one respect, and pleased her in another; she was chagrined at the disagreeable interruption, because it laid her under the necessity of exposing her character to the inquiries of those whom her cries had brought to her assistance; though she was at the same time very well satisfied to find that her lord was ignorant of the adventure, and that it was now in her power to be revenged upon the count, for the severity of his behaviour, when he acted in the capacity of her creditor. She therefore resolved to extort a sum of money from him, by way of composition; and, under pretence of hushing up an affair, which might (otherwise) give scandal an opportunity to be free with her reputation, signified to her hostess, a desire of seeing matters compromised.

The prudent milliner applauded her moderation, by which she foresaw that her own character would escape censure; and being favoured with her ladyship's confidence, went out immediately, in order to communicate her proposals to the prisoner; but while these deliberations were upon the carpet, he had employed his rhetoric so successfully upon his guard, that they were prevailed upon to set him at liberty, and make their own retreat, at the same time. So that her ladyship's scheme proved abortive, and she was fain to retire to her own house, meditating further vengeance upon the fugitive, who did not think proper to stand the brunt of her indignation; but decamped that night for his native country, in which he happily secured his retreat, fully persuaded, that his ruin had been planned by a powerful confederacy in England, of which my lady was the chief instrument.

Mean while, our young gentleman and his tutor enjoyed the consternation and perplexity which they had produced, as an wholesome chastisement bestowed upon a profligate virago, lost to all sense of œconomy and decorum, and a just punishment inflicted upon an infamous adventurer, who not only pillaged, but also disgraced the company by whom he was caressed. It was in consequence of this adventure, that Peregrine conceived a very ludicrous project, the execution of which furnished entertainment and admiration to all the fashionable people in town. The appearance of Cadwallader in a female dress, was so uncouth and preternatural, that the good milliner, who chanced to be favoured with a glimpse of him, as he went up stairs with his supposed gallant, was not only astonished, but affrighted at the peculiarity of his countenance; and notwithstanding her well-tried discretion, which

had never permitted her curiosity to exceed the bounds of complaisance, she could not forbear calling her son Pickle into another
room, after her ladyship's retreat; and asking with manifest marks
of confusion and disquiet, if the person whom he had brought into
her house, was really and *bona fide* a woman and a christian; at the
same time, expressing her suspicion, from the disposition of his
companion's wrinkles, and the bristles that appeared upon her
chin, that she was no better than a witch or a conjurer, whom he
had employed to embroil and expose her customers by the art of
sorcery, for which she prayed God would forgive him. 'Certain
I am (said she) the count and my lady went into the chamber with
the disposition of two lambs, and in the twinkling of an eye, (Lord
have mercy upon us!) there was nothing to be heard but discord
and desperation! Ah! Mr. Pickle, Mr. Pickle! it was for no charitable
end, that you was so anxious to occupy the next room. I thought
there was something unnatural in the case, when I saw you lead
up that old beldame with the beard. You have ruined the reputation
of my house, Mr. Pickle. My good friends the countess of Pepper-
marsh, lady Tickletoe, and Mrs. Riggle, will never enter my doors
again. I shall be deprived of getting an honest livelihood; and all
by the cruelty of one that I loved as well as if I had been the mother
that bore him. O that ever I was born to see this unlucky day!'
These words she accompanied with sundry sobs, and a few *extempore* tears, the nature of which he perfectly understood; and
therefore prescribed a cordial which in a moment set her heart
at ease.

CHAPTER XC

*He persuades Cadwallader to assume the Character
of a Magician, in which he acquires a great Share of
Reputation, by his Responses to three Females of Distinction,
who severally consult the Researches of his Art*

HER suspicion of his associate, while it afforded him subject for
mirth, struck his imagination with an idea which he could not help
indulging; and when he communicated the conceit to Cadwallader,
it in a moment acquired his approbation.[1] This notion he imparted

in a proposal, to subject the town to their ridicule, by giving responses in the character of a professed conjurer, to be personated by the old Misanthrope, whose aspect was extremely well calculated for the purpose. The plan was immediately adjusted in all its parts; an apartment hired in an house accommodated with a public stair; so that people might have free ingress and egress, without being exposed to observation; and this tenement being furnished with the apparatus of a magician, such as globes, telescopes, a magic lanthorn, a skeleton, a dried monkey, together with the skins of an alligator, otter and snake, the conjurer himself took possession of his castle, after having distributed printed advertisements, containing the particulars of his undertaking.

These bills soon operated according to the wish of the projectors. As the price of the oracle was fixed at half a guinea, the public naturally concluded, that the author was no common fortune-teller; and the very next day, Peregrine found some ladies of his quality-acquaintance, infected with the desire of making an experiment upon the skill of this new conjurer, who pretended to be just arrived from the Mogul's empire, where he had learned the art from a Brachman philosopher. Our young gentleman affected to talk of the pretensions of this sage with ridicule and contempt, and with seeming reluctance, undertook to attend them to his apartment, observing, that it would be a very easy matter to detect the fellow's ignorance, and no more than common justice to chastise him for his presumption. Though he could easily perceive a great fund of credulity in the company, they affected to espouse his opinion, and under the notion of a frolic, agreed, that one particular lady should endeavour to baffle his art, by appearing before him in the dress of her woman, who should, at the same time, personate her mistress, and be treated as such by our adventurer, who promised to squire them to the place. These measures being concerted, and the appointment fixed for the next audience-day, Peregrine furnished his friend with the necessary information; and when the hour of assignation arrived, conducted his charge to this oraculous seer.

They were admitted by our hero's valet de chambre, whose visage being naturally meagre and swarthy, was adorned with artificial whiskers; so that he became the Persian dress which he wore, and seemed a very proper master of the ceremonies to an oriental Necromancer. Having crossed his arms upon his breast, with an inclination of the head, he stalked in solemn silence before them into the Penetralia of the temple, where they found the conjurer sitting at a table, provided with pen, ink and paper, divers books and mathematical instruments, and a long white wand lying across the whole. He was habited in a black gown and fur-cap, and his countenance, over and above a double proportion of philosophic gravity which he had assumed for the occasion, was improved by a thick beard white as snow, that reached to his middle, and upon each shoulder sat a prodigious large black cat which had been tutored for the purpose.

Such a figure, which would have startled Peregrine himself, had not he been concerned in the mystery, could not fail to make an impression upon those whom he accompanied. The fictitious chambermaid, in spite of all her natural pertness and vivacity, changed colour when she entered the room, and the pretended lady, whose intellects were not quite so enlightened, began to tremble in every joint, and ejaculate petitions to heaven for her safety. Their conductor advancing to the table, presented his offering, and pointing to the *suivante*, told him, that lady desired to know what would be her destiny in point of marriage. The philosopher, without lifting up his eyes to view the person in whose behalf he was consulted, turned his ear to one of the sable familiars that purred upon his shoulder, and taking up the pen, wrote upon a detached slip of paper these words, which Peregrine, at the desire of the ladies, repeated aloud, 'Her destiny will, in a great measure, depend upon what happened to her about nine o'clock in the morning, on the third day of last December.'

This sentence was no sooner pronounced, than the counterfeit lady uttered a fearful scream, and ran out into the antichamber, exclaiming, 'Christ have mercy upon us! Sure he is the devil incarnate!' Her mistress, who followed her with great consternation, insisted upon knowing the transaction to which the response alluded; and Mrs. Abigail, after some recollection, gave her to understand, that she had an admirer, who, on the very hour and day mentioned by the cunning man, had addressed himself to her in a serious proposal of marriage. This explanation, however, was more ingenious than candid; for the admirer was no other than the identical Mr. Pickle himself, who was a meer dragon among the chambermaids, and, in his previous information communicated to his associate, had given an account of this assignation, with which he had been favoured by the damsel in question.

Our hero seeing his company very much affected with this circumstance of the wizzard's art, which had almost frighted both mistress and maid into hysteric fits, pretended to laugh them out of their fears, by observing that there was nothing extraordinary in this instance of his knowledge, which might have been acquired by some of those secret emissaries whom such impostors are obliged to employ for intelligence, or imparted by the lover himself, who had, perhaps, come to consult him about the success of his amour. Encouraged by this observation, or rather prompted by an insatiable curiosity, which was proof against all sort of apprehension, the disguised lady returned to the magician's own apartment, and assuming the air of a pert chambermaid, 'Mr. Conjurer (said she) now you have satisfied my mistress, will you be so good as to tell me, if ever I shall be married?' The sage, without the least hesitation, favoured her with an answer, in the following words: 'You cannot be married before you are a widow; and whether or not that will ever be the case, is a question which my art cannot resolve, because my foreknowledge exceeds not the term of thirty years.'

This reply, which at once cut her off from the pleasing prospect of seeing herself independent in the enjoyment of youth and fortune, in a moment clouded her aspect; all her good humour was overcast, and she went away, without further inquiry, muttering, in the rancour of her chagrin, that he was a silly impertinent fellow, and a meer quack in his profession. Notwithstanding the prejudice of this resentment, her conviction soon recurred; and when the report of his answers was made to those confederates by whom she had been deputed to make trial of his skill, they were universally persuaded that his art was altogether supernatural, tho' each affected to treat it with contempt, resolving, in her own breast, to have recourse to him in private.

In the mean time, the maid, tho' laid under the most peremptory injunctions of secrecy, was so full of the circumstance which related to her own conduct, that she extolled his prescience, in whispers to all her acquaintance, assuring them, that he had told her all the particulars of her life; so that his fame was almost instantaneously conveyed, thro' a thousand different channels, to all parts of the town; and the very next time he assumed the chair, his doors were besieged by curious people of all sects and denominations.

Being an old practitioner in this art, Cadwallader knew it would be impossible for him to support his reputation in the promiscuous exercise of fortune-telling, because every person that should come to consult him would expect a sample of his skill, relating to things past; and it could not be supposed, that he was acquainted with the private concerns of every individual who might apply to him for that purpose: he therefore ordered his minister, whom he distinguished by the name of Hadgi Rourk, to signify to all those who demanded entrance, that his price was half a guinea; and that all such as were not disposed to gratify him with that consideration would do well to leave the passage free for the rest.

This declaration succeeded to his wish; for this congregation consisted chiefly of footmen, chambermaids, prentices, and the lower class of tradesmen, who could not afford to purchase prescience at such a price; so that, after fruitless offers of shillings and half crowns, they dropped off one by one, and left the field open for customers of an higher rank.

The first person of this species who appeared was dressed like the wife of a substantial tradesman; but this disguise could not screen her from the penetration of the conjurer, who at first sight knew her to be one of the ladies of whose coming he had been apprized by Peregrine, on the supposition that their curiosity was rather inflamed than allayed by the intelligence they had received from his first client. This lady approached the philosopher with that intrepidity of countenance so conspicuous in matrons of her dignified sphere, and in a soft voice, asked with a simper, of what complexion her next child would be? The necromancer, who was perfectly well acquainted with her private history, forthwith delivered his response in the following question, written in the usual form, 'How long has Pompey the black been dismissed from your ladyship's service?'

Endued as she was with a great share of that fortitude which is distinguished by the appellation of effrontery, her face exhibited some signs of shame and confusion at the receit of this oracular interrogation, by which she was convinced of his extraordinary intelligence; and accosting him in a very serious tone, 'Doctor (said she) I perceive you are a person of great abilities in the art you profess; and therefore, without pretending to dissemble, I will own you have touched the true string of my apprehensions. I am persuaded I need not be more particular in my inquiries. Here is a purse of money; take it, and deliver me from a most alarming and uneasy suspence.' So saying, she deposited her offering upon the table, and waited for his answer with a face of fearful expectation, while he was employed in writing this sentence for her perusal: 'Tho' I see into the womb of time, the prospect is not perfectly distinct; the seeds of future events lie mingled and confused: so that I am under the necessity of assisting my divination in some cases, by analogy and human intelligence; and cannot possibly satisfy your present doubts, unless you will condescend to make me privy to all those occurrences which you think might have interfered with the cause of your apprehension.'

The lady having read the declaration, affected a small emotion of shyness and repugnance, and seating herself upon a settee, after having cautiously informed herself of the privacy of the apartment, gave such a detail of the succession of her lovers, as amazed while it entertained the necromancer, as well as his friend Pickle, who from a closet in which he had concealed himself, overheard every syllable of her confession. Cadwallader listened to her story with a look of infinite importance and sagacity, and after a short pause told her, that he would not pretend to give a categorical answer, until he should have deliberated maturely upon the various circumstances of the affair; but if she would take the trouble of honouring him with another visit on his next public day, he hoped he should be able to give her full satisfaction. Conscious of the importance of her doubts, she could not help commending his caution, and took her leave, with a promise of returning at the appointed time; then the conjurer being joined by his associate, they gave a loose to their mirth, which having indulged, they began to concert measures for inflicting some disgraceful punishment on the shameless and insatiate termagant who had so impudently avowed her own prostitution.

They were interrupted, however, in their conference, by the arrival of a new guest, who being announced by Hadgi, our hero retreated to his lurking-place, and Cadwallader resumed his mysterious appearance. This new client, tho' she hid her face in a mask, could not conceal herself from the knowledge of the conjurer, who by her voice recognized her to be an unmarried lady of his own acquaintance. She had, within a small compass of time, made herself remarkable for two adventures, which had not at all succeeded to her expectation: being very much addicted to play, she had, at a certain route, indulged that passion to such excess, as not only got the better of her justice, but also of her circumspection; so that she was unfortunately detected in her endeavours to appropriate to herself what was not lawfully her due. This small slip was attended with another indiscretion, which had likewise an unlucky effect upon her reputation. She had been favoured with the addresses of one of those hopeful heirs who swarm and swagger about town, under the denomination of Bucks; and in the confidence of his honour consented to be one of a partie that made an excursion as far as Windsor, thinking herself secured from scandal by the company of another young lady, who had also condescended to trust her person to the protection of her admirer. The two gallants, in the course of this expedition, were said to use the most perfidious means to intoxicate the passions of their mistresses, by mixing drugs with their wine, which inflamed their constitutions to such a degree, that they fell an easy sacrifice to the appetites of their conductors, who, upon their return to town, were so base and inhuman as to boast among their companions of the exploit they had atchieved. Thus the story was circulated, with a thousand additional circumstances to the prejudice of the sufferers, one of whom had thought proper to withdraw into the country, until the scandal raised at her expence should subside; while the other, who was not so easily put out of countenance, resolved to outface the report, as a treacherous aspersion, invented by her lover as an excuse for his own inconstancy; and actually appeared in public, as usual, till she found herself neglected by the greatest part of her acquaintance.

In consequence of this disgrace, which she knew not whether to impute to the card affair, or to the last *faux pas* she had committed, she now came to consult the conjurer, and signified her errand, by asking whether the cause of her present disquiet was of the town or country? Cadwallader at once perceiving her allusion, answered her question in these terms. 'This honest world will forgive a young gamester for indiscretion at play, but a favour granted to a blabbing coxcomb is an unpardonable offence.' This response she received with equal astonishment and chagrin; and, fully convinced of the necromancer's omniscience, implored his advice touching the retrieval of her reputation: upon which he counselled her to wed with the first opportunity; and she seemed so well pleased with his admonition, that she gratified him with a double fee, and dropping a low curt'sy, retired.

Our undertakers now thought it high time to silence the oracle for the day, and Hadgi was accordingly ordered to exclude all comers, while Peregrine and his friend renewed the deliberations, which had been interrupted, and settled a plan of operations for the next occasion: mean while it was resolved, that Hadgi should not only exercise his own talents, but also employ inferior agents, in procuring general intelligence for the support of their scheme; that the expence of this ministry should be defrayed from the profits of their profession; and the remainder be distributed to poor families in distress.

CHAPTER XCI

Peregrine and his Friend Cadwallader proceed in the
Exercise of the Mystery of Fortune-telling, in the
course of which they atchieve various Adventures

THESE preliminaries being adjusted, our hero forthwith repaired
to a card assembly, which was frequented by some of the most
notable gossips in town, and having artfully turned the conversation upon the subject of the fortune-teller, whose talents he pretended to ridicule, incensed their itch of knowing secrets to such
a degree of impatience, that their curiosity became flagrant, and
he took it for granted, that all or some of them would visit Albu-
mazar on his very first visiting-day. While Peregrine was thus
engaged, his associate made his appearance in another convocation
of fashionable people, where he soon had the pleasure of hearing
the conjurer brought upon the carpet by an elderly gentlewoman,
remarkable for her inquisitive disposition, who addressing herself
to Cadwallader, asked, by the help of the finger-alphabet, if he
knew any thing of the magician that made such a noise in town?
The Misanthrope answered as usual, in a surly tone, 'By your
question you must either take me for a pimp or an ideot. What, in
the name of nonsense, should I know of such a rascal, unless I were
to court his acquaintance with a view to feast my own spleen, in
seeing him fool the whole nation out of their money? Tho', I
suppose, his chief profits arise from his practice, in quality of
pander. All fortune-tellers are bawds, and for that reason are so
much followed by people of fashion. This fellow (I warrant) has
got sundry convenient apartments for the benefit of procreation;
for it is not to be supposed that those who visit him on the pretence
of consulting his supernatural art, can be such fools, such drivelers,
as to believe that he can actually prognosticate future events.'

The company, according to his expectation, imputed his remarks
to the rancour of his disposition, which could not bear to think
that any person upon earth was wiser than himself; and his ears
were regaled with a thousand instances of the conjurer's wonderful
prescience, for which he was altogether indebted to fiction. Some
of these specimens being communicated to him, by way of appeal
to his opinion, 'They are (said he) meer phantoms of ignorance
and credulity, swelled up in the repetition, like those unsubstantial

558

bubbles which the boys blow up in soap-suds with a tobacco pipe. And this will ever be the case in the propagation of all extraordinary intelligence: the imagination naturally magnifies every object that falls under its cognizance, especially those that concern the passions of fear and admiration; and when the occurrence comes to be rehearsed, the vanity of the relater exaggerates every circumstance, in order to inhance the importance of the communication. Thus an incident which is but barely uncommon, often gains such accession in its progress thro' the fancies and mouths of those who represent it, that the original fact cannot possibly be distinguished. This observation might be proved and illustrated by a thousand undeniable examples, out of which I shall only select one instance, for the entertainment and edification of the company: A very honest gentleman, remarkable for the gravity of his deportment, was one day, in a certain coffee-house, accosted by one of his particular friends, who, taking him by the hand, expressed uncommon satisfaction in seeing him abroad, and in good health, after the dangerous and portentous malady he had undergone. Surprised at this salutation, the gentleman replied, it was true, he had been a little out of order over-night, but there was nothing at all extraordinary in his indisposition. "Jesu! not extraordinary! (cried the other) when you vomited three black crows." This strange exclamation the grave gentleman at first mistook for raillery, tho' his friend was no joker; but perceiving in him all the marks of sincerity and astonishment, he suddenly changed his opinion, and, after a short reverie, taking him aside, expressed himself in these words, "Sir, it is not unknown to you, that I am at present engaged in a treaty of marriage, which would have been settled long ago, had not it been retarded by the repeated machinations of a certain person who professes himself my rival. Now I am fully persuaded that this affair of the three crows is a story of his invention, calculated to prejudice me in the opinion of the lady, who, to be sure, would not choose to marry a man who has a rookery in his bowels; and therefore I must insist upon knowing your author of this scandalous report, that I may be able to vindicate my character from the malicious aspersion." His friend, who thought the demand was very reasonable, told him, without hesitation, that he was made acquainted with the circumstance of his distemper by Mr. Such-a-one, their common acquaintance: upon which the person who conceived himself injured went immediately in quest of his supposed defamer, and having found him, "Pray, Sir, (said he, with a peremptory tone) who told you that I vomited three black crows?"

"Three! (answered the gentleman) I mentioned two only."
"Zounds! Sir (cried the other, incensed at his indifference) you
will find the two too many, if you refuse to discover the villainous
source of such calumny." The gentleman, surprised at his heat,
said he was sorry to find he had been the accidental instrument of
giving him offence, but translated the blame (if any there was) from
himself to a third person, to whose information he owed his knowledge of the report. The plaintiff, according to the direction he
received, repaired to the house of the accused; and his indignation
being inflamed at finding the story had already circulated among
his acquaintance, he told him, with evident marks of displeasure,
that he was come to pluck that same brace of crows which he knew
he had disgorged. The defendant seeing him very much irritated,
positively denied that he had mentioned a brace; "One indeed
(said he) I own I took notice of, upon the authority of your own
physician, who gave me an account of it this morning." "By the
Lord! (cried the sufferer in a rage which he could no longer contain)
that rascal has been suborned by my rival, to slander my character
in this manner; but I'll be revenged, if there be either law or equity
in England." He had scarce pronounced these words, when the
doctor happened to enter the room; when his exasperated patient
lifting up his cane, "Sirrah (said he) if I live, I'll make that black
crow the blackest circumstance of thy whole life and conversation."
The physician, confounded at this address, assured him that he
was utterly ignorant of his meaning, and when the other gentleman
explained it, absolutely denied the charge, affirming he had said
no more than that he had vomited a quantity of something as black
as a crow. The landlord of the house acknowledged that he might
have been mistaken; and thus the whole mystery was explained.'

The company seemed to relish the story of the three black crows,
which they considered as an impromptu of Cadwallader's own
invention; but, granting it to be true, they unanimously declared
that it could have no weight in invalidating the testimony of divers
persons of honour, who had been witnesses of the magician's supernatural skill. On the next day of consultation, the necromancer
being in the chair, and his friend behind the curtain, the outward
door was scarce opened, when a female visitant flounced in, and
discovered to the magician the features of one of those inquisitive
ladies, whose curiosity, he knew, his confederate had aroused, in
the manner above described. She addressed herself to him with
a familiar air, observing, that she had heard much of his great
knowledge, and was come to be a witness of his art, which she

desired him to display, in declaring what he knew to be her ruling passion.

Cadwallader, who was no stranger to her disposition, assumed the pen without hesitation, and furnished her with an answer, importing, that the love of money predominated, and scandal possessed the next place in her heart. Far from being offended at his freedom, she commended his frankness with a smile; and, satisfied of his uncommon talents, expressed a desire of being better acquainted with his person: nay, she began to catechise him, upon the private history of divers great families, in which he happened to be well versed; and he, in a mysterious manner, dropt such artful hints of his knowledge, that she was amazed at his capacity, and actually asked if his art was communicable. The conjurer replied in the affirmative; but, at the same time, gave her to understand, that it was attainable by those only who were pure and undefiled in point of chastity and honour; or such as, by a long course of penitence, had weaned themselves from all attachments to the flesh. She not only disapproved, but seemed to doubt the truth of this assertion; telling him, with a look of disdain, that his art was not worth having, if one could not use it for the benefit of one's pleasure: she had even penetration enough to take notice of an inconsistency in what he had advanced; and asked, why he himself exercised his knowledge for hire, if he was so much detached from all worldly concerns. 'Come, come, doctor, (added she) you are in the right to be cautious against impertinent curiosity; but, perhaps, I may make it worth your while to be communicative.'

These overtures were interrupted by a rap at the door, signifying the approach of another client; upon which the lady inquired for his private passage, thro' which she might retire, without the risque of being seen: and when she understood he was deficient in that convenience, she withdrew into an empty room, adjoining to the audience-chamber, in order to conceal herself from the observation of the newcomer. This was no other than the inamorata, who came by appointment to receive the solution of her doubts: and the Misanthrope, glad of an opportunity to expose her to the censure of such an indefatigable minister of fame as the person, who (he knew) would listen from the next apartment; laid her under the necessity of refreshing his remembrance with a re-capitulation of her former confession, which was almost finished, when she was alarmed by a noise at the door, occasioned by two gentlemen who attempted to enter by force.

Terrified at this uproar, which disconcerted the magician

himself, she ran for shelter into the place which was pre-occupied by the other lady, who, hearing this disturbance, had closed the window-shutters, that she might have the better chance of remaining unknown. Here they ensconced themselves, in the utmost consternation, while the necromancer, after some recollection, ordered Hadgi to open the door, and admit the rioters, who (he hoped) would be over-awed by the authority of his appearance. The janitor had no sooner obeyed his instructions, than in rushed a young libertine, who had been for some time upon the town, together with his tutor, who was a worn-out debauchee, well known to the magician. They were both in that degree of intoxication necessary to prepare such dispositions for what they commonly call frolicks, and the sober part of mankind feel to be extravagant outrages against the laws of their country, and the peace of their fellow-subjects. Having staggered up to the table, the senior, who undertook to be spokesman, saluted Cadwallader with 'How do'st do, old Capricorn? Thou seem'st to be a most venerable pimp, and, I doubt not, has abundance of discretion. Here is this young whoremaster (a true chip of the old venereal block his father) and myself, come for a comfortable cast of thy function. I don't mean that stale pretence of conjuring: damn futurity; let us live for the present, old Haly.[1] Conjure me up a couple of hale wenches, and, I warrant, we shall get into the magic circle in a twinkling. What says Galileo? What says the reverend Brahe? Here is a purse, you pimp: hark, how it chinks! This is sweeter than the musick of the spheres.'

Our necromancer, perplexed at this rencounter, made no reply; but taking up his wand, waved it around his head in a very mysterious motion, with a view of intimidating these forward visitants, who, far from being awed by this sort of evolution, became more and more obstreperous, and even threatened to pull him by the beard, if he would not immediately comply with their desire. Had he called his associate, or even Hadgi, to his aid, he knew he could have soon calmed their turbulence; but, being unwilling to run the risque of a discovery, or even of a riot, he bethought himself of chastising their insolence in another manner that would be less hazardous, and rather more effectual. In consequence of this suggestion, he pointed his wand towards the door of the apartment in which the ladies had taken sanctuary; and the two rakes, understanding the hint, rushed in without hesitation.

The females finding their place of retreat taken by assault, ran about the room in great consternation, and were immediately taken prisoners by the assailants, who pulling them towards the windows, opened the shutters at the same instant of time, when (strange to tell!) one of the heroes discovered, in the prize he had made, the very wife of his bosom; and his companion perceived that he had stumbled in the dark upon his own mother. Their mutual astonishment was unspeakable at this eclaircissement, which produced an universal silence for the space of several minutes; and during this pause the ladies having recollected themselves, an expostulation was begun by the elder of the two, who roundly took her son to task for his disorderly life, which laid her under the disagreeable necessity of watching his motions, and detecting him in such an infamous place.

While the careful mother thus exercised her talent for reprehension, the hopeful young gentleman, with an hand in each fob, stood whistling an opera-tune, without seeming to pay the most profound regard to his parent's reproof: and the other lady, in imitation of such a consummate pattern, began to open upon her husband, whom she bitterly reproached with his looseness and intemperance, demanding to know what he had to alledge in alleviation of his present misconduct. The surprize occasioned by such an unexpected meeting had already in a great measure destroyed the effects of the wine he had so plentifully drank, and the first use he made of his recovered sobriety, was to revolve within himself the motives that could possibly induce his wife to give him the rendezvous in this manner. As he had good reason to believe she was utterly void of jealousy, he naturally placed this rencontre to the account of another passion; and his chagrin was not at all impaired by the effrontery with which she now presumed to reprimand him. He listened to her, therefore, with a grave, or rather grim aspect; and to the question with which she concluded her rebuke, answered with great composure, 'All that I have to alledge, madam, is that the bawd has committed a mistake, in consequence of which we are both disappointed: and so, ladies, your humble servant.' So saying, he retired with manifest confusion in his looks; and as he passed through the audience-chamber, eying the conjurer askance, pronounced the epithet of *precious rascal*, with great emphasis. Mean while, the junior, like a dutiful child, handed his mamma to her chair; and the other client, after having reviled the necromancer, because he could not foresee this event, went away in a state of mortification.

The coast being clear, Peregrine came forth from his den, and congratulated his friend upon the peaceable issue of the adventure which he had overheard: but, that he might not be exposed to such inconvenience for the future, they resolved, that a grate should be fixed in the middle of the outward door, through which the conjurer himself should reconnoitre all the visitants, before their admission; so that, to those whose appearance he should not like, Hadgi should, without opening, give notice, that his master was engaged. By this expedient too, they provided against those difficulties which Cadwallader must have encountered, in giving satisfaction to strangers, whom he did not know; for the original intention of the founders was to confine the practice of their art to people of fashion only, most of whom were personally known to the counterfeit magician and his coadjutor.

Indeed, these associates, Cadwallader in particular, notwithstanding his boasted insight into the characters of life, never imagined that his pretended skill would be consulted by any but the weaker-minded of the female sex, incited by that spirit of curiosity which he knew was implanted in their nature: but, in the course of his practice, he found himself cultivated in his preternatural capacity, by people of all sexes, complexions, and degrees of reputation, and had occasion to observe, that when the passions are concerned, howsoever cool, cautious and deliberate, the disposition may otherwise be, there is nothing so idle, frivolous, or absurd, to which they will not apply for encouragement and gratification. The last occurrence, according to the hopes and expectation of the confederates, was whispered about by the ladies concerned, in such a manner, that the whole affair was, in a few days, the universal topic of discourse, in which it was retailed with numberless embellishments, invented by the parties themselves, who had long indulged a pique at each other, and took this opportunity of enjoying their revenge.

These incidents, while they regaled the spleen, at the same time augmented the renown of the conjurer, who was described on both sides as a very extraordinary person in his way; and the alteration in his door was no sooner performed, than he had occasion to avail himself of it, against the intrusion of a great many, with whom he would have found it very difficult to support the fame he had acquired.

Among those who appeared at his grate, he perceived a certain clergyman, whom he had long known an humble attendant on the great, and with some the reputed minister of their pleasures. This Levite had disguised himself in a great coat, boots, and dress quite foreign to the habit worn by those of his function; and being admitted, attempted to impose himself as a country squire upon the conjurer, who calling him by his name, desired him to sit down. This reception corresponding with the report he had heard, touching our magician's art, the doctor said he would lay aside all dissimulation; and after having professed an implicit belief, that his supernatural knowledge did not proceed from any communication with evil spirits, but was the immediate gift of heaven, he declared the intention of his coming was to inquire into the health of a good friend and brother of his, who possessed a certain living in the country, which he named; and, as he was old and infirm, to know what space of time was allotted to him in this frail state of mortality, that he might have the melancholy satisfaction of attending him in his last moments, and assisting him in his preparations for eternity.

The conjurer, who at once perceived the purport of this question, after a solemn pause, during which he seemed absorpt in contemplation, delivered this response to his consulter, 'Tho' I foresee some occurrences, I do not pretend to be omniscient. I know not to what age that clergyman's life will extend, but so far I can penetrate into the womb of time, as to discern, that the incumbent will survive his intended successor.' This dreadful sentence in a moment banished the blood from the face of the appalled consulter, who hearing his own doom pronounced, began to tremble in every joint; he lifted up his eyes in the agony of fear, and saying, 'The will of God be done,' withdrew in silent despondence, his teeth chattering with terror and dismay.

This client was succeeded by an old man about the age of seventy-five, who being resolved to purchase a lease, desired to be determined in the term of years by the necromancer's advice, observing, that as he had no children of his own body, and had no regard for his heirs at law, the purchase would be made with a view to his own convenience only; and therefore, considering his age, he himself hesitated in the period of the lease, between thirty and threescore years.

The conjurer, upon due deliberation, advised him to double the last specified term, because he distinguished in his features something portending extreme old age and second childhood, and he ought to provide for that state of incapacity, which otherwise would be attended with infinite misery and affliction. The superannuated wretch, thunderstruck with this prediction, held up his hands, and, in the first transports of his apprehension, exclaimed, 'Lord have mercy upon me! I have not wherewithal to purchase such a long lease, and I have long outlived all my friends; what then must become of me, sinner that I am, one hundred and twenty years hence!' Cadwallader (who enjoyed his terror) under pretence of alleviating his concern, told him, that what he had prognosticated did not deprive him of the means which he and every person had in their power, to curtail a life of misfortune; and the old gentleman went away, seemingly comforted with the assurance, that it would always be in his power to employ an halter for his own deliverance.

Soon after the retreat of this elder, the magician was visited by one of those worthies known among the Romans by the appellation of *Heredipetes*,[1] who had amassed a large fortune by a close attention to the immediate wants and weakness of raw unexperienced heirs. This honourable usurer had sold an annuity upon the life of a young spendthrift, being thereto induced by the affirmation of his physician, who had assured him his patient's constitution was so rotten, that he could not live one year to an end: he had, nevertheless, made shift to weather eighteen months, and now seemed more vigorous and healthy than he had ever been known; for he was supposed to have nourished an hereditary pox from his cradle. Alarmed at this alteration, the seller came to consult Cadwallader not only about the life of the annuitant, but also concerning the state of his health at the time of his purchasing the annuity, purposing to sue the physician for false intelligence, should the conjurer declare that the young man was sound, when the doctor pronounced him diseased. But this was a piece of satisfaction he did not obtain from the Misanthrope, who, in order to punish his sordid disposition, gave him to understand, that the physician had told him the truth, and nothing but the truth; and that the young gentleman was in a fair way of attaining a comfortable old age. 'That is to say (cried the client, in the impatience of his mortification at this answer) bating accidents; for, thank God, the annuitant does not lead the most regular life: besides, I am credibly informed he is choleric and rash; so that he may be concerned in a duel: then there are such things as riots in the street, in which a rake's skull may be casually cracked; he may be overturned in a coach, overset in the river, thrown from a vicious horse, overtaken with a cold, endangered by a surfeit; but what I place my chief confidence in, is an hearty pox, a distemper which hath been fatal to his whole family. Not but that the issue of all these things is uncertain; and expedients might be found, which would more effectually answer the purpose. I know they have arts in India, by which a man can secure his own interest, in the salutation of a friendly shake by the hand; and I don't doubt that you who have lived in that country, are master of the secret. To be sure, if you was inclined to communicate such a nostrum, there are abundance of people who would purchase it, at a very high price.'

Cadwallader understood this insinuation, and was tempted to amuse him in such a manner as would tend to his disgrace and confusion; but, considering that the case was of too criminal a nature to be tampered with, he withstood his desire of punishing this rapacious cormorant any other way than by telling him, he would not impart that secret for his whole fortune ten times doubled; so that the usurer retired, very much dissatisfied with the issue of his consultation.

The next person who presented himself at this altar of intelligence, was an author, who recommended himself to a gratis advice, by observing that a prophet and poet were known by the same appellation among the antients; and that, at this day, both the one and the other spoke by inspiration. The conjurer refused to own this affinity, which, he said, formerly subsisted, because both species of the *Vates* were the children of fiction; but as he himself did not fall under that predicament, he begged leave to disown all connexion with the family of the poets; and the poor author would have been dismissed without his errand, tho' he offered to leave an ode as security for the magician's fee, to be paid from the profits of his first third night, had not Cadwallader's curiosity prompted him to know the subject of this gentleman's inquiry. He therefore told him, that in consideration of his genius, he would for once satisfy him, without a fee; and desired him to specify the doubts in which he wished to be resolved.

The son of Parnassus, glad of this condescension, for which he thanked the necromancer, gave him to understand, that he had some time before presented a play in manuscript to a certain great man, at the head of taste, who had not only read and approved the performance, but also undertaken to introduce and support it on the stage; that he (the author) was assured by this patron, that the play was already (in consequence of his recommendation) accepted by one of the managers, who had faithfully promised to bring it to light; but that, when he waited on this same manager, to know when he intended to put his production into rehearsal, the man declared he had never seen or heard of the piece: 'Now, Mr. Conjurer (said he) I want to know whether or not my play has been presented, and if I have any sort of chance of seeing it acted this winter?'

Cadwallader, who had, in his younger days, sported among the theatrical muses, began to lose his temper at this question, which recalled the remembrance of his own disappointments; and dispatched the author with an abrupt answer, importing, that the affairs of the stage were altogether without the sphere of his divination, being intirely regulated by the dæmons of dissimulation, ignorance, and caprice.[1]

It would be an endless task to recount every individual response which our magician delivered, in the course of his conjuration. He was consulted in all cases of law, physic, and trade, over and above the ordinary subjects of marriage and fornication; his advice and assistance were sollicited by sharpers who desired to possess an infallible method of cheating, unperceived; by fortune-hunters who wanted to make prize of widows and heiresses; by debauchees who were disposed to lye with other men's wives; by coxcombs who longed for the death of their fathers; by wenches with child, who wished themselves rid of their burthens; by merchants who had insured above value, and thirsted after the news of a wreck; by under-writers who prayed for the gift of prescience, that they might venture money upon such ships only, as should perform the voyage in safety; by Jews who wanted to foresee the fluctuations of stock; by usurers who advance money upon undecided causes; by clients who were dubious of the honesty of their council: in short, all matters of uncertain issue were appealed to this tribunal; and, in point of calculation, *De Moivre*[2] was utterly neglected.

CHAPTER XCII

*The Conjurer and his Associate execute a Plan of
Vengeance against certain Infidels who pretend to
despise their Art; and Peregrine atchieves an
Adventure with a young Nobleman*

B y these means, the whole variety of character undisguised, passed as it were in review before the confederates, who, by divers ingenious contrivances, punished the most flagrant offenders with as much severity as the nature of their plan would allow. At length, they projected a scheme for chastising a number of their own acquaintance, who had all along professed the utmost contempt for the talents of this conjurer, which they endeavoured to ridicule in all companies, where his surprising art was the subject of discourse; not that they had sense and discernment enough to perceive the absurdity of his pretensions, but affected a singularity of opinion, with a view of insulting the inferior understandings of those who were deceived by such an idle impostor.

Peregrine indeed, for obvious reasons, had always espoused their judgment in this case, and joined them in reviling the public character of his friend; but he knew how far the capacities of those virtuosi extended, and had frequently caught them in the fact of recounting their exploits against the conjurer, which were the productions of their own invention only. On these considerations, his wrath was kindled against them, and he accordingly concerted measures with his coadjutor, for overwhelming them with confusion and dismay.

In the first place, a report was spread by his emissaries, that the magician had undertaken to entertain the view with the appearance of any person whom his customers should desire to see, whether dead, or at the distance of a thousand leagues. This extraordinary proposal chancing to be the subject of conversation, in a place where most of those infidels were assembled, they talked of it in the usual stile, and some of them swore, the fellow ought to be pillory'd for his presumption.

Our hero seizing this favourable opportunity, acquiesced in their remarks, and observed with great vehemence, that it would be a meritorious action to put the rascal to the proof, and then toss him in a blanket for non-performance. They were wonderfully pleased with this suggestion, and forthwith determined to try the experiment; though, as they understood the apparition would be produced to one only at a time, they could not immediately agree in the choice of the person who should stand the first brunt of the magician's skill. While each of them severally excused himself from this preference on various pretences, Peregrine readily undertook the post, expressing great confidence of the conjurer's incapacity to give him the least cause of apprehension.

This point being settled, they detached one of their number to Crabtree, in order to bespeak and adjust the hours and terms of the operation, which he insisted upon performing at his own apartment, where every thing was prepared for the occasion. At the appointed time, they went thither in a body, to the number of seven, in full expectation of detecting the impostor; and were received with such gloomy formality, as seemed to have an effect upon the countenances of some among them; though they were encouraged by the vivacity of Pickle, who affected a double share of petulance, for the more effectual accomplishment of his purpose.

Cadwallader made no reply to the interrogations they uttered, in the levity of their insolence, at their first entrance, but ordered Hadgi to conduct them through the next room, that they might see there was no previous apparatus to affright their deputy with objects foreign to his undertaking. They found nothing but a couple of wax-tapers burning on a table that stood with a chair by it, in the middle of the apartment, and returned to the audience-chamber, leaving Peregrine by himself, to encounter the phantom of that person, whom they should (without his knowledge) desire the magician to conjure up to his view.

All the doors being shut, and the company seated, a profound silence ensued, together with a face of dreadful expectation, encouraged by the blue flame of the candles, which were tipt with sulphur for that purpose, and heightened by the dismal sound of a large bell, which Hadgi tolled in the anti-chamber. Cadwallader having thus practised upon their ignorance and fear, desired them to name the person to be produced; and after some whispers among themselves, one of them took the pen, and writing the name of commodore Trunnion upon a slip of paper, put it into the hands of the magician, who rose from his seat, and opening the door of his closet, displayed to their view a scull, with thigh-bones crossed upon a table covered with black cloth.

This melancholy spectacle made a remarkable impression upon the imaginations of the company, already prepossessed by the previous ceremony; and they began to survey one another with looks of consternation, while Cadwallader shutting himself in the closet, that was contiguous to the chamber in which his friend Peregrine was stationed, thrust the label with his uncle's name through a small chink in the partition, according to agreement, muttering all the time a sort of gibberish, that increased the pannic of his audience; then returning to his chair, the knell was knolled again, and Pickle called aloud, 'Damn your mummery, why don't you dispatch?'

This was a signal to Crabtree, who thus certified of his having received the paper, stood up and waved his wand in the figure of an S. The motion being thrice performed, their ears were all of a sudden invaded by a terrible noise in the next room, accompanied with the voice of Peregrine, who exclaimed in a tone of horror and amazement, 'Guard me, heaven! my uncle Trunnion!' This ejaculation had such an effect upon the hearers, that two of them swooned with fear, a third fell upon his knees, and prayed aloud, while the other three, in a transport of dismay and distraction, burst open the door, and rushed into the haunted chamber, where they found the table and chair overturned, and Peregrine extended (in all appearance) without sense or motion, upon the floor.

They immediately began to chafe his temples, and the first symptom of his recovery, which they perceived, was an hollow groan; after which, he pronounced these words: 'Merciful powers! if I live, I saw the commodore with his black patch, in the very cloaths he wore at my sister's wedding.' This declaration compleated their astonishment and terror; they observed a wildness in his looks, which he seemed to bend on something concealed from their view; and were infected by his appearance to such a pitch of superstition, that it would have been an easy matter to persuade them, that the chair and table were apparitions of their forefathers. However, they conducted Peregrine into the council-chamber, where the conjuror and Hadgi were employed in ministring to those who had fainted: and the patients having retrieved the use of their faculties, Cadwallader assuming a double portion of severity in his aspect, asked if they were not ashamed of their former incredulity; declaring, that he was ready to give them more convincing proofs of his art upon the spot, and would immediately recal three generations of their progenitors from the dead, if they were disposed to relish such company. Then turning to one of them, whose great grandfather had been hanged, 'Are you (said he) ambitious of seeing the first remarkable personage of your family? Say the word, and he shall appear.'

This youth, who had been the most insolent and obstreperous of the whole society, and was now depressed with the same proportion of fear, alarmed at the proposal, assured the magician, he had no curiosity of that sort remaining; and that, what he had already seen, would (he hoped) have a good effect upon his future life and conversation. Every one of these heroes made an acknowledgment and profession of the same kind, some of which were attended with tears; and Hadgi having provided chairs for the whole company, they departed exceedingly crest-fallen; and two of the number actually sickened with the agitation they had undergone, while our hero and his associate made themselves merry with the success of their enterprize.

But this scheme of fortune-telling did not engross his whole attention; he still continued to maintain his appearance in the beau monde; and as his expence far exceeded his income, strove to contract intimacies with people of interest and power: he shewed himself regularly at court, paid his respects to them in all places of public diversion, and frequently entered into their parties, either of pleasure or cards. In the course of this cultivation, he happened one evening, at a certain chocolate-house, to overlook a match at piquet, in which he perceived a couple of sharpers making prey of a young nobleman, who had neither temper nor skill sufficient to cope with such antagonists.

Our hero being a professed enemy to all knights of industry, could not bear to see them cheat in publick with such insolent audacity; and therefore, under pretence of communicating some business of importance, he begg'd the favour of speaking to the young gentleman in another corner of the room, and in a friendly manner cautioned him against the arts of his opponents. This hot-headed representative, far from thinking or owning himself obliged to Pickle for his good counsel, looked upon the advice as an insult upon his understanding; and replied with an air of ferocious displeasure, that he knew how to take care of his own concerns, and would not suffer either him or them to bubble him out of one shilling.

Peregrine, offended at the association, as well as at the ingratitude and folly of this conceited coxcomb, expressed his resentment, by telling him, that he expected at least an acknowledgement for his candid intention; but he found his intellects too much warped by his vanity, to perceive his own want of capacity and experience. Inflamed by this reproof, the young nobleman challenged him to play for five hundred pounds, with many opprobrious, or at least contemptuous terms of defiance, which provoked our hero to accept the proposal; and after the other had disengaged himself from the old rooks, who were extremely mortified at the interruption, the two young champions sat down, and fortune acting with uncommon impartiality, Pickle, by the superiority of his talents, in two hours won to the amount of as many thousand pounds, for which he was obliged to take his antagonist's note, the sharpers having previously secured his ready money.

Frantic with his loss, the rash young man would have continued the game, and doubled stakes every time; so that Peregrine might have increased his acquisition to ten times the sum he had gained; but he thought he had already sufficiently chastised the presumption of the challenger, and was unwilling to impower fortune to ravish from him the fruits of his success: he therefore declined my lord's proposal, unless he would play for ready money; and his lordship having in vain tried his credit among the company, our adventurer withdrew, leaving him in an extasy of rage and disappointment.

As the insolence of his behaviour had increased with his ill luck, and he had given vent to divers expressions, which Peregrine took amiss, our young gentleman resolved to augment his punishment, by teazing him with demands which could not, he knew, be immediately satisfied; and next day, sent Pipes to his father's house with the note, which was drawn payable upon demand. The debtor, who had gone to bed half distracted with his misfortune, finding himself waked with such a disagreeable dun, lost all patience, cursed Pickle, threatened his messenger, blasphemed with horrible execrations, and made such a noise, as reached the ears of his father, who ordering his son to be called into his presence, examined him about the cause of that uproar, which had disturbed the whole family. The young gentleman, after having essayed to amuse him with sundry equivocations, which served only to increase his suspicion, and desire of knowing the truth, acknowledged that he had lost some money overnight at cards, to a gamester, who had been so impertinent as to send a message, demanding it that morning, though he had told the fellow, it would not suit him to pay it immediately. The father, who was a man of honour, reproached him with great severity for his profligate behaviour in general, and this scandalous debt in particular, which he believed to be some trifle, and giving him a bank note for five hundred pounds, commanded him to go and discharge it, without loss of time. This well-principled heir took the money, but instead of waiting upon his creditor, he forthwith repaired to the gaminghouse, in hopes of retrieving his loss; and before he rose from the table, saw his note mortgaged for seven eighths of its value.

Mean while, Pickle, incensed at the treatment which his servant had received, and informed of his lordship's second loss, which aggravated his resentment, determined to preserve no medium; and taking out a writ that same day, put it immediately in execution upon the body of his debtor, just as he stepp'd into his chair, at the door of White's Chocolate-house. The prisoner being naturally fierce and haughty, attempted to draw upon the bailiffs, who disarmed him in a twinkling; and this effort served only to heighten his disgrace, which was witnessed by a thousand people, most of whom laughed very heartily, at the adventure of a lord's being arrested.

Such a public transaction could not long escape the knowledge of his father, who (that very day) had the satisfaction to hear that his son was in a spunging-house. In consequence of this information, he sent his steward to learn the particulars of the arrest, and was equally offended, surprized, and concerned, when he understood the nature of the debt, which he imagined his son had already discharged. Unwilling to pay such a considerable sum for a spendthrift, whom he had but too much indulged, and who in less than one week might involve himself in such another difficulty, the old gentleman wrote a letter to Peregrine, representing what a hardship it would be upon him to forfeit such sums by the indiscretion of a son, whose engagements he was not bound to fulfil, and desiring some mitigation in his demand, as it was not a debt contracted for value received, but incurred without subjecting him to the least damage or inconvenience.

Our adventurer no sooner received this letter, than he went in person to wait upon the author, to whom he, in a candid manner, related the particular circumstances of the match, together with the ingratitude and audacity of his son, which he owned had stimulated him to such measures as he, otherwise, would have scorned to take. The nobleman acknowledged, that the revenge was hardly adequate to the provocation, and condemned the conduct of his son with such justice and integrity, as disarmed Peregrine of his resentment, and disposed him to give an undoubted proof of his own disinterestedness, which he immediately exhibited, by producing the note, and tearing it to pieces, after having assured his lordship, that the writ should be withdrawn, and the prisoner discharged before night.

The earl, who perfectly well understood the value of money, and was no stranger to the characters of mankind, stood amazed at this sacrifice which Pickle protested was offered by his esteem for his lordship; and after having complimented him upon his generosity, in a very uncommon strain of encomium, begg'd the favour of his acquaintance, and insisted upon his dining with him next day. The youth, proud of having met with such an opportunity to distinguish himself, in less than an hour performed every article of his promise; and in the morning was visited by the debtor, who came, by the express order of his father, to thank him for the obligation under which he was laid, and ask pardon for the offence he had given.

This condescension was very glorious for our hero, who graciously received his submission, and accompanied him to dinner, where he was caressed by the old earl with marks of particular affection and esteem. Nor was his gratitude confined to exterior civility; he offered him the use of his interest at court, which was very powerful, and repeated his desire of serving him so pressingly, that Peregrine thought he could not dispense with the opportunity of assisting his absent friend Godfrey, in whose behalf he begg'd the influence of his lordship.

The earl, pleased with this request, which was another proof of the young gentleman's benevolence, said, he would not fail to pay the utmost regard to his recommendation; and in six weeks a captain's commission was actually signed for the brother of Emilia, who was very agreeably surprized at the intimation he received from the war-office, though he was utterly ignorant of the canal through which he obtained that promotion.

CHAPTER XCIII

*Peregrine is celebrated as a Wit and Patron,
and proceeds to entertain himself at the
Expence of whom it did concern*

IN the mean time, Peregrine flourished in the gay scenes of life, and (as I have already observed) had divers opportunities of profiting in the way of marriage, had not his ambition been a little too inordinate, and his heart still biassed by a passion, which all the levity of youth could not balance, nor all the pride of vanity overcome. Nor was our hero unmarked in the world of letters and taste: he had signalized himself in several poetical productions, by which he had acquired a good share of reputation; not that the pieces were such as ought to have done much honour to his genius; but any tolerable performance from a person of his figure and supposed fortune, will always be considered, by the bulk of readers, as an instance of astonishing capacity; though the very same production, ushered into the world with the name of an author in less affluent circumstances, would be justly disregarded and despised; so much is the opinion of most people influenced and over-awed by ridiculous considerations.

Be this as it will, our young gentleman was no sooner distinguished as an author, than he was marked out as a patron, by all the starving retainers to poetry: he was solemnized in odes, celebrated in epigrams, and fed with the milk of soft dedication. His vanity even relished this incense; and though his reason could not help despising those that offered it, not one of them was sent away, unowned by his munificence. He began to think himself, in good earnest, that superior genius which their flattery had described; he cultivated acquaintance with the wits of fashion, and even composed in secret a number of *bons mots*, which he uttered in company as the impromptu's of his imagination. In this practice indeed, he imitated some of the most renowned geniuses of the age, who (if the truth were known) have laboured in secret, with the sweat of their brows, for many a repartee which they have vended as the immediate production of fancy and expression. He was so successful in this exercise of his talents, that his fame actually came in competition with that of a great man, who had long sat at the helm of wit; and in a dialogue that once happened between them, on the subject of a cork-screw, wherein the altercation was discharged (according to Bayes) slap for slap, dash for dash,[1] our hero was judged to have the better of his lordship, by some of the minor satellites, that commonly surround and reflect the rays of such mighty luminaries.

In a word, he dipped himself so far in these literary amusements, that he took the management of the pit into his direction, putting himself at the head of those critics who call themselves the town; and in that capacity chastised several players, who had been rendered insolent and refractory by unmerited success. As for the new productions of the stage, though generally unspirited and insipid, they always enjoyed the benefit of his influence and protection; because he never disliked the performance so much as he sympathized with the poor author, who stood behind the scenes in the most dreadful suspence, trembling, as it were, on the very brink of damnation: yet, though he extended his generosity and compassion to the humble and needy, he never let slip one opportunity of mortifying villainy and arrogance. Had the executive power of the legislature been vested in him, he would have doubtless devised strange species of punishment for all offenders against humanity and decorum; but, restricted as he was, he employed his invention in subjecting them to the ridicule and contempt of their fellow-subjects.

It was with that view he set on foot the scheme of conjuration, which was still happily carried on, and made use of the intelligence of his friend Cadwallader; though he sometimes converted this advantage to the purposes of gallantry, being (as the reader may have perceived) of a very amorous complexion. He not only acted the reformer, or rather the castigator, in the fashionable world, but also exercised his talents among the inferior class of people, who chanced to incur his displeasure.[1]

Being one day insulted by a couple of chairmen, who demanded more than their fare, he took particular notice of their number; and next day, Pipes, being dressed in one of his old suits, went by his direction to a coffee-house near their stand, after he had loaded himself with an additional weight, amounting to an hundred pounds at least; and calling the same individual partners who had affronted his master, he took possession of their chair, and ordered them to carry him to a place at the distance of two long miles. The burthen was so extraordinary, that when they attempted to take him up, they imagined the vehicle was detained by some crack or crevice of the pavement, and one of them actually went to disengage it; but finding it clear, he began a song of imprecations upon his fare, who he swore had got a backside of block-tin; but, being obliged to accomplish his undertaking, he bent his shoulders once more to the load, bidding his comrade lift fair and be damn'd. The task was not performed in silence; while they staggered along, he cursed in a strain peculiar to himself, and in vain endeavoured to provoke the patient Pipes with opprobrious language, hoping that he would either dismiss them from his service, or be so incensed at his abuse, as to proceed to manual chastisement; in which case, the fellow would have an opportunity of gratifying his choler upon the author of his present grievance. Finding, however, that the gentleman bore his reproaches with the most philosophic indifference, he lost all patience; and being restrained, by the fear of the law, from an assault upon his fare, he turned the stream of his indignation upon his own partner, who, he alledged, did not bear his share of the burthen. This imputation created a dispute, which was maintained on both sides with such virulence of obloquy, as produced a quarrel, and mutual defiance to single combat, on the spot.

The chair was accordingly set down, without ceremony, the antagonists stripped themselves in a moment; and a fierce battle ensuing, Peregrine, who followed at a distance, enjoyed the pleasure of seeing them both beaten almost to jelly, before the contest was determined. As for Pipes, he sat still, and viewed the engagement with great composure; and perceiving his carriers disabled by their mutual prowess and perseverance, opened the chair, and very deliberately walked home to his master's lodging, where he disincumbered himself of his load.

A few days after the atchievement of this exploit, one of our hero's friends, who lodged at the house of an old peevish puritanical widow, that kept an hosier's shop, was obliged to quit his apartment at a minute's warning, because he had scandalized the house, by treating a female cousin at supper over-night. On this occasion, a great deal of sharp repartee had passed between him and his landlady, who not only subjected him to infinite inconvenience, from such a precipitate removal, but had likewise given her tongue such disagreeable liberties, at his expence, that he vowed revenge, and now sollicited the advice and assistance of his friend. Pickle having inquired into the character of the delinquent, who was hated by her neighbours, for her insolent and fretful disposition, undertook the cause of his companion, to whom he dictated the following advertisement, which was immediately inserted in one of the newspapers: 'Any person possessed of a male black cat, with white feet, and a bushy tail, not exceeding the age of two or three years, will find a purchaser, by carrying it to the sign of the kid near St. James's.'

The projector and his associate having obtained the promise of the publisher, that this intimation should appear next day, went early in the morning to a public house, and occupying a room, the windows of which fronted the hosier's door, sat with joyful expectation to see the effect of their scheme, which soon yielded them all the satisfaction they could desire. The shop was no sooner opened, than it was surrounded by a great number of the Cannaille, who having heard the advertisement read in ale-houses, came (each with a cat under his arm) in hopes of making an advantageous bargain; for though many of them were too inconsiderable to produce such an animal of their own property, they had made free with the first cats they could pick up, and every one repaired with all possible dispatch to the appointed place, with a view of forestalling the market; so that, in disputing the precedence, the whole crew went to loggerheads about the door, to the utter astonishment of the shopkeeper, who could not conceive the meaning of such a congregation.

Nevertheless, she began to harangue them in her usual stile, which was not the mildest sort of expostulation; and one of the multitude, who found means to detach himself from the general uproar and confusion, told her, he had brought a cat, which, he supposed, would answer the marks of her advertisement. 'Here, (said he, presenting the creature) look at him, mistress; I'll be damn'd if you ever saw a finer boar in your life. Do but mind his tusks and his tail; his tail is for all the world like a squirrel's, and yet he's no more than a kitten; I'm the son of a bitch, if he's a day more than six months old.' This address, while it compleated her amazement, kindled her rage to such a degree, that she spit in his face, calling him a cat, and a rat, and a rascal; and shutting the hatch, threatened the whole assembly with Bridewell and imprisonment, if they would not immediately disperse. Her declamation was so shrill, as to command the attention of the whole audience, who finding their hopes frustrated, and hearing themselves so bitterly reviled, put an end to their own jars, and held a momentary conference; in consequence of which, one of them was deputed to ask, whether or not she had advertised for a black cat. This question being answered in the negative, with a string of reproachful epithets, the interrogator approaching the door, 'Why, ye bitch of Babel! (said he) if you won't give money for my cat, you shall have him for love.' With these words he threw it into the shop, and retired; while his brethren, in obedience to this signal, lifted up their hands as one man, and like soldiers at the word of command, discharged about forty cats at the same instant of time, upon the confounded hosier, who finding herself overwhelmed by such a number of animals, which she looked upon as so many fiends sent to torment her, ran aghast into the street with dismal outcries, imploring the assistance of her neighbours, who (as well as our confederates) enjoyed her distress; and after having indulged their animosity, contributed their aid, in ridding her of such a dangerous annoyance.

The next mischievous plan that entered our hero's imagination, was suggested by two advertisements published in the same paper, by persons who wanted to borrow certain sums of money, for which they promised to give undeniable security. Peregrine, from the stile and manner of both, concluded they were written by attornies, a species of people for whom he entertained his uncle's aversion: and in order to amuse himself, and some of his friends, with their disappointment, he wrote a letter signed A. B. to each advertiser, according to the address specified in the news-paper, importing, that if he would come with his writings, to a certain coffee-house near the Temple, precisely at six o'clock in the evening, he would find a person sitting in the right-hand box, next to the window, who would be glad to treat with him about the subject of his advertisement, and, should his security be liked, would accommodate him with the sum which he wanted to raise. Before the hour of this double appointment, Pickle with his friend Cadwallader, and a few more gentlemen, to whom he had thought proper to communicate the plan, went to the coffee-house, and seated themselves near the place that was destined for their meeting.

The hope of getting money had such an evident effect upon their punctuality, that one of them arrived a considerable time before the hour; and having reconnoitred the room, took his station according to the direction he had received, fixing his eye upon a clock that stood before him, and asking of the bar-keeper if it was not too slow. He had not remained in this posture many minutes, when he was joined by a strange figure, that waddled into the room, with a bundle of papers in his bosom, and the sweat running over his nose. Seeing a man in the box to which he had been directed, he took it for granted he was the lender; and as soon as he could recover his breath, which was almost exhausted by the dispatch he had made, 'Sir, (said he) I presume you are the gentleman I was to meet, about that loan.'——Here he was interrupted by the other, who eagerly replied, 'A. B. Sir, I suppose.' 'The same, (cried the last comer) I was afraid I should be too late; for I was detained beyond my expectation, by a nobleman in the other end of the town, that wants to mortgage a small trifle of his estate, about a thousand a year; and my watch happens to be in the hands of the maker, having met with an accident a few nights ago, which set it asleep. But howsomever, there's no time lost, and I hope this affair will be transacted to the satisfaction of us both. For my own part, I love to do good offices myself, and therefore I expect nothing but what is fair and honest of other people.'

His new friend was exceedingly comforted by this declaration, which he considered as a happy omen of his success; and the hope of fingering the cash operated visibly in his countenance, while he expressed his satisfaction at meeting with a person of such candour and humanity. 'The pleasure (said he) of dealing with an easy conscientious man, is, in my opinion, superior to that of touching all the money upon earth; for what joy can be compared with what a generous mind feels, in befriending its fellow-creatures? I was never so happy in my life, as at one time, in lending five hundred pounds to a worthy gentleman in distress, without insisting upon rigid security. Sir, one may easily distinguish an upright man by his countenance; for example now, I think I could take your word for ten thousand pounds.' The other with great joy protested, that he was right in his conjecture, and returned the compliment a thousand fold: by which means, the expectation of both was wound up to a very interesting pitch; and both, at the same instant, began to produce their papers, in the untying of which, their hands shook with transports of eagerness and impatience; while their eyes were so intent upon their work, that they did not perceive the occupation of each other.

At length, one of them, having got the start of the other, and un-rolled several skins of musty parchment, directed his view to the employment of his friend; and seeing him fumbling at his bundle, asked if that was a blank bond and conveyance, which he had brought along with him. The other, without lifting up his eyes, or desisting from his endeavours to loose the knot, which by this time he had applied to his teeth, answered this question in the negative, observing, that the papers in his hand were the security which he proposed to give for the money.

This reply converted the looks of the inquirer into a stare of infinite stolidity, accompanied with the word, *Anan!* which he pronounced in a tone of fear and astonishment. The other, alarmed at this note, cast his eyes towards the supposed lender, and was in a moment infected by his aspect. All the exultation of hope that sparkled in their eyes, was now succeeded by disappointment and dismay; and while they gazed ruefully at each other, their features were gradually elongated, like the transient curls of a Middle-row periwig.

This emphatic silence was, however, broke by the last comer, who, in a faultering accent, desired the other to recollect the contents of his letter. 'Of your letter!' cried the first, putting into his hand the advertisement he had received from Pickle; which he had no sooner perused, than he produced his own, for the satisfaction of the other party: so that another gloomy pause ensued, at the end of which, each uttered a profound sigh, or rather groan, and rising up, sneak'd off, without farther communication; he who seemed to be the most afflicted of the two, taking his departure, with an exclamation of 'Humbugged, egad!'

Such were the amusements of our hero, tho' they did not engross his whole time, some part of which was dedicated to nocturnal riots and revels, among a set of young noblemen, who had denounced war against temperance, œconomy, and common sense, and were indeed the devoted sons of tumult, waste, and prodigality. Not that Peregrine relished those scenes, which were a succession of absurd extravagance, devoid of all true spirit, taste, or enjoyment: but his vanity prompted him to mingle with those who were intitled the choice spirits of the age; and his disposition was so pliable, as to adapt itself easily to the measures of his company, where he had not influence enough to act in the capacity of director. Their rendezvous was at a certain tavern, which might be properly stiled the temple of excess, where they left the choice of their fare to the discretion of the landlord, that they might save themselves the pains of exercising their own reason; and, in order to avoid the trouble of adjusting the bill, ordered the waiter to declare how much every individual must pay, without specifying the articles of the charge; and this proportion generally amounted to two guineas *per* head for each dinner and supper, and frequently exceeded that sum; of which the landlord durst not abate, without running the risque of having his nose slit for his moderation.

But this was a puny expence, compared with that which they often incurred, by the damage done to the furniture and servants, in the madness of their intoxication, as well as the loss they sustained at hazard, an amusement to which all of them had recourse, in the progress of their debauches. This elegant diversion was introduced, encouraged, and promoted by a crew of rapacious sharpers, who had made themselves necessary companions to this hopeful generation, by the talents of pimping and buffoonery: and though they were universally known, even by those they preyed upon, to have no other means of earning their livelihood, than the most infamous and fraudulent practices, they were caressed and courted by these infatuated dupes, when a man of honour, who would not join in their excesses, would have been treated with the utmost indignity and contempt.

Though Peregrine, in his heart, detested those abandoned courses, and was a professed enemy to the whole society of gamesters, whom he considered, and always treated as the foes of human kind, he was insensibly accustomed to licentious riot, and even led imperceptibly into play by those cormorants, who are no less dangerous in the art of cheating, than by their consummate skill in working upon the passions of unwary youth. They are, for the most part, naturally cool, phlegmatic and crafty, and by a long habit of dissimulation, have gained an absolute dominion over the hasty passions of the heart; so that they engage with manifest advantage over the impatience and impetuosity of a warm, undesigning temper, like that of our young gentleman, who, when he was heated with wine, misled by example, invited on one hand, and defied on the other, forgot all his maxims of caution and sobriety, and plunging into the reigning folly of the place, had frequent occasions to moralize in the morning, upon the loss of the preceding night.

These penitential reflections were attended with many laudable resolutions of profiting by the expence which he had so dearly purchased; but he was one of those philosophers, who always put off, till another day, the commencement of their reformation.

CHAPTER XCIV

Peregrine receives a Letter from Hatchway,
in consequence of which he repairs to the Garison,
and performs the last Offices to his Aunt. He is visited
by Mr. Gauntlet, who invites him to his Marriage

IN this circle of amusements our hero's time was parcelled out, and few young gentlemen of the age enjoyed life with greater relish, notwithstanding those intervening checks of reason, which served only to whet his appetite for a repetition of the pleasures she so prudently condemned; when he received the following letter, by which he was determined to visit his estate in the country.

COUSIN PICKLE,

I hope you are in a better trim than your aunt, who hath been fast moored to her bed these seven weeks, by several feet of under-water logging in her hold and hollop, whereby I doubt her planks are rotted, so as she cannot chuse but fall to pieces in a short time. I have done all in my power to keep her tight and easy, and free from sudden squalls that might overstrain her. And here have been the doctors, who have skuttled her lower deck, and let out six gallons of water. For my own part, I wonder how the devil it came there; for you know as how it was a liquor she never took in. But as for those fellows the doctors, they are like unskilful carpenters, that in mending one leak, make a couple; and so she fills again apace. But the worst sign of all is this here, she won't let a drop of Nantz go betwixt the combings of her teeth, and has quite lost the rudder of her understanding, whereby she yaws woundily in her speech, palavering about some foreign part called the New Geereusalem, and wishing herself in a safe birth in the river Geordun. The parson, I must say, strives to keep her steady, concerning the navigation of her soul, and talks very sensibly of charity and the poor, whereof she hath left a legacy of two hundred pounds in her will. And here has been Mr. Gamaliel and your brother my lord, demanding entrance at the gate, in order to see her; but I would not suffer them to come aboard, and pointed my patereroes, which made them sheer off. Your sister Mrs. Clover keeps close watch upon her kinswoman, without ever turning in, and a kind-hearted young woman it is. I should be glad to see you at the garison, if the wind of your inclination sits that way; and mayhap it may be a comfort to your aunt, to behold you along-side of her, when her anchor is apeak. So no more at present, but rests

> Your friend
> And humble servant to command,
> J^{no} HATCHWAY

Next morning, after the receipt of this epistle, Peregrine, in order to manifest his regard to his aunt, as well as his friendship for honest Jack, set out on horseback for their habitation, attended by Pipes, who longed to see his old messmate; but, before he reached the garison, Mrs. Hatchway had given up the ghost, in the threescore and fifth year of her age. The widower seemed to bear his loss with resignation, and behaved very decently upon the occasion, though he did not undergo those dangerous transports of sorrow, which some tender-hearted husbands have felt at the departure of their yoke-fellows. The lieutenant was naturally a philosopher, and so well disposed to acquiesce in the dispensations of providence, that in this, as well as in every other emergency of his life, he firmly believed, that every thing which happened was for the best.

Peregrine's task, therefore, was not so great in comforting him, as in consoling his own sister, who with great poignancy and sincerity of grief, lamented the death of the only relation with whom she had maintained any intimacy of correspondence; for her mother was as implacable as ever, in her enmity against her and Peregrine, and rather more determined in her rancour, that which was originally a sudden transport of indignation, being by this time settled into a confirmed inveteracy of hate. As for Gam, who was now dignified by the country-people with the appellation of the young squire, he still acted in the capacity of minister to the caprice and vengeance of his mother, taking all opportunities of disturbing Julia's peace, slandering her reputation, and committing outrages against the tenants and domestics of her husband, who was a man of a quiet and timorous disposition.

But the chief amusement of young Pickle, in his later years, was the chace, in which he acquired some renown by his intrepidity and remarkable figure, which improved every day in deformity; inso-much, as to suggest a ludicrous scheme of revenge to a gentleman in the neighbourhood, who having been affronted by the insolence of Crookback, cloathed a large baboon that was in his possession, in a dress that resembled the hunting-equipage of Gam; and ordering the animal to be set astride, and tied upon the back of his keenest hunter, turned them out one day after the hounds; and the horse in a little time outstripping all the rest in the field, the rider was mistaken for Gam by the whole company, who saluted him as he passed with a hollow, observing, that the squire had his usual good luck, in being better mounted than his neighbours. Pickle afterwards appearing in his own person, created great astonishment in the spectators, one of whom asked if he had split himself in twain, and pointed out his representative, who was by this time almost up with the hounds: upon which, the identical Gam went in pursuit of the impostor; and when he overtook him was so much enraged at the counterfeit, that he attacked the baboon whip in hand, and, in all probability, would have sacrificed him to his resentment, had not he been prevented by the other fox-hunters, who interposed, in order to make up the difference betwixt two brothers of the sport, and were equally surprised and diverted, when they distinguished the quality of Crookback's antagonist, which they rescued from his rage, and reconveyed to its master.

Peregrine, at the request of his friend Jack, took charge of his aunt's funeral, to which his parents were invited, though they did not think proper to appear, or pay the least regard to his sollicita-tions, when he desired permission to wait upon them in person. Nevertheless, old Gamaliel, at the instigation of his wife, afterwards obtained an order from Doctor's Commons, obliging Hatchway to produce the will of his wife, on the supposition that she had bequeathed to him some part of the money which (she knew) was at her own disposal. But from this step he reaped no other satis-faction than that of finding himself altogether neglected by the testatrix, who had left all her effects to her husband, except one thousand pounds, with her jewels, to Julia's daughter, the bene-faction mentioned in the lieutenant's letter, and some inconsiderable legacies to her favourite domesticks.

A few days after the interment of this good lady, our hero was agreeably surprised with a visit from his friend Godfrey, who had come to England in consequence of that promotion which he owed to his interest, tho' the soldier himself placed it to the credit of a certain courtier who had formerly promised to befriend him, and now finding his advancement unowned, very modestly arrogated the merit of it to himself. He communicated his good fortune to Pickle, who complimented him upon it as an event of which he had no precognition; and at the same time told him, that, in consequence of his preferment, his cousin at Windsor had consented to his being immediately united in the bands of wedlock with his lovely Sophy; that the wedding-day was already fixed; and that nothing would be wanting to his happiness, if Peregrine would honour the nuptials with his presence.

Our hero accepted the invitation with great eagerness, when he learned that Emilia would be there in quality of bride's maid; and now repeated what he had formerly written to his friend, namely, that he was not only willing, but extremely impatient to attone for his mad behaviour to that young lady, by laying himself and his whole fortune at her feet. Godfrey thanked him for his honourable intention, and promised to use his influence, and that of Sophy, in his behalf, tho' he seemed dubious of their success, on account of his sister's delicacy, which could not pardon the least shadow of disrespect. He owned, indeed, he was not certain that she would appear in the same company with Pickle; but as she had made no stipulations on that score, he would interpret her silence in the most favourable manner, and keep her in ignorance of his design, until she should find it too late to retract with any decency. The hope of seeing and conversing with Emilia, and perhaps of being reconciled to her, after having suffered so much and so long from her displeasure, raised a tumult of ideas in his breast, and produced a strange inquietude of joy and perturbation. Gauntlet having stayed with him a few days, and signified the time appointed for his spousals, took his leave, in order to prepare for the occasion; while Peregrine, with his friend Hatchway, made a tour among his acquaintance in the country, with a view of sounding their inclinations touching a project which he had lately conceived, of offering himself as a candidate for a certain borough in the neighbourhood, at the ensuing election for members of parliament.

This scheme, which was suggested to him by one of his quality patrons, would have succeeded according to his wish, had the election taken place immediately; but before that happened, his interest was overbalanced by some small accidents that will be recorded in the sequel. In the mean time, he repaired to Windsor on the eve of his friend's marriage, and understood from Godfrey, that it was with the utmost difficulty he and Sophy could prevail upon his sister to be present at the wedding, when she was informed that her lover was invited, and that her consent had not been obtained until they had promised, on the part of Peregrine, that he should not renew the old topic, nor even speak to her in the stile of a former acquaintance.

Our young gentleman was nettled at this preliminary, to which, however, he said he would adhere; and so well did he think himself fortified with pride and resentment, that he resolved to behave towards her with such indifference, as would, he hoped, mortify her vanity, and thereby punish her for the implacability of her disposition. Armed with these sentiments, he was next day introduced by Godfrey to the bride, who received him with her usual sweetness of temper and affability; and Emilia being present, he saluted her with a distant bow, which she acknowledged with a cold curt'sy, and an aspect of ice. Tho' this deportment confirmed his displeasure, her beauty undermined his resolution; he thought her charms were infinitely improved since their last parting, and a thousand fond images recurring to his imagination, he felt his whole soul dissolving into tenderness and love.

In order to banish those dangerous ideas, he endeavoured to enter into a gay conversation with Sophy, on the subject of the approaching ceremony; but his tongue performed its office very aukwardly, his eyes were attracted towards Emilia, as if they had been subject to the power of fascination; in spite of all his efforts, a deep sigh escaped from his bosom, and his whole appearance indicated anxiety and confusion.

The bridegroom perceiving his condition, abridged the visit, and having conducted his companion to his own lodgings, expressed his concern at having been the innocent occasion of his uneasiness, by exposing him to the sight of Emilia, which he perceived had given him pain. Peregrine, who had by this time recollected the dictates of his pride, assured him, that he was very much mistaken in the cause of his disorder, which was no other than a sudden qualm, to which he had been for some time subject; and to shew him how philosophically he could bear the disdain of Emilia, which, with all deference to her conduct, he could not help thinking a little too severe, he desired, as the bridegroom had made preparations for a private ball in the evening, that he would provide him with an agreeable partner; in which case he would exhibit undoubted proofs of the tranquillity of his heart. 'I was in hopes (answered Godfrey) of being able, with the assistance of Sophy, to make up matters between you and my sister, and for that reason kept her unengaged to any other gentleman for the night; but since she is so peevishly obstinate, I shall take care to accommodate you with a very handsome young lady, whose partner will not be sorry to exchange her for Emilia.'

The thoughts of having an opportunity to coquet with another woman, under the eye of this implacable mistress, supported his spirits during the ceremony which put Gauntlet in possession of his heart's desire; and, by means of this cordial, he found himself so undisturbed at dinner, tho' he sat opposite to his fair enemy, that he was able to pass some occasional jokes upon the new-married couple, with some appearance of mirth and good humour. Nor did Emily any otherwise seem affected by his presence, than by excepting him from the participation of those genial regards which she distributed to the rest of the company. This easiness of behaviour on her side, reinforced his resolution, by giving him pretence to call her sensibility in question; for he could not conceive how any woman of acute feelings could sit unmoved, in presence of a man with whom she had such recent and intimate connexion: not considering, that she had much more reason to condemn his affectation of unconcern, and that her external deportment might, like his own, be an effort of pride and resentment.

This contest, in point of dissimulation, continued till night, when the company was paired for dancing, and Peregrine began the ball by walking a minuet with the bride; then he took out the young lady to whom he was recommended by Gauntlet, being very well pleased to see that her person was such as might have inspired even Emily herself with jealousy, though, at the same time, he perceived his mistress coupled with a gay young officer, whom (with all due deference to his own qualifications) he considered as no despicable rival. However, he himself first began hostilities, by becoming all of a sudden particular with his partner, whom he forthwith assailed with flattering compliments, that soon introduced the subject of love, upon which he expatiated with great art and elocution, using not only the faculty of speech, but also the language of the eyes, in which he was a perfect connoisseur.

This behaviour soon manifested itself to the whole assembly, the greatest part of whom believed that he was in good earnest captivated by the heart of his partner, while Emilia, penetrating into his design, turned his own artillery upon himself, by seeming to listen with pleasure to the addresses of his rival, who was no novice in the art of making love: she even affected uncommon vivacity, and giggled aloud at every whisper which he conveyed into her ear, insomuch that she, in her turn, afforded speculation to the company, who imagined the young soldier had made a conquest of the bridegroom's sister.

Pickle himself began to cherish the same opinion, which gradually invaded his good humour, and, at length, filled his bosom with rage. He strove to suppress his indignation, and called every consideration of vanity and revenge to his aid: he endeavoured to wean his eyes from the fatal object that disturbed him, but they would not obey his direction and command; he wished himself deprived of all sensation, when he heard her laugh, and saw her smile upon the officer; and, in the course of country-dancing, when he was obliged to join hands with her, the touch thrill'd thro' all his nerves, and kindled a flame within him which he could not contain. In a word, his endeavours to conceal the situation of his thoughts, were so violent, that his constitution could not endure the shock; the sweat ran down his forehead in a stream, the colour vanished from his cheeks, his knees began to totter, and his eyesight to fail: so that he must have fallen at his full length upon the floor, had not he retired very abruptly into another room, where he threw himself upon a couch, and fainted.

In this condition he was found by his friend, who seeing him withdraw with such symptoms of disorder, followed him thither; and when he recovered the use of his faculties, pressed him to make use of a bed in that house, rather than expose himself to the night air, by going home to his own lodgings: but not being able to prevail upon him to accept the offer, he wrapped him up in a cloak, and conducting him to the inn where he lodged, helped him to undress and go to bed, where he was immediately seized with a violent fit of the ague. Godfrey behaved with great tenderness, and would have actually bore him company all night, notwithstanding the circumstances of his own situation, had not his friend insisted upon his returning to the company, and making his apology to his partner for his sudden departure.

This was a step absolutely necessary towards maintaining the quiet of the assembly, which he found in great consternation, occasioned by his absence; for some of the ladies seeing the bridegroom follow the stranger in his retreat, the meaning of which they did not comprehend, began to be afraid of a quarrel; and Emilia, upon pretence of that supposition, was so much alarmed, that she could not stand, and was fain to have recourse to a smelling bottle.

The bride, who understood the whole mystery, was the only person that acted with deliberation and composure; she imputed

Emilia's disorder to the right cause, which was no other than concern for the condition of her lover, and assured the ladies there was nothing extraordinary in Mr. Pickle's going off, he being subject to fainting fits, by which he was often overtaken without any previous notice. The arrival of Gauntlet confirmed the truth of this declaration; he made an apology to the company, in the name of his friend, who, he told them, was suddenly taken ill; and they returned to their diversion of dancing, with this variation: Emilia was so disordered and fatigued, that she begged to be excused from continuing the exercise; and Peregrine's partner being disengaged, was paired with the young officer for whom she was originally designed.

Mean while, the bride withdrew into another apartment, with her sister, and expostulated with her upon her cruelty to Mr. Pickle, assuring her, from Godfrey's information, that he had undergone a severe fit on her account, which, in all likelihood, would have a dangerous effect upon his constitution. Tho' Emily was inflexible in her answers to the kind remonstrances of the gentle Sophy, her heart was melting with the impressions of pity and love; and finding herself unable to perform the duty of her function, in putting the bride to bed, she retired to her own chamber, and, in secret, sympathized with the distemper of her lover.

In the morning, as early as decency would permit him to leave the arms of his dear wife, captain Gauntlet made a visit to Peregrine, who had passed a very tedious and uneasy night, having been subject to short intervals of delirium, during which Pipes had found it very difficult to keep him fast belayed. He owned indeed to Godfrey, that his imagination had been haunted by the ideas of Emilia and her officer, which tormented him to an unspeakable degree of anguish and distraction; and that he would rather suffer death than a repetition of such excruciating reflections. He was, however, comforted by his friend, who assured him, that his sister's inclinations would, in time, prevail over all the endeavours of resentment and pride, illustrating this asseveration by an account of the manner in which she was affected by the knowledge of his disorder, and advising him to implore the mediation of Sophy, in a letter which she should communicate to Emilia.

This was an opportunity which our hero thought too favourable to be neglected; and therefore calling for paper, he sat up in his bed, and, in the first transports of his emotion, wrote the following petition to Godfrey's amiable wife.

Dear madam,

The affliction of a contrite heart can never appeal to your benevolence in vain; and therefore I presume to approach you, in this season of delight, with the language of sorrow, requesting that you will espouse the cause of an unhappy lover, who mourns with unutterable anguish over his ruined hope, and interceed for my pardon with that divine creature, whom, in the intemperance and excess of passion, I have so mortally offended. Good heaven! is my guilt inexpiable? Am I excluded from all hope of remission? Am I devoted to misery and despair? I have offered all the atonement which the most perfect and sincere penitence could suggest, and she rejects my humility and repentance. If her resentment would pursue me to the grave, let her signify her pleasure; and may I be branded with the name of villain, and remembered with infamy and detestation to all posterity, if I hesitate one moment in sacrificing a life which is odious to Emilia. Ah! madam, while I thus pour forth the effusions of my grief and distraction, I look around the apartment in which I lie, and every well-known object that salutes my view, recals to my remembrance that fond, that happy day, on which the fair, the good, the tender-hearted Sophy became my advocate, though I was a stranger to her acquaintance, and effected a transporting reconciliation between me and that same inchanting beauty, that is now so implacably incensed. If she is not satisfied with the pangs of remorse and disappointment, the transports of madness I have undergone; let her prescribe what farther penance she thinks I ought to endure; and when I decline her sentence, let me be the object of her eternal disdain.

I commit myself, dear madam! dear Sophy! dear partner of my friend! to your kind interposition. I know you will manage my cause, as a concern on which my happiness intirely depends; and I hope every thing from your compassion and beneficence, while I fear every thing from her rigour and barbarity. Yes! I call it barbarity, a savageness of delicacy altogether inconsistent with the tenderness of human nature; and may the most abject contempt be my portion, if I live under its infliction! But I begin to rave. I conjure you by your own humanity and sweetness of disposition, I conjure you by your love for the man whom heaven hath decreed your protector, to employ your influence with that angel of wrath, in behalf of

Your obliged and

Obedient servant,

P. PICKLE

This epistle was immediately transmitted by Godfrey to his wife, who perused it with marks of the most humane sympathy; and carrying it into her sister's chamber, 'Here is something (said she, presenting the paper) which I must recommend to your serious attention.' Emilia, who immediately guessed the meaning of this address, absolutely refused to look upon it, or even to hear it read, till her brother entering the apartment, reprimanded her sharply for her obstinacy and pride, accused her of folly and dissimulation, and entered so warmly into the interests of his friend, that she thought him unkind in his remonstrances, and bursting into a flood of tears, reproached him with partiality and want of affection. Godfrey, who entertained the most perfect love and veneration for his sister, asked pardon for having given offence, and kissing the drops from her fair eyes, begg'd she would, for his sake, listen to the declaration of his friend.

Thus sollicited, she could not refuse to hear the letter, which when he had repeated, she lamented her own fate, in being the occasion of so much uneasiness, desired her brother to assure Mr. Pickle, that she was not a voluntary enemy to his peace; on the contrary, she wished him all happiness, tho' she hoped he would not blame her for consulting her own, in avoiding any future explanation or connexion with a person whose correspondence she found herself under a necessity to renounce.

In vain did the new-married couple exhaust their eloquence in attempting to prove, that the reparation which our hero had offered was adequate to the injury she had sustained; that in reconciling herself to a penitent lover, who subscribed to her own terms of submission, her honour would be acquitted by the most scrupulous and severe judges of decorum; and that her inflexibility would be justly ascribed to the pride and insensibility of her heart. She turned a deaf ear to all their arguments, exhortations and intreaties, and threatened to leave the house immediately, if they would not promise to drop that subject of discourse.

Godfrey, very much chagrined at the bad success of his endeavours, returned to his friend, and made as favourable a report of the affair, as the nature of his conversation with Emilia would permit; but as he could not avoid mentioning her resolution in the close, Peregrine was obliged to drink again the bitter draught of disappointment, which put his passions into such a state of agitation, as produced a short extasy of despair, in which he acted a thousand extravagancies. This paroxysm, however, soon subsided into a settled reserve of gloomy resentment, which he in secret indulged, detaching himself as soon as possible from the company of the soldier, on pretence of retiring to rest.

While he lay ruminating upon the circumstances of his present situation, his friend Pipes, who knew the cause of his anxiety, and firmly believed that Emilia loved his master in her heart, howsoever she might attempt to disguise her sentiments; I say, Thomas was taken with a conceit which he thought would set every thing to rights, and therefore put it in execution, without farther delay. Laying aside his hat, he ran directly to the house of Sophy's father, and affecting an air of surprize and consternation, to which he had never before been subject, thundered at the door with such an alarming knock, as in a moment brought the whole family into the hall. When he was admitted, he began to gape, stare, and pant at the same time, and made no reply, when Godfrey asked what was the matter, till Mrs. Gauntlet expressed her apprehensions about his master; at whose name being mentioned, he seemed to make an effort to speak, and in a bellowing tone pronounced, 'Brought himself up, split my top-sails!' So saying, he pointed to his own neck, and rose upon his tiptoes, by way of explaining the meaning of his words.

Godfrey, without staying to ask another question, rushed out, and flew towards the inn, with the utmost horror and concern; while Sophy, who did not rightly understand the language of the messenger, addressing herself to him a second time, said with great earnestness, 'I hope no accident has happened to Mr. Pickle!' 'No accident at all, (replied Tom) he has only hanged himself for love.' These words had scarce proceeded from his mouth, when Emilia, who stood listening at the parlour-door, shrieked aloud, and dropped down senseless upon the floor; while her sister, who was almost equally shocked at the intelligence, had recourse to the assistance of her maid, by whom she was supported from falling.

Pipes hearing Emily's voice, congratulated himself upon the success of his stratagem, he sprung to her assistance, and lifting her up into an easy chair, stood by her, until he saw her recover from her swoon, and heard her call upon his master's name, with all the frenzy of despairing love. Then he bent his course back to the inn, overjoyed at the opportunity of telling Peregrine what a confession he had extorted from his mistress, and extremely vain of this proof of his own sagacity.

In the mean time, Godfrey arriving at the house, in which he supposed this fatal catastrophe had happened, ran up stairs to Peregrine's chamber, without staying to make any inquiry below;

and finding the door locked, burst it open with one stroke of his foot. But, what was his amazement, when, upon entrance, our hero starting up from the bed, saluted him with a boisterous exclamation of 'Z——ds! who's there?' He was struck dumb with astonishment, which also rivetted him to the place where he stood, scarce crediting the testimony of his own senses, 'till Peregrine, with an air of discontent which denoted him displeased with his intrusion, dispelled his apprehension by a second address, saying, 'I see you consider me as a friend, by your using me without ceremony.'

The soldier, thus convinced of the falsehood of the information he had received, began to imagine, that Pickle had projected the plan which was executed by his servant; and looking upon it as a piece of unjustifiable finesse, which might be attended with very melancholy consequences to his sister or wife, he answered in a supercilious tone, that he must blame himself for the interruption of his repose, which was intirely owing to the sorry jest he had set on foot.

Pickle, who was the child of passion, and more than half mad with impatience before this visit, hearing himself treated in such a cavalier manner, advanced close up to Godfrey's breast, and assuming a stern, or rather frantic countenance, 'Heark ye, Sir, (said he) you are mistaken if you think I jest; I am in downright earnest I assure you.' Gauntlet, who was not a man to be browbeaten, seeing himself thus bearded by a person of whose conduct he had, he thought, reason to complain, put on his military look of defiance, and erecting his chest, replied with an exalted voice, 'Mr. Pickle, whether you was in jest or earnest, you must give me leave to tell you, that the scheme was childish, unseasonable, and unkind, not to give it an harsher term.' 'Death, Sir, (cried our adventurer) you trifle with my disquiet: if there is any meaning in your insinuation, explain yourself, and then I shall know what answer it will befit me to give.' 'I came with very different sentiments, (resumed the soldier) but since you urge me to expostulation, and behave with such unprovoked loftiness of displeasure, I will, without circumlocution, tax you with having committed an outrage upon the peace of my family, in sending your fellow to alarm us with such an abrupt account of your having done violence upon yourself.' Peregrine, confounded at this imputation, stood silent, with a most savage aspect of surprize, eager to know the circumstance to which his accuser alluded, and incensed to find it without the sphere of his comprehension.

While these two irritated friends stood fronting each other with mutual indignation in their eyes and attitudes, they were joined by Pipes, who without taking the least notice of the situation in which he found them, told his master, that he might up with the top-gallant-masts of his heart, and out with his rejoicing pendants; for as to mistress Emily, he had clapt her helm a-weather, the vessel wore, and now she was upon the other tack, standing right into the harbour of his good will.

Peregrine, who was not yet a connoisseur in the terms of his lacquey, commanded him, upon pain of his displeasure, to be more explicit in his intelligence; and by dint of divers questions, obtained a perfect knowledge of the scheme which he had put in execution for his service. This information perplexed him not a little; he would have chastised his servant upon the spot, for his temerity, had not he plainly perceived, that the fellow's intention was to promote his ease and satisfaction: and on the other hand, he knew not how to acquit himself of the suspicion which he saw Godfrey entertain of his being the projector of the plan, without condescending to an explanation, which his present disposition could not brook. After some pause, however, turning to Pipes, with a severe frown, 'Rascal! (said he) this is the second time I have suffered in the opinion of that lady by your ignorance and presumption; if ever you intermeddle in my affairs for the future, without express order and direction, by all that's sacred! I will put you to death without mercy. Away, and let my horse be saddled this instant.'

Pipes having withdrawn, in order to perform this piece of duty, our young gentleman, addressing himself again to the soldier, and laying his hand upon his breast, said with a solemnity of regard, 'Captain Gauntlet, upon my honour, I am altogether innocent of that shallow device which you impute to my invention; and I don't think you do justice either to my intellects or honour, in supposing me capable of such insolent absurdity. As for your sister, I have once in my life affronted her in the madness and impetuosity of desire; but I have made such acknowledgements, and offered such atonement, as few women of her sphere would have refused; and before God! I am determined to endure every torment of disappointment and despair, rather than prostrate myself again to the cruelty of her unjustifiable pride.' So saying, he stalked suddenly down stairs, and took horse immediately, his spirits being supported by resentment, which prompted him to vow within himself, that he would seek consolation for the disdain of Emilia, in the possession of the first willing wench he should meet upon the road.

While he set out for the garison with these sentiments, Gauntlet, in a suspence between anger, shame and concern, returned to the house of his father-in-law, where he found his sister still violently agitated from the news of Peregrine's death, the mystery of which he forthwith unravelled, recounting at the same time the particulars of the conversation which had happened at the inn, and describing the demeanour of Pickle with some expressions of asperity, which were neither agreeable to Emilia, nor approved by the gentle Sophy, who tenderly chid him, for allowing Peregrine to depart in terms of misunderstanding.

CHAPTER XCV

Peregrine sets out for the Garison, and meets with a
Nymph of the Road, whom he takes into Keeping,
and metamorphoses into a fine Lady[1]

IN the mean time, our hero jogged along in a profound reverie, which was disturbed by a beggar-woman and her daughter, who solicited him for alms, as he passed them on the road. The girl was about the age of sixteen, and notwithstanding the wretched equipage in which she appeared, exhibited to his view a set of agreeable features, enlivened with the complexion of health and chearfulness. The resolution I have already mentioned was still warm in his imagination; and he looked upon this young mendicant as a very proper object for the performance of his vow. He therefore entered into a conference with the mother, and for a small sum of money purchased her property in the wench, who did not require much courtship and intreaty, before she consented to accompany him to any place that he should appoint for her habitation.

This contract being settled to his satisfaction, he ordered Pipes to seat his acquisition behind him upon the crupper, and alighting at the first public house which they found upon the road, he wrote a letter to Hatchway, desiring him to receive this hedge-inamorata, and direct her to be cleaned and cloathed in a decent manner, with all expedition, so that she should be touchable upon his arrival, which (on that account) he would defer for the space of one day. This billet, together with the girl, he committed to the charge of Pipes, after having laid strong injunctions upon him to abstain from all attempts upon her chastity, and ordered him to make the best of his way to the garison, while he himself crossed the country to a market-town, where he proposed to spend the night.

Tom thus cautioned, proceeded with his charge, and being naturally taciturn, opened not his lips, until he had performed the best half of his journey. But Thomas, notwithstanding his irony appearance, was in reality composed of flesh and blood; and his desire being titillated by the contact of a buxome wench, whose right arm embraced his middle as he rode, his thoughts began to mutiny against his master, and he found it almost impossible to withstand the temptation of making love.

Nevertheless, he wrestled with these rebellious suggestions with all the reason that God had enabled him to exert; and that being totally overcome, his victorious passion suddenly broke out in this address. ' 'Sblood! a believe master thinks I have no more stuff in my body than a dried haddock, to turn me adrift in the dark with such a spanker. D'ye think he don't, my dear?' To this question his fellow-traveller replied, 'Swanker! Anan!' And the lover resumed his suit, saying, 'Oons! how you tickle my timbers! Something shoots from your arm, through my stowage, to the very keel-stone. Han't you got quicksilver in your hand?' 'Quicksilver! (said the lady) D—n the silver that has crossed my hand this month. D'ye think if I had silver, I shouldn't buy me a smock?' 'Addsooks! ye baggage, (cried the lover) ye shouldn't want a smock nor a petticoat neither, if you could have a kindness for a true-hearted sailor, as sound and strong as a nine inch cable, that would keep all clear above-board, and every thing snug under the hatches.' 'Curse your gum, (said the charmer) what's your gay balls and your hatchets to me?' 'Do but let us bring to a little, (answered the wooer, whose appetite was by this time whetted to a most ravenous degree) and I'll teach you to box the compass, my dear. Ah! you strapper, what a jolly bitch you are!' 'Bitch! (exclaimed this modern Dulcinea, incensed at the opprobrious term) such a bitch as your mother, you dog. D—n ye, I've a good mind to box your jaws instead of your comepiss. I'll let you know as how I am meat for your master, you saucy blackguard. You are worse than a dog, you old flinty-faced, flea-bitten scrub: a dog wears his own coat, but you wear your master's.'

Such a torrent of disgraceful epithets from a person who had no cloaths at all, converted the gallant's love into choler, and he threatened to dismount and seize her to a tree, when she should have a taste of his cat and nine tails athwart her quarters; but, instead of being intimidated by his menaces, she set him at defiance, and held forth with such a flow of eloquence, as would have intitled her to a considerable share of reputation, even among the nymphs of Billingsgate; for this young lady, over and above a natural genius for altercation, had her talents cultivated among the venerable society of weeders, podders, and hoppers, with whom she had associated from her tender years. No wonder then, that she soon obtained a compleat victory over Pipes, who (as the reader may have observed) was very little addicted to the exercise of speech: indeed he was utterly disconcerted by her volubility of tongue; and being altogether unfurnished with answers to the distinct periods of her discourse, very wisely chose to save himself the expence of breath and argument, by giving her a full swing of cable, so that she might bring herself up; while he rode onwards, in silent composure, without taking any farther notice of his fair fellow-traveller than if she had been his master's cloak-bag.

In spite of all the dispatch he could make, it was late before he arrived at the garison, where he delivered the letter and the lady to the lieutenant, who no sooner understood the intention of his friend, than he ordered all the tubs in the house to be carried into the hall, and filled with water; and Tom having provided himself with swabs and brushes, divested the fair stranger of her variegated drapery, which was immediately committed to the flames, and performed upon her soft and sleek person the ceremony of scrubbing, as it is practised on board of the king's ships of war. Yet the nymph herself did not submit to this purification without repining: she curs'd the director, who was upon the spot, with many abusive allusions to his wooden leg: and as for Pipes the operator, she employed her talons so effectually upon his face, that the blood ran over his nose in sundry streams; and next morning, when those rivulets were dry, his countenance resembled the rough bark of a plum-tree, plastered with gum. Nevertheless, he did his duty with great perseverance, cut off her hair close to the scalp, handled his brushes with dexterity, applied his swabs of different magnitude and texture, as the case required, and lastly, rinsed her whole body with a dozen pails of cold water, discharged upon her head.

These ablutions being executed, he dried her with towels, accommodated her with a clean shift, and acting the part of a valet de chambre, cloathed her from head to foot, in clean and decent apparel which had belonged to Mrs. Hatchway; by which means her appearance was altered so much for the better, that when Peregrine arrived next day, he would scarce believe his own eyes.

He was, for that reason, extremely well pleased with his purchase, and now resolved to indulge a whim which seized him at the very instant of his arrival.

He had (as I believe the reader will readily allow) made considerable progress in the study of character, from the highest rank to the most humble station of life, and found it diversified in the same manner, thro' every degree of subordination and precedency: nay, he moreover observed, that the conversation of those who are dignified with the appellation of polite company, is neither more edifying nor entertaining than that which is met with among the lower classes of mankind; and that the only essential difference in point of demeanor, is the form of an education, which the meanest capacity can acquire, without much study or application. Possessed of this notion, he determined to take the young mendicant under his own tutorage and instruction. In consequence of which he hoped he should, in a few weeks, be able to produce her in company, as an accomplished young lady of uncommon wit, and an excellent understanding.

This extravagant plan he forthwith began to execute with great eagerness and industry; and his endeavours succeeded even beyond his expectation. The obstacle, in surmounting of which he found the greatest difficulty, was an inveterate habit of swearing, which had been indulged from her infancy, and confirmed by the example of those among whom she had lived. However, she had the rudiments of good sense from nature, which taught her to listen to wholsome advice, and was so docile as to comprehend and retain the lessons which her governor recommended to her attention; insomuch, that he ventured, in a few days, to present her at table, among a set of country squires, to whom she was introduced as a niece of the lieutenant. In that capacity she sat with becoming easiness of mien (for she was as void of the *mauvaise honte* as any dutchess in the land) bowed very graciously to the compliments of the gentlemen; and tho' she said little or nothing, because she was previously cautioned on that score, she more than once gave way to laughter, and her mirth happened to be pretty well timed. In a word, she attracted the applause and admiration of the guests, who, after she was withdrawn, complimented Mr. Hatchway upon the beauty, breeding and good humour of his kinswoman.

But what contributed more than any other circumstance to her speedy improvement, was some small insight into the primer, which she had acquired at a day-school, during the life of her father, who was a day-labourer in the country. Upon this foundation did

Peregrine build a most elegant superstructure; he culled out choice sentences from Shakespear, Otway, and Pope, and taught her to repeat them with emphasis and theatrical cadence: he then instructed her in the names and epithets of the most celebrated players, which he directed her to pronounce occasionally, with an air of careless familiarity; and perceiving that her voice was naturally clear, he enriched it with remnants of opera tunes, to be hummed during a pause in conversation, which is generally supplied with the circulation of a pinch of snuff. By means of this cultivation, she became a wonderful proficient in the polite graces of the age; she, with great facility, comprehended the scheme of whist, tho' cribbidge was her favourite game, with which she had amused herself in her vacant hours, from her first entrance into the profession of hopping; and brag[1] soon grew familiar to her practice and conception.

Thus prepared, she was exposed to the company of her own sex, being first of all visited by the parson's daughter, who could not avoid shewing that civility to Mr. Hatchway's niece, after she had made her public appearance at church. Mrs. Clover, who had a great share of penetration, could not help entertaining some doubts about this same relation, whose name she had never heard the uncle mention, during the whole term of her residence at the garison; but as the young lady was treated in that character, she would not refuse her acquaintance, and after having seen her at the castle, actually invited Miss Hatchway to her house. In short, she made a progress thro' almost all the families in the neighbourhood; and, by dint of her quotations, (which, by the bye, were not always judiciously used) she passed for a sprightly young lady, of uncommon learning and taste.

Peregrine having, in this manner, initiated her in the beau monde of the country, conducted her to London, where she was provided with private lodgings and a female attendant; and put her immediately under the tuition of his valet de chambre, who had orders to instruct her in dancing and the French language. He attended her to plays and concerts, three or four times a week; and when our hero thought her sufficiently accustomed to the sight of great company, he squired her in person to a public assembly, and danced with her among all the gay ladies of fashion: not but that there was still an evident air of rusticity and aukwardness in her demeanor, which was interpreted into an agreeable wildness of spirit, superior to the forms of common breeding. He afterwards found means to make her acquainted with some distinguished patterns of her own sex, by whom she was admitted into their most elegant parties, and continued to make good her pretensions to gentility, with great circumspection, till one evening, being at cards with a certain lady, whom she detected in the very fact of unfair conveyance, she taxed her roundly with the fraud, and brought upon herself such a torrent of sarcastic reproof, as overbore all her maxims of caution, and burst open the floodgates of her own natural repartee, twanged off with the appellations of b—— and w——, which she repeated with great vehemence, in an attitude of manual defiance, to the terror of her antagonist, and the astonishment of all present: nay, to such an unguarded pitch was she provoked, that starting up, she snapt her fingers, in testimony of disdain, and, as she quitted the room, applied her hand to that part which was the last of her that disappeared, inviting the company to kiss it, by one of its coarsest denominations.

Peregrine was a little disconcerted at this oversight in her behaviour, which, by the dæmon of intelligence, was in a moment conveyed to all the private companies in town; so that she was absolutely excluded from all polite communication, and Peregrine, for the present, disgraced among the modest part of his female acquaintance, many of whom not only forbad him their houses, on account of the impudent insult he had committed upon their honour as well as understanding, in palming a common trull upon them, as a young lady of birth and education, but also aspersed his family, by affirming that she was actually his own cousin-german, whom he had precipitately raised from the most abject state of humility and contempt. In revenge for this calumny, our young gentleman explained the whole mystery of her promotion, together with the motives that induced him to bring her into the fashionable world; and repeated among his companions, the extravagant encomiums which had been bestowed upon her by the most discerning matrons of the age.

Mean while, the infanta herself being rebuked by her benefactor, for this instance of misbehaviour, promised faithfully to keep a stricter guard for the future over her conduct, and applied herself with great assiduity to the studies, in which she was assisted by the Swiss, who gradually lost the freedom of his heart, while she was profiting by his instruction. In other words, she made a conquest of her preceptor, who yielding to the instigations of the flesh, chose a proper opportunity to declare his passion, which was powerfully recommended by his personal qualifications; and his intentions being honourable, she listened to his proposals of espousing her in private. In consequence of this agreement, they made an elopement together; and being buckled at the fleet, consummated their nuptials in private lodgings, by the Seven Dials, from which the husband next morning sent a letter to our hero, begging forgiveness for the clandestine step he had taken, which he solemnly protested was not owing to any abatement in his inviolable regard for his master, whom he should always honour and esteem to his latest breath, but intirely to the irresistible charms of the young lady, to whom he was now so happy as to be joined in the silken bonds of marriage.

Peregrine, tho' at first offended at his valet's presumption, was, upon second thoughts, reconciled to the event by which he was delivered from an incumbrance; for by this time he had performed his frolick, and begun to be tired of his acquisition. He reflected on the former fidelity of the Swiss, which had been manifested in a long course of service and attachment; and thinking it would be cruelly severe to abandon him to poverty and distress for one venial trespass, he resolved to pardon what he had done, and enable him in some shape to provide for the family which he had intailed upon himself.

With these sentiments, he sent a favourable answer to the delinquent, desiring to see him as soon as his passion would permit him to leave the arms of his spouse, for an hour or two; and Hadgi, in obedience to this intimation, repaired immediately to the lodgings of his master, before whom he appeared with a most penitential aspect. Peregrine, tho' he could scarce help laughing at his rueful length of face, reprimanded him sharply for his disrespect and ingratitude, in taking that by stealth which he might have had for asking; and the culprit assured him, that next to the vengeance of God, his displeasure was that which, of all evils, he dreaded to incur; but that love had distracted his brain in such a manner, as to banish every other consideration but that of gratifying his desire; and he owned, that he should not have been able to preserve his fidelity and duty to his own father, had they interfered with the interest of his passion. He then appealed to his master's own heart for the remission of his guilt, alluding to certain circumstances of our hero's conduct, which evinced the desperate effects of love. In short, he made such an apology as extorted a smile from his offended judge, who not only forgave his transgression, but also promised to put him in some fair way of earning a comfortable subsistence.

The Swiss was so much affected with this instance of generosity, that he fell upon his knees, and kissed his hand, praying to heaven, with great fervour, to make him worthy of such goodness and condescension. His scheme, he said, was to open a coffeehouse and tavern in some creditable part of the town, in hopes of being favoured with the custom of a numerous acquaintance he had made among upper servants and reputable tradesmen, not doubting that his wife would be an ornament to his bar, and a careful manager of his affairs. Peregrine approved of the plan, towards the execution of which he made him and his wife a present of five hundred pounds, together with a promise of erecting a weekly club among his friends, for the reputation and advantage of the house.

Hadgi was so transported with his good fortune, that he ran to Pipes, who was in the room, and having hugged him with great cordiality, and made his obeisance to his master, hied him home to his yokefellow, to communicate his happiness, cutting capers, and talking to himself all the way.

CHAPTER XCVI

He is visited by Pallet ; contracts an Intimacy
with a New-market Nobleman ;
and is by the Knowing-ones taken in

THIS affair being settled, and our adventurer, for the present, free of all female connexions, he returned to his former course of fast living, among the bucks of the town, and performed innumerable exploits among whores, bullies, rooks, constables, and justices of the peace.

In the midst of these occupations, he was one morning visited by his old fellow-traveller Pallet, whose appearance gave him equal surprize and concern. Tho' the weather was severe, he was cloathed in the thin summer-dress which he had wore at Paris, and was now not only threadbare, but in some parts actually patched; his stockings, by a repetition of that practice known among œconomists by the term of *coaxing*, hung like pudding-bags about his ankles; his shirt, tho' new-wash'd, was of the saffron hue, and in divers places appeared through the crannies of his breeches; he had exchanged his own hair for a smoke-dry'd tye-periwig, which all the flour in his drudging-box had not been able to whiten; his eyes were sunk, his jaws lengthened beyond their usual extension;

and he seemed twenty years older than he looked when he and our hero parted at Rotterdam.

In spite of all these evidences of decay, he accosted him with a meagre affectation of content and good humour, struggled piteously to appear gay and unconcerned, professed his joy at seeing him in England, excused himself for having delayed so long to come and present his respects; alledging, that since his return he had been a meer slave to the satisfaction of some persons of quality and taste, who had insisted upon his finishing some pieces with the utmost expedition.

Peregrine received him with that compassion and complaisance which was natural to his disposition, inquired about the healths of Mrs. Pallet and his family, and asked if his friend the doctor was in town. The painter seemed to have resumed his resentment against that gentleman, of whom he spoke in contemptuous terms. 'The doctor (said he) is so much overshadowed with presumption and self-conceit, that his merit has no relief. It does not rise. There is no keeping in the picture, my dear Sir. All the same as if I were to represent the moon under a cloud; there would be nothing but a deep mass of shade, with a little tiny speck of light in the middle, which would only serve to make, as it were, the darkness visible. You understand me. Had he taken my advice, it might have been better for him; but he's bigotted to his own opinion. You must know, Mr. Pickle, upon our return to England, I counselled him to compose a little, smart, clever ode upon my Cleopatra. As Gad shall judge me, I thought it would have been of some service, in helping him out of obscurity; for you know, as Sir Richard observes,

> *Soon will that die, which adds thy fame to mine.*
> *Let me then live, join'd to a work of thine.* [1]

By the bye, there is a most picturesque contrast in these lines, of *thy* and *me*, *living* and *dying*, and *thine* and *mine*. Ah! a pize upon it! Dick, after all, was the man. Ecod! he rounded it off. But, to return to this unhappy young man, would you believe it, he tossed up his nose at my friendly proposal, and gabbled something in Greek, which is not worth repeating. The case was this, my dear Sir, he was out of humour at the neglect of the world. He thought the poets of the age were jealous of his genius, and strove to crush it accordingly, while the rest of mankind wanted taste sufficient to discern it. For my own part, I profess myself one of these; and as the clown in Billy Shakespear says of the courtier's oath, had

I sworn by the doctor's genius, that the pancakes were naught, they might have been for all that very good, yet shouldn't I have been forsworn.[1] Let that be as it will, he retired from town in great dudgeon, and set up his rest near a hill in Derbyshire, with two tops, resembling Parnassus, and a well at the bottom, which he had christened Hyp-o-the-Green. Egad! if he stays in that habitation, 'tis my opinion he'll soon grow green with the hip indeed. He'll be glad of an opportunity to return to the flesh-pots of Egypt, and pay his court to the slighted queen Cleopatra. Ha! well remembered, by this light. You shall know, my good Sir, that this same Egyptian princess has been courted by so many gallants of taste, that as I hope to live, I found myself in some sort of a dilemma, because in parting with her to one, I should have disobliged all his rivals. Now a man would not chuse to give offence to his friends, at least I lay it down as a maxim, to avoid the smallest appearance of ingratitude. Perhaps I may be in the wrong. But every man has his way. For this reason, I proposed to all the candidates, that a lottery or raffle should be set on foot, by which every individual would have an equal chance for her good graces, and the prize to be left to the decision of fortune.[2] The scheme was mightily relished, and the terms being such a trifle as half a guinea, the whole town crouded into my house, in order to subscribe. But there I was their humble servant. Gentlemen, you must have a little patience till my own particular friends are served. Among that number, I do myself the honour to consider Mr. Pickle. Here is a copy of the proposals; and if the list should be adorned with his name, I hope, notwithstanding his merited success among the young ladies, he will for once be shunned by that little vixen called Miss Fortune; he, he, he!'

So saying, he bowed with a thousand apish congês, and presented his paper to Peregrine, who seeing the number of subscribers was limited to one hundred, said he thought him too moderate in his expectations, as he did not doubt that his picture would be a cheap purchase at five hundred, instead of fifty pounds, at which the price was fixed. To this unexpected remark Pallet answered, that among connoisseurs he would not pretend to appraise his picture; but that, in valuing his works, he was obliged to have an eye to the Gothic ignorance of the age in which he lived.

Our adventurer saw at once into the nature of this raffle, which was no other than a begging shift to dispose of a paultry piece, that he could not otherwise have sold for twenty shillings. However, far from shocking the poor man in distress, by dropping the least hint of his conjecture, he desired to be favoured with six chances, if the circumstances of his plan would indulge him so far; and the painter, after some hesitation, condescended to comply with his request, out of pure friendship and veneration; tho' he observed, that in so doing he must exclude some of his most intimate companions. Having received the money, he gave Pickle his address, desiring he would, with his convenience, visit the princess, who, he was sure, would display her most engaging attractions, in order to captivate his fancy; and took his leave, extremely well pleased with the success of his application.

Tho' Peregrine was tempted with the curiosity of seeing this portrait, which he imagined must contain some analogy to the ridiculous oddity of the painter, he would not expose himself to the disagreeable alternative of applauding the performance, contrary to the dictates of conscience and common sense, or of condemning it, to the unspeakable mortification of the miserable author; and therefore never dreamt of returning the painter's visit: nor did he ever hear of the lottery's being drawn.

About this time he was invited to spend a few weeks at the country-seat of a certain nobleman, with whom he had contracted an acquaintance, in the course of his debauches, which we have already described; and his lordship being remarkable for his skill and success in horse-racing, his house was continually filled with the connoisseurs and admirers of that sport, upon which the whole conversation turned, insomuch that Peregrine gradually imbibed some knowledge in horse-flesh, and the diversions of the course; for the whole occupation of the day, exclusive of eating and drinking, consisted in viewing, managing and exercising his lordship's stud.

Our hero looked upon these amusements with an eye of taste, as well as curiosity; he contemplated the animal as a beautiful and elegant part of the creation, and relished the surprising exertion of its speed with a refined and classical delight. In a little time he became personally acquainted with every horse in the stable, and interested himself in the reputation of each; while he also gratified his appetite for knowledge, in observing the methods of preparing their bodies, and training them to the race. His landlord saw and encouraged his eagerness, from which he promised himself some advantage; he formed several private matches for his entertainment, and flattered his discernment, by permitting him to be successful in the first betts he made. Thus was he artfully decoyed into a spirit of keenness and adventure, and disposed to depend upon his own judgment, in opposition to that of people who had made coursing the sole study of their lives. He accompanied my lord to Newmarket, and entering at once into the genius of the place, was marked as fair game, by all the knowing ones there assembled, many of whom found means to *take him in*, in spite of all the cautions and admonitions of his lordship, who wanted to reserve him for his own use.

It is almost impossible for any man, let him be never so fearful or phlegmatic, to be an unconcerned spectator in this busy scene. The dæmon of play hovers in the air, like a pestilential vapour, tainting the minds of all present with infallible infection, which communicates from one person to another, like the circulation of a general pannic. Peregrine was seized with this epidemic distemper to a violent degree; and after having lost a few loose hundreds, in his progress through the various rookeries of the place, entered into partnership with his noble friend in a grand match, upon the issue of which he ventured no less than three thousand pounds. Indeed, he would not have risqued such a considerable sum, had not his own confidence been reinforced by the opinion and concurrence of his lordship, who hazarded an equal bett upon the same event. These two associates engaged themselves in the penalty of six thousand pounds, to run one chaise and four against another, three times round the course; and our adventurer had the satisfaction of seeing his antagonists distanced in the first and second heat; but all of a sudden, one of the horses of his machine was knocked up, by which accident, the victory was ravished almost from his very grasp, and he was obliged to endure the damage and the scorn.

He was deeply affected with this misfortune, which he imputed to his own extravagance and temerity, but discovered no external signs of affliction, because his illustrious partner bore his loss with the most philosophic resignation, consoling himself, as well as Pickle, with the hope of making it up, on some other occasion. Nevertheless, our young gentleman could not help admiring and even envying his equanimity, not knowing that his lordship had managed matters so as to be a gainer by the misfortune; which to retrieve, Peregrine purchased several horses, at the recommendation of his friend; and instead of returning to London, made a tour with him to all the celebrated races in England, at which, after several vicissitudes of fortune, he made shift, before the end of the season, to treble his loss.

But his hopes seemed to increase with his ill luck; and in the beginning of winter he came to town, fully persuaded that fortune must necessarily change, and that next season he should reap the happy fruits of his experience. In this confidence, he seemed to drown all ideas of prudence and œconomy; his former expence was mere parsimony, compared with that which he now incurred: he subscribed to the opera, and half a dozen concerts at different parts of the town; was a benefactor to several hospitals, purchased a collection of valuable pictures, took an house, and furnished it in a most magnificent taste, laid in a large stock of French wines, and gave extravagant entertainments to his quality-friends, who in return loaded him with compliment, and insisted upon his making use of their interest and good-will.

CHAPTER XCVII

He is taken into the Protection of a Great Man ;
sets up for Member of Parliament ; is disappointed in
his Expectation, and finds himself egregiously outwitted

AMONG these professed patrons, the greatest part of whom Peregrine saw thro', there was one great personage, who seemed to support with dignity the sphere in which fortune had placed him. His behaviour to Pickle was not a series of grinning complaisance, in a flat repetition of general expressions of friendship and regard. He demeaned himself with a seemingly honest reserve, in point of profession; his advances to Peregrine appeared to be the result of deliberation and experiment; he chid the young gentleman for his extravagance with the authority of a parent, and the sincerity of a fast friend; and having, by gradual inquiries, made himself acquainted with the state of his private affairs, condemned his conduct with an air of candour and concern. He represented to him the folly and dangerous consequences of the profligate life in which he had plunged himself, counselled him with great warmth to sell off his race-horses, which would otherwise insensibly eat him up; to retrench all superfluous expence, which would only serve to expose him to the ridicule and ingratitude of those who were benefited by it; to lay out his money upon secure mortgages, at good interest; and carry into execution his former design of standing candidate for a borough, at the ensuing election for a new parliament; in which case, this nobleman promised to assist him with his influence and advice; assuring him, that if he could once procure a seat in the house, he might look upon his fortune as already made.

Our adventurer perceived the wisdom and sanity of this advice, for which he made his acknowledgments to his generous monitor, protesting that he would adhere to it in every particular, and immediately set about a reformation. He accordingly took cognizance of his most minute affairs, and after an exact scrutiny, gave his patron to understand, that, exclusive of his furniture, his fortune was reduced to fourteen thousand three hundred and thirty pounds, in Bank and South-Sea annuities, over and above the garison and its appendages, which he reckoned at sixty pounds a year. He therefore desired, that as his lordship had been so kind as to favour him with his friendship and advice, he would extend his generosity still farther, by putting him in a way of making the most advantage of his money. My lord said, that for his own part he did not chuse to meddle in money-matters; that he would find abundance of people ready to borrow it upon land-security; but that he ought to be extremely cautious in a transaction of such consequence; promising at the same time, to employ his own steward, in seeking out a mortgager to whom it might be safely lent.

This agent was accordingly set at work, and for a few days made a fruitless inquiry; so that the young gentleman was obliged to have recourse to his own intelligence, by which he got notice of several people of reputed credit, who offered him mortgages for the whole sum; but when he made a report of the particulars to his noble friend, his lordship started such doubts and objections relating to each, that he was deterred from entering into any engagements with the proposers; congratulating himself, in the mean time, on his good fortune, in being favoured with the advice and direction of such a sage counsellor. Nevertheless, he began to be impatient, after having unsuccessfully consulted all the money-brokers and conveyancers about town, and resolved to try the expedient of a public advertisement. But he was persuaded by my lord to postpone that experiment, until every other method should have failed, because it would attract the attention of all the pettifoggers in London, who (though they might not be able to overreach) would infallibly harrass and teize him out of all tranquillity.

It was on the back of this conversation that Peregrine, chancing to meet the steward near his lord's house, stopped him in the street, to give him an account of his bad luck; at which the other expressed some concern, and rubbing his chin with his hand, in a musing posture, told Pickle, there was a thought just come into his head, pointing out one way of doing his business effectually. The youth, upon this intimation, begg'd he would accompany him to the next coffee-house, in which having chosen a private situation, this grave manager gave him to understand, that a part of my lord's estate was mortgaged, in consequence of a debt contracted by his grand-father, for provision to the younger children of the family; and that the equity of redemption would be foreclosed in a few months, unless the burthen could be discharged. 'My lord (said he) has always lived in a splendid manner, and notwithstanding his ample fortune, together with the profits accruing from the posts he enjoys, he saves so little money, that, upon this occasion, I know he will be obliged to borrow ten thousand pounds, to make up the sum that is requisite to redeem the mortgage. Now, certain I am, that when his design comes to be known, he will be sollicited on all hands, by people desirous of lending money upon such undoubted security; and 'tis odds but he has already promised the preference to some particular acquaintance. However, as I know he has your interest very much at heart, I will (if you please) sound his lordship upon the subject, and in a day or two give you notice of my success.'

Peregrine, ravished with the prospect of settling this affair so much to his satisfaction, thanked the steward for his friendly hint and undertaking, which he assured him should be acknowledged by a more solid proof of his gratitude, provided the business could be brought to bear; and next day, he was visited by this kind manager, with the happy news of his lordship's having consented to borrow ten thousand pounds of his stock, upon mortgage, at the interest of five *per Cent*. This information he received as an instance of the singular esteem of his noble patron; and the papers being immediately drawn and executed, the money was deposited in the hands of the mortgager, who, in the hearing of the lender, laid strong injunctions on his steward to pay the interest punctually at quarter-day.

The best part of our hero's fortune being thus happily deposited, and the agent gratified with a present of fifty pieces, he began to put his retrenching scheme in execution; all his servants (Pipes excepted) were discharged, his chariot and running-horses dis-posed of, his house-keeping broke up, and his furniture sold by auction: nay, the heat of his disposition was as remarkable in this, as in any other transaction of his life; for every step of his saving project was taken with such eagerness, and even precipitation, that most of his companions thought he was either ruined or mad. But he answered all their expostulations with a string of prudent apophthegms, such as, 'The shortest follies are the best;' 'Better to retrench upon conviction than compulsion;' and divers other wise maxims, seemingly the result of experience and philosophic reflection. To such a degree of enthusiasm did his present œconomy prevail, that he was actually seized with the desire of amassing; and as he every day received proposals, from those brokers whom he had employed, about the disposal of his cash, he at length ventured fifteen hundred pounds upon bottomry, being tempted by the excessive premium.

But it must be observed, for the honour of our adventurer, that this reformation did not at all interfere with the good qualities of his heart: he was still as friendly and benevolent as ever, tho' his liberality was more subjected to the restraint of reason; and he might have justly pleaded, in vindication of his generosity, that he retrenched the superfluities in his own way of living, in order to preserve the power of assisting his fellow-creatures in distress. Numberless were the objects to which he extended his charity in private. Indeed, he exerted this virtue in secret, not only on account of avoiding the charge of ostentation, but also because he was ashamed of being detected in such an awkward unfashionable practice, by the censorious observers of this humane generation. In this particular, he seemed to confound the ideas of virtue and vice; for he did good as other people do evil, that is, by stealth; and was so capricious in point of behaviour, that frequently, in public, he wagged his tongue in satirical animadversions upon that poverty, which his hand had, in private relieved. Yet, far from shunning the acquaintance, or discouraging the solicitation of those who, he thought, wanted his assistance, he was always accessible, open, and complacent to them, even when the haughtiness of his temper kept his superiors at a distance; and often saved a modest man the anguish and confusion of declaring himself, by penetrating into his necessity, and anticipating his request, in a frank offer of his purse and friendship.

Not that he practised this beneficence to all the needy of his acquaintance, without distinction; there is always a set of idle profligate fellows, who having squandered away their own fortunes, and conquered all sense of honour and shame, maintain themselves by borrowing from those who have not yet finished the same career, and want resolution to resist their importunate demands. To these he was always inflexible; though he could not absolutely detach himself from their company, because, by dint of effrontery, and such of their original connexions as they have been able to retain, they find admission to all places of fashionable resort.

Several insuccessful attacks had been made upon his pocket, by beggars of this class, one of the most artful of whom, having one day joined him in the Mall, and made the usual observation on the weather, damned the fogs of London, and began a dissertation on the difference of air, preferring that of the county in which he was born, to any climate under the sun. 'Was you ever in Gloucestershire?' (said he to Peregrine) who replying in the negative, he thus went on: 'I have got a house there, where I should be glad to see you. Let us go down together, during the Easter-holidays; I can promise you good country-fare and wholesome exercise; for I have every thing within myself, and as good a pack of fox-hounds as any in the three kingdoms. I shan't pretend to expatiate upon the elegance of the house, which to be sure is an old building; and these, you know, are generally cold, and not very convenient. But, curse the house! the dirty acres about it are the thing; and a damn'd fine parcel they are, to be sure. If my old grandmother was dead—she can't live another season, for she's turned of fourscore, and quite wore out: nay, as for that matter, I believe I have got a letter in my pocket, giving an account of her being despaired of by the doctors. Let me see—No, d—n it, I left it at home, in the pocket of another coat.'

Pickle, who from the beginning of this harangue, saw its tendency, seemed to yield the most serious attention to what he said; breaking in upon it, every now and then, with the interjections, Hum! Ha! The deuce! and several civil questions, from which the other conceived happy omens of success; till perceiving they had advanced as far as the passage into St. James's, the mischievous youth interrupted him all at once, saying, 'I see you are for the end of the walk; this is my way.' With these words he took his leave of the saunterer, who would have delayed his retreat, by calling to him aloud, that he had not yet described the situation of his castle. But Peregrine, without stopping, answered in the same tone, 'Another time will do as well;' and in a moment disappeared, leaving the projector very much mortified with his disappointment; for his intention was to close the description, with a demand of twenty pieces, to be repaid out of the first remittance he should receive from his estate.

It would have been well for our hero, had he always acted with the same circumspection: but he had his unguarded moments, in which he fell a prey to the unsuspecting integrity of his own heart.

There was a person among the number of his acquaintances, whose conversation he particularly relished, because it was frank, agreeable, and fraught with many sensible observations upon the craft and treachery of mankind. This gentleman had made shift to discuss a very genteel fortune, though it was spent with taste and reputation, and now was reduced to his shifts for the maintenance of his family, which consisted of a wife and child. Not that he was destitute of the necessaries of life, being comfortably supplied by the bounty of his friends: but this was a provision not at all suited to his inclination; and he had endeavoured, by divers unsuccessful schemes, to retrieve his former independency.

Peregrine happened one evening to be sitting alone in a coffeehouse, where he over-heard a conversation between this schemer and another gentleman, touching an affair that engaged his attention. The stranger had been left trustee for fifteen hundred pounds bequeathed to the other's daughter by an aunt, and was strongly solicited to pay the money to the child's father, who assured him, he had then an opportunity to lay it out in such a manner, as would greatly conduce to the advantage of his family. The trustee reminded him of the nature of his charge, which made him accountable for the money, until the child should have attained the age of eighteen; but at the same time gave him to understand, that if he could procure such security as would indemnify him from the consequences, he would forthwith pay the legacy into his hands. To this proposal the father replied, that it was not to be supposed he would risque the fortune of his only child, upon any idle or precarious issue; and therefore he thought it reasonable, that he should have the use of it in the mean time; and that, as to security, he was loth to trouble any of his friends about an affair which might be compromised without their interposition; observing, that he would not look upon his condescension as a favour, if obtained by a security, on which he could borrow the same sum from any usurer in town.

After much importunity on one side, and evasion on the other, the money'd gentleman told him, that though he would not surrender the sum deposited in his hands, for the use of his daughter, he would lend him what he should have occasion for, in the mean time; and if, upon her being of age, he should be able to obtain her concurrence, the money should be placed to her account; provided he could find any person of credit, who would join with him in a bond, for the assurance of the lender. This proviso was an obstruction which the other would not have been able to surmount, without great difficulty, had not his cause been espoused by our hero, who thought it was pity a man of honour and understanding should suffer in his principal concerns, on such a paultry consideration. He therefore, presuming on his acquaintance, interposed in the conversation as a friend, who interested himself in the affair; and being fully informed of the particulars, offered himself as a security for the lender.

This gentleman being a stranger to Peregrine, was next day made acquainted with his funds; and, without farther scruple, accommodated his friend with one thousand pounds, for which he took their bond, payable in six months, though he protested that the money should never be demanded, until the infant should be of age, unless some accident should happen which he could not then foresee. Pickle believed this declaration sincere, because he could have no interest in dissembling: but what he chiefly depended upon, for his own security, was the integrity and confidence of the borrower, who assured him, that happen what will, he should be able to stand between him and all danger; the nature of his plan being such, as would infallibly treble the sum in a very few months.

In a little time after this transaction, writs being issued out for electing a new parliament, our adventurer, by the advice of his patron, went into the country, in order to canvass for a borough, and lined his pockets with a competent share of bank-notes for the occasion. But, in this project, he unfortunately happened to interfere with the interest of a great family in the opposition, who, for a long series of years, had made members for that place; and were now so much offended at the intrusion of our young gentleman, that they threatened to spend ten thousand pounds in frustrating his design. This menace was no other than an incitement to Peregrine, who confided so much in his own influence and address, that he verily believed he should be able to baffle his grace, even in his own territories, and by that victory establish his reputation and interest with the minister, who, through the recommendation of his noble friend, countenanced his cause, and would have been very well pleased to see one of his greatest enemies suffer such a disgraceful overthrow, which would have, moreover, in a great measure shaken his credit with his faction.

Our hero, intoxicated with the ideas of pride and ambition, put all his talents to the test, in the execution of this project. He spared no expence in treating the electors; but finding himself rivalled, in this respect, by his competitor, who was powerfully supported, he had recourse to those qualifications in which he thought himself

superior. He made balls for the ladies, visited the matrons of the
corporation, adapted himself to their various humours with surprising facility, drank with those who loved a cherishing cup in
private, made love to the amorous, prayed with the religious,
gossiped with those who delighted in scandal, and with great
sagacity contrived agreeable presents to them all. This was the
most effectual method of engaging such electors as were under the
influence of their wives; and as for the rest, he assailed them in
their own way, setting whole hogsheads of beer and wine abroach,
for the benefit of all comers; and into those sordid hearts that liquor
would not open, he found means to convey himself by the help of
a golden key.

While he thus exerted himself, his antagonist was not idle; his
age and infirmities would not permit him to enter personally into
their parties; but his steward and adherents bestirred themselves
with great industry and perseverance; and the market for votes ran
so high, that Pickle's ready money was exhausted before the day of
election; and he was obliged to write to his patron an account of the
dilemma to which he was reduced; intreating him to take such
speedy measures, as would enable him to finish the business which
he had so happily begun.

This nobleman communicated the circumstances of the case
to the minister, and in a day or two our candidate found credit with
the receiver-general of the county, who lent him twelve hundred
pounds on his personal note, payable on demand. By means of this
new supply, he managed matters so successfully, that an evident
majority of votes was secured in his interest; and nothing could
have obstructed his election, had not the noble peer who set up his
competitor, in order to avoid the shame and mortification of being
foiled in his own borough, offered to compromise the affair with
his honour, by giving up two members in another place, provided
the opposition should cease in his own corporation. This proposal
was greedily embraced; and, on the eve of election, Peregrine
received an intimation from his patron, desiring him to quit his
pretensions, on pain of his and the minister's displeasure; and
promising that he should be elected for another place.

No other disappointment in life could have given him such
chagrin as he felt at the receit of this tantalizing order, by which the
cup of success was snatched from his lip, and all the vanity of his
ambitious hope humbled in the dust. He curs'd the whole chain
of his court connexions, inveighed with great animosity against the
rascally scheme of politicks, to which he was sacrificed; and in

conclusion swore he would not give up the fruits of his own address for the pleasure of any minister upon earth. This laudable resolution, however, was rendered ineffectual by his friend the receiver-general, who was bearer of the message, and (after having, in vain, endeavoured to persuade him to submission) fairly arrested him upon the spot for the money he had advanced; this expedient being performed by virtue of a writ which he had been advised to take out, in case the young man should prove refractory.

The reader, who, by this time, must be pretty well acquainted with the disposition of our adventurer, may easily conceive how he relished this imprisonment. At first, all the faculties of his soul were swallowed up in astonishment and indignation; and some minutes elapsed before his nerves would obey the impulse of his rage, which manifested itself in such an application to the temples of the plaintiff, as laid him sprawling on the floor. This assault, which was committed in a tavern whither he had been purposely decoyed, attracted the regard of the bailiff and his followers, who, to the number of four, rushed upon him at once, in order to over-power him; but his wrath inspired him with such additional strength and agility, that he disengaged himself from them in a trice, and seizing a poker, which was the first weapon that pre-sented itself to his hand, exercised it upon their skulls with incredible dexterity and execution. The officer himself, who had been the first that presumed to lay violent hands upon him, felt the first effects of his fury, in a blow upon the jaws, in consequence of which he lost three of his teeth, and fell athwart the body of the receiver, with which he form'd the figure of St. Andrew's cross: one of his myrmidons seeing the fate of his chief, would not venture to attack the victor in front, but wheeling to one side, made an attempt upon him in flank, and was received obliquely by our hero's left hand and foot, so masterly disposed to the right side of his leg, and the left side of his neck, that he bolted head foremost into the chimney, where his chin was encountered by the grate, which, in a moment, seared him to the bone. The rest of the detachment did not think proper to maintain the dispute, but evacuating the room with great expedition, locked the door on the outside, and bellowed aloud to the receiver's servants, beseeching them to come to the assistance of their master, who was in danger of his life.

Mean while, this gentleman having recollected himself, de-manded a parley; which having with difficulty obtained of our incensed candidate, in consequence of the most submissive application, he complained grievously of the young gentleman's intemperance and heat of disposition, and very calmly represented the danger of his rashness and indiscretion. He told him, that nothing could be more outrageous or idle, than the resistance he had made against the laws of his country, because he would find it impracticable to withstand the whole executive power of the county, which he could easily raise to apprehend and secure him; that over and above the disgrace that would accrue to him from this imprudent conduct, he would knock his own interest on the head, by disobliging his friends in the administration, who were, to his knowledge, at present very well disposed to do him service; that, for his own part, what he had done was by the express order of his superiors, and not out of any desire of distressing him; and that, far from being his enemy, notwithstanding the shocking insult he had sustained, he was ready to withdraw the writ, provided he would listen to any reasonable terms of accommodation.

Peregrine, who was not more prone to anger than open to conviction, being appeased by his condescension, moved by his arguments, and chid by his own reflection for what he had done in the precipitation of his wrath, began to give ear to his remonstrances; and the bailiffs being ordered to withdraw, they entered into a conference, the result of which was our adventurer's immediate departure for London: so that next day his competitor was unanimously chosen, because no body appeared to oppose his election.

The discontented Pickle, on his arrival in town, went directly to the house of his patron, to whom, in the anguish of his disappointment, he bitterly complained of the treatment he had received, by which, besides the disgrace of his overthrow, he was no less than two thousand pounds out of pocket, exclusive of the debt for which he stood engaged to the receiver. His lordship, who was prepared for this expostulation, on his knowledge of the young man's impetuous temper, answered all the articles of his charge with great deliberation, giving him to understand the motives that induced the minister to quit his interest in that borough; and soothing him with assurances that his loss would be amply rewarded by his honour, to whom he was next day introduced by this nobleman, in the warmest stile of recommendation. The minister, who was a pattern of complaisance, received him with the most engaging affability; thanked him very kindly for his endeavours to support and strengthen the interest of the administration; and faithfully promised to lay hold on the first opportunity to express the sense he had of his zeal and attachment; desiring to see him often at his levee, that in the multiplicity of business he might not be in danger of forgetting his services and desert.

CHAPTER XCVIII

Peregrine commences Minister's Dependent ;
meets by Accident with Mrs. Gauntlet ;
and descends gradually, in the Condition of Life

THIS reception, favourable as it was, did not please Peregrine, who had too much discernment to be cajoled with general promises, at a time when he thought himself intitled to the most particular assurance. He accordingly signified his disgust to his introductor, giving him to understand, that he had laid his account with being chosen representative of one of those boroughs for which he had been sacrificed. His lordship agreed to the reasonableness of his expectation, observing, however, that he could not suppose the minister would enter upon business with him, on his first visit; and that it would be time enough, at his next audience, to communicate his demand.

Notwithstanding this remonstrance, our hero continued to indulge his suspicion and chagrin, and even made a point of it with his patron, that his lordship should next day make application in his behalf, lest the two seats should be filled up, on pretence of his inclination's being unknown. Thus importuned, my lord went to his principal, and returned with an answer, importing that his honour was extremely sorry that Mr. Pickle had not signified his request before the boroughs in question were promised to two gentlemen whom he could not now disappoint, with any regard to his own credit or interest; but as several persons who would be chosen were, to his certain knowledge, very aged and infirm, he did not doubt that there would be plenty of vacant seats in a very short time; and then the young gentleman might depend upon his friendship.

Peregrine was so much irritated at this intimation, that in the first transports of his anger he forgot the respect he owed to his friend, and in his presence inveighed against the minister, as a person devoid of gratitude and candour, protesting, that if ever an opportunity should offer itself, he would spend the whole remains of his fortune in opposing his measures. The nobleman having given him time to exhaust the impetuosity of his passion, rebuked him very calmly for his disrespectful expressions, which were equally injurious and indiscreet; assured him that his project of revenge, if ever put in execution, would redound to his own prejudice and confusion; and advised him to cultivate and improve, with patience and assiduity, the footing he had already obtained in the minister's good graces.

Our hero convinced of the truth, tho' not satisfied with the occasion of his admonitions, took his leave in a fit of sullen discontent, and began to ruminate upon the shattered posture of his affairs. All that now remained of the ample fortune he had inherited, was the sum he had deposited in his lordship's hands, together with fifteen hundred pounds he had ventured on bottomry, and the garison, which he had left for the use and accommodation of the lieutenant; and on the per contra side of his account he was debtor for the supply he had received from the receiver-general, and the money for which he was bound in behalf of his friend; so that he found himself, for the first time of his life, very much embarassed in his circumstances: for, of the first half year's interest of his ten thousand, which was punctually paid, he had but fourscore pounds in bank, without any prospect of a farther supply, till the other term, which was at the distance of four long months. He seriously reflected upon the uncertainty of human affairs; the ship with his fifteen hundred pounds might be lost, the gentleman for whom he was security, might miscarry in this, as well as in his former projects, and the minister might one day, through policy or displeasure, expose him to the mercy of his dependant, who was in possession of his notes.

These suggestions did not at all contribute to the ease of our adventurer's mind, already ruffled by his disappointment. He cursed his own folly and extravagance, by which he was reduced to such an uncomfortable situation. He compared his own conduct with that of some young gentlemen of his acquaintance, who, while he was squandering away the best part of his inheritance, had improved their fortunes, strengthened their interest, and increased their reputation. He was abandoned by his gayety and good humour, his countenance gradually contracted itself into a representation of severity and care, he dropped all his amusements and the companions of his pleasure, and turned his whole attention to the minister, at whose levee he never failed to appear.

While he thus laboured in the wheel of dependance, with all that mortification which a youth of his pride and sensibility may be supposed to feel from such a disagreeable necessity, he one day heard himself called by name, as he crossed the Park; and turning, perceived the wife of captain Gauntlet, with another lady. He no sooner recognized the kind Sophy, than he accosted her with his wonted civility of friendship; but his former sprightly air was metamorphosed into such an austerity, or rather dejection of feature, that she could scarce believe her own eyes; and in her astonishment 'Is it possible (said she) that the gay Mr. Pickle should be so much altered in such a short space of time!' He made no other reply to this exclamation, but by a languid smile; and asked how long she had been in town; observing, that he would have paid his compliments to her at her own lodgings, had he been favoured with the least intimation of her arrival. After having thanked him for his politeness, she told him, it was not owing to any abatement of her friendship and esteem for him, that she had omitted to give him that notice; but his abrupt departure from Windsor, and the manner in which he quitted Mr. Gauntlet, had given her just grounds to believe, that they had incurred his displeasure; which suspicion was reinforced by his long silence and neglect from that period, to the present time; when she observed, it was still farther confirmed, by his forbearing to inquire for Emilia and her brother: 'Judge then, (said she) if I had any reason to believe that you would be pleased to hear that I was in town. However, I will not detain you at present, because you seem to be engaged about some particular business; but, if you will favour me with your company at breakfast to-morrow, I shall be much pleased, and honoured to boot, by the visit.' So saying, she gave him a direction to her lodgings; and he took his leave, with a faithful promise of seeing her at the appointed time.

He was very much affected with this advance of Sophy, which he considered as an instance of her uncommon sweetness of temper; he felt strange longings of returning friendship towards Godfrey; and the remembrance of Emilia melted his heart, already softened with grief and mortification. Next day, he did not neglect his engagement, and had the pleasure of enjoying a long conversation with this sensible young lady, who gave him to understand, that her husband was with his regiment; and presented to him a fine boy, the first fruits of their love, whom they had christened by the name of Peregrine, in memory of the friendship which had subsisted between Godfrey and our youth.

This proof of their regard, notwithstanding the interruption in their correspondence, made a deep impression upon the mind of our adventurer, who having made the warmest acknowledgements for this undeserved mark of respect, took the child in his arms, and almost devoured him with kisses, protesting before God, that he should always consider him with the tenderness of a parent. This was the highest compliment he could pay to the gentle Sophy, who again kindly chid him for his disdainful and precipitate retreat, immediately after her marriage; and expressed an earnest desire of seeing him and the captain reconciled. He assured her, nothing could give him greater satisfaction than such an event, to which he would contribute all that lay in his power, though he could not help looking upon himself as injured by captain Gauntlet's behaviour, which denoted a suspicion of his honour, as well as contempt for his understanding. The lady undertook for the concession of her husband, who (she told him) had been extremely sorry for his own heat, after Mr. Pickle's departure, and would have followed him to the garison, in order to solicit his forgiveness, had not he been restrained by certain punctilios, occasioned by some acrimonious expressions that dropt from Peregrine at the inn.

After having cleared up this misunderstanding, she proceeded to give an account of Emilia, whose behaviour, at that juncture, plainly indicated a continuance of affection for her first lover; and desired, that he would give her full powers to bring that matter also to an accommodation: 'For I am not more certain of my own existence (said she) than that you are still in possession of my sister's heart.' At this declaration, the tear started in his eye, while he shook his head, and declined her good offices, wishing that the young lady might be much more happy than ever he should be able to make her.

Mrs. Gauntlet, confounded at these expressions, and moved by the despondent manner in which they were delivered, begg'd to know if any new obstacle was raised, by some late change in his sentiments or situation: and he, in order to avoid a painful explanation, told her, that he had long despaired of being able to vanquish Emilia's resentment, and for that reason quitted the pursuit, which he would never renew, howsoever his heart might suffer by that resolution; though he took heaven to witness, that his love, esteem, and admiration of her were not in the least impaired: but the true motive of his laying aside this design, was the consciousness of his decayed fortune, which, by adding to the sensibility of his pride, increased the horror of another repulse. She expressed her concern for this determination, both on his own account, and in behalf of Emilia, whose happiness (in her opinion) depended upon his constancy and affection; and she would have questioned him more minutely about the state of his affairs, had not he discouraged the inquiry, by seeking to introduce another subject of conversation.

After mutual protestations of friendship and regard, he promised to visit her often, during her residence in town; and took his leave in a strange perplexity of mind, occasioned by the images of love, intruding upon the remonstrances of carking care. He had some time ago forsaken those extravagant companions with whom he had rioted in the heyday of his fortune, and began to consort with a graver and more sober species of acquaintance: but he now found himself disabled from cultivating the society of these also, who were men of ample estates and liberal dispositions; in consequence of which, their parties were too expensive for the consumptive state of his finances; so that he was obliged to descend another degree, and mingle with a set of old batchelors and younger brothers, who subsisted on slender annuities, or what is called a bare competency in the public funds. This association was composed of second-hand politicians and minor critics, who in the forenoon saunter in the Mall, or lounge at shews of pictures, appear in the drawing-room once or twice a week, dine at an ordinary, decide disputes in a coffee-house, with an air of superior intelligence, frequent the pit of the play-house, and once in a month spend an evening with some noted actor, whose remarkable sayings they repeat for the entertainment of their ordinary friends.

After all, he found something comfortable enough in the company of these gentlemen, who never interested his passions to any violence of transport, nor teazed him with impertinent curiosity about his private affairs: for though many of them had maintained a very long, close, and friendly correspondence with each other, they never dreamt of inquiring into particular concerns; and if one of the two who were most intimately connected, had been asked how the other made shift to live, he would have answered, with great truth, 'Really, that is more than I know.' Notwithstanding this phlegmatic indifference, which is of the true English production, they were all inoffensive, good-natured people, who loved a joke and a song, delighted in telling a merry story, and prided themselves in the art of catering, especially in the articles of fresh venison and wild fowl.

Our young gentleman was not received among them on the footing of a common member, who makes interest for his admission; he was courted as a person of superior genius and importance, and his compliance looked upon as an honour to their society. This their idea of his preheminence was supported by his conversation, which, while it was more liberal and learned than that to which they had been accustomed, was tinctured with an assuming air, so agreeably diffused, that instead of producing aversion, it commanded respect. They not only appealed to him, in all doubts relating to foreign parts, to which one and all of them were strangers, but also consulted his knowledge in history and divinity, which were frequently the topics of their debates; and in poetry of all kinds, he decided with such magisterial authority, as even weighed against the opinions of the players themselves. The variety of characters he had seen and observed, and the high spheres of life in which he had so lately moved, furnished him with a thousand entertaining anecdotes; and when he became a little familiarized to his disappointments, so that his natural vivacity began to revive, he flashed among them in such a number of bright sallies, as struck them with admiration, and constituted himself a classic in wit: insomuch that they began to retail his remnants, and even invited some particular friends to come and hear him hold forth. One of the players, who had for many years strutted about the taverns in the neighbourhood of Covent-garden, as the Grand Turk of wit and humour, began to find his admirers melt away; and a certain petulant physician, who had shone at almost all the Port-clubs in that end of the town, was actually obliged to import his talents into the city, where he has now happily taken root.

Nor was this success to be wondered at, if we consider that, over and above his natural genius and education, our adventurer still had the opportunity of knowing every thing which happened among the great, by means of his friend Cadwallader, with whom he still maintained his former intimacy, though it was now checquered with many occasional tifts, owing to the sarcastic remonstrances of the Misanthrope, who disapproved of those schemes which miscarried with Peregrine, and now took unseasonable methods of valuing himself upon his own foresight: nay, he was between whiles like a raven croaking presages of more ill luck from the deceit of the minister, the dissimulation of his patron, the folly of the projector for whom he was bound, the uncertainty of the seas, and the villainy of those with whom he had entrusted his cash: for Crabtree saw and considered every thing through a perspective of spleen, that always reflected the worst side of human nature.

For these reasons, our young gentleman began to be disgusted, at certain intervals, with the character of this old man, whom he now thought a morose cynic, not so much incensed against the follies and vices of mankind, as delighted with the distress of his fellow-creatures. Thus he put the most unfavourable construction on the principles of his friend, because he found himself justly fallen under the lash of his animadversion. This self-accusation very often dissolves the closest friendship: a man, conscious of his own indiscretion, is implacably offended at the rectitude of his companion's conduct, which he considers as an insult upon his failings, never to be forgiven, even though he has not tasted the bitterness of reproof, which no sinner can commodiously digest. The friendship, therefore, subsisting between Crabtree and Pickle, had of late suffered several symptomatic shocks that seemed to prognosticate a total dissolution; a great deal of smart dialogue had passed in their private conversations, and the senior began to repent of having placed his confidence in such an imprudent, headstrong, ungovernable youth.

It was in such paroxysms of displeasure, that he prophesied misfortune to Peregrine, and even told him one morning, that he had dream'd of the shipwreck of the two East-Indiamen on board of which he had hazarded his money. But this was no other than a false vision; for, in a few weeks, one of them arrived at her moorings in the river, and he received a thousand, in lieu of eight hundred pounds which he had lent upon bond to one of the mates. At the same time he was informed, that the other ship, in which he was concerned, had, in all probability, lost her passage for the season, by being unable to weather the Cape. He was not at all concerned at that piece of news, knowing, that the longer he should lie out of his money, he would have the more interest to receive; and finding his present difficulties removed by this supply, his heart began to dilate, and his countenance to resume its former alacrity.

This state of exultation, however, was soon interrupted by a small accident, which he could not foresee: he was visited one morning by the person who had lent his friend a thousand pounds on his security, and given to understand, that the borrower had absconded, in consequence of a disappointment, by which he had lost the whole sum, and all hopes of retrieving it; so that our hero was now liable for the debt, which he besought him to discharge according to the bond, that he (the lender) might not suffer by his humanity. It may be easily conceived, that Peregrine did not receive this intelligence in cold blood. He cursed his own imprudence in contracting such engagements with an adventurer, whom he did not sufficiently know, exclaimed against the treachery of the projector; and having for some time indulged his resentment in threats and imprecations, inquired into the nature of the scheme which had miscarried.

The lender, who had informed himself of the whole affair,

gratified his curiosity in this particular, by telling him that the fugitive had been cajoled by a certain knight of the post, who undertook to manage the thousand pounds in such a manner, as would, in a very little time, make him perfectly independant; and thus he delineated the plan: 'One half of the sum (said he) shall be laid out in jewels, which I will pawn to certain persons of credit and fortune, who lend money upon such pledges at an exorbitant interest. The other shall be kept for relieving them, so that they may be again deposited with a second set of those honourable usurers; and when they shall have been circulated in this manner through a variety of hands, we will extort money from each of the pawn-brokers, by threatening them with a public prosecution, for exacting illegal interest; and I know that they will bleed freely, rather than be exposed to the infamy attending such an accusation.' The scheme was feasible, and though not very honourable, made such an impression upon the needy borrower, that he assented to the proposal; and, by our hero's credit, the money was raised. The jewels were accordingly purchased, pawned, relieved, and re-pledged by the agent, who undertook to manage the whole affair; and so judiciously was the project executed, that he could have easily proved each lender guilty of the charge. Having thus far successfully transacted the business, this faithful agent visited them severally on his own account, to give them intimation, that his employer intended to sue them on the statute of usury; upon which, every one, for himself, bribed the informer to withdraw his evidence, by which alone he could be convicted; and having received these gratifications, he had thought proper to retreat into France, with the whole booty, including the original thousand that put them in motion. In consequence of this decampment, the borrower had withdrawn himself; so that the lender was obliged to have recourse to his security.

This was a very mortifying account to our young gentleman, who in vain reminded the narrator of his promise, importing, that he would not demand the money, until he should be called to an account by his ward; and observed, that long before that period, the fugitive might appear and discharge the debt. But the other was deaf to these remonstrances; alledging, that his promise was provisional, on the supposition that the borrower would deal candidly and fairly; that he had forfeited all title to his friendship and trust, by the scandalous scheme in which he had embarked; and that his treacherous flight from his security was no proof of his honesty and intended return; but on the contrary, a warning, by which he (the lender) was taught to take care of himself. He therefore insisted upon his being indemnified immediately, on pain of letting the law take its course; and Peregrine was actually obliged to part with the whole sum he had so lately received. But this payment was not made without extreme reluctance, indignation, and denunciation of eternal war against the absconder, and the rigid creditor, betwixt whom he suspected some collusion.

CHAPTER XCIX

Cadwallader acts the Part of a Comforter to his Friend;
and is in his turn consoled by Peregrine,
who begins to find himself a most egregious Dupe

THIS new misfortune, which he justly charged to the account of his own folly, recalled his chagrin; and though he endeavoured with all his might to conceal the affair from the knowledge of Cadwallader, that prying observer perceived his countenance overcast; and the projector's sudden disappearance alarming his suspicion, he managed his inquiries with so much art, that in a few days he made himself acquainted with every particular of the transaction, and resolved to gratify his spleen at the expence of the impatient dupe. With this view, he took an opportunity to accost him with a very serious air, saying, a friend of his had immediate occasion for a thousand pounds, and as Peregrine had the exact sum lying by him, he would take it as a great favour, if he would part with it for a few months on undoubted security. Had Pickle known the true motive of this demand, he would, in all likelihood, have made a very disagreeable answer; but Crabtree had wrapt himself up so securely in the dissimulation of his features, that the youth could not possibly penetrate into his intention; and in the most galling suspence replied, that the money was otherwise engaged. The Misanthrope, not contented with this irritation, assumed the prerogative of a friend, and questioned him so minutely about the disposal of the cash, that after numberless evasions, which cost him a world of torture to invent, he could contain his vexation no longer, but exclaimed in a rage, 'Damn your impertinence! 'tis gone to the devil, and that's enough!' 'Thereafter as it may be (said the tormentor, with a most provoking indifference of aspect) I should be glad to know upon what footing; for I suppose you have some expectation of advantage from that quarter.' ' 'Sdeath! Sir (cried the impatient youth) if I had any expectation from hell, I would make interest with you, for I believe from my soul, you are one of its most favoured ministers upon earth.' With these words, he flung out of the room, leaving Cadwallader very well satisfied with the chastisement he had bestowed.

Peregrine having cooled himself with a solitary walk in the park, during which the violence of his choler gradually evaporated, and his reflection was called to a serious deliberation upon the posture of his affairs; he resolved to redouble his diligence and importunity with his patron and the minister, in order to obtain some sine-cure, which would indemnify him for the damage he had sustained on their account. He accordingly went to his lordship, and signified his demand, after having told him, that he had suffered several fresh losses, which rendered an immediate provision of that sort necessary to his credit and subsistence.

His noble friend commended him for the regard he manifested for his own interest, which he considered as a proof of his being at last detached from the careless inadvertency of youth; he approved of his demand, which, he assured him, should be faithfully transmitted to the minister, and backed with all his influence; and encouraged his hope, by observing, that some profitable places were at that time vacant, and, so far as he knew, unengaged.

This conversation helped to restore the tranquillity of Pickle's breast, tho' he still harboured resentment against Cadwallader, on account of the last insult; and on the instant he formed a plan of revenge. He knew the Misanthrope's remittances from his estate in the country, had been of late very scanty, in consequence of repairs and bankruptcies among his tenants: so that, in spite of all his frugality, he had been but barely able to maintain his credit, and even that was engaged on the strength of his running rent. Being therefore intimately acquainted with the particulars of his fortune, he wrote a letter to Crabtree, subscribed with the name of his principal farmer's wife, importing, that her husband being lately dead, and the greatest part of her cattle destroyed by the infectious distemper, she found herself utterly incapable of paying the rent which was due, or even of keeping the farm, unless he would, out of his great goodness, be pleased to give her some assistance, and allow her to sit free for a twelvemonth to come. This intimation he found means to convey by post from a market-town adjoining to the farm, directed in the usual stile to the cynic, who seeing it stamped with the known marks, could not possibly suspect any imposition.

Hackneyed as he was in the ways of life, and steeled with his boasted stoicism, this epistle threw him into such an agony of vexation, that a double proportion of sowering was visible in his aspect, when he was visited by the author, who having observed and followed the postman at a proper distance, introduced a conversation upon his own disappointments, in which, among other circumstances of his own ill-luck, he told him, that his patron's steward had desired to be excused from paying the last quarter of his interest precisely at the appointed term; for which reason, he should be utterly void of cash; and therefore requested, that Crabtree would accommodate him with an hundred pieces out of his next remittance from the country.

This demand galled and perplexed the old man to such a degree, that the muscles of his face assumed a contraction most peculiarly virulent, and exhibited the character of Diogenes with a most lively expression: he knew that a confession of his true situation would furnish Pickle with an opportunity to make reprisals upon him, with intolerable triumph; and that, by a downright refusal to supply his wants, he would for ever forfeit his friendship and esteem, and might provoke him to take ample vengeance for his sordid behaviour, by exposing him, in his native colours, to the resentment of those whom he had so long deceived. These considerations kept him some time in a most rancorous state of suspence, which Peregrine affected to misinterpret, by bidding him freely declare his suspicion, if he did not think it safe to comply with his request, and he would make shift elsewhere.

This seeming misconstruction increased the torture of the Misanthrope, who, with the utmost irritation of feature, 'Oons! (cried he) what villainy have you noted in my conduct, that you treat me like a rascally usurer?' Peregrine very gravely replied, that the question needed no answer; 'for (said he) had I considered you as an usurer, I would have come with a security under my arm; but, all evasion apart, will you stead me? will you pleasure me? shall I have the money?' 'Would it were in your belly, with a barrel of gunpowder! (exclaimed the enraged cynic) since I must be excruciated, read that plaguy paper!—'sblood! why didn't nature clap a pair of long ears and a tail upon me, that I might be a real ass, and champ thistles on some common, independent of my fellow-creatures? Would I were a worm, that I might creep into the earth, and thatch my habitation with a single straw; or rather a wasp or a viper, that I might make the rascally world feel my resentment: but why do I talk of rascality? folly, folly is the scourge of life! Give me a scoundrel (so he be a sensible one) and I will put him in my heart of hearts! but a fool is more mischievous than famine, pestilence and war. The idiotical hag that writes, or causes to be writ, this same letter, has ruined her family, and broke her husband's heart, by ignorance and mismanagement; and she imputes her calamity to providence with a vengeance; and so I am defrauded of three hundred pounds, the greatest part of which I owe to tradesmen whom I have promised to pay this very quarter. Pox upon her! I would she were an horned beast, that the distemper might lay hold on her. The beldame has the impudence too (after she has brought me into this dilemma) to solicit my assistance to stock the farm anew! Before God, I have a good mind to send her an halter, and perhaps I might purchase another for myself, but that I would not furnish food for laughter to knaves and coxcombs.'

Peregrine having perused the billet, and listened to this ejaculation, replied with great composure, that he was ashamed to see a man of his years and pretensions to philosophy, so ruffled by a trifle. 'What signify all the boasted hardships you have overcome (said he) and the shrewd observations you pretend to have made on human nature? Where is that stoical indifference you affirm you have attained, if such a paultry disappointment can disturb you in this manner? What is the loss of three hundred pounds, compared with the misfortunes which I myself have undergone within these two years? Yet you will take upon you to act the censor, and inveigh against the impatience and impetuosity of youth, as if you yourself had gained an absolute conquest over all the passions of the heart. You was so kind as to insult me t'other day in my affliction, by reproaching me with indiscretion and misconduct; suppose I were now to retort the imputation, and ask how a man of your profound sagacity could leave your fortune at the discretion of ignorant peasants? How could you be so blind as not to foresee the necessity of repairs, together with the danger of a bankruptcy, murrain, or thin crop? Why did not you convert your land into ready money, and (as you have no connexions in life) purchase an annuity, on which you might have lived at your ease, without any fear of the consequence? Can't you, from the whole budget of your philosophy, cull one apophthegm to console you in this trivial mischance?'

'Rot your rapidity! (said the cynic, half-choked with gall) if the cancer or the pox were in your throat, I should not be thus tormented with your tongue: and yet a magpye shall speak infinitely more to the purpose. Don't you know, Mr. Wiseacre, that my case does not fall within the province of philosophy? Had I been curtailed of all my members, racked by the gout and gravel, deprived of liberty, robbed of an only child, or visited with the death of a dear friend like you, philosophy might have contributed to my consolation; but will philosophy pay my debts, or free me from the burden of obligation to a set of fellows whom I despise? Speak—pronounce— demonstrate—or may heaven close your mouth for ever!'

'These are the comfortable fruits of your misanthropy, (answered the youth) your laudable scheme of detaching yourself from the bonds of society, and of moving in a superior sphere of your own. Had not you been so peculiarly sage, and intent upon laughing at mankind, you could never have been disconcerted by such a pitiful inconvenience: any friend would have accommodated you with the sum in question. But now the world may retort the laugh; for you stand upon such an agreeable footing with your acquaintance, that nothing could please them better than an account of your having given disappointment the slip, by the help of a noose properly applied. This I mention by way of hint, upon which I would have you chew the cud of reflection; and should it come to that issue, I will use my whole interest with the coroner, to bring in his verdict *Lunacy*, that your carcase may have christian burial.'

So saying, he withdrew, very well satisfied with the revenge he had taken, which operated so violently upon Crabtree, that if it had not been for the sole consideration mentioned above, he would, in all probability, have had recourse to the remedy proposed. But his unwillingness to oblige and entertain his fellow-creatures, hindered him from practising that expedient, till, by course of post, he was happily undeceived with regard to the situation of his affairs; and that information had such an effect upon him, that he not only forgave our hero for the stratagem, which he immediately ascribed to the right author, but also made him a tender of his purse: so that matters, for the present, were brought to an amicable accommodation.

Mean while, Peregrine never slackened in his attendance upon the great; he never omitted to appear upon every levee-day, employed his industry and penetration in getting intelligence of posts that were unfilled, and every day recommended himself to the good offices of his patron, who seemed to espouse his interest with great cordial-ity: nevertheless, he was always too late in his application, or the place he demanded chanced to be out of the minister's gift.

These intimations, tho' communicated in the most warm professions of friendship and regard, gave great umbrage to the young gentleman, who considered them as the evasions of an insincere courtier, and loudly complained of them as such to his lordship, signifying, at the same time, an intention to sell his mortgage for ready money, which he would expend to the last farthing in thwarting his honour, in the very first election he should patronize. His lordship never wanted a proper exhortation upon these occasions: he did not now endeavour to pacify him with assurances of the minister's favour, because he perceived that these medicines had, by repeated use, lost their effect upon our adventurer, whose menaces he now combated, by representing that the minister's purse was heavier than that of Mr. Pickle; that therefore, should he make a point of opposing his interest, the youth must infallibly fail in the contest: in which case he would find himself utterly destitute of the means of subsistence, and consequently precluded from all hope of provision.

This was an observation, the truth of which our young gentleman could not pretend to doubt, tho' it did not at all tend to the vindication of his honour's conduct. Indeed Pickle began to suspect the sincerity of his own patron, who, in his opinion, had trifled with his impatience, and even eluded, by sorry excuses, his desire of having another private audience of the first mover. His lordship also began to be less accessible than usual; and Peregrine had been obliged to dun the steward with repeated demands, before he could finger the last quarter of his interest.

Alarmed by these considerations, he went and consulted the nobleman whom he had obliged in the affair of his son; and had the mortification to hear but a very indifferent character of the person in whom he had so long confided. This new adviser, who (though a courtier) was a rival of the other, gave our adventurer to understand, that he had been leaning upon a broken reed; that his professed patron was a man of a shattered fortune and decayed interest, which extended no farther than a smile and a whisper; that for his own part, he should have been proud of an opportunity to use his influence with the minister in behalf of Mr. Pickle: 'But, since you have put yourself under the protection of another peer, (said he) whose connexions interfere with mine, I cannot now espouse your cause, without incurring the imputation of seducing that nobleman's adherents; a charge which, of all others, I would most carefully avoid. However, I shall always be ready to assist you with my private advice, as a specimen of which, I now counsel you to insist upon having another interview with Sir Steady Steerwell himself, that you may in person explain your pretensions, without any risque of being misrepresented; and endeavour, if possible, to draw him into some particular promise, from which he cannot retract, with any regard to his reputation: for general profession is a necessary armour worn by all ministers in their own defence, against the importunity of those whom they will not befriend, and would not disoblige.'

This advice was so conformable to his own sentiments, that our adventurer seized the first opportunity to demand an hearing; and plainly told his patron, that if he could not be indulged with that favour, he should look upon his lordship's influence to be very small, and his own hopes to be altogether desperate; in which case, he was resolved to dispose of the mortgage, purchase an annuity, and live independant.

CHAPTER C

He is indulged with a second Audience by the Minister,
of whose Sincerity he is convinced.
His Pride and Ambition revive, and again are mortified

If the young gentleman's money had been in other hands, perhaps the peer would have been at very little pains, either in gratifying his demand, or opposing his revenge; but he knew that a sale of the mortgage could not be effected without an inquiry, to which he did not wish to be exposed. He therefore employed all his interest in procuring the solicited audience; which being granted, Peregrine, with great warmth and elocution, expatiated upon the injury his fortune had suffered in the affair of the borough, for which he had stood candidate; he took notice of the disappointment he had sustained in the other election, reminded him of the promises with which he had been amused, and in conclusion, desired to know what he had to expect from his favour.

The minister having patiently heard him to an end, replied with a most gracious aspect, that he was very well informed of his merit and attachment, and very much disposed to convince him of the regard which he paid to both; that till of late, he did not know the nature of his expectations, neither had he the power of creating

Chapter C

posts for those whom he was inclined to serve; but if Mr. Pickle would chalk out any feasible method, by which he could manifest his sentiments of friendship, he should not be backward in executing the plan.

Peregrine laying hold on this declaration, mentioned several places which he knew to be vacant; but the old evasion was still used: one of them was not in his department of business; another had been promised to the third son of a certain earl, before the death of the last possessor; and a third was incumbered with a pension that ate up a good half of the appointments. In short, such obstructions were started to all his proposals, as he could not possibly surmount; though he plainly perceived, they were no other than specious pretexts to cover the mortifying side of a refusal. Exasperated, therefore, at this lack of sincerity and gratitude, 'I can easily foresee, (said he) that such difficulties will never be wanting, when I have any thing to ask; and for that reason, will save myself the trouble of any farther application.' So saying, he withdrew in a very abrupt manner, breathing defiance and revenge. But his patron, who did not think proper to drive him to extremities, found means to persuade his honour, to do something for the pacification of the young man's choler: and that same evening our adventurer received a message from his lordship, desiring to see him immediately.

In consequence of this intimation, Pickle went to his house, and appeared before him with a very cloudy aspect, which signified to whom it might concern, that his temper was at present too much galled to endure reproof; and therefore the sagacious peer forbore taking him to task for his behaviour during the audience he had obtained; but gave him to understand, that the minister, in consideration of his services, had sent him a bank-note for three hundred pounds, with a promise of the like sum yearly, until he could be otherwise provided for. This declaration in some measure appeased the youth, who condescended to accept the present; and next levee-day, made his acknowledgment to the donor, who favoured him with a smile of infinite complacency, which intirely dissipated all the remains of his resentment; for, as he could not possibly divine the true cause of his being temporized with, he looked upon his condescension as an undoubted proof of Sir Steady's sincerity, and firmly believed, that he would settle him in some place with the first opportunity, rather than continue to pay this pension out of his own pocket. In all probability, this prediction would have been verified, had not an unforeseen accident in a moment overwhelmed the bark of his interest at court.

Mean while, this short gleam of good fortune recalled the ideas of pride and ambition, which he had formerly cherished. His countenance was again lifted up, his good humour retrieved, and his mien re-exalted. Indeed, he began to be considered as a rising man by his fellow-dependants, who saw the particular notice with which he was favoured at the public levee; and some of them, for that reason, were at pains to court his good graces. He no longer shunned his former intimates, with whom a good part of his fortune had been spent, but made up to them in all places of public resort, with the same ease and familiarity as he had been used to express, and even reimbarked in some of their excesses, upon the strength of his sanguine expectation. Cadwallader and he renewed their consultations in the court of ridicule; and divers exploits were atchieved, to the confusion of those who had *sailed into the North of their displeasure.*[1]

But these enjoyments were soon interrupted by a misfortune equally fatal and unexpected: his noble patron was seized with an apoplectic fit, from which he was recovered by the physicians, that they might dispatch him according to rule; and accordingly, in two months after they were called, he went the way of all flesh. Peregrine was very much afflicted at this event, not only on account of his friendship for the deceased, to whom he thought himself under many and great obligations, but also, because he feared that his own interest would suffer a severe shock, by the removal of this nobleman, whom he considered as its chief support. He put himself therefore in mourning, out of regard to the memory of his departed friend, and exhibited genuine marks of sorrow and concern; though he had, in reality, more cause to grieve than he as yet imagined.

When quarter day came about, he applied to the steward of his lordship's heir for the interest of his money, as usual; and the reader will readily own he had some reason to be surprized, when he was told he had no claim either to principal or interest. True it is, the manager talked very civilly as well as sensibly on the subject. 'Your appearance, Sir, (said he to Pickle) screens you from all suspicion of an intended fraud; but the mortgage upon those lands you mention, was granted to another person many years before you pretend to have lent that sum; and I have, this very morning, paid one quarter's interest, as appears from this receipt, which you may peruse for your satisfaction.'

Peregrine was so thunder-struck at this information, which

stripped him of his all, that he could not utter one word; a circumstance that did no great honour to his character, in the opinion of the steward, who, in good earnest, began to entertain some doubts of his integrity: for, among the papers of the deceased, which he had examined, there was no writing, memorandum, or receipt, relating to this incumbrance. After a long pause of stupefaction, Peregrine recollected himself so far, as to observe, that either he was egregiously mistaken, or the predecessor of his lord the greatest villain upon earth. 'But, Mr. Whatdyecallum, (said he) you must give me leave to tell you, that your bare assertion, in this affair, will by no means induce me to put up quietly with the loss of ten thousand pounds.'

Having thus expressed himself, he retired from the house, so discontented at this demur, that he scarce knew whether he moved upon his head or heels; and the park chancing to lie in his way, he sauntered about, giving vent to a soliloquy in praise of his departed friend, the burden of which was a string of incoherent curses imprecated upon himself; till his transports, by degrees, giving way to his reflection, he deliberated seriously and sorrowfully upon his misfortune, and resolved to consult lawyers, without loss of time. But, first of all, he proposed to make personal application to the heir, who, by a candid representation of the case, might be inclined to do him justice.

In consequence of this determination, he next morning put his writings in his pocket, and went in a chair to the house of the young nobleman, to whom being admitted by virtue of his appearance, and a small gratification to the porter, he explained the whole affair, corroborating his assertions with the papers which he produced, and describing the disgrace that would be intailed upon the memory of the deceased, should he be obliged to seek redress in a public court of justice.

The executor, who was a person of good breeding, condoled him upon his loss with great good nature, though he did not seem much surprized at his account of the matter; but wished, that since the fraud must have been committed, the damage had fallen upon the first mortgager, who (he said) was a thievish usurer, grown rich by the distresses of his fellow-creatures. In answer to our hero's remonstrances, he observed, that he did not look upon himself as obliged to pay the least regard to the character of his predecessor, who had used him with great barbarity and injustice, not only in excluding him from his countenance and assistance, but also in prejudicing his inheritance, as much as lay in his power; so that it could not be reasonably expected, that he would pay ten thousand pounds of his debt, for which he had received no value. Peregrine, in spite of his chagrin, could not help owning within himself, that there was a good deal of reason in this refusal; and after having given loose to his indignation, in the most violent invectives against the defunct, took his leave of the complaisant heir, and had immediate recourse to the advice of counsel, who assured him that he had an excellent plea, and was accordingly retained in the cause.

All these measures were taken in the first vigour of his exertion, during which his spirits were so flustered with the diversity of passions produced by his mischance, that he mistook for equanimity that which was no other than intoxication; and two whole days elapsed, before he arrived at a due sense of his misfortune. Then indeed he underwent a woeful self-examination; every circumstance of the inquiry added fresh pangs to his reflection; and the result of the whole was a discovery, that his fortune was totally consumed, and himself reduced to a state of the most deplorable dependance. This suggestion alone might (in the anguish of his despondency) have driven him to some desperate course, had not it been in some measure qualified by the confidence of his lawyers, and the assurance of the minister, which (slender as the world hath generally found them) were the only bulwarks between misery and him.

The mind is naturally pliable, and, provided it has the least hope to lean upon, adapts itself wonderfully to the emergencies of fortune, especially when the imagination is gay and luxuriant. This was the case with our adventurer; instead of indulging the melancholy ideas which his loss inspired, he had recourse to the flattering delusions of hope, soothing himself with unsubstantial plans of future greatness, and endeavouring to cover what was past with the veil of oblivion.

After some hesitation, he resolved to make Crabtree acquainted with his misfortune, that once for all he might pass the ordeal of his satire, without subjecting himself to a long series of sarcastic hints and doubtful allusions, which he could not endure. He accordingly took the first opportunity of telling him, that he was absolutely ruined by the perfidy of his patron, and desired that he would not aggravate his affliction, by those cynical remarks which were peculiar to men of his misanthropical disposition. Cadwallader listened to this declaration with internal surprize, which, however, produced no alteration in his countenance; and, after some pause, observed, that our hero had no reason to look for any

new observation from him upon this event, which he had long foreseen, and daily expected; and exhorted him, with an ironical sneer,
to console himself with the promise of the minister, who would
doubtless discharge the debts of his deceased bosom-friend.

CHAPTER CI

*Peregrine commits himself to the Publick,
and is admitted Member of a College of Authors*

THE bitterness of this explanation being passed, our young gentleman began to revolve within himself schemes for making up the
deficiencies of his yearly income, which was now so grievously
reduced, and determined to profit, in some shape or other, by those
talents which he owed to nature and education. He had, in his
affluence, heard of several authors, who, without any pretensions
to genius, or human literature, earned a very genteel subsistence,
by undertaking work for booksellers, in which reputation was not at
all concerned. One (for example) professed all manner of translation, at so much *per* sheet, and actually kept five or six amanuenses
continually employed, like so many clerks in a compting-house;
by which means, he was enabled to live at his ease, and enjoy his
friend and his bottle, ambitious of no other character than that of
an honest man, and a good neighbour.[1] Another projected a variety
of plans for new dictionaries, which were executed under his eye
by day-labourers;[2] and the province of a third was history and
voyages, collected or abridged by understrappers of the same class.

Mr. Pickle, in his comparisons, paid such deference to his own
capacity, as banished all doubts of his being able to excel any of
those undertakers, in their different branches of profession, if ever
he should be driven to that experiment: but his ambition prompted
him to make his interest and glory coincide, by attempting some
performance which should do him honour with the publick, and
at the same time establish his importance among the copy-
purchasers in town. With this view, he worshipped the muse; and,
conscious of the little regard which is, in this age, paid to every
species of poetic composition, in which neither satire nor obscenity
occurs, he produced an imitation of Juvenal, and lashed some
conspicuous characters, with equal truth, spirit, and severity.
Though his name did not appear in the title-page of this production,

he managed matters so, as that the work was universally imputed to the true author, who was not altogether disappointed in his expectations of success; for the impression was immediately sold off, and the piece became the subject of conversation in all assemblies of taste.

This happy exordium not only attracted the addresses of the booksellers, who made interest for his acquaintance, but also roused the notice of a society of authors, who stiled themselves *the college*, from which he was honoured with a deputation, offering to enroll him a member, by unanimous consent. The person employed for this purpose being a bard who had formerly tasted of our hero's bounty, used all his eloquence to persuade him to comply with the advances of their fraternity, which he described in such a manner, as inflamed the curiosity of Pickle, who dismissed the embassador, with an acknowledgement of the great honour they conferred upon him, and a faithful promise of endeavouring to merit the continuance of their approbation.

He was afterwards, by the same minister, instructed in the ceremonies of the college; and, in consequence of his information, composed an ode, to be publickly recited on the evening of his introduction. He understood, that this constitution was no other than a body of authors, incorporated by mutual consent, for their joint advantage and satisfaction, opposed to another assembly of the same kind, their avowed enemies and detractors. No wonder then, that they sought to strengthen themselves with such a valuable acquisition as our hero was like to prove. The college consisted of authors only, and these of all degrees in point of reputation, from the fabricator of a song set to music, and sung at Marybone, to the dramatic bard who had appeared in buskins upon the stage: nay, one of the members had actually finished eight books of an epic poem, for the publication of which, he was, at that time, soliciting subscriptions.

It cannot be supposed that such a congregation of the sons of Apollo would sit a whole evening with order and decorum, unless they were under the check of some established authority: and this inconvenience having been foreseen, they had elected a president, vested with full power to silence any member or members, that should attempt to disturb the harmony and subordination of the whole. The sage, who at this time possessed the chair, was a person in years, whose countenance was a lively portraiture of that rancorous discontent which follows repeated damnation. He had been extremely unfortunate in his theatrical productions, and was (to use the words of a prophane wag, who assisted at the condemnation of his last play) by this time *damn'd beyond redemption*. Nevertheless, he still tarried about the skirts of Parnassus, translating some of the classics, and writing miscellanies; and, by dint of an invincible assurance, insolence untamed, the most undaunted virulence of tongue, and some knowledge of life, he made shift to acquire and maintain the character of a man of learning and wit, in the opinion of people who had neither; that is, thirty-nine in forty of those with whom he associated himself. He was even looked upon in this light by some few of the college; though the major part of those who favoured his election, were such as dreaded his malice, respected his experience and seniority, or hated his competitor, who was the epic poet.

The chief end of this society (as I have already hinted) was to assist and support each other in their productions, which they mutually recommended to sale, with all their art and influence, not only in private conversation, but also in occasional epigrams, criticisms, and advertisements inserted in the public papers. This science, which is known by the vulgar appellation of *puffing*, they carried to such a pitch of finesse, that an author very often wrote an abusive answer to his own performance, in order to inflame the curiosity of the town, by which it had been overlook'd. Notwithstanding this general unanimity in the college, a private animosity had long subsisted between the two rivals I have mentioned, on account of precedence, to which both laid claim, though, by a majority of votes, it had been decided in favour of the present chairman. The grudge indeed never proceeded to any degree of outrage or defiance, but manifested itself at every meeting, in attempts to eclipse each other in smart sayings and pregnant repartee; so that there was always a delicate mess of this kind of wit served up in the front of the evening, for the entertainment and example of the junior members, who never failed to divide upon this occasion, declaring themselves for one or other of the combatants, whom they encouraged by their looks, gestures, and applause, according to the circumstances of the dispute.

This honourable consistory was held in the best room of an ale-house, which afforded wine, punch, or beer, suitable to the purse or inclination of every individual, who separately paid for his own choice: and here was our hero introduced, in the midst of twenty strangers, who, by their looks and equipage, formed a very picturesque variety. He was received with a most gracious solemnity, and placed upon the right hand of the president, who having commanded silence, recited aloud his introductory ode, which met with universal approbation. Then was tendered to him the customary oath, obliging him to consult the honour and advantage of the society, as far as it should lie in his power, in every station of life: and this being taken, his temples were bound with a wreath of laurel, which was kept sacred for such inauguration.

When these rites were performed with all due ceremony, the new member cast his eyes around the place, and took a more accurate survey of his brethren; among whom he observed a strange collection of periwigs, with regard to the colour, fashion, and dimensions, which were such as he had never seen before. Those who sat on each side, nearest the president, were generally distinguished by venerable tyes, the foretops of which exhibited a surprising diversity; some of them rose slanting backwards, like the glacis of a fortification; some were elevated in two distinct eminences, like the hills Helicon and Parnassus; and others were curled and reflected, as the horns of Jupiter Ammon. Next to these, the majors took place, many of which were mere *succedanea*, made by the application of an occasional rose to the tail of a lank bob; and in the lower form appeared masses of hair, which would admit of no description.

Their cloaths were tolerably well suited to the furniture of their heads, the apparel of the upper bench being decent and clean, while that of the second class was thread-bare and soiled; and at the lower end of the room, he perceived divers efforts made to conceal rent breeches and dirty linen: nay, he could distinguish by their countenances, the different kinds of poetry in which they exercised the muse; he saw Tragedy conspicuous in a grave solemnity of regard, Satire louring in a frown of envy and discontent, Elegy whining in a funereal aspect, Pastoral dozing in a most insipid languor of face, Ode-writing delineated in a distracted stare, and Epigram squinting with a pert sneer. Perhaps our hero refined too much in his penetration, when he affirmed, that over and above these discoveries, he could plainly perceive the state of every one's finances, and would have undertaken to have guessed each particular sum, without varying three farthings from the truth.

The conversation, instead of becoming general, began to fall into parties; and the epic poet had actually attracted the attention of a private committee, when the chairman interposed, calling aloud, 'No cabals, no conspiracies, gentlemen.' His rival, thinking it incumbent upon him to make some reply to this rebuke, answered, 'We have no secrets; he that hath ears, let him hear.' This was spoke as an intimation to the company, whose looks were instantly whetted with the expectation of their ordinary meal: but the president seemed to decline the contest; for, without putting on his fighting face, he calmly replied, that he had seen Mr. Metaphor tip the wink, and whisper to one of his confederates; and thence judged, that there was something mysterious on the carpet.

The epic poet, believing his antagonist crestfallen, resolved to take the advantage of his dejection, that he might inhance his own character in the opinion of the stranger; and with that view asked, with an air of exultation, if a man might not be allowed to have a convulsion in his eye, without being suspected of a conspiracy. The president, perceiving his drift, and piqued at his presumption, 'To be sure (said he) a man of a weak head may be very well supposed to have convulsions in his eyes.' This repartee produced a laugh of triumph among the chairman's adherents; one of whom observed, that his rival had got a smart rap on the pate. 'Yes, (replied the bard) in that respect Mr. Chairman has the advantage of me. Had my head been fortified with a horn-work, I should not have been so sensible of the stroke.' This retort, which carried a severe allusion to the president's wife, lighted up the countenances of the aggressor's friends, which had begun to be a little obumbrated; and had a contrary effect upon the other faction, till their chief, collecting all his capacity, returned the salute, by observing, that there was no occasion for an horn-work, when the covered way was not worth defending.

Such a reprizal upon Mr. Metaphor's yoke-fellow, who was by no means remarkable for her beauty, could not fail to operate upon the hearers; and as for the bard himself, he was evidently ruffled by the reflection; to which, however, he, without hesitation, replied, 'Egad! 'tis my opinion, that if your covered way was laid open, few people would venture to give the assault.' 'Not unless their batteries were more effectual than the fire of your wit,' (said the president.) 'As for that matter, (cried the other with precipitation) they would have no occasion to batter in breach; they would find the angle of the *la pucelle* bastion demolished to their hands: he he!' 'But I believe it would surpass your understanding, (resumed the chairman) to fill up the *fossè*.' 'That, I own, is impracticable, (replied the bard) there I should meet with an *hiatus maxime deflendus!*' [1]

The president, exasperated at this insinuation, in presence of the new member, exclaimed with indignation in his looks, 'And yet, if a body of pioneers were set at work upon your skull, they would find rubbish enough to choak up all the common sewers in town.' Here a groan was uttered by the admirers of the epic poet, who taking a pinch of snuff with great composure, 'When a man grows scurrilous, (said he) I take it for an undoubted proof of his over-throw.' 'If that be the case, (cried the other) you yourself must be the vanquished party; for you was the first that was driven to personal abuse.' 'I appeal (answered the bard) to those who can distinguish. Gentlemen, your judgment?'

This reference produced an universal clamour, and the whole college was involved in confusion. Every man entered into dispute with his neighbour, on the merits of this cause. The chairman interposed his authority in vain; the noise grew louder and louder; the disputants waxed warm; the epithets of *blockhead*, *fool*, and *scoundrel* were bandied about. Peregrine enjoyed the uproar, and leaping upon the table, sounded the charge to battle, which was immediately commenced in ten different duels; in consequence of which, the lights were extinguished; the combatants threshed one another without distinction; the mischievous Pickle distributed sundry random blows in the dark; and the people below, being alarmed with the sound of application, the over-turning of chairs, and the outcries of those who were engaged, came up stairs in a body, with lights, to reconnoitre, and, if possible, quell this hideous tumult.

Objects were no sooner rendered visible, than the field of battle exhibited strange groups of the standing and the fallen. Each of Mr. Metaphor's eyes was surrounded with a circle of a livid hue; and the president's nose distilled a quantity of clotted blood. One of the tragic authors, finding himself assaulted in the dark, had, by way of poinard, employed upon his adversary's throat a knife which lay upon the table, for the convenience of cutting cheese; but, by the blessing of God, the edge of it was not keen enough to enter the skin, which it had only scratched in divers places. A satirist had almost bit off the ear of a lyric bard. Shirts and neck-cloaths were torn to rags; and there was such a woeful wreck of periwigs on the floor, that no examination could adjust the property of the owners, the greatest part of whom were obliged to use hand-kerchiefs, by way of night-cap.

The fray, however, ceased at the approach of those who inter-posed; part of the combatants being tired of an exercise, in which they had received nothing but hard blows; part of them being intimidated by the remonstrances of the landlord and his company, who threatened to call the watch; and a very few being ashamed of the scandalous dispute in which they were detected. But though the battle was ended, it was impossible, for that evening, to restore harmony and good order to the society, which broke up, after the president had pronounced a short and confused apology to our adventurer, for the indecent uproar which had unfortunately happened on the first night of his admission.

Indeed, Peregrine deliberated with himself, whether or not his reputation would allow him to appear again among this venerable fraternity: but, as he knew some of them to be men of real genius, how ridiculous soever their carriage might be modified, and was of that laughing disposition, which is always seeking food for mirth, as Horace observes of Philippus,

Risus undique quærit;[1]

he resolved to frequent the college, notwithstanding this accident, which happened at his inauguration; being thereto, moreover, induced by his desire of knowing the private history of the stage, with which he supposed some of the members perfectly well acquainted. He was also visited, before the next meeting, by his introductor, who assured him, that such a tumult had never happened since the institution of the assembly, till that very night; and promised, that for the future, he should have no cause to be scandalized at their behaviour.

Persuaded by these motives and assurances, he trusted himself once more in the midst of their community, and every thing proceeded with great decorum; all dispute and altercation was avoided, and the college applied itself seriously to the purposes of its meeting; namely, to hear the grievances of individuals, and assist them with salutary advice. The first person that craved redress, was a noisy North Briton, who complained (in a strange dialect) that he had, in the beginning of the season, presented a comedy to the manager of a certain theatre, who, after it had lain six weeks in his hands, returned it to the author, affirming there was neither sense nor English in the performance.

The president, (who, by the bye, had revised the piece) thinking his own reputation concerned, declared, in presence of the whole society, that with regard to sense, he would not undertake to vindicate the production; but, in point of language, no fault could be justly laid to its charge: 'The case, however, is very plain, (said he) the manager never gave himself the trouble to peruse the play, but formed a judgment of it from the conversation of the author, never dreaming that it had undergone the revisal of an English writer: be that as it will, you are infinitely obliged to him, for having dispatched you so soon, and I shall have the better opinion of him for it so long as I live; for I have known other-guess authors than you (that is, in point of interest and fame) kept in continual attendance and dependance during the best part of their lives, and after all, disappointed in the expectation of seeing their performances exhibited on the stage.[1] There are only two methods, by which you have any chance of introducing your play upon the theatre; one is compulsive, by the interposition of the great, whom a patentee dares not disoblige; the other, insinuation, by ingratiating yourself with the manager: you must be recommended to his notice; you must cultivate his good graces with all the humility of adulation; write poems in his praise; if he be an actor, support his performance against all censure, though it should be founded upon demonstration; and in public coffee-houses, as well as in private parties, magnify the virtues of his heart, in despite of truth and illustration. This, indeed, is the most effectual expedient, and what I advise you to practise, after you shall have been introduced to his acquaintance, by some person of weight; and if, by these means, and dint of perseverance, you can, in three or four years, see your comedy in rehearsal, you may think yourself extremely fortunate in your application: for a man, without interest or pretension, may present a petition to the captain-general of his majesty's forces, demanding a commission for the first company that shall become vacant, and be as likely to meet with success, as an unsupported author that offers a performance to the stage. Though a patentee had no friends of his own to oblige, why the devil should he put himself to the expence and trouble attending the representation of a new play, and part with three benefit-nights, to please the vanity and fill the pockets of a stranger?'

The northern bard began to argue with great vehemence and vociferation, against the advice and observations of the chairman, undertaking to prove from reason, as well as from experience, that one poet is of greater dignity and importance to the commonwealth, than all the patentees or players that ever existed. But he was over-ruled and silenced in the beginning of his harangue, by a decree of the council, which was unanimously of opinion, that the advice he had received was equally judicious and expedient, and that it would be his own fault, if he did not profit by the admonition.

CHAPTER CII

Further Proceedings of the College

THIS affair was no sooner discussed, than another gentleman exhibited a complaint, signifying, that he had undertaken to translate into English, a certain celebrated author, who had been cruelly mangled by former attempts; and that, soon as his design took air, the proprietors of those miserable translations had endeavoured to prejudice his work, by industrious insinuations, contrary to truth and fair dealing, importing, that he did not understand one word of the language which he pretended to translate. This being a case that nearly concerned the greatest part of the audience, it was taken into serious deliberation: some observed, that it was not only a malicious effort against the plaintiff, but also a spiteful advertisement to the public, tending to promote an inquiry into the abilities of all other translators, few of whom (it was well known) were so qualified, as to stand the test of such examination. Others said, that over and above this consideration, which ought to have its due weight with the college, there was a necessity for concerting measures to humble the presumption of booksellers, who had, from time immemorial, taken all opportunities to oppress and enslave their authors; not only by limiting men of genius to the wages of a journeyman taylor, without even allowing them one sabbath in the week, but also in taking such advantages of their necessities, as were inconsistent with justice and humanity. 'For example, (said one of the members) after I myself had acquired a little reputation with the town, I was caressed by one of those tyrants who professed a friendship for me, and even supplied me with money, according to the exigencies of my situation; so that I looked upon him as the mirrour of disinterested benevolence; and had he known my disposition, and treated me accordingly, I should have writ for him upon his own terms. After I had used his friendship in this manner for some time, I happened to have occasion for a small sum of money, and with great confidence made another application to my good friend; when all of a sudden he put a stop to his generosity, refused to accommodate me in the most abrupt and mortifying style; and though I was at that time pretty far advanced in a work for his benefit, which was a sufficient security for what I owed him, he roundly asked, how I proposed to pay the money which I had already borrowed. Thus was I used like a young whore just come upon the town, whom the bawd allows to run into her debt, that she may have it in her power to oppress her at pleasure; and if the sufferer complains, she is treated like the most ungrateful wretch upon earth; and that too with such appearance of reason, as may easily mislead an unconcerned spectator. "You unthankful drab! (she will say) didn't I take you into my house when you hadn't a shift to your back, a petticoat to your tail, nor a morsel of bread to put into your belly? Ha'n't I cloathed you from head to foot like a gentlewoman, supported you with board, lodging, and all necessaries, till your own extravagance hath brought you into distress; and now you have the impudence, you nasty, stinking brimstone bungaway! to say you are hardly dealt with, when I demand no more than my own." Thus the whore and the author are equally oppressed, and even left without the melancholy privilege of complaining; so that they are fain to subscribe to such terms as their creditors shall please to impose.'

This illustration operated so powerfully upon the conviction and resentment of the whole college, that revenge was universally denounced against those who had aggrieved the plaintiff; and after some debate, it was agreed, that he should make a new translation of some other saleable book, in opposition to a former version belonging to the delinquents, and print it in such a small size, as would enable him to undersell their property; and that this new translation should be recommended and introduced into the world, with the whole art and influence of the society.

This affair being settled to the satisfaction of all present, an author of some character stood up, and craved the advice and assistance of his fellows, in punishing a certain nobleman of great pretensions to taste,[1] who, in consequence of a production which this gentleman had ushered into the world, with universal applause, not only desired, but even eagerly courted his acquaintance. 'He invited me to his house (said he) where I was overwhelmed with civility and professions of friendship. He insisted upon my treating him as an intimate, and calling upon him at all hours, without ceremony; he made me promise to breakfast with him at least three times a week. In short, I looked upon myself as very fortunate, in meeting with such advances from a man of his interest and reputation, who had it in his power to befriend me effectually in my passage through life; and, that I might not give him any cause to think I neglected his friendship, I went to his house in two days, with a view of drinking chocolate, according to appointment: but he had been so much fatigued with dancing at an assembly over night, that his valet de chambre would not venture to wake him so early; and I left my compliments to his lordship, with a performance in manuscript, which he had expressed a most eager desire to peruse. I repeated my visit next morning, that his impatience to see me might not have some violent effect upon his constitution; and received a message from his minister, signifying, that he had been highly entertained with the manuscript I had left, a great part of which he had read, but was at present so busy in contriving a proper dress for a private masquerade, which would be given that same evening, that he could not have the pleasure of my company at breakfast. This was a feasible excuse, which I admitted accordingly, and in a day or two appeared again, when his lordship was particularly engaged. This might possibly be the case; and therefore I returned the fourth time, in hopes of finding him more at leisure; but he had gone out about half an hour before my arrival, and left my performance with his valet de chambre, who assured me, that his lord had perused it with infinite pleasure. Perhaps I might have retired very well satisfied with this declaration, had not I, in my passage through the hall, heard one of the footmen, upon the top of the stair-case, pronounce with an audible voice, "Will your lordship please to be at home, when he calls?" It is not to be supposed that I was pleased at this discovery, which I no sooner made, than turning to my conductor, "I find, (said I) his lordship is disposed to be abroad to more people than me this morning." The fellow (though a valet de chambre) blushed at this observation; and I withdrew, not a little irritated at the silly peer's disingenuity, and fully resolved to spare him my visits for the future. It was not long after this occasion, that I happened to meet him in the park, and being naturally civil, I could not pass him without a salutation of the hat, which he returned in the most distant manner, though we were both solitary, and not a soul within view; and when that very performance, which he had applauded so warmly, was lately published by subscription, he did not bespeak so much as one copy. I have often reflected with wonder upon this ridiculous inconsistency in the man's conduct, which looks like the result of a settled design to render himself odious and contemptible. I never courted his patronage, nor indeed thought of his name, until he made interest for my acquaintance; and if he was disappointed in my conversation, why did he press me so much to further connexion?'

'The case is very clear, (cried the chairman, interrupting him) he is one of those coxcombs who set up for taste, and value themselves upon knowing all men of genius, whom they would be thought to assist in their productions. I will lay an even bet with any man, that his lordship, on the strength of that slender interview, together with the opportunity of having seen your performance in manuscript, has already hinted to every company in which he is conversant, that you solicited his assistance in retouching the piece, which you have now offered to the publick, and that he was pleased to favour you with his advice, but found you obstinately bigotted to your own opinion, in some points relating to those very passages which have not met with the approbation of the town. And as for his caresses, there was nothing at all extraordinary in his behaviour. By that time you have lived to my age, you will not be surprized to see a courtier's promise and performance of a different complexion: not but that I would willingly act as an auxiliary to your resentment,[1] if I thought it was possible to make him repent of his pitiful dissimulation; but, if I guess aright, the person you mean, has long ago conquered all sense of probity and shame, and therefore is effectually shielded against the revenge of an author.'

The opinion of the president was sanctioned by the concurrence of all the members; and all other complaints and memorials being deferred till another sitting, the college proceeded to an exercise of wit, which was generally performed once every fortnight, with a view to promote the expectoration of genius. The subject was occasionally chosen by the chairman, who opened the game with some shrewd remark naturally arising from the conversation; and then the ball was tossed about from one corner of the room to the other, according to the motions of the spirit.

That the reader may have a just idea of this sport, and of the abilities of those who carried it on, I shall repeat the sallies of this evening, according to the order and succession in which they escaped. One of the members observing that Mr. Metaphor was absent, was told by the person who sat next to him, that the poet had foul weather at home, and could not stir abroad. 'What! (said the president, interposing, with the signal upon his countenance) is he wind-bound in port?' 'Wine-bound, I suppose,' (cried another.) 'Hooped with wine! a strange metaphor!' (said a third.) 'Not if he has got into a hogshead,' (answered a fourth.) 'The hogshead will sooner get into him, (replied a fifth) it must be a tun or an ocean.' 'No wonder then, if he should be overwhelmed,' (said a sixth.) 'If he should, (cried a seventh) he will cast up when his gall breaks.' 'That must be very soon, (roared an eighth) for it has been long ready to burst.' 'No, no, (observed a ninth) he'll stick fast at

the bottom, take my word for it; he has a *natural alacrity in sinking*.'[1]
'And yet, (remarked a tenth) I have seen him in the clouds.' 'Then
was he cloudy, I suppose,' (cried the eleventh.) 'So dark, (replied
the other) that his meaning could not be perceived.' 'For all that,
(said the twelfth) he is easily seen through.' 'You talk, (answered a
thirteenth) as if his head was made of glass.' 'No, no, (cried a fourteenth) his head is made of more durable stuff; it will bend before
it breaks.' 'Yet I have seen it broken,' (resumed the president.)
'Did you perceive any wit come out at the hole?' (said another.)
'His wit (replied the chairman) is too subtile to be perceived.'

A third mouth was just opened, when the exercise was suddenly
interrupted by the dreadful cry of fire, which issued from the
kitchen, and involved the whole college in confusion. Every man
endeavouring to be the first in making his exit, the door and passage
were blocked up; each individual was pummelled by the person
that happened to be behind him. This communication produced
noise and exclamation; clouds of smoke rolled upwards into the
apartment, and terror sat on every brow; when Peregrine seeing no
prospect of retreating by the door, opened one of the windows, and
fairly leapt into the street, where he found a crowd of people
assembled to contribute their assistance in extinguishing the
flames. Several members of the college followed his example, and
happily accomplished their escape: the chairman himself being
unwilling to use the same expedient, stood trembling on the brink
of descent, dubious of his own agility, and dreading the consequence of such a leap, when a chair happening to pass, he laid
hold on the opportunity, and by an exertion of his muscles pitched
upon the top of the carriage, which was immediately overturned in
the kennel, to the grievous annoyance of the fare, which happened
to be a certain effeminate beau, in full dress, on his way to a private
assembly.

This phantom of a man, hearing the noise overhead, and feeling
the shock of being overthrown, at the same time, thought that
some whole tenement had fallen upon the chair, and, in the terror
of being crushed to pieces, uttered a scream which the populace
supposed to proceed from the mouth of a woman; and therefore
went to his assistance, while the chairmen, instead of ministring to
his occasions, no sooner recollected themselves, than they ran in
pursuit of their overthrower, who being accustomed to escapes
from bailiffs, dived into a dark alley, and vanishing in a trice, was
not visible to any living soul, until he appeared next day on
Tower-hill.

The human part of the mob, who bestirred themselves for the relief of the supposed lady, no sooner perceived their mistake, in the appearance of the beau, who stared around him with horror and affright, than their compassion was changed into mirth, and they began to pass a great many unsavoury jokes upon his misfortune, which they now discovered no inclination to alleviate; and he found himself very uncomfortably beset, when Pickle pitying his situation, interposed in his behalf, and prevailed upon the chairmen to carry him into the house of an apothecary in the neighbourhood, to whom his mischance proved a very advantageous accident; for the fright operated so violently upon his nerves, that he was seized with a delirium, and lay a whole fortnight, deprived of his senses; during which period he was not neglected in point of medicines, food and attendance, but royally regaled, as appeared by the contents of his landlord's bill.

Our adventurer having seen this unfortunate beau safely housed, returned to the scene of the other calamity, which, as it was no other than a foul vent, soon yielded to the endeavours of the family, and was happily overcome, without any other bad consequence than that of alarming the neighbours, disturbing the college, and disordering the brain of a beau.

Eager to be acquainted with the particular constitutions of a society which seemed to open upon him by degrees, Mr. Pickle did not fail to appear at the next meeting, when several petitions were laid before the board, in behalf of those members who were confined in the prisons of the Fleet, Marshalsea, and King's bench. As those unhappy authors expected nothing from their brethren but advice and good offices, which did not concern the purse, their memorials were considered with great care and humanity; and, upon this occasion, Peregrine had it in his power to manifest his importance to the community; for he happened to be acquainted with the creditor of one of the prisoners, and knew that gentleman's severity was owing to his resentment at the behaviour of the debtor, who had lampooned him in print, because he refused to comply with a fresh demand, after he had lent him money to the amount of a considerable sum. Our young gentleman therefore understanding that the author was penitent, and disposed to make a reasonable submission, promised to employ his influence with the creditor towards an accommodation; and, in a few days, actually obtained his release.

These social duties being discharged, the conversation took a general turn, and several new productions were freely criticised;

those especially which belonged to authors who were either un-connected with, or unknown to the college. Nor did the profession of stage-playing escape the cognizance of the assembly: a deputa-tion of the most judicious members being sent weekly to each theatre, with a view of making remarks upon the performance of the actors. The two censors for the preceding week were accordingly called upon to give in their report; and the plays which they had reviewed were the *Fair Penitent*[1] and the *Revenge*. The person who had examined the former of these tragedies, owned that he had made no material observations upon the principal performers: he said he was, upon the whole, very well entertained, tho' he had, at first, mistaken Lothario, by his dress, for a puppet-shew man, hired for the entertainment of the guests at Calista's wedding; and was afterwards a little surprised at his unreasonable demand, when, in challenging Horatio to single combat, he desired such an unweildy antagonist to meet him a whole mile among rocks; an expedition which could not be performed without imminent danger of broken bones.

Peregrine imagining that this remark proceeded from his ignor-ance of the play, observed that the critick might possibly be misled by the words of the defiance, which run thus;

> *West of the town a mile, among the rocks,*
> *Two hours ere noon to-morrow I expect thee.*[2]

'Sir (answered the censor) I am not acquainted with the text, else I should have placed my observation to the account of the author,[3] instead of the actor, who made a full stop at the word *town*, and then pronounced—*a mile among the rocks*, without the least pause of distinction. Perhaps, indeed, in the researches of his great penetra-tion, he may have discovered that this is the genuine pointing of the poet, and that Lothario had actually a design upon the shins of Altamont's friend: in which case he is to be commended for this, among his other improvements in the art of acting; yet I cannot approve of his refinements in the mystery of dying hard; his fall, and the circumstances of his death, in the character of this gay libertine, being, in my opinion, a lively representation of a tinker oppressed with gin, who staggers against a post, tumbles into the kennel, while his hammer and saucepan drop from his hands, makes divers convulsive efforts to rise, and finding himself unable to get up, with many intervening hiccups, addresses himself to the surrounding mob.'

'I confess (replied Pickle) the action of that same player is not free from unnatural violence and ridiculous gesticulation: a kind of false fire in which he finds his account with the audience, who never fail to honour it with particular marks of applause; but I think the simile of the tinker is too severe, and rather one of those grotesque comparisons which may subject the most grave and solemn incidents to ridicule, than a fair and candid illustration of the fact: as for the perversion of the author's sense, by an impropriety in the declamation, it so commonly occurs, even in the most celebrated actors, that one would think it was an obstacle not to be surmounted: the delightful lullaby of the stage is an established recitative, which seems to have been composed on the supposition that the sentence is always concluded at the end of the line; and when the last word happens to begin a new period, the sense of the whole must suffer accordingly. I have heard the Æsopus of the age,[1] who values himself upon accurate speaking, commit innumerable blunders of this kind, one of which I, at present, recollect, in a passage of a late play, which he repeated in this manner:

> *To beg protection for the men who lie,———*
> *Trembling behind their ramparts.*[2]

Thus he brought the poor Romans under the imputation of falshood as well as fear; for, according to his pause, they told lies, as well as trembled behind their ramparts.'

'These are no other than petty oversights: (said the second censor) that gentleman (take him all in all) is certainly the most compleat and unblemished performer that ever appeared on our stage, notwithstanding the blind adoration which is paid to his rival. I went two nights ago, with an express design to criticize his action: I could find no room for censure, but infinite subject for admiration and applause. In *Pierre* he is great, in *Othello* excellent, but in *Zanga* beyond all imitation.[3] Over and above the distinctness of pronunciation, the dignity of attitude and expression of face, his gestures are so just and significant, that a man, tho' utterly bereft of the sense of hearing, might, by seeing him only, understand the meaning of every word he speaks! Sure nothing can be more exquisite than his manner of telling Isabella how Alonzo behaved when he found the incendiary letter which she had dropt by the Moor's direction; and when, to crown his vengeance, he discovers himself to be the contriver of all the mischief that had happened, he manifests a perfect master piece of action, in pronouncing these four little monosyllables, *Know then, 'twas———I.*[4]

Peregrine having eyed the critick some minutes, 'I fancy (said he) your praise must be ironical, because, in the very two situations you mention, I think I have seen that player out-herod Herod, or, in other words, exceed all his other extravagances. The intention of the author is, that the Moor should communicate to his confidante a piece of information contained in a few lines, which, doubtless, ought to be repeated with an air of eagerness and satisfaction, not with the ridiculous grimace of a monkey, to which, methought, his action bore an intimate resemblance, in uttering this plain sentence:

> ———*he took it up ;*
> *But scarce was it unfolded to his sight,*
> *When he, as if an arrow pierc'd his eye,*
> *Started, and trembling dropt it on the ground.* [1]

In pronouncing the first two words, this egregious actor stoops down, and seems to take up something from the stage, then proceeding to repeat what follows, mimicks the manner of unfolding a letter; when he mentions the simile of an arrow piercing the eye, he darts his forefinger towards that organ, then recoils with great violence when the word *started* is expressed; and when he comes to *trembling dropt it on the ground*, he throws all his limbs into a tremulous motion, and shakes the imaginary paper from his hand. The latter part of the description is carried on with the same minute gesticulation, while he says,

> *Pale and aghast a while my victim stood,*
> *Disguised a sigh or two, and puff'd them from him ;*
> *Then rubb'd his brow, and took it up again.*

The player's countenance assumes a wild stare, he sighs twice most piteously, as if he were on the point of suffocation, scrubs his forehead, and bending his body, apes the action of snatching an object from the floor. Nor is this dexterity of dumb shew omitted, when he concludes his intimation in these three lines:

> *At first, he look'd as if he meant to read it ;*
> *But, check'd by rising fears, he crush'd it thus,*
> *And thrust it, like an adder, in his bosom.*

Here the judicious performer imitates the confusion and concern of Alonzo, seems to cast his eyes upon something, from which they are immediately withdrawn, with horror and precipitation, then shutting his fist with a violent squeeze, as if he intended to make immediate application to Isabella's nose, he rams it in his own bosom, with all the horror and agitation of a thief taken in the manner. Were the player debarred the use of speech, and obliged to act to the eyes only of the audience, this mimickry might be a necessary conveyance of his meaning; but when he is at liberty to signify his ideas by language, nothing can be more trivial, forced, unnatural and antick, than this superfluous mummery. Not that I would exclude from the representation the graces of action, without which the choicest sentiments, cloathed in the most exquisite expression, would appear unanimated and insipid; but these are as different from this ridiculous burlesque, as is the demeanor of a Tully in the rostrum, from the tricks of a Jack-pudding on a mountebank's stage: and for the truth of what I alledge, I appeal to the observation of any person who has considered the elegance of attitude and propriety of gesture, as they are universally acknowledged in the real characters of life. Indeed I have known a Gascon, whose limbs were as eloquent as his tongue: he never mentioned the word sleep without reclining his head upon his hand; when he had occasion to talk of an horse, he always started up and trotted across the room, except when he was so situated that he could not stir without incommoding the company, and in that case he contented himself with neighing aloud: if a dog happened to be the subject of his conversation, he wagged his tail, and grinned in a most significant manner; and one day he expressed his desire of going backwards with such natural imitation of his purpose, that every body in the room firmly believed he had actually overshot himself, and fortified their nostrils accordingly. Yet no man ever looked upon this virtuoso to be the standard of propriety in point of speaking and deportment. For my own part, I confess the player in question would, by dint of these qualifications, make a very good figure in the character of Pantaloon's lacquey, in the entertainment of Perseus and Andromeda,[1] and perhaps might acquire some reputation, by turning the *Revenge* into a pantomime; in which cause, I would advise him to come upon the stage, provided with an handful of flour, in order to besmear his face, when he pronounces *pale and aghast*, &c. and methinks he ought to illustrate the adder with an hideous hiss. But let us now come to the other situation, in which this modern Æsopus is supposed to distinguish himself so much, I mean that same *eclaircissement* comprehended in *Know then 'twas——I*. His manner, I own, may be altered since I was present at the representation of that performance; but certain I am, when I beheld him in that critical conjuncture, his behaviour appeared to me so uncouth, that I really imagined he was visited by some epileptic distemper; for he stood tottering and gasping for the space of two minutes, like a man suddenly struck with the palsy; and after various distorsions and side-shakings, as if he had got fleas in his doublet, heaved up from his lungs the letter *I*, like a huge anchor from foul ground.'

This criticism was acceptable to the majority of the college, who had no great veneration for the player in question; and his admirer, without making any reply, asked in a whisper, of the gentleman who sat next to him, if Pickle had not offered some production to the stage, and met with a repulse.[1] This question was not conveyed so softly, but that it reached the ears of our adventurer, who seemed disposed to make some answer, when he was prevented by the interposition of another member, who begged the opinion and advice of the community, touching a pastoral which he had just composed. Before he had time to produce the performance to the inspection of the society, the chairman observed, with a splenetic air, that he ought to have employed his time in some more profitable amusement, than a species of writing in which he had formerly met with so little success.

'True it is (replied the author) my last production of this kind was not very favourably received; a circumstance intirely owing to the nature of the subject, which did not at all interest the passions of the heart: but here, my dear Sir, the case is otherwise; this pastoral I composed upon the death of my own grandmother,[2] who was a woman, in all respects, worthy of the tears I have shed over her tomb; and this small composition is the genuine offspring of unfeigned sorrow: the blots which are still visible on the paper, indicate the grief with which I wrote it. *Lachrymæ fecêre lituras.* And sure he must have a flinty heart who can hear it read with an unmoistened eye.'

'If that be the case (said the president) I wish you would spare us the affliction of hearing it rehears'd: all of us, I believe, have real grievances of our own; so that we need not hunt after imaginary sorrows.' The poet, notwithstanding this discouragement, begg'd hard that he might exhibit a specimen of his performance; and being restricted to a few lines, he repeated the following stanzas, with the most rueful emphasis.

> Where was thou, wittol Ward, when hapless fate
> From these weak arms mine aged grannam tore:
> These pious arms essay'd too late,
> To drive the dismal phantom from the door.

Could not thy healing drop, illustrious quack,
Could not thy salutary pill prolong her days,
For whom, so oft, to Marybone, alack!
Thy sorrels dragg'd thee thro' the worst of ways?

Oil-dropping Twick'nham did not then detain
Thy steps, tho' tended by the Cambrian maids;
Nor the sweet *environs* of Drury-lane;
Nor dusty Pimlico's embow'ring shades;
Nor Whitehall, by the river's bank,
Beset with rowers dank;
Nor where th' Exchange pours forth its tawny sons;
Nor where to mix with offal, soil and blood,
Steep Snowhill rolls the sable flood;
Nor where the Mint's contaminated kennel runs:
Ill doth it now beseem,
That thou should'st doze and dream,
When death in mortal armour came,
And struck with ruthless dart the gentle dame.

Her lib'ral hand and sympathising breast,
The brute creation kindly bless'd:
Where'er she trod grimalkin purr'd around,
The squeaking pigs her bounty own'd;
Nor to the waddling duck or gabbling goose,
Did she glad sustenance refuse;
The strutting cock she daily fed,
And turky with his snout so red;
Of chickens careful as the pious hen,
Nor did she overlook the tomtit or the wren;
While redbreast hopp'd before her in the hall,
As if she common mother were of all.

For my distracted mind,
What comfort can I find?
O best of grannams! thou art dead and gone,
And I am left behind to weep and moan,
To sing thy dirge in sad funereal lay,
Ah! woe is me! alack! and well-a-day!

These interjections at the close of this pathetic elegy, were not
pronounced without the sobs and tears of the author, who looked

wishfully around him for applause, and having wiped his eyes, asked the chairman's opinion of what he had read. That cynical gentleman, who had no great devotion for the Arcadian, answered with a most equivocal aspect, 'Sad, very sad! sad enough to draw tears from the eyes of a bum-bailiff.' But as the performance was submitted to the criticism of the whole society, the epic poet stood up, and thus communicated his sentiments.

'Without entering upon a minute inquiry into the poetical merits of particular images, I must in general observe, that the stanzas are so irregular in point of measure, as well as in the number of the lines, that they cannot be comprehended under any species of the ancient versification. Then there are many dark allusions in the *Anistrophe*, which no reader can possibly understand, together with a catalogue of the names of places, for which the author seems to have rambled strangely from his subject, more studious of making a silly parade of his skill in poetical geography, than of interesting the passions of the heart. Indeed, one would be apt to conclude from this circumstance, that his grief was mere affectation, did not he blubber so piteously in the last verse. I could have wished, that more dignity had been preserved in the stanza which describes the old gentlewoman's benevolence, and that the last line had been altogether omitted, because it conjures up a most ridiculous image of her having actually hatched that same poultry, which she is said to have tended with such maternal care.'

To these animadversions the censured bard replied, that the verse, in being irregular, the more nearly resembled the natural exclamations of real affliction; and that such irregularity had not only been excused, but even considered as a beauty in many modern productions. He owned, that the allusions might be obscure to some readers, and therefore he intended to explain them in notes, at the bottom of the page. As to the topical descriptions which the critic had censured so severely, he said they were inserted to amuse and relieve the imagination of the reader, that he might not be too much affected with the *Pathos* of the subject; and with regard to the line,

> *As if she common mother were of all,*

far from carrying that ludicrous implication he had mentioned, it certainly conveyed the most amiable and parental idea of the deceased; and he did not doubt, that he should find his own opinion confirmed by that of the public, in a very comfortable sale of the work.

'So, after all this profession of filial tenderness, (cried the epic bard) the world will have some reason to say, you wanted to make a job of your grandmother's death.' 'Perhaps (answered the other) I shall make a present of the copy to my bookseller.' 'If you desire to be thought altogether disinterested in the affair, (resumed the critic) you ought to print a few copies at your own expence, and distribute them *gratis* among your friends; by these means, you will have as good a chance to see your own talents admired, and the memory of your grandame immortalized, as if you had sold the property of the piece for a thousand pounds.'

This proposal seemed to disconcert the elegiac writer; when the chairman interposing, 'Pshaw! (said he) why the devil should he be more delicate in that respect, than those people who sit at the head of taste? In every single circumstance to which you have objected, he has expressly imitated, not to say copied, the celebrated production of the universal patron.' 'What! (replied the other) you mean the famous Gosling Scrag Esq;[1] son and heir of Sir Marmaduke Scrag, who seats himself in the chair of judgment, and gives sentence upon the authors of the age. I should be glad to know, upon what pretensions to genius this preheminence is founded. Do a few flimsy odes, barren epistles, pointless epigrams, and the superstitious suggestions of an half-witted enthusiast, intitle him to that eminent rank he maintains in the world of letters? or did he acquire the reputation of a wit, by a repetition of trite invectives against a minister, conveyed in a theatrical cadence, accompanied with the most ridiculous gestures, before he believed it was his interest to desert his master, and renounce his party? For my own part, I never perused any of his performances, I never saw him open his mouth in public, I never heard him speak in private conversation, without recollecting and applying these two lines in Pope's Dunciad,

Dulness delighted, ey'd the lively dunce,
Remembring she herself was pertness once.[2]

Yet this antick piece of futility will decide dogmatically upon the merits of every new work; and if the author has not previously scratched himself into his favour, will pronounce upon it, with all the insolence and contempt of supercilious presumption. Nor is the levity of his head less provoking than his arrogance and self-conceit; the very performance which he yesterday applauded, will he to-morrow condemn through mere caprice; and that which he yesterday mentioned in terms of disdain, will he to-morrow extol to the skies, provided the author will humble himself so far, as to adore his superior genius, and meanly beg his protection. Never did he befriend a man of poetical merit, who did not court and retain his favour by such slavish prostitution, except one author, lately deceased;[1] and even he extended his complaisance too far, in complimental lines, which the warmth of his gratitude inspired, though he would never submit to the tame criticisms of his patron, or offer such an outrage to his own judgment, as to adopt the alterations which he proposed.'

'One would imagine, (said the chairman) that you had made an unsuccessful application to his patronage; but, notwithstanding all this eloquent declamation, the truth of which I shall not pretend to invalidate, I do aver, that Gosling Scrag Esq; is at this day the best milch-cow that any author ever stroaked: for, over and above his vanity, which lays him open to the necessities of all writers who can tickle, though never so awkwardly, he possesses such a comfortable share of simplicity, or rather lack of penetration, as cannot fail to turn to account with those who practise upon it. Let a scribbler (for example) creep into his notice by the most abject veneration, implore his judgment upon some performance, assume a look of awful admiration at his remarks, receive and read his emendations with pretended extasy, exert himself officiously about his person, make interest to be employed in running upon his errands, bawl for him upon all occasions in common conversation, prose and rhime, sit in presence of this great man, with an apparent sense of his own nothingness, and when he opens his mouth, listen *with a foolish face of praise*;[2] happy! if he has an opportunity to feed him with the soft pap of dedication, or by affecting an idiotical ignorance of the manners of life, to insinuate himself into his opinion, as a person absolutely detached from all worldly pursuits; like a sly brother of the quill, who, in going out, dropped a bank note upon the floor of his apartment, in such a manner, as that it could not escape the notice of Gosling, who viewing it accordingly, "Heavens! (said he, with his hands and eyes lifted up) what philosophical contempt must that man have for the pleasures of wealth!" Yes, I insist upon it, these are arts which will never fail to engage the friendship of Mr. Scrag, which will be sooner or later manifested in some warm sine-cure, ample subscription, post or reversion; and I advise Mr. Spondy[3] to give him the refusal of this same pastoral: who knows but he may have the good fortune of being listed in the number of his beef-eaters: in which case he may, in process of time, be provided for in the customs or church; when he is inclined to marry his own cook-wench, his gracious patron may condescend to give the bride away; and finally settle him in his old age, as a trading Westminster-justice.'

Mr. Spondy thanked the president for his wholesome counsel, which he assured him should not be neglected; and the evening being far advanced, the assembly broke up, without any other remarkable occurrence.

CHAPTER CIII

*The young Gentleman is introduced to a Virtuoso
of the first Order, and commences Yelper*

HITHERTO Peregrine had professed himself an author, without reaping the fruits of that occupation, except the little fame he had acquired by his late satire; but now he thought it high time to weigh *solid pudding against empty praise*;[1] and therefore engaged with some booksellers in a certain translation, which he obliged himself to perform for the consideration of two hundred pounds. The articles of agreement being drawn, he began his task with great eagerness, rose early in the morning to his work, at which he laboured all day long, went abroad with the bats in the evening, and appeared in the coffee-house, where he amused himself with the news-papers and conversation till nine o'clock; then he retired to his own apartment, and after a slight repast, betook himself to rest, that he might be able to unroost with the cock. This sudden change from his former way of life agreed so ill with his disposition, that, for the first time, he was troubled with flatulencies and indigestion, which produced anxiety and dejection of spirits, and the nature of his situation began in some measure to discompose his brain; a discovery which he no sooner made, than he had recourse to the advice of a young physician, who was a member of the college, and at this time one of our hero's most intimate acquaintance.

This son of Æsculapius having considered his case, imputed his disorder to the right cause, namely, want of exercise; dissuaded him from such close application to study, until he should be gradually familiarized to a sedentary life, advised him to enjoy his friend and his bottle in moderation, and wean himself from his former customs by degrees; and, above all things, to rise immediately after his first sleep, and exercise himself in a morning-walk. In order to render this last part of the prescription the more palatable, the doctor promised to attend him in these early excursions, and even to introduce him to a certain personage of note, who gave a sort of public breakfasting to the minor virtuosi of the age, and often employed his interest in behalf of those who properly culti-vated his countenance and approbation.

This proposal was extremely acceptable to our young gentleman, who, besides the advantage which might accrue to him from such a valuable connexion, foresaw much entertainment and satisfaction in the discourse of so many learned guests. The occasions of his health and interest, moreover, coincided in another circumstance, the minister's levee being kept betimes in the morning; so that he could perform his walk, yield his attendance, and breakfast at this philosophical board, without incroaching a great deal upon his other avocations.

Measures being thus preconcerted, the physician conducted our adventurer to the house of this celebrated sage, to whom he recom-mended him as a gentleman of genius and taste, who craved the honour of his acquaintance; but he had previously smoothed the way to this introduction, by representing Peregrine as a young fellow of great ambition, spirit and address, who could not fail to make a figure in the world; that, therefore, he would be a creditable addition to the subordinates of such a patron, and by his qualifica-tions, intrepidity and warmth of temper, turn out a consummate herald of his fame. Upon these considerations, he met with a most engaging reception from the entertainer, who was a well-bred man, of some learning, generosity and taste; but his foible was the desire of being thought the inimitable pattern of all three.

It was with a view to acquire and support this character, that his house was open to all those who had any pretensions to literature; consequently he was surrounded by a strange variety of pretenders; but none were discouraged, because he knew that even the most insignificant might, in some shape, conduce to the propagation of his praise. A babbler, tho' he cannot run upon the scent, may spring the game, and by his yelping help to fill up the cry: no wonder then, that a youth of Pickle's accomplishments was admitted and even invited into the pack. After having enjoyed a very short private audience in the closet, our young gentleman was shewn into another room, where half a dozen of his fellow-adherents waited for their Mæcenas, who in a few minutes appeared, with a most gracious aspect, received the compliments of the morning, and sat down to breakfast, in the midst of them, without any further ceremony.

The conversation at first turned upon the weather, which was investigated in a very philosophical manner by one of the company, who seemed to have consulted all the barometers and thermometers that ever were invented, before he would venture to affirm that it was a chill morning. This subject being accurately discussed, the chief inquired about the news of the learned world; and his inclination was no sooner expressed than every guest opened his mouth, in order to gratify his curiosity: but he that first captivated his attention was a meagre, shrivelled antiquary, who looked like an animated mummy, which had been scorched among the sands of the desert. He told the patron, that he had by accident met with a medal, which, tho' it was defaced by time, he would venture to pronounce a genuine antique, from the ringing and taste of the metal, as well as from the colour and composition of the rust: so saying, he produced a piece of copper coin, so consumed and disguised by age, that scarce a vestige of the impression was to be perceived. Nevertheless this connoisseur pretended to distinguish a face in profil, from which he concluded that the piece was of the Upper empire, and on the reverse he endeavoured to point out the bulb of the spear, and part of the parazonium, which were the insignia of the Roman Virtus, together with the fragment of one fold of the multicium in which she was cloathed. He likewise had discovered one angle of the letter N, and, at some distance, an intire I: from these circumstances conjecturing, and indeed concluding, that the medal was struck by Severus, in honour of the victory he obtained over his rival Niger, after he had forced the passes of mount Taurus. This criticism seemed very satisfactory to the entertainer, who having examined the coin by the help of his spectacles, plainly discerned the particulars which the owner had mentioned, and was pleased to term his account of the matter a very ingenious explanation.

The curiosity was circulated through the hands of all present, and every virtuoso, in his turn, licked the copper, and rung it upon the hearth, declaring his assent to the judgment which had been pronounced. At length, it fell under the inspection of our young gentleman, who, tho' no antiquarian, was very well acquainted with the current coin of his own country, and no sooner cast his eyes upon this valuable antique, than he affirmed, without hesitation, that it was no other than the ruins of an English farthing, and that same spear, parazonium, and multicium, the remains of the

emblems and drapery with which the figure of Britannia is delineated on our copper-money.

This hardy asseveration seemed to disconcert the patron, while
it incensed the medallist, who grinning like an enraged baboon,
'What d'ye tell me of a brass farthing? (said he) Did you ever know
modern brass of such a relish? Do but taste it, young gentleman;
and sure I am, if you have ever been conversant with subjects of this
kind, you will find as wide a difference in the savour between this
and an English farthing, as can possibly be perceived betwixt an
onion and a turnip: besides, this medal has the true Corinthian
ring; then the attitude is upright, whereas that of Britannia is
reclining; and how is it possible to mistake a branch of palm for
a parazonium?'

All the rest of the company espoused the virtuoso's side of the
question, because the reputation of each was concerned; and the
patron finding himself in the same predicament, assumed a
solemnity of feature, dashed with a small mixture of displeasure,
and told Peregrine, that as he had not made that branch of literature
his particular study, he was not surprised to see him mistaken in his
opinion. Pickle immediately understood the reproof; and tho' he
was shocked at the vanity or infatuation of his entertainer and
fellow-guests, asked pardon for his presumption, which was
accordingly excused, in consideration of his inexperience; and the
English farthing dignified with the title of a true antique.

The next person that addressed himself to the chief was a gentleman of a very mathematical turn, who valued himself upon the
improvements he had made in several domestic machines, and now
presented the plan of a new contrivance for cutting cabbages, in
such a manner as would secure the stock against the rotting rain,
and enable it to produce a plenteous after-crop of delicious sprouts.
In this important machine he had united the whole mechanic
powers, with such massy complication of iron and wood, that it
could not have been moved without the assistance of an horse,
and a road made for the convenience of the draught. These objections were so obvious, that they occurred at first sight to the
inspector-general, who greatly commended the invention, which,
he observed, might be applied to several other useful purposes,
could it once be rendered a little more portable and commodious.

The inventor, who had not foreseen these difficulties, was not
prepared to surmount them; but he took the hint in good part, and
promised to task his abilities anew, in altering the constitution of his
design. Not but that he underwent some severe irony from the rest

of the virtuosi, who complimented him upon the momentous improvement he had made, by which a family might save a dish of greens in a quarter, for so trifling an expence as that of purchasing, working and maintaining such a stupendous machine: but no man was more sarcastic in his remarks upon this piece of mechanism than the naturalist, who next appealed to the patron's approbation for a curious disquisition he had made, touching the procreation of muck flies, in which he had laid down a curious method of collecting, preserving and hatching the eggs of these insects, even in the winter, by certain modifications of artificial heat. The nature of this discovery was no sooner communicated, than Peregrine, unable to contain himself, burst into a fit of laughter, which infected every person at the table, the landlord himself not excepted, who found it impossible to preserve his wonted gravity of face.

Such unmannerly mirth did not fail to mortify the philosopher, who, after some pause, during which indignation and disdain were painted in his countenance, reprehended our young gentleman for his unphilosophical behaviour, and undertook to prove, that the subject of his inquiry was of infinite consequence to the progress and increase of natural knowledge: but he found no quarter from the vengeful engineer, who now retorted his ironical compliments, with great emphasis, upon this hot-bed for the generation of vermin, and advised him to lay the whole process before the Royal Society, which would, doubtless, present him with a medal, and give him a place among their memoirs, as a distinguished promoter of the useful arts. 'If (said he) you had employed your studies in finding out some effectual method to destroy those insects which prejudice and annoy mankind, in all probability you must have been contented with the contemplation of the good you had done; but this curious expedient for multiplying maggots, will surely intitle you to an honourable rank in the list of learned philosophers.' 'I don't wonder (replied the naturalist) that you should be so much adverse to the propagation of insects, because, in all likelihood, you are afraid that they will not leave you a cabbage to cut down with that same miraculous machine.' 'Sir (answered the mechanic, with great bitterness of voice and aspect) if the cabbage be as light-headed as some muck-worm philosophers, it will not be worth cutting down.' 'I never dispute upon cabbage with the son of a cucumber,' said the fly-breeder, alluding to the pedigree of his antagonist; who, impatient of the affront, started up with fury in his looks, exclaiming, ' 'Sdeath! meaning me, Sir?'

Here the patron, perceiving things drawing towards a rupture, interposed his authority, rebuking them tor their intemperance, and recommending to them amity and concord against the Goths and Vandals of the age, who took all opportunities of ridiculing and discouraging the adherents of knowledge and philosophy. After this exhortation, they had no pretence for carrying on the dispute, which was dropt, in all appearance, tho' the mechanick still retained his resentment; and after breakfast, when the company broke up, accosted his adversary in the street, desiring to know how he durst be so insolent as to make that scurrilous reflection upon his family: the fly-fancier, thus questioned, accused the mathematician of having been the aggressor, in likening his head to a light cabbage; and here the altercation being renewed, the engineer proceeded to the illustration of his mechanicks, tilting up his hand like a ballance, thrusting it forward by way of lever, embracing the naturalist's nose like a wedge betwixt two of his fingers, and turning it round, with the momentum of a screw or peritrochium. Had they been obliged to decide the dispute, with equal arms, the assailant would have had a great advantage over the other, who was very much his inferior in muscular strength; but the philosopher, being luckily provided with a cane, no sooner disengaged himself from this opprobrious application, than he handled his weapon with great dexterity about the head and shoulders of his antagonist, who, finding this shower of blows very disagreeable, was fain to betake himself to his heels for shelter, and was pursued by the angry victor, who chased him from one end of the street to the other, affording unspeakable satisfaction to the multitude, as well as to our hero and his introductor, who were spectators of the whole scene.

Thus was our adventurer initiated in the society of Yelpers, tho' he did not as yet fully understand the nature of his office, which was explained by the young physician, who chid him for his blunt behaviour in the case of the medal; and gave him to understand, that their patron's favour was neither to be gained, nor preserved by any man that would pretend to convict him of a mistake: he therefore counselled him to respect this foible, and cultivate the old gentleman with all the zeal and veneration, which a regard to his own character would permit him to pay. This task was the easier to one of our young gentleman's pliant disposition, because the virtuoso's behaviour was absolutely free from that insolent self-conceit, which he could not bear without disgust: the senior was, on the contrary, mild and beneficient; and Pickle was rather pleased than shocked at this weakness, because it flattered his vanity with the supposition of his own superior sense.

Cautioned in this manner, Peregrine profited so much by his insinuating qualifications, that, in a very little time, he was looked upon as one of the chief favourites of the patron, to whom he dedicated a small occasional poem; and every body believed he would reap the fruits of his attachment, among the first of the old gentleman's dependants.

CHAPTER CIV

Peregrine finding himself neglected by Sir Steady Steerwell, expostulates with him in a Letter; in consequence of which, he is forbid his House, loses his Pension, and incurs the Reputation of a Lunatick

THIS prospect of success, together with his expectations from the minister, whom he did not neglect, helped to comfort him under the reverse of fortune which he had undergone, and the uncertainty of the law-suit, which he still maintained for the recovery of his ten thousand pounds. The lawyers, indeed, continued to drain his pocket of money, while they filled his brain with unsubstantial hope; and he was actually obliged to borrow money from his bookseller, on the strength of the translation, in order to satisfy the demands of those ravenous harpies, rather than lay the Misanthrope under any difficulties, or have recourse to his friend Hatchway, who lived at the garrison, intirely ignorant of his distress: and this was not at all alleviated by the arrival of the Indiaman, in which he had ventured seven hundred pounds, as we have already observed; for he was given to understand, that the borrower was left dangerously ill at Bombay when the ship sailed, and that his chance for retrieving his money was extremely slender.

So situated, it is not to be supposed that he led a life of tranquillity, tho' he made a shift to struggle with the remonstrances of misfortune: yet such a gush of affliction would sometimes rush upon his thought, as overwhelmed all the ideas of his hope, and sunk him to the very bottom of despondence. Every equipage that passed him in the street, every person of rank and fortune that occurred to his view, recalled the gay images of his former life, with such mortifying reflection as stabbed him to the very soul. He lived, therefore, incessantly exposed to all the pangs of envy and disquiet.

When I say envy, I do not mean that sordid passion, in consequence of which a man repines at his neighbour's success, howsoever deserved; but that self-tormenting indignation which is inspired by the prosperity of folly, ignorance and vice. Without the intervening gleams of enjoyment, which he felt in the conversation of a few friends, he could not have supported his existence; or, at least, he must have suffered some violent discomposure of the brain: but one is still finding some circumstance of alleviation, even in the worst of conjunctures; and Pickle was so ingenious in these researches, that he maintained a good battle with disappointment, till the revolution of the term at which he had received his pension of three hundred pounds.

However, seeing the day elapse, without touching his allowance, notwithstanding his significant method of presenting himself at the minister's levee, when the year was expired, he wrote a letter to Sir Steady, reminding him of his situation and promise, and giving him to understand, that his occasions were such, as compelled him to demand his salary for the ensuing year.

In the morning after this letter was conveyed, the author went to his honour's house, in expectation of being admitted by particular order; but was mistaken in his hope, the minister not being visible. He then made his appearance at the levee, in hopes of being closetted; but though he took all opportunities of watching Sir Steady's eyes, he could not obtain one glance, and had the pleasure of seeing him retire, without being favoured with the least notice. These circumstances of wilful neglect were not over and above agreeable to our hero, who, in the agonies of vexation and resentment, went home, and composed a most acrimonious remonstrance to his honour; in consequence of which, he was not only deprived of all pretensions to a private audience, but expressly denied admittance on a public day, by Sir Steady's own order.

This prohibition, which announced his total ruin, filled him with rage, horror and despair: he cursed the porter who signified the minister's command, threatening to chastise him upon the spot for his presumption, and vented the most virulent imprecations upon his master, to the astonishment of those who chanced to enter during this conference. Having exhausted himself in these vain exclamations, he returned to his lodgings in a most frantic condition, biting his lips so that the blood ran from his mouth, dashing his head and fists against the sides of his chimney, and weeping with the most bitter expressions of woe.

Pipes, whose perception had been just sufficient to let him see, that there was some difference between the present and former situation of his master, over-hearing his transports, essayed to enter his apartment, with a view of administring consolation; and finding the door locked on the inside, desired admittance, protesting, that otherwise he would down with the bulk-head, in the turning of an hand-spike. Peregrine ordered him to retire, on pain of his displeasure, and swore, that if he should offer to break open the door, he would instantly shoot him through the head. Tom, without paying the least regard to this injunction, set himself at work immediately; and his master, exasperated at his want of reverence and respect, which, in his present paroxysm, appeared with the most provoking aggravation, flew into his closet, and snatching up one of his pistols already loaded, no sooner saw his valet enter the apartment, in consequence of having forced the lock, than he presented full at his face, and drew the trigger, but happily the priming flashed in the pan, without communicating with the charge; so that his furious purpose did not take effect upon the countenance of honest Pipes, who disregardful of the attempt, though he knew the contents of the piece, asked, without the least alteration of feature, if it must be foul weather through the whole voyage.

Peregrine, mad as he was, repented of his mischievous intent against such a faithful adherent, in the very moment of execution; and had it proved fatal, according to the design, in all probability he would have applied another to his own head. There are certain considerations that strike upon the mind with irresistible force, even in the midst of its distraction; the momentary recollection of some particular scene, occasioned by the features of the devoted victim, hath often struck the dagger from the assassin's hand. By such an impulse was Pipes protected from any repeated effort of his master's rage; the friendly cause of his present disobedience flashed upon the conviction of Peregrine, when he beheld the rugged front of his valet, in which also stood disclosed his long and faithful service, together with the recommendation of the deceased commodore.

Though his wrath was immediately suppressed, and his heart torn with remorse for what he had done, his brows remained still contracted; and darting a most ferocious regard at the intruder, 'Villain! (said he) how dare you treat me with such disrespect?' 'Why shouldn't I lend a hand for the preservation of the ship, (answered the unruffled Pipes) when there is more sail than ballast aboard, and the pilot quits the helm in despair? What signifies one or two broken voyages, so long as our timbers are strong, and our vessel in good trim: if she loses upon one tack, mayhap she may gain upon another; and I'll be damn'd, if one day or other we don't fetch up our leeway: as for the matter of provision, you have started a pretty good stock of money into my hold, and you are welcome to hoist it up again when you wool?'

Here Tom was interrupted by the arrival of Mr. Crabtree, who seeing Peregrine with a pistol in his hand, and such wild disorder in his looks, his head, hands and mouth besmeared with blood, and, moreover, smelling the gunpowder which had been burnt, actually believed he had either committed, or was bent upon murder, and, accordingly, retreated down stairs with infinite dispatch; though all his speed could not convey him without the reach of Pipes, who overtaking him in the passage, carried him back into his master's apartment, observing by the way, that this was no time to sheer off, when his consort stood in need of his assistance.

There was something so ruefully severe in the countenance of Cadwallader, thus compelled, that at any other time, our hero would have laughed at his concern; but at present, there was nothing risible in his disposition: he had, however, laid aside his pistol, and endeavoured, though in vain, to compose his internal disturbance; for he could not utter one syllable to the Misanthrope, but stood staring at him in silence, with a most delirious aspect, which did not tend to dispel the dismay of his friend, who, after some recollection, 'I wonder (said he) that you have never killed your man before. Pray, how may you have disposed of the body?' Pickle having recovered the faculty of speech, ordered his lacquey out of the room, and in a most incoherent detail, made Crabtree acquainted with the perfidious conduct of the minister.

The confident was very glad to find his fears disappointed; for he had really concluded, that some life was lost: and perceiving the youth too much agitated to be treated by him in his usual stile, he owned that Sir Steady was a rascal, encouraged Pickle with the hope of being one day able to make reprisals upon him; in the mean time, offered him money for his immediate occasions, exhorted him to exert his own qualifications in rendering himself independent of such miscreants, and finally, counselled him to represent his wrongs to the nobleman whom he had formerly obliged, with a view of interesting that peer in his behalf, or at least of obtaining a satisfactory explanation from the minister, that he might take no premature measures of revenge.

These admonitions were so much milder, and more agreeable

than our hero expected from the Misanthrope, that they had a very favourable effect upon his transports, which gradually subsided, until he became so tractable, as to promise that he would conform to his advice; in consequence of which, he next morning waited upon his lordship, who received him very politely, as usual, and with great patience heard his complaint, which, by the bye, he could not repeat without some hasty ebullitions of passionate resentment. This peer, after having gently disapproved of the letter of expostulation, which had produced such unfortunate effects, kindly undertook to recommend his case to the minister, and actually performed his promise that same day, when Sir Steady informed him, to his utter astonishment, that the poor young gentleman was disordered in his brain, so that he could not possibly be provided for in a place of importance, with any regard to the service; and it could not be expected that he (Sir Steady) would support his extravagance from his own private purse: that he had indeed, at the solicitation of a nobleman deceased, made him a present of three hundred pounds, in consideration of some loss that he pretended to have sustained in an election; but, since that time, had perceived in him such indisputable marks of lunacy, both by his distracted letters and personal behaviour, as obliged him to give order, that he should not be admitted into the house. To corroborate this assertion, the minister actually called in the evidence of his own porter, and one of the gentlemen of his houshold, who had heard the execrations that escaped our youth, when he first found himself excluded. In short, the nobleman was convinced, that Peregrine was certainly and *bona fide* mad as a March hare; and, by the help of this intimation, began to recollect some symptoms of distraction which appeared in his last visit; he remembered a certain incoherence in his speech, a violence of gesture and wildness of look, that now evidently denoted a disturbed understanding: and he determined, for his own credit and security, to disentangle himself from such a dangerous acquaintance.

With this view, he, in imitation of Sir Steady, commanded his gate to be shut against our adventurer; so that when he went to know the result of his lordship's conference with the minister, the door was flung in his face, and the janitor told him through an iron grate, that he needed not give himself the trouble of calling again, for his lord desired to be excused from seeing him. He spoke not a word in answer to this declaration, which he immediately imputed to the ill offices of the minister, against whom he breathed defiance and revenge, in his way to the lodgings of Cadwallader; who being made acquainted with the manner of his reception, begg'd he would desist from all schemes of vengeance, until he (Crabtree) should be able to unriddle the mystery of the whole, which he did not doubt of unveiling, by means of his acquaintance with a family, in which his lordship often spent the evening at whist.

It was not long before he had the desired opportunity; the nobleman being under no injunctions or obligation to keep the affair secret, discovered the young gentleman's misfortune, by way of news, to the first company in which he happened to be; and Peregrine's name was not so obscure in the fashionable world, but that his disorder became the general topic of conversation for a day; so that his friend soon partook of the intelligence, and found means to learn the particulars of the minister's information, as above related. Nay, he was in danger of becoming a proselyte to Sir Steady's opinion, when he recalled and compared every circumstance which he knew of Pickle's impatience and impetuosity.

Indeed, nothing more easily gains credit than an imputation of madness fixed upon any person whatsoever: for when the suspicion of the world is roused, and its observation once set at work, the wisest, the coolest man upon earth, will, by some particulars in his behaviour, convict himself of the charge: every singularity in his dress and manner (and such are observable in every person) that before passed unheeded, now rises up in judgment against him, with all the exaggeration of the observer's fancy; and the sagacious examiner perceives distraction in every glance of the eye, turn of the finger, and motion of the head: when he speaks, there is a strange peculiarity in his argument and expression; when he holds his tongue, his imagination teems with some extravagant reverie; his sobriety of demeanour is no other than a lucid interval, and his passion mere delirium.

If people of the most sedate and insipid life and conversation are subject to such criticisms, no wonder that they should take place upon a youth of Peregrine's fiery disposition, which, on some occasions, would have actually justified any remarks of this kind, which his greatest enemies could make. He was accordingly represented as one of those enterprizing Bucks, who, after having spent their fortunes in riot and excess, are happily bereft of their understanding, and consequently insensible of the want and disgrace which they have intailed upon themselves.

Cadwallader himself was so much affected with the report, that for some time he hesitated in his deliberations upon our hero, before he could prevail upon himself to communicate to him the information he had received, or to treat him in other respects as a man of sound intellects. At length, however, he ventured to make Pickle acquainted with the particulars he had learn'd, imparting them with such caution and circumlocution, as he thought necessary to prevent the young gentleman from transgressing all bounds of temper and moderation: but, for once, he was agreeably deceived in his prognostic. Incensed as our hero was at the conduct of the minister, he could not help laughing at the ridiculous aspersion, which, he told his friends, he would soon refute in a manner that should not be very agreeable to his calumniator; observing that it was a common practice with this state pilot, thus to slander those people to whom he lay under obligations which he had no mind to discharge. 'True it is, (said Peregrine) he has succeeded more than once in contrivances of this kind, having actually reduced divers people of weak heads to such extremity of despair, as hath issued in downright distraction, whereby he was rid of their importunities, and his judgment confirmed at the same time: but I have now (thank heaven) attained to such a pitch of philosophical resolution, as will support me against all his machinations; and I will forthwith exhibit the monster to the public, in his true lineaments of craft, perfidy and ingratitude.'

This indeed was the plan with which Mr. Pickle had amused himself during the researches of Crabtree; and by this time it so effectually flattered his imagination, that he believed he should be able to bring his adversary (in spite of all his power) to his own terms of submission, by distinguishing himself in the list of those who, at that period, wrote against the administration. Nor was this scheme so extravagant as it may seem to be, had not he overlooked one material circumstance, which Cadwallader himself did not recollect, when he approved of this project.

While he thus meditated vengeance, the fame of his disorder, in due course of circulation, reached the ears of that lady of quality, whose memoirs have appeared in the third volume[1] of these adventures. The correspondence with which she had honoured our hero had been long broke off, for the reason already advanced, namely, his dread of being exposed to her infatuating charms. He had been candid enough to make her acquainted with this cause of exiling himself from her presence; and she admitted the prudence of his self-restraint, although she could have been very well satisfied with the continuance of his intimacy and conversation, which were not at all beneath the desire of any lady in the kingdom. Notwithstanding this interruption, she still retained a friendship and regard for his character, and felt all the affliction of a humane heart, at the news of his misfortunes and deplorable distemper. She had seen him courted and cultivated in the sun-shine of his prosperity; but she knew from sad experience, how all those insect followers shrink away in the winter of distress. Her compassion represented him as a poor unhappy lunatic, destitute of all the necessaries of life, dragging about the ruins of human nature, and exhibiting the spectacle of blasted youth, to the scorn and abhorrence of his fellow-creatures. Aking with these charitable considerations, she found means to learn in what part of the town he lodged; and laying aside all superfluous ceremony, went in a hackney-chair to his door, which was opened by the ever-faithful Pipes.

Her ladyship immediately recollected the features of this trusty follower, whom she could not help loving in her heart, for his attachment and fidelity, which, after she had applauded with a most gracious commendation, she kindly inquired after the state of his master's health, and asked if he was in a condition to be seen.

Tom, who could not suppose that the visit of a fine lady would be unacceptable to a youth of Peregrine's complexion, made no verbal reply to the question; but beckoning her ladyship with an arch significance of feature, at which she could not forbear smiling, he walked softly up stairs; and she, in obedience to the signal, followed her guide into the apartment of our hero, whom she found at a writing-table, in the very act of composing an eulogium upon his good friend Sir Steady. The nature of his work had animated his countenance with an uncommon degree of vivacity; and being dressed in a neat dishabille, his figure could not have appeared to more advantage, in the eye of a person who despised the tinsel of unnecessary ornament. She was extremely well pleased to see her expectations so agreeably disappointed; for, instead of the squalid circumstances and wretched looks attending indigence and distraction, every thing was decent and genteel; and the patient's aspect such, as betokened internal satisfaction. Hearing the rustling of silk in his room, he lifted up his eyes from the paper, and seeing her ladyship, was struck with astonishment and awe, as at the unexpected apparition of some supernatural being.

Before he could recollect himself from his confusion, which called the blood into his cheeks, she told him, that, on the strength of old acquaintance, she was come to visit him, though it was a long time since he had given her good reason to believe, he had absolutely forgot that there was such a person as she in being. After having made the most warm acknowledgments for this unforeseen honour, he assured her ladyship, that the subject of her reproach was not his fault, but rather his very great misfortune; and that if it had been in his power to forget her so easily, as she seemed to imagine, he should never have given her cause to tax him with want of duty and respect.

Still dubious of his situation, she began to converse with him on different subjects; and he acquitted himself so well in every particular, that she no longer doubted his having been misrepresented by the malice of his enemies; and candidly told him the cause and intent of her coming. He was not deficient in expressions of gratitude for this instance of her generosity and friendship, which even drew tears from his eyes; and as to the imputation of madness, he explained it so much to her ladyship's satisfaction, that she evidently perceived he had been barbarously dealt with, and that the charge was no other than a most villainous aspersion.

Notwithstanding all his endeavours to conceal the true state of his finances, it was impossible for him to give this detail, without disclosing some of the difficulties under which he laboured; and her ladyship's sagacity divining the rest, she not only made him a tender of assistance, but presenting a bank-note for a considerable sum, insisted upon his acceptance of it, as a trifling mark of her esteem, and a specimen of what she was inclined to do in his behalf. But this mark of her benevolence he would by no means receive; assuring her, that though his affairs were at present a little perplexed, he had never felt the least circumstance of distress, and begging that she would not subject him to the burthen of such an unnecessary obligation.

Being obliged to put up with this refusal, she protested she would never forgive him, should she ever hear that he rejected her offer, when he stood in need of her aid; or if in time to come, he should not apply to her friendship, if ever he should find himself incommoded in point of fortune: 'An over-delicacy in this respect (said she) I shall look upon as a disapprobation of my own conduct; because I myself have been obliged to have recourse to my friends, in such emergencies.'

These generous remonstrances and marks of particular friendship, could not fail to make deep impression upon the heart of our hero, which still smarted from the former impulse of her charms: he not only felt all those transports which a man of honour and sensibility may be supposed to feel upon such an occasion, but the sentiments of a more tender passion awaking in his breast, he could not help expressing himself in terms adapted to the emotions of his soul; and at length plainly told her, that were he disposed to be a beggar, he would ask something of infinitely more importance to his peace, than the charitable assistance she had proffered.

Her ladyship had too much penetration to mistake his meaning; but as she did not chuse to encourage his advances, pretended to interpret his intimation into a general compliment of gallantry, and in a jocose manner, desired he would not give her any reason to believe his lucid interval was past. 'In faith, my lady, (said he) I perceive the fit coming on; and I don't see why I may not use the privilege of my distemper, so far as to declare myself one of your most passionate admirers.' 'If you do, (replied her ladyship) I shall not be fool enough to believe a madman, unless I were assured that your disorder proceeded from your love: and that this was the case, I suppose you would find it difficult to prove.' 'Nay, Madam, (cried the youth) I have in this drawer, what will convince you of my having been mad on that strain; and since you doubt my pretensions, you must give me leave to produce my testimonials.' So saying, he opened a scrutore, and taking out a paper, presented her with the following song, which he had written in her praise, immediately after he was made acquainted with the particulars of her story.

I

While with fond rapture and amaze,
On thy transcendent charms I gaze,
My cautious soul essays in vain
Her peace and freedom to maintain:
Yet let that blooming form divine,
Where grace and harmony combine,
Those eyes, like genial orbs, that move,
Dispensing gladness, joy and love,
In all their pomp assail my view,
Intent my bosom to subdue;
My breast, by wary maxims steel'd,
Not all those charms shall force to yield.

II

But, when invok'd to beauty's aid,
I see th' enlighten'd soul display'd;
That soul so sensibly sedate
Amid the storms of froward fate!

Thy genius active, strong and clear,
Thy wit sublime, tho' not severe,
The social ardour void of art,
That glows within thy candid heart;
My spirits, sense and strength decay,
My resolution dies away,
And ev'ry faculty opprest,
Almighty love invades my breast! [1]

Her ladyship having perused this production, 'Were I inclined to be suspicious, (said she) I should believe that I had no share in producing this composition, which seems to have been inspired by a much more amiable object. However, I will take your word for your intention, and thank you for the unmerited compliment, though I have met with it in such an accidental manner. Nevertheless, I must be so free as to tell you, it is now high time for you to contract that unbounded spirit of gallantry, which you have indulged so long, into a sincere attachment for the fair Emilia, who, by all accounts, deserves the whole of your attention and regard.' His nerves thrilled at mention of that name, which he never heard pronounced without agitation; and rather than undergo the consequence of a conversation upon this subject, he chose to drop the theme of love altogether, and industriously introduced some other topic of discourse.

CHAPTER CV

*He writes against the Minister, by whose Instigation
he is arrested, and moves himself by* Habeas Corpus
into the Fleet

My lady having prolonged her stay beyond the period of a common visit, and repeated her protestations in the most frank and obliging manner, took her leave of our adventurer, who promised to pay his respects to her in a few days, at her own house. Mean while, he resumed his task; and having finished a most severe remonstrance against Sir Steady, not only with regard to his private ingratitude, but also to his male-administration of public affairs, he sent it to the author of a weekly paper, who had been long a professed reformer in politics; and it appeared in a very few days, with a note of the publisher, desiring the favour of a further correspondence with the author.

The animadversions contained in this small essay were so spirited and judicious, and a great many new lights thrown upon the subject with such perspicuity, as attracted the notice of the public in an extraordinary manner, and helped to raise the character of the paper in which it was inserted. The minister was not the last who examined the performance, which, in spite of all his boasted temper, provoked him to such a degree, that he set his emissaries at work, and by dint of corruption, procured a sight of the manuscript in Peregrine's own hand-writing, which he immediately recognized; and, for further confirmation of his opinion, compared with the two letters which he had received from our adventurer. Had he known the young gentleman's talents for declamation were so acute, perhaps he would never have given him cause to complain, but employed him in the vindication of his own measures; nay, he might still have treated him like some other authors whom he had brought over from the opposition, had not the keenness of this first assault incensed him to a desire of revenge. He, therefore, no sooner made this discovery, than he conveyed his directions to his dependant the receiver-general, who was possessed of Pickle's notes; and next day, while our author stood within a circle of his acquaintance, at a certain coffee-house, holding forth with great eloquence upon the diseases of the state, he was accosted by a bailiff, who entering the room with five or six followers, told him aloud, that he had a writ against him for twelve hundred pounds, at the suit of Mr. Ravage Gleanum.

The whole company were astonished at this address, which did not fail to discompose the defendant himself, who (as it were instinctively) in the midst of his confusion, saluted the officer across the head with his cane; in consequence of which application, he was surrounded and disarmed in an instant by the gang, who carried him off to the next tavern in the most opprobrious manner. Nor did one of the spectators interpose in his behalf, or visit him in his confinement with the least tender of advice or assistance; such is the zeal of a coffee-house friendship.

This stroke was the more severe upon our hero, as it was altogether unexpected; for he had utterly forgot the debt for which he was arrested. His present indignation was, however, chiefly kindled against the bailiff, who had done his office in such a disrespectful manner: and the first use he made of his recollection in the house to which they conducted him, was to chastise him for the insolence and indecency of his behaviour. This task he performed with his bare fists, every other weapon being previously conveyed out of his reach; and the delinquent underwent his discipline with surprising patience and resignation, asking pardon with great humility, and protesting before God, that he had never willingly and wittingly used any gentleman with ill manners, but had been commanded to arrest our adventurer according to the express direction of the creditor, on pain of forfeiting his place.

By this declaration Peregrine was appeased, and out of a delirium of passion, waked to all the horrors of reflection. All the glory of his youth was now eclipsed, all the blossoms of his hope were blasted, and he saw himself doomed to the miseries of a jail, without the least prospect of enlargement, except in the issue of his law-suit, of which he had, for some time past, grown less and less confident every day. What would become of the unfortunate, if the constitution of the mind did not permit them to bring one passion into the field against another? passions that operate in the human breast, like poisons of a different nature, extinguishing each other's effect. Our hero's grief reigned in full despotism, until it was deposed by revenge; during the predominancy of which, he considered every thing which had happened as a circumstance conducive to its gratification: 'If I must be prisoner for life, (said he to himself) if I must relinquish all my gay expectations, let me at least have the satisfaction of clanking my chains so as to interrupt the repose of my adversary; and let me search in my own breast for that peace and contentment, which I have not been able to find in all the scenes of my success. In being detached from the world, I shall be delivered from folly and ingratitude, as well as exempted from an expence, which I should have found it very difficult, if not impracticable, to support; I shall have little or no temptation to mispend my time, and more undisturbed opportunity to earn my subsistence, and prosecute my revenge. After all, a jail is the best tub to which a cynic philosopher can retire.'

In consequence of these comfortable reflections, he sent a letter to Mr. Crabtree, with an account of his misfortune, signifying his resolution to move himself immediately into the Fleet, and desiring that he would send him some understanding attorney of his acquaintance, who would direct him in the steps necessary to be taken for that purpose. The Misanthrope, upon the receit of this intimation, went in person to a lawyer, whom he accompanied to the spunging-house, whither the prisoner had by this time retired;

and Peregrine was, under the auspices of this director, conducted to the judge's chamber, where he was left in the custody of a tipstaff; and after having paid for a warrant of *Habeas Corpus*, by him conveyed to the Fleet, and delivered to the care of the warden.

Here he was introduced to the lodge, in which he was obliged to expose himself a full half hour to the eyes of all the turnkeys and doorkeepers, who took an accurate survey of his person, that they might know him again at first sight; and then he was turned loose into the place called the master's side, having given a valuable consideration for that privilege. This is a large range of building, containing some hundreds of lodging-rooms for the convenience of the prisoners, who pay so much *per* week for that accommodation. In short, this community is like a city detached from all communication with the neighbouring parts, regulated by its own laws, and furnished with peculiar conveniences, for the use of the inhabitants. There is a coffee-house for the resort of gentlemen, in which all sorts of liquors are kept, and a public kitchen, where any quantity of meat is sold at a very reasonable rate, or any kind of provision boiled and roasted *gratis*, for the poor prisoners: nay, there are certain servants of the public, who are obliged to go to market, at the pleasure of individuals, without fee or reward from those who employ them: nor are they cooped up, so as to be excluded from the benefit of fresh air, there being an open area of a considerable extent adjacent to the building, on which they may exercise themselves in walking, skittles, bowls, and variety of other diversions, according to the inclination of each.

Our adventurer being admitted a denizen of this community, found himself bewildered in the midst of strangers, who, by their appearance, did not at all prepossess him in their favour; and after having strolled about the place with his friend Cadwallader, repaired to the coffee-house, in order to be further informed of the peculiar customs which it was necessary for him to know.

There, while he endeavoured to pick up intelligence from the bar-keeper, he was accosted by a person in canonicals, who very civilly asking if he was a new-comer, and being answered in the affirmative, gave him the salutation of welcome to the society, and, with great hospitality, undertook to initiate him in the constitutions of the brotherhood. This humane clergyman gave him to understand, that his first care ought to be that of securing a lodging; telling him, there was a certain number of apartments in the prison let at the same price, though some were more commodious than others; and that when the better sort became vacant, by the removal of their possessors, those who succeeded in point of seniority, had the privilege of occupying the empty tenements, preferable to the rest of the inhabitants, howsoever respectable they might otherwise be: that when the jail was very much crowded, there was but one chamber allotted for two lodgers; but this was not considered as any great hardship on the prisoners, because, in that case, there was always a sufficient number of males, who willingly admitted the females to a share of their apartments and beds: not but the time had been, when this expedient would not answer the occasion, because, after a couple had been quartered in every room, there was a considerable residue still unprovided with lodging; so that for the time being, the last comers were obliged to take up their habitation in Mount Scoundrel, an apartment most miserably furnished, in which they lay promiscuously amidst filth and vermin, until they could be better accommodated in due course of rotation.

Peregrine hearing the description of this place, began to be very impatient about his night's lodging; and the parson perceiving his anxiety, conducted him, without loss of time, to the warden, who forthwith put him in possession of a paultry chamber, for which he agreed to pay half a crown a week. This point being settled, his director gave him an account of the different methods of eating, either singly, in a mess, or at an ordinary; and advised him to chuse the last, as the most reputable, offering to introduce him next day to the best company in the Fleet, who always dined together in public.

Pickle having thanked this gentleman for his civilities, and promised to be governed by his advice, invited him to pass the evening at his apartment; and in the mean time, shut himself up with Crabtree, in order to deliberate upon the wreck of his affairs. Of all his ample fortune, nothing now remained but his wardrobe, which was not very sumptuous, about thirty guineas in cash, and the garison, which the Misanthrope counselled him to convert into ready money, for his present subsistence. This advice, however, he absolutely rejected, not only on account of his having already bestowed it upon Hatchway, during the term of his natural life, but also with a view of retaining some memorial of the commodore's generosity. He proposed, therefore, to finish in this retreat the translation which he had undertaken, and earn his future subsistence by labour of the same kind. He desired Cadwallader to take charge of his moveables, and send to him such linen and cloaths as he should have occasion for in his confinement. But, among all

Chapter CV

his difficulties, nothing embarassed him so much as his faithful Pipes, whom he could no longer entertain in his service. He knew Tom had made shift to pick up a competency in the course of his ministration; but that reflection, though it in some measure alleviated, could not wholly prevent the mortification he must suffer in parting with an affectionate adherent, who was by this time become as necessary to him as one of his own members, and who was so accustomed to live under his command and protection, that he did not believe the fellow could reconcile himself to any other way of life.

Crabtree, in order to make himself easy on that score, offered to adopt him in the room of his own valet, whom he would dismiss; though he observed, that Pipes had been quite spoiled in our hero's service. But Peregrine did not chuse to lay his friend under that inconvenience, knowing that his present lacquey understood and complied with all the peculiarities of his humour, which Pipes would never be able to study or regard; and therefore determined to send him back to his ship-mate Hatchway, with whom he had spent the fore-part of his life.

These points being adjusted, the two friends adjourned to the coffee-house, with a view of inquiring into the character of the clergyman, to whose beneficence our adventurer was so much indebted; and they learned he was a person who had incurred the displeasure of the bishop in whose diocese he was settled, and, being unequal in power to his antagonist, had been driven to the Fleet, in consequence of his obstinate opposition; tho' he still found means to enjoy a pretty considerable income, by certain irregular practices in the way of his function, which income was chiefly consumed in acts of humanity to his fellow-creatures in distress.

His eulogium was scarce finished, when he entered the room, according to appointment with Peregrine, who ordering wine and something for supper to be carried to his apartment, the triumvirate went thither; and Cadwallader taking his leave for the night, the two fellow-prisoners passed the evening very sociably, our hero being entertained by his new companion with the private history of the place, some particulars of which were extremely curious. He told him, that the person who attended them at supper, bowing with the most abject servility, and worshipping them, every time he opened his mouth, with the epithets of *your Lordship* and *your Honour*, had, a few years before, been actually a captain in the guards; who, after having run his career in the great world, had threaded every station in their community, from that of a buck of the first order, who swaggers about the Fleet in a laced coat, with a footman and whore, to the degree of tapster, in which he was now happily settled. 'If you will take the trouble of going into the cook's kitchen, (said he) you will perceive a beau metamorphosed into a turn-spit; and there are some hewers of wood and drawers of water in this microcosm, who have had forests and fish-ponds of their own: yet, notwithstanding such a miserable reverse of fortune, they are neither objects of regard or compassion, because their misfortunes are the fruits of the most vicious extravagance, and they are absolutely insensible of the misery which is their lot. Those of our fellow-sufferers, who have been reduced by undeserved losses, or the precipitation of unexperienced youth, never fail to meet with the most brotherly assistance, provided they behave with decorum, and a due sense of their unhappy circumstances. Nor are we destitute of power to chastise the licentious, who refuse to comply with the regulations of the place, and disturb the peace of the community, with riot and disorder. Justice is here impartially administered, by a court of equity, consisting of a select number of the most respectable inhabitants, who punish all offenders with equal judgment and resolution, after they have been fairly convicted of the crimes laid to their charge.'

The clergyman having thus explained the œconomy of the place, as well as the cause of his own confinement, began to discover signs of curiosity, touching our hero's situation; and Pickle, thinking he could do no less for the satisfaction of a man, who had treated him in such an hospitable manner, favoured him with a detail of the circumstances which produced his imprisonment: at the same time, gratifying his resentment against the minister, which delighted in recapitulating the injuries he had received. The parson, who had been prepossessed in favour of our youth at first sight, understanding what a considerable part he had acted on the stage of life, felt his veneration increase; and, pleased with the opportunity of introducing a stranger of his consequence to the club, left him to his repose, or rather to ruminate on an event which he had not as yet seriously considered.

I might here, in imitation of some celebrated writers, furnish out a page or two, with the reflections he made upon the instability of human affairs, the treachery of the world, and the temerity of youth; and endeavour to decoy the reader into a smile, by some quaint observation of my own, touching the sagacious moralizer:[1] but, besides that I look upon this practice as an impertinent

Chapter CV

anticipation of the peruser's thoughts, I have too much matter of importance upon my hands, to give the reader the least reason to believe that I am driven to such paultry shifts, in order to eke out the volume. Suffice it then, to say, our adventurer passed a very uneasy night, not only from the thorny suggestions of his mind, but likewise from the anguish of his body, which suffered from the hardness of his couch, as well as from the natural inhabitants thereof, which did not tamely suffer his intrusion.

In the morning he was waked by Pipes, who brought upon his shoulder a portmanteau filled with necessaries, according to the direction of Cadwallader; and tossing it down upon the floor, regaled himself with a quid, without the least manifestation of concern. After some pause, 'You see, Pipes, (said his master) to what I have brought myself.' 'Ey, ey, (answered the valet) once the vessel is ashore, what signifies talking? We must bear a hand to tow her off, if we can: if she won't budge for all the anchors and capstans aboard, after we have lightened her, by cutting away her masts, and heaving our guns and cargo overboard, why then, mayhap, a brisk gale of wind, a tide, or current setting from shore, may float her again in the blast of a whistle. Here is two hundred and ten guineas by the tale, in this here canvas-bag; and upon this scrap of paper——no, avast—that's my discharge from the parish for Moll Trundle——ey, here it is—an order for thirty pounds upon the what-d'ye-call-'em in the city; and two tickets for twenty-five and eighteen, which I lent, d'ye see, to Sam Studding to buy a cargo of rum, when he hoisted the sign of the Commodore at St. Catharine's.' So saying, he spread his whole stock upon the table, for the acceptance of Peregrine; who, being very much affected with this fresh instance of his attachment, expressed his satisfaction at seeing he had been such a good œconomist, paid his wages up to that very day, thanked him for his faithful services, and, observing that he himself was no longer in a condition to maintain a domestick, advised him to retire to the garison, where he would be kindly received by his friend Hatchway, to whom he would recommend him in the strongest terms.

Pipes looked blank at this unexpected intimation, to which he replied, that he wanted neither pay nor provision, but only to be employed as a tender; and that he would not steer his course for the garison, unless his master would first take his lumber aboard. Pickle, however, peremptorily refused to touch a farthing of the money, which he commanded him to put up; and Pipes was so mortified at his refusal, that, twisting the notes together, he threw them into the fire without hesitation, crying, 'Damn the money!' and the canvas-bag, with its contents, would have shared the same fate, had not Peregrine started up, and snatching the paper from the flames, ordered his valet to forbear, on pain of being banished for ever from his sight. He told him, that, for the present, there was a necessity for his being dismissed, and he discharged him accordingly; but if he would go and live quietly with the lieutenant, he promised, on the first favourable turn of his fortune, to take him again into his service. In the mean time he gave him to understand, that he neither wanted, nor would make any use of his money, which he insisted upon his pocketing immediately, on pain of forfeiting all title to his favour.

Pipes was very much chagrined at these injunctions, to which he made no reply; but sweeping the money into his bag, stalked off, in silence, with a look of grief and mortification, which his countenance had never exhibited before. Nor was the proud heart of Pickle unmoved upon this occasion: he could scarce suppress his sorrow in the presence of Pipes, and, soon as he was gone, it vented itself in tears.

Having no great pleasure in conversing with his own thoughts, he dressed himself with all convenient dispatch, being attended by one of the occasional valets of the place, who had formerly been a rich mercer in the city; and this operation being performed, he went to breakfast at the coffee-house, where he happened to meet with his friend the clergyman, and several persons of genteel appearance, to whom the doctor introduced him as a new messmate. By these gentlemen he was conducted to a place, where they spent the forenoon in playing at fives, an exercise in which our hero took singular delight; and about one o'clock a court was held, for the trial of two delinquents, who had transgressed the laws of honesty and good order.

The first who appeared at the bar was an attorney, accused of having picked a gentleman's pocket of his handkerchief; and the fact being proved by incontestible evidence, he received sentence; in consequence of which he was immediately carried to the public pump, and subjected to a severe cascade of cold water. This cause being discussed, they proceeded to the trial of the other offender, who was a lieutenant of a man of war, indicted for a riot, which he had committed in company with a female not yet taken, against the laws of the place, and the peace of his fellow-prisoners. The culprit had been very obstreperous, and absolutely refused to obey the summons, with many expressions of contempt and defiance against the authority of the court; upon which the constables were ordered to bring him to the bar, *vi & armis*; and he was accordingly brought before the judge, after having made a most desperate resistance with a hanger, by which one of the officers was dangerously wounded. This outrage was such an aggravation of his crime, that the court would not venture to decide upon it, but remitted him to the sentence of the warden; who, by virtue of his dictatorial power, ordered the rioter to be loaded with irons, and confined in the strong-room, which is a dismal dungeon, situated upon the side of the ditch, infested with toads and vermin, surcharged with noisome damps, and impervious to the least ray of light.

Justice being done upon the criminals, our adventurer and his company adjourned to the ordinary, which was kept at the coffee-house; and he found, upon enquiry, that his mess-mates consisted of one officer, two under-writers, three projectors, an alchymist, an attorney, a parson, a brace of poets, a baronet, and a knight of the bath. The dinner, tho' not sumptuous, nor very elegantly served up, was nevertheless substantial, and pretty well dressed: the wine was tolerable, and all the guests as chearful as if they had been utter strangers to calamity; so that our adventurer began to relish the company, and mix in the conversation, with that sprightliness and ease which were peculiar to his disposition. The repast being ended, the reckoning paid, and part of the gentlemen withdrawn to cards, or other avocations, those who remained, among whom Peregrine made one, agreed to spend the afternoon in conversation over a bowl of punch; and the liquor being produced, they passed the time very socially in various topicks of discourse, including many curious anecdotes relating to their own affairs. No man scrupled to own the nature of the debt for which he was confined, unless it happened to be some piddling affair; but, on the contrary, boasted of the importance of the sum, as a circumstance that implied his having been a person of consequence in life; and he who had made the most remarkable escapes from bailiffs, was looked upon as a man of superior genius and address.

Among other extraordinary adventures of this kind, none was more romantic than the last elopement atchieved by the officer; who told them, he had been arrested for a debt of two hundred pounds, at a time when he could not command as many pence, and conveyed to the bailiff's house, in which he continued a whole fortnight, moving his lodgings higher and higher, from time to time, in proportion to the decay of his credit; until, from the parlour, he had made a regular ascent to the garret. There while he ruminated on his next step, which would have been to the Marshalsea, and saw the night come on, attended with hunger and cold, the wind began to blow, and the tiles of the house rattled with the storm: his imagination was immediately struck with the idea of escaping unperceived, amidst the darkness and noise of the tempest, by creeping out at the window of his apartment, and making his way over the tops of the adjoining houses. Glowing with this prospect, he examined the passage, which, to his infinite mortification, he found grated with iron-bars on the outside; but even this difficulty did not divert him from his purpose. Conscious of his own strength, he believed himself able to make an hole thro' the roof, which seemed to be slender and crazy; and, on this supposition, he barricadoed the door with the whole furniture of the room: then, setting himself to work with a poker, he in a few minutes effected a passage for his hand, with which he gradually stript off the boards and tiling, so as to open a sally-port for his whole body, thro' which he fairly set himself free, groping his way towards the next tenement. Here, however, he met with an unlucky accident: his hat, being blown off his head, chanced to tumble into the court, just as one of the bailiff's followers was knocking at the door; and this myrmidon recognizing it immediately, gave the alarm to his chief, who, running up stairs to the garret, forced open the door in a twinkling, notwithstanding the precautions which the prisoner had taken, and, with his attendant, pursued the fugitive thro' his own track. 'After this chace had continued some time, (said the officer) to the imminent danger of all three, I found my progress suddenly stopt by a sky-light, through which I perceived seven taylors, sitting at work upon a board. Without the least hesitation or previous notice, I plunged among them, with my backside foremost; and, before they could recollect themselves from the consternation occasioned by such a strange visit, told them my situation, and gave them to understand that there was no time to be lost. One of the number, taking the hint, led me instantly down stairs, and dismissed me at the street-door; while the bailiff and his follower, arriving at the breach, were deterred from entering by the brethren of my deliverer, who presenting their shears, like a range of *chevaux de frise*, commanded them to retire, on pain of immediate death: and the catchpole, rather than risque his carcase, consented to discharge the debt, comforting himself with the hope of making me prisoner again. There, however, he was disappointed: I kept snug, and laughed at his escape-warrant, until I was ordered abroad with the regiment, when I convey'd myself in a hearse to

Gravesend, where I embarked for Flanders; but, being obliged to come over again on the recruiting service, I was nabb'd on another score: and all the satisfaction my first captor has been able to obtain, is a writ of detainer; which, I believe, will fix me in this place, until the parliament, in its great goodness, shall think proper to discharge my debts, by a new act of insolvency.'

Every body owned, that the captain's success was equal to the hardiness of his enterprize, which was altogether in the stile of a soldier: but one of the merchants observed, that he must have been a bailiff of small experience, who would trust a prisoner of that consequence in such an unguarded place. 'If the captain (said he) had fallen into the hands of such a cunning rascal as the fellow that arrested me, he would not have found it such an easy matter to escape; for the manner in which I was caught, is perhaps the most extraordinary that ever was practised in these realms. You must know, gentlemen, I suffered such losses by insuring vessels, during the war, that I was obliged to stop payment, tho' my expectations were such as encouraged me to manage one branch of business, without coming to any immediate composition with my creditors. In short, I received consignments from abroad as usual; and that I might not be subject to the visits of those catchpoles, I never stirred abroad, but, turning my first floor into a warehouse, ordered all my goods to be hoisted up by a crane, fixed to the upper story of my house. Divers were the stratagems practised by those ingenious ferrets, with a view of decoying me from the walls of my fortification. I received innumerable messages from people, who wanted to see me at certain taverns, upon particular business: I was summoned into the country, to see my own mother, who was said to be at the point of death. A gentlewoman, one night, was taken in labour on my threshold: at another time, I was disturbed with the cry of murder in the street; and once I was alarmed by a false fire. But, being still upon my guard, I baffled all their attempts, and thought myself quite secure from their invention; when one of those bloodhounds, inspired, I believe, by the devil himself, contrived a snare by which I was at last entrapped. He made it his business to enquire into the particulars of my traffick; and understanding that, among other things, there were several chests of Florence entered at the custom-house on my behalf, he ordered himself to be inclosed in a box of the same dimensions, with air-holes in the bottom, for the benefit of breathing, and N°. III. marked upon the cover; and being conveyed to my door in a cart, among other goods, was, in his turn, hoisted up to my warehouse, where I stood with a hammer, in order to open the chests, that I might compare the contents with the invoice. You may guess my surprize and consternation, when, upon uncovering the box, I saw a bailiff rearing up his head, like Lazarus from the grave, and heard him declare that he had a writ against me for a thousand pounds. Indeed, I aimed the hammer at his head; but, in the hurry of my confusion, missed my mark: and before I could repeat the blow, he started up with great agility, and executed his office in sight of several evidences, whom he had assembled in the street for that purpose; so that I could not possibly disentangle myself from the toil, without incurring an escape-warrant, from which I had no protection. But, had I known the contents of the chest, by all that's good! I would have ordered my porter to raise it up, as high as the crane would permit, and then have cut the rope by accident.'

'That expedient, (said the knight with the red ribbon) would have discouraged him from such hazardous adventures for the future, and would have been an example *in terrorem* of all his brethren. The story puts me in mind of a deliverance atchieved by Tom Hackabout, a very stout honest fellow, an old acquaintance of mine, who had been so famous for maiming bailiffs, that another gentleman having been ill used at a spunging-house, no sooner obtained his liberty than, with a view of being revenged upon the landlord, he, for five shillings, bought one of Tom's notes, which sold at a very large discount, and taking out a writ upon it, put it into the hands of the bailiff who had used him ill. The catchpole, after a diligent search, had an opportunity of executing the writ upon the defendant, who, without ceremony, broke one of his arms, fractured his skull, and belaboured him in such a manner, that he lay without sense and motion on the spot. By such exploits, this hero became so formidable, that no single bailiff would undertake to arrest him; so that he appeared in all public places, untouched. At length, however, several officers of the Marshalsea-court entered into a confederacy against him; and two of the number, attended by three desperate followers, ventured to arrest him one day in the Strand, near Hungerford-market: he found it impossible to make resistance, because the whole gang sprung upon him at once, like so many tygers, and pinioned his arms so fast, that he could not wag a finger. Perceiving himself fairly overpowered, he desired to be conducted forthwith to jail, and was stowed in a boat accordingly: by that time they had reached the middle of the river, he found means to overset the wherry by accident, and every man disregarding the prisoner, consulted his own safety. As for Hackabout, to whom that

element was quite familiar, he mounted astride upon the keel of the
boat, which was uppermost, and exhorted the bailiffs to swim for
their lives; protesting, before God, that they had no other chance to
be saved.

The watermen were immediately taken up by some of their own
friends, who, far from yielding any assistance to the catch-poles,
kept aloof, and exulted in their calamity. In short, two of the five
went to the bottom, and never saw the light of God's sun, and the
other three, with great difficulty, saved themselves by laying hold
on the rudder of a dung-barge, to which they were carried by the
stream, while Tom, with great deliberation, swam across to the
Surry shore. After this atchievement, he was so much dreaded by
the whole fraternity, that they shivered at the very mention of his
name; and this character, which some people would think an advantage to a man in debt, was the greatest misfortune that could
possibly happen to him; because no tradesman would give him
credit for the least trifle, on the supposition, that he could not
indemnify himself in the common course of law.'

The parson did not approve of Mr. Hackabout's method of
escaping, which he considered as a very unchristian attempt upon
the lives of his fellow-subjects: 'It is enough (said he) that we elude
the laws of our country, without murthering the officers of justice:
for my own part, I can lay my hand upon my heart, and safely say,
that I forgive from my soul the fellow by whom I was made
prisoner, although the circumstances of his behaviour were
treacherous, wicked and profane. You must know, Mr. Pickle,
I was one day called into my chapel, in order to join a couple in the
holy bands of matrimony: and my affairs being at that time so
situated, as to lay me under apprehensions of an arrest, I cautiously
surveyed the man through a lettice which was made for that purpose, before I would venture to come within his reach. He was
cloathed in a seaman's jacket and troussers, and had such an air of
simplicity in his countenance, as divested me of all suspicion: I,
therefore, without further scruple, trusted myself in his presence,
began to exercise the duty of my function, and had actually performed one half of the ceremony, when the supposed woman,
pulling out a paper from her bosom, exclaimed with a masculine
voice, 'Sir, you are my prisoner, I have got a writ against you for
five hundred pounds.' I was thunderstruck at this declaration, not
so much on account of my own misfortune, which (thank heaven!)
I can bear with patience and resignation, as at the impiety of the
wretch, firstly, in disguising such a worldly aim, under the cloak

of religion; and, secondly, in prostituting the service, when there was no occasion for so doing, his design having previously taken effect. Yet I forgive him, poor soul! because he knew not what he did; and I hope you, Sir Sipple, will exert the same christian virtue towards the man by whom you was likewise overreached.'

'O! damn the rascal, (cried the knight) were I his judge, he should be condemned to flames everlasting. A villain! to disgrace me in such a manner, before almost all the fashionable company in town.' Our hero expressing a curiosity to know the particulars of this adventure, the knight gratified his desire, by telling him, that one evening, while he was engaged in a partie of cards, at a drum in the house of a certain lady of quality, he was given to understand by one of the servants, that a stranger, very richly dressed, was just arrived in a chair, preceded by five footmen with flambeaus, and that he refused to come up stairs, until he should be introduced by Sir Sipple. 'Upon this notice (continued the knight) I judged it was some of my quality-friends; and having obtained her ladyship's permission to bring him up, went down to the hall, and perceived a person, whom, to the best of my recollection, I had never seen before. However, his appearance was so magnificent, that I could not harbour the least suspicion of his true quality; and seeing me advance, he saluted me with a very genteel bow, observing, that though he had not the honour of my acquaintance, he could not dispense with waiting upon me, even on that occasion, in consequence of a letter which he had received from a particular friend. So saying, he put a paper into my hand, intimating, that he had got a writ against me for ten thousand pounds, and that it would be my interest to submit without resistance; for he was provided with a guard of twenty men, who surrounded the door in different disguises, determined to secure me against all opposition. Enraged at the scoundrel's finesse, and trusting to the assistance of the real footmen assembled in the hall, 'So, you are a rascally bailiff, (said I) who have assumed the garb of a gentleman, in order to disturb her ladyship's company. Take this fellow, my lads, and roll him in the kennel: here are ten guineas for your trouble.' These words were no sooner pronounced, than I was seized, lifted up, placed in a chair, and carried off in the twinkling of an eye: not but that the servants of the house, and some other footmen, made a motion towards my rescue, and alarmed all the company above: but the bailiff affirming with undaunted effrontery, that I was taken up upon an affair of state, and so many people appearing in his behalf, the countess would not suffer the supposed messenger to be insulted; and he carried me to the county-jail, without further lett or molestation.'

CHAPTER CVI

Pickle seems tolerably well reconciled to his Cage;
and is by the Clergyman entertained with the Memoirs of
a noted Personage, whom he sees by Accident in the Fleet

THE knight had scarce finished this narrative, when our hero was told, that a gentleman in the coffee-room wanted to see him; and when he went thither, he found his friend Crabtree, who had transacted all his affairs, according to the determination of the preceding day; and now gave him an account of the remarks he had overheard on the subject of his misfortune: for the manner of the arrest was so public and extraordinary, that those who were present, immediately propagated it among their acquaintance; and it was that same evening discoursed upon at several tea and card-tables, with this variation from the truth, that the debt amounted to twelve thousand, instead of twelve hundred pounds: from which circumstance it was conjectured, that Peregrine was a bite from the beginning, who had found credit on account of his effrontery and appearance, and imposed himself upon the town as a young gentleman of fortune. They rejoiced, therefore, at his calamity, which they considered as a just punishment for his fraud and presumption, and began to review certain particulars of his conduct, that plainly demonstrated him to be a rank adventurer, long before he had arrived at this end of his career.

Pickle, who now believed his glory was set for ever, received this intelligence with that disdain which enables a man to detach himself effectually from the world, and, with great tranquillity, gave the Misanthrope an entertaining detail of what he had seen and heard since their last parting. While they amused themselves in this manner over a dish of coffee, they were joined by the parson, who congratulated our hero upon his bearing mischance with such philosophic quiet, and began to regale the two friends with some curious circumstances relating to the private history of the several prisoners, as they happened to come in.

At length a gentleman entered,[1] at sight of whom the clergyman rose up, and saluted him with a most reverential bow, which was graciously returned by the stranger, who, with a young man that attended him, retired to the other end of the room. They were no sooner out of hearing, than the communicative priest desired his company to take particular notice of this person to whom he had paid his respects: 'That man (said he) is this day one of the most flagrant instances of neglected virtue which the world can produce. Over and above a cool, discerning head, fraught with uncommon learning and experience, he is possessed of such fortitude and resolution, as no difficulties can discourage, and no danger impair; and so indefatigable is his humanity, that even now, while he is surrounded with such embarassments, as would distract the brain of any ordinary mortal, he has added considerably to his incumbrances, by taking under his protection that young gentleman, who, induced by his character, appealed to his benevolence for redress of the grievances under which he labours from the villainy of his guardian.'

Peregrine's curiosity being excited by this encomium, he asked the name of this generous patron, of which when he was informed, 'I am no stranger (said he) to the fame of that gentleman, who has made a considerable noise in the world, on account of that great cause he undertook in defence of an unhappy orphan; and since he is a person of such an amiable disposition, I am heartily sorry to find that his endeavours have not met with that successful issue which their good fortune in the beginning seemed to promise. Indeed, the circumstance of his espousing that cause was so uncommon and romantic, and the depravity of the human heart so universal, that some people, unacquainted with his real character, imagined his views were altogether selfish; and some were not wanting, who affirmed he was a mere adventurer. Nevertheless, I must do him the justice to own, I have heard some of the most virulent of those who were concerned on the other side of the question, bear testimony in his favour, observing, that he was deceived into the expence of the whole, by the plausible story which at first engaged his compassion. Your description of his character confirms me in the same opinion; though I am quite ignorant of the affair, the particulars of which I should be glad to learn, as well as a genuine account of his own life, many circumstances of which are by his enemies, I believe, egregiously misrepresented.'

'Sir, (answered the priest) that is a piece of satisfaction which I am glad to find myself capable of giving you: I have had the pleasure of being acquainted with Mr. M—— from his youth, and every thing which I shall relate concerning him, you may depend upon as a fact which hath fallen under my own cognizance, or been vouched upon the credit of undoubted evidence.

Mr. M——'s father was a minister of the established church of

Scotland, descended from a very ancient clan,[1] and his mother nearly related to a noble family in the northern part of that kingdom. While the son was boarded at a public school, where he made good progress in the Latin tongue, his father died, and he was left an orphan to the care of an uncle, who, finding him determined against any servile employment, kept him at school, that he might prepare himself for the university, with a view of being qualified for his father's profession.

Here his imagination was so heated by the war-like atchievements he found recorded in the Latin authors, such as Cæsar, Curtius and Buchanan,[2] that he was seized with an irresistible thirst of military glory, and desire of trying his fortune in the army; and his majesty's troops taking the field, in consequence of the rebellion which happened in the year seventeen hundred and fifteen, this young adventurer, thinking no life equal to that of a soldier, found means to furnish himself with a fusil and bayonet, and leaving the school, repaired to the camp near Stirling, with a view of signalizing himself in the field, though he was at that time but just turned of thirteen. He offered his service to several officers, in hope of being inlisted in their companies; but they would not receive him, because they rightly concluded that he was some school-boy broke loose, without the knowledge or consent of his relations. Notwithstanding this discouragement, he continued in camp, curiously prying into every part of the service; and such was the resolution conspicuous in him, even at such a tender age, that after his small finances were exhausted, he persisted in his design; and, because he would not make his wants known, actually subsisted for several days on hips, haws and sloes, and other spontaneous fruits which he gathered in the woods and fields. Mean while, he never failed to be present, when any regiment, or corps of men, were drawn out to be exercised and reviewed, and accompanied them in all their evolutions, which he had learned to great perfection, by observing the companies which were quartered in the place where he was at school. This eagerness and perseverance attracted the notice of many officers, who after having commended his spirit and zeal, pressed him to return to his parents, and even threatened to expel him from the camp, if he would not comply with their advice.

These remonstrances having no other effect than that of warning him to avoid his monitors, they thought proper to alter their behaviour towards him, took him into their protection, and even into their mess; and what above all other marks of favour, pleased the young soldier most, permitted him to incorporate in the battalion, and take his turn of duty with the other men. In this happy situation he was discovered by a relation of his mother, who was a captain in the army, and who used all his authority and influence in persuading M—— to return to school, but finding him deaf to his admonitions and threats, he took him under his own care, and when the army marched to Dumblane, left him at Stirling, with express injunction to keep himself within the walls.[1]

He temporized with his kinsman, fearing that should he seem refractory, the captain would have ordered him to be shut up in the castle; and inflamed with the desire of seeing a battle, no sooner saw his relation marched off the ground, than he mixed in with another regiment, to which his former patrons belonged, and proceeded to the field, where he distinguished himself, even at that early time of life, by his gallantry, in helping to retrieve a pair of colours belonging to M——n's regiment;[2] so that after the affair, he was presented to the duke of Argyle, and recommended strongly to brigadier Grant, who invited him into his regiment, and promised to provide for him with the first opportunity. But that gentleman in a little time lost his command upon the duke's disgrace,[3] and the regiment was ordered for Ireland, being given to colonel Nassau, whose favour, the young volunteer acquired to such a degree, that he was recommended to the king for an ensigncy, which in all probability he would have obtained, had not the regiment been unluckily reduced.

In consequence of this reduction, which happened in the most severe season of the year, he was obliged to return to his own country, thro' infinite hardships, to which he was exposed from the narrowness of his circumstances; and continuing still enamoured of a military life, he entered into the regiment of Scotch greys, at that time commanded by the late Sir James Campbell,[4] who being acquainted with his family and character, encouraged him with the promise of speedy preferment. In this corps he remained three years, during which, he had no opportunity of seeing actual service, except at the affair of Glensheel; and this life of insipid quiet, must have hung heavy upon a youth of M——'s active disposition, had not he found exercise for the mind, in reading books of amusement, history, voyages, and geography, together with those that treated of the art of war ancient and modern, for which he contracted such an eager appetite, that he used to spend sixteen hours a day in this employment. About that time, he became acquainted with a gentleman of learning and taste, who observing his indefatigable application, and insatiable thirst after knowledge, took upon himself the charge of superintending his studies; and by the direction of such an able guide, the young soldier converted his attention to a more solid and profitable course of reading. So inordinate was his desire of making speedy advances in the paths of learning, that within the compass of three months, he diligently perused the writings of Lock, and Malbranche, and made himself master of the first six, and of the eleventh and twelfth books of Euclid's elements. He considered Puffendorf and Grotius with uncommon care, acquired a tolerable degree of knowledge in the French language, and his imagination was so captivated with the desire of learning, that seeing no prospect of a war, or views of being provided for in the service, he quitted the army, and went through a regular course of university education. Having made such progress in his studies, he resolved to qualify himself for the church, and acquired such a stock of school divinity under the instructions of a learned professor at Edinburgh, that he more than once mounted the rostrum, in the public hall, and held forth with uncommon applause. But being discouraged from a prosecution of his plan, by the unreasonable austerity of some of the Scotch clergy, by whom, the most indifferent and innocent words and actions, were often misconstrued into levity and misconduct; he resolved to embrace the first favourable opportunity of going abroad, being enflamed with the desire of seeing foreign countries, and actually set out for Holland, where, for the space of two years, he studied the Roman law, with the law of nature and nations, under the famous professors Tolieu and Barbyrac.[1]

Having thus finished his school education, he set out for Paris, with a view to make himself perfect in the French language, and learn such useful exercises, as might be acquired with the wretched remnant of his slender estate, which was by that time reduced very low. In his journey through the Netherlands, he went to Namur, and paid his respects to bishop Strickland[2] and general Collier, by whom he was received with great civility, in consequence of letters of recomn endation, with which he was provided from the Hague, and the old general assured him of his protection and interest for a pair of colours, if he was disposed to enter into the Dutch Service.

Tho' he was by that time pretty well cured of his military Don Quixotism, he would not totally decline the generous proffer, for which he thanked him in the most grateful terms, telling the general that he would pay his duty to him on his return from France, and then, if he could determine upon returning to the army, should think himself highly honoured in being under his command.

After a stay of two months in Flanders, he proceeded to Paris, and far from taking up his habitation in the suburbs of St. Germain, according to the custom of English travellers, he hired a private lodging on the other side of the river, and associated chiefly with French officers, who (their youthful sallies being over) are allowed to be the politest gentlemen of that kingdom. In this scheme he found his account so much, that he could not but wonder at the folly of his countrymen, who lose the main scope of their going abroad, by spending their time and fortune idly with one another.

During his residence in Holland, he had made himself acquainted with the best authors in the French language, so that he was able to share in their conversation; a circumstance from which he found great benefit; for, it not only improved him in his knowledge of that tongue, but also tended to the enlargement of his acquaintance, in the course of which, he contracted intimacies in some families of good fashion, especially those of the long robe, which would have enabled him to pass his time very agreeably, had he been a little easier in point of fortune: but his finances, notwithstanding the most rigid oeconomy, being, in a few months, reduced to a very low ebb, the prospect of indigence threw a damp upon all his pleasures, tho' he never suffered himself to be thereby, in any degree, dispirited; being in that respect, of so happy a disposition, that conscious poverty or abundance made very slight impressions upon his mind.

This consumption of his cash, however, involved him in some perplexity; and he deliberated with himself whether he should return to general Collier, or repair to London, where he might possibly fall into some business not unbecoming a gentleman; tho' he was very much mortified to find himself incapable of gratifying an inordinate desire which possessed him of making the grand tour, or at least, of visiting the southern parts of France.

While he thus hesitated between different suggestions, he was one morning visited by a gentleman who had sought and cultivated his friendship, and for whom he had done a good office, in supporting him with spirit, against a brutal German, with whom he had an affair of honour. This gentleman came to propose a party for a fortnight, to Fontainebleau, where the court then was; and the proposal being declined by M—— with more than usual stiffness, his friend was very urgent to know the reason of his refusal, and at length, with some confusion, said, "Perhaps your finances are low." M—— replied, that he had wherewithal to defray the expence of his journey to London, where he could be furnished with a fresh supply; and this answer was no sooner made, than the other taking him by the hand, "My dear friend, (said he) I am not unacquainted with your affairs, and would have offered you my credit long ago, if I had thought it would be acceptable; even now, I do not pretend to give you money, but desire and insist upon it, that you will accept of the loan of these two pieces of paper, to be repayed when you marry a woman with a fortune of twenty thousand pounds, or obtain an employment of a thousand a year." So saying he presented him with two actions of above two thousand livres each.

M—— was astonished at this unexpected instance of generosity in a stranger, and with suitable acknowledgment, peremptorily refused to incur such an obligation; but at length, he was, by dint of importunity, and warm expostulation prevailed upon to accept one of the actions, on condition that the gentleman would take his note for the sum; and this he absolutely rejected, until M—— promised to draw upon him for double the value, or more, in case he should at any time want a further supply. This uncommon act of friendship and generosity, M—— afterwards had an opportunity to repay ten-fold, tho' he could not help regretting the occasion, on his friend's account. That worthy man having, by placing too much confidence in a villanous lawyer, and a chain of other misfortunes, involved himself and his amiable lady in a labyrinth of difficulties, which threatened the total ruin of his family; M—— felt the inexpressible satisfaction of delivering his benefactor from the snare.

Being thus reinforced by the generosity of his friend, M—— resolved to execute his former plan of seeing the south of France, together with the seaports of Spain, as far as Cadiz, from whence he proposed to take a passage for London by sea, and with this view, sent forwards his trunks by the diligence to Lyons, determined to ride post, in order to enjoy a better view of the country, and for the conveniency of stopping at those places where there was any thing remarkable to be seen or enquired into. While he was employed in taking leave of his Parisian friends, who furnished him with abundant recommendation, a gentleman of his own country, who spoke little or no French, hearing of his intention, begged the favour of accompanying him in his expedition.

With this new companion, therefore, he set out for Lyons, where he was perfectly well received by the intendant and some of the best families of the place, in consequence of his letters of recommendation; and after a short stay in that city, proceeded down the Rhone, to Avignon, in what is called the *coche d'eau*; then visiting the principal towns of Dauphiné, Languedoc and Provence, he returned to the delightful city of Marseilles, where he and his fellow traveller were so much captivated by the serenity of the air, the good nature and hospitality of the sprightly inhabitants, that they never dreamed of changing their quarters, during the whole winter, and part of the spring. Here he acquired the acquaintance of the marquis D'Argens, attorney-general in the parliament of Aix, and of his eldest son, who now makes so great a figure in the literary world; and when the affair of father Girard and madamoiselle Cadiere began to make a noise, he accompanied these two gentlemen to Toulon, where the marquis was ordered to take precognition of the facts.

On his return to Marseilles, he found a certain noble lord of great fortune, under the direction of a Swiss governor, who had accommodated him with two of his own relations, of the same country, by way of companions, together with five servants in his train. They being absolute strangers in the place, M—— introduced them to the intendant, and several other good families; and had the good fortune to be so agreeable to his lordship, that he proposed, and even pressed him to live with him in England, as a friend and companion; and to take upon him the superintendance of his affairs, in which case, he would settle upon him four hundred a year for life.

This proposal was too advantageous to be slighted by a person of no fortune, or fixed establishment; he, therefore, made no difficulty of closing with it: but as his lordship's departure was fixed to a short day, and he urged him to accompany him to Paris, and from thence to England, M—— thought it would be improper and indecent to interfere with the office of his governor, who might take umbrage at his favour, and therefore excused himself from a compliance with his lordship's request, until his minority should be expired, as he was within a few months of being of age. However, he repeated his importunities so earnestly, and the governor joined in the request, with such appearance of cordiality, that he was prevailed upon to comply with their joint desire; and, in a few days, set out with them for Paris, by the way of Lyons. But before they had been three days in this city, M— perceived a total change in the behaviour of the Swiss and his two relations, who, in all probability, became jealous of his influence with his lordship; and he no sooner made this discovery, than he resolved to withdraw himself from such a disagreeable participation of that young nobleman's favour. He therefore, in spite of all his lordship's intreaties and remonstrances, quitted him for the present; alledging, as a pretext, that he had a longing desire to see Switzerland and the banks of the Rhine, and promising to meet him again in England.

This his intention being made known to the governor and his friends, their countenances immediately cleared up, their courtesy and complaisance returned, and they even furnished him with letters for Geneva, Lausanne, Bern, and Soleure; in consequence of which he met with unusual civilities at these places. Having made this tour with his Scotch friend, (who came up to him before he left Lyons) and visited the most considerable towns on both sides of the Rhine, and the courts of the Electors Palatine, Mentz, and Cologne, he arrived in Holland; and from thence, thro' the Netherlands, repaired to London, where he found my lord just returned from Paris.

His lordship received him with expressions of uncommon joy, would not suffer him to stir from him for several days, and introduced him to his relations.

M— accompanied his lordship from London to his country-seat, where he was indeed treated with great friendship and confidence, and consulted in every thing; but the noble peer never once made mention of the annuity which he had promised to settle upon him; nor did M— remind him of it, because he conceived it was his affair to fulfil his engagements of his own accord. M— being tired of the manner of living at this place, made an excursion to Bath, where he staid about a fortnight, to partake of the diversions; and, upon his return, found his lordship making dispositions for another journey to Paris.

Surprised at this sudden resolution, he endeavoured to dissuade him from it; but his remonstrances were rendered ineffectual by the insinuations of a foreigner, who had come over with him, and filled his imagination with extravagant notions of pleasure, infinitely superior to any which he could enjoy while he was in the trammels, and under the restraints of a governor. He, therefore, turned a deaf ear to all M—'s arguments, and intreated him to accompany him in the journey: but this gentleman, foreseeing that a young man, like my lord, of strong passions, and easy to be misled, would, in all probability, squander away great sums of money, in a way that would neither do credit to himself, or to those who were concerned with him, resisted all his solicitations, on pretence of having business of consequence at London; and afterwards had reason to be extremely well pleased with his own conduct in this particular.

Before he set out on this expedition, M—, in justice to himself, reminded him of the proposal which he had made to him at Marseilles, desiring to know if he had altered his design in that particular; in which case, he would turn his thoughts some other way; as he would not in the least be thought to intrude or pin himself upon any man. My lord protested, in the most solemn manner, that he still continued in his former resolution; and again beseeching him to bear him company into France, promised that every thing should be settled to his satisfaction, upon their return to England. M—, however, still persisted in his refusal, for the abovementioned reasons: and tho' he never heard more of the annuity, he nevertheless continued to serve his lordship with his advice and good offices ever after; particularly in directing his choice to an alliance with a lady of eminent virtue, the daughter of a noble lord, more conspicuous for his shining parts than the splendor of his titles, (a circumstance upon which he always reflected with particular satisfaction, as well on account of the extraordinary merit of the lady, as because it vested in her children a considerable part of that great estate, which, of right, belonged to her grandmother) and afterwards put him in a way to retrieve his estate from a heavy load of debt he had contracted. When my lord set out on his Paris expedition, the money M— had received from his generous friend at Paris was almost reduced to the last guinea. He had not yet reaped the least benefit from his engagements with his lordship; and disdaining to ask for a supply from him, he knew not how to subsist, with any degree of credit, 'till his return.

This uncomfortable prospect was the more disagreeable to him, as, at that time of life, he was much inclined to appear in the gay world, had contracted a taste for plays, operas, and other public diversions, and acquired an acquaintance with many people of good fashion, which could not be maintained without a considerable expence. In this emergency, he thought he could not employ his idle time more profitably than in translating, from foreign languages, such books as were then chiefly in vogue; and upon application to a friend, who was a man of letters, he was furnished with as much business of that kind as he could possibly manage, and wrote some pamphlets on the reigning controversies of that time, that had the good fortune to please. He was also concerned in a monthly journal of literature, and the work was carried on by the two friends jointly, tho' M—— did not at all appear in the partnership. By these means he not only spent his mornings in useful exercise, but supplied himself with money for what the French call the *menus plaisirs*, during the whole summer. He frequented all the assemblies in and about London, and considerably enlarged his acquaintance among the fair sex.

He had, upon his first arrival in England, become acquainted with a lady[1] at an assembly not far from London; and tho', at that time, he had no thoughts of extending his views farther than the usual gallantry of the place, he met with such distinguishing marks of her regard in the sequel, and was so particularly encouraged by the advice of another lady, with whom he had been intimate in France, and who was now of their parties, that he could not help entertaining hopes of making an impression upon the heart of his agreeable partner, who was a young lady of an ample fortune, and great expectations. He, therefore, cultivated her good graces with all the assiduity and address of which he was master; and succeeded so well in his endeavours, that after a due course of attendance, and the death of an aunt, by which she received an accession of fortune, to the amount of three and twenty thousand pounds, he ventured to declare his passion, and she not only heard him with patience and approbation, but also replied in terms adequate to his warmest wish.

Finding himself so favourably received, he pressed her to secure his happiness by marriage; but, to this proposal, she objected the recency of her kinswoman's death, which would have rendered such a step highly indecent, and the displeasure of her other relations, from whom she had still greater expectations, and who at that time importuned her to marry a cousin of her own, whom she could not like. However, that M— might have no cause to repine at her delay, she freely entered with him into an intimacy of correspondence; during which, nothing could have added to their mutual felicity, which was the more poignant and refined, from the mysterious and romantic manner of their enjoying it; for, tho' he publickly visited her as an acquaintance, his behaviour, on these occasions, was always so distant, respectful, and reserved, that the rest of the company could not possibly suspect the nature of their reciprocal attachment: in consequence of which, they used to have private interviews, unknown to every soul upon earth, except her maid, who was necessarily intrusted with the secret.

In this manner they enjoyed the conversation of each other for above twelve months, without the least interruption; and tho' the stability of Mr. M—'s fortune intirely depended upon their marriage, yet as he perceived his mistress so averse to it, he never urged it with vehemence, nor was at all anxious on that score; being easily induced to defer a ceremony which, as he then thought, could in no shape have added to their satisfaction, tho' he hath since altered his sentiments.

Be that as it will, his indulgent mistress, in order to set his mind at ease in that particular, and in full confidence of his honour, insisted on his accepting a deed of gift of her whole fortune, in consideration of their intended marriage; and after some difficulty, he was prevailed upon to receive this proof of her esteem, well knowing that it would still be in his power to return the obligation. Tho' she often intreated him to take upon himself the intire administration of her finances, and upon divers occasions pressed him to accept of large sums, he never once abused her generous disposition, or solicited her for money, except for some humane purpose, which she was always more ready to fulfil than he to propose.

In the course of this correspondence, he became acquainted with some of her female relations; and, among the rest, with a young lady, so eminently adorned with all the qualifications of mind and person, that, notwithstanding all his philosophy and caution, he could not behold and converse with her, without being deeply smitten with her charms. He did all in his power to discourage this dangerous invasion in the beginning, and to conceal the least symptom of it from her relation: he summoned all his reflection to his aid; and thinking it would be base and dishonest to cherish any sentiment, repugnant to the affection which he owed to a mistress, who had placed such unlimited confidence in him, he attempted to stifle the infant flame by avoiding the amiable inspirer of it. But the passion had taken too deep a root in his heart, to be so easily extirpated: his absence from the dear object, increased the impatience of his love. The intestine conflict between that and gratitude, deprived him of his rest and appetite. He was, in a short time, emaciated by continual watching, anxiety, and want of nourishment; and so much altered from his usual chearfulness, that his mistress being surprised and alarmed at the change, which, from the symptoms, she judged was owing to some uneasiness of mind, took all imaginable pains to discover the cause.

In all probability, it did not escape her penetration; for she, more than once, asked if he was in love with her cousin; protesting that, far from being an obstacle to his happiness, she would, in that case, be an advocate for his passion. However, this declaration was never made without manifest signs of anxiety and uneasiness, which made such an impression upon the heart of M—, that he resolved to sacrifice his happiness, and even his life, rather than take any step which might be construed into an injury or insult to a person who had treated him with such generosity and goodness.

In consequence of this resolution, he formed another which was to go abroad, under pretence of recovering his health, but in reality, to avoid the temptation, as well as the suspicion of being inconstant; and in this design he was confirmed by his physician, who actually thought him in the first stage of a consumption, and therefore advised him to repair to the south of France. He communicated his design, with the doctor's opinion, to the lady, who agreed to it with much less difficulty than he found in conquering his own reluctance, at parting with the dear object of his love. The consent of his generous mistress being obtained, he waited upon her with the instrument whereby she had made the conveyance of her fortune to him; and all his remonstrances being insufficient to persuade her to take it back, he cancelled it in her presence, and placed it in that state, upon her toilet, while she was dressing; whereupon she shed a torrent of tears, saying she now plainly perceived that he wanted to tear himself from her, and that his affections were settled upon another. He was sensibly affected by this proof of her concern; and endeavoured to calm the perturbation of her mind, by vowing eternal fidelity, and pressing her to accept of his hand in due form, before his departure. By these means her transports were quieted for the present, and the marriage deferred, for the same prudential reasons which had hitherto prevented it.

Matters being thus compromised, and the day fixed for his departure, she, together with her faithful maid, one morning visited him for the first time at his own lodgings; and after breakfast, desiring to speak with him in private, he conducted her into another room, where assuming an unusual gravity of aspect, "My dear M——, (said she) you are now going to leave me, and God alone knows if ever we shall meet again: therefore, if you really love me with that tenderness which you profess, you will accept of this mark of my friendship and unalterable affection: it will at least be a provision for your journey; and if any accident should befal me, before I have the happiness of receiving you again into my arms, I shall have the satisfaction of knowing that you are not altogether without resource." So saying, she put an embroidered pocket-book into his hand. He expressed the high sense he had of her generosity and affection in the most pathetic terms, and begg'd leave to suspend his acceptance, until he should know the contents of her present, which was so extraordinary, that he absolutely refused to receive it: he was, however, by her repeated intreaties, in a manner compelled to receive about one half, and she afterwards insisted upon his taking a reinforcement of a considerable sum for the expence of his journey.

Having stayed with her ten days beyond the time he had fixed for his departure, and settled the method of their correspondence, he took his leave with an heart full of sorrow, anxiety and distraction, produced from the different suggestions of his duty and love. He then set out for France, and after a short stay at Paris, proceeded for Aix in Provence, and from thence to Marseilles, at which two places he continued for some months: but nothing he met with being able to dissipate those melancholy ideas which still preyed upon his imagination, and affected his spirits, he endeavoured to elude them with a succession of new objects; and with that view, persuaded a counsellor of the parliament of Aix, a man of great worth, learning and good humour, to accompany him, in making a tour of those parts of France which he had not yet seen. On their return from this excursion, they found at Aix an Italian Abbé, a person of character, and great knowledge of men and books, who having travelled all over Germany and France, was so far on his return to his own country.

M—— having, by means of his friend the counsellor, contracted an acquaintance with this gentleman, and being desirous of seeing some parts of Italy, particularly the carnival at Venice, they set out together from Marseilles, in a tartan, for Genoa, coasting it all the way, and lying on shore every night. Having shewn him what was most remarkable in this city, his friend the Abbé was so obliging, as to conduct him thro' Tuscany, and the most remarkable cities in Lombardy, to Venice, where M—— insisted upon defraying the expence of the whole tour, in consideration of the Abbé's complaisance, which had been of infinite service to him, in the course of this expedition. Having remained five weeks at Venice, he was preparing to set out for Rome with some English gentlemen whom he had met by accident, when he was all of a sudden obliged to change his resolution, by some disagreeable letters which he received from London. He had, from his first departure, corresponded with his generous, though inconstant mistress, with a religious exactness and punctuality; nor was she, for some time, less observant of the agreement they had made. Nevertheless, she, by degrees, became so negligent and cold in her expression, and so slack in her correspondence, that he could not help observing and upbraiding her with such indifference; and her endeavours to palliate it were supported by pretexts so frivolous, as to be easily seen through by a lover of very little discernment.

While he tortured himself with conjectures about the cause of this unexpected change, he received such intelligence from England, as, when joined with what he himself had perceived, by her manner of writing, left him little or no room to doubt of her fickleness and inconstancy. Nevertheless, as he knew by experience, that informations of that kind are not to be intirely relied upon, he resolved to be more certainly apprized; and for that end, departed immediately for London, by the way of Tirol, Bavaria, Alsace and Paris.

On his arrival in England, he learned with infinite concern, that his intelligence had not been at all exaggerated; and his sorrow was inexpressible, to find a person, endowed with so many other noble and amiable qualities seduced into an indiscretion, that, of necessity, must ruin the whole plan which had been concerted between them for their mutual happiness. She made several attempts, by letters and interviews, to palliate her conduct, and soften him into a reconciliation; but his honour being concerned, he remained deaf to all her intreaties and proposals. Nevertheless, I have often heard him say, that he could not help loving her, and revering the memory of a person to whose generosity and goodness he owed his fortune, and one whose foibles were over-balanced by a thousand good qualities. He often insisted on a restitution; but, far from complying with that proposal, she hath afterwards often endeavoured to lay him under yet greater obligations of the same kind, and importuned him, with the warmest solicitations, to renew their former correspondence, which he as often declined.

M—— took this instance of the inconstancy of the sex so much to heart, that he had almost resolved, for the future, to keep clear of all engagements for life, and returned to Paris, in order to dissipate his anxiety, where he hired an apartment in one of the academies in the exercises whereof he took singular delight. During his residence at this place, he had the good fortune to ingratiate himself with a great general, a descendant of one of the most ancient and illustrious families in France; having attracted his notice by some remarks he had written on Folard's Polybius,[1] which were accidentally shewn to that great man by one of his aids du camp, who was a particular friend of M——. The favour he had thus acquired, was strengthened by his assiduities and attention. Upon his return to London, he sent some of Handel's newest compositions to the prince, who was particularly fond of that gentleman's productions;

together with Clark's edition of Cæsar;[1] and in the spring of the same year, before the French army took the field, he was honoured with a most obliging letter from the prince, inviting him to come over, if he wanted to see the operations of the campaign, and desiring he would give himself no trouble about his equipage.

M—— having still some remains of a military disposition, and conceiving this to be a more favourable opportunity than any he should ever meet with again, readily embraced the offer, and sacrificed the soft delights of love, which at that time he enjoyed without controul, to an eager, laborious and dangerous curiosity. In that and the following campaign, during which he was present at the siege of Philipsburg, and several other actions, he enlarged his acquaintance among the French officers, especially those of the graver sort, who had a taste for books and literature; and the friendship and interest of those gentlemen were afterwards of singular service to him, tho' in an affair altogether foreign from their profession.

He had all along made diligent inquiry into the trade and manufactures of the countries through which he had occasion to travel, more particularly those of Holland, England and France; and as he was well acquainted with the revenue and farms of this last kingdom, he saw with concern the great disadvantages under which our tobacco-trade (the most considerable branch of our commerce with that people) was carried on; what inconsiderable returns were made to the planters, out of the low price given by the French company; and how much it was in the power of that company to reduce it still lower. M— had formed a scheme to remedy this evil, so far as it related to national loss or gain, by not permitting the duty of one penny in the pound, old subsidy, to be drawn back, on tobacco re-exported. He demonstrated to the ministry of that time, that so inconsiderable a duty could not in the least diminish the demand from abroad, which was the only circumstance to be apprehended, and that the yearly produce of that revenue would amount to one hundred and twenty thousand pounds, without one shilling additional expence to the public: but the ministry having the excise-scheme then in contemplation, could think of no other, till that should be tried; and that project having miscarried, he renewed his application, when they approved of his scheme in every particular, but discovered a surprising backwardness to carry it into execution.

His expectations in this quarter being disappointed, he, by the interposition of his friends, presented a plan to the French company, in which he set forth the advantages that would accrue to themselves, from fixing the price, securing that sort of tobacco which best suited the taste of the public and their manufacture; and finally, proposed to furnish them with any quantity, at the price which they paid in the port of London.

After some dispute, they agreed to his proposal, and contracted with him for fifteen thousand hogsheads a year, for which they obliged themselves to pay ready money, on its arrival in any one or more convenient ports in the south or western coasts of Great Britain, that he should please to fix upon for that purpose. M——— no sooner obtained this contract, than he immediately set out for America, in order to put it in execution; and, by way of companion, carried with him a little French abbé,[1] a man of humour, wit and learning, with whom he had been long acquainted, and for whom he had done many good offices.

On his arrival in Virginia, which opportunely happened at a time when all the gentlemen were assembled in the capital of that province, he published a memorial, representing the disadvantages under which their trade was carried on, the true method of redressing their own grievances in that respect, and proposing to contract with them for the yearly quantity of fifteen thousand hogsheads of such tobacco as was fit for the French market, at a price which he demonstrated to be considerably greater than that which they had formerly received.

This remonstrance met with all the success and encouragement he could expect: the principal planters seeing their own interest concerned, readily assented to the proposal, which, by their influence, was also relished by the rest; and the only difficulty that remained, related to the security for payment of the bills on the arrival of the tobacco in England, and to the time stipulated for the continuance of the contract.

In order to remove these objections, Mr. M— returned to Europe, and found the French company of farmers disposed to agree to every thing he desired for facilitating the execution of the contract, and perfectly well pleased with the sample which he had already sent: but his good friend the abbé, (whom he had left behind him in America) by an unparalleled piece of treachery, found means to overturn the whole project. He secretly wrote a memorial to the company, importing, that he found by experience, M——— could afford to furnish them at a much lower price than that which they had agreed to give; and that, by being in possession of the contract for five years, as was intended according to the proposal, he would have the company so much in his power, that they must afterwards submit to any price he should please to impose; and that if they thought him worthy of such a trust, he would undertake to furnish them at an easier rate, in conjunction with some of the leading men in Virginia and Maryland, with whom, he said, he had already concerted measures for that purpose.

The company were so much alarmed at these insinuations, that they declined complying with Mr. M——'s demands until the abbé's return; and though they afterwards used all their endeavours to persuade him to be concerned with that little traitor in his undertaking, (by which he might still have been a very considerable gainer) he resisted all their solicitations, and plainly told them in the abbé's presence, that he would never prostitute his own principles so far, as to enter into engagements of any kind with a person of his character, much less in a scheme that had a manifest tendency to lower the market-price of tobacco in England.

Thus ended a project the most extensive, simple and easy, and (as appeared by the trial made) the best calculated to raise an immense fortune, of any that was ever undertaken or planned by a private person; a project, in the execution of which, M—— had the good of the public, and the glory of putting in a flourishing condition that valuable branch of our trade, (which gives employment to two great provinces, and above two hundred sail of ships) much more at heart than his own private interest. It was reasonable to expect, that a man, whose debts M—— had paid more than once, whom he had obliged in many other respects, and whom he had carried with him, at a very considerable expence, on this expedition, merely with a view of bettering his fortune, would have acted with common honesty, if not with gratitude: but such was the depravity of this little monster's heart, that on his death-bed he left a considerable fortune to mere strangers, with whom he had little or no connexion, without the least thought of refunding the money advanced for him by M——, in order to prevent his rotting in jail.

When M—— had once obtained a command of money, he, by his knowledge in several branches of trade, as well as by the assistance of some intelligent friends at Paris and London, found means to employ it to very good purpose; and had he been a man of that selfish disposition, which too much prevails in the world, he might have been, at this day, master of a very ample fortune: but his ear was never deaf to the voice of distress, nor his beneficent heart shut against the calamities of his fellow-creatures. He was even ingenious in contriving the most delicate methods of relieving modest indigence, and, by his industrious benevolence, often anticipated the requests of misery.

I could relate a number of examples to illustrate my assertions, in some of which you would perceive the most disinterested generosity; but such a detail would trespass too much upon your time, and I do not pretend to dwell upon every minute circumstance of his conduct. Let it suffice to say, that, upon the declaration of war with Spain, he gave up all his commercial schemes, and called in his money from all quarters, with a view of sitting down, for the rest of his life, contented with what he had got, and restraining his liberalities to what he could spare from his yearly income. This was a very prudential resolution, could he have kept it: but, upon the breaking out of that war, he could not, without concern, see many gentlemen of merit, who had been recommended to him, disappointed of commissions, meerly for want of money to satisfy the expectations of the commission-brokers of that time; and therefore launched out considerable sums for them on their bare notes, great part whereof was lost by the death of some in the unfortunate expedition to the West-Indies.[1]

He, at length, after many other actions of the like nature, from motives of pure humanity, love of justice, and abhorrence of oppression, embarked in a cause,[2] every way the most important that ever came under the discussion of the courts of law in these kingdoms; whether it be considered in relation to the extraordinary nature of the case, or the immense property of no less than fifty thousand pounds a year, and three peerages, that depended upon it.

In the year 1740, the brave admiral[3] who at that time commanded his majesty's fleet in the West-Indies, among the other transactions of his squadron, transmitted to the duke of Newcastle, mentioned a young man, who, tho' in the capacity of a common sailor on board one of the ships under his command, laid claim to the estate and titles of the earl of A——.[4] These pretensions were no sooner communicated in the public papers, than they became the subject of conversation in all companies; and the person whom they chiefly affected, being alarmed at the appearance of a competitor, tho' at such distance, began to put himself in motion, and take all the precautions which he thought necessary to defeat the endeavours of the young upstart. Indeed, the early intelligence he received of Mr. A——y's[5] making himself known in the West-Indies, furnished him with numberless advantages over that unhappy young gentleman: for, being in possession of a plentiful fortune, and lord of many manors in the neighbourhood of the very place where the claimant was born, he knew all the witnesses who could give the most material evidence of his legitimacy; and, if his probity did not restrain him, had, by his power and influence, sufficient opportunity and means of applying to the passions and interests of the witnesses, to silence many, and gain over others to his side: while his competitor, by an absence of fifteen or sixteen years from his native country, the want of education and friends, together with his present helpless situation, was rendered absolutely incapable of taking any step for his own advantage. And although his worthy uncle's conspicuous virtue, and religious regard for justice and truth, might possibly be an unconquerable restraint to his taking any undue advantages; yet the consciences of that huge army of emissaries he kept in pay, were not altogether so very tender and scrupulous. This much, however, may be said, without derogation from, or impeachment of the noble earl's nice virtue and honour, that he took care to compromise all differences with the other branches of the family, whose interests were, in this affair, connected with his own, by sharing the estate with them, and also retained most of the eminent council within the bar of both kingdoms against this formidable bastard, before any suit was instituted by him.

While he was thus entrenching himself against the attack of a poor forlorn youth, at the distance of fifteen hundred leagues, continually exposed to the dangers of the sea, the war, and an unhealthy climate, Mr. M——, in the common course of conversation, chanced to ask some questions relating to this romantic pretender, of one H——,[1] who was at that time the present lord A——y's chief agent. This man, when pressed, could not help owning that the late lord A—m actually left a son, who had been spirited away into America, soon after his father's death; but said he did not know whether this was the same person.

This information could not fail to make an impression on the humanity of Mr. M—, who, being acquainted with the genius of the wicked party who had possessed themselves of this unhappy young man's estate and honours, expressed no small anxiety and apprehension lest they should take him off by some means or other; and, even then, seemed disposed to contribute towards the support of the friendless orphan, and to enquire more circumstantially into the nature of his claim. In the mean time his occasions called him to France; and, during his absence, Mr. A—y arrived in London, in the month of October 1741.——'

Here the clergyman was interrupted by Peregrine, who said there was something so extraordinary, not to call it improbable, in the account he had heard of the young gentleman's being sent into exile, that he would look upon himself as infinitely obliged to the doctor, if he would favour him with a true representation of that transaction, as well as of the manner in which he arrived and was known at the island of Jamaica.

The parson, in compliance with our hero's request, taking up the story from the beginning, 'Mr. A—y (said he) is the son of Arthur late lord baron of A—m,[1] by his wife Mary Sh—d, natural daughter to John duke of B——— and N———by, whom he publickly married on the 21st day of July 1706, contrary to the inclination of his mother, and all his other relations, particularly Arthur late earl of A—y,[2] who bore an implacable enmity to the duke her father, and, for that reason, did all that lay in his power to traverse the marriage: but, finding his endeavours ineffectual, he was so much offended, that he would never be perfectly reconciled to lord A—m, tho' he was his presumptive heir. After their nuptials, they cohabited together in England for the space of two or three years; during which she miscarried more than once: and he being a man of levity, and an extravagant disposition, not only squandered away all that he had received of his wife's fortune, but also contracted many considerable debts, which obliged him to make a precipitate retreat into Ireland, leaving his lady behind him in the house with his mother and sisters; who, having also been averse to the match, had always looked upon her with eyes of disgust.

It was not likely that harmony should long subsist in this family, especially as lady A———m was a woman of a lofty spirit, who could not tamely bear insults and ill-usage from persons, who, she had reason to believe, were her enemies at heart. Accordingly a misunderstanding soon happened among them, which was fomented by the malice of one of her sisters-in-law: divers scandalous reports of her misconduct, to which the empty pretensions of a vain, wretched coxcomb (who was made use of as an infamous tool for that purpose) gave a colourable pretext, were trumped up, and transmitted, with many false and aggravating circumstances, to her husband in Ireland; who, being a giddy, unthinking man, was so much incensed at these insinuations, that, in the first transports of his passion, he sent to his mother a power of attorney, that she might sue for a divorce in his behalf. A libel was thereupon exhibited, containing many scandalous allegations, void of any real foundation in truth; but being unsupported by any manner of proof, it was at length dismissed with costs, after it had depended upwards of two years.

Lord A——m, finding himself abused by the misrepresentations of his mother and sister, discovered an inclination to be reconciled to his lady: in consequence of which, she was sent over to Dublin by her father, to the care of a gentleman in that city;[1] in whose house she was received by her husband, with all the demonstrations of love and esteem. From thence he conducted her to his lodgings, and then to his country-house;[2] where she had the misfortune to suffer a miscarriage, through fear and resentment of my lord's behaviour, which was often brutal and indecent. From the country they removed to Dublin, about the latter end of July, or beginning of August 1714; where they had not long continued, when her ladyship was known to be again with child.

Lord A—m and his issue being next in remainder to the honours and estate of Arthur earl of A—a, was extremely solicitous to have a son; and, warned by the frequent miscarriages of his lady, resolved to curb the natural impatience and rusticity of his disposition, that she might not, as formerly, suffer by his outrageous conduct. He accordingly cherished her with uncommon tenderness and care; and her pregnancy being pretty far advanced, conducted her to his country-seat, where she was delivered of Mr. A—y, about the latter end of April or beginning of May; for none of the witnesses have been able, at this distance, with absolute certainty, to fix the precise time of his birth, and there was no register kept in the parish: and, as an additional misfortune, no gentlemen of fashion lived in that parish; nor did those who lived at any considerable distance, care to cultivate an acquaintance with a man of lord A—m's strange conduct.

Be that as it will, the occasion was celebrated by his lordship's tenants and dependants upon the spot, and in the neighbouring town of New R—ss,[3] by bonfires, illuminations, and other rejoicings; which have made such an impression upon the minds of the people, that, in the place where they happened, and the contiguous parishes, several hundred people have already declared their knowledge and remembrance of this event, in spite of the great power of the claimant's adversary in that quarter, and the great pains and indirect methods taken by his numberless agents and emissaries, as well as by those who are interested with him, in the event of the suit, to corrupt and suppress the evidence.

Lord A——m, after the birth of this son, who was sent to nurse in the neighbourhood, according to the custom of the country,

(where people of the highest distinction put their children out to
nurse into farm-houses and cabbins) lived in harmony with his
lady for the space of two years: but having, by his folly and
extravagance, reduced himself to great difficulties, he demanded
the remainder of her fortune from her father the duke of B——,
who absolutely refused to part with a shilling, until a proper settlement should be made on his daughter, which by that time he had
put out of his own power to do, by his folly and extravagance.

As her ladyship, by her endeavours to reform the œconomy of
her house, had incurred the displeasure of some idle, profligate
fellows, who had fastened themselves upon her husband, and
helped to consume his substance, they seized this opportunity of
the duke's refusal; and, in order to be revenged upon the innocent
lady, persuaded lord A—m, that the only means of extracting
money from his grace would be to turn her away, on pretence of
infidelity to his bed, for which, they hinted, there was but too much
foundation. At their suggestions, a most infamous plan was projected; in the execution of which, one P——,[1] a poor, unbred,
simple, country booby, whom they had decoyed into a snare, lost
one of his ears, and the injured lady retired that same day to New
R——ss, where she continued several years. She did not, however,
leave the house, without struggling hard to carry her child along
with her; but, far from enjoying such indulgence, strict orders were
given, that the boy should not, for the future, be brought within
her sight. This base, inhuman treatment, instead of answering the
end proposed, produced such a contrary effect, that the duke of
B——, by a codicil to his will, in which he reflects upon lord
A——m's evil temper, directed his executors to pay to his daughter
an annuity of one hundred pounds, while her lord and she should
continue to live separate; and this allowance ceased on lord A—m's
death.

While she remained in this solitary situation, the child was universally known and received as the legitimate son and heir of her
lord, whose affection for the boy was so conspicuous, that in the
midst of his own necessities, he never failed to maintain him in the
dress and equipage of a young nobleman. In the course of his
infancy, his father having often changed his place of residence, the
child was put under the instruction of a great many different school-
masters, so that he was perfectly well known in a great many different parts of the kingdom; and his mother seized all opportunities
(which were but rare, on account of his father's orders to the
contrary) of seeing, and giving him proofs of her maternal tenderness,

until she set out for England, after having been long in a declining
state of health, by a paralytical disorder; upon the consequence of
which, such dependance was placed by her inconsiderate husband,
who was by this time reduced to extreme poverty, that he actually
married a woman whom he had long kept as a mistress;[1] and this
creature no sooner understood that lady Al—m was departed from
Ireland, than she openly avowed her marriage, and went about
publickly with lord A———m, visiting his acquaintances in character
of his wife.

From this æra may be dated the beginning of Mr. A———y's
misfortunes: this artful woman, who had formerly treated the
child with an appearance of fondness, in order to ingratiate herself
with the father, now looking upon herself as sufficiently established
in the family, thought it was high time to alter her behaviour with
regard to the unfortunate boy; and accordingly, for obvious
reasons, employed a thousand artifices to alienate the heart of this
weak father from his unhappy offspring: yet, notwithstanding all
her insinuations, nature still maintained her influence in his heart;
and though she often found means to irritate him by artful and
malicious accusations, his resentment never extended farther than
fatherly correction; and she would have found it impossible to
accomplish his ruin, had not her efforts been reinforced by a new
auxiliary, who was no other than his uncle, the present usurper of
his title and estate; yet even this confederacy was over-awed, in
some measure, by the fear of alarming the unfortunate mother, till
her distemper increased to a most deplorable degree of the dead
palsy, and the death of her father had reduced her to a most forlorn
and abject state of distress. Then they ventured upon the execution
of their projects; and (though their aims were widely different)
concurred in their endeavours to remove the hapless boy, as the
common obstacle to both.

Lord Al—m, who (as I have already observed) was a man of weak
intellects, and utterly void of any fixed principle of action, being,
by this time, reduced to such a pitch of misery, that he was often
obliged to pawn his wearing-apparel, in order to procure the
common necessaries of life; and having no other fund remaining,
with which he could relieve his present necessities, except his sale
of the reversion of the A———a estate, to which the nonage of his son
was an effectual bar, he was advised by his virtuous brother, and
the rest of his counsellors, to surmount this difficulty, by secreting
his son, and spreading a report of his death. This honest project he
the more readily embraced, because he knew that no act of his could

frustrate the child's succession. Accordingly, the boy was removed from the school at which he was then boarded, to the house of one K——gh,[1] an agent and accomplice of the present earl of A——a, where he was kept for several months closely confined; and in the mean time, it was industriously reported that he was dead.

This previous measure being taken, lord A—m published advertisements in the gazettes, offering reversions of the A——a estate to sale; and emissaries of various kinds were employed, to inveigle such as were ignorant of the nature of the settlement of these estates, or strangers to the affairs of his family. Some people, imposed upon by the report of the child's death, were drawn in to purchase, thinking themselves safe in the concurrence of his lordship's brother, upon presumption that he was next in remainder to the succession; others, tempted by the smallness of the price, (which rarely exceeded half a year's purchase, as appears by many deeds) though they doubted the truth of the boy's being dead, ran small risques on the contingency of his dying before he should be of age, or in hope of his being prevailed upon to confirm the grants of his father; and many more were treating with him on the same notions, when their transactions were suddenly interrupted, and the scheme of raising more money, for the present, defeated by the unexpected appearance of the boy, who being naturally sprightly and impatient of restraint, had found means to break from his confinement, and wandered up and down the streets of Dublin, avoiding his father's house, and choosing to encounter all sorts of distress, rather than subject himself again to the cruelty and malice of the woman who supplied his mother's place. Thus debarred his father's protection, and destitute of any fixed habitation, he herded with all the loose, idle, and disorderly youths in Dublin, skulking chiefly about the college, several members and students of which, taking pity on his misfortunes, supplied him at different times with cloaths and money. In this unsettled and uncomfortable way of life did he remain, from the year 1725 to the latter end of November 1727; at which time his father died so miserably poor, that he was actually buried at the public expence.

This unfortunate nobleman was no sooner dead, than his brother Richard, now earl of A——a,[2] taking advantage of the nonage and helpless situation of his nephew, seized upon all the papers of the defunct, and afterwards usurped the title of lord A——m, to the surprize of the servants, and others who were acquainted with the affairs of the family. This usurpation, bold as it was, produced no other effect than that of his being insulted by the populace as he went through the streets, and the refusal of the king at arms to enrol the certificate of his brother's having died without issue. The first of these inconveniences he bore without any sense of shame, tho' not without repining, conscious that it would gradually vanish with the novelty of his invasion; and as to the last, he conquered it by means well known and obvious.

Nor will it seem strange, that he should thus invade the rights of an orphan with impunity, if people will consider, that the late lord A——m had not only squandered away his fortune, with the most ridiculous extravagance, but also associated himself with low company; so that he was little known, and less regarded, by persons of any rank and figure in life; and his child, of consequence, debarred of the advantages which might have accrued from valuable connexions. And tho' it was universally known, that lady A——m had a son in Ireland, such was the obscurity in which the father had lived, during the last years of his life, that few of the nobility could be supposed to be acquainted with the particular circumstances of a transaction in which they had no concern, and which had happened at the distance of twelve years before the date of this usurpation. Moreover, as their first information was no other than common fame, the public clamour occasioned by the separation, might inspire such as were strangers to the family affairs, with a mistaken notion of the child's having been born about or after the time of that event. The hurry and bustle occasioned by the arrival of the lord lieutenant about this period, the reports industriously propagated of the claimant's death, the obscurity and concealment in which the boy was obliged to live, in order to elude the wicked attempts of his uncle, might also contribute to his peaceable enjoyment of an empty title: and lastly, lord chancellor W—m,[1] whose immediate province it was to issue writs for parliament, was an utter stranger in Ireland, unacquainted with the descents of families, and consequently did not examine farther than the certificate enrolled in the books of the king at arms. Over and above these circumstances, which naturally account for the success of the imposture, it may be observed, that the hapless youth had not one relation alive, on the side of his father, whose interest it was not to forward or connive at his destruction; that his grand-father the duke of B—— was dead; and that his mother was then in England, in a forlorn, destitute, dying condition, secreted from the world, and even from her own relations, by her woman Mary H——,[2] who had a particular interest to secrete her, and altogether dependant upon a miserable and precarious allowance from the dutchess of B——, to whose caprice she was moreover a most wretched slave.

Notwithstanding these concurring circumstances in favour of the usurper, he did not think himself secure while the orphan had any chance of finding a friend who would undertake his cause; and therefore laid a plan for his being kidnapped, and sent to America as a slave. His coadjutor in this humane scheme, was a person who carried on the trade of transporting servants to our plantations, and was deeply interested on this occasion, having, for a meer trifle, purchased of the late lord A——m the reversion of a considerable part of the A—a estate; which shameful bargain was confirmed by the brother, but could never take place, unless the boy could be effectually removed.

Every thing being settled with this auxiliary, several ruffians were employed in search of the unhappy victim; and the first attempt that was made upon him, in which his uncle personally assisted, happening near one of the great markets of the city of Dublin, an honest butcher,[1] with the assistance of his neighbours, rescued him by force from their cruel hands. This, however, was but a short respite; for (tho', warned by this adventure, the boy seldom crept out of his lurking places, without the most cautious circumspection) he was, in March 1727, discovered by the diligence of his persecutors, and forcibly dragged on board of a ship bound for Newcastle on Delaware river in America,[2] where he was sold as a slave, and kept to hard labour, much above his age or strength, for the space of thirteen years, during which he was transferred from one person to another.

While he remained in this servile situation, he often mentioned, to those in whom he thought such confidence might be placed, the circumstances of his birth and title, together with the manner of his being exiled from his native country; although, in this particular, he neglected a caution which he had received in his passage, importing, that such discovery would cost him his life. Mean while the usurper quietly enjoyed his right; and to those who questioned him about his brother's son, constantly replied, that the boy had been dead for several years. And Arthur earl of A——a dying in April 1737, he, upon pretence of being next heir, succeeded to the honours and estate of that nobleman.

The term of the nephew's bondage, which had been lengthened out beyond the usual time, on account of his repeated attempts to escape, being expired in the year 1739, he hired himself as a common sailor in a trading vessel bound to Jamaica; and there, being entered on board of one of his majesty's ships under the command of admiral Vernon, openly declared his parentage and pretensions. This extraordinary claim, which made a great noise in the fleet, reaching the ears of one lieutenant S—n,[1] nearly related to the usurper's Irish wife, he believed the young gentleman to be an impostor; and thinking it was incumbent upon him to discover the cheat, he went on board of the ship to which the claimant belonged, and, having heard the account which he gave of himself, was, notwithstanding his prepossessions, convinced of the truth of what he alledged: and, on his return to his own ship, chanced to mention this extraordinary affair upon the quarter-deck, in the hearing of Mr. B—n,[2] one of the midshipmen, who had formerly been at school with Mr. A—y. This young gentleman not only told the lieutenant, that he had been school-fellow with lord A———m's son, but also declared that he should know him again, if not greatly altered, as he still retained a perfect idea of his countenance.

Upon this intimation, the lieutenant proposed that the experiment should be tried; and went with the midshipman on board the ship that the claimant was in for that purpose. After all the sailors had been assembled upon deck, Mr. B—n, casting his eyes around, immediately distinguished Mr. A—y in the croud, and laying his hand on his shoulder, "This is the man," said he; affirming at the same time, that, while he continued at school with him, the claimant was reputed and respected as lord A—m's son and heir, and maintained in all respects suitable to the dignity of his rank. Nay, he was, in like manner, recognized by several other persons in the fleet, who had known him in his infancy.

These things being reported to the admiral, he generously ordered him to be supplied with necessaries, and treated like a gentleman; and, in his next dispatches, transmitted an account of the affair to the duke of Newcastle, among the other transactions of the fleet.[3]

In September or October 1741, Mr. A—y arrived in London; and the first person to whom he applied for advice and assistance was a man of the law,[4] nearly related to the families of A———a and A—m, and well acquainted with the particular affairs of each, who, far from treating him as a bastard and impostor, received him with civility and seeming kindness, asked him to eat, presented him with a piece of money, and, excusing himself from meddling in the affair, advised him to go to Ireland, as the most proper place for commencing a suit for the recovery of his right.

Before the young gentleman had an opportunity, or indeed any inclination, to comply with this advice, he was accidentally met in the street by that same H—n, who, as I have mentioned, gave Mr. M——r the first insight into the affair. This man immediately knew the claimant, having been formerly an agent for his father, and afterwards a creature of his uncle's, with whom he was, not without reason, suspected to be concerned in kidnapping and transporting his nephew. Be that as it will, his connexions with the usurper were now broke off by a quarrel, in consequence of which he had thrown up his agency; and he invited the hapless stranger to his house, with a view of making all possible advantage of such a guest.

There he had not long remained, when his treacherous landlord, tampering with his inexperience, effected a marriage between him and the daughter of one of his own friends, who lodged in his house at the same time: but afterwards, seeing no person of consequence willing to espouse his cause, he looked upon him as an incumbrance, and wanted to rid his hands of him accordingly. He remembered that Mr. M—r had expressed himself with all the humanity of apprehension, in favour of the unfortunate young nobleman, before his arrival in England; and being well acquainted with the generosity of his disposition, he no sooner understood that he was returned from France, than he waited upon him with an account of Mr. A—y's being safely arrived. Mr. M——r was sincerely rejoiced to find, that a person who had been so cruelly injured, and undergone so long and continued a scene of distress, was restored to a country where he was sure of obtaining justice, and where every good man (as he imagined) would make the cause his own: and, being informed that the youth was in want of necessaries, he gave twenty guineas to H—n for his use, and promised to do him all the service in his power; but had no intention to take upon himself the whole weight of such an important affair, or indeed to appear in the cause, until he should be fully and throughly satisfied that the claimant's pretensions were well founded.

In the mean time, H—n insinuating that the young gentleman was not safe in his present lodging, from the machinations of his enemies, M—r accommodated him with an apartment in his own house; where he was at great pains to remedy the defect in his education, by rendering him fit to appear as a gentleman in the world: and having received from him all the intelligence he could give, relating to his own affair, laid the case before council, and dispatched a person to Ireland, to make further enquiries upon the same subject; who, on his first arrival in that kingdom, found the claimant's birth was as publickly known as any circumstance of that kind could possibly be, at so great a distance of time.

The usurper and his friends gave all the interruption in their power to any researches concerning that affair; and had recourse to every art and expedient that could be invented, to prevent its being brought to a legal discussion: privilege, bills in chancery, orders of court surreptitiously and illegally obtained, and every other invention, was made use of to bar and prevent a fair and honest trial by a jury. The usurper himself, and his agents, at the same time that they formed divers conspiracies against his life, in vain endeavoured to detach Mr. M——r from the orphan's cause by innumerable artifices, insinuating, cajoling, and misrepresenting with surprising dexterity and perseverance.

His protector, far from being satisfied with their reasons, was not only deaf to their remonstrances, but, believing him in danger from their repeated efforts, had him privately conveyed into the country; where an unhappy accident (which he hath ever since sincerely regreted) furnished his adversary a colourable pretext to cut him off in the beginning of his career.

A man happening to lose his life, by the accidental discharge of a piece, that chanced to be in the young gentleman's hands,[1] the account of this misfortune no sooner reached the ears of his uncle, than he expressed the most immoderate joy at having found so good a handle for destroying him, under colour of law. He immediately constituted himself prosecutor, set his emissaries at work to secure a coroner's inquest suited to his cruel purposes; set out for the place in person, to take care that the prisoner should not escape; insulted him in jail, in the most inhuman manner; employed a whole army of attornies and agents, to spirit up and carry on a most virulent prosecution; practised all the unfair methods that could be invented, in order that the unhappy gentleman should be transported to Newgate, from the healthy prison to which he was at first committed; endeavoured to inveigle him into destructive confessions; and, not to mention other more infamous arts employed in the affair of evidence, attempted to surprize him upon his trial, in the absence of his witnesses and council, contrary to a previous agreement with the prosecutor's own attorney: nay, he even appeared in person upon the bench at the trial, in order to intimidate the evidence, and brow-beat the unfortunate prisoner at the bar, and expended above a thousand pounds in that prosecution. In spite of all his wicked efforts, however, which were defeated by the spirit and indefatigable industry of Mr. M——r, the young gentleman was honourably acquitted, to the evident satisfaction of all the impartial; the misfortune that gave a handle for that unnatural prosecution, appearing to a demonstration to have been a mere accident.

In a few months, his protector, who had now openly espoused his cause, (taking with him two gentlemen to witness his trans-actions)[1] conducted him to his native country, with a view to be better informed of the strength of his pretensions, than he could be by the intelligences he had hitherto received, or by the claimant's own dark and almost obliterated remembrance of the facts which were essential to be known. Upon their arrival in Dublin, applica-tion was made to those persons whom Mr. A——y had named as his schoolmasters and companions, together with the servants and neighbours of his father. These, though examined separately, without having the least previous intimation of what the claimant had reported, agreed in their accounts with him, as well as with one another, and mentioned many other people as acquainted with the same facts to whom Mr. M——r had recourse, and still met with the same unvaried information. By these means, he made such progress in his inquiries, that in less than two months no fewer than one hundred persons, from different quarters of the kingdom, either personally, or by letters, communicated their knowledge of the claimant, in declarations consonant with one another, as well as with the accounts he gave of himself. Several servants who had lived with his father, and been deceived with the story of his death, so industriously propagated by his uncle, no sooner heard of his being in Dublin, than they came from different parts of the country to see him; and though great pains were taken to deceive them, they, nevertheless, knew him at first sight; some of them fell upon their knees, to thank heaven for his preservation, embraced his legs, and shed tears of joy for his return.

Although the conduct of his adversary, particularly in the above-mentioned prosecution, together with the evidence that already appeared, were sufficient to convince all mankind of the truth of the claimant's pretensions, Mr. M——r, in order to be further satisfied, resolved to see how he would be received upon the spot where he was born; justly concluding, that if he was really an impostor, the bastard of a kitchen-wench, produced in a country intirely pos-sessed by his enemy and his allies, he must be looked upon in that place with the utmost detestation and contempt.

This his intention was no sooner known to the adverse party, than their agents and friends, from all quarters, repaired to that place with all possible dispatch, and used all their influence with the people, in remonstrances, threats, and all the other arts they could devise, not only to discountenance the claimant upon his arrival, but even to spirit up a mob to insult him. Notwithstanding these precautions, and the servile awe and subjection in which tenants are kept by their landlords in that part of the country, as soon as it was known that Mr. A——y approached the town, the inhabitants crowded out in great multitudes to receive and welcome him, and accompanied him into town with acclamations and other expressions of joy, insomuch that the agents of his adversary durst not shew their faces. The sovereign of the corporation, who was a particular creature and favourite of the usurper, and whose all depended upon the issue of the cause, was so conscious of the stranger's right, and so much awed by the behaviour of the people, who knew that consciousness, that he did not think it safe, even to preserve the appearance of neutrality upon this occasion, but actually held the stirrup while Mr. A——y dismounted from his horse.

This sense of conviction in the people, manifested itself still more powerfully, when he returned to the same place in the year 1744, about which time lord A——a being informed of his resolution, determined again to be before-hand with him, and set out in person with his agents and friends, some of whom were detached before him, to prepare for his reception, and induce the people to meet him in a body, and accompany him to town, with such expressions of welcome as they had before bestowed on his nephew: but in spite of all their art and interest, he was suffered to pass through the street in a mournful silence; and though several barrels of beer were produced, to court the favour of the populace, they had no other effect than that of drawing their ridicule upon the donor; whereas, when Mr. A——y, two days afterwards, appeared, all the inhabitants, with garlands, streamers, music, and other ensigns of joy, crowded out to meet him, and ushered him into town with such demonstrations of pleasure and good-will, that the noble peer found it convenient to hide himself from the resentment of his own tenants, the effects of which he must have severely felt, had not he been screened by the timely remonstrances of Mr. M—r, and the other gentlemen who accompanied his competitor.

Nor did his apprehension vanish with the transactions of this day; the town was again in uproar on the Sunday following, when it was known that Mr. A——y intended to come thither, from Dunmain, to church: they went out to meet him as before, and conducted him to the church-door with acclamations, which terrified his uncle to such a degree, that he fled with precipitation in a boat, and soon after intirely quitted the place.

It would be almost an endless task to enumerate the particular steps that were taken by one side to promote, and by the other to delay the trial: the young gentleman's adversaries finding that they could not, by all the subterfuges and arts they had used, evade it, repeated attempts were made to assassinate him and his protector, and every obstruction thrown in the way of his cause which craft could invent, villany execute, and undue influence confirm. But all these difficulties were surmounted by the vigilance, constancy, courage and sagacity of M——r; and, at last, the affair was brought to a very solemn trial at bar, which being continued, by several adjournments, from the eleventh to the twenty-fifth day of November, a verdict was found for the claimant, by a jury of gentlemen, which, in point of reputation and property, cannot be easily paralleled in the annals of that or any other country;[1] a jury that could by no means be suspected of prepossessions in favour of Mr. An——y, (to whose person they were absolute strangers) especially if we consider that a gentleman in their neighbourhood, who was nephew to the foreman, and nearly related to some of the rest of their number, forfeited a considerable estate by their decision.

This verdict (said the parson) gave the highest satisfaction to all impartial persons that were within reach of being truly informed of their proceedings, and of the different genius and conduct of the parties engaged in the contest; but more especially to such as were in court (as I was) at the trial, and had an opportunity of observing the characters and behaviour of the persons who appeared there to give evidence.——To such it was very apparent, that all the witnesses produced there on the part of the uncle, were either his tenants, dependents, pot-companions, or persons some way or other interested in the issue of the suit, and remarkable for a low kind of cunning: that many of them were persons of profligate lives, who deserved no credit: that (independent of the levity of their characters) those of them who went under the denomination of colonels, (colonel L——fts[2] alone excepted, who had nothing to say, and was only brought there in order to give credit to that party) made so ridiculous a figure, and gave so absurd, contradictory and inconsistent an evidence, as no court or jury could give the least degree of credit to.—On the other hand, it was observed, that the nephew and Mr. M——r his chief manager, (being absolute strangers in that country, and unacquainted with the characters of the persons they had to deal with) were obliged to lay before the court and jury such evidence as came to their hand, some of whom plainly appeared to have been put upon them by their adversaries, with a design to hurt.—It was also manifest, that the witnesses produced for Mr. A——y were such as could have no manner of connexion with him, nor any dependence whatsoever upon him, to influence their evidence; for the far greatest part of them had never seen him from his infancy, till the trial began; and that many of them (though poor and undignified with the title of colonels) were people of unblemished character, of great simplicity, and such as no man in his senses would pitch upon to support a bad cause.—It is plain that the jury, (whose well-known honour, impartiality and penetration must be revered by all who are acquainted with them) were not under the least difficulty about their verdict; for they were not inclosed above half an hour, when they returned with it.—These gentlemen could not help observing the great inequality of the parties engaged, the great advantages that the uncle had in every other respect (except the truth and justice of his case) over the nephew, by means of his vast possessions, and of his power and influence all round the place of his birth; nor could the contrast between the different geniuses of the two parties escape their observation.—They could not but see and conclude, that a person who had confessedly transported and sold his orphan-nephew into slavery, who, on his return, had carried on so unwarrantable and cruel a prosecution to take away his life, under colour of law, and who had also given such glaring proofs of his skill and dexterity in the management of witnesses for that cruel purpose, was in like manner capable of exerting the same happy talent on this occasion, when his all was at stake; more especially, as he had so many others who were equally interested with himself, and whose abilities, in that respect, fell nothing short of his own, to second him in it.— The gentlemen of the jury had also a near view of the manner in which the witnesses delivered their testimonies, and had from thence an opportunity of observing many circumstances and distinguishing characteristics of truth and falshood, from which a great deal could be gathered, that could not be adequately conveyed by any printed account, how exact soever; consequently, they must have been much better judges of the evidence on which they founded their verdict, than any person, who had not the same opportunity, can possibly be.

These, Mr. Pickle, were my reflections on what I had occasion to observe concerning that famous trial; and on my return to England two years after, I could not help pitying the self-sufficiency of some people, who, at this distance, pretended to pass their judgment on that verdict with as great positiveness, as if they had been in the secrets of the cause, or upon the jury who tried it; and that from no better authority, than the declamations of lord An——a's emissaries, and some falsified printed accounts, artfully cooked up, on purpose to mislead and deceive.

But to return from this digression, lord A——a, the defendant in that cause, was so conscious of the strength and merits of his injured nephew's case, and that a verdict would go against him, that he ordered a writ of error to be made out before the trial was ended; and the verdict was no sooner given, than he immediately lodged it, though he well knew he had no manner of error to assign. This expedient was practised merely for vexation and delay, in order to keep Mr. A—y from the possession of the small estate he had recovered by the verdict; that, his slender funds being exhausted, he might be deprived of other means to prosecute his right; and, by the most oppressive contrivances and scandalous chicanery, it has been kept up to this day, without his being able to assign the least shadow of any error.

Lord A——a was not the only antagonist that Mr. A——y had to deal with; all the different branches of the A——a family, who had been worrying one another at law ever since the death of the late earl of A——a, about the partition of his great estate, were now firmly united in an association against this unfortunate gentleman; mutual deeds were executed among them, by which many great lordships and estates were given up by the uncle to persons who had no right to possess them, in order to engage them to side with him against his nephew, in withholding the unjust possession of the remainder.

These confederates having held several consultations against their common enemy, and finding that his cause gathered daily strength since the trial, by the accession of many witnesses of figure and reputation, who had not been heard of before; and that the only chance they had to prevent the speedy establishment of his right, and their own destruction, was by stripping Mr. M——r of the little money that yet remained, and stopping all further resources whereby he might be enabled to proceed; they, therefore, came to a determined resolution to carry that hopeful scheme into execution; and, in pursuance thereof, they have left no expedient or stratagem, how extraordinary or scandalous soever, unpractised to distress Mr. An—y and that gentleman. For that end, all the oppressive arts and dilatory expensive contrivances that the fertile invention of the lowest pettifoggers of the law could possibly devise, have with great dexterity been played off against them in fruitless, quibbling, and malicious suits, intirely foreign to the merits of the cause. Not to mention numberless other acts of oppression, the most extraordinary and unprecedented proceedings, by means whereof this sham writ of error hath been kept on foot ever since November 1743, is to me (said the doctor) a most flagrant instance, not only of the prevalency of power and money, (when employed, as in the present case, against an unfortunate, helpless man, disabled, as he is, of the means of ascertaining his right) but of the badness of a cause, that hath recourse to so many iniquitous expedients to support it.

In a word, the whole conduct of lord A——a and his party, from the beginning to this time, hath been such, as sufficiently manifests, that it could proceed from no other motives than a consciousness of Mr. A—y's right, and of their own illegal usurpations, and from a terror of trusting the merits of their case to a fair discussion by the laws of their country: and that the intention and main drift of all their proceedings plainly tends to stifle and smother the merits of the case from the knowledge of the world, by oppressive arts and ingenious delays, rather than trust it to the candid determination of an honest jury. What else could be the motives of kidnapping the claimant, and transporting him when an infant? of the various attempts made upon his life since his return? of the attempts to divest him of all assistance to ascertain his right, by endeavouring so solicitously to prevail on Mr. M—r to abandon him in the beginning? of retaining an army of counsel, before any suit had been commenced? of the many sinister attempts to prevent the trial at bar? of the various arts made use of to terrify any one from appearing as witness for the claimant, and to seduce those who had appeared? of the shameless, unprecedented, low tricks now practised, to keep him out of the possession of that estate for which he had obtained the verdict, thereby to disable him from bringing his cause to a further hearing, and of the attempts made to buy up Mr. M——'s debts, and to spirit up suits against him? Is it not obvious from all these circumstances, as well as from the obstruction they have given to the attorney-general's proceeding to make a report to his majesty, on the claimant's petition to the King for the peerage, which was referred by his majesty to that gentleman, so far back as 1743; that all their efforts are bent to that

one point of stifling, rather than suffering the merits of this cause
to come to a fair and candid hearing; and that the sole consideration
at present between them and this unfortunate man is not, whether
he is right or wrong, but whether he shall or shall not find money
to bring this cause to a final determination.

Lord A——a and his confederates not thinking themselves safe
with all these expedients, while there was a possibility of their
antagonist's obtaining any assistance from such as humanity,
compassion, generosity, or a love of justice might induce to lay open
their purses to his assistance, in ascertaining his right, have, by
themselves and their numerous emissaries, employed all the arts
of calumny, slander and detraction against him, by traducing his
cause, vilifying his person, and most basely and cruelly tearing his
character to pieces, by a thousand misrepresentations, purposely
invented and industriously propagated in all places of resort, which
is a kind of cowardly assassination that there is no guarding against:
yet, in spite of all these machinations, and the shameful indifference of mankind, who stand aloof unconcerned, and see this unhappy gentleman most inhumanely oppressed by the weight of
lawless power and faction, M——r, far from suffering himself to
be dejected by the multiplying difficulties that croud upon him,
still exerts himself with amazing fortitude and assiduity, and will
(I doubt not) bring the affair he began and carried on with so much
spirit, while his finances lasted, to an happy conclusion.

It would exceed the bounds of my intention, and perhaps
trespass too much upon your time, were I to enumerate the low
artifices and shameful quibbles, by which the usurper has found
means to procrastinate the decision of the contest between him
and his hapless nephew, or to give a detail of the damage and
perplexity which Mr. M— has sustained and been involved in, by
the treachery and ingratitude of some who listed themselves under
him in the prosecution of this affair, and by the villainy of others,
who, under various pretences of material discoveries they had
to make, &c. had fastened themselves upon him, and continued
to do all the mischief in their power, until the cloven foot was
detected.

One instance, however, is so flagrantly flagitious, that I cannot
resist the inclination I feel to relate it, as an example of the most
infernal perfidy that perhaps ever entered the human heart. I have
already mentioned the part which H—n acted in the beginning of
M—'s connection with the unfortunate stranger, and hinted that
the said H—n lay under many obligations to that gentleman, before

Mr. A—y's arrival in England. He had been chief agent to lord A——y, and, as it afterwards appeared, received several payments of a secret pension which that lord enjoyed, for which he either could not, or would not account. His lordship, therefore, in order to compel him to it, took out writs against him, and his house was continually surrounded with catchpoles for the space of two whole years.

Mr. M—— believing, from H—n's own account of the matter, that the poor man was greatly injured, and persecuted on account of his attachment to the unhappy young gentleman, did him all the good offices in his power, and became security for him on several occasions: nay, such was his opinion of his integrity, that after Mr. A—y was cleared of the prosecution carried on against him by his uncle, his person was trusted to the care of this hypocrite, who desired that the young gentleman might lodge at his house for the convenience of air, M——'s own occasions calling him often into the country.

Having thus, by his consummate dissimulation, acquired such a valuable charge, he wrote a letter to one of lord A—y's attornies, offering to betray Mr. An—ey; provided his lordship would settle his account, and give him a discharge for eight hundred pounds of the pension, which he had received, and not accounted for. Mr. M—, informed of this treacherous proposal, immediately removed his lodger from his house into his own, without assigning his reasons for so doing, until he was obliged to declare it, in order to free himself from the importunities of H—n, who earnestly solicited his return. This miscreant finding himself detected, and disappointed in his villainous design, was so much enraged at his miscarriage, that, forgetting all the benefits he had received from M— for a series of years, he practised all the mischief that his malice could contrive against him; and at length entered into a confederacy with one G—tr-y,[1] and several other abandoned wretches, who, as before said, under various pretences of being able to make material discoveries, and otherwise to serve the cause, had found means to be employed in some extra-business relating to it, tho' their real intention was to betray the claimant.

These confederates, in conjunction with some other auxiliaries of infamous character, being informed that Mr. M—r was on the point of securing a considerable sum, to enable him to prosecute Mr. An—y's right, and to bring it to a happy conclusion,[2] contrived a deep laid scheme to disappoint him in it, and at once to ruin the cause. And previous measures being taken for that wicked purpose, they imposed upon the young gentleman's inexperience and credulity, by insinuations equally false, plausible, and malicious; to which they at length gained his belief, by the mention of some circumstances that gave what they alleged an air of probability, and even of truth. They swore that Mr. M—— had taken out an action against him for a very large sum of money; that they had actually seen the writ; that the intention of it was to throw him into prison for life, and ruin his cause, in consequence of an agreement made by him with lord A——ey, and his other enemies, to retrieve the money that he had laid out in the cause.

This plausible tale was enforced with such an air of truth, candor, and earnest concern for his safety, and was strengthened by so many imprecations, and corroborating circumstances of their invention, as would have staggered one of much greater experience, and knowledge of mankind, than Mr. A—ey could be supposed at that time. The notion of perpetual imprisonment, and the certain ruin they made him believe his cause was threatened with, worked upon his imagination to such a degree, that he suffered himself to be led like a lamb to the slaughter, by this artful band of villains; who secreted him at the lodgings of one Pr—nt—ce,[1] an intimate of G——y's, for several days, under colour of his being hunted by bailiffs employed by Mr. M—, where he was not only obliged by them to change his name, but even his wife was not suffered to have access to him.

Their design was to have sold him, or drawn him into a ruinous compromise with his adversaries, for a valuable consideration to themselves. But as no ties are binding among such a knot of villains, the rest of the conspirators were jockied by G—st—ey; who, in order to monopolize the advantage to himself, hurried his prize into the country, and secreted him even from his confederates, in a place of concealment one hundred miles from London, under the same ridiculous pretence of M——'s having taken out a writ against him, and of bailiffs being in pursuit of him every where round London.

He was no sooner there than G—st—ey, as a previous step to the other villany he intended, tricked him out of a bond for six thousand pounds, under colour of his having a person ready to advance the like sum upon it, as an immediate fund for carrying on his cause; assuring him, at the same time, that he had a set of gentlemen ready, who were willing to advance twenty-five thousand pounds more for the same purpose, and to allow him five hundred pounds a year for his maintenance, 'till his cause should be made an end of, provided that Mr. M— should have no further concern with him or his cause.

Mr. A—ey, having by this time received some intimations of the deceit that had been put upon him, made answer, that he should look upon himself as a very ungrateful monster, indeed, if he deserted a person who had saved his life, and so generously ventured his own, together with his fortune, in his cause, until he should first be certain of the truth of what was alleged of him, and absolutely rejected the proposal. G—st—ey, who had no other view in making it than to cover the secret villany he meditated against him, and to facilitate the execution thereof, easily receded from it, when he found Mr. A—ey so averse to it, and undertook neverthe- less to raise the money; adding, that he might, if he pleased, return to Mr. M—— whenever it was secured. The whole drift of this pretended undertaking to raise the twenty-five thousand pounds, was only to lay a foundation for a dexterous contrivance to draw Mr. A—ey unwarily into the execution of a deed, relinquishing all his right and title, under a notion of its being a deed to secure the repayment of that sum.

G—st—ey having, as he imagined, so far paved the way for the execution of such a deed, enters into an agreement with an agent, employed for that purpose by Mr. A—ey's adversaries, purporting, that in consideration of the payment of a bond for six thousand pounds, which he, G—st—ey, had, as he pretended, laid out in Mr. A—ey's cause, and of an annuity of seven hundred pounds a year, he was to procure for them from Mr. A—ey a deed, ready executed, relinquishing all right and title to the An—ey estate and honours. Every thing being prepared for the execution of this infernal scheme, unknown to Mr. A—ey, G—st—ey then thought proper to send for him to town from his retirement, in order, as he pretended, to execute a security for twenty-five thousand pounds.

This intended victim to that villain's avarice, no sooner arrived in town, full of hopes of money to carry on his cause, and of agreeably surprising his friend and protector Mr. M—— with so seasonable and unexpected a reinforcement, than an unforeseen difficulty arose, concerning the payment of G—st—ey's six thousand pound bond. That money was to have been raised out of the estate of a lunatic, which could not be done without the leave of the Court of Chancery, to whom an account must have been given of the intended applica- tion of it. While preparations were making to rectify this omission, G—st—ey immediately carried Mr. A—ey again into the country, lest he should happen to be undeceived by some means or other.

Chapter CVI

In the mean time, this wicked machination was providentially discovered by Mr. M——r, before it could be carried into execution, by means of the jealousies that arose among the conspirators themselves; and was, at the same time, confirmed to him by a person whom the very agent for an An—ey party had entrusted with the secret. M—r no sooner detected it than he communicated his discovery to one of Mr. A—ey's council, a man of great worth; and immediately thereupon, took proper measures to defeat it. He then found means to lay open to Mr. A—ey himself, the treacherous scheme that was laid for his destruction: he was highly sensible of it; and could never afterwards reflect on the snare that he had so unwarily been drawn into, and had so narrowly escaped, without a mixture of horror, shame, and gratitude to his deliverer.

The consummate assurance of the monsters who were engaged in this plot, after they had been detected, and upbraided with their treachery, is scarce to be parallelled; for they not only owned the fact of spiriting Mr. A—ey away, in the manner abovementioned, but justified their doing it, as tending to his service. They also maintained, that they had actually secured the twenty-five thousand pounds for him, tho' they never could name any one person who was to have advanced the money. No man was more active in this scheme than H—n; nor any man more solicitous to keep Mr. A—ey up in the false impressions he had received, or in projecting methods to ruin his protector, than he.

Among many other expedients for that purpose, a most malicious attempt was made to lodge an information against him, for treasonable practices, with the secretary of state, notwithstanding the repeated proofs he had given of his loyalty; and, as a preparatory step to this accusation, a letter, which this traitor dictated, was copied by another person, and actually sent to the earl of C——d,[1] importing, that the person who copied the letter had an affair of consequence to communicate to his lordship, if he would appoint a time for receiving the information. But that person, upon full conviction of the villany of the scheme, absolutely refused to proceed further in it; so that his malice once more proved abortive: and before he had time to execute any other contrivance of the same nature, he was imprisoned in this very jail for debt.

Here, finding his creditors inexorable, and himself destitute of all other resource, he made application to the very man whom he had injured in such an outrageous manner, set forth his deplorable case in the most pathetic terms, and intreated him, with the most abject humility, to use his influence in his behalf. The distress of this varlet immediately disarmed M——r of his resentment, and even excited his compassion; and, without sending any answer to his remonstrances, he interceded for him with his creditors: and the person to whom he was chiefly indebted, refusing to release him without security, this unwearied benefactor joined with the prisoner in a bond for above one hundred and forty pounds, by which he obtained his release.

He was no sooner discharged, however, than he entered into fresh combinations with G—y and others, in order to thwart his deliverer in his schemes of raising money, and otherwise to distress and deprive him of liberty; for which purpose, no art or industry (perjury not excepted) hath been spared. And, what is still more extraordinary, this perfidious monster having found money to take up the bond, in consequence of which he regained his freedom, hath procured a writ against M——r, upon that very obligation; and taken assignments to some other debts of that gentleman, with the same christian intention. But, hitherto, he hath, by surprising sagacity and unshaken resolution, baffled all their infernal contrivances, and retorted some of their machinations on their own heads: and at this time, when he is supposed by some, and represented by others, as under the circumstances of oblivion and despondence, he proceeds in his design with the utmost calmness and intrepidity, meditating schemes, and ripening measures, that will one day confound his enemies, and attract the notice and admiration of mankind.'

Peregrine, having thanked the priest for his obliging information, expressed his surprize at the scandalous inattention of the world to an affair of such importance; observing, that, by such inhuman neglect, this unfortunate young gentleman, Mr. A—ey, was absolutely deprived of all the benefit of society; the sole end of which is, to protect the rights, redress the grievances, and promote the happiness of individuals. As for the character of M—r, he said it was so romantically singular in all its circumstances, that, tho' other motives were wanting, curiosity alone would induce him to seek his acquaintance: but he did not at all wonder at the ungrateful returns which had been made to his generosity by H—n, and many others, whom he had served in a manner that few, besides himself, would have done; for he had been long convinced of the truth conveyed in these lines of a celebrated Italian author:

Li beneficii, che per la loro grandezza, non puonno esser guiderdonati, con la scelerata moneta dell' ingratitudine, sono pagati.[1]

Chapter CVI

'The story which you have related of that young gentleman, (said he) bears a very strong resemblance to the fate of a Spanish nobleman, as it was communicated to me by one of his own intimate friends at Paris. The countess d'Alvarez died immediately after the birth of a son, and the husband surviving her but three years, the child was left sole heir to his honours and estate, under the guardianship of his uncle, who had a small fortune and a great many children. This inhuman relation, coveting the wealth of his infant ward, formed a design against the life of the helpless orphan, and trusted the execution of it to his valet de chambre, who was tempted to undertake the murder by the promise of a considerable reward. He accordingly stabbed the boy with a knife, in three different places, on the right side of his neck: but, as he was not used to such barbarous attempts, his hand failed in the performance; and he was seized with such remorse, that, perceiving the wounds were not mortal, he carried the hapless victim to the house of a surgeon, by whose care they were healed: and in the mean time, that he might not forfeit his recompence, found means to persuade his employer, that his orders were performed. A bundle being made up for the purpose, was publickly interred as the body of the child, who was said to have been suddenly carried off by a convulsion; and the uncle, without opposition, succeeded to his honours and estate. The boy being cured of his hurts, was, about the age of six, delivered, with a small sum of money, to a merchant just embarking for Turkey; who was given to understand, that he was the bastard of a man of quality; and that, for family reasons, it was necessary to conceal his birth.

While the unfortunate orphan remained in this deplorable state of bondage, all the children of the usurper died one after another; and he himself being taken dangerously ill, attributed all his afflictions to the just judgment of God, and communicated his anxiety on that subject to the valet de chambre, who had been employed in the murder of his nephew. That domestic, in order to quiet his master's conscience, and calm the perturbation of his spirits, confessed what he had done, and gave him hopes of still finding the boy, by dint of industry and expence. The unhappy child being the only hope of the family of Alvarez, the uncle immediately ordered a minute inquiry to be set on foot; in consequence of which he was informed, that the orphan had been sold to a Turk, who had afterwards transferred him to an English merchant, by whom he was conveyed to London.

An express was immediately dispatched to this capital, where he

733

understood that the unhappy exile had, in consideration of his faithful services, been bound apprentice to a French barber-surgeon; and after he had sufficiently qualified himself in that profession, been received into the family of the count de Gallas, at that time the emperor's embassador at the court of London. From the house of this nobleman, he was traced into the service of count d'Oberstorf, where he had married his lady's chamber-maid, and then gone to settle as a surgeon in Bohemia.

In the course of these inquiries, several years elapsed; his uncle, who was very much attached to the house of Austria, lived at Barcelona, when the father of this empress queen resided in that city, and lent him a very considerable sum of money in the most pressing emergency of his affairs: and when that prince was on the point of returning to Germany, the old count finding his end approaching, sent his father confessor to his majesty, with a circumstantial account of the barbarity he had practised against his nephew, for which he implored forgiveness, and begg'd he would give orders, that the orphan, when found, should inherit the dignities and fortune which he had unjustly usurped.

His majesty assured the old man, that he might make himself easy on that score, and ordered the confessor to follow him to Vienna, immediately after the count's death, in order to assist his endeavours in finding out the injured heir. The priest did not fail to yield obedience to this command: he informed himself of certain natural marks on the young count's body, which were known to the nurse and women who attended him in his infancy; and, with a gentleman whom the emperor ordered to accompany him, set out for Bohemia, where he soon found the object of his inquiry, in the capacity of major domo to a nobleman of that country, he having quitted his profession of surgery for that office.

He was not a little surprized, when he found himself circumstantially catechised about the particulars of his life, by persons commissioned for that purpose by the emperor. He told them, that he was absolutely ignorant of his own birth, though he had been informed, during his residence in Turkey, that he was the bastard of a Spanish grandee, and gave them a minute detail of the pilgrimage he had undergone. This information agreeing with the intelligence which the priest had already received, and being corroborated by the marks upon his body, and the very scars of the wounds which had been inflicted upon him in his infancy, the confessor, without further hesitation, saluted him by the name of count d'Alvarez, grandee of Spain, and explained the whole mystery of his fortune.

If he was agreeably amazed at this explanation, the case was otherwise with his wife, who thought herself in great danger of being abandoned by an husband of such high rank; but he immediately dispelled her apprehension, by assuring her, that as she had shared in his adversity, she should also partake of his good fortune. He set out immediately for Vienna, to make his acknowledgements to the emperor, who favoured him with a very gracious reception, promised to use his influence, so that he might enjoy the honours and estate of his family; and, in the mean time, acknowledged himself his debtor for four hundred thousand florins, which he had borrowed from his uncle. He threw himself at the feet of his august protector, expressed the most grateful sense of his goodness, and begg'd he might be permitted to settle in some of his imperial majesty's dominions.

This request was immediately granted; he was allowed to purchase land in any part of the hereditary dominions of the house of Austria, to the amount of the sum I have mentioned; and made choice of the country of Ratibor in Silesia, where, in all probability, he still resides.'

Peregrine had scarce finished this narrative, when he perceived Mr. M——r slip something into the hand of the young man with whom he had been conversing at the other end of the room, and rise up from the table, in order to take his leave. He at once understood the meaning of this conveyance, and longed for an opportunity to be acquainted with such a rare instance of primitive benevolence; but the consciousness of his present situation hindered him from making any advance, that might be construed into forwardness or presumption.

CHAPTER CVII

He is surprised with the Appearance of Hatchway
and Pipes, who take up their Habitation in
his Neighbourhood, contrary to his Inclination and
express Desire

BEING now regularly initiated in the mysteries of the Fleet, and reconciled in some measure to the customs of the place, he began to bear the edge of reflection without wincing; and thinking it

would be highly imprudent in him to defer, any longer, the purposes by which only he could enjoy any ease and satisfaction in his
confinement, he resolved to resume his task of translating, and
every week compose an occasional paper, by way of revenge upon
the minister, against whom he had denounced eternal war. With
this view he locked himself up in his chamber, and went to work
with great eagerness and application; when he was interrupted by
a ticket-porter, who, putting a letter in his hand, vanished in a
moment, before he had time to peruse the contents.

Our hero, opening the billet, was not a little surprised to find
a bank-note for fifty pounds, inclosed in a blank sheet of paper;
and having exercised his memory and penetration on the subject of
this unexpected windfall, had just concluded, that it could come
from no other than the lady who had so kindly visited him a few
days before, when his ears were suddenly invaded by the well-
known sound of that whistle which always hung about the neck of
Pipes, as a memorial of his former occupation; and this tune being
performed, he heard the noise of a wooden leg ascending the stair;
upon which he opened his door, and beheld his friend Hatchway,
with his old ship-mate at his back.

After a cordial shake of the hand, with the usual salutation of
'What cheer, cousin Pickle?' honest Jack seated himself without
ceremony; and casting his eyes around the apartment, 'Split my
topstay-sail! (said he, with an arch sneer) you have got into a snug
birth, cousin. Here you may sit all weathers, without being turned
out to take your watch, and no fear of the ship's dragging her
anchor. You ha'n't much room to spare, 'tis true: an' I had known
as how you stowed so close, Tom should have slung my own
hammock for you, and then you mought have knocked down this
great lubberly hurricane house. But, mayhap, you turn in double,
and so you don't chuse to trust yourself and your doxy to a clue
and canvas.'

Pickle bore his jokes with great good-humour, rallied him in his
turn about the dairy-maid at the garrison, enquired about his
friends in the country, asked if he had been to visit his niece, and,
finally, expressed a desire of knowing the cause of his journey to
London. The lieutenant satisfied his curiosity in all these particulars; and, in answer to the last question, observed, that understanding, from the information of Pipes, that he was land-locked,
he had come from the country in order to tow him into the offing.
'I know not how the wind sits (said he); but if so be, as three
thousand pounds will bring you clear of the cape, say the word,

736

and you shan't lie wind-bound another glass, for want of the money.'

This was an offer which few people, in our hero's situation, would have altogether refused; especially as he had all the reason in the world to believe, that, far from being a vain, unmeaning compliment, it was the genuine tribute of friendship, which the lieutenant would have willingly, ay and with pleasure, paid. Nevertheless, Peregrine peremptorily refused his assistance, tho' not without expressing himself in terms of acknowledgment suitable to the occasion; and told him, it would be time enough to make use of his generosity, when he should find himself destitute of all other resource. Jack employed all his rhetorick, with a view of persuading him to take this opportunity to procure his own enlargement; and, finding his arguments ineffectual, insisted upon his accepting an immediate supply for his necessary occasions; swearing, with great vehemence, that he would never return to the garison, unless he would put him upon the footing of any other tenant, and receive his rent accordingly.

Our young gentleman as positively swore, that he never would consider him in that light; remonstrating, that he had long ago settled the house upon him for life, as a pledge of his own esteem, as well as in conformity with the commodore's desire; and beseeching him to return to his usual avocations, protested that, if ever his situation should subject him to the necessity of borrowing from his friends, Mr. Hatchway should be the first man to whom he would apply himself for succour. To convince him that this was not the case at present, he produced the bank-note, which he had received in the letter, together with his own ready money; and mentioned some other funds, which he invented *extempore*, in order to amuse the lieutenant's concern. In the close of this expostulation, he desired Pipes to conduct Mr. Hatchway to the coffee-house, where he might entertain himself with the newspapers for half an hour; during which he would put on his cloaths, and bespeak something for dinner, that they might enjoy each other's company, as long as his occasions would permit him to stay in that place.

The two sailors were no sooner gone, than he took up the pen, and wrote the following letter, in which he inclosed the bank-note, to his generous benefactress:

MADAM,

Your humanity is not more ingenious than my suspicion. In vain

737

you attempt to impose upon me by an act of generosity, which no person upon earth, but your ladyship, is capable of committing. Tho' your name was not subscribed on the paper, your sentiments were fully displayed in the contents, which I must beg leave to restore, with the same sense of gratitude, and for the same reasons I expressed, when last I had the honour to converse with you upon this subject. Tho' I am deprived of my liberty, by the villainy and ingratitude of mankind, I am not yet destitute of the other conveniences of life; and, therefore, beg to be excused from incurring an unnecessary addition to that load of obligation you have already laid upon,

Madam,

Your ladyship's most devoted,

Humble servant,

PEREGRINE PICKLE

Having dressed himself, and repaired to the place of appointment, he dispatched this epistle by the hands of Pipes, who was ordered to leave it at her ladyship's house, without staying for an answer; and in the mean time gave directions for dinner, which he and his friend Hatchway ate very chearfully in his own apartment, after he had entertained him with a sight of all the curiosities in the place. During their repast, Jack repeated his kind offers to our adventurer, who declined them with his former obstinacy, and begged he might be no more importuned on that subject: but, if he insisted upon giving some fresh proofs of his friendship, he might have an opportunity of exhibiting it in taking Pipes under his care and protection; for nothing affected him so much as his inability to provide for such a faithful adherent.

The lieutenant desired he would give himself no trouble upon that score; he being, of his own accord, perfectly well disposed to befriend his old ship-mate, who should never want, while he had a shilling to spare. But he began to drop some hints of an intention to fix his quarters in the Fleet, observing, that the air seemed to be very good in that place, and that he was tired of living in the country. What he said did not amount to a plain declaration, and therefore Peregrine did not answer it as such, tho' he perceived his drift; and took an opportunity of describing the inconveniences of the place, in such a manner, as he hoped would deter him from putting such an extravagant plan in execution.

This expedient, however, far from answering the end proposed, had a quite contrary effect, and furnished Hatchway with an argument against his own unwillingness to quit such a disagreeable place. And, in all probability, Jack would have been more explicit, with regard to the scheme he had proposed, if the conversation had not been interrupted by the arrival of Cadwallader, who never failed in the performance of his diurnal visit. Hatchway, conjecturing that this stranger might have some private business with his friend, quitted the apartment, on pretence of taking a turn: and meeting Pipes at the door, desired his company to the Bear, by which name the open space is distinguished; where, during a course of perambulation, these two companions held a council upon Pickle: in consequence of which it was determined, since he obstinately persisted to refuse their assistance, that they should take lodgings in his neighbourhood, with a view of being at hand to minister unto his occasions, in spite of his false delicacy, according to the emergency of his affairs.

This resolution being taken, they consulted the bar-keeper of the coffee-house about lodging, and she directed them to the warden; to whom the lieutenant, in his great wisdom, represented himself as a kinsman to Peregrine, who, rather than leave that young gentleman by himself to the unavoidable discomforts of a prison, was inclined to keep him company, 'till such time as his affairs could be put in order. This measure he the more anxiously desired to take, because the prisoner was sometimes subject to a disordered imagination, upon which occasion he stood in need of extraordinary attendance; and therefore he (the lieutenant) intreated the warden to accommodate him with a lodging for himself and his servant, for which he was ready to make any reasonable acknowledgment. The warden, who was a sensible and humane man, could not help applauding his resolution; and several rooms being at that time unoccupied, he put him immediately in possession of a couple, which were forthwith prepared for his reception.

This affair being settled to his satisfaction, he dispatched Pipes for his portmanteau; and returning to the coffee-house, found Peregrine, with whom he spent the remaining part of the evening. Our hero, taking it for granted that he proposed to set out for the garison next day, wrote a memorandum of some books which he had left in that habitation, and which he now desired Jack to send up to town by the waggon, directed for Mr. Crabtree; and cautioned him against giving the least hint of his misfortune in the neighbourhood, that it might remain, as long as possible, concealed from the knowledge of his sister, (who, he knew, would afflict herself immoderately at the news) nor reach the ears of the rest of his family, who would exult and triumph over his distress.

Hatchway listened to his injunctions with great attention, and promised to demean himself accordingly: then the discourse shifted to an agreeable recapitulation of the merry scenes they had formerly acted together; and the evening being pretty far advanced, Peregrine, with seeming reluctance, told him that the gates of the Fleet would in a few minutes be shut for the night, and that there was an absolute necessity for his withdrawing to his lodging. Jack replied, that he could not think of parting with him so soon, after such a long separation; and that he was determined to stay with him an hour or two longer, if he should be obliged to take up his lodging in the streets. Pickle, rather than disoblige his guest, indulged him in his desire, and resolved to give him a share of his own bed. A pair of chickens and 'sparagus were bespoken for supper, at which Pipes attended with an air of internal satisfaction; and the bottle was bandied about in a jovial manner 'till midnight, when the lieutenant rose up to take his leave, observing, that being fatigued with riding, he was inclined to turn-in. Pipes, upon this intimation, produced a lanthorn ready lighted; and Jack, shaking his entertainer by the hand, wished him good-night, and promised to visit him again betimes in the morning.

Peregrine, imagining that this behaviour proceeded from the wine, which he had plentifully drank, told him, that if he was disposed to sleep, his bed was ready prepared in the room, and ordered his attendant to undress his master; upon which Mr. Hatchway gave him to understand, that he had no occasion to incommode his friend, having already provided a lodging for himself: and the young gentleman demanding an explanation, he frankly owned what he had done, saying, 'You gave me such a dismal account of the place, that I could not think of leaving you in it without company.' Our young gentleman, who was naturally impatient of benefits, and foresaw that this uncommon instance of Hatchway's friendship would encroach upon the plan which he had formed for his own subsistence, by engrossing his time and attention, so as that he should not be able to prosecute his labours; closeted the lieutenant next day, and demonstrated to him the folly and ill consequences of the step he had taken. He observed, that the world in general would look upon it as the effect of mere madness; and, if his relations were so disposed, they might make it the foundation of a statute of lunacy against him; that his absence from the garison must be a very great detriment to his private affairs; and, lastly, that his presence in the Fleet would be a very great hindrance to Pickle himself, whose hope of regaining his liberty altogether depended upon his being detached from all company and interruption.

To these remonstrances Jack replied, that, as to the opinion of the world, it was no more to him than a rotten net-line; and if his relations had a mind to have his upper works condemned, he did not doubt but he should be able to stand the survey, without being declared unfit for service; that he had no affairs at the garison, but such as would keep cold; and with regard to Pickle's being interrupted by his presence, he gave him his word, that he would never come alongside of him, except when he should give him the signal for holding discourse. In conclusion, he signified his resolution to stay where he was, at all events, without making himself accountable to any person whatsoever.

Peregrine seeing him determined, desisted from any further importunity; resolving, however, to tire him out of his plan by reserve and supercilious neglect; for he could not bear the thought of being so notoriously obliged by any person upon earth. With this view he quitted the lieutenant, upon some slight pretence; after having told him, that he could not have the pleasure of his company at dinner, because he was engaged with a particular club of his fellow-prisoners.

Jack was a stranger to the punctilios of behaviour, and therefore did not take this declaration amiss; but had immediate recourse to the advice of his counsellor Mr. Pipes, who proposed that he should go to the coffee-house and kitchen, and give the people to understand that he would pay for all such liquor and provisions as Mr. Pickle should order to be sent to his own lodging. This expedient was immediately practised; and, as there was no credit in the place, Hatchway deposited a sum of money, by way of security, to the cook and the vintner, intimating, that there was a necessity for taking that method of befriending his cousin Peregrine, who was subject to strange whims, that rendered it impossible to serve him any other way.

In consequence of these insinuations, it was that same day rumoured about the Fleet, that Mr. Pickle was an unhappy gentleman disordered in his understanding, and that the lieutenant was his near relation, who had subjected himself to the inconvenience of living in a jail, with the sole view of keeping a strict eye over his conduct. This report, however, did not reach the ears of our hero till next day, when he sent one of the runners of the Fleet, who attended him, to bespeak and pay for a couple of pullets, and something else, for dinner, to which he had already invited his friend Hatchway, in hope of being able to persuade him to retire into the country, after he had undergone a whole day's mortification in the place. The messenger returned with an assurance, that the dinner should be made ready according to his directions, and restored the money, observing that his kinsman had paid for what was bespoke.

Peregrine was equally surprized and disgusted at this information, and resolved to chide the lieutenant severely, for his unseasonable treat, which he considered as a thing repugnant to his reputation. Mean while, he dispatched his attendant for wine to the coffee-house, and finding his credit bolstered up in that place by the same means, was enraged at the presumption of Jack's friendship, and questioned the valet about it, with such manifestation of displeasure, that the fellow, afraid of disobliging such a good master, frankly communicated the story which was circulated at his expence. The young gentleman was so much incensed at this piece of intelligence, that he wrote a bitter expostulation to the lieutenant, wherein he not only retracted his invitation, but declared that he would never converse with him, while he should remain within the place.

Having thus obeyed the dictates of his anger, he gave notice to the cook, that he should not have occasion for what was ordered; and repairing to the coffee-house, told the landlord, that whereas he understood the stranger with the wooden leg had prepossessed him and others with ridiculous notions, tending to bring the sanity of his intellects in question; and, to confirm this imputation, had, under the pretence of consanguinity, undertaken to defray his expences; he could not help (in justice to himself) declaring, that the lame person was, in reality, the madman, who had given his keepers the slip; that, therefore, he (the landlord) would not find his account in complying with his orders, and encouraging him to frequent his house; and that, for his own part, he would never enter the door, or favour him with the least trifle of his custom, if ever he should, for the future, find himself anticipated in his payments by that unhappy lunatic.

The vintner was confounded at this retorted charge; and, after much perplexity and deliberation, concluded, that both parties were distracted; the stranger, in paying a man's debts against his will, and Pickle, in being offended at such forwardness of friendship.

CHAPTER CVIII

These Associates commit an Assault upon Crabtree,
for which they are banished from the Fleet.
Peregrine begins to feel the Effects of Confinement

OUR adventurer having dined at the ordinary, and in the afternoon
retired to his own apartment, as usual, with his friend Cadwallader;
Hatchway and his associate, after they had been obliged to discuss
the provision for which they had paid, renewed their conference
upon the old subject; and Pipes giving his mess-mate to understand, that Peregrine's chief confident was the old deaf batchelor,
whom he had seen at his lodging the preceding day, Mr. Hatchway,
in his great penetration, discovered, that the young gentleman's
obstinacy proceeded from the advice of the Misanthrope, whom,
for that reason, it was their business to chastise. Pipes entered
into this opinion the more willingly, as he had all along believed the
senior to be a sort of wizzard, or some caco-dæmon, whom it was
not very creditable to be acquainted with. Indeed, he had been
inspired with this notion by the insinuations of Hadgi, who had
formerly dropped some hints touching Crabtree's profound knowledge in the magic art; mentioning, in particular, his being possessed of the philosopher's stone; an assertion to which Tom had
given implicit credit, until his master was sent to prison for debt,
when he could no longer suppose Cadwallader lord of such a
valuable secret, else he would have certainly procured the enlargement of his most intimate friend.

With these sentiments he espoused the resentment of Hatchway;
and they determined to seize the supposed conjurer, with the first
opportunity, on his return from his visit to Peregrine, and, without
hesitation, exercise upon him the discipline of the pump. This plan
they would have executed that same evening, had not the Misanthrope luckily withdrawn himself, by accident, before it was dark,
and even before they had intelligence of his retreat. But, next day,
they kept themselves upon the watch 'till he appeared, and Pipes
lifting his hat, as Crabtree passed, 'O damn ye, old Dunny, (said
he), you and I must grapple by and by; and, a'gad! I shall lie so
near your quarter, that your ear-ports will let in the sound, tho'f
they were double caulked with oakum.'

The misanthrope's ears were not quite so fast closed, but that they received this intimation; which, tho' delivered in terms that he did not well understand, had such an effect upon his apprehension, that he signified his doubts to Peregrine, observing, that he did not much like the looks of that same ruffian with the wooden leg. Pickle assured him, he had nothing to fear from the two sailors, who could have no cause of resentment against him; or, if they had, would not venture to take any step, which they knew must block up all the avenues to that reconcilement, about which they were so anxious; and, moreover, give such offence to the governor of the place, as would infallibly induce him to expel them both from his territories.

Notwithstanding this assurance, the young gentleman was not so confident of the lieutenant's discretion, as to believe that Crabtree's fears were altogether without foundation: he forthwith conjectured that Jack had taken umbrage at an intimacy, from which he found himself excluded, and imputed his disgrace to the insinuations of Cadwallader, whom, in all likelihood, he intended to punish for his supposed advice. He knew his friend could sustain no great damage from the lieutenant's resentment, in a place which he could immediately alarm with his cries, and therefore wished he might fall into the snare, because it would furnish him with a pretence of complaint; in consequence of which, the sailors would be obliged to shift their quarters, so as that he should be rid of their company, in which he at present could find no enjoyment.

Every thing happened as he had foreseen; the Misanthrope, in his retreat from Peregrine's chamber, was assaulted by Hatchway and his associate, who seized him by the collar without ceremony, and began to drag him towards the pump, at which they would have certainly complimented him with a very disagreeable bath, had not he exalted his voice in such a manner, as in a moment brought a number of the inhabitants, and Pickle himself to his aid. The assailants would have persisted in their design, had the opposition been such, as they could have faced with any possibility of success; nor did they quit their prey, before a dozen, at least, had come to his rescue, and Peregrine, with a menacing aspect and air of authority, commanded his old valet to withdraw: then they thought proper to sheer off, and betake themselves to close quarters, while our hero accompanied the affrighted Cadwallader to the gate, and exhibited to the warden a formal complaint against the rioters, upon whom he retorted the charge of lunacy, which was supported by the evidence of twenty persons, who had been eye-witnesses of the outrage committed against the old gentleman.

The governor, in consequence of this information, sent a message to Mr. Hatchway, warning him to move his lodging next day, on pain of being expelled; and the lieutenant contumaciously refusing to comply with this intimation, was in the morning, while he amused himself in walking upon the bear, suddenly surrounded by the constables of the court, who took him and his adherent prisoners, before they were aware, and delivered them into the hands of the turnkeys, by whom they were immediately dismissed, and their baggage conveyed to the side of the ditch.

This expulsion was not performed without an obstinate opposition on the part of the delinquents, who, had they not been surprized, would have set the whole Fleet at defiance, and, in all probability, acted divers tragedies, before they could have been over-powered. Things being circumstanced as they were, the lieutenant did not part with his conductor, without tweaking his nose, by way of farewel; and Pipes, in imitation of such a laudable example, communicated a token of remembrance, in an application to the sole eye of his attendant, who, scorning to be out-done in this kind of courtesy, returned the compliment with such good will, that Tom's organ performed the office of a multiplying glass. These were mutual hints for stripping; and accordingly, each was naked from the waist upwards in a trice. A ring of butchers from the market was immediately formed; a couple of the reverend Flamens, who, in morning-gowns, ply for marriages in that quarter of the town, constituted themselves seconds and umpires of the approaching contest, and the battle began without further preparation. The combatants were, in point of strength and agility, pretty equally matched; but the jailor had been regularly trained to the art of bruising: he had more than once signalized himself in public, for his prowess and skill in this exercise, and lost one eye upon the stage, in the course of his exploits. This was a misfortune of which Pipes did not fail to take the advantage: he had already sustained several hard knocks upon his temples and jaws, and found it impracticable to smite his antagonist upon the victualling-office, so dexterously was it defended against assault: upon which he changed his battery, and being ambi-dexter, raised such a clatter upon the turnkey's blind side, that this hero, believing him left-handed, converted his attention that way, and opposed the unenlightened side of his face to the right-hand of Pipes, which being thus unprovided against, slily bestowed upon him a peg under the fifth rib, that in an instant laid him senseless on the pavement, at the feet of his conqueror, who was congratulated upon his victory, not only by his friend Hatchway, but also by all the by-standers, particularly the priest who had espoused his cause, and now invited the strangers to his lodging in a neighbouring alehouse, where they were entertained so much to their liking, that they determined to seek no other habitation while they should continue in town: and notwithstanding the disgrace and discouragement they had met with, in their endeavours to serve our adventurer, they were still resolved to persevere in their good offices, or, in the vulgar phrase, to see him out.

While they settled themselves in this manner, and acquired familiar connexions round all the purlieus of the ditch, Peregrine found himself deprived of the company of Cadwallader, who signified by letter, that he did not chuse to hazard his person again in visiting him, while such assassins occupied the avenues through which he must pass; for he had been at pains to inquire into the motions of the seamen, and informed himself exactly of the harbour in which they were moored.

Our hero had been so much accustomed to the conversation of Crabtree, which was altogether suitable to the singularity of his own disposition, that he could very ill afford to be debarred of it at this juncture, when almost every other source of enjoyment was stopped. He was, however, obliged to submit to the hardships of his situation; and as the characters of his fellow-prisoners did not at all improve upon him, he was compelled to seek for satisfaction within himself. Not but that he had an opportunity of conversing with some people, who neither wanted sense, nor were deficient in point of principle; yet there appeared in the behaviour of them all, without exception, a certain want of decorum, a squalor of sentiment, a sort of jailish cast contracted in the course of confinement, which disgusted the delicacy of our hero's observation. He, therefore, detached himself from their parties as much as he could, without giving offence to those among whom he was obliged to live, and resumed his labours with incredible eagerness and perseverance, his spirits being supported by the success of some severe *Philippics*, which he occasionally published against the author of his misfortune.

Nor was his humanity unemployed in the vacations of his revenge: a man must be void of all sympathy and compassion, who can reside among so many miserable objects, without feeling an inclination to relieve their distress. Every day almost presented to his view such lamentable scenes, as were most likely to attract his notice, and engage his benevolence. Reverses of fortune, attended with the most deplorable circumstances of domestic woe, were continually intruding upon his acquaintance; his ears were invaded with the cries of the hapless wife, who from the enjoyment of affluence and pleasure, was forced to follow her husband to this abode of wretchedness and want; his eyes were every minute assailed with the naked and meagre appearances of hunger and cold; and his fancy teemed with a thousand aggravations of their misery.

Thus situated, his purse was never shut, while his heart remained open. Without reflecting upon the slenderness of his store, he exercised his charity to all the children of distress, and acquired a popularity which, though pleasing, was far from being profitable. In short, his bounty kept no pace with his circumstances, and in a little time he was utterly exhausted. He had recourse to his bookseller, from whom, with great difficulty, be obtained a small reinforcement; and immediately relapsed into the same want of retention. He was conscious of his infirmity, and found it incurable: he foresaw, that by his own industry he should never be able to defray the expence of these occasions; and this reflection sunk deep into his mind: the approbation of the public, which he had earned or might acquire, like a cordial often repeated, began to lose its effect upon his imagination; his health suffered by his sedentary life and austere application; his eyesight failed, his appetite forsook him, his spirits decayed; so that he became melancholy, listless, and altogether incapable of prosecuting the only means he had left for his subsistence; and (what did not at all contribute to the alleviation of these particulars) he was given to understand by his lawyer, that he had lost his cause, and was condemned in costs. Even this was not the most mortifying piece of intelligence he received; he at the same time learn'd, that his bookseller was bankrupt, and his friend Crabtree at the point of death.

These were comfortable considerations to a youth of Peregrine's disposition, which was so capricious, that the more his misery increased, the more haughty and inflexible he became. Rather than be beholden to Hatchway, who still hovered about the gate, eager for an opportunity to assist him, he chose to undergo the want of almost every convenience of life, and actually pledged his wearing-apparel to an Irish pawnbroker in the Fleet, for money to purchase those things, without which he must have absolutely perished. He was gradually irritated by his misfortunes into a rancorous resentment against mankind in general, and his heart so alienated from the enjoyments of life, that he did not care how soon he quitted his miserable existence. Though he had shocking examples of the vicissitudes of fortune continually before his eyes, he could never be reconciled to the idea of living like his fellow-sufferers, in the most abject degree of dependance. If he refused to accept of favours from his own allies and intimate friends, whom he had formerly obliged, it is not to be supposed that he would listen to proposals of that kind from any of his fellow-prisoners, with whom he had contracted acquaintance: he was even more cautious than ever of incurring obligations: he now shunned his former mess-mates, in order to avoid disagreeable tenders of friendship; and imagining that he perceived an inclination in the clergyman, to learn the state of his finances, he discouraged and declined the explanation, and at length secluded himself from all society.

CHAPTER CIX

He receives an unexpected Visit ; and the Clouds of Misfortune begin to separate

WHILE he pined in this forlorn condition, with an equal abhorrence of the world and himself, captain Gauntlet arrived in town, in order to employ his interest for promotion in the army; and, in consequence of his wife's particular desire, made it his business to inquire for Peregrine, to whom he longed to be reconciled, even at the expence of a slight submission. But he could hear no tidings of him, at the place to which he was directed; and, on the supposition that our hero had gone to reside in the country, applied himself to his own business, with intention to renew his enquiries, after that affair should be transacted. He communicated his demands to his supposed patron, who had assumed the merit of making him a captain, and been gratified with a valuable present on that consideration; and was cajoled with hopes of succeeding in his present aim, by the same interest.

Mean while, he became acquainted with one of the clerks belonging to the war-office, whose advice and assistance, he was told, would be a furtherance to his scheme; and as he had occasion to discourse with this gentleman, upon the circumstances of his expectation, he learned that the nobleman, upon whom he depended, was a person of no consequence in the state, and altogether incapable of assisting him in his advancement. At the same time, his counsellor expressed his surprize that captain Gauntlet did not rather interest in his cause the noble peer, to whose good offices he owed his last commission.

This remark introduced an explanation, by which Godfrey discovered, to his infinite astonishment, the mistake in which he had continued so long, with regard to his patron; tho' he could not divine the motive which induced a nobleman, with whom he had no acquaintance or connection, to interpose his influence in his behalf. Whatsoever that might be, he thought it was his duty to make his acknowledgment; and for that purpose, went next morning to his house, where he was politely received, and given to understand, that Mr. Pickle was the person to whose friendship he was indebted for his last promotion.

Inexpressible were the transports of gratitude, affection, and remorse, that took possession of the soul of Gauntlet, when this mystery was unfolded. 'Good heaven! (cried he, lifting up his hands) have I lived so long in a state of animosity with my benefactor? I intended to have reconciled myself to him, at any rate, before I was sensible of this obligation; but now I shall not enjoy a moment's quiet, until I have an opportunity of expressing to him my sense of his heroic friendship. I presume, from the nature of the favour conferred upon him, in my behalf, that Mr. Pickle is well known to your lordship; and I should think myself extremely happy, if you could inform me in what part of the country he is to be found: for the person with whom he lodged, some time ago, could give me no intelligence of his motions.'

The nobleman, touched with this instance of generous self-denial in Peregrine, as well as with the sensibility of his friend, lamented the unhappiness of our hero, while he gave Gauntlet to understand that he had been long disordered in his intellects, in consequence of having squandered away his fortune; and that his creditors had thrown him into the Fleet-prison: but whether he still continued in that confinement, or was released from his misfortunes by death, his lordship did not know, because he had never enquired.

Godfrey no sooner received this intimation, than (his blood boiling with grief and impatience) he craved pardon for his abrupt departure; and quitting his informer on the instant, reimbarked in his hackney-coach, and ordered himself to be conveyed directly to the Fleet. As the vehicle proceeded along one side of the market, he was surprised with the appearance of Hatchway and Pipes, who stood cheapening collyflowers at a green-stall, their heads being cased in worsted nightcaps, half covered with their hats, and a short tobacco-pipe in the mouth of each. He was rejoiced at sight of the two seamen, which he took for an happy omen of finding his friend; and, ordering the coachman to stop the carriage, called to the lieutenant by his name. Jack replying with an *Hilloah*, looked behind him, and recognizing the face of his old acquaintance, ran up to the coach with great eagerness, and shaking the captain heartily by the hand, 'Odd's heart! (said he) I'm glad thou ha'st fallen in with us: we shall now be able to find the trim of the vessel, and lay her about on the other tack. For my own part, I have had many a consort in my time, that is, in the way of good-fellowship, and I always made shift to ware 'em at one time or another: but this headstrong toad will neither obey the helm nor the sheet; and, for aught I know, will founder where he lies at anchor.'

Gauntlet, who conceived part of his meaning, alighted immediately; and being conducted to the sailor's lodging, was informed of every thing that had passed between the lieutenant and Pickle. He, in his turn, communicated to Jack the discovery which he had made, with regard to his commission; at which the other gave no signs of surprize: but taking the pipe from his mouth, 'Why, look ye, captain, (said he) that's not the only good turn you have owed him. That same money you received from the commodore, as an old debt, was all a sham, contrived by Pickle for your service; but a' wool drive under his bare poles, without sails and rigging, or a mess of provision on board, rather than take the same assistance from another man.'

Godfrey was not only amazed, but chagrined at the knowledge of this anecdote; which gave umbrage to his pride, while it stimulated his desire of doing something in return for the obligation. He enquired into the present circumstances of the prisoner; and understanding that he was indisposed, and but indifferently provided with the common necessaries of life, tho' still deaf to all offers of assistance, began to be extremely concerned at the account of his savage obstinacy and pride, which would, he feared, exclude him from the privilege of relieving him in his distress. However, he resolved to leave no expedient untried, that might have any tendency to surmount such destructive prejudice; and, entering the jail, was directed to the apartment of the wretched prisoner. He knocked softly at the door, and when it was opened, started back with horror and astonishment: the figure that presented itself to his view, was the remains of his once happy friend; but so miserably altered and disguised, that his features were scarce cognizable. The florid, the sprightly, the gay, the elevated youth, was now metamorphosed into a wan, dejected, meagre, squalid spectre; the hollow-eyed representative of distemper, indigence and despair: yet his eyes retained a certain ferocity, which threw a dismal gleam athwart the cloudiness of his aspect, and he, in silence, viewed his old companion with a look betokening confusion and disdain. As for Gauntlet, he could not, without emotion, behold such a woful reverse of fate, in a person for whom he entertained the noblest sentiments of friendship, gratitude and esteem: his sorrow was at first too big for utterance, and he shed a flood of tears before he could pronounce one word.

Peregrine, in spite of his misanthropy, could not help being affected with this uncommon testimony of regard; but he strove to stifle his sensations: his brows contracted themselves into a severer frown, his eyes kindled into the appearance of live coals; he waved with his hand, in signal for Godfrey to be gone, and leave such a wretch as him to the miseries of his fate; and finding nature too strong to be suppressed, uttered a deep groan, and wept aloud.

The soldier, seeing him thus melted, unable to restrain the strong impulse of his affection, sprung forwards, and clasping him in his arms, 'My dearest friend, and best benefactor, (said he) I am come hither to humble myself for the offence I was so unhappy as to give, at our last parting; to beg a reconciliation, to thank you for the ease and affluence I have enjoyed through your means, and to rescue you, in spite of yourself, from this melancholy situation; of which, but an hour ago, I was utterly ignorant. Do not deny me the satisfaction of acquitting myself, in point of duty and obligation. You must certainly have had some regard for a person, in whose favour you have exerted yourself so much; and if any part of that esteem remains, you will not refuse him an opportunity of approving himself, in some measure, worthy of it. Let me not suffer the most mortifying of all repulses, that of slighted friendship; but kindly sacrifice your resentment and inflexibility to the request of one, who is at all times ready to sacrifice his life for your honour and advantage. If you will not yield to my intreaties, have some regard to the wishes of my Sophy, who laid me under the strongest injunctions to solicit your forgiveness, even before she knew how much I was indebted to your generosity; or, if that consideration should be of no weight, I hope you will relax a little for the sake of poor Emilia, whose resentment hath been long subdued by her affection, and who now droops in secret at your neglect.'

Every word of this address, delivered in the most pathetic manner, made an impression upon the mind of Peregrine: he was affected with the submission of his friend, who, in reality, had given him no just cause to complain. He knew that no ordinary motive had swayed him to a condescension, so extraordinary in a man of his punctilious temper: he considered it, therefore, as the genuine effect of eager gratitude and disinterested love, and his heart began to relent accordingly. When he heard himself conjured in the name of the gentle Sophy, his obstinacy was quite overcome; and when Emilia was recalled to his remembrance, his whole frame underwent a violent agitation. He took his friend by the hand, with a softened look; and soon as he recovered the faculty of speech, which had been overpowered in the conflict of passions that transported him, protested, that he retained no vestige of animosity, but considered him in the light of an affectionate comrade, the ties of whose friendship, adversity could not unbind. He mentioned Sophy in the most respectful terms; spoke of Emilia with the most reverential awe, as the object of his inviolable love and veneration; but disclaimed all hope of ever more attracting her regard; and excused himself from profiting by Godfrey's kind intention, declaring, with a resolute air, that he had broke off all connection with mankind, and that he impatiently longed for the hour of his dissolution, which, if it should not soon arrive by the course of nature, he was resolved to hasten with his own hands, rather than be exposed to the contempt, and more intolerable pity, of a rascally world.

Gauntlet argued against this frantic determination with all the vehemence of expostulating friendship; but his remonstrances did not produce the desired effect upon our desperate hero, who calmly refuted all his arguments, and asserted the rectitude of his design from the pretended maxims of reason and true philosophy.

While this dispute was carried on with eagerness on one side, and deliberation on the other, a letter was brought to Peregrine, who threw it carelessly aside unopened, tho' the superscription was in an hand-writing to which he was a stranger; and, in all probability, the contents would never have been perused, had not Gauntlet insisted upon his waving all ceremony, and reading it forthwith. Thus solicited, Pickle unsealed the billet, which, to his no small surprize, contained the following intimation:

Mr. P. Pickle,

Sir,

This comes to inform you, that, after many dangers and disappointments, I am, by the blessing of God, safely arrived in the

Downs, on board of the Gomberoon Indiaman, having made a
tolerable voyage; by which I hope I shall be enabled to repay, with
interest, the seven hundred pounds which I borrowed of you before
my departure from England. I take this opportunity of writing by
our purser, who goes express with dispatches for the company,
that you may have this satisfactory notice, as soon as possible,
relating to one whom I suppose you have long given over as lost.
I have inclosed it in a letter to my broker, who, I hope, knows your
address, and will forward it accordingly: and I am, with respect,
Sir,

Your most humble servant,
BENJAMIN CHINTZ

He had no sooner taken a cursory view of this agreeable epistle,
than his countenance cleared up, and reaching it to his friend, with
a smile, 'There (said he) is a more convincing argument, on your
side of the question, than all the casuists in the universe can
advance.' Gauntlet, wondering at this observation, took the paper,
and casting his eyes greedily upon the contents, congratulated him
upon the receit of it, with extravagant demonstrations of joy: 'Not
on account of the sum (said he) which, upon my honour, I would,
with pleasure, pay three times over for your convenience and
satisfaction; but because it seems to have reconciled you to life,
and disposed your mind for re-enjoying the comforts of society.'
The instantaneous effect which this unexpected smile of fortune
produced in the appearance of our adventurer, is altogether inconceivable! it plumped up his cheeks in a moment, unbended and
enlightened every feature of his face; elevated his head, which had
begun to sink, as it were, between his shoulders; and from a
squeaking, dispirited tone, swelled up his voice to a clear, manly
accent. Godfrey, taking advantage of this favourable change, began
to regale him with prospects of future success: he reminded him
of his youth and qualifications, which were certainly designed for
better days than those he had as yet seen; he pointed out various
paths, by which he might arrive at wealth and reputation; he importuned him to accept of a sum for his immediate occasions; and
earnestly begged, that he would allow him to discharge the debt
for which he was confined: observing, that Sophy's fortune had
enabled him to exhibit that proof of his gratitude, without any
detriment to his affairs; and protesting, that he should not believe
himself in possession of Mr. Pickle's esteem, unless he was permitted to make some such return of good-will to the man, who had

not only raised him from indigence and scorn to competence and reputable rank, but also impowered him to obtain the possession of an excellent woman, who had filled up the measure of his felicity.

Peregrine declared himself already overpaid for all his good offices, by the pleasure he enjoyed in employing them, and the happy effects they had produced, in the mutual satisfaction of two persons so dear to his affection; and assured his friend, that one time or other he would set his conscience at ease, and remove the scruples of his honour, by having recourse to his assistance: but, at present, he could not make use of his friendship, without giving just cause of offence to honest Hatchway, who was prior to him in point of solicitation, and had manifested his attachment with surprising obstinacy and perseverance.

CHAPTER CX

Peregrine reconciles himself to the Lieutenant ;
and renews his Connection with Society.
Divers Plans are projected in his Behalf ; and he has
Occasion to exhibit a remarkable Proof of Self-denial

THE captain, with reluctance, yielded the preference in this particular to Jack, who was immediately invited to a conference, by a note subscribed with Pickle's own hand. He was found at the prison-gate waiting for Gauntlet, to know the issue of his negotiation; and no sooner received this summons than he set all his sails, and made the best of his way to his friend's apartment; being admitted by the turnkey, in consequence of Peregrine's request, communicated by the messenger who carried the billet. Pipes followed close in the wake of his shipmate; and, in a few minutes after the note had been dispatched, Peregrine and Gauntlet heard the sound of the stump, ascending the wooden stair-case with such velocity, that they at first mistook it for the application of drumsticks to the head of an empty barrel. This uncommon speed, however, was attended with a misfortune: he chanced to overlook a small defect in one of the steps, and, his prop plunging into a hole, he fell backwards, to the imminent danger of his life. Tom was luckily at his back, and sustained him in his arms, so as that he escaped without any other damage than the loss of his wooden leg, which was snapt in the middle, by the weight of his body, in falling: and such was his impatience, that he would not give himself the trouble to disengage the fractured member; but unbuckling the whole equipage in a trice, left it sticking in the crevice, saying a rotten cable was not worth heaving up, and, in this natural state of mutilation, hopp'd into the room with infinite expedition.

Peregrine taking him cordially by the hand, seated him upon one side of his bed; and after having made an apology for that reserve, of which he had so justly complained, asked, if he could conveniently accommodate him with the loan of twenty guineas. The lieutenant, without opening his mouth, pulled out his purse; and Pipes, who overheard the demand, applying the whistle to his lips, performed a loud overture, in token of his joy. Matters being thus brought to an accommodation, our hero told the captain, that he should be glad of his company at dinner, with their common friend Hatchway, if he would in the mean time leave him to the ministry of Pipes; and the soldier went away for the present, in order to pay a short visit to his uncle, who, at that time, languished in a declining state of health, promising to return at the appointed hour.

The lieutenant, having survey'd the dismal appearance of his friend, could not help being moved at the spectacle, and began to upbraid him with his obstinate pride, which (he swore) was no better than self-murder. But the young gentleman interrupted him in the course of his moralizing, by telling him he had reasons for his conduct, which, perhaps, he should impart in due season; but, at present, his design was to alter that plan of behaviour, and make himself some amends for the misery he had undergone. He accordingly sent Pipes to redeem his cloaths from the pawnbroker's wardrobe, and bespeak something comfortable for dinner. And when Godfrey came back, he was very agreeably surprised to see such a favourable alteration in his externals; for, by the assistance of his valet, he had purified himself from the dregs of his distress, and now appeared in a decent suit, with clean linnen, while his face was disencumbered of the hair that overshadowed it, and his apartment prepared for the reception of company.

They enjoyed their meal with great satisfaction, entertaining one another with a recapitulation of their former adventures at the garison; and in the afternoon, Gauntlet taking his leave, in order to write a letter to his sister, at the desire of his uncle, who finding his end approaching, wanted to see her without loss of time, Peregrine made his appearance on the bear, and was complimented on his coming abroad again, not only by his old mess-mates, who had not seen him for many weeks, but by a number of those objects whom his liberality had fed, before his funds were exhausted. Hatchway was, by his interest with the warden, put in possession of his former quarters, and Pipes dispatched to make inquiry about Crabtree at his former lodging, where he learn'd, that the Misanthrope, after a very severe fit of illness, was removed to Kensington Gravel-pits, for the convenience of breathing a purer air than that of London.

In consequence of this information, Peregrine, who knew the narrowness of the old gentleman's fortune, next day desired his friend Gauntlet to take the trouble of visiting him, in his name, with a letter, in which he expressed great concern for his indisposition, gave him notice of the fortunate intelligence he had received from the Downs, and conjured him to make use of his purse, if he was in the least hampered in his circumstances. The captain took coach immediately, and set out for the place, according to the direction which Pipes had procured.

Cadwallader having seen him at Bath, knew him again at first sight; and, though reduced to a skeleton, believed himself in such a fair way of doing well, that he would have accompanied him to the Fleet immediately, had not he been restrained by his nurse, who had been, by his physician, invested with full authority to dispute and oppose his will, in every thing that she should think prejudicial to his health; for he was considered, by those who had the care of him, as an old humourist, not a little distempered in his brain. He inquired particularly about the sailors, who (he said) had deterred him from carrying on his usual correspondence with Pickle, and been the immediate cause of his indisposition, by terrifying him into a fever: and understanding that the breach between Pickle and Hatchway was happily cemented, and that he was no longer in any danger from the lieutenant's resentment, he promised to be at the Fleet with the first convenient opportunity; and, in the mean time, wrote an answer to Peregrine's letter, importing, that he was obliged to him for his offer, but had not the least occasion for his assistance.

In a few days, our adventurer recovered his vigour, complexion and vivacity; he mingled again in the diversions and parties of the place; he received, in a little time, the money he had lent upon bottomry, which, together with the interest, amounted to upwards of eleven hundred pounds. The possession of this sum, while it buoyed up his spirits, involved him in perplexity. Sometimes he thought it was incumbent upon him, as a man of honour, to employ the greatest part of it, in diminishing the debt for which he suffered; on the other hand, he considered that obligation effaced, by the treacherous behaviour of his creditor, who had injured him to ten times the value of the sum; and in these sentiments, entertained thoughts of attempting his escape from prison, with a view of conveying himself, with the shipwreck of his fortune, to another country, in which he might use it to better advantage.

Both suggestions were attended with such doubts and difficulties, that he hesitated between them, and for the present, laid out a thousand pounds in stock, the interest of which, together with the fruits of his own industry, he hoped, would support him above want in his confinement, untill something should occur, that would point out the expediency of some other determination. Gauntlet still insisted upon having the honour of obtaining his liberty, at the expence of taking up his notes to Gleanum, and exhorted him to purchase a commission with part of the money which he had retrieved. The lieutenant affirmed, that it was his privilege to procure the release of his cousin Pickle, because he enjoyed a very handsome sum by his aunt, which of right belonged to the young gentleman, to whom he was, moreover, indebted for the use of his furniture, and for the very house that stood over his head; and that, although he had already made a will in his favour, he should never be satisfied, nor easy in his mind, so long as he remained deprived of his liberty, and wanted any of the conveniences of life.

Cadwallader, who by this time assisted at their councils, and was best acquainted with the peculiarity and unbending disposition of the youth, proposed, that seeing he was so averse to obligations, Mr. Hatchway should purchase of him the garison with its appendages, which, at a moderate price, would sell for more money than would be sufficient to discharge his debts; and that, if the servile subordination of the army did not suit his inclinations, he might, with his reversion, buy a comfortable annuity, and retire with him to the country, where he might live absolutely independent, and entertain himself, as usual, with the ridiculous characters of mankind.

This plan was, to Pickle, less disagreeable than any other project which had as yet been suggested; and the lieutenant declared himself ready to execute his part of it, without delay: but the soldier was mortified at the thoughts of seeing his assistance unnecessary, and eagerly objected to the retirement, as a scheme that would blast the fairest promises of fame and fortune, and bury his youth and talents in solitude and obscurity. This earnest opposition on the part of Gauntlet, hindered our adventurer from forming any immediate resolution: which was also retarded by his unwillingness to part with the garrison upon any terms, because he looked upon it as a part of his inheritance, which he could not dispose of, without committing an insult upon the memory of the deceased commodore.

CHAPTER CXI

He is engaged in a very extraordinary Correspondence,
which is interrupted by a very unexpected Event

WHILE this affair was in agitation, the captain told him, in the course of conversation, that Emilia was arrived in town, and had enquired about Mr. Pickle with such an eagerness of concern, as seemed to proclaim that she was in some measure informed of his misfortune: he, therefore, desired to know if he might be allowed to make her acquainted with his situation, provided he should be again importuned by her on that subject, which he had at first industriously waved.

This proof, or rather presumption of her sympathising regard, did not fail to operate powerfully upon the bosom of Peregrine, which was immediately filled with those tumults which love, ill stifled, frequently excites. He observed, that his disgrace was such as could not be effectually concealed; therefore he saw no reason for depriving himself of Emilia's compassion, since he was for ever excluded from her affection; and desired Godfrey to present to his sister the lowly respects of a despairing lover.

But, notwithstanding his declaration of despondence on this head, his imagination involuntarily teemed with more agreeable ideas: the proposal of Crabtree had taken root in his reflection, and he could not help forming plans of pastoral felicity, in the arms of the lovely Emilia, remote from those pompous scenes, which he now detested and despised. He amused his fancy with the prospect of being able to support her in a state of independency, by means of the slender annuity which it was in his power to purchase, together with the fruits of those endeavours, which would profitably employ his vacant hours; and foresaw provision for his growing family in the friendship of the lieutenant, who had already constituted him his heir. He even parcelled out his hours, among the necessary cares of the world, the pleasures of domestic bliss, and the enjoyments of a country life; and spent the night in ideal parties with his charming bride, sometimes walking by the sedgy bank of some transparent stream, sometimes pruning the luxuriant vine, and sometimes sitting in social converse with her, in a shady grove of his own planting.

These, however, were no more than the shadowy phantoms of imagination, which, he well knew, would never be realized: not that he believed such happiness unattainable by a person in his circumstances; but because he would not stoop to propose a scheme, which might, in any shape, seem to interfere with the interest of Emilia, or subject himself to a repulse from that young lady, who had rejected his addresses in the zenith of his fortune.

While he diverted himself with these agreeable reveries, an unexpected event intervened, in which she and her brother were deeply interested. The uncle was tapped for the dropsy, and died in a few days after the operation; having bequeathed, in his will, five thousand pounds to his nephew, and twice that sum to his niece, who had always enjoyed the greatest share of his favour.

If our adventurer, before this occurrence, looked upon his love for Emilia as a passion which it was necessary, at any rate, to conquer or suppress; he now considered her accession of fortune as a circumstance which confirmed that necessity, and resolved to discourage every thought on that subject, which should tend to the propagation of hope: when one day, in the midst of a conversation calculated for the purpose, Godfrey put into his hand a letter directed to Mr. Pickle, in the hand-writing of Emilia; which the youth no sooner recognized, than his cheeks were covered with a crimson dye, and he began to tremble with violent agitation: for he, at once, guessed the import of the billet, which he kissed with great reverence and devotion, and was not at all surprised when he read the following words.

S IR,

I have performed a sufficient sacrifice to my reputation, in retaining hitherto the appearance of that resentment, which I had long ago dismissed; and as the late favourable change in my situation, impowers me to avow my genuine sentiments, without fear of censure, or suspicion of mercenary design, I take this opportunity to assure you, that if I still maintain that place in your heart, which I was vain enough to think I once possessed, I am willing to make the first advances to an accommodation; and have actually furnished my brother with full powers to conclude it, in the name of your appeased   EMILIA

Pickle, having kissed the subscription with great ardour, fell upon his knees, and lifting up his eyes, 'Thank heaven! (cried he, with an air of transport) I have not been mistaken in my opinion of that generous maid. I believed her inspired with the most dignified and heroic sentiments, and now she gives me a convincing proof of her magnanimity: it is now my business to approve myself worthy of her regard. May heaven inflict upon me the keenest arrows of its vengeance, if I do not, at this instant, contemplate the character of Emilia with the most perfect love and adoration; yet, amiable and inchanting as she is, I am, more than ever, determined to sacrifice the interest of my passion to my glory, tho' my life should fail in the contest; and even to refuse an offer, which, otherwise, the whole universe should not bribe me to forego.'

This declaration was not so unexpected as unwelcome to his friend Gauntlet, who represented that his glory was not at all interested in the affair; because he had already vindicated his generosity, in repeated proffers to lay his whole fortune at Emilia's feet, when it was impossible that any thing selfish could enter into the proposal: but that, in rejecting her present purpose, he would give the world an opportunity to say that his pride was capricious, his obstinacy invincible, and his sister undeniable reason to believe, that either his passion for her was dissembled, or the ardour of it considerably abated.

In answer to these remonstrances, Pickle observed, that he had long set the world at defiance; and as to the opinion of Emilia, he did not doubt that she would applaud, in her heart, the resolution he had taken, and do justice to the purity of his intention.

It was not an easy task to divert our hero from his designs, at any time of life; but, since his confinement, his inflexibility was become almost insurmountable. The captain, therefore, after having discharged his conscience, in assuring him that his sister's happiness was at stake, that his mother had approved of the step she had taken, and that he himself should be extremely mortified at his refusal, forbore to press him with further argument, which served only to rivet him the more strongly in his own opinion; and undertook to deliver this answer to Emilia's letter.

MADAM,

That I revere the dignity of your virtue with the utmost veneration, and love you infinitely more than life, I am at all times ready to demonstrate: but the sacrifice to honour, it is now my turn to pay; and such is the rigour of my destiny, that, in order to justify your generosity, I must refuse to profit by your condescension. Madam, I am doomed to be for ever wretched; and to sigh, without ceasing, for the possession of that jewel, which, tho' now in my offer, I dare not enjoy. I shall not pretend to express the anguish that tears my heart, whilst I communicate this fatal renunciation; but appeal to the delicacy of your own sentiments, which can judge of my sufferings, and will, doubtless, do justice to the self-denial of your forlorn

P. PICKLE

Emilia, who knew the nicety of our hero's pride, had foreseen the purport of this epistle, before it came to her hands: she did not, therefore, despair of success, nor desist from the prosecution of her plan; which was no other than that of securing her own happiness, in espousing the man upon whom she had fixed her unalterable affection. Confident of his honour, and fully satisfied of the mutual passion with which they were inspired, she gradually decoyed him into a literary correspondence, wherein she attempted to refute the arguments on which he grounded his refusal; and, without doubt, the young gentleman was not a little pleased with the enjoyment of such delightful commerce, in the course of which he had (more than ever) an opportunity of admiring the poignancy of her wit, and the elegance of her understanding.

The contemplation of such excellency, while it strengthened the chains with which she held him enslaved, added emulation to the other motives that induced him to maintain the dispute; and much subtlety of reasoning was expended upon both sides of this very particular question, without any prospect of conviction on either part: 'till, at last, she began to despair of making him a proselyte to her opinion by dint of argument; and resolved, for the future, to apply herself chiefly to the irresistible prepossessions of his love, which were not at all diminished or impaired by the essays of her pen. With this view she proposed a conference, pretending that it was impossible to convey all her reflections, upon this subject, in a series of short letters; and Godfrey undertook to bail him for the day: but, conscious of her power, he would not trust himself in her presence, tho' his heart throbbed with all the eagerness of desire to see her fair eyes disrobed of that resentment which they had wore so long, and to enjoy the ravishing sweets of a fond reconciliation.

Nature could not have held out against such powerful attacks, had not the pride and caprice of his disposition been gratified to the full in the triumph of his resistance: he looked upon the contest as altogether original, and persevered with obstinacy, because he thought himself sure of favourable terms, whenever he should be disposed to capitulate. Perhaps he might have overshot himself, in the course of his perseverance: a young lady of Emilia's fortune and attractions, could not fail to find herself surrounded by temptations, which few women can resist. She might have misinterpreted the meaning of some paragraph, or taken umbrage at an unguarded expression in one of Peregrine's letters: she might have been tired out by his obstinate peculiarity, or, at the long run, construed it into madness, slight, or indifference; or, rather than waste her prime in fruitless endeavours to subdue the pride of an headstrong humorist, listen to the voice of some admirer, fraught with qualifications sufficient to engage her esteem and affection. But all these possibilities were providentially prevented by an accident, attended with more important consequences than any we have hitherto recounted.

Early one morning, Pipes was disturbed by the arrival of a messenger, who had been sent express from the country by Mr. Clover, with a packet for the lieutenant, and arrived in town overnight; but as he was obliged to have recourse to the information of Jack's correspondent in the city, touching the place of his abode, before he demanded entrance at the Fleet, the gate was shut; nor would the turnkeys admit him, altho' he told them, that he was charged with a message of the utmost consequence; so that he was fain to tarry 'till day-break, when he, at his earnest solicitation, was allowed to enter.

Hatchway, opening the packet, found a letter inclosed for Peregrine, with an earnest request, that he would forward it to the hands of that young gentleman with all possible dispatch. Jack, who could not dive into the meaning of this extraordinary injunction, began to imagine that Mrs. Clover lay at the point of death, and wanted to take her last farewel of her brother; and this conceit worked so strongly upon his imagination, that, while he huddled on his cloaths, and made the best of his way to the apartment of our hero, he could not help cursing, within himself, the folly of the husband in sending such disagreeable messages to a man of Peregrine's impatient temper, already soured by his own uneasy situation.

This reflection would have induced him to suppress the letter, had not he been afraid to tamper with the ticklish disposition of his friend, to whom, while he delivered it, 'As for my own part, (said he) mayhap I may have as much natural affection as another; but, when my spouse parted, I bore my misfortune like a British man and a Christian: for, why? he's no better than a fresh-water sailor, who knows not how to stem the current of mischance.'

Pickle being waked from a pleasant dream, in which the fair Emilia was principally concerned, and, hearing this strange preamble, sat up in his bed, and unsealed the letter, in a state of mortification and disgust: but what were the emotions of his soul, when he read the following intimation!

DEAR BROTHER,

It hath pleased God to take your father suddenly off, by a fit of the apoplexy; and as he has died intestate, I give you this notice, that you may, with all speed, come down and take possession of your right, in despite of master Gam and his mother, who, you may be sure, do not sit easy under this unexpected dispensation of providence. I have, by virtue of being a justice of the peace, taken such precautions as I thought necessary for your advantage; and the funeral shall be deferred until your pleasure be known. Your sister, tho' sincerely afflicted with her father's fate, submits to the will of heaven with laudable resignation, and begs you will set out for this place without delay; in which request she is joined by, Sir,

Your affectionate brother, and

Humble servant,

CHARLES CLOVER

Peregrine, at first, looked upon this epistle as a meer illusion of the brain, and a continuation of the reverie in which he had been engaged. He read it ten times over, without being persuaded that he was actually awake: he rubbed his eyes, and shook his head, in order to shake off the drowsy vapours that surrounded him: he hemm'd thrice with great vociferation, snapp'd his fingers, tweak'd his nose, started up from his bed, and, opening the casement, took a survey of the well-known objects that appeared on each side of his habitation. Every thing seemed congr'ous and connected, and he said, within himself, 'Sure this is the most distinct dream that ever sleep produced.' Then he had recourse again to the paper, which he carefully perused, without finding any variation from his first notion of the contents.

Hatchway, seeing all his extravagance of action, accompanied with a wild stare of distraction, began to believe that his head was

at length fairly turned, and was really meditating means for securing
his person; when Pickle, in a tone of surprize, exclaimed, 'Good
God! am I, or am I not awake?' 'Why, look ye, cousin Pickle,
(replied the lieutenant) that is a question which the deep sea-line
of my understanding is not long enough to sound: but, howsomever, tho'f I can't trust to the observation I have taken, it shall
go hard but I will fall upon a way to guess whereabouts we are.'
So saying, he lifted up a pitcher full of cold water, that stood behind
the outward door, and discharged it in the face of Peregrine, without ceremony or hesitation.

This remedy produced the desired effect: unpalatable as it was,
the young gentleman no sooner recovered his breath, which was
endangered by such a sudden application, than he thank'd his
friend Jack for the seasonable operation he had performed; and
having no longer any just reason to doubt the reality of what
appealed so convincingly to his senses, he shifted himself on the
instant, not without hurry and trepidation; and putting on his
morning-dress, sallied forth to the bear, in order to deliberate
with himself on the important intelligence he had received.

Hatchway, not yet fully convinced of his sanity, and curious to
know the purport of the letter, which had affected him in such an
extraordinary manner, carefully attended his footsteps in this excursion, in hope of being favoured with his confidence, in the
course of their perambulation. Our hero no sooner appeared at the
street-door, than he was saluted by the messenger, who having
posted himself in the way for that purpose, 'God bless your noble
honour, squire Pickle, (cried he) and give you joy of succeeding to
your father's estate.' These words had scarce proceeded from his
mouth, when the lieutenant hopping eagerly towards the countryman, squeezed his hand with great affection, and asked if the old
gentleman had actually taken his departure: 'Ay, master Hatchway,
(replied the other) in such a woundy haste, that he forgot to make
a will.' 'Body of me! (exclaimed the seaman) these are the best
tidings I have heard since I first went to sea. Here, my lad, take my
purse, and stow thyself chocque-full of the best liquor in the land.'
So saying, he tipped the peasant with ten pieces, and immediately
the whole place ecchoed with the sound of Tom's instrument; while
Peregrine, repairing to the walk, communicated the billet to his
honest friend, who, at his desire, went forthwith to the lodgings of
captain Gauntlet, and returned in less than half an hour with that
gentleman, who (I need not say) was heartily rejoiced at the
occasion.

CHAPTER CXII

Peregrine holds a Consultation with his Friends,
in consequence of which he bids adieu to the Fleet.
He arrives at his Father's House, and asserts
his Right of Inheritance

NOR did our hero keep the Misanthrope in ignorance of this happy turn of fortune: Pipes was dispatched to the senior, with a message requesting his immediate presence; and he accordingly appeared, in obedience to the summons, growling with discontent, for having been deprived of several hours of his natural rest. His mouth was immediately stopped with the letter, at which he *smiled a horrible ghastly grin*; and, after a compliment of congratulation, they entered into close divan, about the measures to be taken in consequence of this event.

There was no room for much debate: it was unanimously agreed, that Pickle should set out, with all possible dispatch, for the garison, to which Gauntlet and Hatchway resolved to attend him; and Pipes was accordingly ordered to prepare a couple of post-chaises, while Godfrey went to procure bail for his friend, and provide them with money for the expence of the expedition, but not before he was desired by Peregrine to conceal this piece of news from his sister, that our youth might have an opportunity to surprise her in a more interesting manner, after he should have settled his affairs.

All these previous steps being taken in less than an hour, our hero took his leave of the Fleet, after he had left twenty guineas with the warden for the relief of the poor prisoners, a great number of whom conveyed him to the gate, pouring forth prayers for his long life and prosperity; and he took the road to the garison, in the most elevated transports of joy, unallayed with the least mixture of grief at the death of a parent whose paternal tenderness he had never known; so that his breast was absolutely a stranger to that boasted Στοργὴ, or instinct of affection, by which the charities are supposed to subsist.

Of all the journeys he had ever made, this, sure, was the most delightful: he felt all the extasy that must naturally be produced in a young man of his imagination, from such a sudden transition, in point of circumstance; he found himself delivered from confinement and disgrace, without being obliged to any person upon earth for his deliverance; he had it now in his power to retort the contempt of the world, in a manner suited to his most sanguine wish; he was reconciled to his friend, and enabled to gratify his love, even upon his own terms; and saw himself in possession of a fortune more ample than his first inheritance, with a stock of experience that would steer him clear of all those quicksands among which he had been formerly wrecked.

In the middle of their journey, while they halted at an inn for a short refreshment and change of horses, a postilion ran up to Peregrine in the yard, and falling at his feet, clasped his knees with great eagerness and agitation, and presented to him the individual face of his old valet de chambre. The youth perceiving him in such an abject garb and attitude, commanded him to rise, and tell the cause of such a miserable reverse in his fortune. Upon which Hadgi gave him to understand, that he had been ruined by his wife, who having robbed him of all his cash and valuable effects, had eloped from his house, with one of his own customers, who appeared in the character of a French count, but was in reality no other than an Italian fidler; that, in consequence of this retreat, he (the husband) was disabled from paying a considerable sum which he had set apart for his wine-merchant, who being disappointed in his expectation, took out an extent against his effects; and the rest of his creditors following his example, hunted him out of house and home: so that, finding his person in danger at London, he had been obliged to escape into the country, skulking about from one village to another, till being quite destitute of all support, he had undertaken his present office, to save himself from starving.

Peregrine listened with compassion to his lamentable tale, which too well accounted for his not appearing in the Fleet, with offers of service to his master in distress, a circumstance that Pickle had all along imputed to his avarice and ingratitude; and he assured him, that as he had been the means of throwing in his way the temptation to which he fell a sacrifice, he would charge himself with the retrieval of his affairs: in the mean time, he made him taste of his bounty, and desired him to continue in his present employment, until he should return from the garison, when he would consider his situation, and do something for his immediate relief.

Hadgi attempted to kiss his shoe, and wept, or affected to weep, with sensibility, at this gracious reception; he even made a merit of his unwillingness to exercise his new occupation, and earnestly begged that he might be allowed to give immediate attendance upon his dear master, from whom he could not bear the thoughts of a second parting. His intreaties were reinforced by the intercession of his two friends, in consequence of which the Swiss was permitted to follow them at his own leisure, while they set forwards, after a slight repast, and reached the place of their destination before ten o'clock at night.

Peregrine, instead of alighting at the garison, rode straightway to his father's house; and no person appearing to receive him, not even a servant to take care of his chaise, he dismounted without assistance, and being followed by his two friends, advanced into the hall, where perceiving a bell-rope, he made immediate application to it, in such a manner as brought a couple of footmen into his presence. After having reprimanded them, with a stern look, for their neglect, in point of attendance, he commanded them to shew him into an apartment; and, as they seemed unwilling to yield obedience to his orders, asked if they did not belong to the family?

One of them, who took upon himself the office of spokesman, replied with a sullen air, that they had been in the service of old Mr. Pickle, and now that he was dead, thought themselves bound to obey no body but their lady, and her son Mr. Gamaliel. This declaration had scarce proceeded from his mouth, when our hero gave them to understand, that since they were not disposed to own any other master, they must change their quarters immediately; and ordered them to decamp without further preparation: and as they still continued restiff, they were kicked out of doors by the captain and his friend Hatchway. Squire Gam, who overheard every thing that passed, and was now more than ever inflamed with that rancour which he had sucked with his mother's milk, flew to the assistance of his adherents, with a pistol in each hand, bellowing *Thieves! thieves!* with great vociferation, as if he had mistaken the business of the strangers, and actually believed himself in danger of being robbed. Under this pretence he discharged a piece at his brother, who luckily escaping the shot, closed with him in a moment, and wresting the other pistol from his gripe, turned him out into the court-yard, to the consolation of his two dependants.

By this time, Pipes and the two postilions had taken possession of the stables, without being opposed by the coachman and his deputy, who quietly submitted to the authority of their new sovereign; but the noise of the pistol had alarmed Mrs. Pickle, who running down stairs, with the most frantic appearance, attended by two maids and the curate, who still maintained his place of chaplain and ghostly director in the family, would have assaulted our hero with her nails, had not she been restrained by her attendants, who, tho' they prevented her from using her hands, could not hinder her from exercising her tongue, which she wagged against him with all the virulence of malice. She ask'd, if he was come to butcher his brother, to insult his father's corpse, and triumph in her affliction; she bestowed upon him the epithets of spendthrift, jailbird, and unnatural ruffian; she begg'd pardon of God for having brought such a monster into the world, accused him of having brought his father's grey hairs with sorrow to the grave; and affirmed, that were he to touch the body, it would bleed at his approach.

Without pretending to refute the articles of this ridiculous charge, he allowed her to ring out her alarm; and then calmly replied, that if she did not quietly retire to her chamber, and behave as became a person in her present situation, he should insist upon her removing to another lodging, without delay; for he was determined to be master in his own family. The lady, who, in all probability, expected that he would endeavour to appease her with all the tenderness of filial submission, was so much exasperated at his cavalier behaviour, that her constitution could not support the transports of her spirits; and she was carried off by her women, in a fit, while the officious clergyman was dismiss'd after his pupil, with all the circumstances of disgrace.

Our hero having thus made his quarters good, took possession of the best apartment in the house, and sent notice of his arrival to Mr. Clover, who, with his wife, visited him in less than an hour, and was not a little surprised to find him so suddenly settled in his father's house. The meeting of Julia and her brother was extremely pathetic. She had always loved him with uncommon tenderness, and looked upon him as the ornament of her family; but she had heard of his extravagancies with regret, and tho' she considered the stories that were circulated at his expence, as the malicious exaggerations of his mother and her darling son, her apprehension had been grievously alarmed by an account of his imprisonment and distress, which had been accidentally conveyed to that country by a gentleman from London, who had been formerly of his acquaintance: she could not, therefore, without the most tender emotions of joy, see him, as it were, restored to his rightful inheritance, and re-established in that station of life which she thought he could fill with dignity and importance.

After their mutual expressions of affection, she retired to her mother's chamber, with a view to make a second offer of her service and attendance, which had been already rejected with scorn since her father's death; while Peregrine consulted his brother-in-law, about the affairs of the family, so far as they had fallen within his cognizance and observation.

Mr. Clover told him, that though he was never favoured with the confidence of the defunct, he knew some of his intimates, who had been tampered with by Mrs. Pickle, and even engaged to second the remonstrances by which she had often endeavoured to persuade her husband to settle his affairs by a formal will; but that he had from time to time evaded their importunities with surprising excuses of procrastination, that plainly appeared to be the result of invention and design, far above the supposed pitch of his capacity; a circumstance from which Mr. Clover concluded, that the old gentleman imagined his life would not have been secure, had he once taken such a step as must have rendered it unnecessary to the independence of his second son. He moreover observed, that, in consequence of this information, he no sooner heard of Mr. Pickle's death, which happened at the club, than he went directly, with a lawyer, to his house, before any cabal or conspiracy could be formed against the rightful heir; and, in presence of witnesses provided for the purpose, sealed up all the papers of the deceased, after the widow had, in the first transports of her sorrow and vexation, fairly owned, that her husband had died intestate.

Peregrine was extremely well satisfied with this intelligence, by which all his doubts were dispelled, and having chearfully supped with his friends on a cold collation which his brother-in-law had brought in his chariot, they retired to rest, in different chambers, after Julia had met with another repulse from her capricious mother, whose overflowing rage had now subsided into the former channel of calm inveteracy.

Next morning the house was supplied with some servants from the garison, and preparations made for the funeral of the deceased; and Gam having taken lodging in the neighbourhood, came with a chaise and cart to demand his mother, together with his own cloaths, and her personal effects.

Our hero, tho' he would not suffer him to enter the door, allowed his proposal to be communicated to the widow, who eagerly embraced the opportunity of removing, and was, with her own baggage, and that of her beloved son, conveyed to the place which he had prepared for her reception; whither she was followed by her woman, who was desired by Peregrine to assure her mistress, that, until a regular provision could be settled upon her, she might command him, in point of money, or any other accommodation in his power.

CHAPTER CXIII

He performs the last Offices to his Father, and returns
to London, upon a very interesting Design

SUITS of mourning being provided for himself, his friends and adherents, and every other previous measure taken, suitable to the occasion, his father was interred, in a private manner, in the parish-church; and his papers being examined, in presence of many persons of honour and integrity, invited for that purpose, no will was found, or any other deed, in favour of the second son, tho' it appeared by the marriage settlement, that the widow was intitled to a jointure of five hundred pounds a year. The rest of his papers consisted of East-India bonds, South-sea annuities, mortgages, notes and assignments, to the amount of fourscore thousand seven hundred and sixty pounds, exclusive of the house, plate and furniture, horses, equipage and cattle, with the garden and park adjacent, to a very considerable extent.

This was a sum that even exceeded his expectation, and could not fail to entertain his fancy with the most agreeable ideas. He found himself immediately a man of vast consequence among his country neighbours, who visited him with compliments of congratulation, and treated him with such respect as would have effectually spoiled any young man of his disposition, who had not the same advantages of experience as he had already purchased at a very extravagant price. Thus shielded with caution, he bore his prosperity with surprising temperance; every body was charmed with his affability and moderation; and when he made a circuit round the gentlemen of the district, in order to repay the courtesy which he owed, he was caressed by them with uncommon assiduity, and advised to offer himself as a candidate for the county, at the next election, which, they supposed, would soon happen, because the present member was in a declining state of health. Nor did his person and address escape unheeded by the ladies, many of whom did not scruple to spread their attractions before him, with a view of captivating such a valuable prize: nay, such an impression did this legacy make upon a certain peer, who resided in this part of the country, that he cultivated Pickle's acquaintance with great eagerness, and, without circumlocution, offered to him in marriage his only daughter, with a very considerable fortune.

770

Our hero expressed himself, upon this occasion, as became a man of honour, sensibility and politeness; and frankly gave his lordship to understand, that his heart was already engaged. He was pleased with the opportunity of making such a sacrifice to his passion for Emilia, which, by this time, inflamed his thoughts to such a degree of impatience, that he resolved to depart for London, with all possible speed; and for that purpose industriously employed almost every hour of his time in regulating his domestic affairs. He paid off all his father's servants, and hired others, at the recommendation of his sister, who promised to superintend his houshold in his absence: he advanced the first half-yearly payment of his mother's jointure; and as for his brother Gam, he gave him divers opportunities of acknowledging his faults, so as that he might have answered to his own conscience for taking any step in his favour; but that young gentleman was not yet sufficiently humbled by misfortune, and not only forbore to make any overtures of peace, but also took all occasions to slander the conduct and revile the person of our hero, being, in this practice, comforted and abetted by his righteous mamma.

Every thing being thus settled for the present, the triumvirate set out on their return to town, in the same manner with that in which they had arrived in the country, except in this small variation, that Hatchway's chaise-companion was now the valet de chambre refitted, instead of Pipes, who, with another lacquey, attended them on horseback. When they had performed two thirds of their way to London, they chanced to overtake a country squire, on his return from a visit to one of his neighbours, who had entertained him with such hospitality, that (as the lieutenant observed) he rolled himself almost gunwale to, at every motion of his horse, which was a fine hunter; and when the chaises pass'd him at full speed, he set up the sportsman's hollow, in a voice that sounded like a French horn, clapping spurs to Sorrel at the same time, in order to keep up with the pace of the machine.

Peregrine, who was animated with an uncommon flow of spirits, ordered his postilion to proceed more softly; and entered into conversation with the stranger, touching the make and mettle of his horse, upon which he descanted with so much learning, that the squire was astonished at his knowledge, and so engaged with his manner of discourse, that, when they approached his habitation, he invited the young gentleman and his company to halt, and drink a bottle of his ale; and was so pressing in his solicitation, that they complied with his request. He accordingly conducted them through a spacious avenue, that extended as far as the highway, to the gate of a large *chateau*, of a most noble and venerable appearance, which induced them to alight and view the apartments, contrary to their first intention of drinking a glass of his October at the door.

The rooms were every way suitable to the magnificence of the outside, and our hero imagined they had made a tour through the whole sweep, when the landlord gave him to understand that they had not yet seen the best apartment of the house, and immediately led them into a spacious dining-room, which Peregrine did not enter without giving manifest signs of uncommon astonishment. The pannels all round were covered with portraits, at full length, by Vandyke; and not one of them appeared without a ridiculous tye-perriwig, in the style of those that usually hang over the shops of two-penny barbers. The strait boots in which the figures had been originally painted, and the other circumstances of attitude and drapery, so inconsistent with this monstrous furniture of the head, exhibited such a ludicrous appearance, that Pickle's wonder, in a little time, gave way to his mirth, and he was seized with a violent fit of laughter, which had well nigh deprived him of his breath.

The squire, half pleased and half offended at this expression of ridicule, 'I know (said he) what makes you laugh so woefully: you think it strange to zee my vorefathers booted and spurred, with huge three-tailed perriwigs on their pates. The truth of the matter is this: I could not abide to zee the pictures of my vamily, with a parcel of loose hair hanging about their eyes, like zo many colts; and zo I employed a painter vellow from London to clap decent perriwigs upon their skulls, at the rate of vive shillings a head, and offered him three shillings a-piece to furnish each with an hand-zome pair of shoes and stockings: but the rascal, thinking I must have 'em done at any price, after their heads were covered, haggled with me for vour shillings a picture; and zo, rather than be imposed upon, I turned him off, and shall let 'em stand as they are, 'till zome more reasonable brother of the brush comes round the country.'

Pickle commended his resolution, tho', in his heart, he blessed himself from such a barbarous Goth; and, after they had dispatched two or three bottles of his beer, they proceeded on their journey, and arrived in town about eleven at night.

CHAPTER THE LAST

*He enjoys an Interview with Emilia, and makes
himself ample Amends for all the
Mortifications of his Life*

GODFREY, who had taken leave of his sister, on pretence of making a short excursion with Peregrine, whose health required the enjoyment of fresh air, after his long confinement, sent a message to her, that same night, announcing his arrival, and giving her notice that he would breakfast with her next morning; when he and our hero, who had dressed himself for the purpose, taking a hackney-coach, repaired to her lodging, and were introduced into a parlour, adjoining to that in which the tea-table was set. Here they had not waited many minutes when they heard the sound of feet, coming down stairs; upon which our hero's heart began to beat the alarm, and he concealed himself behind the screen, by the direction of his friend, whose ears being saluted with Sophy's voice from the next room, he flew into it with great ardour, and enjoyed upon her lips the sweet transports of a meeting so unexpected; for he had left her in her father's house at Windsor.

Amidst these emotions, he had almost forgot the situation of Peregrine; when Emilia, assuming an enchanting air, 'Is not this (said she) a most provoking scene to a young woman like me, who am doomed to wear the willow, by the strange caprice of my lover? Upon my word, brother, you have done me infinite prejudice, in promoting this jaunt with my obstinate correspondent; who, I suppose is so ravished with this transient glimpse of liberty, that he will never be persuaded to incur unnecessary confinement for the future.' 'My dear sister, (replied the captain, tauntingly) your own pride set him the example; so you must e'en stand to the consequence of his imitation.' ''Tis a hard case, however, (answered the fair offender) that I should suffer all my life, by one venial trespass. Heigh ho! who would imagine that a sprightly girl, such as I, with ten thousand pounds, should go a begging? I have a good mind to marry the next person that asks me the question, in order to be revenged upon this unyielding humourist. Did the dear fellow discover no inclination to see me, in all the term of his releasement? Well, if ever I can catch the fugitive again, he shall sing in his cage for life.'

It is impossible to convey to the reader a just idea of Peregrine's transports, while he overheard this declaration; which was no sooner pronounced, than, unable to resist the impetuosity of his passion, he sprung from his lurking place, exclaiming, 'Here I surrender;' and rushing into her presence, was so dazzled with her beauty, that his speech failed: he was fixed, like a statue, to the floor; and all his faculties were absorpt in admiration. Indeed, she was now in the full bloom of her charms, and it was nearly impossible to look upon her without emotion. What then must have been the extasy of our youth, whose passion was whetted with all the incitements which could stimulate the human heart! The ladies screamed with surprize at his appearance, and Emilia underwent such agitation as flushed every charm with irresistible energy: her cheeks glowed with a most delicate suffusion, and her bosom heaved with such bewitching undulation, that the cambrick could not conceal or contain the snowy hemispheres, that rose like a vision of paradise to his view.

While he was almost fainting with unutterable delight, she seemed ready to sink under the tumults of tenderness and confusion; when our hero, perceiving her condition, obeyed the impulse of his love, and circled the charmer in his arms, without suffering the least frown or symptom of displeasure. Not all the pleasures of his life, had amounted to the ineffable joy of this embrace, in which he continued for some minutes totally entranced. He fastened upon her pouting lips, with all the eagerness of rapture; and, while his brain seemed to whirl round with transport, exclaimed in a delirium of bliss, 'Heaven and earth! this is too much to bear!'

His imagination was accordingly relieved, and his attention in some measure divided, by the interposition of Sophy, who kindly chid him for his having overlooked his old friends: thus accosted, he quitted his delicious armful, and, saluting Mrs. Gauntlet, asked pardon for his neglect; observing, that such rudeness was excuseable, considering the long and unhappy exile which he had suffered, from the jewel of his soul. Then turning to Emilia, 'I am come, madam, (said he) to claim the performance of your promise, which I can produce under your own fair hand: you may, therefore, lay aside all superfluous ceremony and shyness, and crown my happiness without farther delay; for, upon my soul! my thoughts are wound up to the last pitch of expectation, and I shall certainly run distracted, if I am doomed to any term of probation.'

His mistress, having by this time recollected herself, replied with a most exhilerating smile, 'I ought to punish you, for your obstinacy, with the mortification of a twelve-months' trial; but 'tis dangerous to tamper with an admirer of your disposition, and therefore, I think, I must make sure of you while it is in my power.' 'You are willing, then, to take me for better for worse, in presence of heaven and these witnesses?' cried Peregrine, kneeling, and applying her hand to his lips. At this interrogation, her features softened into an amazing expression of condescending love; and while she darted a side-glance, that thrilled to his marrow, and heaved a sigh more soft than zephyr's balmy wing, her answer was, 'Why—ay——and heaven grant me patience to bear the humours of such a yoke-fellow.' 'And may the same powers (replied the youth) grant me life and opportunity to manifest the immensity of my love. Mean while, I have eighty thousand pounds, which shall be laid immedi-ately in your lap.'

So saying, he sealed the contract upon her lips, and explained the mystery of his last words, which had begun to operate upon the wonder of the two sisters. Sophy was agreeably surprised with the account of his good fortune: nor was it, in all probability, unacceptable to the lovely Emilia; tho', from this information, she took an opportunity to upbraid her admirer with the inflexibility of his pride, which (she scrupled not to say) would have baffled all the suggestions of his passion, had not it been gratified by this providential event.

Matters being thus happily matured, the lover begged that immediate recourse might be had to the church, and his happiness ascertained before night. But the bride objected, with great vehemence, to such precipitation, being desirous of her mother's presence at the ceremony; and she was seconded in her opinion by her brother's wife: upon which Peregrine, maddening with desire, assaulted her with the most earnest intreaties, representing, that, as her mother's consent was already obtained, there was surely no necessity for a delay, that must infallibly make a dangerous impres-sion upon his brain and constitution. He fell at her feet, in all the agony of impatience; swore that his life and intellects would actually be in jeopardy by her refusal; and when she attempted to argue him out of his demand, began to rave with such extravagance, that Sophy was frightened into conviction: and Godfrey enforcing the remonstrances of his friend, the amiable Emilia was teized into compliance.

After breakfast the bridegroom and his companion set out for the Commons for a licence, having first agreed upon the house at which the ceremony should be performed, in the lodgings of the bride: and the permission being obtained, they found means to engage a clergyman, who undertook to attend them at their own time and place. Then a ring was purchased for the occasion; and they went in search of the lieutenant, with whom they dined at a tavern, and not only made him acquainted with the steps they had taken, but desired that he would stand god-father to the bride: an employment which Jack accepted with demonstrations of particular satisfaction; 'till chancing to look into the street, and seeing Cadwallader approach the door, in consequence of a message they had sent to him by Pipes, he declined the office in favour of the senior; who was accordingly ordained for that purpose, on the supposition that such a mark of regard might facilitate his concurrence with a match, which, otherwise, he would certainly oppose, as he was a professed enemy to wedlock, and, as yet, ignorant of Peregrine's intention.

After having congratulated Pickle upon his succession, and shook his two friends by the hand, the Misanthrope asked whose mare was dead, that he was summoned in such a plaguy hurry from his dinner, which he had been fain to gobble up like a cannibal. Our hero gave him to understand, that they had made an appointment to drink tea with two agreeable ladies, and were unwilling that he should lose the opportunity of enjoying an entertainment which he loved so much. Crabtree, shrivelling up his face, like an autumn leaf, at this intimation, cursed his complaisance, and swore they should keep their assignation without him; for he and letchery had shook hands many years ago.

The bridegroom, however, likening him unto an old coachman, who still delights in the smack of the whip, and dropping some flattering hints of his manhood, even at these years, he was gradually prevailed upon to accompany them to the place of rendezvous; where, being ushered into a dining-room, they had not waited three minutes when they were joined by the parson, who had observed the hour with great punctuality.

This gentleman no sooner entered the room, than Cadwallader, in a whisper to Gauntlet, asked if that was not the cock-bawd; and before the captain could make any reply, 'What an unconscionable whoremaster the rogue is! (said he) scarce discharged from confinement, and sweetened with a little fresh air, and yet he wenches with a pimp in canonicals in his pay.' The door again opened, and Emilia broke in upon them, with such dignity of mien, and divinity of aspect, as inspired every spectator with astonishment and admiration. The lieutenant, who had not seen her since her charms were ripened into such perfection, expressed his wonder and approbation in an exclamation of 'Add's zooks! what a glorious galley!' and the Misanthrope's visage was instantly metamorphosed into the face of a mountain-goat; he licked his lips instinctively, snuffed the air, and squinted with a most horrible obliquity of vision.

The bride and her sister being seated, and Hatchway having renewed his acquaintance with the former, who recognized him with particular civility, Peregrine withdrew into another apartment with his friend Crabtree, to whom he imparted the design of this meeting, which the latter no sooner understood, than he attempted to retreat, without making any other reply than that of 'Pshaw! rot your matrimony! can't you put your neck in the noose, without my being a witness of your folly?'

The young gentleman, in order to vanquish this aversion, stepped to the door of the next room, and begged the favour of speaking with Emilia, to whom he introduced the testy old batchelor, as one of his particular friends, who desired to have the honour of giving her away. The bewitching smile with which she received his salute, and granted his request, at once overcame the disapprobation of the Misanthrope, who with a relaxation in his countenance which had never been perceived before that instant, thanked her in the most polite terms for such an agreeable mark of distinction. He accordingly led her into the dining-room, where the ceremony was performed without delay; and after the husband had asserted his prerogative on her lips, the whole company saluted her by the name of Mrs. Pickle.

I shall leave the sensible reader to judge what passed at this juncture, within the bosoms of the new-married couple: Peregrine's heart was fired with inexpressible ardour and impatience; while the transports of the bride were mingled with a dash of diffidence and apprehension. Gauntlet saw it would be too much for both, to bear their present tantalizing situation till night, without some amusement to diverge their thoughts; and therefore proposed to pass part of the evening at the public entertainment in Marybone-gardens, which were at that time frequented by the best company in town. The scheme was relished by the discreet Sophy, who saw the meaning of the proposal, and the bride submitted to the persuasion of her sister; so that, after tea, two coaches were called, and Peregrine was forcibly separated from his charmer, during the conveyance.[1]

While they stood before the orchestra, listening to an English ballad, which was sung in a very agreeable manner, our hero perceived a taudry Frenchman leaning against a post, and entertaining himself with a soliloquy upon the barbarous want of taste in England, so conspicuous in the applause which was given to that miserable performance; and as his remarks were not made without some insolent reflections upon the nation, he marked him as a proper object for his ridicule, and began to project some scheme for exposing him to the mirth of the company, because he looked upon him as some pert valet de chambre, who assumed the character of a gentleman, by the night; when he was saved the trouble of inventing by an accident which the foreigner of himself incurred.

One of the waiters belonging to the place, had marked with chalk the score of a company whom he attended, on the very post which the Frenchman had thought proper to occupy: so that, when he walked away, he carried off the greatest part of the reckoning upon his bag and shoulders. The servant coming to add another bottle to the account, perceived almost the whole particulars of the bill effaced, and began to raise an hideous outcry against the people that stood nearest him: upon which our hero told him how the misfortune had happened, and pointed out the person who bore the impression upon his back. This intelligence was no sooner communicated, than the waiter, calling some of his brethren to his assistance, went in pursuit of the delinquent (while Pickle desired his company to take notice) and telling him, that he had carried off part of a reckoning, desired he would return, that they might compare the marks upon his bag with the fragment which remained upon the post.

The Frenchman, who did not understand one word of the English language, seeing himself accosted in a very petulant manner by this attendant, at first imagined that he and his companions came with a design to affront him, because he was a foreigner; and therefore thinking it incumbent upon him to support the dignity of his nation, began to talk very big in his native tongue, and, in order to inforce his words, laid his hand upon his sword, in a very menacing posture: upon which the confederates flew upon him, and securing both his arms, led him backward through a lane of people, who laughed heartily at his captivity, which he now believed to be the effect of an information laid against him, for some trespass upon our laws, and, with a most ludicrous expression of fear, protested, that he was utterly ignorant and innocent of the crime for which he was apprehended.

Chapter the Last

Being conducted to the spot, his back was applied to the post, and the separate parts of the score matched like two exchequer tallies; by which means they were able to ascertain the reckoning, and then dismiss'd the counterpart, who had stood under their hands, with a most rueful face of expectation, and afforded merriment to a whole crowd of spectators, a great part of whom gave him a convoy to the gate, by which he made his retreat with great expedition.

The new-married couple and their company having made shift to spend the evening, and supped on a slight collation in one of the boxes, Peregrine's patience was almost quite exhausted; and taking Godfrey aside, he imparted his intention to withdraw in private from the sea-wit of his friend Hatchway, who would, otherwise, retard his bliss, with unseasonable impediments, which, at present, he could not possibly bear. Gauntlet, who sympathized with his impatience, undertook to intoxicate the lieutenant with bumpers to the joy of the bride, and, in the mean time, desired Sophy to retire with his sister, under the auspices of Cadwallader, who promised to squire them home.

The ladies were accordingly conducted to the coach, and Jack proposed to the captain, that, for the sake of the joke, the bridegroom should be plied with liquor, in such a manner as would effectually disable him from enjoying the fruits of his good fortune for one night at least. Gauntlet seemed to relish the scheme, and they prevailed upon Pickle to accompany them to a certain tavern, on pretence of drinking a farewel glass to a single life; there the bottle was circulated, till Hatchway's brain began to suffer innovation, and as he had secured our hero's hat and sword, he felt no apprehension of an elopement, which, however, was effected; and the youth hastened on the wings of love to the arms of his enchanting bride. He found Crabtree in a parlour, waiting for his return, and disposed to entertain him with a lecture upon temperance; to which he paid very little attention, but ringing for Emilia's maid, desired to know if her mistress was a-bed. Being answered in the affirmative, he sent her up stairs to announce his arrival, undressed himself to a loose gown and slippers, and wishing the Misanthrope good-night, after having desired to see him next day, followed in person to the delicious scene, where he found her elegantly dished out, the fairest daughter of chastity and love.

When he approached, she was overwhelmed with confusion, and hid her lovely face from his transported view; while Mrs. Gauntlet, seeing his eyes kindled at the occasion, kissed her charming sister, who, throwing her snowy arms about her neck, would have detained her in the room, had not Peregrine gently disengaged her confidante from her embrace, and conducted her trembling to the door; which having bolted and barricadoed, he profited by his good fortune, and his felicity was perfect.

Next day he rose about noon, and found his three friends assembled, when he learned that Jack had fallen in his own snare, and been obliged to lie in the same tavern where he fell: a circumstance of which he was so much ashamed, that Peregrine and his wife escaped many jokes, which he would have certainly cracked, had he not lain under the predicament of this disgrace. In half an hour after he came down, Mrs. Pickle appeared with Sophy, blushing like Aurora or the goddess of health, and sending forth emanations of beauty unparallelled: she was complimented upon her change of situation by all present, and by none more warmly than by old Crabtree, who declared himself so well satisfied with his friend's fortune, as to be almost reconciled to that institution, against which he had declaimed during the best part of his life.

An express was immediately dispatched to Mrs. Gauntlet, with an account of her daughter's marriage; a town-house was hired, and an handsome equipage set up, in which the new-married pair appeared at all public places, to the astonishment of our adventurer's fair-weather friends, and the admiration of all the world: for, in point of figure, such another couple was not to be found in the whole united kingdom. Envy despaired, and detraction was struck dumb, when our hero's new accession of fortune was consigned to the celebration of public fame: Emilia attracted the notice of all observers, from the pert templar to the Sovereign himself, who was pleased to bestow encomiums upon the excellence of her beauty. Many persons of consequence, who had dropped the acquaintance of Peregrine, in the beginning of his decline, now made open efforts to cultivate his friendship anew: but he discouraged all these advances with the most mortifying disdain; and one day, when the nobleman, whom he had formerly obliged, came up to him in the drawing-room, with the salutation of 'Your servant, Mr. Pickle', he eyed him with a look of ineffable contempt, saying, 'I suppose your lordship is mistaken in your man,' and turned his head another way, in presence of the whole court.

When he had made a circuit round all the places frequented by the beau-monde, to the utter confusion of those against whom his resentment was kindled; paid off his debts, and settled his money-matters in town; Hatchway was dismissed to the country, in order to prepare for the reception of his fair Emilia; and in a few days after his departure, the whole company (Cadwallader himself included) set out for his father's house, and, in their way, took up Mrs. Gauntlet the mother, who was sincerely rejoiced to see our hero in the capacity of her son-in-law. From her habitation they proceeded homewards at an easy pace, and, amidst the acclamations of the whole parish, entered their own house, where Emilia was received in the most tender manner, by Mr. Clover's wife, who had provided every thing for her ease and accommodation, and, next day, surrendered unto her the management of her own houshold affairs.

FINIS

NOTES

FOR continued help I am deeply grateful to Professor Lewis M. Knapp and to Professor Herbert Davis, the General Editor of this series. I am indebted also to Professors Robert Alter, Moses Hadas, Robert Halsband, Allen T. Hazen, Benjamin Hunningher, Joseph Mazzeo, and to Mrs. Lillian de la Torre, Miss Emily Cloyd, Miss B. J. Rahn, Mr. Robert Elmer, Mr. John Frayne, and Dr. George Lam, for the explication of individual passages. Occasionally I cite from the edition of 1872, prepared by David Herbert (indicated by the initials 'D. H.') and, for a few terms, the Blackwell edition of 1925. Some translations of Latin and Greek quotations have kindly been provided by Professor Moses Hadas; others have been taken from the standard Loeb editions. No attempt has been made to provide a complete list of passages omitted in the second edition in 1758 (cited as '2'), but major changes of a sentence or more have been noted. For a complete collation see H. S. Buck, *A Study in Smollett* (1925), pp. 123–207 (cited as 'Buck'). Dr. John Moore, *Life of Smollett* (1797) is referred to as 'Moore', and George M. Kahrl, *Tobias Smollett Traveler-Novelist* (1945) as 'Kahrl'.

Title-page. On the title-page of the first edition there were two lines from Horace, *Ars Poetica*, 317–18:

> Respicere exemplar vitae morumque jubebo
> Doctum imitatorem, & veras hinc ducere voces
>
> [And I still bid the learned maker look
> On life, and manners, and make those his book
> trans. Ben Jonson]

Page 1. A slang term for £100,000.

Page 2. Thomas Creech's translation of Horace appeared in 1684. Smollett, however, quotes Pope's rendering (*Epistles*, I. vi. 1–2), which reduces Creech's triplet to a couplet. See Twickenham ed., iv. 236–7.

Page 4. Hawser Trunnion, according to Edward Hinchliffe in *Barthomley* (1856), was based on Admiral Daniel Hore, who about 1750 built at Hull, near Warrington, a house like a ship, with cabins where the officers slept in hammocks, and bells sounded the time of day; where the lawn served as a quarter-deck and the conversation was always nautical. See *Notes and Queries*, 11th series, ii. 421; and Kahrl, pp. 28–35.

Page 5. (1) *Pederero*, a short piece of chambered ordnance.

(2) Perhaps drawn from Captain John Bover. For details of his career see Kahrl, pp. 30–35.

(3) Perhaps drawn from Admiral Hore's servant, Thomas Smale. See Kahrl, pp. 32–35.

Page 6. Probably meaning a few casks of good old brandy from Nantes.

Page 8. Not identified. A Captain in the Navy, William Bower, died 23 July 1733 (*Gent. Mag.*, July 1733, p. 380; *L.M.*, p. 370).

Page 9. (1) Sir George Rooke (1650–1709) and Sir John Jennings (1664–1743), famous naval commanders.

(2) *Fleur de Lys*. This name had been used by several French ships. Other ships' names which follow were well known at the time.

Page 12. A variant of 'The Boatswain's Whistle'. See Charles N. Robinson, *The British Tar in Fact and Fiction* (1909), pp. 347–8.

Page 21. (1) Nicholas Culpeper, *A Directory for Midwives : or, a Guide for Women in their Conception, Bearing and Suckling Their Children, &c.* (1651). For *Aristotle's Compleat and Experienced Midwife* (1700) see Sir D'Arcy Power, *The Foundations of Medical History* (1931), pp. 176–7.

(2) John Quincy, *Pharmacopoeia Officinalis et Extemporanea : or, a Compleat English Dispensatory* (1718). There were twelve editions by 1742.

Page 22. This phrase omitted in 2.

Page 23. What follows to the end of the chapter summarized in a single sentence in 2.

Page 27. (1) The rest of this paragraph omitted in 2.

(2) Samuel Johnson in his *Dictionary* (1755) defined 'peregrine' as 'foreign; not native; not domestick', and 'to peregrinate' as 'to travel; to live in foreign countries'. One of the meanings of 'to pickle' (verb) was given as 'to season or imbue highly with any thing bad; as, a *pickled* rogue, or one consummately villainous'.

Page 28. (1) Smollett was particularly interested in the medicinal use of water, and in 1752 published *An Essay on the External Use of Water* (48 pages), which showed his independent views.

(2) *Comfit*—a candied fruit or sweetmeat—and *colocynth*, from which was produced a bitter purgative drug.

Page 48. The modern Dutch phrase is 'Hans in den Kelder', referring to an unborn child.

Page 58. (1) The first eight paragraphs and the beginning of the ninth omitted in 2. The rest of the chapter was attached to Chap. XII in the revised version. The numbering of chapters is never thereafter the same. For the regrouping of material and renumbering of chapters see Buck, pp. 128 ff.

(2) Roman historian (*c.* 100–25 B.C.), who wrote biographies in clear, simple Latin.

Page 63. Davit—a curved piece of timber or iron used as a ship's crane.

Page 65. The following six paragraphs omitted in 2. For the substituted material and regrouping of chapters see Buck, pp. 128–31.

Page 66. A purgative drug.

Page 72. The source of this description of Davy Jones is uncertain. There is no formal legend, and the name, which personifies the danger of the sea, may come from Jonah.

Page 78. A *jolthead* is a dolt, a blockhead.

Page 80. Echoes Falstaff in *I Henry IV*, II. ii. 19–21. See Kahrl, p. 34.

Page 81. The following episode omitted in later editions.

Page 83. 'The Asses' Bridge', the fifth proposition in Euclid, a test of ability imposed on the inexperienced or ignorant.

Page 86. Peter Kolben (1675–1726), *The Present State of the Cape of Good Hope* (published in German at Nürnberg, 1719, and translated into English by Mr. Medley, 2 vols., 1731).

Page 87. From this point to the end of the chapter, and the first five paragraphs in Chap. XX omitted in 2. See Buck, pp. 131–6.

Page 103. For a discussion of Smollett's verses see Howard S. Buck, *Smollett as Poet* (1927).

Page 104. Substituting for another.

Page 113. Corrected to 'immodest' in 2.

Page 117. Aeneid, xi. 715–16. 'Foolish Ligurian, vainly puffed up in pride of heart, for naught hast thou tried thy slippery native tricks.' (Loeb.)

Page 118. See Buck, *Smollett as Poet.*

Page 119. The tune of 'Death and the Cobbler' is given in W. Chappell, *Popular Music of the Olden Time* (1859), i. 348–53.

Page 134. Perhaps a mixture of Leibniz, and Pope's 'Whatever is, is right'.

Page 137. See note to p. 63. Used for flogging.

Page 153. High-pitched.

Page 156. *The Taming of the Shrew*, IV. i. 59-60.

Page 166. All the rest of this chapter and the beginning of the next omitted in 2. See Buck, pp. 138-43.

Page 181. (1) Morgan, the Welsh apothecary in *Roderick Random*.

(2) Professor Knapp suggests a Welsh distortion of Poll Bayard (i.e. polled Bayard), the magic horse given by Charlemagne to Renaud. Poll, meaning hair cut short.

Page 182. *Satan's Invisible World Discovered: Detailing the Particulars of Strange Pranks Played by the Devil, together with a Particular Account of Several Apparitions, Witches, and Invisible Spirits* was published as a chap-book well into the nineteenth century. *A System of Magick; or, A History of the Black Art* (1726), was attributed in advertisements to Andrew Moreton, one of Defoe's pseudonyms. See J. R. Moore, *Checklist of Defoe* (1960), No. 487.

Page 184. The laughable.

Page 185. See final paragraph of *Roderick Random*.

Page 186. *King Lear*, IV. vi. 11-24.

Page 189. The rest of the paragraph omitted in 2.

Page 190. Apparently this was not an unusual imposition. *The Gentleman's Guide in His Tour through France. Wrote by an Officer* (4th ed. enlarged, 1770), pp. 15-16, advised: 'When a gentleman hires a packet-boat from Dover to Calais, let him insist upon being carried into the harbour in the ship, without paying the least regard to the representations of the master; when he tells you it is low water, or the wind is in your teeth, say, you will stay on board till it is high water . . . the boatmen will demand almost as much for rowing you to shore as you gave for your whole passage.'

Page 191. Kahrl (p. 40) suggests that 'the second quarter of *Peregrine Pickle* is one great, sustained prose satire on the Grand Tour, every detail of which can be fully substantiated from contemporary books on Continental travel', and cites William E. Mead, *The Grand Tour in the Eighteenth Century* (1914) as a useful authority. See in particular pp. 29-31, 44-45, 78-84, 103-39, and 364-74.

Page 192. Last part of sentence omitted in 2.

Page 194. For Father Graham, or Graeme, see Smollett's *Travels* (World's Classics), pp. 19-20.

Page 195. The Jacobite rebellion of 1745.

Page 196. Moore, I. cxxv, stated that 'Mr. Hunter, of Burnside [David Hunter of Monifieth, Forfarshire], was the individual among them who is mentioned as having wept bitterly . . . [and] cursed his own fate with frantic imprecations. I myself heard Mr. Hunter express himself in this manner to Dr. Smollett, and at the same time relate the affecting visit which he and his companions daily made to the sea-side, when they resided at Boulogne.'

Page 199. Not mentioned in 2.

Page 202. In the revised version Peregrine's 'guilty passion was not gratified'.

Page 205. (1) Smollett describes the *traiteur* [restaurant-keeper] and his wife in his later *Travels* (World's Classics), pp. 58–59.

(2) This episode is largely omitted in 2. See Buck, pp. 146–7.

Page 207. (1) Annibale Antonini, *Memorial de Paris et de ses environs à l'usage des voyageurs* (new ed. Paris, 1734), gives lists of paintings and other details.

(2) These were the usual sights recommended in the contemporary guide books.

Page 211. Writing of 1750, Moore commented: 'The story of the king's ecuyer, who stabbed a barber for having accidentally cut his face in shaving, I remember, was much talked of at that time in Paris. Whether the barber actually died of his wound I do not recollect.' (I. cxxv.)

Page 224. (1) Drawn from Dr. Mark Akenside (1721–70), author of *The Pleasures of Imagination* (1744). Moore definitely makes the identification, adding 'I have been told that Smollett's pique at him arose from some reflections Akenside had thrown out against Scotland, after his return from Edinburgh, where he had studied.' (I. cxxiii.) Yet Akenside may not have been in Paris in 1750. Wholly convincing proof of the ascription may be found in Howard S. Buck, 'Smollett and Akenside', *Journal of English and Germanic Philology*, January 1932, pp. 10–26. See also Isaac D'Israeli, *Calamities of Authors* (1812), ii. 5–6; and James J. Abraham, *Lettsom* (1933), p. 41.

(2) Until recently no convincing identification of the original for this character has been made. In a recent article in *Studies in English Literature*, Summer 1964, pp. 351–9, Ronald Paulson convincingly shows that many of the qualities of Pallet clearly resemble those of Hogarth. In places there are even close parallels to Hogarth's troubles at Calais in 1748. Moreover, the name may well have been intended to suggest Hogarth, who in 1749 had issued an engraved self-portrait showing himself with his dog Trump and a prominently displayed palette. An artist's palette had almost become his trade-mark, having been used as his seal on

the subscription tickets for his engravings. Yet there are difficulties in such an interpretation. Moore, op. cit., claimed that Pallet burlesqued an actual English painter whom Smollett met in Paris in 1750, and Hogarth is not known to have visited the Continent that summer. Moreover, neither Hogarth nor his friends resented the caricature, and there is no evidence that Smollett actively disliked the artist. Perhaps the character represents a conflation of traits, largely drawn from Hogarth, but with some from another English painter met in Paris, and the whole enlivened with Smollettian fictional details.

Page 225. (1) Horace, *Satires*, I. i. 69: 'Change but the name, of you the tale is told.' (Conington.)

(2) Condensed in 2.

(3) *Iliad*, xiv. 90. 'Be silent lest any other of the Achaeans should hear this word.'

(4) *Iliad*, xviii. 249 ff.

Page 227. 'Abrodiaitos, or *the Beau*' in later editions. Aeschylus, *Persians*, line 41.

Page 228. The following quotations from Euripides' *Ion* appear in lines 192, 203, 210, 212-13, 218.

Page 230. (1) *Iliad*, i. 4-5. 'To all dogs and fowl.'

(2) Probably 'Je ne sais quois.'

Page 232. (1) The beautiful, the fair.

(2) Shaftesbury's *The Moralists: a Philosophical Rhapsody* (1709) was included in his *Characteristics* (1711).

(3) Something divine.

Page 233. (1) Colley Cibber was made poet laureate in 1730. His official odes were much derided.

(2) For a detailed analysis of this dinner see Kahrl, pp. 44-49. There are some resemblances to Trimalchio's dinner party in Petronius' *Satyricon*.

Page 234. (1) The last clause omitted in 2.

(2) This sentence omitted in 2.

Page 235. The arrangement of the dining-room.

Page 236. (1) Perfumed powder.

(2) Roman emperor (A.D. 218-22), murdered in a Praetorian uprising.

Page 239. Marcus Gabius Apicius, Roman gourmet of the first century A.D. His name was given to a Latin cookery book containing recipes stemming from as late as the third century. Martin Lister's London edition appeared in 1705, and another by Almeloveen in Amsterdam in 1709. For details see Kahrl, op. cit.

Page 240. (1) Horace, *Satires*, II. viii. 42. 'Then is brought in a lamprey in the midst of swimming prawns.'

(2) *Hypotrimma*—a sauce made of all sorts of condiments. Hesychius of Alexandria, lexicographer.

(3) Gabriel Humelbergius, sixteenth-century physician. Martin Lister (1638–1712), English naturalist and physician. Both men had edited Apicius.

Page 241. (1) S. Baring-Gould in *English Minstrelsie* (1895), III. vii. gives the title as 'A Bumper, Squire Jones'.

(2) *The Merchant of Venice*, IV. i. 49–50.

Page 242. (1) From 'and the count' to Peregrine 'being rendered frolicksome', three paragraphs later, omitted in 2.

(2) Act III, scene vi. MIRTILLO: 'Like the thirsty sick man, who long desired the forbidden liquor, such am I, a long-time ill, burning and consumed with amorous thirst.' (trans. J. Mazzeo). Omitted in the middle is 'If you ever reach the liquor, poor one, drink rather of death, extinguish your life rather than your thirst.'

Page 244. The rest of this paragraph and the next, up to 'and attempted to plunge his hand', omitted in 2.

Page 248. Sixth-century B.C. Athenians, who plotted to kill the tyrant Hippias. Though unsuccessful, they were later called Liberators.

Page 252. For various later changes in phraseology in this paragraph, see Buck, p. 152.

Page 253. (1) Italian male soprano (*c.* 1680–1750). His name was Francesco Bernardi, but he took the name of his native city, Siena.

(2) Unidentified. Perhaps meant to be Giuseppe Monticelli of Venice, medical writer, or Angelo Maria Monticelli, male soprano, who was singing in London in the 1740's.

Page 256. (1) Howard S. Buck, in *Journal of English and Germanic Philology*, Jan. 1932, p. 13, shows that this is a direct quotation from two lines of Akenside's *Ode to the Earl of Huntingdon* (Strophe III, stanza 3).

(2) Act II, scene i.

> PHYSICIAN: . . . like impregnate Clouds, hover o'er our heads, will (when they once are grasped but by the eye of reason) melt into fruitful showers of blessings on the people.
> BAYS: Pray mark that Allegory. Is not that good?

Page 258. *Iliad*, ii. 246–7. 'Of reckless speech, clear-voiced talker though thou art, refrain thee, and be not minded to strive singly against kings.' The quotation was omitted in later versions.

Page 259. Book x, chap. xii. The muleteer refers to the common practice among innkeepers of substituting tom-cat for rabbit in their stews. Scipio's appetite suddenly disappears and he leaves the table.

Page 264. The four and a half paragraphs before this omitted in 2.

Page 270. Jean Charles Folard (1669-1752), writer on tactical history. His *Histoire de Polybe . . . avec un commentaire ou un corps de science militaire* (1727) was well known.

(2) Sheds for sheltering besiegers, walls, and ditches, battering rams, and various engines for throwing rocks and missiles.

Page 271. *Testudo*—overlapping shields of soldiers held over their heads for protection.

Page 272. (1) First performed in 1637. George de Scudéry wrote a letter to the Academy criticizing the play. For an account of the whole affair see H. Carrington Lancaster, *A History of French Dramatic Literature in the Seventeenth Century* (1932), part ii, vol. i, pp. 118-51.

(2) Perhaps Susannah Maria Cibber (1714-66), who was famous as Belvidera.

Page 273. (1) Heroine's of Otway's *The Orphan* (1680) and *Venice Preserved* (1682); and of Henault's *Cornélie Vestale* (1713), and Marmontel's *Cléopâtre*. Smollett may have seen the latter, first performed on 20 May 1750, with La Clairon in the title part, and probably Grandval as Anthony.

(2) David Garrick. The following attack was changed in the second edition to a short compliment. See Buck, pp. 154-6.

Page 274. (1) Character of the young rake in Nicholas Rowe's *The Fair Penitent* (1703).

(2) James Quin, Garrick's chief rival. For Smollett's quarrel with him see Buck, pp. 65-81, 91.

Page 275. (1) *Hamlet*, III. ii. 38.

(2) A character in Vanbrugh's *The Provoked Wife* (1697).

(3) La Clairon (Claire Josèphe Hippolyte Léris, 1723-1803) whose acting was of the declamatory school. See note (1), p. 273.

Page 276. Perhaps Charles-François Nicolas Racot de Granval (1710-84), one of the leading performers in the 1740's before Lekain's appearance on the scene. See note (1), p. 273.

Page 277. *The Dance* (Loeb Classical Library, v (1936), 285-7).

Page 283. From *Aesop's Fables*. In the fable an inundation overflows a farmer's stable. Swift, in his poem 'On the Words Brother Protestants', thus described what happened:

> A Ball of new-dropt Horse's Dung,
> Mingling with Apples in the Throng,
> Said to the Pippin, plump and prim,
> *See Brother, how we apples swim.*
>
> (*The Poems of Jonathan Swift*, ed. H. Williams (1937), iii. 811.)

Page 284. Perhaps referring to Genesis xlix. 14: 'Issachar is a strong ass.' See H. R. S. van der Veen, *Jewish Characters in Eighteenth-Century English Fiction and Drama* (Groningen, 1935), 46. (Cited by Strauss, p. 43.)

Page 288. This sentence was shortened in 2.

Page 291. Cf. *Travels* (World's Classics), p. 38. Smollett had himself had a similar argument at Ghent with a Frenchman.

Page 292. This sentence omitted in 2.

Page 300. Last part of sentence omitted in 2.

Page 302. Persius, *Satires*, iii. 64. 'Meet misfortune half way.'

Page 304. *Gil Blas*, book vii, chap. 13. Professor Knapp points out that in the 1750 edition of Smollett's translation there is this note: 'Eleazar, a famous magician, who cast out devils, by tying to the nose of the possessed, a certain mystical ring, which the demon no sooner smelled, than he overturned and abandoned the patient. . . .'

Page 310. Charles Alexander of Lorraine (1712–80), Governor-General of the Netherlands.

Page 323. The beautiful, the fair.

Page 324. (1) *I Henry IV*, v. iv. 115.
(2) See p. 303.

Page 325. This entire chapter omitted in 2. For other revisions see Buck, pp. 160–6.

Page 333. *Oedipus at Colonus* by Sophocles.

Page 334. 'Some other time.'

Page 336. Hamlet, I. iv. 38–39.

Page 342. (1) Roman throwing-spear and small round shield.
(2) *Pythian Odes*, i. 41. 'From the Gods come all the means of mortal exploits.'
(3) Spoils won by a Roman general who had slain an enemy leader in single combat.

Notes

Page 343. *Pythian Odes*, i. 13. 'But all the beings that Zeus hath not loved, are astonied when they hear the voice of Pierides.'

Page 344. Much of this sentence is paraphrased from Akenside's notes to his *Ode to the Earl of Huntingdon* (stanza ii. 2). See article by Buck listed in note (1), p. 256.

Page 346. The last half of this sentence omitted in 2.

Page 347. (1) Sir Hans Sloane (1660–1753). His collections of specimens, books, and manuscripts later formed the nucleus of the British Museum.

(2) Don Saltero's coffee-house museum, 18 Cheyne Walk, Chelsea, was satirically described by Steele in *The Tatler*, No. 34. After the proprietor died in 1728 it was run by his daughter. Smollett was a patron. See Knapp, pp. 111–12.

(3) Transportation ships pulled by horses through canals.

Page 348. (1) A house of correction for lewd women. Gentlemen could pay to observe their indecent actions. See T. Nugent, *The Grand Tour* (3rd ed. 1778), i, pp. 83–84 and 114; also W. E. Mead, *The Grand Tour* (1914), pp. 368–9.

(2) The specific performer not identified. Yet see J. Fransen, *Les Comédiens Français en Hollande au xviie et au xviiie siècles* (Paris, 1925).

Page 349. Book xxvi, Chap. 50.

Page 350. (1) Thomas Nugent, in *The Grand Tour* (3rd ed., 1778), i. 83, commented: 'It is also customary for strangers to see something of the famous *spiel* houses, or music houses in this city. These are a kind of taverns and halls where young people of the meaner sort, both men and women, meet two or three times a week, for dancing. Here they only make their rendezvous, but the execution is done elsewhere. Those who choose to satisfy their curiosity in this respect, should take care to behave civilly, and especially not to offer familiarities to any girl that is engaged with another man, otherwise the consequences might be dangerous, for the *Dutch* are very brutish in their quarrels.'

(2) A notorious resort in Covent Garden, portrayed by Hogarth in *Four Times of the Day* (1738), begun by Tom King and later run by his widow. It was patronized by the most unruly rakes. See H. B. Wheatley, *Hogarth's London* (1909), pp. 133–6, 287; and *Nocturnal Revels: the History of King's Place and Other Modern Nunneries . . .* (1779).

Page 360. A large single-sheaved block employed in heaving up the anchor.

Page 378. Everything in this chapter up to this point omitted in 2.

Notes

Page 385. *Hamlet*, II. ii, 396–8.

Page 386. See Robert Alter, *Rogue's Progress* (1964), p. 58.

Page 388. (1) The chapter-heading and all except the first two sentences of this chapter omitted in 2. See Buck, p. 169.

(2) Gyges, King of Lydia, *c*. 685–653 B.C., who was reputed to have found in a hollow horse of bronze a magic ring which could render the wearer invisible.

Page 392. (1) Turns of the sand glass (of 14 or 28 seconds' period), used as a measure of time when ascertaining a vessel's speed by the log.

(2) Plunger or piston of a ship's pump, which was sometimes driven by a small windmill with canvas sails.

Page 393. There were a number of French ships named the *Renommée*.

Page 394. Sometimes written 'futtock' or 'puttock' shrouds—leading from the upper part of the lower mast, or of the main shrouds, to the edge of the top, or through it, and connecting the topmast rigging with the lower mast.

Page 401. A coarse kind of snuff made from the darker and ranker tobacco leaves (*OED*).

Page 402. Probably Charles Fitzroy, 2nd Duke of Grafton, grandson of Charles II, at one time Chamberlain of the Household of George II. Perhaps Ethelreda, or Audrey Harrison, wife of Charles, Viscount Townshend. Undoubtedly Philip Stanhope, Earl of Chesterfield. (D. H.)

Page 424. From here to end of chapter omitted in 2. For adjustments see Buck, pp. 173–5.

Page 425. A game of chance, having a ball which could fall into niches marked E or O.

Page 430. *II Henry IV*, IV. iv. 31–34. The quotation is somewhat garbled.

Page 431. Lady Vane. See next note.

Page 432. Frances Anne Hawes, born *c*. 1715, the daughter of Francis Hawes, Esq., of Purley Hall, near Reading in Berkshire, who was one of the South Sea Directors in 1720. His London house was in Winchester St. She died in London, 31 Mar. 1788. The general chronology of her memoirs can be established through comments of other people. See subsequent notes.

Page 433. (1) *Henry V*, IV, Prologue.

(2) Second daughter of George II. In *An Apology for the Conduct of a Lady of Quality* (1751), pp. 15–16, the author stated that on Miss Hawes's

first appearance at Bath, among her admirers was a gentleman who later published his adventures under the name of Loveit, and a Col. O—.

Page 434. Lord William Hamilton, second son of James Douglas, 4th Duke of Hamilton. The Princess Royal was Anne (1709–59), who married the Prince of Orange in 1734.

Page 435. Charles Colyear, 2nd Earl of Portmore, known as a patron of the turf. See also note (1), p. 443 (1).

Page 436. (1) Although masquerades at the Opera House in the Haymarket had been suppressed by royal proclamation, they were still carried on under the name of Ridottos or Balls, and Heidegger, the manager, was appointed master of the revels by George II.

(2) Charles, Earl of Selkirk, brother of the 4th Duke of Hamilton, Lord William's father.

Page 438. (1) Henry Beauclerk, fourth son of Charles, 1st Duke of St. Albans, who was the son of Charles II by Nell Gwyn. There was a printed *Erratum* in vol. iii of the first edition reading 'for Lord H. B. read Lord S. B.', but this correction was not made in later editions, and was erroneous.

(2) Lord Henry Beauclerk.

Page 440. This sentence was expanded and made more rapturous in 2. The marriage occurred in May 1733. See *Gent. Mag.* iii. 268: 'Ld Wm Hamilton, married to Miss Haws, Daughter of Francis Haws, Esq.: a South Sea Director in 1720. able to give her 40,000£.'

Page 441. (1) Lady Susan Hamilton (died 1755), who in 1736 married Tracy Keck.

(2) Hamilton.

Page 443. (1) Juliana, third wife and widow of Peregrine Hyde, 3rd Duke of Leeds, married Charles, 2nd Earl of Portmore, on 7 Oct. 1732. See *Gent. Mag.* ii (Oct. 1732), 1030.

(2) Maria [Molly] Skerrett, whom Sir Robert Walpole finally married in 1738.

(3) Sir William Yonge, 4th baronet (died 1755), who was Secretary of War in 1735.

Page 445. Hamilton near Glasgow.

Page 448. Leeds. See note to p. 443. She later presented Lady Vane at Court.

Page 449. William Holles, 2nd Viscount Vane (1714–89).

Page 450. Oxford Chapel (Marylebone). The marriage took place on 19 May 1735 (*Gent. Mag.* v. 275). Perhaps the officiating clergyman was

Benjamin Hoadly, Bishop of Winchester, or John Hough, Bishop of Worcester.

Page 451. In later editions the statement, transferred from the end of the memoirs, that she had paid Lord W—m's debts, was inserted at this point. See Buck, p. 176.

Page 452. (1) Perhaps George, 3rd Earl of Cholmondeley. He had married Mary, the only legitimate daughter of Sir Robert Walpole, but this lady had died in 1731. Horace Walpole lamented his 'profusion'. (D. H.)

(2) The Hon. Sewallis Shirley (1709–65), son of Robert, 1st Earl of Ferrers. He afterwards married Margaret, Dowager Countess of Orford.

(3) This fervent description did not meet with universal acceptance. Thus Lady Mary Wortley Montagu later wrote to Lady Bute (16 Feb. 1752): 'He appear'd to me gentile, well bred, well shap'd and sensible, but the charms of his Face and Eyes, which Lady V describes with so much warmth, were, I confess, allwaies invisible to me, and the artificial part of his character very glareing, which I think her story shows in a strong light.' (W. Moy Thomas ed. (1893), ii. 216–17: corrected from manuscript.) A few years later, when Shirley and his wife separated, Horace Walpole commented ironically to Sir Horace Mann (5 July 1754): 'The testimonials which Mr. Shirley had received in print from that living academy of love-lore, my Lady Vane, added to this excessive tenderness of one, little less a novice, convinced everybody that he was a perfect hero.' (*Yale Walpole Ed.*, xx. 439.)

Page 453. Probably Lord Charles Hay of Linplum, third son of Charles, 3rd Marquis of Tweeddale.

Page 457. (1) Prince of Wales.

(2) Lord Vane's supposed impotence was much talked about. It was hinted at in *A Letter to the Right Honourable the Lady V—ss V—* (1751). For Horace Walpole's remarks see note to page 485. In *The Tell-Tale* (1756), i. 157–8, there was a story about Lord Vane's finding Lady Vane asleep with *Peregrine Pickle* before her. He slyly puts *The Practice of Piety* in its place. Upon waking she discovers the trick. When Lord Vane congratulates her on her reformation, she replies: 'Nay, nay, let our reformation go hand in hand, I beseech you; when you, my Lord, practice the Whole Duty of Man, then I'll read the Practice of Piety.'

Page 458. Hamilton, brother of her first husband.

Page 459. (1) Evelyn Pierrepont, 2nd Duke of Kingston (1711–73).

(2) Conti.

(3) Touche. Her sister was Madame d'Arthy, the Prince of Conti's first mistress. (D. H.)

Page 462. (1) In later editions it was stated that plans had been made in Paris. Exactly what happened is not clear. For example, Patrick Guthrie wrote to James Gibbs on 10 Aug. 1736, from Boulogne-sur-Mer: 'My Lord Vane rid several times post through this town. I did not see him. I hear he is gone from Calais to London. He was in search of his wife, and had forty or fifty people riding over France in quest of her. I hear she run from him at Paris with one of the Shirleys, who carried her to Brussels; he came post here as a courier, hired a ship, one Mirlton master, for Dover, but went to Ostend, where he landed, from thence went to Brussels and brought my Lady Vane to Ostend, and thence carried her to London in Mirlton's ship. . . .' (Portland Manuscripts (*Historical Manuscripts Commission*, 1901), vi. 63.)

(2) Orford. See notes (2) and (3), p. 452; and *Yale Walpole Ed.*, xix. 309; xx. 239.

(3) Philip Yorke, Lord Hardwicke. In the British Museum there are two letters from Lady Vane to Lord Hardwicke perhaps written about this time (Add. MS. 35597, ff. 364, 368).

Page 467. The 1st Earl of Egmont wrote in his diary on 27 Jan. 1737 (*H.M.C.* (1923), ii. 335-6): 'I read this day in the newspapers my Lord Vane's advertisement offering 100£ reward to him that should discover his lady, who for some time has eloped from him. One would think he had lost some favourite spaniel bitch, for he describes her person very particularly, even to the clothes she wears. . . . But the advertisement makes sport to the town. He is a very silly young man, half mad, half fool.' The actual advertisement first appeared in the *Daily Journal*, 24 Jan. 1737. It ran in the *Grub-Street Journal* from 27 Jan. to 24 Feb., and in other papers. After mentioning the reward, threatening prosecution for anyone concealing his wife, and promising good treatment if she should return, Lord Vane added this description: 'She is about 22 Years of Age, tall, well-shaped, has light brown Hair, is fair complexioned, and has her upper Teeth placed in an irregular manner. She had on when she absented a red Damask French Sack, and was attended by a French Woman who speaks very bad English.'

Page 468. Thoresby, at Thoresby in Sherwood. On 31 Mar. 1737, the 1st Earl of Egmont wrote in his diary (*H.M.C.* (1923), ii. 381): 'I learned this day that Lady Vane, who has so long eloped from my lord her husband, is in the country with the Duke of Kingston, who has still in keeping the French mistress he stole out of France.' See notes to p. 459.

Page 473. Thomas Villiers, second son of William, 2nd Earl of Jersey, and later Earl of Clarendon, was for several years British Minister at Dresden and other courts of the Empire. (D. H.)

Page 474. (1) Possibly a member of the royal family. She later refers to her aversion to selling herself to a prince.

(2) Cholmondeley.

Page 475. Robert Knight (1675–1744), Cashier to the South Sea Co. See John Carswell, *The South Sea Bubble* (1960), pp. 266–7.

Page 476. (1) Augustus, 4th Earl of Berkeley (1716–55).

(2) Cholmondeley.

(3) Not identified. Perhaps this was the lady referred to by Lady Lucy Wentworth in a letter to her father on 29 Dec. 1737: 'Lord Vane keeps a Lady in the country, so he's now easy without my Lady, but she's comeing to town from the Bath, and says she's sure she can behave in a manner that will make her be esteem'd as well as ever.' (*Wentworth Papers*, ed. James J. Cartwright (1883), p. 534.)

Page 477. (1) Henry St. John, Lord Bolingbroke, had a house at Chanteloup in Touraine. He had married, in 1720, Marie Claire Deschamps de Marcilly, who had been the second wife of a cousin of Mme. de Maintenon.

(2) John Christie of Baberton. He died 30 Apr. 1789, aged about 80. He had been in the Foot-guards, but left the army on winning a large lottery prize. He attended the Earl of Berkeley on his travels in Europe. (D. H.)

Page 478. (1) Lady Mary Wortley Montagu wrote to Lady Pomfret in Jan. 1739: 'Lady Vane is returned hither in company with Lord Berkeley, and went with him in publick to Cranford, where they remain as happy as love and youth can make them. I am told that though she does not pique herself upon fidelity to any one man (which is but a narrow way of thinking), she boasts that she has always been true to her nation, and notwithstanding foreign attacks, has always reserved her charms for the use of her own countrymen.' (Thomas. ed. (1893), ii. 36–37, corrected.)

(2) Henry Berkeley, a cousin of Lord Berkeley.

(3) Perhaps Capt. Benjamin Rudyard, of West Woodhay, Berks., aide-de-camp to Lord Stair at Dettingen. So identified by Aucher Warner in *Sir Thomas Warner* (1933), p. 125.

Page 479. Four different doctors have been suggested: Smollett himself, John Shebbeare, Peter Shaw, and William Smellie. Because neither Smollett nor Shebbeare were fashionable physicians in 1739, when the event occurred, they may be eliminated. The case for Shaw was presented by Judd Kline in *Philological Quart.*, July 1948, pp. 219–28. Knapp (p. 140) argues cogently for Smellie. See also John Glaister, *Dr. William Smellie* (Glasgow, 1894), pp. 12 and 360.

Page 480. Sir Thomas Aston. See note to p. 482.

Page 481. (1) Holdman. His character is vindicated in *A Letter to the Right Honourable the Lady V—ss V—* (1751).

(2) William Anne, 2nd Earl of Albemarle, was Lord Berkeley's uncle by marriage. (D. H.)

Page 482. Sir Thomas Aston, 4th baronet of Aston, Staffordshire. He was a brother of Dr. Johnson's friend, Molly Aston. The identification is rendered certain by a comment by Horace Walpole. See note to p. 485.

Page 483. Christie. See note (2), p. 477.

Page 485. Andrew Cantwell (died 1764). He had settled in Paris in 1733, and became one of the severest opponents of inoculation against smallpox. Evidently gossip about Lady Vane and Sir Thomas was widespread. Among unpublished manuscripts of Horace Walpole now in the collection of Mr. W. S. Lewis, and cited with his kind permission, there is *Sunday or the Presence Chamber : a Town Eclogue*. To this Walpole added a note: 'This Eclogue was wrote at Florence [summer–autumn 1740], as a Sequel to Lady Mary Wortley's Six. She was then there, & Lady Vane was expected there with Sir Thomas Aston, for whom She had quitted Earl Berkeley. . . .' In this 'Eclogue' Lady Vane appears as 'Liquorissa'. Included are such lines as:

> Zounds! are you mad my Lord? Your *Liquorissa*
> In other Countries follows her Blissa.

A footnote to this added: 'Lord Vane was said to be Impotent, yet at any time woud give his Wife great Sums to return to Him, which as soon as She had got, She always ran away again. 'Tis of this Lord Pope says:

> The Fool, whose Wife elopes some twice a quarter
> For Matrimonial Solace dies a Martyr.'
>
> (*First Epistle of the First Book of Horace Imitated*, 150–1.)

In another poem, 'Patapan or the Little White Dog', Walpole again referred to Lady Vane: 'See fair Vanella browse a lustful goat.' (*Yale Walpole Ed.* xxx. 295.)

Page 486. (1) Apparently Lady Vane had continued with Lord Berkeley until late in 1741. On 23 Nov. 1741 Horace Walpole wrote to Sir Horace Mann: 'You can't imagine what an entertaining fourth act of the opera we had t'other night—Lord Vane in the middle of the pit, making love to my Lady! The Duke of Newcastle has lately given him three-score thousand pounds to consent to cut off the entail of the Newcastle estate; the fool immediately wrote to his wife to beg she would return to him from Lord Berkeley, that he had got so much money, and now they might live *comfortably* . . . she is at Lord Berkeley's house; whither go divers after her [Lord Berkeley was then living in Spring Garden].' Walpole also reported an anecdote about Lady Vane and the Blessed Sacrament. (*Yale Walpole Ed*. xvii, 209–10.)

(2) Henry Berkeley.

Page 488. Hugh Fortescue, 13th Baron Clinton, created in 1746 Lord Fortescue and Earl of Clinton. He died in 1751. (D. H.)

Page 489. (1) In the later revision there was added here: 'I remembered that his former attachment began in the season of my prosperity, when my fortune was in the zenith, and my youth in its prime; and that he had forsaken me in the day of trouble, when my life became embarrassed, and my circumstances were on the decline. I foresaw nothing but continual persecution from my husband, and feared that once the keener transports of our reconciliation should be over, his affection would sink under the severity of its trial.'

(2) Thomas, 4th Duke of Leeds, stepson of the Duchess of Leeds, mentioned earlier.

(3) Probably Henry Vane, later Earl of Darlington, Lord Vane's first cousin.

Page 490. On 9 June 1742 Lieut.-Col. Charles Russell reported from Ghent to his wife in London: 'The greatest beauty we have here has followed us from England, which is Lady Vane, who arrived here last Monday night, and in reality has followed the brigade of Guards, which, as soon as she is tired with, intends to proceed to Brussels. She has no woman with her, and walks about each evening with an officer on each side of her.' (Russell–Astley Manuscripts, *H.M.C.* lii (1900), 215.) On 17 June 1742 Horace Walpole wrote to Sir Horace Mann: 'The troops continue going to Flanders, but slowly enough. Lady Vane has taken a trip thither after a cousin of Lord Berkeley, who is as simple about her as her own husband is, and has written to Mr. Knight at Paris to furnish her with what money she wants. He says, she is vastly to blame, for he was trying to get her a divorce from Lord Vane, and then would have married her himself. Her adventures are worthy to be bound up with those of my good sister-in-law, the German Princess [Mary Moders], and Moll Flanders.' (*Yale Walpole Ed*. xvii, 459.)

Page 492. (1) Lord Robert Bertie, third son of Robert, Duke of Ancaster. He was not the youngest brother. (D. H.)

(2) Countess of Calemberg, Princess of Chemay, M. D'Harrach. See p. 500.

(3) Robert Manners, third son by his second wife of John, 2nd Duke of Rutland. The family seat was at Belvoir, Lincolnshire. (D. H.) Perhaps the others of the triumvirate were Lieut.-Col. William Henry Ker, Earl of Ancram; and Capt. George Waldegrave, both close friends

and messmates of Lord Robert Manners and Henry Berkeley in this campaign. (See *H.M.C.* (1900), lii. 214, 236, &c.)

Page 497. (1) Probably near Grimsthorpe in Lincolnshire. (D. H.)
(2) Lionel Vane.

Page 499. She was there on 26 Feb. 1743, when Lieut.-Col. Charles Russell wrote from the Hotel de Flandre to his wife in London: 'and who should be amongst 'em ever since we have been here but Lady Vane, who keeps Lent with the family, has a lodging near and is well received in this town, but whilst we've been here is chiefly with us. Berkeley shuns her much and assured me he would never be with her but in my company. She behaves extremely modest and very agreeable.' (Russell–Astley Manuscripts, *H.M.C.* (1900), lii. 224.)

Page 500. (1) The Duke of Newcastle was maternal grand-uncle of Lord Vane. See also next note.
(2) John Dalrymple, 2nd Earl of Stair (1673–1747). In the Stair Manuscripts at Lochinch Castle, vol. xxvii (made available through the kindness of the present Earl of Stair), there are two letters from Lady Vane in 1743. In the first from Brussels, 14 Aug., she writes of her continued misfortunes caused by her husband's persecution. 'But as he is Endeavouring by all methods at Viena to procure a Grant from the Queen to Empower him to take me. What I have to beg of your Lordship is your Interest with the King, to prevent Mr Robinson's Soliciting in behalf of Lord Vane, in his Majesty's name; Mr Robinson as I am inform'd refused Ld Vane His Services when my Lord first applied to him; but Upon receiving a Letter afterwards from the Duke of Newcastle to desire it of him, he now acts for Ld Vane tho as yet with Little Success; nor do I fear any thing Unless his Majesty was to interfere. . . .' All she desires, she insists, is 'to remain in Safety of my Life'. In the second letter, from Paris, two weeks later, on 28 Aug., she refers again to her 'Unhappy Situation; Which is render'd much more so, by Lord Vane's having Obtain'd Permission to take me at Brusselles, by Mr Robinson's Soliciting for him (in the Kings name as I am told) . . .'. She begs Lord Stair's help in securing from the King permission for her to live quietly at Brussels 'Whilst I can finnish my law Suits in England because till such time they can be decided, I am not Secure from Lord Vane's Insults. . . . All I desire is to be heard, before the Judges of England; and to be safe from Lord Vane till I am heard; after Which I shall readily Submit. . . .'
(3) Probably Granville. At this time he was still Lord Carteret. He was abroad with George II at the time. (D. H.)

Page 503. (1) See note to p. 479. This would have been in 1743.
(2) In *Gent. Mag.* xiii (Nov. 1743), 612, there is the notice: 'The Lady

V— exhibited in the King's Bench, Articles of the Peace against her Husband for ill Usage.'

Page 510. John James Heidegger (1659?-1749), famous opera manager, a notoriously ugly man. No one expected this situation to last. Fanny Russell wrote to her brother, Lieut.-Col. Charles Russell, on 27 Aug. 1744: 'Lord and Lady Vane keep mighty well still, but 'tis not supposed she will stay long with him.' (Russell-Astley Manuscripts, *H.M.C.* (1900), lii. 338.)

Page 512. Henry Berkeley was killed in the battle of Fontenoy in May 1745. (*Yale Walpole Ed.* xix. 43.)

Page 520. Fortescue. See note to p. 488.

Page 533. Leaf L-12 in vol. iii of the first edition was a cancel. Instead of the preceding sentence the original ran: 'This declaration was a mystery at that time, but is now explained; for I have been credibly informed, and think his conduct since that time has plainly demonstrated, that he was inadvertently drawn into a promise of marriage, from which his honour would not allow him to recede. Upon that supposition, I heartily acquit him of all injustice to me.' See catalogue of Elkin Mathews Ltd. (June 1929), item 165, which lists a copy in its uncancelled state.

Page 536. Probably William Pulteney, Earl of Bath; Philip Dormer Stanhope, Earl of Chesterfield; and Henry Vane, active in the political Opposition.

Page 537. Perhaps Lionel Cranfield, 1st Duke of Dorset. In 1724 he had been constituted Custos Rotulorum of the County of Kent, and was also Warden and Admiral of the Cinque Ports and Constable of Dover. (D. H.)

Page 538. (1) Alexander Pope, *Epistle to a Lady*, line 114. Smollett's rendering changes the meaning. Pope has 'For true No-meaning puzzles more than wit'.

   (2) The rest of the paragraph omitted in 2. The points in Lady Vane's favour were put back in her own narrative. See notes to pp. 451 and 489 (1).

Page 540. The rest of the chapter omitted in 2.

Page 551. Opening changed in 2 to bridge the gap caused by omission of virtually all of preceding chapter.

Page 562. Referring to Edmund Halley (1656-1742) and Tycho Brahe (1546-1601), famous astronomers.

Page 566. *Heredipeta*—'one who seeks after inheritances'—a word used by Petronius.

Notes

Page 568. (1) Doubtless reflecting Smollett's own unhappy experiences with *The Regicide*. See Buck, pp. 54–112.

(2) Abraham de Moivre (1667–1754), mathematician. One of his well-known works was *The Doctrine of Chances: or, a Method of Calculating the Probability of Events in Play* (London, 1718).

Page 576. A combination of terms used in *The Rehearsal*. See Act I, scene ii: 'I'll give you dash for dash'; and Act III, scene i: '. . . t'others upon him, slap, with a Repartee; then he at him again, dash with a new conceipt.'

Page 577. The next five paragraphs omitted in 2.

Page 596. See E. S. Noyes, 'A Note on *Peregrine Pickle* and *Pygmalion*', *Modern Language Notes*, May 1926, pp. 327–30, for resemblances to Shaw's later play.

Page 600. A game of cards, something like modern 'poker'.

Page 604. The last couplet of Richard Steele's 'Verses to the Author of the Tragedy of *Cato*' (*Occasional Verse of Richard Steele*, ed. Rae Blanchard (1952), p. 15). Steele has 'Name' instead of 'fame'.

Page 605. (1) *As You Like It*, I. ii. 66–70, somewhat garbled.

(2) For resemblances of this lottery scheme to Hogarth's, see article by Ronald Paulson listed in note (2), p. 224.

Page 634. Echoes *Twelfth Night*, III. ii. 28.

Page 637. (1) Smollett himself later employed helpers of this sort on some of his larger projects.

(2) Perhaps Samuel Johnson, who, in 1750, had a number of amanuenses working for him in the garret of his house in Gough Square.

Page 641. A gap greatly to be lamented.

Page 643. *Epistles*, I. vii. 79. 'Seek laughter from any source.'

Page 644. The rest of the chapter omitted in 2.

Page 646. The Earl of Chesterfield. See Buck, pp. 84–86.

Page 648. The rest of the sentence omitted in 2.

Page 649. See *Peri Bathous*, chap. iii.

Page 651. (1) The criticism of *The Fair Penitent* omitted altogether in 2.

(2) Speech of Lothario in Nicholas Rowe's *The Fair Penitent*, II. ii.

(3) David Garrick. He had played Lothario in 1747, with Quin as Horatio. See *The London Stage*, part III, vol. ii.

Page 652. (1) James Quin.

(2) James Thomson's *Coriolanus*, IV. iv.

(3) Pierre in Otway's *Venice Preserved* and Zanga in Edward Young's *The Revenge*. Quin's best Shakespearian roles were Othello, Falstaff, and the ghost in *Hamlet*.

(4) *The Revenge*, V, last scene.

Page 653. The Revenge, III. i.

Page 654. Lewis Theobald's *Perseus and Andromeda* was one of Rich's most popular afterpieces at Covent Garden during the season of 1749–50 (*The London Stage, 1660–1800*, part IV, vol. i, pp. lxv and 136).

Page 655. (1) The rest of the chapter omitted in 2. The question suggests Smollett's acknowledgement of personal reasons behind his attacks.

(2) A burlesque of Lord Lyttelton's monody on the death of his wife. See Buck, pp. 107–9.

Page 658. (1) George, Lord Lyttelton.

(2) *Dunciad* (second version), i. 111–12. 'Delighted' is 'with transport' in the original.

Page 659. (1) Probably James Thomson, who died in 1748.

(2) Pope's *Epistle to Dr. Arbuthnot*, line 212 (in the Atticus portrait).

(3) Henry Fielding. His second wife had been his first wife's maid.

Page 660. Dunciad, i. 54.

Page 672. Of the original edition.

Page 676. See Buck, pp. 29–30.

Page 682. An obvious jibe at Fielding's technique in *Tom Jones*.

Page 691. Daniel MacKercher (see Knapp, pp. 70–71, 121–2), referred to as the 'melting Scot' in Smollett's satire *Reproof* (1747). He was born about 1702 and died 2 Mar. 1772.

Page 693. (1) MacKercher is a form of Mac Fearacher, or Farquhar, so that he was a member of the warlike clan of Farquharson (A. Lang).

(2) George Buchanan (1506–82), author of *Rerum Scoticarum Historia* (1582). According to Moore, Smollett had founded his tragedy of *The Regicide* on the assassination of James I of Scotland, which had much affected him in Buchanan's account.

Page 694. (1) This was just before the battle of Sheriffmuir, 13 Nov. 1715, in which the outnumbered Hanoverians under John Campbell, 2nd Duke of Argyll, were able to hold off the rebel Jacobites under John Erskine, Earl of Mar. Although technically indecisive, this engagement in effect crushed the rebellion.

(2) Morison's.

(3) Despite his success in putting down the Jacobite rising, Argyll was

deprived of his offices in 1716, possibly because of the enmity of the Duke of Marlborough.

(4) Born 1667, Campbell had fought with distinction at Malplaquet and was made Colonel of the Scots Greys in 1717. He was killed at Fontenoy in 1745.

Page 695. (1) Jean Barbeyrac (1674–1744), world-famous legal authority, appointed professor at University of Groningen in 1717.

(2) Thomas John Francis Strickland was made Bishop of Namur in 1727. He kept the Ministry in London informed of Jacobite movements on the Continent. Collier—perhaps Gen. David Colyear, Earl of Portmore.

Page 701. There have been suggestions that this might represent Lady Vane, here disguised as unmarried. See Buck, pp. 21–26. MacKercher was reputed to have been one of her lovers.

Page 705. Jean Charles Folard (1669–1752), *Histoire de Polybe* (1727).

Page 706. Samuel Clarke's edition appeared in 1712.

Page 707. Perhaps named J. J. Huber (see Lewis M. Knapp and Lillian de la Torre in *English Language Notes*, Sept. 1963, pp. 31–32). The episode of the 15,000 hogsheads appears confirmed by items in the *Virginia Gazette*, 5 Aug. 1737, and in issues from 31 Mar. to 6 May 1738.

Page 709. (1) The war of Jenkins's Ear. Smollett had sailed as a surgeon's mate in 1740.

(2) This was the celebrated Annesley case. For an older account see Andrew Lang, *The Annesley Case* (English Notable Trials) (1912), pp. 1–79. In a forthcoming volume Lillian de la Torre will provide a thorough analysis of all the evidence. Meanwhile Knapp and de la Torre (see note to p. 707) suggest that Smollett's version in *Peregrine Pickle* was derived from a manuscript account prepared by the Annesley faction and later used as the source of *An Abstract of the Case of James Annesley*, published in 1751, and of another independent recension in 1754.

(3) Admiral Edward Vernon. There is no evidence that he intervened in the matter. See Knapp and de la Torre, loc. cit., p. 32.

(4) Anglesey.

(5) James Annesley, the claimant.

Page 710. William Henderson.

Page 711. (1) Arthur Annesley, Baron Altham, in July 1706 married Mary Sheffield, illegitimate daughter of the Duke of Buckingham.

(2) Anglesey (or Anglesea).

Page 712. (1) Capt. Temple Briscoe.

(2) Dunmaine, County Wexford.

(3) New Ross in County Wexford.